Charles de Lint

MOONHEART

PAN FANTASY

PAN BOOKS

London, Sydney and Auckland

First published in Great Britain 1990 by Pan Books Ltd
This edition published 1991 by Pan Books Ltd,
Cavaye Place, London SW10 9PG
1 3 5 7 9 8 6 4 2
© Charles de Lint 1984
ISBN 0 330 31576 5

Grateful acknowledgement is made to Robin Williamson
for permission to use a portion of "For the Three of Us", from the
album *Songs of Love and Parting*, © 1981 by Robin Williamson

Printed in England by Clays Ltd, St Ives plc

for
MaryAnn

who helps it happen

CONTENTS:

PART ONE

The Wren's Thistle Cloak

Tell me where is fancy bred,
Or in the heart or in the head?

—WILLIAM SHAKESPEARE

Chapter One

SARA KENDELL once read somewhere that the tale of the world is like a tree. The tale, she understood, did not so much mean the niggling occurrences of daily life. Rather it encompassed the grand stories that caused some change in the world and were remembered in ensuing years as, if not histories, at least folktales and myths. By such reasoning, Winston Churchill could take his place in British folklore alongside the legendary Robin Hood; Merlin Ambrosius had as much validity as Martin Luther. The scope of their influence might differ, but they were all a part of the same tale.

Though in later years she never could remember who had written that analogy of tale to tree, the image stayed with her. It was so easy to envision:

Sturdily rooted in the past, the tale's branches spread out through the days to come. The many stories that make up its substance unfold from bud to leaf to dry memory and back again, event connecting event like the threadwork of a spider's web, so that each creature of the world plays its part, understanding only aspects of the overall narrative, and perceiving, each with its particular talents, only glimpses of the Great Mystery that underlies it all.

The stories on their own are many, too myriad to count, and their origins are often too obscure or inconsequential on their own to be recognized for what they are. The Roman statesman Marcus Tullius Cicero said it best: "The beginnings of all things are small."

Though he lived and died some two thousand years before Sara was born, and though the tale was so entangled by the time she came into it that it would have been an exercise in

3

futility to attempt to unravel its many threads, Sara herself came to agree with Cicero. Years later she could pinpoint the exact moment that brought her into the tale. It was when she found the leather pouch with its curious contents in one of the back storerooms of her uncle's secondhand shop.

The Merry Dancers Old Book and Antique Emporium was situated on Bank Street, between Third Avenue and Fourth in the area of Ottawa called the Glebe. It was owned by Jamie Tams who took his inspiration for the name from the aurora borealis, the northern lights that the French call *les chèvres dansantes*. The dancing goats.

"It's quite appropriate," he told Sara one day. He was leaning on the long display case that supported the relic of a cash register which worked by turning a crank on its side. "Think about it. The Arctic's what? Ice and snow. Tundra and miles of nothing at best. Who'd expect a treasure like the Dancers in a place like that?"

Sara smiled. "Are you implying that somewhere in all this junk there're similar treasures to be found?"

"Implying? Nope. It's a straight fact. When was the last time you went through the jumble of boxes in the back rooms? There could be anything in them—not valuable, mind, but treasures all the same."

He stared pointedly at Sara's typewriter, an IBM self-correcting Selectric, and the pile of paper that was stacked beside it.

"If you weren't so busy writing the Great Canadian Novel . . ."

"What sorts of things?" Sara wanted to know. "Like Aladdin's lamp?"

"You never can tell."

"I suppose not."

"And," Jamie finished triumphantly, "if you never look, you'll never know either!"

Sara tried, but she couldn't keep a straight face any longer. They both broke into laughter.

Neither of them needed to work—at least not for financial considerations. Jamie in his time, and now Sara in hers, ran The Merry Dancers as a hobby. That it showed any sort of a profit at all at the end of each fiscal year was as much due to luck as through any particular effort on their part, though Sara was more conscientious in her management than Jamie'd ever been. ("Comes with being young," Jamie warned her darkly.

"Wait'll you get older. The whole place'll fall to pieces around you as you go doddering about. You'll see.")

It was a standing joke between them that whenever Jamie visited the store, at one point or another, he'd play the concerned proprietor. But for all the teasing, they both knew that if they ever made the shop as tidy as some of the newer ones on the street, it would lose half of its charm.

The Merry Dancers was cluttered, certainly somewhat dusty, but not dirty. Leaning bookshelves stuffed with fat, leatherbound volumes took up two walls, while the bay windows in front held a curious sampling of items the store offered, set out in a confusing array that put off as many people as it attracted. There were treasures to be found, indeed, but not for the fastidious. Clutter swirled like autumn leaves around old chairs, dressers, sideboards, desks, rockers, wicker tables and an umbrella stand overflowing with rolled-up maps, knobby-ended walking sticks and an African shaman's staff.

Behind the cash area it was no tidier. A walnut-paneled door led to the storerooms, a washroom, and a tiny kitchen meant only for someone without a trace of claustrophobia in their mental make-up. There were more shelves on the walls, laden with everything from books and calendars stacked a foot high to more curious wonders. To one side, set up so that she could look out the front windows when she was thinking, was Sara's desk holding her typewriter, paper, ashtray, coffee mug, tottering piles of reference books, a stuffed brown bear called Mr. Tistle with a plaid patched stomach, a stack of *National Geographic*s and a copper-and-brass pencil holder—all in a four-by-three-foot surface area.

That didn't include the pigeonholes at the back of the desk, stuffed with letters (answered and unanswered), envelopes, more paper, her driver's license (that she never remembered to take with her when she used the car), a small Aiwa cassette player, that was connected to a pair of Monitor Audio speakers balanced precariously on wrought iron brackets above the bay windows, and the filing system for her fledgling writing career that included notes (hundreds of them on anything from matchbook covers to the small sheets torn out of her spiralbound notebook), information on who had what story and how often it'd been rejected, a list of her accepted stories (eleven of them!), and the addresses for all her correspondents that had started out being in alphabetical order but somehow degenerated into catch-as-catch-can.

On the day that Sara found the pouch she'd been thinking of the storeroom and all those unopened boxes gathering dust. It was easier to think of them than to decide if she was writing a thriller, a Gothic, a fantasy, or some bizarre permutation of the three. The boxes came from rummage sales, estates, country auctions and Lord knew where. Her writing hadn't been going well that day so she decided to make a start on them.

Perched on a stool behind the counter, her typewriter covered with a piece of velvet with frayed edges and moth-holes to keep the dust from it, she was working on her third box. Like the first two it had decidedly more junk and dust in it than any sort of treasure. Sighing, she ignored the grime that coated her hands and entrenched itself under her fingernails and tried to make the best of it. She tapped her foot along with Silly Wizard, a Scots folk group that were playing on the cassette machine, her thoughts lost in daydreams.

While Sara was one of that exiguous segment of the world's population that views the commonplace through a screen of whimsy, she was not flighty. She could dream about the history of a particular knick-knack, creating in her mind all sorts of implausible origins for it at the same time as she decided on a price, neatly printed the amount on a small sticker, and attached it to the bottom of the item in question.

Rummaging through the box that day, she was, if not a candidate for the next cover of *Chatelaine*, at least a study of enterprise. Her thick brown curls fell past her shoulders with all the unruly orderliness of a hawthorn thicket. She was small and thin, with delicate bones and intensely green eyes, her features not so much classically beautiful as quirky. She was, as usual, dressed in a pair of faded jeans and a shapeless old sweater and a pair of practical brown leather shoes in desperate need of a polish.

"I've got to feel real," she would respond wearily to whichever well-intentioned friend was the latest to ask why she couldn't be a little more fashionable. "It's hard enough the way things are, without walking around like a mannequin."

"But..." the intrepid soul might start to argue.

"What I'd really like to be," Sara'd say then, "is a genuine tatterdemalion. You know—all patches and loose bits?"

Blowing the dust off the newest layer that the box had to offer, she certainly felt real, if not a complete ragamuffin. She'd just managed to put three finger-wide streaks of dirt on her cheek and breathed in a cloud of dust at the same time. Coughing, she dug out the latest treasure—a wind-up plastic bear that would have beaten its tiny drum if its drumsticks weren't broken off, its key lost, and—she rattled it speculatively—its innards not a jumble of loose bits. She considered throwing it out, glanced at Mr. Tistle, then found she didn't have the heart. She wrote 10¢ on a sticker, stuck it on the bottom of its foot, and tried again. A brass ashtray joined the bear (75¢), then a saucerless teacup (50¢), a tin whisk (15¢), and a postcard of the Chateau Laurier in a wooden frame ($2.50—because of the frame).

It must be time for lunch, she thought as she reached in again.

This time she came up with a parcel wrapped in brown paper. The Scotch tape that held the end flaps down were yellow and brittle with age. Pretending it was Christmas, or her birthday, she squeezed and shook it about a bit. Then, when she couldn't guess, she opened it.

Inside was a framed picture and a small leather bag that looked like it was made of tanned moosehide. Its drawstrings were tied in a knot. Well, this was nice, she thought, looking the bag over. She could use it as a changepurse, seeing how she'd lost her old one last night somewhere between leaving the store and reaching home.

She set the bag aside to look at the picture. It was a pen-and-ink line drawing that had been painted with watercolors. The frame was a white wood that she couldn't place—a hardwood, at any rate, with a very fine grain. The picture was of two men sitting across from each other in a woodland glade. Though the painting was small, there was a lot of detail packed into it. The forest reminded Sara of Robert Bateman's work—the tree trunks were gnarled and had a barky texture; the leaves seemed separate and exact. The grass blades, the rough surface of the big stone at the edge of the clearing were all intricately rendered.

She turned her attention to the men. One was an Indian. He sat cross-legged, with a small ceremonial drum on his knee, his thick black hair hanging down either side of a square-featured face in two beaded braids. His leggings and shirt were of a plain doeskin; an ornamental band of colored beads and dentalium shells formed the shirt's collar. His eyes, against the coppery tan of his skin, were a startling blue.

Sara sat back and held the painting farther away for a moment. The detail was incredible. Each bead in the Indian's braids was a different color. She was amazed at the artist's skill, for she'd tried painting once and had given it up as a hopeless cause. But the experience left her with a sense of awe whenever she came across something this good. Bending closer again, she studied the Indian's companion.

He was obviously Caucasian, for all that the artist had given him a dark tan, and didn't look anything like the first explorers or *coureurs de bois* that Sara remembered from her history books (though why she thought to date the scene didn't occur to her at that moment). He looked older than the Indian, with grey streaks in his red hair. His clothing was leather as well— as primitive as his companion's but obviously of a different culture. Around his neck was a leather thong holding a curious Y-shaped object. By his knee was what looked for all the world like a small Celtic harp. His eyes, Sara noted with a sense of satisfaction, were as green as her own, though why that should please her, she couldn't say.

The two men were sharing a pipe—the Indian held it, smoke streaming upward in a long spiral, and was passing it to the red-haired man. It was probably a peacepipe, Sara decided. She searched for a signature, but could find nothing to identify the artist. Sighing, she laid it aside and had a look at the pouch that had shared the painting's package. Maybe something in it would give her a clue.

Untying the knot, she shook the pouch's contents onto the countertop. Curious, she thought, examining the objects that came to light. There was a curved claw, its pointed end too dull to be a cat's. More like a dog's . . . or a wolf's. She turned it over in her fingers and decided from its size that it had belonged to something smaller. Like a fox.

Next was a bundle of tiny brown feathers, tied together with leather. Then kernels of dried corn, ranging in color from a very dark brown through rust to yellow, that were threaded on another bit of leather. A rounded pebble, with thin layers of what looked like quartz running through it, followed. The last two objects were the strangest yet.

One was a flat disc made of bone. Holding it up to her eyes, she could make out a faint trace of design on either side. On one was a pair of stag's horns, each point carefully delineated, on the other a quarter moon. Around the edge of each side ran a design that was worn so much it was almost impossible to make out. She held it under the lamp that served to light her desk and squinted, then finally dug a magnifying glass out of

a drawer and studied the disc properly. The designs jumped
out under magnification. They were intertwining bands of Celtic
ribbonwork.

She sat back and thought about that, laying both magnifying
glass and disc on the counter in front of her. Now here was
something to dream about if ever there was. The disc was about
the size of a checker and well worn, rounded like a fat button.
What had it been used for?

The last object was a small ball of hardened clay, about the
size of the large marbles she used to play with in grade school.
Poking experimentally at the clay, a piece flaked off to reveal
a dull gleam like brassy metal. A little pinprick of excitement
ran up Sara's spine as she carefully broke away the clay. When
she was done, she held in her hand a tiny ring, about a quarter-
inch wide, with, she discovered when she investigated it under
the magnifying glass, the same spiraling ribbonwork that she'd
found on the bone disc. Weird. She hefted the ring in her hand,
decided it was made of gold and tried it on. It was a perfect
fit for the ring finger of her left hand.

She admired it for a moment or two, then had a sudden
vision of cursed rings that couldn't be removed and tugged it
off. When it lay in her hand again, she laughed at her overactive
imagination and set the ring down with the rest of the pouch's
contents. What a strange find, she thought, smiling at her luck.

Sara was the sort of person who thought a lot about luck.
"Find a penny, pick it up; all the day you'll have good luck."
She always did, no matter how tarnished or grungy the coin
was. She never walked under ladders, nor let a black cat cross
her path, sometimes circling a whole block just to avoid that
invisible trail of ill chance. She always sent all twenty copies
of a chain letter on, for all that she was sure it was a con job.
Walking along a streambed, she'd pick one smoothed pebble
out of hundreds and keep it in her pocket for months. For luck.

And now there was this.

What it looked like was someone's collection of luck. The
claw, the pebble, the feathers, corn and bone disc—they were
the sorts of things you might expect to find in an Indian's
medicine bag. Except Indians didn't use Celtic ribbonwork,
nor did they have gold rings. At least not in those days.

This time she stopped and wondered why she assumed it
was so old. There was really no way that she could put a date
to either the painting or the pouch . . . but she *knew* they were
old. She just did. The intensity of that knowing gave her a

queer feeling. She glanced at the painting again. A shaman and a Celtic bard, she thought.

Looking away, she blinked rapidly a few times and took a deep breath. Okay, it was old. Time to move on to more practical things. Whatever else the pouch had offered, there hadn't been a clue to the identity of the artist. She looked at the side of the box to see if Jamie had bothered to note where they'd gotten the box. Printed in his neat handwriting, with a magic marker, was:

FROM THE ESTATE OF
DR. ALED EVANS

Aled Evans. A Welshman, if the name was anything to go by. Sara tried to picture what he'd looked like. Sort of Albert Schweitzerish? She shrugged and studied the painting again, bending so close that her nose was just a few inches away from it.

For a moment everything wavered around her. She had the decidedly weird sensation that the store had vanished, to be replaced by the forest in the painting. The feeling came over her with a razor-sharp acuteness—so suddenly that it took her breath away. She could sense the gnarled cedar thickets and the thick grass of the glade, the tall pines sweeping skyward on every side of her, their dark green points stabbing the clouds. The rich pungent odor of dark loam filled her nostrils.

Startled, she looked up, half expecting the image to remain and the store to be gone. But the shop was still there, as cluttered as ever. Outside, the afternoon drizzle continued to mist down, slicking the streets and spraying the windows with a million tiny droplets. Silly Wizard were just finishing off a selection of jaunty reels. Nothing had changed. Except maybe in her, for to her eyes the store seemed vague, lacking the clear definition of the forest she'd just seen, felt, smelled. . . .

Her pulse beat a quick tattoo. She glanced at the painting again, expecting the sensation to return, but the painting remained what it was—an image of ink lines and watercolor in a wooden frame. Strange. She pushed the pouch's contents around with a finger and shook her head. Just for a moment there, it'd seemed that she'd really been someplace else. Maybe she was coming down with the flu.

At that moment the tiny bell above the front door jingled

and the real world intruded on her speculations in the unmistakable shape of Geraldine Hathaway. She stood in the doorway with her back to Sara, shaking out her umbrella, then closing it up with a snap. Sara stifled a groan.

"Well, Ms. Kendell," Miss Hathaway said. Her glasses clouded up with condensation and she took them off, rummaged in her purse for a handkerchief, and wiped them before continuing. "How is business today?"

"Quiet," Sara said. Or at least it had been.

"Ah, well. The weather, you know." The glasses returned to her nose and the handkerchief to its purse. "I see," she added, studying the litter on the countertop, "that you have some new stock. Anything that might be of interest to me?"

"Hard to say," Sara replied. "It's mostly junk."

"Well, you know what they say. What's junk to some . . ." Her voice trailed off as she neared the counter.

Sara stifled another groan. She'd yet to figure out what made Geraldine Hathaway tick. The only time she ever seemed to want to purchase something was when it was being held for someone else. Then she'd wave her checkbook about and argue until Sara felt like wringing her neck.

"Oh, I say. What's this?" Miss Hathaway picked up the gold ring that had come from the medicine bag. "How much is this?"

"Its not for sale," Sara said and braced herself for the worst.

"Nonsense. Everything is for sale in an establishment such as this. There's no need to play coy with me. I'll give you a good price for it. Say fifteen dollars?"

I'm not angry, Sara told herself, and I won't get angry. The customer's alway's right. It pays to be polite. God, what rubbish! If she never saw Miss Hathaway again it'd be too soon.

"Well?" Miss Hathaway demanded. "Don't grit your teeth, girl. It's an irritating habit. Have you got a box for it?"

"I'm afraid it's not for sale," Sara replied evenly. "First off, it's solid gold—"

"Why so it is! Twenty dollars then, and not a penny more."

"And secondly, it's mine, and I don't want to sell it."

"That's hardly a very businesslike attitude."

One, two, three. Deep breath. "Look," Sara tried. "I don't want to sell it."

"Well then, you shouldn't have it on display in your store."

"It wasn't on display. I was sitting at the counter here while

I was—" She shook her head. "It doesn't matter what I was doing with it. I'm not selling it and that's final."

Miss Hathaway glared at her. "Well, that's a fine way to talk. I've got a good mind to report you to the Better Business Bureau. First you have merchandise offered for sale and you refuse to sell it. Then—"

"That's my right!" Sara cried, her voice rising with her temper. "If I don't want to sell something, I don't have to. I don't care if you go to Parliament Hill and get a bill passed saying I've got to sell it. You still won't get it."

"And then," Miss Hathaway continued, "you're extremely rude in the bargain."

"Rude? *Me?*"

Sara put a sudden clamp on her temper. She breathed slowly to steady herself and began again.

"Miss Hathaway," she said as politely as she could, "I'm not going to sell this ring and there's no point in arguing about it." She pried the ring from the woman's hands. "Thank you. And now in future, perhaps you'd care to do your shopping someplace else? I really don't need this sort of aggravation."

"Aggravation? Why!" For one blessed second Miss Hathaway was speechless. Then: "I demand to see the manager."

"I am the manager."

"The owner then."

"I'm the owner as well," Sara lied.

She could just imagine Jamie being confronted with an enraged Geraldine Hathaway. He wouldn't speak to her for a week.

"Then . . . then . . ."

Sara came around from behind the counter and, taking the woman by the arm, steered her towards the door.

"We're just closing," she said.

"It's only two o'clock!"

"For lunch. Goodbye, Miss Hathaway."

They got as far as the door before the woman made her final stand.

"I demand to be treated with some respect!" she cried.

Sara couldn't hold back any longer. "Out, out, out!" she shouted, opening the door and almost bodily shoving Miss Hathaway through it.

On the sidewalk, Miss Hathaway opened her umbrella with an angry snap and glared at Sara. "You won't see me in here again," she said loudly, hoping to attract the attention of a passerby. Unfortunately, the drizzle was keeping most people off the streets and the sidewalk was empty.

"Well, thank God for that," Sara replied and slammed the door shut.

She locked it, turned the "Open" sign around so that it read "Closed" from outside and stomped back to her stool. She sat there fuming for long moments until the whole scene had repeated itself in her mind. Then she began to giggle. Well! She never thought she'd have the nerve to do that. Wait'll she told Jamie.

She opened her hand and looked down at the ring that had caused the whole fuss. It *was* hers, she decided. That was one of the nice things about operating The Merry Dancers. Her rooms at home were as cluttered as the store, filled with odd things that'd caught her fancy. The painting and the pouch's contents would be right at home there. She ran a finger along the frame of the painting. Who *had* the artist been? She looked at the side of the box once more.

"Dr. Aled Evans," she murmured, and decided to give Jamie a call to see if he remembered where he'd gotten the box or if he knew who Dr. Evans had been.

She remembered Jamie saying something this morning about *having* to get that damned article for *International Wildlife* finished, so he'd probably be at his desk in the Postman's Room. She dug the phone out from the shelf it shared with her coffee thermos and a stack of old historicals that she'd meant to give away ages ago, but never quite got around to. Setting the phone down on the countertop, she dialed the number and started to put the pouch's contents back as she waited for Jamie to answer.

"Mmm?" he said, seven rings later.

"Hi, Jamie. Finished that article yet?"

"Oh, hello, Sairey. Almost. I'm having trouble summing up. How the hell do you sum up mushrooms?"

"You have them for dinner."

"Fun-nee."

"Guess who I threw out of the store today."

Jamie laughed. "David Lindsay, the well-known Australian explorer?"

"Nope. Geraldine Hathaway."

"You didn't."

"I did."

"Good for you!" he said."

"*And* I've been working hard all afternoon—cleaning out the storerooms."

"For this you interrupt a genius at his labor?"

"A genius would know how to sum up an article on mushrooms."

"Keep it up and we'll have you for dinner, you little wretch."

Sara laughed. She rolled the ring back and forth in the palm of her hand and, checking the side of the box to make sure she had the name right, asked:

"Jamie, do you know a Dr. Aled Evans? That's A-L-E-D."

"I knew a Dr. Evans. He was a history professor at Carleton who died a few years ago. In '76. Why do you ask?"

"Well, one of the boxes that I'm going through has 'From the Estate of Dr. Aled Evans' written on its side. Was he Welsh?"

"Born in Wales, but he grew up in Toronto. He moved up here when the university offered him a position in '63."

"How come we've got a box of his effects in the back of the store?"

"Ah, well. I got to know Aled quite well, as it happens. When he died he left me everything he had. He didn't have any close family, except for some distant cousins in Wales, and he didn't want to leave a lifetime's treasures with total strangers. Most of it—the furniture and books and the like— are scattered through the House, but there were a few boxes of junk that I just stored in the back of the shop.

"I'd planned to sell them, but I didn't have the heart to go through them. I'd forgotten they were even there. I haven't thought of Aled in a long time. Funny you should mention him. He used to love mushrooms."

"Would you rather I just left all this stuff in the back, then?"

"No. There's no real point in keeping it around. I'm sure Aled wouldn't have wanted me to hang onto that stuff. It was the books and artifacts that he was most concerned about. There can't be much of interest in those boxes anyway."

"Even in the desolate Arctic tundra, there are treasures to be found. . . ." Sara said with a smile.

"What?"

"I said, you'd be surprised. I've found the most beautiful painting—pen and ink with a watercolor wash. Was he an artist?"

"Not that I knew."

"And there was something else—the neatest thing. It looks like an Indian medicine bag. You know. A little leather pouch with all sorts of odd things in it. A fox's claw, some feathers and corn kernels. But the most interesting things are a bone disc with some designs carved on it and a little gold ring."

"A *gold* ring?"

"Umhmm. It was inside a ball of clay. When I picked away at it, the ball fell apart and there it was."

"Strange. Though Aled always did have a bent for curiosities—especially anything with an anthropological slant to it. He loved old things—*really* old things—like Aztec pottery and arrowheads and the like. That weird clay demon-gourd you've got in your sitting room came from his collection."

Something clicked in Sara's mind.

"I remember," she said. "I just didn't connect it till now. I think I met him—just before I went to Europe. Was he the tall, reedy sort of fellow with a big bushy moustache like Yosemite Sam's?"

"Yosemite Sam? Such a lyrical description. For this I put you through college?"

"I never went to college, ninnyhammer."

"Well, you can't blame me for that."

There was a pause in the conversation that lasted for the space of a few heartbeats.

"Well?" Sara asked. "Was it him?"

"Indeed it was," Jamie replied. "I was just thinking about him. He used to come around the House quite a lot in the old days—to use the Library and play chess. He won fifty-three consecutive games from me."

Sara gazed idly at the knick-knacks spread across the countertop. "Did you know that he had a plastic wind-up bear?" she asked.

"Did *you* know," Jamie replied, "that I've still got to get this bloody article done? At the risk of seeming rude. . . ."

"Very rude. But that's okay. Just don't come down to the shop or I'll toss you out on your ear like I did Miss Hathaway. I'm feeling very fierce today."

Jamie laughed. "Will you be home for dinner? Blue's been in the kitchen all day concocting some wild Mexican dish."

"Without mushrooms?"

"I don't want to look at another mushroom for at least a year."

"Then I'll be home. I think I might close up early again. It's shitty outside and the only customer I've had all afternoon's been dear Miss Hathaway."

"Okay. Bring the painting with you, if you would. I'd like to have a look at it. And bring that 'medicine bag' or whatever it is."

"Will do. See ya."

"'Bye."

Sara cradled the phone and regarded her find once more. She finished returning everything to the pouch except for the ring. As she went to put it away as well, she shrugged, then slipped it on her finger. For luck.

Going to the front door, she unlocked it and, after looking up and down the street to make sure Geraldine Hathaway wasn't lurking somewhere, turned the sign around so that it read "Open." She might as well finish the box she was working on before she went home. She put a new tape in the cassette machine and the soft tones of Pachelbel's *Canon* drifted through the store. Humming along, she went back to her chore. The box, which grew progressively dustier with each subsequent layer, had no more wonders like the medicine bag in it. At one point she paused long enough to roll a cigarette, light it, take a couple of puffs, then set it aside as she plunged back into her work. Unlike a ready-made cigarette, it promptly went out.

As she was nearing the second-to-last layer, the bell above the door jingled. Sara started, then smiled when she saw that it wasn't Geraldine Hathaway come back for round two, but Julie Simms, a waitress who worked at Kamals, a restaurant at the corner of Third and Bank.

"Are you on your break?" Sara asked, taking the opportunity to relight her cigarette.

"Mmhmm. A big fifteen minutes. God, but it's dull today."

Sara laughed. Julie was her best friend. When Sara'd first met her, she'd thought Julie a little cynical—mostly because she had a look in her eyes that lent a certain sardonic quality to everything she said—but Sara soon discovered that this was far from the case.

Julie worked hard, dividing her time between Kamals, two morning courses at Carleton, and supporting an eight-year-old son. She had a madcap sense of humor and a willingness to give just about anything at least one try. They'd taken all sorts of artsy crafts courses together and took a perverse delight in giving each other their latest creations for Christmas and birthdays. This peaked last year when Julie gave Sara a four-by-two-foot macramé wall hanging of an owl with big polished wooden beads for eyes. Sara had yet to forgive her and was still planning her revenge.

"You look busy for a change," Julie said, shrugging off her raincoat. "Jamie been cracking down on you?" She looked around for a place to hang it and settled on the knob of the door that led to the storerooms.

Sara shook her head. "I'm just sorting through junk." She pushed aside her work and set two coffee mugs down on the counter. "Want some?"

"Anything. So long as I can get off my feet for a few minutes. God, I hate the day shifts. You stand around just as much, only you don't get nearly the same tips."

"I haven't any cream. Forgot to pick some up on my way in this morning."

"That's okay." Julie settled down in the visitor's chair behind the counter and stretched out her legs. "Ah! I think I'll just vegetate here for the rest of the afternoon. Mind?"

"Be my guest." Sara poured coffee from her thermos, handed Julie a cup, and relit her cigarette for the third time. "The tips are even shittier here, though."

"Talking about dung—I saw old Miss Hathaway stomping by the restaurant earlier. Was she in to visit you?"

"I threw her out."

"You . . . ?" Julie broke into laughter and spilled her coffee before she could set it down on the counter. "I don't believe it."

"It's true. She drives me crazy."

"She drives everybody crazy."

"This time I had to do it. It was either that or wring her neck."

"I think I'd settle on wringing her neck. It's so much more permanent." She waited expectantly for a moment, then added: "Well? Aren't you going to give me the scoop?"

Sara moved her chair conspiratorially closer and did just that.

"Serves her right!" Julie said when Sara was done. "And what a find! Can I have a look?"

Sara tugged the ring off and passed it over.

"It's definitely gold," Julie said, turning it around in her palm. "It looks old."

"The box came from the estate of a history professor that Jamie knew."

"But this looks *really* old. And look at the color. It must be eighteen karat at least."

She held it up beside the wedding band she wore to forestall being asked out for dates while she was on the job. It had a fifty percent success rate. Beside the wedding band, Sara's ring had a positive glow of richness to it.

"It looks kind of brassy," Sara said.

"That's because the gold content's so high. Mine's only ten karat." Julie hefted the ring before passing it back. "It's heavy, too. I wonder how old it is?"

"A hundred years?"

Julie shrugged. "You should get it dated. I wonder where you can get that done. At a jeweler's, I suppose. Or the museum."

"I'll ask Jamie," Sara said. "He'd know."

Julie nodded. She picked up her coffee, then glanced at her watch. "Oh, no! Look at the time!"

She took a gulp and bustled to her feet, pulling a face as she dragged her raincoat from the doorknob.

"I don't know if I'll last the day," she moaned, then brightened. "What're you doing on Saturday?"

"I don't know. Why?"

"I've got the night off. I thought I'd spring for a sitter for Robbie and take in a couple of sets at Faces."

"Who's playing?"

"Who cares? I just want to go out and have somebody get *me* a beer for a change. I can't stay late though. I'm taking Robbie to my mum's on Sunday."

"I'll let you know before the end of the week. Okay?"

"Sure. See ya."

The doorbell jingled again and she was gone.

Sara stared at the clutter that was taking over the countertop and wished she'd asked Julie what the time was. She went on a quest for her clock and found it behind her typewriter. Three-thirty. She'd give it another half-hour and then go home. Flipping over the cassette to the side with Delius on it, she got back to work.

When she'd reached the bottom of the box and put everything away on its appropriate table, it was four-thirty. She stuffed the painting and medicine bag into her knapsack, buttoned up her coat and left the store.

Halfway down the block she paused, trying to remember if she'd tested the front door after she'd locked it. Whenever she left the store she invariably stopped somewhere in the first few blocks to think about it. Convincing herself that she had, indeed, tested the door, she went on. By the time she reached home, the momentary sensation of dislocation she'd experienced with the painting had been relegated to a cobwebby corner of her mind. But the painting itself and the medicine bag were still fascinating curiosities and she was looking forward to showing them to Jamie.

Chapter Two

HOME was Tamson House.

It took up a large city block and was designed at the turn of the century by Anthony Tamson, Jamie's grandfather, who, according to his journals, had been looking for "a curious home, reminiscent of a labyrinth, if you will, but with a sense of warmth. Gothic, but not severely so. And it must have towers." It had, in fact, three of them. Sara's rooms were in the northwest tower, where Patterson Avenue first touches Central Park.

From O'Conner Street, one of the main downtown thoroughfares that as it approaches Tamson House takes on a more residential attitude, the House appeared to be a block of old-fashioned townhouses set kittycorner to each other with not so much as a fraction of an inch between them. They were a facade, for inside the House ran the length of the block in one long tumble of rooms and hallways, two stories high (in some places three, not including the attics), with steep gables from cornice to ridge, well worn eaves overhung in places with vines, and the odd dormer window. Each front door was serviceable and opened into a hall.

Along the sides of the block, following Patterson on the north and Clemow Avenue on the south, similar facades were presented. The House was not so wide here and, though only one or two of these doors opened, all the mail slots worked. Jamie delighted in the use of many names for his correspondence and used an equal number of addresses with them. Behind these facades were still more rooms that ran the length of the block, connecting the front of the House facing O'Connor, with the back that looked out on Central Park and beyond it, Bank Street.

Central Park was a curiosity in itself, though the Tamsons

weren't responsible for its vagaries. It was a riverlike width of green that had its start at Chamberlain Avenue near the Queensway, and ran southeasterly towards the Rideau Canal, broken only once by Bank Street and again by Clemow, before driving under O'Connor to the canal. Because of the purposefulness of its route, it cut a corner from the rectangle that Tamson House would have made, giving it, from a bird's perspective, the semblance of a crookedly cut piece of pie with the point end broken off.

The park was home to pigeons and sparrows, joggers, sunworshipers, winos, at least one bag lady and shrill-voiced children in the summer. In the winter it took on an austerity that was both lonely and contemplative. Snow covered the benches and trees like the white sheets on a deserted house's furniture, and the few hardy birds that managed to eke out a living subsisted more on the neighborhood's generosity in the way of bread crumbs and bird seed than through any particular talents of their own.

There was a park in the center of the House's block as well, though this wasn't open to the public and, indeed, few even knew it existed. Tamson House was one of those curiosities that was only noticed by out-of-towners. Locals rarely gave it a second glance. The park took up four acres, surrounded on all sides by the walls of the House. There were birch and oak growing in it, juniper and cedar, some apple trees and berry bushes, tended undergrowth that included hawthorns, lilacs and roses, a vegetable garden, and a plethora of flowering plants.

The whole of it was lovingly cared for by a live-in gardener named Theodore Burchin who insisted that everyone call him Fred. He was a tall, awkward-looking individual, cut from the same cloth as Cervantes's Don Quixote, complete with an unruly mane of grey-white hair and a wispy handlebar moustache, stork-thin neck and limbs, and a proclivity to tilt at his own personal windmills—which included anything and anyone who didn't tender plants the considerable respect he felt was their due.

The garden had the disconcerting tendency, once one was in it, to appear much larger than its actual acreage and Fred was the only person who knew it thoroughly. He could often be seen apologizing to shrubs as he was trimming them, or wandering along the cobblestoned paths that connected the House's many garden-side doors. The paths met together at a grassy knoll in the center of the garden where a fountain was surrounded by benches, like royalty surrounded by its courtiers. Statues hid in amongst the greenery, gnomes and nymphs and fabulous beasts that peeped out from between the leaves or appeared suddenly around a turn in a path to startle a newcomer.

Sara had grown up in Tamson House. Her parents, Jamie's sister Gillian and John Kendell of Kendell Communications, had died in a car crash when she was six and left a stipulation in their will that she was to be left in her uncle's care. Jamie, once the initial shock of their death, and the fact they had entrusted Sara to him, had worn off, had taken to his new duties like a doting father.

As the years went by their relationship progressed from a father/daughter affinity, through the difficulties of Sara's puberty and her subsequent need for self-discovery, to what they were now: good friends. Jamie had always made time for Sara; he knew the importance of this from his own boyhood. His father Nathan, a widower soon after Gillian's birth, had always had time for his children. He had also known when to leave them alone, giving them a chance to grow. With Sara, Jamie thought he could have done worse than follow his father's example.

The surviving Kendells, John's brother Peter and the matriarch Norma, had tried to take Sara from Tamson House at first ("To give her a decent, *Christian* upbringing"), but the case never went to court once they found that neither Jamie nor Sara displayed any interest in the Kendell empire and were content simply to let any accrued stipends and interests be reinvested in the companies in question.

Jamie had no need for their money as he had both his father's inheritance and his own publishing efforts to pay his way. To his thinking, the various schemes and projects that the Kendells busied themselves with were nothing more than the moves in some sprawling game of Monopoly. He signed a paper naming Peter Kendell trustee of Sara's holdings, while Peter signed one waiving all claims to Sara's guardianship. Jamie, watching the Kendell family lawyer gather up the papers in his briefcase, could almost feel their relief from where he sat.

Sara, nine at the time, was so obviously cut from the same cloth as her uncle that the Kendells knew they'd have trouble coping with her upbringing. Having successfully negotiated for what they'd really come for, they quietly bowed out of Sara's life to reappear only on birthdays, her high school graduation day, and the odd time during the Christmas holidays.

Sara's rooms in the northwest tower were her private refuge from the world at large, as well as from the constant influx of houseguests that helped to fill the endless rooms of Tamson House. She had a sitting room that she, surprisingly, kept neat as a pin, with a working fireplace, comfortable chairs, a sideboard and a china cabinet, her stereo components along with a haphazard collection of records stored in three apple crates, a Persian rug with matching drapes courtesy of The Merry Dancers, and a scattering of small tables. Windows overlooked Patterson Avenue, the Bank Street side of Central Park as well as that portion that bordered Clemow. A door led off into her workshop-cum-studio that was as cluttered as the shop. Its main furnishing was a long worktable running along one wall with a window above it overlooking the House's gardens.

Two other doors led out of her workroom—one to a washroom, complete with an antique bathtub and brass fixtures to match the tub's clawed feet, the other to her bedroom.

This was her sanctum. In it was a cedar chest that held all her treasures and luck, a four-poster bed with two pillows and a flower-patterned comforter, a Laskin classical guitar in its case by the window with a Martin D-35 steel-string guitar balanced on top, a highbacked oak chair with a cushioned seat, a large wardrobe filled with jeans, sweaters, Danskins and the odd Indian-print skirt, and a dresser. A solid wall of bookcases was half full of books ranging from popular bestsellers through mysteries and fantasies to turn-of-the-century Irish authors and fairytale collections, the other half crammed with the friends of her childhood—a ragged-eared stuffed bear, a doll whose eyes didn't close anymore no matter how often you tipped her, and a thin-limbed patched rabbit—as well as an array of knick-knacks and curios.

It was there that she arrived after work, breathless from taking the stairs two at a time. She divested herself of her coat, exchanged her shoes for a pair of moccasins; then, rolling up and lighting a cigarette, she dug about in her knapsack for her latest treasures. Smoke wreathed about her head as she waltzed about the room, holding up the painting to see where she'd put it.

She had a print of Bateman's "Bull Moose" hanging in her bedroom, across from a copy of Gainsborough's "Market Cart." The remaining wall was covered with a haphazard collage of photographs of Julie, Blue, Jamie and sundry houseguests and friends. The walls of the workroom were plastered with posters for folk festivals, craft fairs and various pop groups. In the sitting room was a copy of Waterhouse's "Lady of Shallot," an untitled watercolor by Blue of a fox peering through a hedge, Durer's "Hare"—torn from an old art book and stuck in a frame that she'd commandeered from the shop—a picture of Jamie and herself when she was fourteen and all tangle-haired and awkward, and a photo of her cat Tuck when he was still a kitten.

She finally decided to hang the painting over the night table in her bedroom. With that decision out of the way, she went looking for Jamie, wondering as she did who she'd run into. You could meet almost anyone in Tamson House.

At various times there'd been a swarm of poets in the left-wing study; a conjurer in the garden trying to charm roses from a lilac bush—much to Fred's dismay; a professor of folklore from the University poring through her uncle's library, making small excited sounds under his breath as he came across some out of print volume that the University library didn't even have a reference to; a stripper and a ballet dancer who, having moved all the furniture out of one of the second-floor sitting rooms, were comparing moves; a Bible student who'd mistaken "Tamson" for "Samson" and wandered around for a few days looking for relics.

One evening a whole troupe of carnies descended on the House, baffling everyone with their conversation, a studied mixture of L.A. aphorisms and metaphors from the circus, all delivered completely deadpan. It wasn't until weeks later that Sara discovered they'd all been higher than kites having, earlier in the day, partaken of some silvery tablets formulated by a Swedish scientist and left behind in his makeshift laboratory in one of the pantries before he'd moved on. The carnies' room had tenaciously held onto the distinctive smell of greasepaint for weeks until Sara found the broken jars of theater makeup behind the sofa and cleaned them up.

Tamson House, she'd decided, was like Fear & Loathing in Ottawa. Hunter S. Thompson would have been very much at home. In fact, if all they said about him was true, she was surprised that she hadn't already run into him in one room or another.

Without her rooms as a refuge, she would have gone quietly mad a long time ago. But there weren't always Houseguests— at least not always the stranger ones—and most stayed only briefly. Weeks at a time might go by with only the regulars to be found in their usual haunts. Only a very few had stayed so long that, for all intents and purposes, they lived there.

These few ended up taking some duty or another. Fred was the gardener. Blue, an ex-biker, had become Security Chief. He was living in the Firecat's Room these days with an artist from Ohio who specialized in Japanese brushwork. Completing the present roster was Sam Pattison, an author who, like Sara, had sold short stories that had yet to appear in print. He had the air of a delicatessen owner about him. He was a short bustling man in his mid-forties with a rounded balding head and frizzy black hair. He took care of the Library, though he spent most of his time making tiptap typewriter sounds on his Olympia and filling the wastebaskets with sheets of crumpled-up manuscripts. Lately he'd taken to writing scripts for the CBC Television series *The King of Kensington*, and wouldn't listen to anyone who told him that it had been taken off the air.

·Jamie paid little attention to the Houseguests unless they sought him out and Sara soon learned to do the same. When she asked him about them once, he'd only shrugged.

"They need some place to be," he'd replied. "Lord knows, the House is big enough. They come for the same reason that you and I and the regulars stay. To get away from the world outside for awhile.

"I can't deny them that. They're like us, Sairey. Different from the norm. And, as this is a place where difference is the norm, they can relax. There's no need to try and fit in because everything fits in here."

That was what Sara liked best about Tamson House: that it didn't seem to be a part of the world outside its walls. Stepping over its threshold was like stepping into a place where everything you knew had to be forgotten to make way for new rules. It was here, when the world outside lost all its secrets and seemed to unfold around her, flat and unending, every surprise and wonder ironed out of it, here in the maze of rooms that she could find mystery again and rejuvenate her own sense of wonder.

And somehow, for all that it seemed a place where only chaos could govern, some unspoken rule had people cleaning up after themselves and making sure that nothing in the House was damaged, be it fixture or guest. The broken jars in the carnies' room had been the exception rather than the rule. Sara doubted that they even realized that they'd left them behind.

As Blue put it: "It's like the House takes care of itself, you know? It does weird things to people so that nobody messes up. It's funny how it works out that way."

All in all, Tamson House with its twisting corridors, endless rooms and secret passageways and stairwells, the facades it presented to the world at large and the hidden garden inside its walls, was a curious place, suited to its curious owner.

"Curious," Jamie said, hearing Sara out.

She'd found him in the Postman's Room. It was called that because once during a postal strike, their postman had spent three weeks in it sorting old letters and muttering to himself about the need for order and how greed and avarice were deadly sins, though he later accepted his raise and the resumption of his normal duties without protest. Jamie was just getting ready for a before-dinner cup of tea that was steeping in a pot at his desk when Sara came in. His article on mushrooms was stacked in a tidy pile of manuscript pages on a table beside his chair.

Jamie was a small man, but what he lacked in height he made up for in intensity. His clear grey eyes were as piercing as a peregrine's and the impression he usually gave was of a tightly coiled spring about to burst loose. His hair was grey and thinning on top, his full beard bushy and still retaining some of its original chestnut color. He tended to wear brown corduroys, a peculiarly Irish tweed vest—basically a sports jacket without sleeves—a cotton shirt and loafers. He had an obsession for knowledge—not simply clear and provable facts, but other, more tenuous knowledge that was more intuitive than studied and therefore open to question . . . at least by those who might dispute the validity of any matter "not manifest or detectable by clinical methods alone." He'd been studious even as a boy, losing himself to the twists and turns of old riddles and older lore, living in his father's rambling House—inhabiting the tower where Sara now lived when Nathan was alive and inheriting the whole maze upon the old man's death. The stipends paid to him on the securities his father had left him were enough to keep the House in good repair and, with saving a bit here and there, he was able to travel when the fancy took him, broadening his world view in his endless quest for knowledge. Then he began to publish and earn a second income that tended to accumulate in the bank, garnering interest and growing year by year like a forest gone wild.

What those fat bank accounts proffered, to Jamie's way of thinking, was freedom. The freedom to worry away at the gigantic jigsaw puzzle that was the Great Mystery of the world without the need to waste valuable time providing for the roof over his head.

When he began, he wrote down every scrap he learned, first filling spiralbound notebooks, then a series of cloth journals the contents of which, like some Wiccan's Book of Shadows, would have had him up before the Inquisition were it still around. Finally he acquired a home computer. Among other uses, it stored past and present findings in its memory banks— a perplexity of information that only its electronic circuitry could hope to retain in any semblance of order, and then present on its viewscreen exactly this or that bit of data with all the cross-references appropriate to the given question.

He gave everything names. So the computer became Memoria. The file name for his findings was Aenigma. His code to reach that file was Rogare. The Latin names gave the whole affair, to his mind, a sense of order. Latin, he maintained, no longer a living language, had over the years atrophied into an irrevocable stability, degenerating into a stuffy warehouse of words for all the world's sciences. So why not his own? He called it Arcanology—the study of secrets.

His interest never flagged because he always felt himself to be on the verge of discovering the key that would unlock it all. The possibility that *an* answer, if not *the* answer, was close at hand kept him at his work. He had only to find it. It became his quest, his Grail. And what he did with his work was continue a Tamson tradition, for in the library, stored in glassed shelves, were his grandfather's journals—book upon book filled with a spidery, close handwriting—and his father's typewritten manuscripts bound together in folders.

His sister Gillian had never had an interest in anything esoteric. Always afraid of standing out or being different, and deeply embarrassed at the image her family presented to the world, she made it her life's work to cling to style and the swift vagaries of fashion. It still puzzled Jamie that she'd left Sara in his care. The only solution that came to his mind was that it was the one time she'd allowed some Tamsonishness to come to the fore and intuitively understood that for someone like Sara, even as a toddler, life in the House would be far more beneficial than the life Gillian had chosen for herself.

So, because Gillian was what she was, it was Jamie who inherited the House and a safety deposit box filled with securities—and other objects more curious and more valuable—while Gillian received the bulk of Nathan's considerable wealth. Neither of them found fault in their father's wisdom.

Combining her inheritance with the Kendell family fortune, Gillian and John's financial worth had had to be measured in terms of nine digits and employed the better part of Sourial & Landeau, Chartered Accountants, on a year-round basis simply to keep solvent. Much of this had been left to Sara upon their deaths who, tending more to Tamson temperament than the matter of fact business acumen of the Kendells, was baffled by it all. When she turned twenty-one she gained legal control of the Kendell empire, but she only went in to the offices a couple of times a year to put her signature on this or that form. Sizable payments appeared in her bank account on the 5th of every month in return for that small effort.

Now in the Postman's Room, Jamie's eyes glittered with interest as he studied the motley collection of objects that was Sara's find. He picked them up, one by one, and carefully scrutinized each for a long moment before going on to the next. At last he set them all down and began to refill his pipe.

Tea steamed in mugs on a low table between their chairs. Sara waited patiently, busying herself with the makings of a cigarette. She knew there was no rushing Jamie once he started pondering something.

The Postman's Room lent itself to contemplation. The walls were cloaked behind bookshelves, except for the west where a hearth and a mantle shared space with a sideboard and a rolltop desk, and part of the east where a window overlooked O'Connor. Set in the back of the desk was the viewscreen of Jamie's computer and, in front of it, the terminal with which he communicated to that mass of circuitry and micro-chips. Inside the desk, where the lefthand drawers had been, the main body of the computer hummed quietly through air vents, reviewing its storage perhaps, muttering to itself like an old man.

"I don't know what to make of this," Jamie said, once he had his pipe comfortably going again. "This alone is remarkable." He tapped the frame of the painting with the stem of his pipe. "Together with the contents of the medicine bag . . ." He shook his head and sent a stream of smoke drifting upward.

Sara sighed. She looked out the window and wondered, not for the first time, why she couldn't hear any of the street traffic from outside when the window was open. "There are some odd acoustics in this place," Jamie'd told her once, "and some odder rooms, when you come right down to it. I'm never sure when I open a door whether the room that's supposed to be there will be there. Though over the years I've learned to deal with it. Usually, or so I've found, the room you find yourself in is the one you really wanted in the first place."

Looking away from the window, she picked up the ring from the table and returned it to her finger.

"I suppose it's just a collection of curios," she ventured.

Jamie shook his head again. "No. There's more to them than that. It has the feeling of—I don't know—meaning, I suppose. The painting seems to draw one into it."

"That's exactly what I felt! Only it was more like the painting becoming more real than the store—just for that moment."

"So you said." Jamie puffed steadily at his pipe. "I suppose," he added, "I could take it 'round to Potter's in the morning. He might be able to identify the artist—or at least date it. I wonder, though. . . ."

"How so?"

Jamie raised his eyebrows. "A blue-eyed Indian? Sharing a pipe with what, to all intents and purposes, seems like a Celtic bard? While it would make a great illustration for one of Barry Fell's books. . . ." He frowned to himself. "I'm just not sure if our mystery painter has used some artistic license in his subject material, or if he was painting from life. You see—and I can't explain why I feel this way—to my mind, it seems as though it was painted from life."

A shiver of excitement played up Sara's spine.

"Who's Barry Fell?" she wanted to know.

"An American with the interesting theory that the Celts discovered North America long before even the Vikings did."

"And you think that somehow this artist—"

"Went back into time to capture a meeting between an Indian shaman and a Celtic bard?" Regretfully, Jamie shook his head. "I know it has the *feel* of both age and truth about it, but I'm afraid that's a little too farfetched—for all that it appeals to my sense of mystery. No. It's more likely he was at something like a Renaissance Faire and got a couple of fellows to pose for him. Let's wait and see what Potter says about it before we go scrabbling about for theories."

"What about the ring?"

"We'd have better luck with the bone disc," Jamie replied.

"I can take that to the museum to be carbon dated. The ring hasn't a jeweler's mark. Nothing. Just that design."

Sara twirled the ring around on her finger and looked thoughtful.

"Why do you think," she asked, "that someone'd go through all that trouble to hide it in a ball of clay?"

"Perhaps it was a ritual of some sort."

"I think it's a weird thing to do."

"That depends," Jamie said, "on your outlook. If the pouch is, in fact, a medicine bag, then everything in it is a charm of some sort. The other objects are reasonable enough in that respect. And as for the ring, well, I've never heard of anything like it. I'd have to do some research on it."

"What would you look under? Gold rings hidden in clay?"

"Lord knows." Jamie laughed and tapped the ashes from his pipe bowl. "I'll look into it after I've seen Potter and taken a run by the museum." Returning the bag's contents to their container, he added: "Want to have a look at my article?"

When she was done, Sara straightened the sheets and laid them on the table. "It's very good. Very tight. Informative." She grinned. "I loved the bit on page six where you were talking about 'mushrumps.' Adds a bit of piquancy. Or was that a typo?"

Jamie laughed. "You're an incorrigible snippet and I'll get you back for this. If you ever publish a book, I'll slip the publishers that photo of you with your crewcut for the dust-jacket."

"You wouldn't dare! Besides, I burned the negative."

"But not all the copies. *I* have one, hidden away for an occasion such as this."

"Oh, God! I give up. I confess. I'll do anything. Just throw it out, okay?"

Jamie put his article away and shrugged noncommittally.

"Perhaps," he said. "Let's go down to dinner and see what culinary delights Blue's concocted for us."

"About the photo, Jamie . . ."

"Did I tell you I ran into Russell today? He got that grant and starts rehearsals on Monday. I've been thinking of instituting a Tamson Grant, you know, and—"

Sara stamped her foot. "The picture!"

"I don't have a copy."

"You . . . ?"

Jamie grinned. "But I wish I did. We'll not see the likes of that again for a long time. How long did you wear that scarf on your head?"

"Oooh!" Words failed her.

Jamie attempted a repentant expression.

"Temper, temper," he murmured.

"I don't think I'm talking to you anymore," she replied and huffed out of the study, but by the time they made it down to the Silkwater Kitchen, they'd decided to settle their differences in a game of Go after dinner.

They found Blue busy at the stove, stirring the contents of a frying pan that filled the kitchen with a spicy smell. Sally Timmons, the Ohio artist, was busy setting the table. Sara stifled a grin at the incongruous picture Blue presented at the stove. He stood six two in his boots, wore faded grease-stained jeans with a T-shirt that said "Harley Davidson" pulled tight around his big shoulders, had a pierced left ear, six o'clock shadow that was about three days old, and long black hair pulled back in a ponytail. In contrast, Sally was petite, about Sara's size. She had shoulder-length brown hair, with bangs that touched her eyebrows, a heart-shaped face and what Sara called artist's eyes—shadowed and haunted-looking. She was wearing a print dress with an off-white smock overtop.

"Want to get the beer from the fridge?" Blue asked over his shoulder. He put the finishing touches on his hamburger in hot sauce and brought it to the table.

"Sure," Sara said. "Is there any juice?"

"Some pineapple on the second shelf. Behind the apples."

Then Fred and Sam showed up and they sat down to a dinner of tacos and spinach salad. Tacos were one of Blue's specialties, picked up when he lived on the Texas/Mexico border in the early seventies. The filling was so spicy that besides the beer and the juice they killed a big pitcher of ice water. Jamie insisted, as he always did, that he'd have scar tissue in his throat for the rest of his life, but they all agreed the meal was fabulous.

It was Sara's turn to wash up. Afterwards, she and Jamie had their game of Go. Sara had the white stones, Jamie the black. The game took almost three hours and ended with Sara forcing Jamie into a position where he could only give up his stones and not attack.

"I want a five-stone handicap next time," he said and Sara laughed.

Fred and Sam had returned to their own rooms and Sally

and Blue watched an old Bette Davis movie on the TV that ended about the same time as the Go game. While Sally went up to the Firecat's Room and Jamie to his study, Sara accompanied Blue on his rounds. Having accepted the position of Security Chief on his own initiative (it wasn't really necessary, but if it made him happy), Blue took his self-imposed duties very seriously. Every night before he went to bed, he went around the House to check things out.

"You don't know how easy a place like this would be to burgle," he told Sara.

"But if someone really wants to," Sara said, "a locked door or latched window isn't going to stop them. And besides, anyone's welcome here anyway."

"Not anyone," Blue insisted.

"Well, Jamie's never turned anyone away."

"The House makes its own decisions about who stays and who goes," Blue said.

It really seemed that way sometimes, Sara admitted to herself, but she took the opportunity to pounce on Blue's logic.

"Then there's no real need for you to do your rounds, is there?" she asked.

"Yeah, well . . . it makes me feel like I'm contributing something, you know? And if there ever *is* any trouble. . . ."

In recent memory, there'd only been trouble once. But Blue had handled it with frightening efficiency. An English woman had been staying with them—one of Jamie's literary contacts in London. She'd gone out in the evening and been followed back to the House by a couple of men who gave Darwin's theory of evolution undeniable credence. They'd hardly had a chance to lay a hand on her before Blue was there to convince them of the error of their ways. Both of them ended up in the hospital. The most surprising thing was that, for all Blue's biker image, he was normally as gentle as a lamb. Until something he cared for was threatened.

Sara thought about Blue as she got ready for bed. It was kind of scary knowing there was that capacity in him, even though he kept it in check. She'd watched him working out with his weights, the sweat glistening on his tattooed arms and his broad chest, the way his muscles corded and knotted as he worked the bench press. When he went at the punching bag, she was sure it was going to split under his blows. But scary or not, it was comforting to have him there should the need ever arise for his particular talents. And besides, she loved him like a big brother.

She'd had some of her best times with him, sitting around and talking, or watching a movie. He loved movies, from the old silent screen gems to *Raiders of the Lost Ark*. There was a true artistic streak in him as well. Whenever Sara took one of her courses with Julie, she ended up tutoring him as well, which helped her grasp the techniques better herself. There's nothing like teaching someone to see how much you know about something, Sara discovered. He'd tried everything from macrame to soft sculpture. He'd made the floppy-eared rabbit for her one Easter that was her favorite plush toy next to Mr. Tistle who now guarded The Merry Dancers for her.

He'd settled on watercolors as his best medium of expression, which probably explained why he and Sally got along so well. It was an odd sight to see the big galoot hunched over a delicate watercolor, the paintbrush looking like a toothpick in his big hands. His painting of the fox that hung in her room was as good as any professional could do.

She looked at it now, then remembered this afternoon's find. She'd forgotten to show it to him. Well, tomorrow was soon enough, she decided, and a huge yawn settled the matter. She went around flicking off the lights in her sitting room and the washroom, and headed for bed. Pulling the comforter up to her chin, her head no sooner hit the pillow than she was asleep.

Sara didn't dream often, of if she did, she rarely remembered more than the odd snatch. People who had long interesting dreams and remembered every detail the next day were a source of envious irritation to her. Julie was like that.

Be that as it may, she was no sooner asleep that night, than she found herself smack in the middle of one. She found herself in the glade depicted in the painting she'd discovered that afternoon. But where the painting was sharp-edged in its clarity, her dream had a murky texture to it and she moved through it in the way a swimmer might move through molasses.

The two men from the painting weren't present. In their place was a piece of brightly woven cloth, perhaps a foot square in size. There were designs woven into the material and, making her way slowly against the heavy air that dragged at her every movement, she finally stood close enough to crouch down and investigate it.

Dead center was a large circle with a symbol in it that she

recognized as a Celtic motif. She tried to think of what it was called. She even had an album cover with that design on it—some Breton group. An . . . An Triskell. As the name came to her she smiled. The symbol was a triskell, or triskellion, three curved branches radiating from a central triangular shape, enclosed by a circle. On the cloth, four bars came out of the circle making the whole thing look like some elaborate Celtic cross. A border of ribbonwork went around the edge of the cloth with intricate knotwork in each corner. She nodded to herself. It was like the ribbonwork on her ring.

In the way of dreams, Sara felt that she had all the time in the world, and yet not a second to spare. Strangely enough, she knew that she was dreaming as well—something she'd never experienced before. Weren't you supposed to wake up when you realized you were dreaming? At least that was what happened when she was daydreaming, an exercise that she had a lot of experience at.

The sense of calm urgency lifted her attention from the cloth to look around the glade. Empty, it still had a presence to it, as though the two figures from the painting were there, only not visible to her. Trying to recall the details of their features, all she came up with was a stag's head for the bard, and a bear's for the shaman. And no sooner had she pictured them, than they were on either side of her, oblivious to her presence, intent on each other.

Sara felt the first premonition that she might be in some sort of danger. It had nothing to do with the two men. (Men? Did you call things men when they had the heads of animals on top of their bodies instead of their own?) It was something else that set her nerves on edge. She searched the glade, but could find nothing. As her gaze returned to the men, she saw that the bear-headed one had taken a bag from his belt. He drew out a handful of small bone discs that were exact replicas of the one that Sara had found that afternoon.

The bear/shaman knelt by the cloth and, setting the bag aside, held the discs in his cupped hands. As Sara watched, he let them fall onto the cloth. They tumbled and spun, around and over, slow as drifting leaves, not a handful, but hundreds of yellowed bone discs. They filled her sight—a long tumble of ivory flickers, a never-ending stream that blurred into brown-grey, and she found herself standing alone in a featureless place.

There was nothing but mist all around her, above and below

hear Blue's record. It was a far-offish sound that had as much volume as the last of autumn's leaves rustling overhead, but was clear enough so that she could follow the melody. Humming along with it, she ambled on, nodding to statues when she came upon them, going where her feet led her and trying not to think anymore. The walking and humming were easy. Stopping herself from thinking was less so.

She reached the center of the garden and sat down on one of the benches. It was quiet here. Not even the guitar music reached this far. The fountain was still, turned off with the coming of colder weather. She looked up into the night sky, found Orion, Canis Major and the Little Dipper without much effort. The moon was too low for her to see now, lost somewhere in the west.

Gazing skyward helped calm her. Or at least it put things into perspective. She went over the day's events, from finding the painting and medicine bag through her evening in the House to her dream. Laid out before her like that, she saw that she'd been letting herself get carried away. Or at least letting her imagination run a little too freely. Which explained her nightmare.

There was something special about this afternoon's find. She twiddled the ring on her finger as she pondered it. There was no denying that this was one of those treasures that Jamie was always harping on about. The painting was a prize. The bag was a fascinating riddle. Its contents were both curious and, in the case of the ring, valuable. But that was as far as it went.

Still, she couldn't shake the niggling thought that it was all connected and that something else was about to happen, that some final key would appear to join all her half thoughts into something that, while it might not be understandable, would at least be in its entirety. Remembering her dream-monster, she had second thoughts about how desirable that might actually be. Now she understood a little better what kept Jamie at his studies. There was always that moment of sensing that an answer lay just within reach. Was it worth trying for?

Back in her bedroom, she exchanged her clothing for a fresh nightgown and climbed into bed. *Was* it worth trying to understand? She remembered a line of Francis Bacon's that Jamie loved to quote: "Whatever deserves to exist, deserves to be known." Well, she thought sleepily as she curled up against her pillow, what she had to find out was whether anything did exist in the first place. Then she could go about trying to understand it.

She knew that in the morning everything would be, if not clearer, at least not so intense. Too tired to worry about a repetition of her nightmare now, she searched for sleep and found it with a suddenness that dissolved any further thought. And, thankfully, it was deep and dreamless.

Chapter Three

Kieran Foy woke just as his train pulled into Ottawa Station. He gathered up his knapsack, bedroll and guitar case, and propped them up on the seat beside him. Shrugging into his old pea jacket, he waited patiently for the hiss and clatter of the train to stop and the announcement that they'd reached their destination to crackle over the train's intercom.

He hoped Jean-Paul had driven out to meet him like he'd said he would. He didn't feel like taking a bus and didn't think he had enough for cab fare left over after the price of his ticket. That was the trouble with not paying attention to money. It was never there when you needed it. If it was nice tomorrow, he'd go up to the Mall and busk for a few hours. If the Mall was still there. Lord lifting Jesus, how long had it been since he'd been in Ottawa? Only three, four years? How come it seemed like a place from another life?

Rolling a cigarette, he had just enough time to light it and stuff his tobacco pouch back into his pocket before the announcement came. He shouldered his pack and roll, picked up his guitar case, and swung into the aisle, going down it with the long, loose gait of someone more used to open country than the city. He nodded to the Jesuit priest he'd shared the car with all the way from Halifax and studiously ignored the scattering of other passengers.

Outside, he looked up at the sky. The stars weren't much different here, though the sky didn't have the same clarity as a Nova Scotian night. He missed the smell of the sea already, the raucous cries of gulls and terns, the Maritime scents, the feeling that the world was real—stone and wood instead of plastic and metal and Lord knew what else they made buildings

39

out of these days. *Nom de tout*. He was only gone a day and a half and it felt like a year.

He found Jean-Paul waiting for him in the reception area and set down his guitar to return his friend's embrace.

"Hey, Kieran!" Jean-Paul said, stepping back. "*Ça va?*"

"*Ça va.*"

"*Ton voyage, ç'est bien passé?*"

"*Oui.*" Kieran grinned. "You've put on weight, my friend."

Jean-Paul Gagnon was basically a compact man in his late thirties, thickening a little around the waist, black-haired and smooth shaven, and dark of complexion. He was wearing tan trousers, a heavy knit sweater and a dark blue ski jacket.

"And what would you expect?" Jean-Paul asked, patting his stomach. "I sit around my office all day doing important government work. I have no time for frivolities such as exercise."

"But time enough for the beer, *non?*"

Jean-Paul shrugged eloquently. "*Certainement*. But look at yourself. Are you a musician still, or a fisherman? And your French! Your accent is atrocious."

Kieran eyed his reflection in a window. His blue woolen touque pushed down a mat of black hair in desperate need of a wash; two days worth of stubble darkened his cheeks and chin, and his clothing had seen better days. His old pea jacket was patched at the elbows, his corduroys were worn threadbare at the knees and on the rear, and in another month or so his workboots would probably give up the ghost and die. As it was, when it rained they let in more water than they kept out.

"I've been working the boats as much as the clubs," he said, switching to English.

Jean-Paul took his hands and regarded the calluses critically.

"You have ruined your hands, my friend, *n'est-ce pas?*" he said. "Your hands, your French—ah, what is to be done with you? Had I known the East would do this to you, I would never have let you go. You said nothing in your letters!"

Kieran laughed. His first feelings of alienation dissolved as Jean-Paul fussed over him. It was people that made a place, he decided. So long as he had a friend like Jean-Paul here in Ottawa, he could never feel too out of place.

"*Allons-y,*" Jean-Paul said, taking Kieran's guitar case and steering him towards the door. "We should stand here, chatting like homeless sparrows, when we could be comfortable at home? Come, come."

"Are you still living on Powell?" Kieran asked as they stowed his gear in the backseat of Jean-Paul's old Volkswagen.

He admired the bug, which was becoming as rare these days as it had been plentiful five or six years ago. Most of the old VW drivers had traded their bugs in for Rabbits, or switched to Hondas.

"*Mais oui*," Jean-Paul replied. "Why should I move?"

"Why indeed?" Kieran murmured as the VW roared into life.

After Kieran had showered, shaved and changed into a new set of clothes which, while no less threadbare than what he'd been wearing, were at least clean, the two of them sat down to a midnight meal of mushroom omelet and beer. Not until the plates were swabbed clean with the last chunks of toast and pushed aside, and Kieran had a cigarette rolled and lit, did their conversation turn to what had brought him back.

"What has it been?" Jean-Paul asked, opening a second beer.

He offered it to Kieran who shook his head. Kieran was still nursing his first. Jean-Paul smiled.

"Three years?" he wondered aloud. "Four? Nothing but a few letters and cards, then a cable comes yesterday and *voila!* You are here. The cable said the matter was urgent, but not what the matter was. Will you tell me of it?"

"*Bien sûr, mon ami.*"

Only where did he begin? He tapped some ash from his cigarette and took a pull from his beer.

"Do you remember Tom Hengwr?" he asked at last, setting the bottle back on the table.

"That man? *Mais oui*. He was a strange one, *non?* Always so mysterious. So calm seeming, but his eyes. . . . He could be dangerous, that one, he was like . . . like that Don Juan in those books you sent me last Christmas. *Un sorcier*."

Kieran hid his surprise. Castaneda's books were vague at best, alluding to mysteries rather than revealing them. So much so that Kieran had wondered while he read them if Castaneda really knew anything about the Yaqui Way. He preferred the Wilson book he'd sent Jean-Paul the previous year, but hadn't really expected his friend to read any of them. Jean-Paul hadn't spoken of the books in his letters except to thank Kieran for them.

"You believe in such things?" he asked, regarding Jean-Paul in a new light.

"A little." Jean-Paul shrugged. "There is much in the world

for which there is no explanation, *n'est-ce pas?* I do not say that such things exist, but I am willing to be convinced. *Mais, ça ne fait rien.* We spoke of Thomas Hengwr, not of sorcery."

"The two are, perhaps, more entwined than you might imagine, my friend."

Jean-Paul settled back into his chair and regarded Kieran steadily.

"Then it seems," he said, "that the time has come for me to be convinced."

Kieran sighed. He knew, from his own experience, that there was only one way to convince someone and that was by showing them. Only the thought of doing so made him uneasy. From across a span of years, it seemed he could hear the old man scolding him.

"You want to impress people with tricks?" Tom had demanded. "Then take up juggling oranges or something. A mage has no time for conjuring and parlor tricks. Let me tell you what happens when you piss away your powers on them: First you lose respect for your skills and that debilitates them. And then, when a time comes that you really need them, you lose control and there's hell to pay. And let me tell you one more thing: secrecy in itself is a source of power."

"But what's the point of it all, then?" Kieran had asked.

"What you really want to know is why can't you use these powers to lift yourself to great heights in the eyes of the world, isn't it?" The old man spat and stared out across the Gatineau Mountains for a long moment, green eyes glittering with anger. Then he sighed. "You follow the Way to ennoble yourself so that you can do some good in the world, Kier. The powers are secondary—more defense than anything else. For as you come into contact with benevolent forces, so you come into contact with malevolent ones as well. Your powers are to protect you against the latter—not to make your journey any easier. Does that make any sense to you?"

"I think so," he'd replied, not really understanding then.

But in the years that followed, the old man's little speech stayed with him, clearer in his memory than many other incidents that had, at the time of their occurrence, seemed of far greater import. And in the end he *had* come to understand. Following the Way was a responsibility, not only to himself, but to the harmony he strove to create in his relationship with the world.

Weighty words, he thought, looking up to find Jean-Paul still regarding him curiously, but filled with truth all the same. In light of them, perhaps he'd been too harsh on Castaneda. If Castaneda knew the secrets, he hid them well, in between the lines of his books. Just as Kieran knew he had to hide them in between the lines of what he said to Jean-Paul now. There were times when truth was too dangerous—especially to the uninitiated. For they had no defense.

He stubbed out his cigarette and rolled another.

"I guess I was exaggerating," he said as he lit the cigarette. "Oh?"

"There was a bond between us," Kieran explained, not wanting to lie to his friend, but not wanting to touch on matters best left unspoken either. "It was . . . mystical. No matter how far apart we'd be, I'd always know that he was . . . all right, I suppose. It was like we were in constant contact. You know what they say about twins? Tom and I were like twins, despite the age difference between us. I'd never met anyone like him before."

"You speak of him in the past tense," Jean-Paul said.

There was an intent look hidden behind the Frenchman's casual attitude, but Kieran was too caught up in what he was saying to notice it.

"I was working on a boat in Fox Point," he said. "That's a little village on St. Margaret's Bay. I knew Tom was in Ottawa— there was that bond between us, you see. Then two days ago . . . nothing. It was like he'd vanished from the face of the earth or . . . or . . . ."

"That he'd died?"

"He can't be dead. I'd *know* if he was dead."

Jean-Paul shook his head. He pointed to the phone on the kitchen wall.

"You could call him, *non?*"

"He doesn't have a phone. I don't even know where he was staying. He was never one to have a home or to own things. . . ."

"You two sound much the same," Jean-Paul said. "What was he doing here in Ottawa?"

"Looking for something. An answer to an old riddle."

Jean-Paul's eyebrows lifted quizzically.

"I know. It doesn't make much sense. I just don't know how to explain it. I said he didn't own things, only he did. He collected information in here." Kieran tapped his temple. "That was his wealth. I don't know exactly what he was looking for in Ottawa—not specifically. But whatever it was, he knew it was here."

Jean-Paul sighed. "I don't pretend to understand, *mon ami*. It all sounds too fantastic. This bond between you. Some mysterious quest. Your friend's disappearance. I would help you if I could, *n'est-ce pas?* But I don't know what help I can give."

Kieran looked around the kitchen.

"This is help enough," he said. "If I could stay here while I look for him. . . ."

"Bien sûr! That is little enough for me to do. But what will you do? Where will you begin? It seems to me that you have set an impossible task for yourself. If all you have to go on is this—what? A broken bond?"

"I'll start by asking around. He had other friends in town."

"From what I remember of him, he knew many people, but had few friends, *non?*"

"There's that," Kieran agreed, but he remembered something else the old man'd told him once.

"I have enemies," Tom had said. "Not many, but the few I have are powerful. It's a regrettable thing, but when you follow the Way. . . ." He shrugged. "The deeper you delve, the more chance there is that you'll make enemies. Not all mages seek the same knowledges, nor do we all wish to share what we've found with each other. Where there is light, there is also darkness. As it is in the souls of mankind, so it is in the soul of a mage. For are we not all men and women as well?

"You frown, Kier, but you will see. I wish you didn't have to, but you will see. I only hope you have the needed strength of purpose when the time of your challenge comes."

Kieran stubbed out his cigarette. A sense of bleakness rose up inside him. Was this his time? Lord dying Jesus, he wished it didn't have to be so.

"You seem tired, *mon ami*," Jean-Paul said. "We should retire. The night grows late. I must be up early tomorrow and you have had a long trip. You must be weary, *non?*"

"Oui."

Jean-Paul took their plates to the sink and stacked them beside the frying pan. As he reached to flick off the light above the sink, Kieran spoke softly.

"Jean-Paul?"

"Oui?"

"Have you seen or heard anything of the old man lately?"

Jean-Paul paused a moment before replying. He turned and leaned against the sink to face Kieran.

"Not since the days of The Celt's Room—above that restaurant."

"The Lido," Kieran said.

Jean-Paul nodded. "That was it. They call it Christopher's now. It has become a McDonald's for the smarter set, *n'est-ce pas?* They still have a liquor license, only now they sell their hamburgers for four ninety-five. I think Thomas Hengwr would be as out of place in such a place as I was when you played in The Celt's Room."

He's lying, Kieran knew with sudden insight. He felt a pang of guilt at the unfair thought. Why should Jean-Paul lie to him? What could he have to hide? They were friends.

Friends, yes, he answered himself, but four years is a long time. Much can happen in four years. People change. And whatever the reasons, whether he had changed or not, Kieran knew Jean-Paul was lying.

He began to roll another cigarette to cover his confusion. As his fingers twisted the paper around the tobacco, his features remained calm. But anger and sorrow fought in his mind.

Nom de tout! he wanted to shout. Why are you doing this? Why do you lie? How can you be the enemy?

As though in response to the sudden turmoil in his guest, Jean-Paul said: "You must remember, Kieran. Thomas Hengwr and I were never friends, *n'est-ce pas?* He would have no reason to contact me."

Kieran nodded, fighting down his anger and the need to know why Jean-Paul was dissembling. He studied his friend and saw, with that sixth sense that the old man had awoken in him, the telltale nervousness that he hadn't noticed before, the tightening around the corners of Jean-Paul's eyes, the very wavering in the air between them that said so much more than the words they spoke.

But knowing did nothing towards helping him understand. Nor did it ease the pain. And most confusing of all, he could still sense Jean-Paul's honest affection for him.

"Go to bed, *mon ami*," Jean-Paul said. Kieran heard his voice as though from a great distance. "You remember the room? Second on the right from the top of the stairs. We will speak again in the morning when we are both more rested, *non? Bonsoir.*"

"Bonsoir," Kieran murmured and watched him go.

He listened to the creak of Jean-Paul's footsteps on the stairs and wanted to run after him and shake the truth from him. But now was not the time. First he needed some other answers, then he would confront Jean-Paul. Where was the old man? What part, if any, had Jean-Paul played in his disappearance?

Kieran knew he couldn't go off half cocked like some fisherman with one too many tots of rum in him. Taking a last drag from his cigarette, he butted it out and went to find his room.

It was the one he had always used when he stayed with Jean-Paul. Not a thing in it had changed. There was the double bed against one wall. It had a dark green quilt on it that hung over each side to brush the floor. His pack lay on the foot of the bed, his guitar on the floor beside. The room made Kieran sad, for it reminded him of better times when there'd been no suspicion between them.

Is this what you mean, Tom? he asked the empty room. That I should suspect my oldest friend of duplicity?

The sense of urgency that had sent him from Fox Point to catch the train in Halifax returned. Tom was gone. Not dead, but gone. But everything he'd ever taught Kieran remained. Light and dark. Black and white. Were things ever so clear cut? He saw himself in shades of grey. Jean-Paul . . . might he not be lying for some reason or other, but still not be an enemy? Kieran eyed his reflection in the mirror on top of the dresser and frowned. He turned to the window.

Kieran remembered hanging the flower print curtains that still hung across the window. Tugging them open, he looked out on Powell Avenue for long moments. It was a stately street—all old houses, brick and wood, with dormer windows and enclosed verandas, gardens and well kept lawns, tall elms and maples. It was the sort of area that was home to lawyers and architects and Assistant Deputy Ministers like Jean-Paul. Those that owned the houses. But, like any facade, many of these old mansions hid the fact that they'd been divided into apartments and housed everybody from prim old ladies to the odd whole-earth person who could afford the exorbitant rents.

The street filled Kieran's vision but could do nothing to lull his mind. Was he overreacting? Seeing conspiracies where none existed? He had nothing to go on but that extra sense the old man had taught him how to use.

"Think of it as a . . . a deep sight," Tom'd told him. "It's good for many things—stripping illusions and going to the heart of a matter. When you're dealing with people, it can act as a lie detector of sorts. And, when properly cultivated, it's far more efficient than any machine devised by man. We've got it all in here," he said, tapping his skull. "All we've got to do is learn how to use it."

Kieran sighed and turned from the window. He stretched out on the bed, not bothering to take off his clothes or unpack. It was possible that he was misjudging Jean-Paul, but things had changed. While it might not be dangerous for him to stay here, he couldn't take the chance that it might turn out to be so. With the old man missing and no one to find him except for Kieran. . . . He'd wait until Jean-Paul was sleeping. Then he'd go. If he was wrong, he could aways apologize later.

He set a mental alarm clock to wake himself an hour later, closed his eyes and slept.

Sixty-three minutes later, Kieran was drifting ghostlike down the stairs, as soft-footed as any smuggler making landfall on Scotia's rocky coasts. His pack was on his back, his guitar case in hand.

He paused at the front door, holding the moment of leaving in his mind with sadness, then slipped out into the night, easing the door closed behind him. It shut with a barely audible click. Standing on the stoop, he surveyed the street with deepsight more than his tangible senses. So it was that he discovered the man watching from a car before he was spotted himself.

He melted back into the shadows by the house. The man's car was across the street and three houses down. A black humor settled on him as he regarded what could only be a confirmation of his hitherto unproven fears. Had he needed tangible proof of Jean-Paul's duplicity, here it was, big as life. He felt no sense of triumph in being right.

He had two choices. He could make his way through Jean-Paul's backyard to Clemow and possible safety—temporary safety at any rate—or he could confront the watcher now and perhaps learn something of what was going down.

"There are times to retreat from danger," Tom would have said, "and times it must be faced head on. If you choose to face it—go boldly. Remember that no matter how strong your enemy might be, you too have power."

Shifting his guitar case from right hand to left, he stepped from the shadows and headed for the car. He walked calmly, with his loose stride, crossed the street, and was almost at the car before the man noticed him. Daydreaming, Kieran thought. Bored more than likely. Kieran reached inside himself to find where his strength lay and drew it up. He leaned against the window on the driver's side, his eyes blazing in the darkness with a strange feral glow—like the reflection of a cat's eyes caught in a car's headlights.

"Don't call in," he said.

He spoke softly, but his words penetrated the thick glass. The man's finger hesitated on his radio's control. The witchlight flickered in Kieran's eyes and before the man knew what he was doing, he'd taken his hand from the radio's controls and used it to roll down his window. A fine sheen of sweat beaded his brow.

"I . . . I won't call in," he said slowly, his voice slightly slurred.

He was a large man, broad-faced and thick-shouldered, with short dark-brown hair and the look of a policeman stamped into his features. He wore a quilted ski-jacket and pressed brown trousers—his disguise, Kieran decided. Kieran smiled. He'd been lucky with this one. It wasn't easy to bend someone to your will this quickly. You had to catch them off guard, otherwise it took considerable preparation. Or power.

"Who do you work for?" Kieran demanded, holding the man's gaze with his own. "The horsemen?"

The man nodded. "Special Branch."

"What kind of Special Branch?"

"PRB—the Paranormal Research Branch."

Lord dying Jesus! What did the horsemen want with him? And what were they doing with a Special Branch studying the paranormal? This was something out of a bestseller. It didn't have any place in real life and Kieran found it hard to put into any sort of reasonable perspective. But if it *was* true, how had they keyed on to him?

The horsemen were the RCMP—the Royal Canadian Mounted Police. The Federal police. Canada's finest with their Musical Ride and fancy red coats. The Mounties who always get their man. The horsemen. But—

"What do you want with me?" Kieran asked.

"Nothing. You're to be kept under surveillance."

"Why?"

There was no reply. Kieran wanted to shake the man by the throat to get an answer, but forced himself to stay calm.

"When's your relief?" he asked.

"Six AM."

Kieran did a rapid calculation. That left him about two and a half hours. No—he'd have more than that. No one would know he was gone until Jean-Paul woke up and whistled them down on him again. No one, except his man here.

"Do you know a Thomas Hengwr?" Kieran asked.

Again there was no reply. The witchlight in Kieran's eyes burned dangerously, but either the man truly didn't know, or it would take a deeper probe to dig the information out of him. Kieran didn't have the time for a deeper probe.

Well, this was great. He'd really learned a lot. The old man was still gone without a trace, and now he had the Mounties on his ass as well. The witchlight intensified momentarily as he spoke again.

"You never saw me leave," Kieran said.

The man nodded.

Kieran sighed and broke eye contact. There was a tiny ache in his temples that came from the abrupt use of energies he'd utilized. As he stepped back, the Mountie rolled up the window again and returned to studying Jean-Paul's house as though Kieran was no longer present.

Kieran set off east on Powell, heading for Bank Street. He kept a wary eye open on the off chance that his horseman had some backup with him, but sensed nothing out of the ordinary. Ottawa, unlike most big cities, seemed to shut down around eleven most nights. After twelve, all you saw cruising the streets were police cars and taxis. There was a seamier underside to the nation's capital—Kieran knew that all too well— but it required a firmer sense of purpose to uncover it than it did in most cities. Like anywhere, if you wanted something badly enough, it could be found.

Like a place to stay? Kieran asked himself.

He had to decide what he was going to do. He could scratch Jean-Paul. Was there anyone else he could call up? What? At three or so in the morning? And who was to say that anybody could be trusted now? He would've bet his life on Jean-Paul. . . .

He paused as he reached Bank. Across the street, the thin strip of Central Park lay peaceful in the darkness. Beyond it rose the dark bulk of Tamson House. As his gaze rested on that curious building, a queer sense of disquiet settled upon him.

He knew a little more about the House and its owners than

most people might, but that wasn't very much. There was an older man, a patriarch of sorts, and his niece. They were the owners. They were filthy rich, but spent most of their time playing at being "of the people." The man, James Tamson, was some sort of an authority on the anthropological aspects of the paranormal, but the one time Kieran had mentioned him to the old man, Tom had laughed him off.

"He means well, Jamie does," Tom had said, "and you'll rarely find a nicer or more obliging fellow, but he's as close to following the Way as you were before I met you. Though that's not entirely fair. It's not that he's a charlatan. Its just that he doesn't *know*, and without that *knowing*, he'll never be more than a collector of curiosities. You should meet him sometime, Kier. You'd probably like his niece."

Kieran recalled laughing at the teasing look in the old man's eyes, and that had been the end of it. Except now he remembered the stories that used to go around about Tamson House—that odd things happened in it, that it was run as a commune of sorts and every sort of character who came through Ottawa eventually made their way through its doors.

He regarded the building thoughtfully. He'd never been in the place himself, but if all he'd heard was true, it could well be the safe harbor he was looking for. Except. . . . There was that queer sensation that had come to him when he first viewed it, that there was something wrong about Tamson House, as though there was an evil abroad tonight and it had settled upon those strange gabled eaves before moving on.

Kieran felt overcautious, but perhaps justly so. Because there was this: he didn't have only the horseman outside of Jean-Paul's and all the implications of RCMP surveillance to worry about. There was also the fact that the old man was missing and Kieran was sure of one thing. Whatever was involved in Tom's disappearance, it was something beyond the pale of the herenow. Less corporeal than the horsemen, to be sure, but no less real or dangerous for that. Understanding that, it made no sense to seek shelter in a place that seemed so disquieting.

He watched the House for a few minutes longer. The feeling was gone now, but he was no more inclined to go into Tamson House than if it had remained. "Someone's stepped on my grave," Tom used to say about a feeling like that. There was a sense of ill luck about it, like seeing a raven at sea before starting a voyage. Fisherman's superstition. But he had the east coast in his blood now, for all his growing up in Ontario.

His best bet, he decided, putting aside any further considerations of Tamson House, was to head up the few blocks to the bus depot on Catherine Street, stash his guitar and knapsack in a locker, and then make the best of it for the rest of the night. He needed to keep a low profile for now. With the streets empty, he'd stand out too much. But later, when they filled up with people going off to work or whatever, he'd merge with the crowds. Then he could put out some feelers about finding a new place to stay.

Well, hello, Ottawa, he thought as he headed north on Bank. Nice to be back.

5:15, Wednesday morning.

Kieran sat nursing his third coffee in a twenty-four hour Italian restaurant called Tomorrow's on the corner of Bank and Frank Street. His pocket was heavier by the weight of one locker key and he was getting a little wired on caffeine. He rolled a cigarette, lit it, and set it on the edge of a filled ashtray. Except for the bored waitress with the beehive hairdo and the short-order cook in back, he had the place to himself.

He could remember—it was what? Five, six years ago?— when there'd been a folk club downstairs and he'd played there with a couple of fellows on St. Patrick's Day. Tim Anderson on fiddle and big smiling Eamon Mulloy on accordian. He couldn't remember what the place'd been called then. Later it'd been turned into a punk rocker's bar—The Rotter's Club. He wondered what it was now. Probably a wine bar that played loud Euro-pop music and aimed itself at the singles set. That seemed to be happening to most live bars these days.

Things changed. They always did. Sometimes it seemed too much, or too inexplicable. Like with Jean-Paul. Kieran could remember the old days when it seemed that every second pub had a single act or small band playing in it. He'd enjoyed those times, gigging around town, playing everything from C&W and "Mr. Bojangles" to traditional Celtic music, weekends up in the Gatineau with the old man, learning the Way.

He hadn't planned on coming back. At least not so soon, and not like this. But, he supposed, he should have expected it. Nothing lasted forever.

When he and the old man'd moved to Nova Scotia, Kieran had felt he was home for the first time in his life. There was something about those rocky seascapes and rolling farmlands that struck a chord in him. He had a room in Billy Field's farmhouse near Peggy's Cove, southwest of Halifax, and spent his time wandering around, taking the odd job on a fishing boat when they were short-handed, gigging with Billy's group The Islanders or on his own. He'd been content. Even after the old man left. He'd missed Tom, but they'd kept in touch. With the bond that lay between they were never far from each other.

That bond was important—not just for the affection between them. Kieran had a long way to go still, following the Way, and the old man was his mentor. He smiled, thinking of him.

"Hengwr" literally meant "old man" in some language or other—or so Tom insisted. Tom looked like a gremlin out of a fairy tale, standing a head shorter than Kieran's five-eleven, with a hooked nose, grizzled beard and hair, and bird-bright eyes that protruded alarmingly, like the British comedian Marty Feldman's.

But for all his comical appearance, accentuated by his penchant for floppy hats and baggy overcoats, the old man surely knew his stuff. That had become apparent from their first meeting across a table in the visiting rooms of St. Vincent de Paul Penitentiary outside of Montreal. The old man had been the visitor.

It was in late '69 and Kieran was serving two years for B&E and another two years for possession of cannabis with intent to traffic. The sentences ran concurrently. In real time, he'd do sixteen months. He had two left to go, having been passed over in his parole review.

He met the old man in the middle of three days of solitary confinement—having been sent there for talking out of turn with a guard. The detention cell, called the hole, was six feet by ten, with a pallet on the floor, an enamel sink and potty, and little else. They took away all your clothes except for your underwear and gave you a pair of white overalls. Then, when they locked the big iron door that took up almost the whole of one wall of your cell, you sat there for however long a term you'd pulled. He'd been surprised when the guard came for him. Naturally the guard hadn't told him anything; just as naturally, Kieran hadn't asked where they were going. He changed from overalls to grey pants and shirt, put on his jacket and boots, and silently preceded the guard across the compound to the buildings that housed the prison's offices. It wasn't until they were inside that the guard finally spoke.

"You've got a visitor, Foy. Go on through."

A visitor? You didn't get visitors when you were in the hole. You lost all your privileges. He opened his mouth to ask what was going on, then thought better of it. What the hell. A visitor? He couldn't think of who it might be, but went on down the hall, stopped to be frisked by another guard before going into the visitors' room, then went in and saw Thomas Hengwr for the first time.

That first view made him reconsider his earlier thought of, well, whatever was going on, at least it was a break in the monotony. He'd never seen such a weird-looking individual before, but what stopped him from laughing outright, or even smiling at the old man's appearance, was the uncomfortable sense of. . . . In retrospect years later, he realized it was the sense of power that hung over the old man that'd kept him from laughing. He learned later that few people saw Tom in that light.

"Kieran Foy?" were the old man's first words. "Come in, come in. Have a seat. I'm very pleased to meet you."

Kieran stayed by the door.

"Who're you?" he demanded.

"Thomas Hengwr," the old man replied, bowing comically. "At your service. Sit, sit! Don't be shy."

Shaking his head, Kieran crossed the room and sat across the table from him. Before he could speak again, Tom'd dug a sheaf of ratty-looking paper from one of the voluminous side pockets of his overcoat. He showed Kieran a picture of himself, taken before he was busted.

"Not a bad likeness, don't you think?" Tom asked.

"Sure. But listen—"

"Now," Tom interrupted, studying his papers. "Let's see. You became a ward of the Children's Society in . . . hmm. Sixty-four. Is that correct? Quit school as soon as you legally could—you were quite a troublemaker, weren't you? Then. . . ." He riffled through the pages. "There's not a whole lot more really, except for hearsay and rumors. Fascinating material, though. A couple of vagrancy charges. Drugs, nothing major. One conviction—you pulled probation on that one. What was it? A year? Then you were arrested in Hull for breaking and entering and drew time on both charges."

"Is there a point to all this?"

The old man straightened the papers, laid them on the table between them and lifted his gaze to meet Kieran's. There was something eerie about his eyes.

"Are you very happy with the way your life seems to be going?" Tom asked.

Kieran shook his head—not so much in reply, as for amusement.

"What's it to you?" he asked. "Are you a social worker or something?"

"A question for a question," the old man said. "Well, here's another: do you know Alice Sherwin?"

"Alice . . . ?"

But then he remembered. Mrs. Sherwin. She ran a second-hand bookstore down in the Glebe that he used to frequent—as much for her company and their long talks over tea as for the books that he never seemed to get enough of. She'd been like . . . like an aunt to him, he supposed. She was a little flaky, what with her Tarot cards and horoscopes and all, but nothing too serious.

"Look," he said at last. "I don't know what you're after, but I think you're barking up the wrong tree. If you're offering me parole, I'd rather do my time. All I've got is two months left, for Christ's sake. If you're writing a book or something, I'm not really not worth your time. Joe master criminal I'm not. And if you're here to save my soul, I'm not interested."

"Your soul," the old man murmured.

He said it in such a way, with his deep green eyes glittering, weirdly, that a spooky chill ran up Kieran's spine.

"It's curious that you should mention that," Tom said, "because that's exactly why I *am* here. No Bible-thumping, I assure you. Nothing fancy. It's just that I happened to mention to Alice—she's a mutual acquaintance, you see, my suspicious friend—I happened to mention to her that I was looking for a . . . how should I put it? An apprentice would be the best term."

"Apprentice in what?"

"In the Way."

When the old man spoke that word, sudden vistas seemed to open before Kieran. It was as though he saw his life unfold before him in a multitude of possibilities. He saw himself going on as he was, in and out of jail, living in squalor, then dressed in a slick suit like some Mafiosa underling. It was a gritty view, from the underbelly of life, and he already had a foot half in it. Then he saw himself going straight—nine-to-five job, drifting in a morass of boredom from which there was no escape because the mortgage payments had to be made, content to be one of many drones in a secure world that held no surprises.

There were other views—variations on those two for the most part. They were like roads undulating into the distant days to come, some straight and narrow, confining, others broad and painted in broad gaudy strokes. Then his attention centered on one that ran in and out of the others like a twisting footpath. On it he saw himself as himself, unassuming but fulfilled. For no reason he could articulate, that road in particular drew him, for in it he saw his potential flourishing. He seemed to hear music and a distant voice singing. Barely, he made out the words:

> *Don't you see yon bonny, bonny road*
> *that lies across the ferny brae,*
> *that is the road to fair Elfland,*
> *where you and I this night maun gae....*

The singer had the same voice as that of the old man who sat across from him and the realization of this brought him back down to earth. He blinked, trying to bring Tom's face into focus.

"No illusions," the old man said. "If you follow the Way, it'll be the hardest thing you'll ever do. And the most rewarding."

Kieran hardly heard what he said. He had no pretensions concerning his worth, present or future. He'd never thought of looking for a way out of what he'd become. With little education except for the patchy results of his eclectic reading, no formal training nor any productive interests, there wasn't a whole lot he could aim for. But now. . . . He felt he was being offered something that was all he could ever want. Later he could never find the words to describe how he'd known this, or how he'd felt at that moment. Nor what made him choose what he chose.

"Alice recommended you," Tom said, "and now that I've met you myself, I have to concur with her. You're a rough diamond, Kieran Foy, but a diamond all the same. Will you come with me?"

Kieran came all the way down to reality.

"What?" he asked.

His thoughts were still somewhat blurred and he wasn't able to bring the old man's features into focus completely.

"You mean right now?" he added. "I mean, I can't. That is, I don't want to break out or anything. . . ."

Tom laughed. "I'd hardly ask that."

"What exactly are you asking?"

"I want someone to teach, someone to study with me. A companion, a friend." He tapped his head. "I've so much stored away in here. I want to pass some of it on before I go." He smiled. "It all seems strange, doesn't it? The Way is a wordless thing—a concept that's hard to shape words around. But . . . you sensed it, didn't you? Despite your lack of knowledge, you still *knew* something, didn't you?"

Kieran nodded slowly, remembering the . . . vision?

"Trust what you felt," the old man said. "Trust that knowledge. For now it's intuitive, but it will become clearer in time. That, at least, I can promise you."

Kieran looked around the visitors' room, looked down at the prison clothes he was wearing, and remembered what lay ahead of him. Another day and a half in the hole. Two more months in the pen. Those were the hard facts. But faced with the certainty of some mystic promise that was reflected in the old man's curious eyes, none of it seemed important. He had the feeling at that moment that nothing was impossible to the individual who faced him across the table and found that he wanted that same sense of . . . purpose for himself. That serenity.

"Are you with me?" Tom asked.

Kieran had no choice. It was like being asked do you want to be nothing, or everything?

"Yes," he said. "Only how . . . ?"

Tom shook his head. "Leave that to me."

He returned his sheaf of papers to his pocket and stood up to call the guard.

"There seems to be some sort of mistake," Tom said to the guard when he came. "My friend was supposed to be discharged today."

Kieran wasn't sure he'd heard right. He looked into the guard's face and saw his own confusion reflected there. Then the guard nodded.

"We'd better go talk to the warden," he said.

Turning, he led the way.

No one stopped them or questioned them. Kieran wasn't

frisked coming out of the visitors' room. Everything passed in a blur. They reached the warden's office and before Kieran really knew it, he was given back his personal effects, had changed into some clothes that the old man had brought with him—jeans, a flannel shirt, boots and a tweed sports jacket— and they were standing outside the prison.

"That's it?" Kieran asked. "Is it . . . is it even legal?"

"Oh, quite so. There's still some paperwork to be done, but that won't take them long."

"But . . . how did you get them to do that?"

The old man shrugged. "I think we'll go to Ottawa, what do you say? I've a place up in the Gatineau—a ski lodge that a friend's letting me have for awhile. We can work there on weekends. You can do what you like during the week."

"But. . . ."

Tom led him to an old beat-up Chevy that was parked in the lot. Kieran remembered standing by the car, hand on the hood, and looking back at the grey walls of St. Vincent de Paul Penitentiary. The sky was blue, and there were no walls around him. He could go anywhere, do anything.

"Let's go," the old man said. "This place depresses me. We can talk on the way."

That was how it all began.

"More coffee?"

The waitress' voice startled him out of his reverie. He looked up and saw that the restaurant was filling up with people. The clock above the door that led to the kitchen read 7:10.

"Non, merci," he murmured. "Just the bill."

Three coffees, one-twenty. Whatever happened to the bottomless cup? Kieran wondered as he paid at the cash register. The waitress smiled briefly as she handed him his change and told him to have a nice day.

"I'll give it a try," he said.

With his change, Kieran had a grand total of a dollar-eighty left in his pocket. He needed money and a place to stay. But most of all he needed to find the old man. This was, if nothing else, his chance to repay him for that day in St. Vince and all the years since.

"Why did you want a student?" he'd asked Tom once.

"For immortality."

"Immortality?"

The old man had smiled. "You'd have to be as old as I am to fully appreciate what I mean, Kier. Everyone has the need

to leave their mark on the world. The old craftsfolk took on
apprentices so that their own skills lived on. They still do this
in places like Japan. Civilized country, Japan. You'll find traces
of that in the Maritimes and the backwoods of Quebec, too,
though the skills are mostly passed down through the family."

"Like an inheritance?"

"Somewhat. But it's more the sense that all I've worked on
won't go to waste. When I'm dead, I'll live on—in you. You'll
amend what I've taught you, add to it, drop things that don't
work so well for you, but the core will still be my teachings.
That's my immortality. And not only mine, but my teacher's
before me, and his before him. It goes back a long way."

A long way. The Way.

Kieran's method of dealing with the horseman outside of
Jean-Paul's was just a side effect of that learning. It was a
flashier aspect, for, as with the martial arts of the East, the
visible manifestations cloaked the true heart of the matter. The
old man's Way wasn't much different from the teachings of
Taoism or the writings of Thoreau. It had a basic truth to it as
important in this day and age when so much more existed to
diffuse it as it had in the lost years of its shaping. Such a thing
was worth preserving. It deserved immortality.

Kieran had hardly understood any of it that afternoon in the
visitors' room in St. Vincent de Paul. It had taken the old man
to show him that the Way was something he'd been looking
for all his life, but had had no point of reference to, so that he
might have recognized it himself. He owed Tom Hengwr more
than he could ever repay.

Buttoning up his jacket, he stood in the doorway of Tomorrow's for a moment, surveying the street with more than
his eyes, weighing the vibes. He was new to this cloak and
dagger game. Who was to say that the construction worker
waiting at the bus stop wasn't watching for him? Or that the
businessman with his vinyl briefcase and trendy moustache
wasn't a horseman?

Kieran sighed. Was it still paranoia when you *knew* someone
was after you? He stepped out onto Bank Street. At the corner
he looked around once more, then set off east on Frank, heading
for Sandy Hill. What he needed now was some information.
He only hoped that some of the old crowd was still hanging
around.

Chapter Four

8:30, Wednesday morning.

RCMP Special Inspector John Tucker was not happy. He sat in his office, elbows propped on his desk, chin cupped in his hands, frowning at his coffee. He was a big man—206 pounds on a six-foot frame—with short-cropped brown hair that was greying at the temples, a squared moustache and pale grey eyes. He had the sort of skin that didn't tan, though it reddened when he was in the sun—or when his blood pressure went up. Last week he'd celebrated his forty-fifth birthday. Today there wasn't anything to celebrate. His face was flushed and Dr. Lawrence Hogue, who was sitting across the desk from him, was all too aware of that fact.

Tucker had been only a little irked when he was put in charge of the security for Project Mindreach. (Project Spook was more appropriate. Christ, who thought up these code names anyway?) It had seemed like a simple enough operation at the outset: Project Mindreach would specialize in documenting the viability of psychic resources, should they exist. But the whole thing had soured from the word go. That always happened when you put a CM—Civilian Member of the Force—in charge. The trouble was, if it all fell apart now, it was going to be his ass in the sling. Not the Superintendent's. Not Hogue's. His.

He sat up and glared across the desk.

"Any more bright ideas?" he demanded.

Hogue shifted uneasily in his chair. He was a portly man in his early forties, uncomfortable when not in the familiar confines of his laboratory. His heavy jowls and mournful eyes reminded Tucker of a cow. Brilliant in the lab; Tucker had no arguments there. But outside of it, stripped of his white smock and clipboard, he barely passed muster.

"I've got a meeting with Superintendent Madison at noon," Tucker said, "and he's got an appointment with Williams at two. The Honorable Minister is going to want more than a handful of surveillance reports for his eight mill'. Surveillance reports don't mean shit. We need some results."

"Foy should have led us to the old man," Hogue said.

"Foy's looking for the old man as well."

"What?"

"You heard me."

Tucker leaned back in his chair to stare out the window. He could see the Rideau River from his office.

"Gagnon picked Foy up at Ottawa Station a little before midnight," he said wearily. "They went back to his place on Powell, had something to eat and shot the shit for awhile. When Gagnon got up this morning, Foy was gone."

"Who was on the stakeout?" Hogue liked using words like that. It made him feel like he was part of a television show SWAT team. "Didn't he see anything?"

"He saw lots of things—old ladies walking their dogs, kids making out . . . but he didn't see Foy. He's filling out a report downstairs if you want to talk to him. Constable Thompson. Paul Thompson. He's a good man. I worked with him on an operation in Vancouver this summer."

"But not good enough, it seems."

Tucker frowned. "If these guys are really the spooks you make them out to be, it's not too surprising, is it?"

"You don't believe it's possible, do you?"

"It doesn't matter what I believe. It doesn't even matter if they've got three eyes and four arms. What I need is some results, and I need them yesterday."

"But—"

"Look," Tucker said wearily. "We've been through this before. I think something weird's going on. Sure. But I'm not about to call in the exorcist, okay? You show me some proof, and we'll talk about it again. I just want to get on with my job and sitting around on my ass isn't doing my job."

Hogue nodded. He cleared his throat. "What about Gagnon?" he asked. "Did you speak to him?"

"Did I?" Tucker tapped his fingers irritatably on his desktop as he thought back over his recent telephone conversation with Jean-Paul Gagnon. "He's all set to raise hell. Wants to call the papers, his MP—whatever it takes. A Royal Commission. I have to go out and see him this morning and try to calm him down."

"Did you find out why Foy was here? Was it because of Thomas Hengwr?"

"I had trouble getting much out of him. He was too worked up. He wanted to know why we'd lied to him. Wanted to know why we had a man staked out in front of his house. Wanted to know why his phone was tapped. Christ only knows how he found out about that!

"Here's what he had to say about Foy: He was in some little dump in Nova Scotia when he suddenly got this feeling that there was something wrong with Hengwr. He immediately dropped what he was doing—which was scraping the barnacles off of a fishing boat for some old geezer. . . . Say, tell me. If these spooks are so powerful, why's one of them no better than a derelict and the other a fucking beach bum? No. Never mind. I don't think I'm up for one of your philosophical lectures at this time of the morning."

He took a swig of coffee. It was cold. Grimacing, he pushed the Styrofoam cup aside.

"So, anyway. He drops what he's doing and takes the first train to Ottawa. That all checks with the man we had on him. Then he goes to Gagnon's place. They talk about old times and whatnot. Foy springs the question: Heard anything about Tom Hengwr? Gagnon gives him the lie like we told him to and Foy clams up. Goes all cold on Gagnon. They head off to their rooms for the night and bingo! Gagnon gets up in the morning and Foy's gone. Out the back door, I'd guess. Like he *knew* we had a man out front."

"Did Gagnon say what kind of a feeling Foy had?" Hogue's eyes betrayed his excitement. They'd gone from placid to calculating. "This is what we've been looking for."

"Re-lax," Tucker said. "It was just a feeling, you know? You never get one like that? Everyone has 'em from time to time."

"But not everyone travels a thousand miles to check one out. No. There's something between them. An intangible something—like a telepathic union. It fits!"

"Yeah, well, if we ever catch up with either of them, you can ask them how it works, okay? I've put out an APB on both of them. You'll have someone to play around with soon enough. Right now I'm more worried about Gagnon."

"You have to make him understand how important this is."

"He doesn't give a shit about its importance. Not anymore. All he knows is we've fucked up a ten-year friendship for him and left him feeling like a heel, you know? He doesn't buy the story about trying to entrap the master criminal Thomas Hengwr anymore. He wants to see warrants for both of them. Wants— oh shit! He wants the moon delivered to him on a silver platter." Tucker shook his head. "What I can't see is why he waited so long before jumping on the legality bandwagon. I know he didn't care that much for Hengwr. I suppose when it came to his friend Foy...."

"Can't you stop him from talking?"

"How?"

Hogue shrugged. "I thought you people had your methods."

"Like filling his pants with cement and dropping him in the Ottawa River? What do you think we are? The C-I-fucking-A? No. I'll go out and talk to him. See what I can do. Lay it on him like it is, I suppose. I don't know. I just hope we can keep the press out of it."

The press would cut them to ribbons. The press would have a field day. It'd be on the front pages and the six o'clock news in all its spectacular detail. They'd be screaming for another commission. It pissed Tucker off just thinking about it.

He believed in the Force, what it stood for, the job it could do. What it had to do. But the image of the true blue Mountie in his red coat and flat-brimmed hat was getting a little tarnished. What kept the RCMP above so many of its counterparts throughout the world was the respect that they'd earned. That respect made their job easier, made them more efficient. Made the men proud of their work. A man with pride worked well.

Tucker was a career man himself. He'd joined the Force when he was nineteen. In '54. He'd done his bit with the horse and dress uniform, pulled the two-year backwater shifts from Newfoundland to the Yukon. Made corporal when he was twenty-four and worked his way up to where he was now. He wouldn't go any further. Not because the commissions weren't offered to him, but because he felt if he got any higher up in the hierarchy, he'd lose touch with his reason for joining up in the first place: helping people.

It was a somewhat naive attitude for this day and age, and Tucker knew it. But he'd played it straight this far. He'd never been involved in anything that compromised his personal sense of honor, though it wasn't as easy now as it had been when he'd first joined. Everything was getting too complicated. Narcotics, terrorism, just general crime itself. It was all building up. It couldn't be handled on the municipal or provincial levels. And it was getting hard on the federal level as well. The whole world was coming apart at the seams and Canada was going straight down the tubes with the rest of them.

Project Mindreach was a perfect example. He understood the ramifications—if the theories of Hogue and his colleagues held up. But it just seemed like so much bullshit. There were more important things that needed to be dealt with and Tucker couldn't figure out why he'd been assigned to this operation.

Tucker was a troubleshooter, sent in when a situation got too sticky, or put on an operation that the brass was afraid could turn bad on them. But whatever his own thoughts on Project Spook, he was in charge for the duration—liaison and advisor, head of security, but his hands tied as he watched Hogue and his lab boys blow it, left, right, and center.

The Paranormal Research Branch was a dismal failure. At least so far. They had an eight-million-dollar budget, unlimited access to computer time, half a floor of offices and labs, Hogue and his assistants, and a six-man squad on stand-by. And what had they come up with? Zilch. Without subjects, they had only speculation to work on. They should have picked up Hengwr immediately, but Hogue was convinced that the old man was only a go-between. Too shabby to be a leader himself. There had to be someone above him and *that* was who Hogue wanted in his lab. Right now, with the pressure coming down from above, Hogue'd settle for anybody. Even this Foy, if need be. If the PRB was closed down before it ever got on its feet, Hogue would have a hell of a time selling anybody on a new project.

"You've got to stop Gagnon from talking," Hogue said.

Tucker shook his head. "I'm not going to force him. This is still a democracy. The private citizen still has some rights, for Christ's sake. At least he does in my books. I'm going to reason with Gagnon and we'll see what comes out."

He checked his watch. Five to nine. If he took the Queensway from Headquarters, he should be able to make Tunney's Pasture in, say, fifteen minutes. Opening his desk drawer, he took out a snub-nosed .38 and clipped it to his belt. He wasn't likely to need it, he just felt naked going out without it. Putting on his coat, he left it unbuttoned to hide the bulge the pistol made.

"I'll go now," he told Hogue, "and try to calm him down."

"You were willing to pick up Hengwr," Hogue said. "And Foy. We've got nothing on either of them. What makes their rights any different from Gagnon's?"

Tucker paused at the door and looked back.

"I'll tell you something," he said. "It's because I've read the reports on both of them. They're bums, and one of them's got a criminal record. Gagnon's different. He holds down a responsible position. He's earned the right to be treated with some respect. And it wouldn't matter to me if Gagnon was a farmer or the president of I-B-fucking-M. He's productive, and that's what counts. Your two spooks haven't shown themselves to be that yet. Does that answer your question?"

"Yes, but—"

"Look. I'm in charge of this operation, remember? I know what you're thinking. 'He's going to spill his guts and blow the whole shebang.' Well, I've got some news for you. Sometimes you try and trust people, okay? That's what I should have done in the beginning with Gagnon, instead of pussyfooting around with that crock of bullshit you talked me into. Master criminal. Jesus H. Christ!"

"Inspector—"

"You don't like it? Go cry to the Superintendent then. When he takes me off, *that*'s when I'm off. But not till then. Got it?"

He didn't calm down until he was in his '79 Buick, cruising down the Queensway, listening to General Grant cracking stupid jokes on CFRA.

9:30, Wednesday morning.

Gagnon wasn't as old as Tucker had expected. At thirty-eight, he seemed young to be the Assistant Deputy Minister in charge of the Health Protection Branch. To get there at that age, Tucker reasoned, he had to be more than competent. They'd only met over the phone before. In person, Gagnon was the picture of a high-placed civil servant. He wore an expensive tweed suit, tailor-fitted, a cream shirt and a narrow brown tie. In his lapel was a small Canadian flag pin—two red bars and a red maple leaf in a field of white.

Tucker had checked into Jean-Paul when they'd learned of his connection to Foy, but hadn't come up with anything sinister—either in his background or his present lifestyle. He was French Canadian, from St. Jérôme, a small town north of

Montreal that had the honor of being home to the largest church in the Laurentians—the Cathédrale de St. Jérôme, built between 1897 and 1899. He'd taken his Ph.D. and M.D. at McGill University and worked for the Department of Health and Welfare from '70 onwards. He led a quiet life. He was not, so far as Tucker could see, a candidate for any sort of criminal activity. Unless he'd just never been caught.

"Before you say anything," he said as the secretary showed him into Gagnon's office, "I want to apologize for your treatment so far and assure you that I'll make every effort to explain exactly what we're dealing with. After that, you make your decision, okay?"

Jean-Paul blinked, unprepared for the Inspector's opening remark. He'd been steeling himself to an uncomfortable confrontation.

"*Bonjour, inspecteur,*" he said. Needing a moment to gather his thoughts, he added: "Did you have any trouble finding my office?"

Tucker shook his head. "No. I just detected my way here."

Jean-Paul smiled politely at the Inspector's attempt at humor.

Tucker settled into a chair and leaned forward. "Why don't you let me tell it through and you can grill me all you like afterwards, okay? It'll save time."

"As you wish, *inspecteur.*"

"The name's John. John Tucker."

Jean-Paul shrugged. Settling back in his chair, Tucker tapped his fingers together for a moment, then plunged into his explanation. Jean-Paul sat quietly throughout it, his features giving away nothing. When Tucker was done, Jean-Paul shook his head thoughtfully.

"*C'est incroyable,*" he said at last. "this Project Mindreach...all you have told me. I think I preferred your first explanation. It was, at least, more believable, *n'est-ce pas?*"

"I haven't bought the whole show myself, to tell you the truth. But that's what's been going down so far."

"And you think Kieran is one of these...spooks?"

Tucker shrugged. "Let's just say we have reason to suspect that he's got some kind of—I don't know. Special powers, I suppose. That's *if* Hogue's theories are valid. Let's face it. The whole thing's a little farfetched when you come right down to it. But just suppose it *was* true...."

Jean-Paul thought back to his conversation with Kieran last

night. If what the Inspector said was true, it explained much that had been left unsaid—avoided even. But all he said was:

"Is that still a reason to persecute him?"

"Look. I know he's your friend. . . ." Tucker's voice trailed off and he sighed. "What I'm asking for is your cooperation in keeping this to yourself. Not your help. Just . . . can you keep it out of the papers?"

Jean-Paul shook his head. *"Je regrette*. . . . I cannot agree with your methods, *inspecteur*. I wished no part of it. Now I am involved. And, as you mentioned earlier, Kieran *is* my friend—no matter how he might feel about my part in this at the moment."

"Yeah. Well, I kind of thought you'd say something like that. Say, how'd you two ever get together anyway? I mean, you don't exactly move in the same circles."

"We met at a friend's lodge in the Gatineau. Pierre was having a party and had hired a folk group to play at it—fiddle tunes and the like. Kieran was a member of the group. They called themselves The Humors of Tullycrine—the name comes from an Irish tune, I think. I knew nothing of Kieran at the time. But we had the opportunity to speak later and I enjoyed his company very much. We—how do you say it? We 'hit it off' from the beginning, *n'est-ce pas?*

"You would not know this—you would not even care, I should think. But Kieran is a very warm person, a loyal friend. That is why I feel so . . . sick with what I have done to him. Such an injust betrayal. I will tell you: I never liked Thomas Hengwr very much. There was something . . . *étrange* . . . strange about him. Feeling as I did, I did not find it hard to believe your story of his criminal activities and how you needed my help to capture him. Also, you were very convincing, *non?*

"I suckered you," Tucker admitted. "But if we ever get ahold of Foy I'll tell him the truth about your part in all this."

"'Get ahold of him.' And what will you do with Kieran, once you 'get ahold of him'?"

"That's not really up to me."

Jean-Paul sighed. "You have given me this explanation because you respected me, is that not so?"

"Yes."

"Why do you have so little respect for Kieran? His values are, perhaps different, but does that make him a criminal?"

Tucker thought about that for a moment, recalling his own tirade against Hogue.

"Okay," he said. "I'll give you that. But now you listen to this: Suppose—just suppose—that Hogue's theories are valid, that powers like that do exist. Don't you understand why we have to get a handle on them ourselves? Imagine such power in the hands of terrorists. Or . . . or anyone to whom human life means nothing. Then where are we?"

"Once again you make a strong argument, *inspecteur.*"

Jean-Paul looked away. He felt uncomfortable. For all the Inspector's brash mannerisms, he had a golden tongue. He wondered if Tucker lost very many arguments. He went over the Inspector's explanation, trying to convince himself that it was only so much imagination, but was not able to. Thomas Hengwr—the old man *was* odd. And Kieran—for several years now he'd been sending Jean-Paul occult books for Christmases and birthdays. The Don Juan series. Colin Wilson's *The Occult* and *Mysteries.* The books hadn't convinced him of anything. But what if they were a way of preparing him for . . . for what? Admittance into some secret sect? Jean-Paul found that hard to believe. But surely even the RCMP would not make up such an outlandish story to cover up some more sinister plot?

"I will do this, *inspecteur,*" Jean-Paul said at last. "I will keep my information to myself. For now. But you must promise me: If you find Kieran, you will get in touch with me immediately. You will let me speak to him, before you do anything to him."

"That I can promise you," Tucker said, his relief evident. "And if for some reason Foy gets in touch with you?"

"That will be my affair. I will speak with him first. Who knows? Perhaps he will agree to meet with you. But I find the thought unlikely. He will not overcome his feeling of betrayal so easily, I think."

"Then it's a deal," Tucker said.

He stood up and offered his hand. Sighing, Jean-Paul shook it.

"And the wiretap, *inspecteur?*"

"Perfectly legal. We ran it by Judge Peterson for authorization. I'll have it taken off. Say, how did you pick up on it?"

Jean-Paul smiled. "I didn't. It was an educated guess."

"Well, I'll be damned!"

"I hope not, *inspecteur.* Also, there is a man who followed me to work and another watching my house."

"I'll take them off. But listen up, Mr. Gagnon. Don't blow this on me. I'm trusting you. If I'm wrong about this...."

"I, too, am trusting you, *non?*"

"Yeah. I guess you are at that."

"*D'accord.* And now...we both have work that requires our attention, is that not so?"

Tucker nodded. "Thanks, Jean-Paul. Do you mind if I call you that?"

Jean-Paul shook his head. "No...John. Now please. I have much to think on."

When the Inspector was gone, Jean-Paul sat staring into nothing. Had he made a mistake in agreeing to go along with the Inspector? The man was...persuasive. Ah, Kieran, he thought. *Q'est-ce que tu fais?* What are you doing?

12:10, Wednesday afternoon.

RCMP Superintendent Wallace Madison shook his head as Tucker finished his report. Madison was sixty-three, due to retire in a couple of years. His life, like Tucker's, was the Force. Period. He was tall and distinguished looking and needed a cane because of a hip injury in '69 that hadn't been treated properly.

"I don't know, John," he said.

"Know what?"

"Whether to promote or demote you sometimes. I really didn't think you'd have any luck with this Gagnon over at Health Protection. When Hogue came crying to me...."

Tucker lifted his gaze despairingly.

"What can I say, Wally?"

Madison sighed. "Not much." The bantering tone left his voice. "I need something hard for the Minister, John."

Tucker shook his head. "You've got to stall him. Give us a couple of days. Foy can't have gone far. Hengwr disappeared in Ottawa and, unless what Foy told Gagnon was a crock of shit, he's gonna hang around here looking for him. Then we pick him up."

"You've got a way with words, John. No doubt about it." Madison shoved the operation's file into his briefcase. "I'll do what I can. Do you have time for some lunch?"

"'Fraid not. I've got to check out a couple of leads. You remember that stuff we found in Hengwr's room? The stuff Benson's been checking out?"

"Ted's got something?"

"Not exactly. What he *has* got is some guy that came into the museum with a bone disc that he wants to get dated. Thing is, it matches the set from Hengwr's room."

Madison nodded. "I can use that with the Minister. Following some hot leads."

Tucker grinned at the Superintendent's sarcasm.

"It's the only break we've got so far, Wally. I'm going to take a run down and have a talk with this guy. Benson's stalling him for us."

"If you get anything. . . ."

Tucker smiled. "I know where to reach you. Kissing ass in the Solicitor General's office."

"Get out of here!"

"Yes, *sir!*"

They both laughed.

Chapter Five

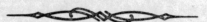

On Wednesday morning, Sara woke up feeling better than she had in ages. She wasn't normally a morning person; even with ten hours sleep, it took her two coffees and as many cigarettes just to creak her eyes open and start the gears turning. But today she woke up vibrant and alert.

Her alarm clock informed her that it was eight-thirty. But instead of burrowing her head back under the pillows, she jumped out of bed and set about getting dressed. A few minutes later, she headed down the stairs to the Silkwater Kitchen wearing jeans, moccasins and a pink sweatshirt with a picture of David Bowie in his "Ashes to Ashes" clown makeup on the front.

There was a fresh pot of coffee simmering on the stove—a sure sign that she wasn't the first up, she deduced with what she thought was a splendid show of deduction for this hour of the morning. She poured herself a mugful and settled down at the table that overlooked the garden to roll her first cigarette of the day. She leaned back in her chair and contentedly blew a wreath of silvery-grey smoke up to the ceiling.

She was seriously considering even having some breakfast, when she happened to glance out the window. Blue's new friend Sally was in the garden, wearing a burgundy Danskin top, leotards, leg warmers and black Chinese slippers. She was performing some esoteric warm-up ritual that looked like a cross between ballet and Kung Fu. Her movements were slow and deliberate and she spent as much time holding a pose as getting to it.

Sara watched until Sally finished, then got up to get more coffee as Sally headed for the kitchen.

"Morning!" Sara called and motioned to the pot. "What do you take in it?"

"Just black, thanks."

"You must be freezing."

"It's not so bad, once you get going." Sally slid into a seat across from Sara's. "You're up early. Blue said to go up and give you a shake if you hadn't dragged yourself down by nine-thirty. Said it was the only way to get you up."

"Usually is," Sara replied, pushing Sally's mug across the table to her. "I don't know what's come over me today. I just feel great. Alive! I'll probably collapse around noon when my brain finally realizes how long it's been awake." She looks so serene, Sara thought, studying Sally over the brim of her mug.

"What was that you were doing?" she asked.

"Tai chi. It's a meditation of sorts."

"Oh, yeah? Looks like something Bruce Lee would do." Sara made a couple of quick chopping motions in the air with the flats of her hands. "Slowed down."

"They're quite similar, actually. Only I like to think that the martial arts are just tai chi speed up."

They both laughed.

"So what're you up to today?" Sara asked.

"We're going for a ride up the Gatineau. If Blue ever wakes up."

"Brrr." Sara shivered. "You'd think he'd put his bike away by this time of year. But he never does."

"Not till the first snowfall, he told me. It won't be that bad."

"Wanna bet? I can lend you a parka. Then again, the way you were prancing around outside just now...."

Sally shook her head. "I don't feel the temperature when I'm doing tai chi."

"My offer still stands, then. For the parka."

"I think Blue'd be insulted. I've convinced him that I'm terribly hardy. It wouldn't do to blow the image too soon. Are you working today?"

"Umhmm."

"At the risk of seeming very snoopy, I've been wondering about something. You don't really *have* to work. So why do you?"

"Oh, I don't know. Gets me out, I suppose. The House can get such a grip on you that if you didn't *have* to go out, you could spend the rest of your life here, wandering aimlessly through the halls like a ghost. Sometimes I'm not so sure that there aren't ghosts in here, you know, doing just that."

Sara glanced at the old Coca-Cola clock that hung above the kitchen door. The time was nine-thirty.

"Speaking of work," she said, "I've got to get going and open up. You should drop by sometime. I'll show you the wonders of the antiquarian business—sure to dazzle your mind and baffle your senses. Or something like that."

Sally laughed. "Okay. I'll take you up on that."

"Are you going to be around for awhile?" Sara asked. "I mean in Ottawa."

"I think so. I've only been here a few months, but I really like it here—being with Blue and everything."

"I hope it works out," Sara said. "Blue's never had much luck with relationships. Most nice ladies don't look any further than his biker image. And as for the women who *are* are attracted by it—" She put her hand over her mouth. "I didn't mean..."

"That's okay. I know what you meant."

"How'd you guys meet, anyway? All I know is one day you weren't here, and the next you were. With Blue."

"We met in the National Art Gallery, of all places. It was so unexpected. I noticed him—how can you miss him?—standing and staring at some piece of modern art, just shaking his head, and I couldn't figure him out. There he was in his jean jacket and T-shirt, pierced ear and ponytail, going through the gallery like the art critic from *The New York Times* or something. Very serious."

"He gets like that."

"Well, I know that now. I suppose it's not very fair judging people by their appearances, but it just seemed so strange. I was feeling very bold, I suppose, so I marched up to him and introduced myself. I just *had* to know what he was doing there. I suppose I was expecting a cocky answer or something, but he started talking very earnestly about this painting—I forget who it was by, but it was one of those dreadful Impressionistic things that I've never cared for—and what with one thing and another, we ended up going for lunch. And then, after a"—Sally smiled—"whirlwind romance, I ended up here."

"That's perfect! It's like the plot of one of those Hollywood musicals—you know, with Bing Crosby and Marjorie Reynolds. So. Are you going to stay?"

"In the House? I'm not sure. I think so. I'd like to. It depends on how it all works out. Everything's happened kind of suddenly."

"Well, *I* hope it works out. I think it's just great." Sara looked at the clock again. "Oh, Lord. I've got to run. I'll see you later. Maybe you can show me some of that tai chi of yours—if you don't mind someone who's a total klutz and stumbles all over herself."

"I'd love to. It'll give me someone to work with."

Sara smiled. "I don't know. If it entails getting up this early every morning... Today's the exception more than the rule, you see. But I'd like to give it a try. See you tonight. That is if you make it back from your adventure in the frozen wilderness."

"I think I'll survive."

Sara raced up to her room, grabbed her coat, a scarf and her knapsack, and headed for the store, her hair blowing every which way in the wind. She was a couple of blocks from the House before she realized that she was still wearing her moccasins, but by then she decided she was too far along to go back and get her boots. The sky was overcast, but maybe it wouldn't rain. She grinned to herself. Today was the sort of day where nothing could go wrong. Last night's dream was as far from her thoughts as her old beau Stephan was. And she wasn't thinking of him at all.

Sara was sitting in front of her Selectric in The Merry Dancers, with Alan Stivell's harp music trickling from the speakers above the door. The sense of heightened awareness, or clarity, that she'd woken up with hadn't deserted her yet. In fact she'd just figured out what to do with her main protagonist—something that had been holding her up for a week or so.

She was in the middle of typing up the reactions of her lead female character when the phone rang.

"Damn," she muttered, missing the 'T' key so that "heart" came out reading "heary". She frowned at the phone, willing it to stop ringing, gave up after the fifth shrill jangle and picked it up. "The Merry Dancers, good afternoon," she said. "This is a recording. If you would like to leave a message, please speak clearly and—"

"Sairey?"

"Oh, hi, Jamie. What's up?"

"I'm afraid we've got a bit of a problem."

"What do you mean?"

"I don't know where to begin. Remember I said I'd take your painting into Potter's this morning? I decided to go up to the museum and show Ted Benson your little bone button first. I knew he'd have to send out to Energy, Mines and Resources on Booth Street, so I thought I'd get that done right away."

"Jamie, what's happened? Your voice sounds all jittery."

"I. . . ." He cleared his throat. "I've just finished an interview with an Inspector Tucker from the RCMP. It seems that your bone button was stolen from an art exhibit and—"

"Stolen? But that's impossible! I found it in that box in the back of the shop. It'd been there for years."

"Well, *I* know that. I tried to tell this Inspector and he—he's a real thug, Sairey. Talks like he stepped out of a Mickey Spillane novel."

Sara's heartbeat had picked up.

"What happened?" she asked. "What did you tell them? Did you tell them about the other stuff I found?"

She stared at her ring and closed her fist protectively around it.

"Let me start at the beginning," Jamie said. "I went up to Ted's office and told him what I needed done. He just smiled and said, 'No problem,' until I took the button out of my pocket. I knew something was wrong right away, because he got this strained look on his face as though I'd—I don't know. Pulled down my pants. He went all white and asked me where I'd gotten it. I started to tell him, but then he said never mind and asked me to wait in his office for a moment. I guess that's when he called the police—or this Inspector Tucker at any rate.

"When he came back he seemed more normal. Offered me a tea and what not. He was quite casual, asked to have a look at the button, how you were, how was my writing going. He managed to kill a half hour or so with all that—not that I was suspicious at the time. I realized all this after. Anyway, a knock came at the door and then the Inspector was there—filling the bloody doorway, Sairey! He's a big man—the sort that has 'authority' stamped all over his face."

Sara had a sudden vision of a policeman with the word "authority" stamped on his forehead in red ink. It didn't make her smile.

"He laid right into me," Jamie said. "Wanted to know where I'd gotten it, why had I brought it in to Ted—I think I'll ask

Blue to stomp on him for me. Do you think Blue would do that?"

"Don't ask him," Sara said. Because Blue would. If Jamie or she asked him to.

"But imagine," Jamie said. "Calling the police on me. It just goes to show you. You can't trust anyone anymore."

"Why did he want to know all about the bone disc?" Sara asked.

"Well, that's what I asked him, but he wouldn't tell me. 'Confidential,' he said pompously, then gave me a look as though I was some sort of common criminal. After that he wanted to know who I was, what I did for a living, and kept asking Ted to confirm whether I was telling the truth or not. I got mad then. I refused to talk to either of them anymore and demanded a call to my lawyer. The Inspector just looked at me strangely, then said: 'Go ahead. I'm not booking you yet, so it might be a wasted trip for him.'"

"Oh, God! Jamie, are you in jail now?"

"No. I'm at a pay phone. I wanted to call you right away in case this Inspector Tucker decides to go see you at the store. In fact, I'm sure he'll be down there."

"What for?"

"For more information. You know he wouldn't give the button back? 'I can't do that, I'm afraid,' he says, all official-like. Then he writes me a receipt for it. A receipt!"

"Jamie? What am I going to say if he shows up here?"

"Nothing! Don't tell him anything. Call MacNabb. You have the right to have a lawyer present. In fact, you should probably call Phillip right now. We'll sue them for . . . for . . . I don't know. Harassment."

Sara kept glancing at the door, expecting to see a police car pull up outside, siren wailing, light flashing. They'd rush in with their guns out and take her away. They'd ask her about the ring and the painting and everything. But they were her treasures, and they didn't have any right to them. Jamie's friend had left them to him, and Jamie'd told her she could keep them.

"Sairey? Are you still there?"

"I was just thinking. They can't really do anything, can they, Jamie? I mean, we know that stuff's been sitting in the back room for years."

"But we can't prove it."

"Why should we have to?"

"The last thing the Inspector told me was that your button was part of an art exhibit that had been stolen en route from Toronto to the museum here in Ottawa. Apparently they recovered all of it except for that one artifact. Your button."

"But that's impossible!"

"That's what I told him. I don't think he cared what I said. You know, Sairey, I'm not sure what's going on, but I do know this: It's something very strange. I have a bad feeling about it—a very bad feeling."

Sara felt the same way. As though in answer to that foreboding, the bell above the shop's door tinkled and she looked up to see a large man entering. There was no red ink on his forehead, but she knew immediately who he was.'

"I . . . I think he's . . . here," she mumbled into the phone.

"Who is? Inspector Tucker?"

Sara nodded, then realized that Jamie couldn't see her. "If not him, then his brother."

"Don't say anything to him! Nothing. I'll call MacNabb and we'll be down as soon as we can. Okay?"

"Okay."

Sara cradled the phone. The man was looking idly about the store and she wondered for a moment if she hadn't been mistaken. But then the man approached the counter.

"Are you Ms. Sara Kendell?" he asked.

There was no mistaking that tone of voice. Although she'd never had any personal experience with it, she knew it from a hundred cop shows on TV. She nodded and tried to figure out why she felt guilty. She hadn't done anything wrong, but her hands wouldn't stop trembling. Maybe policemen just made you feel that way, she thought. Maybe it was a special ingredient in their cologne.

"I'd like to ask you a few questions, if I may. My name's John Tucker. I'm an Inspector with the RCMP."

As though they were playing out a scene in a movie, he put his hand in the inner breast pocket of his jacket and showed her his ID. The badge gleamed like a mirror.

"About what? I mean, no. I'm not supposed to talk to you until my . . . uh . . . lawyer gets here."

She felt stupid saying that. What if he arrested her for being uncooperative?

"Your lawyer?" Tucker glanced at the phone, then back at Sara and sighed. "Was that your uncle on the phone just now?"

Sara nodded.

"He's a little excitable, isn't he?" Tucker nodded to Sara's visitor's chair. "Mind if I sit down?"

"I can't stop you, can I?"

"Jesus H. Christ! What is it with you people?" Tucker glared at her. "What do you think I am? The neighborhood ogre?"

Sara shook her head numbly. She was frightened by the vehement tone of his voice and nervously started to twist her ring on her finger until she remembered that she didn't want to call attention to it. Then she clasped her hands together on her lap and stared wide-eyed at the policeman to see what he'd say next.

Tucker sat down.

"Look," he said. "I'm sorry. I've just come from an interview with your uncle who is a most exasperating man. I'm not here to arrest anyone. I'm not here to powertrip. I just want to ask a couple of simple questions and then be on my way, okay?"

Sara swallowed, then gathered her courage.

"Why did you lie to him?" she asked.

"To who?"

"To Jamie. About the bone disc. You know it was never stolen from some exhibit. It couldn't have been. I only found it yesterday in a box of junk."

"I don't know if the bone disc was stolen or not. I . . ."

He paused, reviewing his earlier interview with Jamie Tams. Then he thought of Jean-Paul Gagnon. Maybe he should just stop playing games.

"Look," he said. "I'm going to level with you as best I can. I can't tell you everything, but . . . well, we'll see how it goes.

"We're looking for a couple of men—I can't tell you why, but it's important that we find them. One of them left behind a bag of these bone things in the room he was renting before he disappeared. There were sixty of the discs in it. Each one has a design on it—a different image on either side and all the designs are different. The one your uncle brought into the museum seems to be a part of the same set of . . . whatever they are.

"Ted Benson's been working for us—trying to figure out what they are, where they're from. To try and get a clue on the old fellow who owned them. One of the two men we're looking for. Do you follow me so far?"

Sara nodded, a little mollified. She found herself listening to the Inspector's explanation with interest and she wasn't frightened of him any more. But she still had that sense of foreboding—the little warning light in the back of her head was still flashing. She remembered—

—A spill of bones, clicking and clacking against each other as they tumbled and fell . . . and she was falling too . . . through a mist of grey and brown . . . one more bone . . . until the face reared up with its ursine features and fierce eyes, jaws gaping—

—her dream. She shivered, but the Inspector didn't appear to notice it, nor the sense of evil that seemed to fill the shop for a moment. She thought she saw something move in the shadows that lay between two kitchen hutches that stood against a wall behind the Inspector. She looked quickly away and tried to concentrate on what Tucker was saying.

"When your uncle brought that bone disc in to Benson, he didn't know what to think. This is a very . . . volatile investigation that we're involved in. Highly secure. No one's supposed to know anything about it, but here comes your uncle waltzing in with another piece to the same puzzle we've been working on without any luck. Benson called me and I came down to see what was up."

Sara glanced at the shadows, but there was nothing there—if there ever had been.

"I mean, put yourself in our position," Tucker was saying. "Here's something we've been working on for a couple of weeks—without much success, I might as well add—and here comes what might be a vital clue. Okay. So I blew it talking to your uncle. He got me a little hot with his accusations and I had to think to myself: What's he trying to hide?"

"He just gets a little excited," Sara said.

Tucker shrugged. "And it was the same thing with you when I first walked in. Even now you're looking like I'm going to bite you or something."

"I . . . I had a bad dream last night," Sara said, "and something made me remember it just now. You're right about Jamie, but he's not a criminal. He gets worked up pretty quickly and you as much as called him a liar. And with all you read in the papers about . . . you know. . . ."

"Royal Commissions and the like?"

"Well. . . ."

"You've been reading too many thrillers."

"Who are these men you're looking for?" Sara asked. "What did they do?"

"They haven't done anything yet. We just want to talk to them."

He reached into his pocket and took out a couple of pictures. Laying them on the counter in front of Sara, he asked:

"Ever seen either of them before?"

Sara had a look.

"Him," she said, putting her finger on a picture of Thomas Hengwr.

"Do you know him then?"

"Not really. He's been in the shop a few times and I think I even saw him at the House once or twice. But not recently."

"Could he have secreted the disc in here, without your knowing it?"

Sara thought about how she'd found it—wrapped in a brown paper parcel, inside the medicine pouch.

"I don't see how he could've," she said. "I found it at the bottom of a box that I got out of the storeroom. It was covered with dust and I never let anyone back there anyway."

Tucker nodded. He indicated the picture of Kieran.

"How about him?"

"He looks sort of familiar—not someone I know, but like I've seen him around." She squeezed her eyes shut, trying to remember. "I think he might've played in a band—a folk band. That was a long time ago—three or four years at least. They were called the Humors of something or other. It was a long name. I think he sang, maybe played guitar too." She looked up. "I'm not being much of a help, am I?"

"At least you're trying. You haven't seen either of them around, have you? I mean lately?"

Sara shook her head. "I'm not sure about him—" she pointed to Kieran's picture—"but I'd remember if I'd seen the other fellow. I used to have long talks with him every few weeks or so. He was a funny sort. He seemed younger than he looked, but older at the same time. Did you show these pictures to Jamie?"

"I didn't think there'd be much point."

Tucker put the pictures away and took out a pen and notepad. He wrote down his name and both home and business phone numbers on a piece of paper, tore it from the pad, and handed it to Sara.

"If you remember anything else—anything at all—give me a call, would you?"

"Okay. You can't tell me why you're looking for them?"

"'Fraid not. Does it matter?"

"Of course it matters. He seemed like such a nice old man. I liked him a lot. I'd hate to think of him being in trouble."

"If he's in trouble, it's not because of us. We're just trying to find him."

"Oh," Sara said.

"I'm sure he'll turn up all right." Tucker stood up. "Look. Thanks for your help. It's appreciated. And I'm sorry for coming on so heavy before."

"That's okay. I guess I was a little on edge." She looked down at the paper he'd given her. "I just call up and ask for you?"

"Night or day."

Sara stuffed the note into the pocket of her jeans and stood up with him. At that moment the front door burst open and Jamie thundered in, dragging Phillip MacNabb, their family lawyer, behind him. MacNabb, a man in his fifties, seemed a little out of breath. He had a broad open face, the honest lines of which had stood him in good stead before many a jury.

"That's him! That's him!" Jamie cried.

"Easy, Jamie." MacNabb turned his attention to the Inspector and they exchanged smiles.

"Hey, Phil. How's it going?"

"Well enough, Tucker. How's Maggie?"

"Okay, I guess. Haven't seen her for awhile."

At the pained look in the Inspector's eyes, MacNabb quickly changed the subject. "So what seems to be the problem here?" he asked.

"It's okay," Sara said. "We got it all straightened out."

"I've got to get back to the office," Tucker said. He tipped his hand against his forehead in a casual salute. "Thanks again for your help, Ms. Kendell. Keep in touch."

He stepped past a flustered Jamie and was through the door before Jamie could think to stop him. Jamie grabbed MacNabb's sleeve.

"Can't you serve him a writ or whatever it is you lawyers do?" he asked.

"Jamie!" Sara said. "It's all right."

"What happened?" MacNabb asked.

"Sit down and I'll tell you all about it."

Sara dug up her thermos and peered inside to see how much coffee was left.

"Anyone want some?" she asked.

MacNabb took the seat that Tucker had so recently vacated. Jamie hovered around looking like a disgruntled rooster until Sara steered him into a chair and set a mug in his hands.

"He seemed like a nice enough man," she said as she perched on the stool behind the counter. "He's looking for these two men, you see...."

Okay, Tucker thought as he climbed into his Buick.

It was parked on Fourth Avenue, around the corner from The Merry Dancers. He put his hands on the steering wheel and stared out the windshield.

So what did he have? Something. Maybe nothing to do with Project Spook, but then again.... Tucker didn't believe in co-incidences. The thing he had to figure out was what Tams was doing with the bone disc in the first place. He considered himself a pretty good judge of character, and he figured Sara was being straight with him.

So, if she had found the disc where she said she had, how had it gotten there in the first place? And what was it doing there? Obviously Tams had access to the storerooms, but Tucker just couldn't figure out what the point of it all was. If Tams was involved, why had he come waltzing into Benson's office with the disc?

Tucker scratched his head. He wasn't going to get any further sitting here. He'd have to put a tail on both Sara and her uncle and get back to headquarters to see what he could dig up on them in the files. Maybe things were coming together. Something had to give. Maybe even the elusive Mr. Hengwr.

He started up the engine and headed down Fourth to the Driveway. On the way he radioed headquarters and had a couple of men put on Sara Kendall and Jamie Tams.

"Yeah," he responded to a question from the man on dispatch. "It's in the Glebe. Between Third and Fourth. If you shake your asses, maybe you can still pick them up there."

Shaking his head, he hooked the mike back onto the dashboard. His squad was getting a little lazy. Too much sitting around. Well, if the feeling he had was right, things'd pick up pretty soon. And if they didn't? Well, he'd just have to push a little harder.

"So that's it," Sara said.

"I'd like to see those other discs," Jamie said.

He was still somewhat miffed at Tucker's treatment of him, but the Inspector's explanation to Sara had set his curiosity in motion, smoothing his ruffled feelings.

Sara laughed. "Good luck."

"Well, we've still got the other stuff you found," Jamie said. "I'll be a little more discreet in my inquiries after today."

MacNabb stood up. "I don't think I want to hear about this. I might as well head back to the office."

"I'm sorry to have dragged you all the way down for nothing," Jamie said. He was looking a bit sheepish. "I guess I got a little worked up."

MacNabb smiled. "I'm used to it. Wait till you see my bill. 'Bye, Sara. It was nice seeing you again. Try and stay out of trouble, would you, Jamie?"

"Well, now what?" Sara asked when the lawyer was gone.

"Now what what?"

Sara held up her hand and the ring sparkled.

"What about this and the painting and the other stuff? Do you think it's all connected with the bag of bone discs at the museum?"

"Can't be." Jamie pursed his lips. "Aled died in '76 and that stuff's been sitting in the storerooms since then."

"Inspector Tucker seems to think that they'd been planted there. Either by you, or one of the men he's looking for."

"Well *I* didn't put them there. At least not the way the Inspector means."

"I know that."

Sara pulled out her tobacco pouch and rolled a cigarette.

"It's funny though," she said around her cigarette as she lit it. "Them finding a whole bag of the same kind of artifacts. What do you think they are?"

Jamie shrugged. "All the designs were different, he said, didn't he?"

"Umhmm."

"It's hard to say. A game of some sort?"

"I wonder if they were planted in the storerooms," Sara said.

"To what purpose?"

Sara pointed her cigarette at Jamie.

"*That*'s what'd be interesting to find out," she said.

"Are you going to play sleuth?"

"Maybe."

"Sairey, be careful." Jamie's face wrinkled with worry.

"That man Tucker doesn't look like anyone to fool around with."

"He's not out to get *us*, Jamie. We haven't done anything wrong."

"He doesn't know that."

But her vague premonition hadn't left her yet. Nor had her dream. She remembered the discs falling over each other in a long tumble. It was too much of a coincidence that she'd dreamed that last night after only seeing one of the bone discs, and today was told there were sixty more. She remembered the cloth with the Celtic cross and ribbonwork on it. The shaman/bear had dropped the discs onto it as though they were some sort of... oracular device maybe?

After Jamie left she couldn't get back to her novel. She just sat, smoking cigarettes and drinking coffee, going over the odd happenings of the past couple of days. A little chill touched her every time she thought of the gaping jaws of whatever creature it had been that sent her clawing her way out of her nightmare last night. The nightmare itself seemed like a warning of some sort. A warning about what? That she shouldn't get involved? Or that if she didn't get involved something terrible would happen to her?

That, she told herself, was taking it a little far.

She thought about the two photographs that Tucker had shown her. She'd forgotten to ask him their names. He probably wouldn't have told her anyway. She'd never learned the old man's, even though he'd been in the shop often enough. For all his friendliness, he never came across as the sort of person you could ask personal questions of. As for the younger fellow...

She tried to think of who might know him. Who else had played in that band? Julie might know.

She dialed the number and waited through a few rings.

"Hello?"

"Hi, Julie. Are you busy?"

"Nope. You calling about Saturday? I found out who's playing at Faces. Cobbley Grey."

"Who?"

"Cobbley Grey. That's Toby Finnegan's new band. Don't you remember him? He's that fiddle player that Linda had a mad crush on. He used to play in The Humors of Tullycrine."

Something went click in Sara's mind. The chances of it being coincidence had just dropped by a few more percentage points. It happened that way. Synchronicity. You never thought of someone, but when you did, all of a sudden the name kept coming up.

"Are they playing there all week?" Sara asked.

"Supposed to. They opened last night. Beth went and saw them and said they were pretty good. They're right up your alley—all jigs and reels and stuff."

"Julie, remember that guitar player in Toby's old band—the quiet fellow with the dark hair?"

"Vaguely. Why?"

"You don't remember his name, do you?"

"No. Is it important? Linda would know. Or we could ask Toby on Saturday. Have you got Linda's number?"

"No. But that's okay. It's not very important."

"I'm feeling snoopy. Why'd you want to know his name?"

"It's a long story. Are you working tomorrow?"

"I start at four."

"Drop in before you go in to work and I'll tell you all about it."

Sara cradled the phone and stared at it thoughtfully. She dug out her clock and checked the time. Five to five. Would Toby be at the club yet? Setting up maybe, or doing a sound check? Probably not. They'd have gone through all that last night. Well, there was Linda then.

Sara stopped and asked herself, why am I doing this? Even if she did find out the fellow's name, what would that get her? Nothing, she supposed, but she'd be doing something. It had started with finding that package in the storeroom. She was involved now, and she had to be doing something.

She pulled out the phonebook and looked up Linda Deverell's number. She might be home from work by now. Rolling another cigarette after she dialed, she waited for Linda to answer.

Johnnie Too-bad was listening to the new Black Uhuru album. The reggae sound blasted from two big Tanoy speakers, bass thumping in time to the ganja buzz that he was floating on. He was a thin, reedy black man, with red-brown dreadlocks and wide brown eyes, who'd taken his name from an old Slickers song. He had a set of scales on the floor in front of him and was weighing out ounces of ganja. Hemp, weed, marijuana, ganja, call it what you will—as Jah made ganja for men to get high, he made Johnnie Too-bad to sell it.

There was a big spliff stuck between the index and middle

fingers of his right hand. In between weighing the ganja and bagging it in one-ounce plastic baggies, he took long tokes on the spliff.

Besides the sound system, two plastic milk crates filled with reggae albums and a few pillows strewn across the floor, the room was devoid of furnishings. There was a poster of Bob Marley on one wall, Gregory Isaacs and Bunny Wailer looked down from a second. The third had travel posters for "Sunny Jamaica," one on either side of the door leading into the room. Behind him, the curtainless window was open a crack, held open by a stack of cigarette paper packages.

When the knock came at the door, he hardly heard it over the sound of the music. It came again, between cuts, and he raised his head to stare at the door, the first whispers of paranoia knifing through his drug-fuzzed mind.

"Who is that, mon?" he called out.

He stared at the piles of ganja—half of it in neat little baggies, the other half a brown mound on a spread-out newspaper. He held up his spliff and wondered, mournfully, if this was going to be his last toke.

"It's Kieran. Kieran Foy."

Johnnie Too-bad's tension drained away under a flood of relief. He took a long toke, then went to the door, opening it a crack. Ganja smoke drifted from his nostrils as he looked Kieran over.

"What you want, mon?"

"Can we talk?"

Kieran smiled, eyeing the spliff and Johnnie's dilated pupils.

"Sure, mon. I and I have time to talk. How's it you find I?"

"I ran into Larry on Rideau Street."

Johnny shook his head. "That mon needs to learn a t'ing or two. He knew I busy."

"I won't take long. I need a little help, that's all."

Johnny stepped aside so that Kieran could enter, then closed the door. He offered Kieran the spliff.

"No thanks."

"It's good smoke, mon. Straight from Ja-mai-ca, you know? There's a man there has a connection wid I. No problem. Only here. Babylon is the problem."

Kieran pulled up a cushion and sat down across from Johnnie. The Rastaman turned over the record as it ended and Black Uhuru came roaring from the speakers again.

"You got trouble wid the po-lice, hey, mon? What you want wid I?"

"Two things. Have you seen Tom around? Thomas Hengwr?"

Johnnie shook his head. "He is very hot, that mon. Po-lice want him bad. You, too. There is trouble, you know, mon? I and I don't want no trouble. What is this other t'ing you want wid I, mon?"

"I need a place to stay. A safe place."

"That will cost, mon." Johnnie rubbed his fingers together. "Cost plenty, you know? You very hot, mon."

"I haven't got any money. I . . ." Kieran sighed. "Okay. Thanks anyway, Johnnie."

"Wait up, mon," Johnnie said as Kieran stood up.

The Rastaman dug into his pocket and came up with a wad of money. He peeled off three twenties and handed them over.

"I and I will help you, but. . . ." He shrugged, indicating the ganja. "I tell you this. I and I hear you are in town, hear you are in bad trouble, you know? I feel bad, mon. Too-bad." He grinned. "But t'ings are bad wid I, too mon. Po-lice watch I too much, you know? I and I give you this money. Other t'ing is too much risk, mon. You understand I?"

Kieran nodded.

"Thanks," he said, pocketing the money. "I'll get this back to you as soon as I can. I . . . Stay cool, *mon ami.*"

"I be cool, mon. Always cool. You keep the money, mon. Jah know that we are friends. What is money, then? Is only Babylon. Poor or rich, I and I be happy. Give I the smoke and the reggae, you know, mon? Let the baldheads keep Babylon."

Does that make me a Rasta as well? Kieran wondered. He too had left the cities, the "Babylon," for the simpler life down east. He took Johnnie's hand and squeezed it tightly.

The Rastaman smiled and took another hit from his spliff. "You remember your friend To-by, mon?" he asked.

"Sure. What about him?"

"He too is in town, you know? He plays the music."

Johnnie mimed playing a fiddle.

"Where's he playing?"

"In the club Faces, mon. Is down Bank, you know? Maybe he can help you where I and I can not, hey?"

"It's a thought."

Kieran hadn't seen Toby for a long time. Not since the days of The Humors, with Eamon and Tim and John Sanders.

"You have a lively time, mon."

Kieran smiled.

"*Salut,*" he said as he stepped into the hall.

The music from Johnnie Too-bad's stereo followed him down the stairs.

Kieran Foy, Sara repeated to herself for about the hundredth time after she finished talking to Linda. It was five-thirty and she was locking up the store. Well, now she had a name to go with the face, but it didn't help any. She wasn't really sure what knowing his name should do. Perhaps she should go to Faces tonight and try to find something out about him from Toby. She didn't know Toby all that well. Enough to say hello to and that was about it. Still, he'd have no reason not to talk to her, would he?

She decided to have dinner at Patty's Place, the small Irish restaurant across the street from Faces. That way she'd be able to see Toby as soon as he showed up at the club. She'd rather talk to him before he started his first set.

She set off south on Bank. It wasn't a long walk. Just past Lansdowne Park and across the bridge. At the corner of Fifth and Bank she paused, stopped by the usual question of whether or not she'd actually locked up the store when she left. Looking back, she never noticed the plainclothes RCMP officer who slipped into the doorway of the Herb and Spice Shop, waiting there for her to turn around and cross the street before he set off after her once more.

RCMP Constable Paul Thompson was determined not to blow this assignment. He was still pissed at how Foy had got by him last night. They should've had a man on the back door. . . . He shrugged. Well, that was then and this was now. He kept to an easy pace, letting his subject gain a fair-sized lead on him. *She* wasn't going to get away on him.

6:30, Wednesday evening.

Tucker was in his office, just starting on his dinner. He pulled the plastic lid off his coffee and unwrapped a ham and cheese sandwich. He had had time for one bite when Hogue came into his office.

"Am I disturbing you, Inspector?"

Always, Tucker thought. He motioned Hogue to take a seat and took another bite.

"It's about your report," Hogue said. "How accurate are the conversation transcripts?"

Tucker frowned. "What do you want to know for?"

"There's no need to be so antagonistic, Inspector. We're supposed to be on the same team."

Like shit we are. Tucker attempted a smile.

"What's your question, Hogue?"

"When you were taking Miss Kendell's statement she mentioned something about a dream. A bad one. 'Something made me remember it just now,' you have her down as saying. Can you recall what it was that keyed her in? Something you said?"

"What's the difference?"

Hogue sighed. "The difference is, we're looking for people with special powers. You obviously thought her remark about her dream was important enough to enter into your report. I think it's important too. Remember Foy with his 'feeling'?"

"It's hardly the same thing, Hogue. I make out those reports in such detail to give myself something to think about. If I wanted real accuracy, I'd have them make out statements and sign them, see?"

Hogue tapped the report against his knee.

"I want that girl in here," he said.

"No."

"What do you mean, 'no'? I've got this feeling about her—"

"You got a *feeling*, Hogue? Then run your fucking tests on yourself. You've got enough controls to fill up ten file drawers. You don't need another."

"I don't want her as a control. I want her because she might be—"

"Look, Hogue. She's not one of your spooks, okay? I've talked to her. *And* to Tams. Now they might be hiding something, I'll grant you that, but what it is is my business. Not yours. Stick to your lab. You've already fucked up this operation enough as it is."

"I've already spoken to the Superintendent," Hogue said. "He agrees with me. Apparently—"

"Oh, yeah?"

Tucker slammed his sandwich down and punched Madison's number on his phone, wishing the pushbuttons were Hogue's face.

"Wally?" he said when he got through. "Who do you want handling this Project? Me or that bright-eyed lab bunny that's parked his ass in my office?"

"What do you mean, John? He has a pretty good idea there.

The Minister's making nervous noises and this woman looks like the perfect thing to allay him with. Something hard, you know? To explain our budget."

"Fuck the Minister. And his budget. We've been running this operation Hogue's way. That's why we're in the position we're in now. We pick up that woman now and you'll blow what I've been working on."

Madison sighed on the other end of the line and Tucker knew what he was doing. He was weighing the problem he had with the Minister right now, against the previous problems that Tucker had pulled him out of. Tucker wasn't worried about which'd come out on top. He knew Madison too well.

"Okay, John," Madison said. "I'll give you twenty-four hours."

"I need till the end of the week."

"I can't wait that long. Williams wants results—last week."

"I need till the end of the week."

"What am I supposed to tell Williams?"

"The end of the week, Wally."

Madison sighed again. "Okay, John. You've got it. But don't let me down."

"I won't." Tucker hung up and regarded Hogue. "Get the fuck out of my office, asshole."

Hogue's face went red. "I've had just about as much of your abuse as I can take, Inspector."

"So go fill out a grievance. Just leave me alone."

Hogue looked as if he was going to say something else, but under Tucker's glare he only stalked out of the Inspector's office. Tucker shook his head.

It probably hadn't been such a good idea to verbalize his feelings about Hogue, but it certainly made him feel better. Besides, it wasn't like it was coming as a surprise to the jerk. But enough fun and games. Now he had to get some results. Picking up his sandwich, he headed for the radio room to see if either of his men had called in. Under his arm was a thick set of files containing all that the RCMP had on James Stewart Tamson (aka Jamie Tams), his father, his grandfather, and Tamson House.

There was a lot of money happening in the Tamson circle of influence. Kendell Communications. Tamson's own money. And that house. From a skim through the files, it appeared that the place was a clearing house for all the weirdos that came through Ottawa. Investigations had proven there was nothing sinister happening there, but that didn't sit right with Tucker. Maybe the previous investigators had been looking for the wrong kind of things. To Tucker's way of thinking, Tamson House seemed the perfect place for someone like Hengwr or Foy to hide out. Indefinitely, if need be. But before he cracked down on that place, he wanted a little more information on Tamson himself. And his niece Sara Kendell.

There was nothing for him in the radio room. Laying the files on the desk in a corner of the room, he settled down to give them another serious study.

Chapter Six

THE first thing Kieran did after leaving Johnnie Too-bad's apartment was get himself something to eat. He left Sandy Hill, crossing the Rideau Canal by way of the Laurier Avenue Bridge, and made his way down to Elgin Street. He ended up at Pepper's, a small restaurant near the corner of Frank Street that did a booming business with the hip crowd that had made Elgin Street their own during the past year or so. Sitting near the window, he reviewed what he had to go on so far.

It wasn't, he admitted, a whole lot. Tom was gone and the horsemen wanted him. Wanted both of them. Why? The face of the Mountie he'd questioned last night popped into his mind. He'd said something about paranormal research, that the horsemen had set up a special branch to investigate those mysteries that science couldn't explain. Kieran shook his head. Lord lifting Jesus! The Way might have some outward psychokinetic trappings, but it went far beyond that. You might as well pick up a couple of Zen monks or a Norindian shaman and give them a good going over while you were at it.

Kieran could just imagine the old man in the horsemen's labs.

"The Way is real, but it has no form. It is attainable by any who dare to follow it, but the journey is long and the rewards cannot be weighed by your present values. First you must attain an inner stillness—attain it and *maintain* it. Without conscious effort. That is the heart of the Way: inner silence. The old language has a word to describe it: taw. It means the silence that is like music. Strength through harmony. Once you have attained it, nothing is impossible."

What would the Mounties have to say about that? It was what the old man had told him . . . at least ten years ago now.

Tom had described the journey as similar to the twenty-one years it took one of the old harpers to become a true bard. Seven years learning. Seven years practice. Seven years playing. Kieran still had another eleven years to go himself by that reckoning. And then? When it was done?

"Why you begin again," Tom had told him. "There is never an end. But with each step you take on the journey, your heart will become more pure, your taw will grow more still. And the silent music inside you will become more profound. Understand this, Kier. The Way is the world, and you travel it to attain harmony with and within the greater all. Nothing more.

"But harmony—that is not such a little thing in itself, now is it? Peace. A balance. They are only words. Only when you begin to achieve that harmony will you understand. And then— why then the words won't matter anymore."

When Kieran had begun to understand, he found himself no more able than the old man to put his feelings into words. The Way *was* beyond words. And this the horsemen wanted to put in their lab and study? *Nom de tout!* Why not try to harness moonlight while they were at it?

But Kieran knew the reasons behind this research. They saw power in it. *If* they even believed, they saw only the power. They would never understand that that power could not and should not be possessed without a commensurate inner strength. Oh, there were aspects that could be utilized without that deeper understanding, but in the end they led only to destruction. Self-destruction. But misguided or not, the Mounties were a hindrance to his search, and a danger. Kieran was only interested in finding Tom. He didn't need the man on his tail, making what was turning into a difficult task more difficult.

As he finished his meal, he came to a decision. He had little to go on, true enough. But he did have something. Johnnie Too-bad had given him the lead: Toby Finnegan. Though none of the old band had fully understood the relationship between Kieran and Tom (how did one explain a sorcerous tutorship in twentieth century terms?), they'd all come to know the old man pretty well. If Toby was gigging again, he might have heard something.

It wasn't much, but it was worth a shot. Kieran paid his bill with one of Johnnie Too-bad's twenties, pocketed the change, and stepped out onto Elgin. The area between his shoulder-blades prickled in anticipation. He expected to be stopped at any moment. Sighing, he set off down Elgin, heading for Ottawa South.

Sara pushed the empty fish and chips basket across the table. She had a window seat in Patty's Place that commanded a good view of the front entrance to Faces. So far she hadn't seen Toby go in, but it was still early. Just going on to a quarter of seven.

What was she going to accomplish? she asked herself for the umpteenth time. Nothing. Everything. The more she thought of it, the more foolish she felt. She toyed with her ring, following the ridge of its ribbonwork with the pad of her thumb. What would Inspector Tucker think if he knew where the ring had come from?

She sighed. Nothing. Everything. Those two words seemed to sum up her whole feeling on the situation. They were diametrically opposed, but their very contradiction bound them together in her mind. She thought of Sally's tai chi, which in turn made her think of the Chinese philosophy of yin and yang. Which was what tai chi meant, she realized, dredging the information up from her memory. She'd read a book on it once. The two ch'i. Heaven and Earth. The mountain and the valley.

She sighed. Her mind was wandering. Either her one draft had affected her more than it had any right to, or that sense of clarity that she'd woken up with this morning was wearing off. *Or* . . . growing stronger.

She was, she realized, feeling a little high. It had nothing to do with the lift she got from drugs or alcohol. It wasn't a big rushy thing—no colors or special effects. Just a subtle heightening of her awareness.

This is silly, she told herself. She was just getting carried away. Except . . . she *did* feel different. And ever since that moment when she'd found the ring and the other stuff, unusual things had been happening to her. From the feeling that she was going to fall into the painting to her dream last night and today's decidedly bizarre events. RCMP manhunts and . . . the dream. . . .

If she closed her eyes she could still see the bones tumbling, the weird faces of the strange beasts/men who were using them to do . . . what? Bear and stag and . . .

She shivered. And something else. Something that had lunged at her with gaping jaws. Dreams and fancies, she told herself,

that's all. That was what she got for playing detective and
trying to tie a myriad unassociated events and objects together.
Except—

At that moment the front door of the restaurant opened and
a sensation like an electric shock went through her. Scratch all
chance for this to be other than coincidence, she said to herself,
for there in the doorway, dressed in a dark blue pea jacket with
a blue touque to match, was the younger man from the Inspector's pictures. Kieran Foy.

His gaze met hers, then dropped to her ring hand, his eyes
widening. A look touched his eyes, like that of a beast at bay.
She thought he was going to twist back through the door and
escape, so she jumped to her feet and pushed through the tables
towards him.

"Please!" she called. "I have to talk to you."

Now his eyes narrowed. He was looking past her, over her
shoulder. But she had almost reached him and didn't notice.

"Your name's Kieran Foy, isn't it?"

She tried to ignore the amused smiles of the restaurant's
other patrons, but then she was looking into Kieran's face and
cold fear replaced her excitement at finding him. His eyes were
starting to glow.

It was as he was crossing Lansdowne Bridge that Kieran
realized he was no longer alone. Dusk had fallen and the city
was lit from within now. Porchlights, streetlamps, the yellow
lights that spilled from windows and between half-drawn curtains, the bright glare of headlights from passing cars and buses.
The sky above Ottawa was paled with an electrically charged
aura that could be seen from miles away. Inside the city, it
lightened shadows, added to the general glitter of storewindow
displays, neon lighting, traffic lights.

In the country, where night's darkness was more complete,
night vision was deeper, more focused. The city tended to
diffuse that, just as noise pollution muffled the ear's natural
sensitivity. Kieran, who had become naturalized to the ways
of the country and lonely stretches of uninhabited coastlines of
the Maritimes, felt like he was walking with blinkers and ear-
plugs when he was in a city.

Now as the feeling of being shadowed came to him, he
paused on the bridge and looked down at the water in the Rideau
Canal. It had been lowered in anticipation of winter when it
became the world's longest ice rink. With the cessation of his

own movement, the constant agitation of the city came over him in a rush. He took a couple of deep breaths, quieted the patter of his heart and drew on the stillness inside.

Heightened senses threaded through the jungle of impressions that assailed him. It was not a policeman he sensed, closing in. Nor anything mortal. It was something from beyond the herenow. He couldn't pinpoint it—neither its position, nor exactly what it was. There was just something sharing the night with him, something that had as much in common with city streets as a wolf might have with the plains of the air.

Kieran reassessed his position. Go on, or. . . . Or what?

He went on, taking up his pace once more as though nothing untoward had made him pause to look down from the top of the bridge. He was nearing Faces now, knew he was still early. Knowing Toby, he'd not show up until a half hour or so before the first set. Until then . . . Kieran saw the yellow and green sign of Patty's Place across the street. A place to wait, within view of the club, but off the street.

He crossed Bank, sensing his unseen watcher follow. It was pointless to turn and look for it. He knew, if he turned, there'd be nothing there. Nothing for even his deepened sight to view.

"There are beings," Tom had told him once, "who, though they are not of this world, this here and now, still manifest in this reality from time to time. The original inhabitants of this land called them manitous—the little mysteries. Europeans call them elves. Use the terms if you will, but only for the sake of convenience, for they are of many kinds.

"You'll sense them rarely. Rarer still will you see them. They are drawn here by power and the display of strong emotions. Witches and mages are their primary interest, though you will find them often in times of great sorrows, joys, angers and fears. They are drawn by the use of magic, or by the knowledge that magic is about to be used. So you will feel them from time to time, *know* their presence; but without their consent, that is as close to them as you will ever get."

"Are they dangerous?" Kieran had asked.

The old man shrugged. "Everything has the potential to be dangerous. Mostly the manitous are curious, but be wary in your dealings with them, Kier, should the occasion arise. It's best to ignore them—at least until they wish to be known by you. And remember this: No matter how humanlike they might appear, they are not of this world. Their ways are different from ours."

It was such a being Kieran sensed now. He hesitated in front of Patty's Place, for he heard sounds now. Whatever watched him had grown in number. There were rustlings—leather against leather, bead clicking against quill. Murmurs that sounded like wind, but he knew them to be voices. The old man had taught him many old tongues and he found that he could almost make out individual words. A soft tapping, muffled and eerie like the pads of fingers brushing against the leather skin of a drum, reached his ears.

They were all around him, he realized. And something else was present as well—though this was more a premonition of a presence than the actual presence itself. It reminded him of the feeling he'd had last night when he'd been looking at the strange gables and rooftops of Tamson House from across Bank Street. A sense of maleficence. A warning prickle settled along his spine, though whether the danger was represented by his hidden watchers, this other presence, or from something inside the restaurant, he wasn't sure.

Standing here, he told himself, was doing no good. Maintaining a calmer show than he felt inwardly, he entered the restaurant, pausing in the doorway to give the place a look over. He'd been here before—many times, in fact. But that had been three years ago.

His earlier premonition began to scrape a raw pattern down his spine. Get out! his senses were screaming. Now! Before it's too late. There was something in the shadows at the back of the restaurant that drew him. A familiar face, or . . . Before he had a chance to investigate it, a young woman who'd been sitting at a windowside table stood up. Power emanated from her. From her . . . No. From her ring. As she stood up to get his attention, his gaze locked on that tiny band of gold. He knew that ring. He heard Tom's voice in his head.

"There's so much to tell you," the old man was saying. "I wonder sometimes how my own master knew what to give and what to pass on. Does no good to give it all, Kier. You'll see that when it's your own turn to take on an apprentice. There's things best learned on your own, in your own way. Others that need to be shown. Take this ring." He held up a gold band, a twin to the one on Sara's finger. "Looks to be plain gold—except for the ribboned design. But there's more to it than that. Can you feel it?"

Tom had passed the ring over to Kieran then. Kieran almost

dropped it. He was startled by the intensity of . . . what? The emotion locked in it?

"We in the craft," Tom explained, "who follow the Way, no matter which path . . . we call it a gifting ring, Kier. It is for friends who are more than friends, who are . . . special. When you meet someone wearing one of these you'll know you can trust them. There is much locked in that metal—love, power, knowledge. Those who wear them often grow to follow the Way themselves—the ring acting as a catalyst of sorts."

"Where do the rings come from?" Kieran had asked.

"We make them. Later . . . when your studies are more advanced, I'll show you how it's done. It entails metalwork— oh, yes. But so much more. A balanced heart, a deep taw, silent as a mountain tarn, and one more thing."

"What's that?"

"A friend. Someone worthy to wear it. Without that, the ring is nothing."

"What happens when the owner of a ring dies and it gets passed on to someone else?"

The old man smiled. "Gifting rings have a knack of finding their way into the right hands. Or should I say onto the right fingers?"

The right fingers . . .

Kieran stared, from the ring on the woman's finger to her face. Then he saw the man behind her, rising from his table. Friend? His gaze flicked back to Sara and he shook his head slowly, witchlights blossoming in his eyes. Friends didn't set you up.

Constable Paul Thompson had been nursing a cup of cold tea for the past three-quarters of an hour. He'd taken a seat further back in the restaurant where he could keep an eye on Sara without being too conspicuous. He wasn't really worried about her noticing him. Most people couldn't spot a tail if their life depended on it. Which was too bad, because if you *were* being tailed, your life just might be on the line.

Thompson figured this to be pretty much of a routine assignment, but he wasn't going to take any chances. After last night, he was determined to stick as close to the subject as he could, no matter how innocent she seemed. He knew she'd come here for more than dinner. She was waiting for someone. That was obvious from the way she kept checking the street through the window. The thing was who was she waiting for? When he answered that, he might just come up with the break they were looking for.

Policework can be tedious. No one knew that better than Thompson. He'd seen enough of its tedium on his seven years on the Force. It wasn't all car chases and shoot-outs like TV and the movies made it out to be. In fact it rarely was. Though being assigned to Tucker's special squad had certainly increased the likelihood of things getting a little more interesting than they might, say, on an assignment in the Territories.

He was about to order a second tea when the front door of the restaurant opened. Ho-lee shit! he thought, recognizing Kieran at the same time as Sara. So this was who she'd been waiting for.

His reaction, however, was different from hers.

While she was starting from her table, he lunged to his feet, drawing his .38 from under his coat. The big steel barrel centered on Kieran as Thompson braced his left hand on his right wrist, assuming the tried and true position that had been drummed into him during his early days of training at the Academy in Regina.

"Freeze!" he cried out.

His voice boomed in the small restaurant. He felt his palm slicken. "You move, and you're gone—got it?"

Sara never heard the constable's command. Looking into Kieran's eyes, the restaurant lost its reality for her. The light grew dimmer and the air shivered like a heat mirage. She sensed invisible presences all around her, watching. She heard the sound of muffled drumming mixed with the click of beads and quills. As the light in the restaurant grew fainter still, she began to make out shapes—tall slender beings dressed in buckskins and rough-woven cloth. The swirling beadwork on their shirts was as intricate as the ribbonwork on her ring. But the designs weren't Celtic.

Her throat grew tight and she was finding it hard to breathe. She could make out the faces of the watchers now. Their features were pinched, the skin drawn tight across their facial bones, their eyes large and vaguely owl-like. The tips of their ears rose higher than eartips should. A few had headdresses made from long feathers and dangling quills. One had two tiny pronged horns on his brow. Oh, God! They were *growing* from its brow, she realized.

Her legs started to shake. She could see the drums. Every second being held one under its arm. Slender fingers tapped their rhythms. The sound came from all around. The smell of a forest was in the air—a rich, dark scent of cedar and pine. The restaurant began to sway in her sight and she put out a hand to keep her balance. Her trembling fingers came into contact with Kieran's arm and gripped it tightly.

A spark seemed to fly up her own arm at the contact—like static electricity, only stronger. Suddenly she was seeing through Kieran's eyes, sharing his thoughts. She understood his anger/fear/sorrow in a confusing rush, then was swept under the deluge of his emotions. He was thinking simultaneously on many levels:

The watchers were not dangerous, for all that their drumming and clicking was building up tension like the cheap soundtrack of some grade B horror flick. The woman hadn't set him up—on the other hand, she couldn't help him either. The visible danger was the constable with his big .38 pointed at them. The prime danger was something else, that indefinable essence of evil he'd first sensed hovering over Tamson House and later recognized outside the restaurant.

He searched for it, found it in the shadows at the back of the restaurant, behind the constable, outside the circle that the drumming watchers had made around the woman and himself. It was a vague shape, a barely definable outline of . . . what? Some creature. Bear . . . but not-bear. He felt the touch of a taw far more powerful than his own—a silence that was dark with the promise of power. It was old, very old, and twisted like the roots of a willow. Merciless.

The drummers quickened their tempo and a shiver ran up Kieran's spine. As though that were a starter's pistol, signaling the beginning of some bizarre contest, the tableau broke. Sara screamed, seeing the monster from her dreams through Kieran's eyes. The constable took a step forward, then the shadows lunged from the wall and fell upon him. He twisted out of shape—man into creature. The .38 fell from talons that could no longer hold it. His shirt and jacket tore apart as his chest swelled, corded muscle growing on corded muscle, matted fur covering his skin. His mouth gaped and yellow canines protruded an inch from his gums.

The momentum of his forward motion carried him through the circle of drummers, claws lashing out. One of the drummers caught a blow and was smashed to the floor, pale blood issuing from the ruin of its chest. The drumming stopped with an abruptness that was threatening in itself. Kieran could hear the world of the here and now for a moment—the screams of the restaurant's patrons as they fought to get out the small exit. The rattle of chairs as they were knocked to the floor. The smash of beer mugs as they spilled, rolled off the tables and exploded in showers of thick glass.

The monster that the constable had become howled and charged forward. Kieran pushed Sara aside and met the beast's rush with outstretched hands. As his fingers touched the matted fur, he loosed his power. Red-gold magefire blossomed from his hands. The smell of the beast's fetid breath was overcome by the rank stink of burned flesh and fur that filled the air. One paw scraped down Kieran's side, the claws ripping through the thick cloth of his pea jacket and shirt to tear the flesh underneath, but Kieran's defense had been too quickly executed for the monster to do more.

As it began to fall toward him, Kieran sidestepped, pulling Sara with him. When it hit the floor, the furry bulk dissolved, and the constable lay there—his shirt and jacket torn, his flesh seared black. His features were twisted into a mask that plainly showed the horror of his death.

Kieran stumbled against a table. Bile rose in his throat. His side felt like it was on fire and he could feel his own blood seeping down his leg. As he went to his knees, the drumming started up once more. He jerked his head up to stare at the strange beings, but the manitous paid him no mind. They went out of focus and the restaurant spun in his sight. Sara trembled with the burden of the bond she still shared with him. She'd seen all he'd seen, felt all he'd felt. The earlier confusion of his emotions was compounded now by a terrible guilt at what he'd done. He'd taken a life. Never before . . . Lord dying Jesus! Never before. . . .

The drumming increased its tempo. The figures of the drummers were vague outlines that stamped about them, encircling them, feet moving in time, moving faster with each step. Deep at the back of the restaurant, like a clot of darkness blacker still than the shadows around it, the evil presence watched. Through his blind despair Kieran, and Sara through him, could sense it mocking them. Then, with a rumble that shook the foundations of the restaurant, it was gone.

Its disappearance did nothing to ease their shared pain and grief. The shadows, rather than growing lighter with the evil's absence, closed in on all sides. These were like the bulk of tall trees now, pines with needles that whispered as the wind rasped them, one against the other. The herenow they knew was gone. Restaurant, the street outside, the city itself—all gone.

They could still hear the sound of drumming, faintly against the whisper of the pines. The shadows of the trees pressed closer, enveloping them, until only the darkness existed. The last thing they heard was the silence that followed the abrupt cessation of the drumming.

When the barman finally dared to step back into Patty's Place and looked in, he saw only the shambles of the restaurant and, in the midst of a cleared space, the corpse of the constable, his limbs splayed awkwardly like the cotton arms of a rag doll. His clothing lay about him like a tattered pall. His skin was charred black and his eyes stared sightlessly into unknown distances.

The contents of the barman's stomach rose up in his throat and he turned away to throw up. In the distance, strident sirens could be heard approaching.

11:45, Wednesday evening.

Tucker sat in his office, his desk lit only by a tabletop lamp. The yellow glare mercilessly highlighted the black on white of the statements he was reading. The rest of the room was in darkness. He reread snatches of the barman's statement:

"There was this sound . . . sorta like drumming. It came from all around. And then these . . . I don't know. Shapes. Vague shapes seemed to be everywhere. Then the . . . the constable stood up, pulling out his gun. I didn't know he was a cop then. . . ."

Tucker leaned back in his chair and wearily rubbed his eyes. Vague shapes. What the hell was that supposed to mean? For that matter, what the hell was Thompson doing pulling his piece in a crowded restaurant, for Christ's sake? Tucker looked back at the statement.

"Then he changed into something . . . like Lon Chaney Jr. in *The Wolf Man*, you know? I swear! I never saw anything like it!"

Tucker had interviewed the barman himself and remembered the fear etched in the man's face. His name was Timothy Driver. Thirty-six years old. Married. One child. He'd been employed at Patty's Place for fourteen months. No criminal record. No record of psychiatric problems. Just a plain joe. Not the kind of a guy to make up, a bullshit story like this.

Bullshit story? Tucker sighed. He had another twenty-some witnesses to corroborate Driver's story. Not to mention the restaurant itself. The place was in shambles. Not to mention Thompson's body. Je-*sus!* He'd looked like someone had taken a blowtorch to him.

"He was growling like some kinda animal," Driver's statement continued. "Then he attacked this guy in the doorway." Driver had identified Foy from one of the photographs they had of him on file. "The same guy he was pointing the gun at, you know? He howled and just went for him. I never saw anything like it. This other guy just waited with his arms outstretched. And when the—what the fuck do you call something like that? When the monster got near him, this guy's hands just lit up. I tell ya, I was out that door so fucking fast..."

Just what were they dealing with here?

Tucker tapped his fingers against each other and went through what they had. Facts. They had twenty-three witnesses' statements corroborating Driver's. Facts. Thompson was tailing Sara Kendell. Obviously she'd been waiting there for a meeting with Foy. (Wait'll he got his hands on her! Swearing she didn't know anything....) Facts. Thompson pulls his gun, then turns into the fucking wolfman. Foy blasts him with—what? Then both he and the Kendell woman split.

These weren't facts. From the moment Thompson pulled his piece, the whole thing turned surreal. Except what had happened to Kendell and Foy?

"They never came out," Driver's statement read. "I'll swear to that. I was standing where I could see both the front door and the one on the side, and they never came out. I was the first one in—it couldn't have been more than a couple of minutes after...you know, it all started to happen. But they weren't there. I can't figure it out. That Foy guy took a bad hit. He wasn't going to be traveling anywhere very far. Or very fast."

Foy took a hit. But by the time Tucker got there, there wasn't even any evidence that Thompson had ever turned into this monster. They just had the statements of the witnesses to go on. Who was to say that Foy's wound was real? Who was to say that any of this was real? He'd talked to Hogue after the first few statements were taken, and Hogue was just as baffled as the rest of them. Some sort of mass hallucination, he tagged it.

"Like UFO sightings," Hogue had explained. "There's no way we can know exactly what it was they *did* see. What has happened is, somehow, they've convinced themselves that Constable Thompson turned into some sort of a monster. The recent glut of movies like *The Wolfen* and *An American Werewolf in London* are as much to blame as anything."

"Twenty-four people all dreaming they saw the wolfman?" Tucker had asked. "How the hell's that possible?"

The antagonism between them had been set aside. This was so far outside the boundaries of his own experience that Tucker was suffering from a sense of helplessness.

"What we're obviously dealing with," Hogue said, "is a very powerful telepath. To be able to project his will on that many people..."

Tucker massaged his temples as he thought back on their conversation. Maybe telepathy explained what the witnesses saw, but it didn't explain how Foy and Kendell had pulled their disappearing act. At least he'd managed to keep it away from the press, swearing the witnesses to silence in the interests of national security. He doubted the cock-and-bull story about an armed robbery foiled by an off-duty policeman would hold up for very long. But it might hold up long enough for them to get a handle on the situation themselves.

The trouble was they just didn't have anything hard. The facts were Thompson was dead and Hengwr, Foy and now Sara Kendell were missing. Everything else was just speculation and weirdness. The coroner's report was in on Thompson. He'd died of massive burns. Concentrated burns. Jesus. What a way to go. Fried. Like a goddamned slab of beef that someone had taken a torch to.

Opening his desk drawer, Tucker shook a couple of aspirin from a bottle, looked for something to wash them down with, then swallowed them dry, grimacing at the taste. As he was replacing the bottle, his gaze went to the four warrants that Madison had dropped off earlier in the evening. He'd dragged Judge Peterson from a dinner party to get them signed. Now all Tucker had to do was serve them.

He pulled them out and spread them on his desk, one by one. Thomas Hengwr. Kieran Foy. James Stewart Tamson, aka Jamie Tams. Sara Kendell.

Where did he start? With Tamson, he supposed. But if he

was anything like Foy. . . . How do you pick up someone who can vanish? Someone who can fry you with—what the hell did Hogue call it? Some kind of pyrokinetic power. Shit. Dealing with this was like trying to take out a houseful of terrorists, armed to the teeth, while all you had was a fucking peashooter.

Tucker stared into the darkened corners of his office. Was one of them sitting there right now, watching him? What were their capabilities? Better still, what were their weaknesses? This had gone a little beyond grabbing a couple of spooks so that Hogue and his pals could give them a once over in the lab. Now one of his men was dead.

Tucker had a privileged position on the Force. He made as much as a Deputy Commissioner, for all his rank of Special Inspector. He was a troubleshooter—something the brass would never admit existed in the first place. He kept the rank of Inspector, but didn't work out of an office like his colleagues. He was on the street more often than not. He was answerable only to Madison, who in turn bypassed the Commissioner and reported directly to the Solicitor General.

He had a Corporal and five Constables under him. That was his squad. He had access to the rest of the force's manpower and resources, but he and his squad did the main work. Their specialties were big drug busts, terrorists, organized crime, security on visits from foreign heads of state (where they worked in conjunction with the Secret Service), stop-gapping security leaks—international, national, or internal.

It was work Tucker liked. He felt he was accomplishing something. And even though three got off for every one he put away, he was still doing something. But this . . . this Project Spook. The whole fucking operation stank. Thompson's features swam into his mind's eye—the way he'd looked this morning when Tucker had debriefed him, and the way he was now: a stiff in the morgue. Vacant. Empty. Nobody home.

Tucker gathered up the warrants and stuffed them in the inside breast pocket of his jacket. He'd go down and pick up one of his squad and have a little chat with Jamie Tams. Collins would do nicely. After all, he'd been Thompson's partner. Tucker flexed his fingers. Remembering his two meetings with Tams earlier in the day, he doubted that Jamie had any of the paranormal attributes that Hogue claimed Foy and Hengwr did. And if he did . . . Tucker decided that at this point he just didn't give a shit. Tams was simply going to have to have some fucking good explanations. At least he'd better if he knew what was good for him.

Jamie was worried. Normally Sara rang up when she wasn't going to be home for dinner. It was getting very late—going on midnight—and after the past day's events . . .

He turned from the window overlooking O'Connor Street and crossed the study to his desk, following one of the well worn paths that had left faded trails in the Persian carpet his grandfather had covered the floor with those many years ago. Sitting at the desk, he regarded Memoria's terminal for long moments. The word PROCEED flickered blue on the screen.

Jamie thought for a moment, typed in the word BONES, then thought some more. He was trying to run a check through Memoria's banks to see what references she could come up with on Sara's artifacts, but was having a hard time concentrating. Blue had taken his bike down to the store around six-thirty and returned with the report that the place was all locked up, and no, there didn't seem to be anything unusual around the shop, and no, he hadn't seen Sara along the way, and no, she wasn't in Kamal's with Julie nor at the smoke shop. Nor, Jamie had ascertained, was she at the apartment of any of her small circle of friends.

So where was she?

He sighed, typed out a qualifier ANTLERS. Nothing. QUARTER MOON. Nothing. What were the designs that ran along the rim of the bone disc? He scratched his chin through his beard, then typed in CELTIC RIBBONWORK.

Data from his files flashed by on the screen and Jamie scanned it half-heartedly. He kept his finger depressed on a key and a small white cursor sped rapidly down the screen.

Maybe he should try the hospitals, he thought. Or the police. . . . No. Scratch that.

A light beside the computer began to blink and the screen darkened. When the light stopped blinking, BONES remained at the top of the screen. Under it were the symbols: ???

Jamie frowned, finding it hard to divide his attention between what was happening in Memoria and what was going around in his head. He knew he wasn't going about this right, but theoretically working on this puzzle should have kept him from thinking about Sara. Should have, but didn't.

He expected her to come bounding into his study at any

moment. Or at least call. He didn't like feeling like a worried old hen—the image didn't suit him. Except here he sat, brooding like a father with his daughter out on her first date. Except *that* father didn't have on his mind what Jamie had on his. And—

What was he doing? Jamie asked himself. It was getting bad when he started having conversations with himself.

He entered GAMES and diligently went through the long list that appeared on the screen. What else could he qualify "bones" with? The refrain to an old song ran through his head: "Take off your skin and dance around in your bones...." Right. Just the thing. It was probably something very simple. Or it could just be something that wasn't entered in Memoria's voluminous memory banks. His Aenigma files were incredibly bulky, storing not only what information he'd garnered for himself over the years, but also much of his father's and grandfather's findings as well, though he was not nearly finished sifting through their journals. Plus there was the information that his correspondents sent him. Unfortunately, the information he wanted was probably something he had no reference to at all.

He tapped his finger on the desktop. What if that Inspector *had* arrested Sara? How could he find out? Look up the RCMP in the yellow pages and give them a ring? Sure. And they'd just answer whatever he had to ask them. Why not ask for a crystal ball while he was at it?

His finger stopped tapping. Crystal ball. For a moment his worries dropped from him. Feeling the first taste of excitement he'd had since he started this search, he typed out ORACULAR DEVICES.

Bingo! Now here was a meaty list. He ran the cursor down it, pausing at an unfamiliar word. WEIRDIN. He did a reference check and came up with the definition: ADJ./SCOTS ORIGIN/ EMPLOYED FOR THE PURPOSE OF DIVINATION. That wasn't good enough. First of all, it was in a list of oracular devices—as a noun, not an adjective. Secondly, he wasn't familiar with the term—at least not in this particular connotation. Curious now, he asked the computer for more information.

The screen shimmered, like an old man clearing his throat before expounding on some anecdote, then a new body of print appeared. Jamie grew more puzzled as he read it through.

WEIRDIN. ORACULAR DEVICE SIMILAR TO EGYPTIAN
TAROT OR CHINESE BOOK OF CHANGES. COMPRISED OF
SIXTY-ONE TWO-SIDED FLAT ROUND DISCS MADE OF
BONE, WITH AN IMAGE CARVED ON EITHER SIDE: ONE
HUNDRED AND TWENTY-TWO IMAGES IN ALL. DIVIDED
INTO THIRTEEN PRIME; TWENTY-THREE SECONDARY
(FIFTEEN FIRST RANK AND EIGHT SECOND RANK); AND
TWENTY-FIVE TERTIARY (NINE STATIC AND SIXTEEN
MOBILE).

Screened images began to appear on the screen, showing
either side of a round disc with a description to the right of the
image. As they started at the bottom of the screen and slowly
drifted upwards to disappear into the topmost portion, Jamie
stared. He typed a request and Memoria started the images
again from the beginning. As the first hit center screen, Jamie
pushed hold. There it was. The ribbonwork, antlers on one
side, quarter moon on the other. Sara's bone disc.

The legend to the right read:

PRIME ONE

A] THE HORNED LORD—LORD OF ANIMALS AND THE
WORLD'S WOOD; ASPECT OF CERNUNNOS, PAN, ETC.;
SUPERNATURAL POWER, PROTECTION.

B] THE MOON MOTHER—THE WHITE GODDESS IN ALL
HER ASPECTS; IMMORTALITY, PERPETUAL RE-
NEWAL, ENLIGHTENMENT.

Jamie released the hold and the image went drifting upwards. He read the others as they went by.

THE GREY MAN/THE BLUE MAIDEN.
THE QUEEN OF OTTERS/THE OLD FERN MAN.
THE HARPER, OR WREN/THE PIPER.

The computer ran through all thirteen Prime bones, then
started on the Secondary ones.

THE HAZEL STAFF/THE IRON SWORD.
THE THISTLE CLOAK/THE MIRROR.

Reaching out, Jamie blacked the screen, saw that his hand
was trembling and sat back in his chair, staring at nothing.

He had never entered that information into Memoria. He *knew* that. He was the only person who used it, storing *his* findings. Anything else, whether from his correspondents or the journals of his father and grandfather, was entered only by him. No one else touched it. And if he hadn't entered the information . . .

And such information. The images struck right to the heart. The Hazel Staff was magic power, journeying, wisdom. What else could it be if you correlated it with mythological symbolism? The Iron Sword was justice, courage, authority.

This was it—the key he'd been searching for for all these years. Leaning forward, he reactivated the screen. He typed in WEIRDIN, then SOURCE? Moments later the answer was on the screen. Pale blue letters against the dark background spelled out the name: THOMAS HENGWR.

"Hengwr?" Jamie said aloud. "But when could he have had access to Memoria?"

"Must have been around seventy-three."

Jamie sat very still, then slowly turned. Sitting in one of the chairs near the fireplace was a curious individual with pronounced and definite features that seemed to have been carved by a craftsperson more interested in details than the work as a whole. Hawk's nose, bulging eyes. High forehead, gaunt cheeks.

"I'm surprised it took you so long to find it," Tom said. "Though I can see that you already understand what that information can mean to your studies."

Jamie just stared. Click-click-click. His mind correlated incidents from the past few days.

"You're the one the police are looking for," he said at last.

"But not for any criminal activity," Tom explained. "It's more because of what I know and what they hope to do with what I know. It's a rather complicated state of affairs—especially at this particular time."

"How did you get in here?" Jamie demanded. "What are you doing here?"

Another thought occurred to him. How could he have forgotten?

"Sara! What've you done with her?"

Tom Hengwr's hand drifted lazily up to stroke the air between them. With the slow movement of those gnarled fingers, Jamie felt an easing of the sudden pressure that had been building up in his temples.

"I came through the door," Tom said, "though I entered the House from the gardens. Most amazing gardens."

Jamie swallowed, wondering where the electricity in the air had come from. The whole room seemed to be charged with static. "Do you know where Sara is, Tom?"

"With my apprentice Kieran. She's safe enough for now, Jamie, have no fear. Neither Inspector Tucker nor...others that might harm her can reach her."

Jamie tugged at his beard, then, to give himself something calming to do, began to fill his pipe. His hands were still trembling. "*Where* is she?"

"That's more difficult to explain." Tom drew his legs up under him and leaned against the arm of his chair. "Turn off old man computer there and come have a seat by the fireplace with me. It's a long story, you see. It has its start about fifteen hundred years ago. In Wales."

"Aled Evans," Jamie said.

"He too had a part to play—though not the one I thought. To be honest, the whole matter's out of our hands now. I'll tell you, Jamie, I thought it would be you and me that would see the end to the story, but now it seems as though our part is done. Your niece and my apprentice will have to see it through."

Jamie blackened Memoria's screen again and, taking his pipe and matches with him, took the chair opposite his uninvited guest.

"I haven't a clue what you're talking about," he said.

"I'll try to explain."

Tucker pulled his Buick up to the Bank Street curb near the corner of Powell. Turning off the ignition, he got out and pocketed the keys. In the passenger's seat, Constable Daniel Collins shook a Pall Mall from a crumpled pack, lit it, then joined the Inspector where he stood staring at the dark bulk of Tamson House.

Collins was tall and lean, with a thick bush of light brown hair and a small moustache. His face was long and angular, his eyes dark. For all Collins's chain smoking, Tucker knew he was in better physical shape than any man in his squad. But the smoking was going to catch up to him, sooner or later, Tucker thought, and he'd be sorry.

The width of Bank Street and a section of the park were between them and the House, but even from where they stood, the building seemed to go on forever. A great big sprawl of rooms like nothing else in the city. It was funny how there wasn't more attention paid to the place. It dated back to the early part of the century and should have been classified as a heritage home by now. Should have been turned into a block of apartments, or a museum, or *something*. Not just a big private house, more empty than not.

Collins took a drag from his cigarette and stole a glance at the Inspector. It was almost one o'clock and the Glebe night was very still. The shadows in the park had an eeriness about them, as though strange shapes were moving through their dark tangles. Tucker's features were hard, and his whole body gave off tension. Collins knew just what he was feeling. Paul Thompson had been his partner. He still couldn't believe Paul was dead, except he'd seen the body and. . . .

He felt like shit over what had gone down earlier this evening. The worst thing was knowing that, no matter what you did, you couldn't make what had happened go away. Activity might ease the pain somewhat, but it wouldn't make it go away. And reading that shit in the paper, the lies that the brass had used for the cover-up. . . .

He sighed. At least it made Paul out to be a hero. Taking another drag, Collins flicked his half-smoked butt across the street. It landed in a shower of sparks in the middle of the road.

"Are we going in?" he asked.

"Who's on the stakeout?" Tucker replied.

"Bailey. He took over at midnight. He should be parked about halfway down Patterson."

"Have you been following the reports?" Tucker asked.

"Not much in 'em," Collins replied.

"There's fuck-all in them!"

Tucker turned away at last and leaned on the car, arms folded on the roof to prop up his chin.

"You read the file on this place?" he asked. "There must be fifteen fucking front doors. What kind of a house is that? How the hell can we keep tabs on a place like that? Jesus H. Christ! I'm so sick of this operation."

Collins shook another cigarette loose and dug in his pocket for his lighter. He said nothing. He hadn't worked with hard-ass Tucker before this project, but he'd heard stories. The one thing you didn't do was shoot off your mouth when he was in one of his moods. They said a rabid dog was friendlier.

They stood by the car, neither speaking. When his new cigarette was half smoked, Collins flipped it away, started to reach for another, then just stuck his hands in his pockets. He was remembering Paul Thompson's face. He hadn't enjoyed going down to the morgue earlier tonight. But he'd had to go. He just felt he owed Paul that much. But remembering, a coldness started up in his bowels. What the hell was it that killed a man like that? Paul had been heeled, too. Had his piece out and ready to fire. He'd never even got off a shot.

Tucker stirred.

"Let's go," he said and opened the driver's door.

Collins started to speak, then thought better of it. Wordlessly, he went around to his own side of the car and got in.

"I want to see what he does tomorrow," Tucker said as he turned over the engine. "I want to know who he talks to, where he goes, what he has for lunch, how many shits he takes. If he's involved, something'll break. Of all of them, he'll break first."

"What about the girl?"

"I don't know about her. I know she was meeting Foy at Patty's Place, but somehow I just didn't read her as a part of all this. If she is involved, she's going to be tougher to crack. *If* we can even find her. But I'll tell you this, Collins. We'll get those fuckers. Whoever's responsible for offing Thompson, we'll get them. Right now I don't want to do something that'll let some smart-assed lawyer get him off on a technicality. When we go for him, I want him dead to rights."

Putting the car into gear, he floored the gas pedal and took off with a squeal of rubber. Beside him Collins just stared through the windshield, his own feelings mirroring Tucker's. They needed something hard, something that'd stick. They just had to be patient. But there was one thing Collins promised himself. When they finally brought somebody in, he was going to go a few rounds with him in the interrogation room.

PART TWO

The Dancer and the Drum

As kingfishers catch fire,
Dragonflies draw flame.
—GERARD MANLEY HOPKINS

CHAPTER ONE

I'M dreaming again, Sara thought.

She had to be. Tall pines and larches reared on all sides of her, filling the night air with the pungent scent of their resin. A carpet of needles cushioned each step she took. Each step. . . .

Sara stopped abruptly. Where was she? The last thing she remembered was being in Patty's Place when— She shivered. Had that been a dream, too? Where did one stop and the other begin? Leaning against a tree, she slid down, drawing her knees up to her chin, hugging her legs to stop trembling.

Dreams weren't supposed to be like this. Not . . . this real. Not with trees whose rough bark poked at her through her sweatshirt. Or sap that stuck to her fingers where she touched it, or the lonely sound of the wind traveling through the topmost branches. She squeezed her eyes shut, willing herself to wake, but nothing changed. The realization that she had no control over the situation raised goosebumps on her skin.

When had she started this dream? Before she found the ring? She held up her hand to look at it. Even in the dim light of the forest it was clearly visible, for a dull light seemed to emanate from it. Was it real? Or had the dream started after she'd found it?

She remembered the beast men, one like a stag and one like a bear, and then the other thing—like a bear, too, but with fetid breath and gaping jaws. . . . She'd seen, no, sensed it twice. She'd only seen it once, and that was to the accompaniment of the bear/shaman's bone discs. Then she'd sensed it— once when the RCMP Inspector was questioning her in The Merry Dancers, fleetingly, and again in the restaurant.

She buried her face in her hands. What was happening to

her? Oh, God. What if nothing was? What if she was just losing her mind?

She lifted her head, wiping the unshed tears from her eyes. The forest was too real to be a dream. She had to accept that, somehow, she'd been transported to it, though for what reason still remained a mystery. It was probably in Quebec somewhere. In the Gatineau Hills. She had to start walking until she got to a road and could find her way back home. She'd figure out what direction she should be heading in by taking a reading from the stars. All those nights of staring dreamily into the night skies might just pay off.

She stood up, but hesitated again. If someone *had* dropped her off here, there had to be a reason for it. They were probably close by still, watching for her reactions. That, or it was some sicko who was waiting for her to freak out completely before coming after her with an axe. Her legs began to tremble again.

Kneeling, she scrabbled through the pine needle carpet until she came up with a length of wood thick and long enough to serve as a club. She broke off the twigs that stuck out from it and stood up again, hefting it. It didn't make her feel much better.

The forest was awfully quiet. Her own breathing sounded ragged and harsh to her ears—a sure signal to anyone who was stalking her. Stalking. Why did she have to use that word? She held her breath, then let it out slowly, repeating that until she felt a little calmer. She took a couple of steps, being careful not to snap a twig, and was surprised at how soundlessly she moved.

What if this was a dream? Nothing seemed to make sense anymore. If it was a dream, nothing could really hurt her then, could it? Didn't you just wake up when things got too scary? That was comforting, except for the small voice at the back of her head that asked: What about all those people who die in their sleep? Maybe that was what happened when you *didn't* wake up in time.

Move, she told herself. Start moving. It's not doing you any good to be hanging around here.

Again the actual motion was more a glide than her normal pace. She bit back questions as they formed in her mind and just kept going. She sped through the forest, as sinuously as a panther, like a ghost, like water flowing downhill, making its own pathway. She avoided the trees and protruding branches with an unnatural grace. It didn't even seem as though she was using her legs. She was just flowing, faster and faster, until her surroundings started to mist and blur in her sight.

It *is* a dream, she thought thankfully. Soon I'll wake up and everything'll be all right.

The forest was thinning, or disappearing. She refused to let it bother her. This was a dream. If she just went with the flow she'd wake up soon enough. Dreams didn't last forever. Most of them were only a few moments long in actual time, however lengthy they seemed when you were in the middle of them. At least that was what she remembered reading somewhere.

She slowed down to see where she was. She was still traveling through woodlands, but the forest was now made up of black spruce and groundcover of reindeer moss that spread a greenish-mauve color over broken stumps and windfallen trees. Moving slowly forward, she stepped out on a high ridge and looked out over a wide expanse of water. The headland on which she stood was a fractured limestone cliff that towered some three hundred feet above the shoreline. Below her, along the shore, were sand dunes, beaches, and salt marshes.

The beauty of the scene held her spellbound for long moments. The wind brought the tang of salt to her nostrils and she breathed deeply. The rude wooden club that she was still holding fell from limp fingers.

At length, something tugged at her and she headed to the right, south along the coast. She passed cliffs laden with wild rose bushes, more spruce, some cedar. The feeling of being drawn grew stronger and she began to hurry again. There was a sound in the air that she couldn't recognize. It was soft and distant, but as insistent as a summoning bell. The clarity of its tone was bell-like as well, but it wasn't a bell. Not until she reached a long sweep of shingled beach did she recognize it for what it was. Harping.

She paused to listen. The sound of the sea, waves lapping gently to shore, mingled with the bittersweet lament of the harp notes. She saw in the distance a large lump of limestone lifting from the beach and suddenly knew where she was. She and Jamie had spent a few weeks down here one summer. That was Percé Rock, supposedly named by Champlain, a great shiplike rock that surveyed the Gulf of St. Lawrence like a beached whale. She remembered seeing the Rock by day and being impressed. By moonlight, it filled her with awe.

By moonlight. It wasn't just that. It was the feeling that had been growing in her all day, that subtle heightening of her senses, now mixed with the strangeness of her dream. She listened to the harping. It was fey and resonant, and she thought of Alan Stivell's rendition of "Ys," complete with the sounds of the sea—but this was deeper, more solemn, more magical.

She wasn't frightened anymore. Heading across the shingles she never gave a thought to why she couldn't see the lights of Percé village or the statue of the saint on top of Mont Saint-Anne that was a landmark for fishermen at sea. She saw only the Rock and the sea and the play of moonlight on the shore. Heard only the sound of the waves and the soft, fey harping. Sought only the harper.

She found him at the foot of the Rock, seated with his back against that limestone monolith. Nearby was a leather coracle like the kind she'd seen in old picture books of historical Ireland. At his feet was a thin dog, all fur and eyes. It lifted its head as she approached and whined softly. The harper let his hands fall from the strings of his instrument and looked up.

With a shock, Sara recognized him. It was the man from her painting. Younger, but the same man. She paused where she stood, suddenly shy, and a little frightened.

The harper's eyes had narrowed as he studied her. When he spoke, his voice was clear and ringing, but the words were in no language that Sara knew. She shook her head, then took a step back as the harper laid his instrument aside and stood up. He held his hands open before him in the universal gesture of peace. His hands said, Look, I have no weapons. I offer only peace.

Still unsure, Sara let him approach. He lifted his hands towards her—slowly so as not to startle her—and laid a palm on either side of her head. A pain like fire pierced her mind. She reeled and would have fallen, but he supported her, eyes suddenly filled with concern.

"Easy," he said. "I meant no harm. It was just—"

Sara tore herself free of his grip and staggered backward. She shook her head slowly. The pain was gone, but she was still a little shaky. Then suddenly she realized something.

"I...I can understand you," she said.

"I am a bard," he said as though that explained it all. When she said nothing, he added: "We have the gift of tongues. It is a gift that can also be given to another."

"A gift of..." Sara repeated in a murmur.

She looked away from him, back to the cliffs, and saw for

the first time that there was nothing there but the wild head-
lands. No village, no statue, nothing.

"Percé," she said almost to herself. "What happened to the
village?"

"I saw no village," the harper replied. "You are the first I
have met in this land, m'lady. What is its name?"

"Its name?" She looked from him to his coracle. "You didn't
arrive here in that, did you? From across the sea?"

The harper nodded. "It was a long journey, and not one of
my own choosing. My gifts sustained me, but only barely. If
there is shelter near . . . ?"

It's just a dream, Sara told herself. Nothing to panic about.
Percé doesn't have to be here in a dream. Men who looked
like they stepped from a history book can cross the ocean in a
coracle with nothing but a harp and a dog. Why not?

"Are you ill?" the harper asked. "The giving of the gift of
tongues is not a powerful spell, but had I known it would pain
you so . . ."

"No. I'm fine. I mean, I appreciate being able to understand
what you're saying and all. It's just that . . . the last time I was
here it was . . . different."

For one thing, she'd been awake.

"Different? How so?"

He was still having some trouble understanding her, Sara
decided. Must be her accent or something. God! Her accent?
She was worrying about accents? Why not just wake up instead?
Or should she tell him that she was dreaming him, complete
with harp, coracle and dog. And magic gifts. Maybe she should
have taken up writing fantasy novels instead of the mystery
she was working on.

He was still waiting for her answer. She swallowed, but
with difficulty. Her throat was too dry.

"It's hard to explain," she said at last. "I'm not from around
here, you see."

"Then why are you here? A maid alone on a deserted shore.
Is this land so peaceful that such a thing can be?"

Maybe not the land, Sara thought, but in my dream, yes.
Why not? It's my dream isn't it? Unless this was someone
else's dream and— No. She didn't want to start thinking along
those lines.

"My name's Sara," she said to change the subject. "Sara
Kendell. What's yours?"

"Sara," the harper repeated, saying her name as though he was tasting it. "It is an unfamiliar name, but has a lovely ring to it." He smiled. "You do not guard your names here, as we do in my homeland. But as you have entrusted me with yours, so will I give you mine. I am called Taliesin, once of Gwynedd, for all the long roads I've trod, but now of no land. Or of all lands."

"Taliesin."

She knew the name, but before she could remember from where, her gaze lit on the ring finger of his left hand. There, all gold and bright, was a twin to the ring on her own finger. She held up her hand to compare them, then felt herself grow dizzy. She remembered who Taliesin was. He was the most famous of all the Welsh bards—a magician as well as a harper who supposedly wrote the druidical "Battle of the Trees" that Robert Graves had based his book *The White Goddess* on.

"How can this be?" Taliesin said, echoing Sara's thoughts, though he referred to the ring on her hand and not what his name meant to her.

Too weird, Sara thought and her dizziness grew. She felt a touch on her arm, as though the harper had reached for her, but that touch turned to mist, or she did, for it was gone, and the spinning grew fiercer. She lost all sense of equilibrium. Darkness swelled and then—

Sara was someplace else.

Her dream was still too jumbled to make sense out of. She blinked, feeling that sensation of dislocation that comes when you don't wake up in your own bed, but she wasn't quite sure what bed she'd gone to sleep in last night, so she couldn't even tell herself to relax. Her eyes opened and she gave a small cry of dismay.

It was starting all over again. The pines and larches reared about her. The smell of resin was thick in the air. She was lying on a thick carpet of pine needles and the air was very still, except for high above where the wind murmured through the treetops.

She sat up, willing her surroundings away. But with a sense of déja vu that set her nerves on edge, the forest stayed where it was, and she stayed in it. Alone, except for the sound of the wind and— Sitting up, her hand brushed something that was neither pine branch nor cone. Pulse drumming, she looked down upon the still white features of Kieran Foy.

He lay stretched out on the pine needles beside her, face ashen. There was a rude bandage on his side through which a faint red stain of dried blood could be seen. Sara remembered the scene in the restaurant, the flash of the monster's talons. . . . And if Kieran was here, and she was here, and that wound was here—then might it not all be real?

She started to shake all over. Backing away from Kieran's still form, she knocked something over. Twisting with surprise, she discovered it was only a clay jug. Water spilled from it and soaked into the pine needles until she had enough presence of mind to pick it up and set it upright. Beside the jug, on a rudely woven and dyed cloth, were strips of dried meat and flat things that looked like unleavened cornbread or cakes.

Who had left these things? Who had bound Kieran's wound? She stared wildly through the trees, but found no answer in them. It's morning, she realized then, sensing the sun more than seeing it through the thick canopy of pine boughs above them. Morning where? At that moment, Kieran stirred.

His eyelids fluttered, then opened wide. At first he didn't seem to focus on anything. Then his gaze cleared and he looked directly into Sara's eyes, his own confusion mirroring hers. His lips parted, but no sound issued forth. He reached for her hand, but when their skin touched, Sara knew a dizzying surge of displacement. Suddenly they were sharing minds again. His sickness and confusion became her own and she saw herself through his eyes.

"Don't touch me!" she cried, tugging her hand free. "Don't ever touch me!" She couldn't bear to feel that again, and she backed away from him.

"W-water," Kieran croaked. "Please. . . ."

The jug was right behind her. She picked it up and edged closer. His jacket lay beside him, neatly folded. Careful not to touch him, she bunched up his jacket and managed to work it under his head, and then she was able to trickle water into his mouth. More fell down his chin than went in, but it was enough. His eyes began to clear. Sara sat back on her heels and regarded him critically.

"How're you feeling?" she asked.

Close up as she was, she could see the changes that the few years since she'd seen him playing with Toby Finnegan's band had brought. Beyond the chalky pallor of his face, she saw strong lines. It was the face of a man who was usually sure of himself, a determined face, but not without a touch of gentleness. He returned her look with frank curiosity.

"Not so good," he said at last.

He sat up. One hand went to his side at the effort.

"Nom de tout! I feel like I was hit by a truck."

When his fingers came in contact with his bandage, he looked down, shocked. His own memory of what had happened in Patty's Place flooded his mind. Physically, he was feeling stronger by the minute. But his head reeled with the images that came to him. Lord dying Jesus!

"A shaper," he murmured, fingering his bandage.

"A what?"

"A shapechanger. That's what gave me this."

"Do you know what's going on?"

There was an edge to Sara's voice that brought Kieran's gaze sharply to her. He remembered through the haze of his confused waking her crying something about not touching her.

"I didn't try to . . . take advantage of you or something, did I?"

"What?" Then Sara realized what he was talking about. She shook her head. "It's when you caught hold of my hand . . . when you were waking. All of a sudden I wasn't in myself anymore. I was seeing everything through you. . . ."

Not the best of explanations, she realized as she was speaking. But lucidity was beyond her reach just now.

"You must be an empath," Kieran said. "When people are under stress, they tend to project more strongly than usual. Physical contact heightens it—feeds it directly to you. I'll damp my projecting so it won't happen again." He concentrated for a moment then reached out his hand. "Give it a try now."

Sara shook her head. "No, thank you." She paused, then added: "It's never happened to me before."

Kieran shrugged and dropped his hand. He still felt weak. Just the effort of holding out his hand had drained him.

"How did you get us out of the restaurant?" he asked. Looking around, he added: "And where did you get us to?"

"Me? I didn't have anything to do with it. I thought it was you. You or those weird drummers. Don't *you* know what's going on?"

Kieran seemed to be accepting all of it fairly calmly, Sara thought. But then, after what she'd seen him do in the restaurant . . . why shouldn't he?

"Who are you?" she asked. "I mean, I know your name—

it's Kieran Foy—but *who* is Kieran Foy? Why are the RCMP looking for you—for you and that old man?"

"You seem to know as much as I do already."

"I don't know anything. All I know is that in the last couple of days, my whole world's been turned topsy-turvy and I haven't a clue what's going on."

Kieran wasn't prepared to go into anything with her, at least not until he understood a little more himself. But he saw that Sara wasn't going to be satisfied with some vague answer.

"Let's start with this," he said. "You know who I am. Who are you? Maybe if we pool what we know, we can come up with something."

It wouldn't hurt, she decided. "My name's Sara Kendell." She had a faint flash of her dream harper as she spoke. She almost wished she was back under the Rock with him. At least then she'd *known* she was dreaming. Right now she wasn't sure of anything.

Kieran regarded her strangely. Sara Kendell. She was Jamie Tams' niece. He recalled the feeling he'd had looking at Tamson House the other night—was it only last night?—that sense of some evil presence that had showed up again at Patty's Place. He couldn't sense it now, so perhaps it wasn't directly tied to her, but she was still involved. In some way. Now all he had to do was discover in what way.

"The ring," he said. "Where did you get it?"

Sara looked down at her hand. She traced the ribbonwork with a finger, then glanced up.

"I think that's where it all began," she said. "It's an inheritance of sorts, I suppose. A man named Evans—Aled Evans— left it to my uncle in a box of other junk. I found it a few days ago and that's when it all started."

A few days ago, Kieran thought. That was when the old man had disappeared. Her involvement, no matter how involuntary, was becoming more certain. But so far he only had pieces to try and fit together, and the full picture still eluded him. He listened to her tell of what she'd found in the box, of the RCMP Inspector, her feelings, Once started, the whole story spilled out of her, as though the simple telling of it to him would somehow make it all better, make all the strangeness go away.

"Sounds to me," he said, "as though it's just a matter of your being in the wrong places at the wrong times."

Sara shook her head. "It's all real, isn't it? This is all really happening! And if it's real—then my feelings are real too. I can't just step away from it now."

"You have to. You're totally unprepared for...for anything. Look at you! You're shaking like a leaf."

"Do you think I *wanted* to be involved? I haven't been given a choice in the matter. I'd jump at the chance to have it all just go away."

Or would she? She realized that, for all that she was scared, really scared, she was also feeling very much alive.

"How did you get involved?" she asked.

"It seems I've been involved in this for all my life," Kieran replied.

What was he to do now? Tell her how he first met Tom in St. Vincent de Paul? How he'd studied and trained since then? There was no way she could understand.

"That doesn't tell me much," she said.

"There isn't anything to tell, really."

"Oh? What happened to pooling our knowledge?"

"None of this concerns you," Kieran said. "You're just an innocent bystander that somehow got pulled into the action. Get out while you've got the chance."

"And how am I supposed to do that?"

Kieran rubbed his temples. This wasn't going right at all. He didn't even know where they were. Her recollections of what had happened in the restaurant were much clearer than his own. His pain blocked out a lot of it.

The strange beings with their drums—they were what Tom called manitous. Elves. If they were a part of whatever was going on, it made sense that, for whatever their reasons were, the manitous had brought Sara and him into their own realm. The Otherworld. Now all he had to do was figure out a way to get Sara back. When that was done, he could get on with his own business.

"Well?" she demanded.

"Understand," he said. "Things aren't the same here as they were before—in our own world."

"Our *own* world? What do you mean—"

"Let me finish. You're in over your head here. You've been very protected, living as you have in Tamson House. You and your uncle are rich. You can go slumming when you want, because if the going ever gets rough, you can just step away from any problems that might arise. Money does that. Well,

in what you're involved in now, money doesn't mean shit."
He pulled out what he had left of the three twenties that Johnny
Too-bad had given him and tossed it onto the pine needles
between them. "You can't buy your way out of trouble here.
It just won't work. What's required here are skills that you
simply don't have. Nor is there the time to train you in them."

Sara stood up and glared at him.

"Of all the pig-ignorant things I've ever heard! Slumming?
Buying our way out of problems? What do you know about
us? Here you are, nothing more than some common thug that's
wanted by the police for God knows what crimes, and you're
telling me *I* don't run my life properly? What about you? I
didn't choose to get involved in this. But you say you've been
involved in it for most of your life and where's it gotten you?
You don't seem to know any more than I do about what's going
on."

"You don't understand," Kieran tried to explain. *Nom de
tout*. You'd think he could take one foot out of his mouth
before he put the other in.

"You're right!" Sara said. "I *don't* understand. But at least
I'm willing to admit it."

With that she turned and started to walk away.

"Where are you going?" Kieran tried to stand up, but a lance
of pain ran down his side.

Sara paused to give him a scathing look.

"I'm not as stupid as you obviously think I am," she said.
"It's plain enough you don't want me around, so I'm going
where I won't bother you."

"But you don't know what you're getting into. You—"

"I didn't know before, but that didn't stop things from hap-
pening to me. I think my big mistake was trying to find you.
God knows why I bothered. Don't you worry about me, Mr.
Know-it-all-wizard or whatever it is you think you are."

"Wait a second!"

"Piss off!"

With that she ran off into the trees.

Kieran tried to get up again and managed to make it to his
knees. He called out after her, but there was no reply. Fine,
he thought, settling weakly down. His side throbbed. Take off
if you want. That just gets rid of one problem for me. Except,
he realized, he hadn't been at all fair to her.

He didn't really know anything about her. And just because
she and her uncle were loaded, that didn't automatically make

them useless as human beings. He pounded a fist into the ground. Lord lifting Jesus! Why couldn't he have tried to be just a bit more reasonable? She'd seemed like a sensible enough person. She'd handled the bizarreness of this situation rather well—maybe better than he had when he'd first been introduced to the strangeness that lay side by side with the more mundane world of the here and now. If anything happened to her now, it'd be his fault. He was responsible for her being here.

Wearily, he made his way to the bole of a tall pine and leaned against it. This was great. Just great. So where did he go from here? He could hardly take a step, yet somehow he had to make sure Sara didn't get hurt *and* find the old man. No problem. All he had to do was hike into the woods after her and then the two of them could blithely go tripping off to find Tom. Sure. How did the old song go? *And if apple trees grew in the ocean. . . .*

God damn!

Her cheeks streaked with tears of frustration and anger, Sara ran until she thought she could run no more, then forced herself to run further. Low-hanging boughs slapped her in the face, tree trunks seemed to jump into her way, roots reached out to trip her, and she kept rushing down corridors that ended abruptly in impassable thickets. It wasn't at all like her dream. There was none of that sense of liquid gliding, the effortless passage of moving through the forest like a ghost.

When she tripped over a root and went flying headlong onto the thick carpet of mulch, she stayed where she fell. Sitting up, she rubbed a bruise on her knee and a lump on her head, and looked around.

This had gotten her nowhere. Not only did she have no idea as to where she was, but she no longer knew how to get back to where she'd come from. She'd half a notion that if she ran hard and far enough, she'd find herself on that beach where she'd met Taliesin. Why not? If dreams could be real—or at least dreamworlds seemed to be—why couldn't she pick the one she was going to be in? Which was all well and good in theory, but hadn't quite panned out like she'd hoped it would. There was probably some trick to it that she didn't know. Yet. She'd learn. And then she'd show Kieran Foy who could handle themselves and who couldn't.

Having caught her breath, she suddenly found herself wanting a cigarette. Funny. She hadn't thought about smoking for
what seemed ages. Now she had a craving that wouldn't stop.
She patted her pockets half-heartedly and was happy to find
her tobacco pouch nestled in the back pocket of her jeans, safe
and sound, if a little flat. Taking it out, she rolled a cigarette
and . . . no lighter. Typical. Maybe if she rubbed two sticks
together? Sure. Or maybe a convenient bolt of lightning would
drop from the sky and give her a light.

Sighing, she stuck the tobacco pouch back in her pocket.
She was about to throw her cigarette away, then thought better
of it and stuck it behind her ear. Trying not to think of smoking
or cigarettes, she drew up her knees and rested her chin on top
of them. It didn't do much good. She thought of Taliesin and
could only see his fire.

A light, a light. A kingdom for a light! I'm sinking, she
thought, irrevocably into a state of madness brought on by
nicotine withdrawal. They'll find me here someday, white bones
lying in amongst the pine needles, skeletal fingers holding the
remnants of a cigarette. . . .

Sense of humor—intact. Shall we do a quick check on the
rest of me? Better not. Hate to find out I was missing something.
Quick shift of gears: seashore and harper. And how do I get
myself there?

She was here due to some sort of magic. Obviously, to get
from here to where Taliesin was would require more of the
same. How spells work was the next question. Having until
very recently not even believed that they existed, it was hard
to work with the idea now. The best way to start, she supposed,
was to look at what magics she'd actually seen work.

When Kieran had killed the monster, what had he done?
There hadn't been any incantation or waving of hands. One
minute he'd just been standing there and the next . . . But just
before that moment . . . he'd been so still. Then his eyes'd begun to glow and when she laid her hand on his arm, she'd
felt . . . stillness. He'd been like silence itself, inside.

That had to be it. Like an actor or musician preparing for
their moment on stage, or a martial artist's motionless concentration. A gathering of inner forces. Because whatever the
magic was, it had come from inside. And it made sense that
you had to be completely absorbed in it. Kieran, seeing how
he claimed to be some sort of adept, probably could tune into

a previously attained state where he was keyed into the power. It had to be something like that. Unless you were born with it and just had to snap your fingers?

Sara shook her head. Nope. That just didn't . . . *feel* right.

She remembered reading a discussion in one of Jamie's books on the differences between natural or intuitive magic and ritual magic. Kieran hadn't gone through any ritual. She started to feel excited, as though she was on the brink of some great discovery.

If it was intuitive . . . if she could just focus on where she wanted to be and will herself there as forcefully as she could. . . . Well, it was worth a try. Better than running through the woods and ramming her head against trees. So how did she start?

The silence . . . the inner quiet . . . was probably the most important thing. And meditating, like with TM, was probably the best way to attain it. Although her TM instructor had told her that position wasn't important, she'd always liked to assume a half lotus and pretend she was a Buddha. It made it all seem more . . . important somehow. So, with a grimace of effort, she pulled her legs into position.

Okay. Hands on knees. Relax. Eyes closed. Her mantra, individually chosen for her by her instructor and never to be revealed—because then they wouldn't get the $45 from some other hopeful initiate—rose up from her memory. She concentrated on the mantra, repeating it silently to herself.

Gai-eng-ga. Gai-eng-ga.

($15 a syllable. . . .)

Gai-eng-ga.

(I wonder what Jamie's thinking right now. . . .)

Gai-eng-ga.

(What if I get stuck in this half lotus? Who's going to get me out of it?)

Gai-eng-ga.

The extraneous little thoughts kept intruding and ruining her concentration. Every time that happened she got a little more frustrated, then remembered that she was supposed to be relaxing, found herself thinking about that instead of concentrating on what she was supposed to. . . .

After fifteen minutes or so, she sighed and opened her eyes. This wasn't going at all the way it should. How was she supposed to work up some magic if she couldn't even relax? She looked down at her ring and traced the design with her finger, frowning.

Kieran was probably right. This sort of thing required skills that she just didn't have. And she certainly didn't have the time to learn them. Who'd teach her anyway? Kieran? Not likely. If she could even find him again.

She twisted the ring back and forth on her finger. The touch of its metal was soothing. She leaned her head back against the tree and closed her eyes again. She thought of the Rock. And the ocean. The fire. The harper and his dog. Taliesin. Harp music like Stivell's. Liquid notes falling, one by one into the tide.

A Breton tune filled her head, one of those gavottes that didn't have more than a dozen notes all told and just went on and on, and she found herself humming it. Back and forth she twisted the ring, a half smile playing on her lips. In amongst the tune she heard the ocean, wave against wave against shore.

After a while, she was no longer thinking of going anywhere. She drifted in a dreamy state. Her breathing eased. The air passed between her lips like the gentlest of breezes. She smelled the sea in the air. Heard the cry of a distant gull.

The souls of sailors take the form of gulls, she thought, but the thought was a distant thing.

Her chin dropped to her chest. She heard the murmur of waves breaking against a shore . . . stronger now. Felt the wind in her hair. Tasted it. Tangy. Salty. The forest around her dissolved and she was—

—drowning.

For a moment she panicked. She was over her head in water. The weight of her jeans and sweatshirt was dragging her down. Her legs, still assuming the half lotus, were a dead weight and felt like they were glued together. Flailing her arms, she fought her way to the surface. As her head broke from the water, she managed to disentangle her legs. Air! She gulped lungfuls, then paused, treading water, to look around.

What she saw stunned her. She'd done it! She'd actually done it!

A moccasined foot touched bottom just then and she realized that the water she was in wasn't all that deep. The tide had come back in and she'd plunked herself down in the middle of it. But that didn't matter—she'd done it. It didn't matter that she couldn't remember how; it was enough for now that she was here.

She stood up, feeling like a drowned rat, and stared up at the bulk of Percé Rock as it reared high in the morning skies. Turning, she looked shoreward. There was no village of Percé. No statue of a saint on top of the cliff. The trouble was . . . She looked back at the base of the Rock where the tide waters were foaming around the limestone. The trouble was there was no harper either.

She half swam, half waded closer to shore. The tidal current, though not strong, still worked hard at drawing her out into the ocean. When the water was up to her waist, it kept trying to tip her over. The shingle made an uneven footing and wet jeans had to be the heaviest things in the world. The water sank to her thighs, to her knees, her ankles.

She shivered when she was standing on solid ground once more; it wasn't exactly balmy this morning. She tried to wring herself dry, but it was impossible. Pushing her wet hair back from her face, she shaded her eyes and looked right, then left. Where was her harper?

Far along the left shore, under an overhang of limestone overgrown with black spruce, she saw a thin tendril of smoke that could only come from a fire. It had to be his. She took a few soggy steps in that direction, made out both man and dog by squinting her eyes, and broke into a run. Her moccasins squished unpleasantly with each step and she knew she must look a sight, but she didn't care. All she could think of was that the fire meant warmth and a chance to dry out. It wasn't until she was a half dozen yards from the fire that she gave a thought as to what her welcome might be.

The dog started yapping and Taliesin lifted his head, scrambling to his feet when he saw who it was. Feeling a little self-conscious, she continued on until only a few yards separated them.

"Hi," she said.

Taliesin gave her an odd look, then raised his face to the sky. Sara wondered what he was doing, then realized that the "gift of tongues" had translated her greeting literally.

"I meant, hello," she said. "How's it going?" She shifted uncomfortably, feeling very cold and wet. Wasn't he even going to invite her to sit by his fire?

"M'lady," he said formally, continuing to regard her curi-

ously. "If I offended you in some way yestereven, I beg your
pardon. It was not intentional. I am unused to your ways
and—"

"Hold it a sec'," Sara broke in. "You didn't offend me."

"But you disappeared. So suddenly. I thought..."

"Ah. Well..."

This was where she was supposed to tell him that he was
just a figment of her imagination. A part of a dream she was
having.

"I didn't exactly disappear," she said. "I mean, it might
have seemed that way to you, but what actually happened was
I just woke up. This is—this isn't making much sense, is it?"

But Taliesin nodded. "I think I understand. You are not
here in body, but in spirit? Like a sending? Yet..." His brow
furrowed. "Last night I touched you and you seemed solid
enough to me then."

"But this is just a dream," Sara said, feeling more awkward
every moment. "My dream, you see?"

The harper smiled.

"You are dreaming this?" he asked. He made a sweeping
motion with his arms that encompassed the whole of the shore,
the cliffs and the sea. "You are dreaming me?"

"Well, I...."

"I thought you were of the Middle Kingdom, perhaps. One
of Gwyn ap Nudd's people or some spirit come to walk the
world awhile—visiting from the Otherworld."

"Well, no. That is I *do* come from the Otherworld. *An*
Otherworld, at any rate."

"You are awfully wet...for a dreamer," he said, still smiling. "Yestereven, I mistook you for one of the fey folk by the
way you vanished. Your apparel seemed odd to me. Becoming,
to be sure, but not a style that the maidens in my homeland
wear. But I thought to myself: 'This is a strange land, Taliesin.
The garments, the very customs will be different. Make no
judgments, lest you judge unwisely.' Yet now that I have learned
that it is all but a dream, well...."

He shrugged.

"You're making fun of me!"

"And you are not? Playing the jester with me?"

"I'm not!"

"And yet you speak of dreams...."

"Oh, this is absurd!"

"Come," Taliesin said. "Dreaming or not, you are still dis-

comforted. I have tea brewing—do you know of tea in this
land? It comes from the far east, they say, or at least the learning
of it did. What I have steeping here are the last of the rosehips
I dried ere I was exiled from Gwynedd. Share it with me and
we will speak of dreams or whatever you will. I've been a long
time at sea and in strange circumstances. For all that I had
Hoyw here as my companion, I've been lonely, m'lady—"

"My name's Sara."

She didn't feel comfortable being called "m'lady"—especially not when she looked like a ragamuffin. Which, she admitted, she usually did, but right now more than usual. She'd
had to smile at the dog's name. Her new knowledge in lan-
guages had translated it for her: "Alert." The old dog seemed
anything but.

"Yes," Taliesin said, nodding. "I'd not forgotten your name.
But I had not thought to presume in using it." His shoulders
lifted and fell easily. "New customs and all. Have a seat, Sara.
Would you be averse to another small spell?"

"What do you mean?"

"Just this."

He stepped before her and gently, so as not to startle her,
took her by the shoulders. He hummed under his breath and a
warm tingle ran down Sara's arms from his touch and she
realized that her clothes were drying. Sara took a startled step
back. The scent of apple blossoms filled the air.

"How did you do that?" she asked.

"How? Do you wish a lesson in magics?"

"Yes. No. I mean, not now. But how did you so it? Where
did the . . . ability . . . power to do it come from?"

The harper tapped his chest.

"From within," he said. "From the deep silences within the
magics grow."

I was right, Sara thought with a certain sense of satisfaction.
*It's something inside. And I must have it too, or I wouldn't
have been able to return here.*

So enrapt was she at digesting this new knowledge, that she
let Taliesin steer her to a flat rock and sit her down. He took
and extra cloak from his pack and settled it across her shoulders,
fixing it at her throat with a simple silver clasp, but her chill
had left her. Not until the harper handed her a mug of tea did
she remember where she was. And who she was with.

"Thanks."

She cupped her hands around the mug. It was made from

a plain reddish clay, fired without a glaze and made without a handle, but the lip of it was smooth when she brought it up to her mouth and it held the tea's heat well.

"I have the feeling," Taliesin said, "that there is a tale to be told in your arrival here. You are as much a stranger to this shore as I am, is that not so?"

"Sort of. I've been here before—but it was different."

Taliesin nodded. "You mentioned a village yestereven."

"It used to be over there," Sara said, pointing back the way she'd come, and tugged the cloak back around her.

"I saw no sign of it. No ruins—nothing."

"That's because it hasn't been built yet."

"A riddle?" Taliesin asked. "I'll warn you. I'm more than a good match when it comes to the telling of riddles."

"Well, maybe you can figure this one out, then."

Sara fished in her back pocket to see how her tobacco pouch had fared from its dip in the sea and Taliesin's subsequent drying magic. Miraculously, even the papers were dry. She rolled a cigarette, leaned forward and took up a twig from the fire to light it, then gratefully blew a wreath of blue-grey smoke into the morning air.

"Different customs," Taliesin murmured, his eyes widening.

"It's called a cigarette."

The word came out in English, there being no translation for what it was in the Welsh she assumed they were speaking. She wondered briefly what year it was that Sir Walter Raleigh came back to England with tobacco. Jamie would know.

"Is it part of the riddle?"

"Indirectly, I suppose it is. You see, Taliesin—" That was the first time she'd spoken his name aloud. It had a nice ring to it, she decided.

"You see," she continued, "I know all about you. Well, not everything. It's just that, where I come from . . . you're a legend. You lived some fifteen hundred years ago. So . . . I have to make up my mind: either I'm dreaming, or, somehow, I've gone back in time."

She shot him a glance to see how he was taking this information and saw that he was taking it very well. He didn't even seem . . . well, shocked or anything. Curiosity was there, in those deep green eyes, but that was all.

"Doesn't that even surprise you?" she had to ask.

"I find it strange," he replied, seeming to choose his words with care, "but perhaps you forget that I have dealt with faerie for most of my life. It seems to me that of the two of us, you should be the most startled."

"I am. It's ... an adventure and all, I guess, but it scares the hell out of me at the same time."

She didn't say anything for awhile, just stared out over his shoulder at the sea, smoking her cigarette.

"I don't even know how to describe where I come from," she said at last. "I'd have to—to explain how I got here—but I don't think your language has words for any of it. Yet."

Taliesin nodded thoughtfully, then glanced at her ring.

"Perhaps you should begin with that," he said. "It seems a twin to my own. In fact, it could be mine."

Sara looked from her finger to his and shook her head.

"They're hardly the same size," she said.

Taliesin removed his. "Mine has the strange property of fitting whatever finger it is placed on. It was a gift—from one of my teachers. A man named Myrddin. And yours?"

"I sort of inherited mine."

"May I see it?" Taliesin asked.

When she'd pulled it off and handed it to him, he passed his own to her. She tried it on, while he tried on hers. She'd expected it to be about twice the size of her own ring, but found that it fit snugly. And hers ... hers fit the harper's finger as though it had been made for it. Taliesin removed her ring and studied it closely. When he looked at Sara finally, there was an odd look in his eyes.

"This could be my ring," he said slowly, "given the wear of the years. It has the same ... resonance as my own, save that yours is older. I find it ... disquieting."

"What does it mean?"

"I'm not sure."

They returned each other's rings and sat quietly, considering.

"Tell me your tale," Taliesin said, "for all that you think you won't find the proper words. Perhaps if we exchange tales, we might make some sense out of our strange meeting on this lonely shore."

Where've I heard that before? Sara thought, then decided that the harper would be different from Kieran. He seemed to genuinely want to understand. So she told him everything she knew, from when she found the ring straight on through to the present moment. It took two more cigarettes and another mug of tea—and surprisingly, her new vocabulary had enough words for the telling.

"And before?" Taliesin asked. "Before you found the ring? What was your life like? Did it prepare you for these events?"

"No. At least not intentionally, I'm sure. Or—Oh, I don't know."

So she told him about Tamson House, which was a difficult concept to exchange with one who knew smoky halls, peat huts and leather tents; and about her uncle Jamie. Then she recounted what she could remember of the legends that surrounded the poet Taliesin in her own time—from the story of Gwion Bach and the magical cauldron, to that day in Maelgwn's court when he put to shame all of the king's bards.

"It is strange what the years can do to a man's name," he said when she was done.

"Those stories aren't true?" Sara asked, feeling vaguely disappointed.

"Not so much untrue as garbled."

"You didn't write 'The Battle of the Trees'?"

"'Câd Godden'?" Taliesin repeated and the words stayed in their Welsh. "Not I, though I know it well. Those verses hold all the secrets of bardic lore in their riddling lines, Sara. They are the magic and the mystery of the world."

"But what does it mean?"

"'I was in many shapes before I was released,'" Taliesin quoted. "The first line tells all. Such is the Way we follow through life. Many shapes. The knowledge gained through wearing them. And one day comes the release that is the harmony—attained when one is one with all."

"I'm not sure I followed all of that."

Taliesin smiled. "If you did, you wouldn't need to ask. And if you need to ask, then those verses remain the riddle that they are. That is the bard's Way, Sara. To become a master of riddles and then step beyond them."

"Is that what you are—what you've done?"

"No. But I am trying. Let me tell you of my beginnings— for we promised each other the sharing of tales—and then we can try to unravel what meaning 'Câd Godden' holds for our meeting. This will be the true tale—not my life as the legends would have it. You are not too tired?"

Sara shook her head. She had known he wouldn't cop out like Kieran, and the thought made her feel good. Like she'd just found a friend. Taliesin shifted his long legs in the sand before him and laid his hand on Hoyw's head, ruffling the thick fur around the old dog's ears.

"Taliesin am I," he began. "Chief bard in the west was I and my original country was the Region of the Summer Stars. The tale has it I was a foundling, cast up on the shores of Gwynedd by Dylan Eil Ton, he who rules the waves and is Aranrhod's son, who knows the sea as most men know their palms—" He paused, looking at her. "Why are you smiling?"

"I don't know. It all sounds so formal."

Taliesin grinned ruefully. "I am used to telling the tale in the halls of kings—not to friends. I will try to leave out the bardic resonances."

So he told her how Elphin, the son of Gwyddon, found him cast up on the shore in a wicker and leather coracle, how he brought the babe home and how his wife and he raised the foundling as though he was their own son.

"If ever I was named Gwion Bach," he said, "as the legends would have it, that memory is long gone from me. Much knowledge have I gathered, but it was twenty-one long years of tutorship under the bard Myrddin that made me what I am—not three drops from the cauldron of Ceridwen. Hard work it was, that learning, for I was lazy as a boy and preferred wandering the woodlands to learning in the sacred groves. Many a day and night I sat under the boughs of the Red-Branch, the central tree in Myrddin's grove that was sacred to the Moonmother and her Horned Lover, and many a longer year I walked the roads with him, from high moors of Alba to Arthur's Caerlleon upon Usk. And still, to this day, that process of learning goes on."

A long charmed life he'd led, with adventures that ranged from the land of the faerie folk in their Middle Kingdom, to nights spent in thatch-roofed inns in the company of brigands and thieves; from king's courts to the lonely wildlands. He told her how he won Maelgyn's enmity.

"It was not a fair contest," he explained. "His bards were not true bards—not in the old sense of the word. They did not follow the Way. Theirs was the poetry untouched by the Moonmother—more bound in histories, often false histories, with never a spark of Her fey light in what they recited or sang.

"She was with me that day I sang their tongues mute and cast the skill from their harpers' fingers. I freed my fosterfather Elphin that day, but the deed came back to haunt me for, when at last I wearied of the road and longed to settle down in the only homeland I knew as my own, Maelgyn had his druids bind me and cast me, my harp and my dog and all, adrift on the sea."

"And here you are."

"Here I am, a foundling once more, cast again upon a shore by the will of Dylan Eil Ton."

"How did you survive the journey?" Sara asked.

"My magics sustained me. I turned inward, focused on the heart of my being—my taw, the inner stillness that is like magic, or more like the silence between the notes than actual music itself."

"Phew!" Sara murmured. "If I hadn't already been through some weird things myself, I'd find it hard to believe you."

Neither of them said much for a while. Sara looked seaward and tried to imagine Taliesin's voyage, but only ended up shaking her head with the wonder of it all.

"What's it like," she asked at last, "this...taw?"

"Do you play an instrument?" Taliesin asked.

"A little bit. Not wholeheartedly. I guess I don't really do anything wholeheartedly."

"Have you ever felt as one with your instrument? That moment when nothing stood between you and what your heart bade you play?"

"A couple of times—I think."

Taliesin smiled. "That is what your taw is like. When you can maintain your contact with it, you have taken a long step along the bard's Way. To learn the inner magic of a thing, always to have your taw close at hand, you must pursue your calling wholeheartedly. It need not be through music. That is the bard's Way. Other Wayfarers have their own methods.

"But for me—the harmony between player and instrument—that was the key to unlocking the primary magic. Magic that stayed in my music and shaped my life. It is like touching the Moon's heart, Sara. There is no other feeling like it. Imagine that celestial ship rising above a forest. That first moment when she lifts from the trees, that moment filled with promise and wildness and potent magics...that is what my life is, following the Way. That is what my taw holds for me."

"You make it sound...perfect." Sara sighed. "I wish I could get in touch with myself like that."

"What makes you think you cannot?" Taliesin pointed to the ring on her finger. "That ring—it is a gifting ring. My master Myrddin gave mine to me. Such a ring does not find its way to the finger of one without the potential to be a Way-farer."

"Nobody gave it to me. I found it in a box in the back of my uncle's store."

Like a Crackerjack box, she thought. *"Free Gift Inside!"*

But Taliesin shook his head.

"It is still a gift," he said, "no matter how it came to you. Such rings have a kenning—a sense of their wearer's right-ness."

"I don't know. I think it's just a fluke that I found it—that I'm here. There's no meaning in all this for me. Take yourself. You're someone important with magic powers and everything."

"Magic is just a side road along the Way."

"Its a pretty wild side road. No. I'd just be kidding myself and I know it. There's something wonderful going on and I'm sure you're a part of it. But me? I think I just lucked into it, that's all."

Taliesin frowned. "That is your friend Kieran speaking."

"He's not my friend."

"Nevertheless, you are merely repeating the words you told me he spoke to you. I know this, Sara: There is no such thing as chance in the workings of the world. While it is true that we make our own decisions, those decisions are there to be made because a greater power than we may ken has placed them there. Over such moments we have no control. But we *do* control the decision of which path we will take. If you step away from this now. . . ." He sighed. "You will never know, will you?"

"Well, what do you think I should do?"

"The choice must be yours."

"Then at least tell me what you think's going on. Why am I here? What is my choice?"

"I remember," Taliesin said, "asking Myrddin that same question once. He looked at me and told me I could do one of two things. Accept the challenge and fulfill my potential, or spend the rest of my days wondering what I had passed by." He shook his head. "I have said too much, I think."

"No. You've said just enough. I'm going to . . . to take this road and see where it leads me."

"Don't follow blindly," the harper warned. "Fare with your eyes open and a willingness to learn."

"I'll remember."

A kestrel cried overhead and Sara followed its flight with her gaze. When she looked back at Taliesin, she asked:

"How old are you? You don't look more than a young forty, but from all you've said you've done. . . . And then there's that painting of you I have. You look a lot older in it."

Taliesin shrugged. "Time is a strange master and to those of us who walk the Middle Kingdoms—these Otherworlds— it has a tendency to turn in upon itself, twisting forward and backward until it becomes impossible to reckon. I was older when I planned to retire in Gwynedd than I am now. You speak of a painting, but I have never met the man that is in it with me. At least I do not recognize his description nor his garb from what you've told me.

"I have long given up following the workings of time. Myrddin once told me that he lived backwards—that he knew much of what was to come, but little of what had been. At the time I thought it yet another of his riddles. But now I think I understand him better."

Myrddin—who must be Merlin. King Arthur. The Welsh bard Taliesin. Personages out of legend come to life, discussed as though they were flesh and bone, one of them sitting across the fire from her. If this wasn't all just a dream. . . . Sara shook her head.

"What instrument do you play?" Taliesin asked her suddenly. "The harp?"

"No. I wish I did. I just fool around with the guitar some."

"Git-arr?"

"It's a . . ."

Oh, boy. Here they were back to describing things that the language they were using had no words for.

"You left it behind when you . . . journeyed here?"

Sara nodded. "In my room. It's shaped like this." She made a figure eight using both her hands. "At least the body is. Then it has a neck that sticks out here." She took a stick and drew a rough shape in the sand. "The strings—there are six of them—are attached to pegs up here and resonate across the soundhole."

"I would like to see it," Taliesin said.

"I'll bring it the next time I come." The next time. She had to smile.

"No," Taliesin said. "Think of it now and I will bring it to you."

"You can do that?"

Taliesin nodded. He reached for his harp and set it on his knee. With a Y-shaped key that hung from his neck he tuned the strings. Trailing his fingers across them, he awoke a scatter of notes that seemed to sparkle in the air between them. Sara shivered with pleasure.

"Picture the instrument," Taliesin said. "Hold its image in your mind."

She drew up an image of her Laskin—the classical guitar with its slotted head, curly maple back and front and rosewood sides, the silver lengths of the three wound strings and the taut gut strings. . . . The more she thought of the instrument, the more she longed to have it in her hands. She always felt like that when she heard someone else playing. Her fingers would get all itchy and—

Her eyes snapped open. There was a weight on her knees and, half fearfully, she looked down at her guitar case. She ran a hand along its smooth surface, then grinned at Taliesin, her eyes shining.

"You did it!" she cried.

Popping the clasps, she set the case down on the sand beside her and took out the guitar.

"I don't know if it'll be in tune. . . ." she began, but it was.

Taliesin set his harp aside and took the guitar in his hands, holding it awkwardly. He plucked a string or two, setting his fingers on the fretboard as he'd seen Sara do while she was testing its tuning, then shook his head and passed it back to her.

"I'm too old to learn a new instrument," he said. He took out a small six-holed bone whistle and laid it on the sand in front of him, then set his harp on his knee again. "The whistle and harp will have to do. But I would like to hear you play."

"I don't really know anything that's . . . you know . . . good." Sara was suddenly shy again.

"Try this," Taliesin said. He began a simple air and Sara stumbled along behind him, trying to pick up the tune. Patiently he repeated it until she began to get the knack of it.

"Now we will see," the harper said, "what affinity you have for the bard's Way. It's little enough that I will show you this time, but enough to start you on your journey. This tune will be your key—composed now, this moment, between you and me on this beach, leagues from my homeland and years from yours.

"We will call it 'Lorcalon'—'The Moon's Heart'—for that is what you will be in time, Sara. A moonheart. A follower of the Way. Two things this air will bestow upon you. It will be your stepping-stone to your own silences within, your own taw, and it will be a protection against those who would bind you with their magic. For such is the method of mages—they bind you with their eyes, with their thoughts, and make your will theirs.

"Against a strong spell, this will avail you little. But against a normal binding spell, you have but to call up this tune in your mind, and your will remains your own. Play it through. Again with me."

He put aside his harp and took up the tune on his whistle, playing across the turns of the air that Sara drew from her guitar. To Sara it seemed as if her fingers were doing a slow dance along her fretboard. The tune was simple, but its resonances stretched deeply inside her, awaking feelings she never knew were there. The tune became all. Her fingers played it, her ears heard it, her eyes saw dancing notes of gold and green that stepped in time to its rhythm. She smelled the scent of apple blossoms, strong and heady, and her pulse beat to its timing.

"Farewell," she heard Taliesin say as though from a great distance. Again the word seemed to drop into her mind without passing first through her ears. "Your own time calls you. Return to me, when and how you can. I will be waiting."

She wanted to cry: "No! I don't want to go! Not yet!"

But it was too late. She could feel the shore fading around her, heard only the sound of her own music. The sea and the sound of the bone whistle were gone. And then she opened her eyes—

—she was sitting in a glade with tall pines around her, playing Taliesin's air on her guitar. She dropped her hands from the instrument and for a few moments echoes remained, then all was still. A deep surge of disappointment went through her, but then she pushed the ache away. She had things to do in this world.

Humming the tune the harper had given her, she put her guitar back into its case and stood up. She looked around herself, then set off, certain, though she couldn't have said how, of which way to go. Twenty minutes of walking brought her back to the glade where she'd left Kieran. He was sitting up against a tree, staring off into space. When he caught sight of her, his eyes widened and he reached out a hand.

"Sara!" he called. "Before you take off again, I just want to say I'm sorry for the hard time I gave you earlier. I was being a prick. It's just that everything's been so weird lately and I—hey! Where did you get the guitar? And the cloak? Where did you go?"

Because she was feeling in an expansive mood, Sara regarded him with some measure of affection. It was nice that he'd apologized. Maybe there was hope for the lug yet. Fingering her cloak, she sat down near him. She placed her guitar case beside her and wondered where to begin. She didn't want to tell him about Taliesin. That was going to be *her* secret. So what would she tell him? She decided to give him a taste of his own medicine and treat the whole thing mysteriously.

"I was with a friend," she said.

"A friend? Lord dying Jesus! Where did you find a friend here?"

But then he remembered the way he'd behaved to her earlier. He'd just taken what information he could from her and given her nothing in return. Nothing but a hard time.

"I'm sorry," he said. "Can we start again?"

"How so?" She wasn't going to make it easy for him.

"How about if I start with telling you where all this started for me?"

Sara grinned. "That sounds more like it," she said.

"I should've done this right away," Kieran said.

Sara thought of how she'd spent her morning. She could still feel a tingle deep inside—a tingle that was an echo of the tune Taliesin had taught her. "You should have," she said, "but I'm kind of glad that things turned out the way they did."

"What do you mean?"

Sara shook her head, enjoying her secret.

"Nom de tout!" Kieran muttered, then sighed. "Okay. I guess I deserve that."

He leaned his head back against the tree and stared up into the network of branches above. "I was serving two years in St. Vincent de Paul Penitentiary when I first met Thomas Hengwr. That's the other fellow that the horsemen are looking for, you see . . ."

Chapter Two

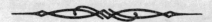

12:30, Thursday morning.

Lawrence Hogue was in the kitchenette of his apartment making a last cup of tea before he went to bed when the rap came at his door. He shot an irritated glance down the hall, hoping whoever it was—probably Mrs. Simpson from two doors down, reeking of alcohol and looking for tonic water— would simply go away. But a moment later the rapping was repeated, more insistently. Sighing, Hogue set down the copy of this week's *MacLean's* and heaved his bulk from the chair.

He didn't care much to be disturbed at any time—whether he was working on a complicated calculation in the lab, or simply relaxing at home, it never failed to irritate him. So he wasn't prepared to be intimidated when he reached the door.

"Who's there?" he demanded.

"Gannon," came the soft-spoken reply.

Hogue's fingers trembled as he unlocked the door. Phillip Gannon pushed past him into the apartment with the assurance of someone who was very rarely denied anything he wanted. He reminded Hogue of Tucker. Like the Inspector, Gannon was a big, self-confident man who knew how to intimidate without appearing overtly threatening. As such, he was the antithesis of Hogue, whose bullying was reserved for the few men in the lab who had to work under him and was based only on Hogue's placement in the bureaucratic structure.

Gannon was very much like Tucker, except that Gannon's street origins were cloaked under a veneer of civilized behavior that was all the more disquieting when one was aware of his capability for sudden violence. Tonight he wore a light beige overcoat on top of a tailored three-piece suit, patent leather

143

shoes, a Christian Dior shirt and a narrow black tie. He was the picture of an elegant businessman standing in Hogue's hallway, leaning casually against the doorway as though he belonged there, his voice cultured and soft; but he had the body of a weight-lifter and the cold, dead eyes of a fish.

"What are you doing here?" Hogue asked.

He didn't like the way he felt when confronted by men like Gannon and Tucker. It made him too aware of how his overweight and out-of-shape body betrayed the same softness within as was displayed without.

"Mr. Walters would like to speak with you," Gannon said. "Better get your coat."

"Tell him I'll . . . I'll call him in the morning."

Gannon shook his head. "Mr. Walters would like to see you in person. Tonight. No discussion."

As always, Hogue capitulated immediately. His sense of self was abysmally low. It had been like that for him in public school and carried over through college and medical school. By now it was so firmly entrenched in his mental make-up that he could not stand up for himself without a complete reversal of what thirty-four years of bowing and scraping and pettyminded unrealized dreams had turned him into. His only solace was his profession. He showed a certain brilliance amidst the straightforwardness of scientific logistics, and within the power structure of the bureaucracy—where he was amongst the upper echelons—he was one who "got things done." Nevermind that the greater part of such work was largely conceived and carried out by his understaff. In the lab he was an authority. A mover and a doer. Everything his life otherwise lacked. Outside those white-washed walls . . .

"Let's *go*, Dr. Hogue."

Gannon gave him a small push and Hogue stumbled to the closet to get his coat. The simple fear he felt in Gannon's presence escalated and was replaced with a more chilling one. What did Walters want with him tonight?

His hands were shaking as he put on his coat and he wished right then that he'd never gotten involved with this affair in the first place. Unfortunately, the time for such a decision was long past. And to be fair, given the way his life had been going, how could he have chosen otherwise? The additional financial considerations aside, Walters' interest in his career was a stepping-stone to greater things. He'd been shocked and impressed with his own importance when J. Hugh Walters had first called to discuss some articles he'd had published. Hogue had been eager to help then.

But in the months that followed, he'd become enmeshed in a nightmare from which there was no escape. It was then that he first learned about how much control one man could have over another. But by then it was too late to back out. There was no place for him in the world of men like Walters and Gannon.

"There's a car waiting downstairs," Gannon said when Hogue finally had his coat on.

He ushered Hogue out before him and closed the door to the apartment. The lock caught with a small click and Hogue shivered. The sound was an ominous reminder of how he'd closed the doors on all his options. He tried to remember what the turning point had been. When had a good student, and later a good researcher, become the man who could be taken from his own home in the middle of the night by some Gestapo-like goon?

Sometimes Hogue thought that if he could figure that out, there might still be a way out for him. Mostly he knew that for the wishful thinking it was. Walters had too strong a hold on him. The RCMP were unforgiving when it came to one of their own leaking secrets—even if that one was only a CM, a Civilian Member. And Hogue didn't even want to think about what Walters would do with him if Project Mindreach was closed down. He'd read enough spy novels to know how loose ends like himself were usually tied off.

Tucker pulled his Buick up to the curb at the corner of Waverly and Elgin and shifted into neutral. Beside him, Collins took a final drag from his cigarette and stubbed it out in the ashtray.

"Thanks for the lift."

"S'okay. See you in the morning."

"Yeah."

Collins reached for the doorhandle, then turned to regard Tucker.

"Everybody feels like shit about what happened to Paul," he said. "It was a piss-poor way to buy it. Not that there's a good way, only..."

Tucker stared straight ahead. "Only what?"

"Maybe you should take it easy, you know? Get some sleep, maybe."

"Yeah. Sure. Until the next guy buys it."

Collins shrugged.

"Look," Tucker said as he was getting out. "I appreciate the concern, okay? But I can't let it rest. Nobody gets away with wasting one of my team."

"Paul was my friend."

Tucker turned. "Then maybe you understand."

"Yeah. I guess I do."

Collins shut the door and watched the Buick pull away before heading for his apartment. He wasn't going to sleep much himself. But until they had something hard to go on, what the fuck could they *do?* But, goddamn. When they got hold of the guy that did it. Then . . . oh, yes. Then.

In the foyer of his building he shook out another Pall Mall, lit it and checked his mailbox. As he went up the stairs with his phone bill in hand, he wondered how much he had left of that fifth of Scotch he'd picked up on the weekend. He hoped there was enough it put a haze across the knife-edged loss that was cutting up his gut.

After dropping Collins off, Tucker headed up Elgin and took the Laurier Bridge across the Rideau Canal. He shot a glance over his shoulder at the big clock on the Peace Tower that was part of the Parliment Buildings, but they still hadn't gotten it working. Hell of a way to run the capital of the country. Fucking Peace Tower clock didn't even work. It was about as much use as the bozos they'd voted into office that debated in the Commons below it.

His wristwatch told him it was just going on one. Hell of a way to spend a Wednesday night. Hell of a way to spend any kind of a night. Not that he had a whole lot else to do—at least not since he'd broken up with Maggie again.

Tucker sighed. He had neither family nor very many close friends. It was hard to get to know people when your job took you back and forth across country, twenty-four hours a day, 365 days a fucking year. He had about four months vacation leave piled up and double that again in sick leave. What he should do was just take the whole lot of it and go some place like Jamaica or Greece and let someone else shovel this shit for awhile. Christ, anything was better than this.

He smiled bitterly. Well, Tucker, he told himself. You've got 'em again. Them old mid-operation blues.

On an impulse, he turned left on King Edward, drove the

three blocks to Daly, and turned right, coming to a stop across from the house where Thomas Hengwr had kept a room. He switched off the ignition and stared at the darkened building, not bothering to check the windows in the building on his side of the street where one of his men was holding down the stakeout on Hengwr's place.

So where are you now, Hengwr? he asked the shadows that spilled between the old houses. Was it your idea to have my man blown away? Or did your boy do it on his own time?

He sat in silence for a long time, waiting for some inspiration to come to him. Then, sighing, he started up the Buick and headed up to Rideau Street. He decided it was time to have another look through the files back at the office. Christ knew he could just about quote the fuckers word for word as it was. But he couldn't just sit around and do nothing, waiting for a break that might never come. He might come across something he'd missed before. Yeah, and maybe Hengwr and Foy'd waltz in and turn themselves in.

But that wasn't the way it worked in the real world. Real world? Hell, with the speculations on which this Project was founded, who was to say where the real world even fit in?

Meeting J. Hugh Walters in his private study wasn't quite the same thing as being dined by him in the Chateau Laurier, Hogue decided. For one thing there was no one to see how important you were. And for another, there was a palpable sense of danger floating in the air. The sudden realization came to him that at some point between the last time he'd met with Walters and tonight, he'd been thrust across the boundary that separated colleague from employee. He wondered if he'd ever get a chance to work his way back.

"Sit down, Lawrence, sit down," Walters greeted him. "Would you care for a drink?" But once Walters took his chair behind his big desk, little time was wasted in getting to the matter at hand.

"I'm not at all pleased with your handling of Project Mindreach, Lawrence."

"I . . . I can explain," Hogue began, trying to relax so that his trembling hands wouldn't spill his cognac.

"I'm sure you can," Walters replied wearily. "But I don't pay you for explanations. I pay you for results. The latter, it seems, are beyond your capabilities."

Walters frowned and Hogue wanted to crawl under the rug.

He felt like a nobody, compared to his host, who had controlling stocks in a half dozen multi-national consortiums, who chaired a number of important advisory boards as a favor to friends in the Senate, who was on a first name basis with both the Prime Minister and the Leader of the Opposition, whose actual political interests were of a far greater scope than simply the country of his birth and present residence, who when he traveled abroad was as welcome in the war-torn Middle East or in the Eastern Block as he was amongst the member nations of NATO.

"I could get better results if it wasn't for Inspector Tucker," Hogue said.

"I understood that the strategies were yours. He simply implemented them."

"Yes. That's true. But since then—since we lost Hengwr, and now Foy—he's taken over."

"I don't understand what you're driving at," Walters said.

"No," Hogue explained. "It's I who didn't understand. When you first brought him up, I thought he'd be perfect for the job. We needed tight, absolute security. And we have that. But now that we've had a couple of setbacks—based on my strategies, I'll admit—he's taken over the Project."

"That won't do." Walters tapped his fingers on the blotter before him. "If it's true, we'll have to have him stopped."

"I don't think you fully appreciate the uniqueness of Tucker's position on the Force," Hogue said. "I didn't myself until just recently. They simply turn him loose on the problem and don't check up on him again until the operation's finished. He doesn't get told so much as he tells. He's answerable only to Superintendent Madison, who in return reports directly to the Solicitor-General's office. I don't think even the Commissioner is aware of Tucker's position."

"I don't believe he is," Walters agreed. "But then again, when I recommended that such a position be set up, there were good reasons for it—reasons that no longer apply as that old problem has since been rectified. In the meantime, there seemed to be no reason to change Tucker's status. He has been doing an exemplary job."

"You recommended . . . ?"

"That was some time ago—around the time of the APLQ fiasco."

Walters was referring to the burglary of the Agence de Presse Libre du Quebéc offices in 1972. The APLQ was a politico-journalist organization that, along with the Mouvement Pour la Défense de Prisoniers Politiques du Quebéc, was sympathetic to the FLQ cause and alleged to have lent assistance to jailed "political prisoners." The affair, like a low-key Watergate, didn't become public knowledge until some three and a half years later with the arrest of an RCMP Constable involved in a bombing attempt on the Mount Royal home of a Steinberg's supermarket chain executive in Montreal. Subsequent evidence pointed to the first time that the RCMP had been implicated in methodical illegal activity.

Tucker had been assigned to assist the Royal Commission that was established in the summer of 1977 to determine the scope and frequency of those activities.

Seeing Hogue's baffled look, Walters shrugged.

"At any rate," he said, "when it was decided that we needed the tightest security available, I naturally thought of Tucker."

"And does he. . . ." Hogue licked his lips nervously. "Does he know anything about the arrangement between us?"

"Heavens, no. He doesn't even know that I recommended him in the first place. But that's rather irrelevant. You were telling me how he was obstructing the positive flow of the Project. How so, exactly?"

"It's not something that's easy to explain."

"Try," Walters urged dryly.

"Yes. Well. It's more a number of small things than anything major. But you know as well as I that in research, great discoveries are made not from major efforts, but—"

"Spare me the lecture. How is he hindering the Project?"

"We lost Hengwr. Then—"

"I understood that Hengwr's loss was due to your miscalculations, not Tucker's."

"Yes. Perhaps. But tell me this then: why wouldn't he bring in this Sara Kendell? She had potential. Not to mention that he refused to cover up a loud-mouthed ADM out in Tunney's Pasture who was threatening to go to the papers. Not to mention that he lost one of his men—"

"Yes," Walters broke in again. "That interested me. How was he attacked? Are any of the statements of the witnesses available? I didn't receive any with your earlier report."

"I have them in my office. I'll send them over with a courier first thing in the morning."

"Now this woman. What's your interest in her?"

"Did you read the reports?" Hogue asked.

"Yes. They hardly seemed to warrant further investigation."

"Tucker seemed to think she was important enough to have followed. He put a man on both her and her uncle."

"Ah," Walters murmured, nodding to himself. "Because of the bone artifact?"

"I think it's something more. Tucker's been studying the files on Tamson House. He's spending more time with those files than he is on his so-called security."

Walters smiled thinly. "But you are secure, are you not?"

"Yes. But—"

"Then how is he being lax?"

"He . . . that is. . . ."

"I think if there is any laxness to be discussed, it is yours, Lawrence. Only yours. Your pathetic attempt to pass the blame over to Tucker is scarcely laudable. You had your chance, and you've failed. And, I will admit, some of the blame for that failure is mine as well. I saw only your work in the laboratory and didn't consider what values of leadership you might have— or that you lacked. Unfortunately for both of us, it's too late now. My quarry is long gone and, with him, any reasons I might have had in continuing to support Project Mindreach."

"Hengwr's just one man," Hogue protested. "There are others. Many others."

"Others who are gifted to some degree," Walters agreed. "Yes. There are those. Ones who can guess the draw of a card from another room. Who can make a matchbox feebly twitch on a tabletop, or who can find some missing object after three or four false starts. And there might even be others like Hengwr—truly gifted men. But I'm afraid, with him warned, we'll not see their like soon—either in the world at large, openly showing their gifts, or in our lab, spilling their secrets from drug-loosened tongues. No, Lawrence. I'm afraid it's over."

"You're going to close up? Just like that?"

The fear returned and sweat beaded Hogue's brow. He knew too much for Walters simply to let him go. So long as the Project was operative, he was safe. Without it . . . when Walters had no more use for him. . . .

"It will be more gradual than—" Walters snapped his fingers. "After all, we're dealing with the government, aren't we?"

"Then I still have a chance," Hogue murmured.

"How so?"

"To find him. Your Thomas Hengwr. If I find him, the Project won't be closed down, will it?"

"No. Of course not. But—"

"Then I'll find him. And I'll get his secrets for you."

He had to, Hogue realized. If he redeemed himself, if he could give Walters what he wanted, the implicit threat in Gannon's cold eyes need never be realized.

Walters seemed to take a long while to consider. When he finally nodded, Hogue felt himself let go of a breath that he hadn't realized he'd been holding.

"Why not?" Walters said. "It certainly won't hurt. We'll go on for awhile—but with one small difference."

"What's that?"

"Tucker will be removed. I don't want to have to listen to you blaming the poor man for all your failures any more."

"How do you plan to...remove him?" Hogue asked.

The word, coming from Walters and hard on the heels of Hogue's own fears, carried an ominous ring.

Walters regarded him and smiled. "For God's sake, Lawrence," he said, reading the look in Hogue's eyes. "Get a hold of yourself. He'll be transferred. Removed from the Project. Not from his place here amongst the living. What do you take us for? Butchers?"

He glanced at Gannon as he spoke. His assistant gave him a thin smile in return, then returned to his feigned indifference. Hogue, still flustered, missed the exchange.

"No," he was saying. "I didn't think that. At least...that is, I wasn't thinking at all."

"Well," Walters said dryly, "see that you at least make an attempt to in the future. And now, if you've nothing more to add?"

Hogue shook his head.

"Then Phillip will see you home."

Walters watched his assistant lead Hogue from the room and slowly shook his head. It was strange how wrong a first impression could be. When he'd been looking for someone to head up Project Mindreach, someone whose research followed his own interests but who could also be controlled, Hogue had seemed perfect. He'd summed up the thrust of his studies succinctly during that first interview, ending with an observation that had decided Walters.

"These people," Hogue had said. "If they have even half of the abilities that have been attributed to them, their potential is unlimited. In fact, it's conceivable that they might even be immortal, for with such a finely attuned control over body and mind, it's only a few steps further to the development of a regenerative cellular structure that neither ages nor suffers the permanent loss of an appendage. If they lost a limb, they could simply grow another."

"Do you really believe this?" Walters had asked.

"I believe in the potential for such abilities. Whether or not there are men and women in the world who possess them is another matter. I would need firsthand case studies to satisfy my own doubts, let alone allay the skepticism of the scientific community at large. And to be honest, I have no hope of finding such subjects to document. The only ones who ever step forth are fools and charlatans."

"If I could provide you with a subject?"

"If you could. . . ." Hogue had smiled. "The sky would be the limit. *If* you could provide me with a subject."

Walters shook his head again, remembering. Oh, he'd had a subject all right. It merely needed careful handling.

He'd first met Thomas Hengwr at a faculty party at the home of a history professor from the University of Toronto. That was in 1954. Hengwr had been introduced to him as Roger Shipley—a philosophy prof who was a colleague of Dr. Aled Evans in whose home the party was being held. He'd been an odd little man then, comical in appearance, but a brilliant conversationalist. They'd spent that night and many a night throughout that semester discussing and comparing their own fields of expertise: Walters's was the world of finance, but his interests matched Aled's specialty, anthropology. Hengwr had been well versed in both pre-history and other more arcane applications of philosophy, particularly pre-Christian religions.

The three of them were almost inseparable that winter of '54–'55. But in the spring, Walters was transferred to New York City where he began his quick rise from prodigy to the presidency of his first multi-national. He lost touch with both Evans and Hengwr until, moving to Ottawa, he'd read Evans's obituary in the local paper. Coincidentally, that same week he attended a luncheon sponsored by the National Museum. The guest speaker was Thomas Hengwr.

Walters had recognized him at once; the man hadn't changed during the twenty-five years that had passed since those days in Toronto. Which struck Walters as mildly curious. What interested him more, however, was that when he was speaking to Hengwr after the luncheon, the man had been polite and appreciative of Walters's interest in his talk, but totally denied knowing him, denied ever having taught at U of T, in fact, denied being the man Walters insisted he was.

Faced with the conflicting reality of his memories versus Hengwr's denials, Walters had acquiesced amiably enough, but vowed to satisfy, if nothing else, his own curiosity.

He instigated a private investigation that, by the very ambiguity of its results, fascinated him all the more. The man giving the talk that day, the man he'd spoken to, did not exist, at least not in any official records. Nor did the professor Walters remembered in Toronto. On top of that, what little information he did acquire pointed to something so bizarre that at first Walters was prepared to dismiss the entire affair out of hand. But as further tantalizing snippets of information were added, and a crude picture began to form, he realized he was on the track of something far more important than the salving of his curiosity.

Thomas Hengwr was a sorcerer, and had been for many years.

Walters now initiated a serious study of the paranormal, combining what little data he had on Thomas Hengwr with the most up-to-date speculations that the scientific community was prepared to consider. What had begun as a means of assuaging that unfamiliar sensation of being brushed off had become a mild obsession.

It was easy enough to rationalize. If such powers existed, he wanted them for his own. If Hengwr was an immortal, then Joseph Hugh Walters would be an immortal as well. And once immortal . . . what could be denied a man who lived forever? Neither wealth, nor political power, nor anything. If one had all of eternity to work with, what could not be acquired, given time?

But then—when everything appeared to be going well— Thomas Hengwr simply disappeared. Had he sensed the approaching entrapment? For a man with his capabilities, it would be child's play to circumvent a simple police investigation. That was why they'd gone about their own investigation so circumspectly. But however Hengwr'd come to see through their ploys, he was gone now. And with him, all hope of Walters's acquiring those extraordinary powers for himself.

"Rankles, doesn't it?"

Walters shook off his reverie and nodded to Gannon who'd

returned from seeing Hogue off in his cab.

"It comes from playing it all so low key," Walters said. "This town does it to one."

"Does what?"

"Puts a small-town mentality on everything you do."

Gannon shrugged. "I don't think it's a lack of our professionalism that spooked Hengwr."

"You hadn't mentioned that before."

"I've had to think about it," Gannon said. "But the more I do, the more it seems that something else spooked him."

"Such as?"

"Well, if you grant him the capabilities that you do, isn't it highly probably that there are others like him? And if you're with me that far, isn't it conceivable that he might have an enemy amongst those others?"

"It's possible, I suppose."

"Look at it this way," Gannon explained. "He lived like he was on the run. Look how he covered up when you met him at that luncheon. And when we backtracked him—nothing. No, I think he was on the run and someone got close and spooked him."

"Which leaves us where?"

"With two choices. We either find Hengwr and help him out against whoever's after him, or we find out who's after him and see what we can learn from them."

Walters nodded. "I like that."

"About Hogue. . . ."

"He's a liability."

A cold smile flickered in Gannon's eyes. "How do you want it handled?" he asked.

"Make it look accidental."

"And Tucker?"

"No. I don't want Tucker out of it. That speech was for Hogue's benefit. But I want the Inspector prodded. He could very well find Hengwr for us. The man has a certain tenacity that won't let him give up until he's finished what he's set out to do."

Gannon frowned. "That could be dangerous. I don't think Tucker's someone we can play out on a line and then cut off when we don't need him."

"Then you'll just have to be careful, Phillip. After all—that's what I pay you for."

Gannon nodded. "Do you have any ideas on how we can prod him?"

"No. I'll leave that up to you. Only keep it clean." As Gannon stood up, Walters added: "One more thing, Phillip. I think you should check into this Sara Kendell that Hogue mentioned. And her uncle. We can't afford to pass anything up at this point. I've heard a lot of strange talk about Tamson House over the years and it could be that we've been ignoring the very thing we've been looking for simply because it's been under our noses all along."

"And how do you want that handled?" Gannon asked.

"Very carefully. Perhaps you could tag one of them and bring them in."

"Okay, Mr. Walters. But Hogue first?"

"Oh, yes," Walters said with a nod. "Hogue first."

Personnel had brought him the files on two other up and coming researchers, either one of whom would be a good replacement for Hogue. All things considered, anything would be a good replacement for Hogue. He watched Gannon leave the study and picked up the files as the door closed. But while his eyes scanned the computer-generated printouts his mind was still following its old train of thought. Where *was* Thomas Hengwr?

2:00, Thursday morning.

It was curious, Tucker thought, sitting in his office. Curious how Lawrence Hogue, a nobody researcher with a small firm in Toronto, had suddenly been put in charge of something as prestigious as Project Spook. Having reviewed the case files and found nothing again, Tucker had started on the files of PRB's personnel, looking for he knew not what, just trying to keep busy. Hogue's file made him pause.

It seemed that it was Hogue who'd fouled up whenever they were close to something. Tucker'd put that down to inexperience, coupled with the man's need to be "in charge." It was that, or plain incompetence. Tucker favored the latter. Unfortunately, there were no revelations hidden away in his file. It was simply the dull history of a dull man who'd just happened to be involved in the appropriate research when Operation Mindreach had been initiated.

Tucker made a mental note to ask Wally about him in the morning. Maybe he had something on Hogue, though what that might be, or what bearing it would have on the problem at hand, was anybody's guess.

Hogue had to be given credit where credit was due, though. His theories were certainly imaginative. The problem was if the reports of what had happened at Patty's Place earlier this evening were accurate, they weren't dealing with super-brained spooks so much as wizards out of one of those hobbit books that he'd tried to read a few years back. Tucker sighed. Maybe he should have stuck with those books. He might've picked up something he could use now, instead of running around in circles, dodging reporters who had enough instinct to smell a cover-up but nothing hard to even speculate with.

Fuck, he was tired. What he really needed was some rest. Or at least a breather.

He pushed the stack of files to one side of the desk and reached for the phone. Dialing a familiar number, he listened to it ring on the other end of the line. A half-dozen strident rings later, a woman answered, her voice heavy with sleep.

"Hello?"

"Hey, Maggie. What're you doing?"

"Doing? I *was* sleeping until— Is that you, Tucker?"

"Yeah. I thought if you weren't doing anything, maybe we could—"

"Do you have any idea what time it is? What time *is* it?"

"Going on quarter past two. It's a little late. I know."

"Why are you calling, Tucker? I thought we'd worked things out the last time we talked and decided that this sort of thing wasn't going to happen any more."

"Yeah. Well, that was a few weeks ago. I thought maybe we'd have a new perspective on it by now."

"The only perspective we need is some sort of a commitment, John. From you."

Tucker sighed. He always liked the way she called him Tucker. Had a nice ring to it. She only called him John when she was upset with him.

"Maybe we could talk about commitment now," he said.

"I think we've talked the whole thing through once too often. I don't want to argue with you anymore. Especially not in the middle of the bloody night. I'd rather we just stayed friends."

"So would I. That's why I called you. To talk to a friend."

There was a moment's silence on the line.

"Are you still there?" Tucker asked.

"I'm here. I'm wondering about you. Are you all right? You sound a little strange."

"No. I'm just a little tired, that's all. Look, I'm sorry I woke you up and—"

"Are you still assigned to that Special Branch?"

"'Fraid so."

"There was a story on the news tonight—something about an armed robbery in a restaurant of all places. An RCMP officer was killed. Does that have anything to do with the way you're feeling right now?"

"Yeah. Thompson was one of my men. I put him on that assignment before it blew up in his face."

"I thought as much. When they named Madison as the RCMP spokesperson, I sort of figured you were involved." She sighed. "Shit. I don't know if I want to hear any more."

"Well, that's okay. Look, I've gotta run, Maggie. It's been great talking to you."

"Uh-uh, Tucker. Not so fast. I know just where your head's at about now. All mixed up with morality and mortality and what's the point. Why don't you come over for a little while and we'll talk. I'll make you some cocoa."

"I don't want to impose. . . ."

"Bullshit. Then why'd you call? I'm going to get dressed. Do you remember the address?" There was a smile in her voice.

"I'm going to forget it in three weeks?"

"I hope I don't regret that you didn't. Drive carefully, Tucker."

She hung up and Tucker regarded the receiver with the faintest trace of a smile softening his grim features.

"You look terrible."

Tucker leaned against the doorframe and tried on his best Bogart expression.

"Here's lookin' at you, kid. You look great."

"Get out of the hall before one of my neighbors sees you. I've been trying to convince them that I've given up hanging around with the likes of you. It's done wonders for my reputation."

Tucker headed for the living room and sank into the sofa, stretching his legs out before him. The apartment was in Tower A of Riverside Place. The living room window gave a good view of the downtown area—a patchwork of lights like some giant's quilt. While Maggie was in the kitchen fixing their cocoa, Tucker unclipped his .38, stuck it in the pocket of his jacket, and shoved the rolled-up bundle under the sofa. Leaning back, he stared out the window, trying to blank his mind.

Maggie came out of the kitchen with a steaming mug of hot chocolate in each hand. "Well, don't you look comfortable," she said.

"I'm trying," Tucker said.

Maggie set his mug down within easy reach and settled in the chair opposite him.

"So how was your day, dear?" she asked.

Tucker laughed.

He'd first met Margaret Finch about four years ago when he was involved with a case of internal sabotage in the Department of Indian Affairs. She was a lawyer and had been representing their main suspect—a young Ojibway brave. Through sheer stubbornness and strength of will, she'd managed to hold Tucker off long enough to clear her client, solving Tucker's case for him in the bargain. Somewhere along the way they'd become involved with each other on a more personal level, starting an on again, off again relationship that had lasted the better part of three and a half years.

Three weeks ago they'd called it quits and they'd both expressed relief that the question between them had finally been resolved. They were attracted to each other, but their personalities clashed more often than they complemented one another. By calling Maggie tonight, Tucker knew that he'd started the ball rolling all over again.

Funny thing, though. Just thinking that maybe they could work something out made him feel better than he had in a while. The three weeks apart had only served to remind him of what he was losing when he lost her. It *was* time for them to make a commitment—at least for him to. He wasn't sure if this would help or hinder his current problems with Project Spook, then decided that he really didn't give a shit. He needed a couple of hours away from the whole mess anyway—and when the whole thing was over with maybe it was about time he seriously considered some other career options, ones that would allow them to make a life together.

"Why'd we ever call it quits?" he asked suddenly. "I mean, it feels so good, just sitting here with you. . . ."

"Let's not talk about us right now. There's no easy solution and I don't think I'm ready to get into it just now."

Tucker sat up and regarded her seriously. "Let's get married," he said.

"Jesus! That's a solution?"

"You don't want to?"

"That's not it." Maggie frowned. "Or at least that's only partly it. I mean. . . ." She sighed and shook her head.

"Okay," Tucker said. "We'll talk about something else."

He took a sip of his hot chocolate, watching her over the rim of his mug. She was a tall lithe woman who could easily have been a model if she hadn't chosen a more cerebral profession, the sort of person who looked good in whatever she wore, from an evening gown to the flannel shirt and jeans she was wearing right now. Her thick brown hair was pulled back into a ponytail, accentuating the lines of her cheekbones and brow. Pale green eyes regarded him steadily. Wide lips shaped a smile.

Christ! Tucker thought. How could he ever have just walked away?

"How does an armed robbery in a restaurant have anything to do with your PRB?" she asked, then paused, frowning slightly. "Maybe I shouldn't have asked that. I'm not sure I even want to know. Highly classified, right?"

"Right. But your security clearance is still operative. I checked before I came over."

"You would. I'm still not sure I want to know." She shrugged. "Don't get me wrong. I'm as curious as the proverbial cat. I'm just not sure it's something I want to be involved in. You know what I mean?"

"Sure. It's getting pretty weird. So. That's two things we don't talk about."

Maggie reached over, closing her hand around his fingers. "Will it help if you talk about it?" she asked.

"Always does."

They looked at each other for long moments, then Maggie smiled and seemed to come to a decision. Moving around the coffee table, she sat beside him on the couch.

"So tell me," she said, her hand resting lightly on his knee.

Chapter Three

THE old brass-rimmed clock that straddled the mantle in the Postmans' Room was edging its hour hand to the Roman numeral "XII." Midnight, Jamie thought. The witching hour. Wednesday's last breath, Thursday's first intake of air. The circle of the seasons, of time itself, in microcosm. He looked from the clock to where Thomas Hengwr sat across from him, the big chair swallowing his diminutive form. Puffing on his pipe, Jamie sent a wreath of smoke spiraling up to the ceiling.

"You and I," Tom said, "are much the same, Jamie. Two old men attempting to unravel the riddles of the unseen world."

"The same?" Jamie asked. "I always got the impression that you looked down on my studies."

"I never looked down. I merely questioned your methods and your apparent inability to perceive the reality of what waits for all of us just beyond the here and now. I have the advantage there, Jamie, for not only do I believe in that magic Otherworld, but I have walked its roads, I can draw on its powers."

Jamie shook his head. "Tell me about Sara," he said. "I'm not interested in a discussion of the reality or unreality of magic."

Though that wasn't entirely true. With every word, his guest set the blood trembling in Jamie's veins and, strangely, he had the sudden curious impression that Tamson House was listening as avidly as he was. He understood a bond between himself and the House at that moment that he'd never fully appreciated before. This was his forefather's true heritage—what his father Nathan, and his father Anthony had left him.

It was as though he was a part of its walls, shutting away the outside world, leaning closer so as not to miss a single word that their odd guest might utter. He was a part of the

160

towers that overlooked Ottawa's skyline, the cellars that sank
their stony roots deep into the land that supported the city. His
eyes were like the House's windows at that moment—looking
inward and outward at the same time.

"The magic cannot be ignored," Tom said. "It is because
of it that I sit here speaking with you, that your niece walks
the Otherworld, that so much has been set in motion."

"Why *are* you here?"

"Because of events that have their beginning fifteen hundred
years ago."

Jamie sighed and set his pipe aside. "All right," he said.
"I'll listen. I'm not saying that I'll believe anything. I just want
some answers. And if that means a history lesson. . . ."

He let the sentence hang there unfinished and Tom nodded.
"I will be as brief as possible, Jamie."

He folded his hands on his lap and regarded his host for
long moments. "There was a king in Wales by the name of
Maelgwn who had a druid and an enemy. The enemy was the
bard Taliesin. Are you familiar with their history?"

"I think so. Taliesin won a riddle contest, didn't he? And
in the process managed to make fools of Maelgwn's bards,
druids, and the king himself. Is that right?"

"That and more. Maelgwn was a vindictive man. Though
honor forbade his retaliating at the time, he did not—*could
not*—forget that Taliesin had made fools of them all. He was
determined to have his revenge. But bards could not be dealt
with as ordinary men in those times—especially not a bard
such as Taliesin was. Yet while one could not physically harm
them, one could banish them.

"Maelgwn's chief druid forced the bard into a coracle and
set him adrift. It was a fitting fate, he thought—for from the
sea in a coracle Taliesin was cast up on those same shores
many years before. How better to deal with him than return
him to the sea from whence he came? In this way they—
Maelgwn and his druid—could not be held responsible for the
bard's fate. It was in the hands of Dylan Eil Ton. They thought:
Let the sea's god decide what must be done with him.

"But a price was paid for that deed. As the tide dragged
Taliesin's coracle out to sea, he cried forth a curse and the
king's druid was turned to stone. He became a menhir and for
a thousand years he stood on that desolate stretch of coastline,
a tall grey-backed standing stone pointing westward across the
great seas."

"Like some Welsh Merlin," Jamie remarked.

Tom shook his head. "Myrddin, who you call Merlin, *was* Welsh, Jamie. And he was neither turned to stone nor trapped in one, despite all the tales that say otherwise. He was both bard and druid, a powerful combination that made him the greatest wizard that the Green Isles ever knew. When his work in the Isles was done, Ninane, the Lady of the Lake, led him back to the Summer Country—the same land that birthed Taliesin, though he never returned to it."

"Fascinating," Jamie said. "If true."

"Oh, it is true enough."

"Though what bearing it has on Sara's disappearance remains oblique. At least to my humble understanding. *Where is she*, Hengwr?"

"You have listened to me this much. Allow me to finish. Imagine that those two—Taliesin and the king's druid—imagine that they survived the span of all those years. Survived, but were changed. That the druid had taken up the Way of Light and the bard now walked the realms of shadow. In a time such as this, technological achievements soar, new wonder piling on new wonder with bewildering ease. But imagine such men warring with magic now, when the gods have retreated from the world and nothing remains to check their struggle.

"They could make a ruin of this world, for who could stop them? Can a bullet kill a man who can become a wind? Can imprisonment hold a man who can become shadow?"

Jamie shook his head—not in reply, but in disbelief.

"Earlier this evening," Tom replied, "Taliesin attacked my apprentice in a restaurant. Kieran was with your niece. Taliesin changed a man into some terrible werebeast and it was only through Kieran's quick defense that Sara's and his own deaths were averted. Taliesin has changed, Jamie. He has become evil. Though it was Kieran who slew the werebeast—slew an innocent man shapechanged by that bard—I lay the onus for that deed at Taliesin's feet. He will stop at nothing now, Jamie. And unless he *is* stopped, there will be many more deaths."

"Just . . . just suppose I believed any of it," Jamie said. "What has that got to do with me? Or Sara? What does this Taliesin want?"

"Power. And the death of the druid."

"Where's the druid?"

"In hiding."

"God!" Jamie rubbed his face. "And you're on the druid's side, I take it? What makes him right and Taliesin wrong?"

"As Taliesin changed, so did the druid. He became a force for good, Jamie. Believe me. I would not aid such a man if he was still evil. In the passage of years, their roles have reversed. I admit that Taliesin was wronged. He had just cause to lay his curse on the druid. But the druid paid his price; a thousand years locked in stone. Surely he has suffered enough?"

Jamie took a couple of long breaths and tried to think. It was obvious that Tom believed what he was saying. Impossible though it all was, Tom believed. So what was he supposed to do? Play along?

"You said that you thought that I'd be able to help you," Jamie said at last. "That you thought you and I would . . . finish all this. But that now it's up to Sara and your . . . what? Apprentice?" Did people still have apprentices? He supposed people like Thomas Hengwr might. "What are they supposed to do? What are you doing here?"

"After the attack in the restaurant . . . friends of mine took them into the Otherworld."

"That's the second or third time you've mentioned this 'Otherworld.' What is it?" He paused, but before Tom could reply, Jamie held up his hand. "Never mind. I assume it's just more of this magic, right? But tell me what sort of friends took them away. Was it this druid?"

"If I told you, you would not believe me. Just as you find everything I have said thus far unbelievable."

"Try me."

"The manitous took them, Jamie. North American cousins of those beings called elves that figure so prominently in European folk tales."

"Jesus!"

Tom shrugged wearily. He met Jamie's questioning gaze steadily.

"So," Jamie said at length. "What are they supposed to do there?"

"They will meet with a shaman who knew Taliesin when he first arrived on these shores. His name is A'wa'rathe—He-Who-Walks-With-Bears. They had wandering folk in North America then as well, Jamie. They were solitary Shaman/bards who were part of no tribe, but yet of all tribes. Like the European bards. Musicians, magic workers, healers. They were called rathe'wen'a—the Drummers-of-the-Bear—for their totem was the bear. The manitous that brought Kieran and Sara into the Otherworld will in turn bring A'wa'rathe to them."

"To do what?"

"A'wa'rathe holds the key as to how Taliesin may be stopped."

"So why aren't you there? Why is Sara involved? Christ, why am *I* involved?"

"Sara was unfortunate enough to be in the wrong place at the wrong time. She seems to have certain... abilities of her own. Rather than let her come under Taliesin's influence, for he is attracted to both magic users and those with the potential to become magic users, I had her taken with Kieran. She will be safe there."

"And meanwhile? Where's your druid?"

"Working—even as I am. We lead Taliesin astray. While he follows us, he won't be following Kieran and Sara."

"By us, do you mean me as well?"

Tom shook his head. "I need but one thing from you. The same thing that Taliesin has already sought here."

"Taliesin's been here already?"

"Not inside, no. But I have sensed an aftertrace of his presence about the House. Something kept him at bay—perhaps the House itself."

"What's the thing you want?"

"I left a few objects in Aled Evans's keeping, Jamie. I need them now. The keybone of my Weirdin is one."

"I don't have it anymore," Jamie said. "I took it to the museum, where the RCMP confiscated it. They've also got the rest of them."

"Then that solves one problem," Tom said. "It will take no great skill to retrieve them."

"What do you use them for?"

"As guideposts along the Way. Normally, at least. They are also an oracle of sorts. For my present purposes, I will use them to discover the most auspicious time and place to deal with Taliesin."

"Why did you enter them in Memoria?"

"I thought if I put them in your computer that you would discover them and use them. As I said, they are more than an oracle, Jamie. They are all that survives from the ancient druidic alphabet of the trees. Mine once belonged to Taliesin, but he left them with the rathe'wen'a and they came into my hands.

I thought that with them, you would begin to follow the Way. The Craft of Silence.

"I tell you once again, Jamie. There is magic, though it is not, perhaps, what you think it to be. All the trappings of power are just that. Trappings. The Way itself is a strengthening of the spirit, a growing closer to the balance that governs the world. Progress is slow along the Way, but every step of the journey is like a note in the oldest tune of all. When you have the tune complete, you are complete yourself. Every potential becomes realized. Then you can move beyond this existence. No longer will you be reborn, for your time on this earth will be done."

"Where do you go?"

"To the Summer Country, Jamie. But its like I could never describe to you. I have seen only glimpses of it myself, but what I have seen remains burned into my soul. I yearn for my time there. How I yearn."

"Why didn't you just tell me about these Weirdin and the Way?" Jamie asked. "Why did you have to hide them like you did?"

Tom sighed. "Secrecy itself is a source of power, Jamie. And also—in many ways you are different from those in the world around you, but in many ways you are the same. Most people will not accept a gift—most will not allow it its true worth if it is given freely."

A therapist, Jamie decided, could make a life's work of Thomas Hengwr. But that wasn't what concerned him just now. His feelings were mixed. He wanted to believe. But unfortunately, Jamie was also pragmatic. No matter how much he studied the paranormal and *wanted* to believe in it, he also had to accept that there simply wasn't any solid evidence.

Case in point: Thomas Hengwr. He couldn't think of anyone more unreliable. But that judgment didn't bring him any closer to his main concern, which was finding out what Tom had done with Sara. Jamie believed that wherever Sara was—and it wasn't in some airy-fairy Otherworld—Tom had something to do with it. Until he found out, he meant to keep his curious guest talking.

"Who did the painting?" he asked.

"I did."

"You? I never knew you could paint."

Tom smiled. "There is a great deal you don't know about me, Jamie. But I did not physically craft the painting. I created it with magics as a gift for Aled. The concept of a meeting between an European bard and one of the rathe'wen'a fascinated him."

"The red-haired man is Taliesin?"

Tom nodded. "And the other is A'wa'rathe. They were both handsome men—Taliesin especially. But every rose hides a thorn."

"Do you want the painting?" Jamie asked. "Or was it just the . . . ah, what did you call it? The keybone?"

"Not the painting," Jamie said, "but there is one other thing. A small golden ring like this."

He lifted his hand and Jamie saw there on his finger a ring similar to the one Sara had found in the storeroom of The Merry Dancers.

"It is called a gifting ring," Tom explained, "and it is an object of power. The one I seek—the one Aled had—once belonged to Taliesin. A normal gifting ring serves to mark someone under the protection of a Wayfarer—one who follows the Way. They are given in friendship and have some small magic about them. Enough so that those who receive them often take to the Way themselves.

"But the ring I seek, Taliesin's ring, is more than that. He received it from his tutor Myrddin who in return received it from the Lady of the Lake. It was forged by Gwyn ap Nudd, the King of the Faeries in the Summer Country, and has this additional property: it enhances one's magical potentials. It was because of the ring that Taliesin was able to turn Maelgwn's druid to stone. It was the ring that let him survive the long voyage from Gwynedd to North America in nothing but a coracle."

"You'd think," Jamie said, "if the ring is that powerful, that he would have used it to stop his banishment."

"Not necessarily. If I had to hazard a guess, I would say that Taliesin knew that he was no longer welcome in his homeland and so, in his own heart, chose exile. Either that, or the gods withdrew their protection from him for that moment. All that I know is that he no longer has it, but seeks it, and if he were to regain it. . . ."

"That ring sat in the storeroom of The Merry Dancers for three years or better," Jamie said. "And before that, Aled had it for God knows how many years."

"Twenty-two," Tom said.

"All right. Twenty-two. What's taken Taliesin so long to

come looking for it? How did you get it in the first place? And you've known where it was for all that time. If you needed it, why didn't you get it sooner?"

"I had no need for it. As to where I got it—that was at the same time that I acquired Taliesin's Weirdin. The tale went around that Taliesin had died. A'wa'rathe had his effects and gave them to me when I asked for them. All he kept was a six-holed bone whistle."

"What about his harp?" Jamie asked.

Tom shrugged. "It vanished. A'wa'rathe thought it was claimed by Dylan Eil Ton and returned to the Summer Country."

Jamie took up his pipe and tapped the ashes from its bowl into an ashtray. He began to fill it with fresh tobacco. "So he was just pretending to be dead?" he asked.

"Truly I do not understand what he meant to accomplish with that tale. All I know is that for years there was peace, and then an evil was abroad once more—an evil that Maelgwn's druid recognized as the spirit of Taliesin, but changed. From bard to horror. The manitous named it Mal'ek'a—the Dread-That-Walks-Nameless. But Maelgwn's druid can give it a name: Taliesin."

"And the ring . . . ?"

"Is important as much as a defense against Taliesin as is keeping it out of his hands."

Jamie nodded. "I see," he said. "Only I don't have it."

"You don't—" Tom's face blanched. "Then where . . . ?"

"Sara has it."

"Then she is in terrible danger. The ring will draw Taliesin to her—or her to him—like a bee to a flower. We may be already too late."

Jamie stared at Tom's shocked features and a feeling of dread crept up his spine. He hadn't been willing to accept much of Tom's wild story, but now the reality at least of Sara's peril struck him like a physical blow. "Well, don't just sit there!" he cried. "Get her back here!"

Tom stood up and the air crackled around him, like static jumping from a shirt when it is pulled from the dryer. Jamie regarded him numbly, not knowing what to expect. Would Sara suddenly appear here—pop in out of nowhere like a special effect in a movie? A long minute slipped by and nothing happened.

"What are you waiting for?" Jamie demanded.

Tom's shoulders slumped. "I have been too clever for my

own good," he replied slowly. "I asked the manitous to take her—both Kieran and her—deep and far away, to a place even I don't know, in case I should be trapped by Taliesin and the knowledge taken from me. There are a hundred hundred pockets of the Otherworld—each layered one against the other like the layers of an onion. They could be in any one of them."

Totally forgotten now was the impossibility of the situation. All Jamie cared about was Sara and getting her back. He didn't even stop to think that if none of this was real, then she wasn't in any danger. "Sara," he said softly. His gaze remained on Tom. "What have you done to her?"

"I only meant to protect her. Please, believe me."

Jamie nodded without much enthusiasm. Then a thought came to him. "The ring! You can find her through the ring."

Tom shook his head. "Taliesin can—because he has a bond with it. A bond I do not share. It was his ring. Not mine."

"Do something!" Jamie cried.

A hard look came into Tom's eyes. "I will try," he said, and then he was gone in a *whuft* of displaced air.

Jamie half rose from his chair, staring at the place Tom had occupied moments earlier, then slowly sank back into the cushions. Oh, God, he thought. It *was* all true. There were powers beyond the here and now and somehow he and Sara were caught up in the middle of them.

His pulse pounded. I'm too old for this, he thought. What if my heart goes on me?

He tried breathing, slow and deep. In, out . . . in, out. Calm down. He wanted to get up and go running through the House in the forlorn hope that Sara had somehow gotten back on her own and even now was fast asleep in her bed. Safe and sound. He had only to get up and go look for himself to see that everything was all right. There was no weird Tom Hengwr appearing and disappearing, no threat of some long-dead bard come haunting, no magic ring.

But he knew that the hope was no more than a futile wish. Sara wasn't in her bed, nor in a kitchen, an attic, the cellar, nor anywhere. She was no longer on this world, if Thomas Hengwr could be believed. And with what he'd just seen— one minute standing in front of him as solid as the desk or a chair, in the next second gone—how could he not believe?

When he stopped trembling, Jamie told himself, he'd get up from this chair and go find Blue. He had to talk to someone, someone normal. It was that or quietly turn to jelly here in the

Postman's Room. But whatever courage he could normally claim seemed to have vanished and it was all he could do to just sit where he was with his knees knocking together and his jaws clamped shut to keep his teeth from rattling against each other.

He sat there for a long while and slowly the thunder of his heartbeat quieted. Something in the House, that steadfast presence of a building that had stood so many years, a patient presence that came as much from the actual timber and stone that made it up as it did from the House itself, settled over him. He waited until he could unclench his hands from his knees and light his pipe without spilling tobacco all over himself, then stood up, feeling like an invalid just out of sickbed, and went looking for Blue.

In the Firecat's Room, the House seemed to whisper to Jamie. That's where you will find him.

He set off in that direction, wondering how he was even going to begin to tell Blue what was going on. What would he say? Look out for a dead Welsh bard named Taliesin? Sara's gone to faeryland, but that's okay. A wizard went off to get her back.

He shook his head. Smoke streamed from his pipe and trailed along behind him as he stalked off down the hallway. Moving, Jamie felt better, though it didn't do much for straightening out this weird mess they'd managed to get themselves into. He wondered why Aled had never told him the importance of what he'd left Jamie as an inheritance, then remembered something Tom had said earlier: "Secrecy itself is a source of power...."

Jamie sighed.

"If you've got any pull up there, Aled," he said, lifting his gaze to the ceiling, "have someone give us a hand, okay?"

Which was a strange thing for a man who didn't believe in God or Heaven to say. But right now Jamie was willing to call on anyone, so long as they were willing to help.

The stars of the Otherworld spilled a winter-sharp light into the glade where Thomas Hengwr stood. He watched them silently and gave the constellations their bardic names: the Wren, who was the mage's guide to the Otherworld. Left of it, the constellation of the Queen of Otters and her consort the Bearded King. Under them swam the Salmon, who hid or revealed knowledge, depending on its whims. And lifting from the eastern horizon, hidden for the time being by the tall spruce and pine that encircled the glade, was the Weaver at her Loom who held all their fates.

They were each a part of a bardic mage's symbolic measure of the world through which he or she moved. And whether named in the stars or in a druid's alphabet of the trees, hidden in the turns of ritual music or carved on Weirdin bones, they were always the same: one hundred and twenty-two images, sixty-one dualities that likened the motions of one's soul to the riddling steps of the world's balance that a mage took on his or her journey to the Summer Country. Tom sighed and brought his thoughts back to the matter at hand.

As the deep silence of his taw filled him, he slowly knelt in the grass. The stillness that came from inside him seemed to seep out of his body, pore by pore, until what wind there was in the glade died away and even the stars above paused in their solemn dance. When the silence was so profound that it hung from every blade of grass, poised like an inheld breath, he brought out the pouch of Weirdin that he had retrieved from the museum.

That at least had been as simple to accomplish as he'd told Jamie it would be. But the ring and Jamie's niece were another matter entirely. There were a hundred hundred layers of the Otherworld and she could be in any one of them. Close at hand in the realms nearest the herenow, or deep in those worlds where the boundaries between space and time were so thin as to be transparent. A hundred hundred worlds. Where in them would the manitous have taken her? Where would A'wa'rathe be meeting Kieran? His only hope was that the bones could guide him, for even his bond with Kieran was severed by the distance of the Otherworld between them.

He took a cloth from the bag and laid it on the grass in front of him, then withdrew twelve of the Weirdin at random and held them above the cloth in cupped hands.

"Speak to me," he whispered to the night and breathed across the bones.

Then he let them fall.

Avidly, he bent down to read their placement. The reading cloth had a triskellion shape in the center of a Celtic cross. Each arm of the triskell, the cross, and the outsides of the cross's circle had a meaning, dependent on the fall of the bones and their placement to each other. The bone symbolizing the Maiden fell on the east arm of the cross. Beside it was the Hazel Staff and the Lake. He took the Maiden to be Sara. The

Staff could mean either wisdom or journeying; the Lake, receptive wisdom.

Tom stared at them for a long time, shaking his head as he tried to make sense out of the reading. Was Kieran teaching Sara magics? He was still an apprentice himself so that seemed unlikely. Surely Kieran knew better. Tom turned to the fall of the remaining nine bones to see what light they could shed on this new riddle.

So intent was he on the reading, that he failed to sense a deepening of the shadows in the surrounding woods. The dark between the trees grew darker still.

The symbol of the Wren was in the top right-hand corner of the cloth, in the area that designated present allies or adversaries. That was plain enough. The Wren was also called the Harper, so that was Taliesin. But did the bone's placement mean that Taliesin had already contacted Sara? Perhaps he'd even acquired the ring?

The shadows coalesced and eased out of the wood, sliding across the glade with a sly, almost imperceptible motion. It was as subtle as the shadow of a tree moving with the passage of the sun across the sky.

Tom looked at the bottom right corner of the cloth where the course of action, if one was to be recommended, would be. There were two Weirdin there. The Drum and the Lizard, or Salamander. Revelation and silence. Opposites. And yet the same—if the Lizard's silence were taken as one's taw.

The shadow was at Tom's shoulder now, rising from the ground like a castaway cloak suddenly taking shape. As it gained stature, Tom's concentration on the reading shattered. Abruptly aware of his danger, he threw himself forward, turning as he fell so that he faced the threat as he rolled to his feet. He cursed himself for a novice and raised his hands to begin a protective warding. Then the blood drained from his face as he recognized what he faced. His hands fell limply to his side.

"You!" he cried, his throat tightening to choke the word.

Then the shadow was upon him.

From shapelessness, it had taken an all too familiar shape. A hand like a claw raked across Tom's face, cutting to the bone. The force of the blow threw him backward. He tried to roll aside, tried to shape a spell, but his magics and strengths had deserted him, running away like water as recognition of his attacker hit home. His assailant closed the distance between them with a swift motion and lifted him with ease. Strong hands closed on his arms. His feet sought purchase, but kicked only air. His attacker shook him until his neck snapped, then cast him aside as though he was nothing more than a child's broken toy.

It turned then to regard the fall of the Weirdin for long moments, memorizing each position. When it was done, it retrieved Tom's corpse and, hoisting it under an arm, set off into the forest where the shadows swallowed it once more.

Behind in the glade, the silence of Tom's spell dissolved. Movement came as a wind stirred the grasses. The sudden violence was forgotten. Only the stars that looked down on the Weirdin cloth, and the bones that lay in a white scatter upon it, remembered, until they too moved on to follow their ancient trails across the sky.

"Far out," Blue said. "That must be some pretty hot shit you're on."

He was sitting on his bed in the Firecat's Room, wearing a T-shirt and jeans. Sally was under the covers, head propped up against a pillow, sheet and blankets pulled up to her chin.

"What do you mean?" Jamie asked.

Blue grinned. "Drugs, my man. Dope. Tripping. What else?"

"It's the truth, Blue. He just vanished. And if that could happen, what's to say the rest of it isn't true?"

The humor fled Blue's face. Jamie showed none of his usual fluster, but Blue realized that that was because the crisis was so serious. The panic was there—at the back of Jamie's eyes.

"You're serious," Blue said. "I mean, you really believe this."

Jamie nodded. "I know what it sounds like, but... what else can I think?"

"Shit. So what're we going to do?"

"I don't know."

Sally stirred. She looked from one to the other, not believing what she'd just heard.

"Blue," she said. "You don't believe any of this, do you?"

"I know it sounds weird, but if Jamie says that's what happened, then that's what happened, no matter how off the wall it might sound."

"But—"

"You don't understand, Sally. You see some strange things living in the House. This is just a little weirder than usual, that's all." He looked back at Jamie. "Thing I don't understand is why you're so surprised, Jamie. I mean, aren't you the one who does all the studying about stuff like this?"

"I never really thought of it as real before. I wanted to, but I just couldn't accept it without some sort of proof. And now..." He rubbed his face. "Thanks for believing me, Blue."

"Hey! What else can I do? You're my main man, Jamie."

"I think you're both being taken for a ride," Sally said.

"Then where's Sara?" Blue demanded. "And how'd this guy Hengwr manage to just pop in and out of the House like he did? I checked every window and door before we went to bed...." He paused, thinking a moment. "Maybe I should go check them again."

"Did you ever stop to think that maybe Sara just met herself some nice guy and went home with him?" Sally asked. "It does happen, you know."

Blue smiled, remembering their meeting in the National Art Gallery. Then he shook his head.

"Sara would've called," he said. "Maybe not to tell us that, but to tell us she wouldn't be home for supper."

"I give up!" Sally said and rolled over, pulling the covers over her head. "Go off and look for elves and wizards," she added, her voice muffled by the covers. "Just let me get some sleep."

Blue looked at Jamie and shrugged as if to say, She hasn't been here long enough to really understand.

"Maybe we should all try to get some sleep," Jamie said, knowing full well that sleep was the furthest thing from his mind at the moment.

"I think we should each have a hot milk toddy first," Blue said. "You want one, Sally?"

"I'm asleep."

"Okay. C'mon, Jamie. Let's see what we can rustle up."

Jamie nodded thankfully. He didn't want to be alone just now. He couldn't shake the feeling of dread that lay over him. If that harper hurt her, he'd...he'd what? God! He felt like he was losing his mind.

"Jamie?"

He looked up to see Blue waiting for him by the door.

"I just keep worrying about Sara, Blue. I know nothing seems to make sense, but if Tom wasn't lying, she's in terrible danger and there's nothing we can do about it."

"We'll think of something," Blue said reassuringly. He still wasn't sure how much he could accept as real. That Jamie had experienced something out of the ordinary, he did believe. That there were . . . wizards and elves involved was a little harder to swallow. Besides, whenever he'd thought about that kind of thing, he'd always pictured Jamie as the wizard. As the doer. Not the victim. And Sara . . . Blue shook his head. He didn't want to think of anything happening to her.

"C'mon, Jamie," he said.

Wearily, Jamie pushed himself out of the chair he'd been sitting in and followed Blue down to the Silkwater Kitchen.

8:10, Thursday morning.

Lawrence Hogue stood at the bus stop at the corner of Bank and Somerset Street, waiting for a #2. He was reading the morning edition of *The Citizen*—Thompson's death was covered on the first page, under a headline that blazoned: RCMP OFFICER SLAIN. The accompanying copy was sketchy. There was no mention of the PRB. The gist of the story was that Thompson had been off-duty and stopped for dinner at Patty's Place. When the armed gunman entered, he'd tried to foil the robbery attempt. The gunman shot him three times before Thompson even drew his own weapon.

Hogue stared at the photograph of a stretcher being wheeled out of Patty's Place. Nowhere in the article did he see the questions that should have been asked. Why was a gunman attempting to rob a piddly little restaurant like Patty's Place in the first place? Where were the interviews with the witnesses? The restaurant had been almost full. Had no one *seen* the incident? The very effectiveness of the lie frightened Hogue. It reminded him too much of the control that Walters had over him.

"Excuse me. Do you have a light?"

Hogue looked up, startled. The man who'd addressed him was dressed in a beige overcoat, open to show a dark blue business suit. In his hand he held a cigar. He put it into his mouth and leaned forward. Before Hogue had a chance to reply to the man's request, he heard a faint *whiff* of displaced air and felt a pinprick stinging in his neck. He lifted his hand to brush at the spot and knocked the small fléchette from his skin. But he was too late. The cardiovascular poison coating the fléchette had already begun to work. A concentrated derivative of asp toxin was collapsing his vascular system and stopping his heart. His gaze swam and there was a sharp pain in his chest. The man with the cigar regarded him with obvious concern.

"Hey," he said. "Are you all right? I think there's something wrong with this guy," he added as others in the crowd approached.

The man supported Hogue; his vice-like grip on Hogue's arms were all that kept him upright. Hogue seemed to see hundreds of faces staring at him, whirling around in a kaleidoscope of features. He thought—Walters . . . you bastard . . .

The man with the cigar lowered him gently to the pavement. "Somebody better call a cop or an ambulance," he said over his shoulder. "I think he's having a heart attack or something." The cigar vanished under his overcoat, into the breast pocket of his suit coat.

"Who's got some change?" a man in a tweed coat called from the phone booth.

The man who'd held the cigar stepped back into the crowd. Around him people were digging in their pockets for coins. By the time a uniformed policeman arrived, the man was walking briskly north on Bank Street. As he reached the corner of Cooper Street, a tan Chevy pulled up to the curb. The man got in and the car pulled away.

"How'd it go?" Gannon asked, shifting gears.

Serge Morin leaned back against the seat. "Piece of cake," he replied with a smile.

"Coffee?"

Tucker opened a bleary eye and looked across Maggie's bedroom. She was standing at the door, her hair pinned up and looking far too awake for the way he was feeling.

"Well, it's on the counter," she said, turning away. "I've got to finish washing up. I'm due to meet an anxious client on Nicholas Street at nine-thirty."

"What time's it now?"

"Quarter past eight."

Shit, Tucker thought, staring at the ceiling. Time to up and about. Throwing back the covers, he padded into the kitchen and poured himself a mug of black coffee and took it back to the bedroom while he dressed.

"How are you feeling, Tucker?"

"Better." He was sitting on the edge of the bed admiring her. "Why don't we both play hookey today?"

Maggie smiled. "No can do. But I'm not booked for the weekend."

"You're on."

He ran his fingers over the stubble on his chin.

"Top shelf, on the right," Maggie said. "I never did get around to throwing them out."

Tucker headed for the bathroom and found his razor and shaving cream where she said they'd be. He had his face lathered and was about to start shaving, when Maggie slipped in between him and the mirror to put on her eyeshadow. Looking over her shoulder, he grinned and started on one cheek.

"What are you going to do today?" Maggie asked.

"Hit the office first. See if anything's up. Then I guess I'll take a run 'round to the Tamson House. I've got a better perspective on the whole thing now . . . thanks to you."

"You're welcome. What you should do is keep an open mind."

"An open mind? About werewolves? Or wizards?"

"Not *that* open a mind. But you've a tendency to see things one way."

She paused and lying unspoken between them was: such as why she sometimes defended people she knew were guilty.

"From all you've told me," she added, "it doesn't seem that you're dealing with the common criminal element here."

"Yeah. Only what the hell *am* I dealing with?"

Maggie shook her head and stepped out of his way. "I don't know, Tucker. It scares me to think there could be people out there with those kinds of . . . abilities." She regarded him earnestly. "What would they be like? Would they even be human? They probably wouldn't even think like you or me. Good and bad might not have any meaning for them."

"Yeah. I know. It scares me too." He rinsed the remaining lather off his face and ran his fingers through his hair. "You want a lift to Nicholas?"

"Sure. But no sirens, okay?"

Jamie awoke from a nightmare of clawing shadows and monstrous shifting faces. He sat up, his nightshirt clinging to his sweaty skin, and stared out the window of his bedroom. The clock by his bed read eight-thirty and the sky was a bright blue. He thought for a moment of lying down again, then decided he couldn't face another nightmare. Swinging his feet out of bed, he arose and dressed. He met Blue and Sally in the Silkwater Kitchen where Tuck was raising his usual fuss to be fed.

Sally offered him some coffee which he accepted gratefully.

"We were thinking of having some apple pancakes," Blue said. "Ohio-style—whatever that is. You want some?"

Sally laughed. "I take it by 'Ohio-style,' you want me to make them?"

"Did I, or did I not serve up the most delicious tacos you ever tasted last night?"

"That you did. And most humbly too, I must admit."

"I rest my case, dear lady."

Sally regarded him with exaggerated amazement. "Humble *and* polite!"

"House-trained, too."

Jamie smiled weakly, appreciating their attempt at levity. He was about to get up and head for the Postman's Room and his studies, when he noticed the fading light outside, as though the sky had suddenly grown overcast.

"Anyone hear a weather forecast for today?" he asked.

"Yeah. Clear skies and . . ." Blue's voice trailed off as he too looked out the window. "What the . . . ?"

The light continued to fail until it was as dark outside as though the day had never come. Leaving the table, Blue fumbled until he found the light switch. The overhead light in the kitchen's ceiling blossomed. Blue opened the door that led out into the garden and stared at the sky. The dark was absolute. No stars. No clouds visible. If it was a storm, it had come without wind and it was going to be a real mother. The air was charged with static.

Blue stepped back into the kitchen and met Jamie's gaze. The skin between his shoulder blades prickled and he knew Jamie was thinking of the same thing he was: last night's strange guest and his story.

"It's not natural," Sally said.

Then she paused as she too remembered. She'd pooh-poohed it last night, but now a chill skittered up her spine and she shivered.

"Let's check the other side of the House," Blue said.

As they started for the O'Connor side of the House, a huge bang came from the side that faced Patterson on the North. The floor trembled underfoot and they looked at each other with mounting fear.

"What the fuck was that?" Blue muttered, then led off in that direction.

The windows they passed all showed the same view: darkness. The sound that had brought them around to the north face of the House wasn't repeated, but the anticipation of a second set them all on edge.

"Maybe they're blasting somewhere?" Sally offered in a small voice.

"Yeah," Blue said. "And I guess they threw a sheet over the House so that it wouldn't get dusty."

For all that they were anticipating another bang, they still weren't prepared for the second one. It boomed all around them like a crack of thunder. The doorway they passed rattled in its hinges and a vase toppled over on a sideboard by the wall. The vibration almost knocked them from their feet.

"I don't believe this," Blue said, recovering first. "It's like we're—"

"Under siege," Jamie finished, remembering what Thomas Hengwr had told him about the harper Taliesin and his dark strength. If this was the harper attacking them and he was this powerful, how could they possibly hope to hold him off? Where was Tom when they could use him?

"I'm going to have a look," Blue said, starting for the door.

"Wait!" As Blue turned to him, Jamie added: "Tom said— something about the House itself being a protection against Taliesin. What if by opening a door, you leave a breach in whatever it is that's protecting us?"

Blue was about to protest that there had to be a rational explanation for what was going on, when a third crash came, this time knocking them all to the floor. As they started to get to their feet, a succession of crashes rattled the House as though a giant hand was shaking it. Pictures leaped from the walls, their glass shattering as they hit the floor. Vases and knick-knacks bounced from tables and sideboards, adding to the din. The three human inhabitants huddled together on the floor, each trying to cope with the situation as best each could, not one of them willing to accept what was happening, but unable to refute it either.

When the last of the thunder and shaking died away, Blue sat up to take stock. "Anybody hurt?" he asked.

Jamie and Sally shook their heads dully. Jamie started to get up, but Blue waved him back.

"Not yet," he said. "No use in . . . in just getting knocked down again."

Jesus, he thought. What the fuck was going on? He wanted to put it down to an earthquake—scary enough on its own— but the skies didn't go black when the earth moved. This kind of thing just didn't happen. Except it was happening and, by the faces of his companions, he knew someone had to take charge and it looked like he'd gotten himself elected. It didn't matter that the same fear was thudding in his heart—someone had to stay on top of it.

"Who all's in the House?" he asked.

The question gave them something else to think about.

"Fred," Jamie said. "And Sam."

"No one else?" A weird image came into Blue's head, of Jamie standing behind the desk of a hotel, counting the missing room keys on the hooks behind him.

Jamie shook his head. "Not that I know of."

"Well, first off we've got to get hold of them before one of them tries to go outside. I think you're right, Jamie. Some-how the House is our protection against whatever it is that's trying to get in. Shit, if some fucking monster of Tom Hengwr's can exist, why can't the House have powers too?"

Jamie nodded. Inside the House he felt safe—no matter how furious the blows came from what was attacking them. His bond, that sense of being a part of its walls, of the double-sided eyes of its windows that looked out on a black void now, and in on their terror, seemed to promise security. So long as they stayed inside. Once beyond its walls, the House seemed to warn, and it could no longer protect them.

"Well, you two stay here," Blue said, "and I'll go have a look-see for the others. Okay?"

Neither Sally nor Jamie wanted Blue to go off on his own, but they realized the sense of his plan.

Nodding to them, Blue set off. The halls echoed strangely with his footfalls. The darkness beyond the windows seemed more liquid then gaseous. In his imagination, he could see the windows bulging under the pressure of that darkness, saw shad-ows seeping and dripping through the cracks where sill met wall. He tried to shake the feeling of dread that hung over him.

"Just hang on," he whispered to the House. "For Christ's sake, don't let whatever's out there in."

The hairs on the back of his neck were prickled. The last

time he'd been this close to something that wasn't quite of this
world was during the half year or so when he'd lived with
Charlie Nez on the Navajo Reservation near Flagstaff in New
Mexico. He'd been doing a lot of mescal and mushrooms in
those days and sometimes it got a little hard. trying to separate
the real from the drug visions.

He could remember strange nights out on dry rock plateaus
just staring at the stars and listening to stories, or night hunts
when they went soft-stepping in a single file—five or six of
them—down shallow arroyos, looking for porcupines or kan-
garoo rats. There was the pinch of sacred pollen that Charlie'd
given him to ward off witches, the chanting in the firelight at
a Sing (he could still hear that eerie "Ya Ha He Ya Ha He"
drifting off into the night), the great green slopes of the
Lukachukai Mountains, the puffs of dust that Charlie'd tell him
were dust devils—kicked up by one of the Hard Flint Boys to
play a trick on the Wind Children. They built sweat baths,
looked for turquoise to make totems from, and Charlie'd taught
him sign language—finger-speak. "This is how First Man and
First Woman talked, when they didn't want Snake to hear what
they were saying, Blue."

And always the stories, about Changing Woman and the
Sun, about Diving Heron bringing witchcraft and giving some
to Snake and how it turned to poison in Snake's mouth, about
Coyote and the Hero Twins. They were just stories, except
Charlie's eyes never smiled as they did when he was putting
you on.

Blue frowned. He didn't like the way his thoughts were
going because it made everything that was happening *now* too
real. Still, his fingers twitched at his side as he hurried down
the halls, shaping a Blessing Way, and he wished he still had
that sacred pollen that Charlie'd given him, or even the turquoise toad totem that he'd chipped out himself and carried in
his pocket for years.

He found Fred in the west wing, just about to go out into
the gardens.

"I've got to go out," the gardener protested as Blue took
his arm. "With this storm, the plants will be frantic...."

"It's not a storm, Fred."

"What do you mean?"

"There's no time to explain. Just wait for me here and *don't*
open a door or a window. Is Sam still staying in the West
Library?" There was a small room, more like a large closet

really, set off the library that Sam Pattison had laid claim to by the simple expedient of putting in a cot and a chair to pile his clothes on.

Fred shook his head. "I don't know, Blue."

"Well, wait for me here, okay? I'll go have a look."

He found Sam outside the door of his room, trying to staunch an ugly wound on the left side of his head with a shirt. He was sitting on the floor, his back against the wall, and his eyes had a somewhat glazed look to them when he glanced up. His frizzy hair was matted with blood around the wound. The once-white shirt was red.

"You okay?" Blue asked, kneeling beside him.

"I think so." He indicated a small brass figurine of the Cornish piskie Jan Penalurick that lay on the floor nearby. "That bloody thing leaped off the shelf and gave me a good whack on the head. What's going on, Blue? Are we in the middle of an earthquake?"

"Worse."

Brushing aside Sam's hands, Blue investigated the wound. It wasn't as bad as it looked. Tearing two strips from the shirt, he made a pad of one and used the second to tie it in place. They'd get it patched up properly when they had a chance.

"Come on," he said, helping Sam to his feet.

With Sam leaning on his arm, he led the way back to where Fred was waiting. The gardener was staring out a window, trying to make out how his wards were surviving the bizarre weather.

"Just for a moment," he said to Blue, but the biker shook his head.

"No way. Let's go."

Halfway back to the Patterson side of the House where Jamie and Sally were waiting for them, the sudden sharp clamor of thunder heralded another attack. Blue pulled Sam down to the floor. Fred tumbled, the shaking knocking his feet from under him. Under the roar of the attack, they could hear the crash of falling tables, vases smashing, books falling from their shelves. Then the lights went dead, silence fell, and it was as black inside the House as it was outside.

Blue crouched like an animal at bay, his gaze darting left and right, trying to penetrate the stygian dark. He felt utterly helpless. When the sound of scratching—like Tuck's claws on wood only magnified a hundred times—came from the nearest door, he jumped nervously. He turned in the direction he thought the sound was coming from, then blinked, because he could suddenly see again. But the light—

"Jesus!" he murmured.

A vague illumination crept up from the baseboards—a pale blue-green, faint and shimmering, but more than welcome after the empty black that had left him thinking they were in limbo. He reached a hand out towards it, not touching it, just close enough to feel the heat if there was any. It wasn't hot or cold.

The scratching set his teeth on edge. When it finally faded and died, he let out a breath he hadn't been aware of holding. He stared at the weird light. More of the House's power? He didn't even want to think about it.

He got up, helped Sam to his feet, and started them off down the corridor again. From time to time, they heard the odd clawing at doors they passed. Blue clamped his teeth tightly and hurried them on. The next bout of shaking and thunder was mild compared to the previous one and Blue began to hope that whatever was trying to get in was weakening. By the time they reached Sally and Jamie, everything was quiet again.

"Now what?" Jamie asked when they were all gathered together.

Blue shook his head, trying to think. Sara's cat Tuck had found its way down to where they were and was crouched in a corner, hissing, his orange fur standing on end. Blue was very aware of everyone looking to him. They expected him to do something. Which was fine, except what was he supposed to do?

"The phone?" he asked, thinking aloud.

"We tried it while you were gone," Sally replied. "It's dead."

None of them spoke of the pale illumination, nor where it was coming from. Nor did they wonder what had caused the scratching sounds—at least not aloud. The scratching was the worst of all, because if you stopped to picture what it might be that was making it, the size of the creature's claws and the power in its limbs. . . .

Blue took a deep breath. Okay. So far they'd ascertained that there was something outside trying to get in, that it had cut the electricity and phone lines, that it couldn't get in because somehow the House was stopping its entry. So why hadn't the auxiliary generator cut in? That at least was easy to figure out, Blue realized. Nobody'd gone down to switch the sucker on. And in the meantime, the House'd been nice enough to provide some light for them—creepy light, no doubt about that, but it was better than shitting bricks in the dark waiting for God knows what to come busting in on them.

"We've got to find out what we're up against," he said at last, "before we can do anything about it."

"We *know* what it is," Jamie said.

Blue shook his head. "We've got a vague idea from what Tom Hengwr told you but that's no man—sorcerer or not—scratching at the doors."

"You're not going to go out there and find out, are you?" Sally asked.

"Dunno. Let me think a minute."

While he did, Jamie tried to explain to Sam and Fred, but gave up halfway through. He kept getting mixed up and ended up feeling as confused as they were. The besieger chose that moment to start up the next round. Thunder boomed. The doors sounded like they were being clawed to ribbons. A side table turned over and crashed on the floor, narrowly missing Fred. The remaining paintings were flung from the walls. Anything that wasn't bolted down hopped and shifted and fell.

It dragged on and on, a cacophony of sound and motion that left them in a helpless tangle against one wall, shielding themselves as best they could from the broken glass and shifting furniture. Then finally it died away.

"Okay," Blue said.

Their heads were all ringing, the blood pounding in their ears. Blue crawled over to a side table and broke off one of its legs with a well-placed kick. With the jagged end held out before him, he advanced on the door.

"No more fucking around," he said.

"Blue!" Sally and Jamie cried at the same time.

Ignoring them both, he slipped the chain onto the door, took a deep breath, and slowly opened it. He thought he was prepared for anything, but when the door suddenly smashed against him, opening to the end of the chain's limit, he thought his heart was going to stop. Something that was a cross between an animal's furred paw and a man's arm thrust through the opening. It reached in as far as its shoulder, the taloned paw raking the air.

Recovering from the first shock of the attack, though not from the horror of it, Blue jabbed the paw with the sharp edge of his club and was rewarded with a howling withdrawal. Before he lost his chance, he slammed the door shut with his

shoulder and bolted it. The shaking and pounding returned with
a renewed fury. Blue turned from the door and, knocked to
his knees, crawled back to where the others crouched. His
knuckles were white around the end of his club.

"I don't believe it," he kept saying. "It was some kind of—
what the fuck *was* it?"

The pale faces of his companions held no enlightenment.
They looked sickly in the weird light and for a moment Blue
was sure he was just having a very, *very* bad nightmare.

They huddled together as though they were the component
parts of one organism, gazes fixed on the door, each praying
in his or her own way that whatever strength it was that had
let the House prevail against their attacker thus far would not
now fail. Slowly, the attack fell off, but still they clung to each
other, not able to believe that it was over, even though the
silence dragged into minutes, then into a full half hour. It was
Blue who first noticed the change.

"Look," he said, gently disengaging himself from Sally and
Fred.

The House's supernatural illumination was fading as light
began to come through the windows once more. Blue stood
up, the club still in his hand, and made his way to a window.
For a moment he thought he saw the expanse of a great wide
field with a dark pine forest behind it; then all there was outside
was Patterson Avenue, lying calm and peaceful in the morning
light. There was no sign of their attacker, no way to tell that
any of it had ever happened.

"It . . . it's gone," Sally said wonderingly.

"It'll be back," Blue warned.

Jamie tried a switch and light from the overhead fixture
joined the sunlight that washed the room. He looked down the
hall and saw that the other lights—the ones whose switches
they hadn't been flicking back and forth—were all on as well.

"Electricity's back," he said blankly. Somehow hearing it
said aloud seemed to comfort them.

Blue turned to the door.

"It could just be a ploy," Jamie said.

"I know. But I'm ready for it this time."

The others stayed back from the door as he stepped forward.
His own hand trembled as he reached for the knob, but he was
the only one aware of that. To the others he seemed unnaturally
calm. The lock disengaged with a click and then the door slowly
opened. Blue peered out. The first shock was that the outside

of the door was unmarred—it didn't have even a scratch on it. Then his shoulders stiffened and from behind him, the others could hear him murmur: "Je-*sus!*"

"What is it?" Sally asked.

Blue shut the door before anyone could look and rested his back against it. He felt sick.

"Someone better call the cops," he said.

"What is it? Sally repeated, a hint of hysteria in her voice.

"There's a body out there," Blue replied dully. "It looks like it was torn apart by whatever it was that tried to get through the door. But there's not even a mark on the fucking door!"

"A body?" Jamie took a step forward. "Whose?"

"I don't know. Just call the cops. Jesus! How are we going to explain any of this?"

Jamie didn't really want to see, but he had to know. A vague premonition was stirring in him. Gently he pushed Blue aside, opened the door and looked for himself.

"Oh, God!" he said, recognizing the clothing. Slowly he closed the door, his face paler than before, the features tight.

Blue swallowed. "You . . . know him?"

Jamie nodded. "It's Tom Hengwr. Or at least what . . . what's left of him."

He felt nauseous. Crossing the room, he headed for the phone, paused with his hand on the receiver. Blue was right. What *could* they say to the police? They'd all be taken in for questioning and then, away from the protection of the House. But they couldn't just leave the body lying there. Someone was going to see it and— God! Why hadn't the police shown up already? With the tumult out there. . . .

Blue tossed his club into a corner where it clattered before lying still. Everyone started and Tuck jumped, spitting, and took off down the hall. The others just looked at the table leg, then at Jamie.

"You want me to do it?" Blue asked.

Jamie shook his head. He knew whom he had to call now. He pulled out the phonebook, looked up a number, then dialed. "Hello?" he said when the phone was picked up at the other end of the line. "I'd like to speak to an Inspector Tucker."

The news hit Tucker hard. It wasn't as though he'd liked Hogue or anything, but it was weird the way he'd just keeled over like that.

"What a way to go, Wally."

Madison, who was sitting across from Tucker's desk, nodded.

"I got our own men onto it as soon as word came in," he said. "The preliminary reports all point to a heart attack."

"Did he have a history of heart trouble?"

"You've got the file, John."

"Yeah. I guess I do."

And besides, Tucker thought, fat men were always susceptible to coronary problems—especially uptight fat men like Hogue had been. His gaze dropped to the desktop and fell upon a small three by five card that he hadn't noticed when he first came in. He glanced at it idly, then stopped in shock, picking it up.

"John?" Madison said. "What is it?"

Silently, Tucker handed over the card. Typed on it was the message: "you could be next." Just that. No capitals, no punctuation.

"Je-sus!" Madison said, looking from the card to Tucker. "So Hogue was. . . ."

"What else? Him first. Me next."

"How did this get here?" Madison asked.

"Christ! How should I know? I just got here myself."

"But this means there's someone inside involved—"

"I know what the fuck it means!" Tucker clenched his fists, staring at the small card in Madison's hand. He took a breath, trying to steady the anger that was burning in him.

"Look, I'm sorry, Wally. I didn't mean to snap like that. But don't worry. We'll find the sucker that left that here."

Madison dropped the card on the desk.

"I forgot," he said. "There might've been some prints on it."

Tucker shook his head. "No. They're too slick for that."

It was hard to keep the anger from boiling over. He hadn't cared too much for Hogue, that was true. But it had just become a whole new ball game. First Thompson, then Hogue. Now this card. Someone was playing games and they were playing for keeps. Well, they were going to find that Tucker played for keeps too—and he didn't play by any rules.

"Inspector?"

Tucker looked up.

"What is it?" he asked the constable standing in the doorway of his office.

"We can't raise Warne."

"Warne?"

"He's on the Tamson stakeout. He took over from Bailey at eight and hasn't checked in yet."

"Jesus. What's next?"

At that moment the phone rang. "Call for you, Inspector. It's a Jamie Tams. He says its urgent."

Tucker stared blankly across his office. He'd felt so fucking calm coming in this morning. How come it all had to fall apart in five minutes? So Jamie Tams was calling, was he? Calling to make some demands, maybe? To see if his fucking note was found? Well, let's see just what it was that he wanted.

"Put him on," he said.

Chapter Four

THE Otherworld forest was alive with sounds. Above them a lazy wind stirred the pines. In the distance a jay—the self-appointed rumor-monger of the eastern woodlands— could be heard scolding. All around them insects hummed. Kieran leaned against the trunk of a tree as he spoke, the rough bark catching in his hair when he moved his head. His story made a stark counterpoint to the peaceful background.

Sara lay on her stomach, her head propped up on her arms as she listened to him. She proved—much to Kieran's surprise after their heated exchange earlier this morning—to be a good listener. But she seemed so unsurprised with what he was telling her that Kieran wondered from time to time if she really was listening. When he'd brought her up to date, she looked off into the forest for a long time and said nothing.

"Well?" he asked finally.

"Well what?"

He shrugged. "You're taking it all very well. You don't seem the least bit startled by anything I've said."

Sara sat up, a rueful smile on her lips.

"You've told me a lot of weird stuff," she said, "but after all I've been through in the past twenty-four hours, I'm not sure anything'd surprise me anymore." She pulled up her legs, resting her chin on her knees, and regarded him critically. "There's some things I don't understand though."

"Like what?"

"Well, this telepathic power you have for one thing. Doesn't your head get filled up with a lot of noise?"

Kieran shook his head. "You learn to tune it—like a radio. But I'll admit that there's nothing nicer than psilence some-times. That's silence with a 'p.'"

188

"Can you read my mind right now? Do you know what I'm thinking?"

"Doesn't work that way. I can project thoughts—to a receptive mind. The rest of it, the 'noise'... well, to use the radio analogy again, it's like being just off the station. You know there's something there—another person or what have you—but not what it's actually thinking. Emotions come through the clearest."

"And what about... like when we were in the restaurant? When I could feel everything you were feeling."

"That was because I was projecting too hard and you have some degree of psychic empathy."

He held out his hand to her again. "Try touching me again," he said.

Sara hesitated, then finally stretched out a hand to meet his. She flinched when their skin came into contact, but nothing happened.

"Weird," she said, drawing back her hand. She bit at her lip, thinking. "Okay. What about this mentor of yours? I'll go along with his being a... a wizard, I suppose. But do you really believe he's the reincarnation of some long-dead Welsh druid?"

"Not the reincarnation. He's the same druid. Maelgwn's druid. His name was Tomasin Hengwr t'Hap then."

"And he was the one who... banished the bard Taliesin?"

Kieran nodded. "Banished him, and was turned into stone for a thousand years for his trouble."

Since finding the ring, Sara had given up on coincidence. Everything that happened to her since then fit into place too well, like the pieces of some gigantic jigsaw puzzle. It wasn't a comforting feeling. Neither was hearing the same story that Taliesin had told her from the other side at all comforting. For all that she'd kept her features blank, she was still surprised that Kieran hadn't sensed her shock at that point in the story. Perhaps magic powers weren't all they were cracked up to be. Either that, or it was simply that Kieran wasn't an adept yet and nuances slipped past him. Either way, Kieran made her uneasy.

"Your Thomas Hengwr doesn't sound like a very nice person," she said.

"Why? Because he banished Taliesin? The king *made* him do it."

Sara frowned. "Bullshit. That's like the Nazis saying they

weren't guilty because they 'ver only following orders, ja?' He's responsible for what he did. He could have said no."

"He was different then."

"How so?"

Kieran felt the first touch of his temper returning. "You don't understand," he said. "You haven't met him. If he was an evil man once, he's changed. *Nom de tout!* Do you think he likes to remember those days? There isn't a kinder or more gentle man alive."

"You just say that because you're close to him. That's the same reason why you've accepted his story about Taliesin being some terrible monster out to get him." ·

"And I suppose you know better?"

"I . . ." Sara shook her head. This was definitely not the time to tell him about who she'd met by Percé Rock. "I just don't believe that part of it, that's all."

"Look," Kieran said slowly, trying to keep a rein on his temper. He'd never met anyone who could frustrate him as much as this woman. "Just as Tom changed, so did the harper. It's as simple as that. Taliesin wants revenge. It's been festering inside of him for fifteen hundred years or better. Lord dying Jesus! That would change anybody."

"Okay, okay." Sara refused to meet his gaze. "I don't want to talk about it anymore."

"Well, what *do* you want to talk about?"

"Nothing!"

For a moment they glared at each other, then Sara looked away again.

"Where do you think your mentor is?" she asked, striving for a level tone of voice.

Kieran sighed. "I don't know. I'm not even sure he's . . . alive anymore. When our contact broke, when I came to Ottawa looking for him I thought—well, I thought I'd just find him, you know? Or see that he'd left some word for me. Something. Now I think—now I don't know what I think."

"I think we should get out of this place."

"And just how do you propose we do that?"

"Same way we got here."

Sara thought about how she'd reached out for Taliesin, that second time. It was just a matter of focusing, wasn't it? Of concentrating on Tamson House and humming the moonheart tune Taliesin had given her. Then she remembered the moment in Patty's Place, just before she'd blacked out. There'd been the sound of drums all around them, and those dancing shapes. . . .

"Someone brought us here," she said. "They fixed your wound and left us that stuff." She indicated the provisions that their benefactors had provided. "Can't you get a fix on them? You know. Sort of find them with your thoughts or however it is that you do it?"

"I've tried," Kieran said. "There's just an . . . emptiness beyond this glade. Like we're enclosed in a bubble of psilence."

"I got out," Sara said. "I went quite a ways. We could try just walking for a while," she added, "and see what we can find. That depends on you though, I guess. How're you feeling?"

"Stiff." Kieran prodded his bandage gently. "But better than I should be—considering how badly I got hit, and how bad I felt earlier. I'm ready to give it a go."

"You look a bit better. Not so peaked, if you know what I mean."

"Thanks a lot."

Sara shrugged. "What can I say?"

She stood up, feeling good as she straightened the fall of Taliesin's cloak around her shoulders. Picking up her guitar case, she looked down at Kieran. "Well?" she asked.

But Kieran was looking behind her. Following his gaze, Sara turned and slowly set her guitar down. Standing between two pines was a silvery-grey wolf the size of a large German shepherd. A *very* large German shepherd, she amended. It regarded them with amber eyes that discomfortingly seemed to reflect far more intelligence than an animal should have. Sara, trying to keep one eye on the wolf, looked around for something to use as a weapon, though if the wolf attacked she wasn't sure what she'd actually do with a weapon. She settled on the clay jug and was edging towards it, when Kieran spoke.

"I don't think it means to harm us."

"Oh, no?"

Kieran was shaking his head, but Sara wasn't looking in his direction. She'd reached the jug and slowly bent to pick it up, expecting the huge beast to come lunging at her any second.

"It's just here to make sure we don't leave," Kieran guessed.

"Then where was it when I took off before?"

"I'm not sure. . . ."

"Well," Sara said, swallowing. She didn't feel nearly as brave as she was acting. "We can test your theory easily enough, I guess. You stay put."

"Sara! Don't do anything stupid."

She turned to regard him icily. "Don't you tell me what to do, Kieran Foy."

Hefting the jug, she started for the forest, crossing the glade as far from where the wolf stood as she could. It made no move to follow her, did nothing, in fact, except sit on its haunches and watch.

"Now you get up," Sara called back.

No sooner did Kieran start to rise to his feet than the wolf stood as well, taking a few paces forward. A low warning growl rumbled deep in its chest and the guard hairs around its neck bristled. Sara froze. Not until Kieran lowered himself down once more did the wolf relax.

"Looks like it's you he wants," Sara said, far more lightly than she felt.

Her pulse was drumming. She wanted to take to her heels and run as far and as fast as she could. She glanced at Kieran, thinking, We're not even on the same side. Because there were sides drawn up: those who stood with Taliesin and those who stood with Kieran's mentor, Thomas Hengwr. Which was all well and good, except she wanted no part in some centuries-old war. On the other hand, just as Kieran was beholden to his mentor, so had she claimed Taliesin as her own, making her beholden to him. But all she wanted to do was learn the magics and musics that the bard had to offer. Not become a soldier in some struggle that didn't concern her.

For long moments she considered, then sighed, tossed the jug onto the grass and returned to sit by her guitar case.

"I thought you were going to leave," Kieran said.

"I was."

"Why didn't you?"

Sara shrugged. It wasn't something she was prepared to go into right now, so she ignored the question. She turned so that she could watch Kieran's guard. The wolf, seemingly satisfied that his charge was no longer intent on leaving, faded back into the forest. But though it was no longer in sight, its presence remained.

"Well, now what?" Sara asked.

"It looks like we wait."

"For what?"

"For whatever's going to happen. I don't *know*, Sara."

Sara nodded. She felt irritated, now that the initial fear had subsided. They waited. Fine. For what?

Frowning, she reached for her guitar case and snapped open its clasps. She had to get her mind off of everything for a moment.

"It's funny," Kieran said as she was taking the Laskin from its case.

"What is?"

"Well, you are, I suppose. I get the feeling that you know far more about what's going on than you let on."

"I should be so lucky."

Kieran cleared his throat, but he didn't say anything else. Picking up her guitar, she removed herself to the far side of the glade, sitting down at an equal distance from where Kieran sat and where the wolf had vanished. She pulled out her tobacco, rolled a cigarette, then remembered that she didn't even have a match on her. She shot a glance over to Kieran.

"Have you got a light?" she asked.

"Have you got a smoke? I lost my tobacco pouch somewhere along the way."

Moments later, they were both puffing away. I should give these things up, Sara thought as she took in a long drag. Sticking the smoking butt into the wedge that her bass E string made between the nut and its tuning peg she started to play. Whether it was the cigarette, or the music, or some combination of the two, she started to relax almost immediately. Closing her eyes, she took up the tune that Taliesin had taught her.

"Lorcalon," she murmured to herself as her fingers found the notes.

A stepping-stone, he'd called it. To her own inner silences. Her taw. Kieran had talked a little about that as well and while she still wasn't clear on what it meant exactly, the more she played the piece, the closer she felt to some immense place of quiet strength. Got to be careful, she thought, that I don't let it take me away.

She smiled, wondering what Kieran would think if she just upped and vanished. Probably wouldn't surprise him at all. Then again, it wouldn't be that good an idea to let on what she had done. At least not now. He might not be aware of it, but there was a truce between them for the moment. Sooner or later they would be clearly standing on opposite sides of this struggle. Until then it seemed best to let him think she was just what he thought she was now: a persnickety little ninny-hammer who'd just happened to stumble into the middle of it all.

And who says you're not? she asked herself. Good question. She'd have to give that a good think someday. But not right now. Right now belonged to the music and the stillness it found inside her.

Noon came and went. The sun held itself directly overhead for the passage of one long breath and then began its descent towards evening. Sara had put her guitar away and the two of them tried some of the little cakes that had been left for them by their unknown hosts. They proved to be chewy and somewhat dry and Sara ended up regretting that she'd tossed the water jug aside so casually. When she'd gone to retrieve it, it was empty.

They didn't talk much. Once Sara mentioned something that had been troubling her: that Jamie would be worrying about her. Kieran replied with something Tom had told him once.

"Time doesn't pass the same here," he said. "We could spend a week and find we were only gone a few minutes."

Sara nodded. She remembered spending the entire morning with Taliesin on the beach and coming back to find it only around ten o'clock or so in the glade. Then she thought of Rip Van Winkle.

"Doesn't it sometimes work the other way as well?" she asked.

What if she got back to Ottawa and a hundred years had passed?

Kieran nodded, but didn't say anything.

Just before it got fully dark, they tried leaving once more. The only success they had to show for their efforts was the return of the silvery-grey wolf. It faced back into the woods once they settled down again.

"Why doesn't someone *come?*" Sara cried, but Kieran had no answer for that either.

Eventually they slept and Sara dreamed of her harper, but this time she was like a ghost and could only view him from a distance. He was wandering up and down the beach near the Rock, as though searching for something . . . or someone, she thought. Maybe he was waiting for her. She called to him, and his head lifted and he looked about, but he never saw her. Humming the moonheart tune, she tried to go to him physically once more, but all that happened was that she woke up and it was morning in the glade.

They spent a quiet day and discovered that, barring their

disagreeing views on Taliesin, they had a fair amount in common. Given different circumstances, Sara thought, she might have gone for him, but every time that thought came up, she saw Taliesin's features in her mind's eye and remembered her dream last night of him walking the coastline, searching. And now she was sure he'd been searching for her. She tried to will herself back to him again to no avail. She wanted to ask Kieran how exactly that sort of thing worked, but that would have entailed explaining where and why she was going, and she couldn't do that.

The minutes became hours and the day drifted on. Later in the afternoon, Sara took her guitar across the glade once more and played the moonheart tune some more—not trying to go anywhere anymore, just looking for some peace and that quiet that rose up inside her when she woke the notes from her instrument. After a while she put her guitar away again and, feeling like she was mentally wrapped in a cocoon as close and warm as Taliesin's cloak, dozed in the shade of one of the tall pines.

Her eyes snapped open when Kieran suddenly sat up, and she looked around, searching for what had disturbed him. She crossed the glade as quietly as she could to sit beside him.

"What is it?" she asked.

Staring into the forest, Kieran shook his head. "I don't know," he said. "All of a sudden, everything seems different."

Sara suddenly sensed it too. There was a stillness in the air that was startling only by its sudden presence. It was as though the forest was waiting for something, or someone.

"Nom de tout!" Kieran murmured.

She came out of the forest like a ghost,.a tall Indian woman riding a great bull moose, a pair of silver-furred wolves padding along either side. The bull stood a good seven feet at the shoulders, with an antler spread of five and a half feet from tip to tip. Its coat was a dark brown and its bell, the fold of skin that hung down from its throat, was darker still. Though the animal weighed close to a ton, it stepped out from amongst the trees with as delicate and soft a step as its small African cousin the roebuck.

The woman sat behind the hunch of the bull's front shoulders and regarded Sara and Kieran appraisingly as they scrambled to their feet. Her hair hung in two long black braids on either side of her face that were entwined with beadwork and lacing. She wore a sleeveless dress of doeskin, its collar a twin to the one the shaman wore in Aled Evans's painting, with the same intricate pattern of colored beads and dentalium shells. And her eyes, too, were like the shaman's—a sudden blue against the deep coppery hue of her skin.

"God, she's beautiful," Sara said.

Kieran made no reply. Sara felt a charge building up in the air, like static electricity, only finer. Magical tension, she realized, not really sure how she knew.

The tableau held for a few minutes longer, then the woman slid gracefully from the back of her mount and approached them. In her bare feet, she still topped Kieran's height by a few inches. The moose stayed where she'd left it, but the wolves followed on her heels, sitting on their haunches when she paused a half dozen feet from where Sara and Kieran stood waiting. She raised her right hand, palm outward, in the time-honored gesture that meant, "I come in peace; see I bear no weapon." Sara almost expected her to say "How," like in some bad B-grade western, but when the woman spoke, her voice was clear and melodious.

"Which of you is the craftson of Toma'heng'ar?" she asked.

Sara shot a glance at Kieran. She understood whatever language it was that the woman was speaking, thanks, no doubt, to the expediency of having a bard give her the gift of tongues, but she wasn't sure if it would be intelligble to him. Kieran, however, seemed to have no trouble understanding her.

"I am," he said. "My name is Kieran Foy."

"And your companion?"

"Sara Ken—" Sara started to reply, then remembered what Taliesin had told her about giving names freely. "Don't pay me any mind," she added. "I'm just baggage on this trip. Kieran, here, is the magic man."

The woman inclined her head to them. "My name is Ha'kan'ta," she said. "I give you greeting, Kieranfoy and Saraken."

"Was it you that had us brought here?" Kieran asked.

"Not I. You are the guests of the quin'on'a." At their puzzled expressions, she explained. "They are the spirits-of-the-wild. The manitous. Surely your craftfather spoke of them to you?"

"He didn't have a whole lot to say about them."

Ha'kan'ta smiled. "The quin'on'a are a secret people. One privileged to be named their friend may tend towards secrecy when referring to them."

Sara eyed the wolves nervously.

"Those pets of yours," she asked. "Are they tame?"

"They are not my pets," Ha'kan'ta said stiffly. "Would you tame the wild?"

"Where we come from it seems like they've tamed everything."

"Then it is a sorry world you come from."

"Depends. There's a lot of good things in it too."

Sara knew she was being a little snarky, but couldn't help it. They'd been sitting around twiddling their thumbs for a couple of days and now this woman waltzes in all magical and beautiful while the pair of them were as grubby as a couple of rubbies on the streets back home. She looked past Ha'kan'ta to where the bull moose stood placidly chewing its cud, then back at the wolves with their clear, overly-intelligent eyes.

"I just wanted to know if they were dangerous," she said.

"Do not be alarmed, Saraken. Approach them with respect and they will respect you in turn."

Easy for you to say, Sara thought. Before she could ask the question that was most on her mind, Kieran voiced it for her.

"Why were we brought here, Ha'kan'ta?"

"To meet my father, A'wa'rathe. But He-Who-Walks-With-Bears walks with them in the Place of Dreaming Thunder now, so I have come in his place. The message that the quin'on'a sent me was that Toma'heng'ar wished my father to teach you the Beardance. That is a gift not lightly given, but there are bonds between my father and your craftfather that reach back across the passing of many summers, so I have come where he could not."

She paused, eyeing Kieran curiously. "Tell me, does your craftfather still pursue his foe, the thing of shadows that the manitou have named Mal'ek'a?" At Kieran's nod, she sighed. "Hunter and hunted. The one hunts and in turn is hunted. And in the end, will either survive? My father told me once that should either one of them succeed, the survivor would have nothing left to live for. They are bound to each other, like the caribou to the wolf. The wolf keeps the caribou strong, weeding out the weak stock, while the caribou sustains the wolf. But what when the balance is broken?"

"Tom only wants peace," Kieran said.

"And his foe?" Ha'kan'ta asked. "The thing of shadows that he will not name? Who can say that it does not seek peace as well?"

"I can give it a name," Kieran said. "Taliesin."

"You don't know that!" Sara protested.

Before Kieran could reply to Sara's outburst, Ha'kan'ta shaped a ward against ill luck and took a step back. The wolves, startled at the sudden movement, arose bristling to flank her.

"Taliesin?" she said. "Toma'heng'ar seeks Taliesin Red-hair's death?"

"But only because Taliesin seeks his! Tom wants peace. Nothing more."

"Then peace he has," Ha'kan'ta said, "for Taliesin is long dead, Kieranfoy. The little mysteries still sing their laments for his passing. If you seek him, you must seek him in the Place of Dreaming Thunder, for he no longer walks the worlds we know. He is with my father now, for they were drum-brothers. As were *your* craftfather and mine. And by such reckoning, Toma'heng'ar and Taliesin were drum-brothers as well. Mother Bear will only bring bad medicine to your craft-father if he continues on this path."

Kieran shook his head stubbornly. "Maybe his body's buried somewhere, but a part of him still lives. A part of him's out to get the old man."

"Dead men do not hunt—save in the Place of Dreaming Thunder, young warrior, and what is done there is of no concern to the living. Believe me."

"Then how do you explain. . . ." Kieran began, then he shook his head.

He'd already been through this argument with Sara. Why was it that everyone he met couldn't understand what danger Taliesin was?

Standing beside him, Sara said nothing. She was still mulling over the fact that Taliesin *was* dead. It was something she'd never really stopped to think about before. This whole time-travel paradox was bewildering. It had been different when she was with him, knowing that she could reach out and touch him and he'd be real. Then she could talk about him being a long-dead legend and they could both laugh about it. But the fact was: he *was* dead. Just because through some magic she could reach back into time and be with him didn't change the fact that in her own time he didn't exist anymore. He was only so much dust, gone to this Place of Dreaming Thunder that Ha'kan'ta had spoken of.

She had the strongest urge to will herself back to him right now, but knew that the attempt would be doomed to failure. It wasn't as though she hadn't tried already. But she just couldn't accept the fact of his death. Not when just yesterday she'd been with him. Been with him, listened to him play his harp, heard his voice, watched the way his red hair caught the sun and his green eyes sparkled with light. . . .

She blinked, surprised at the intensity of emotion that just thinking about him woke in her. To give her trembling hands something to do, she rolled a cigarette, lighting it with Kieran's lighter that he'd left rolled up in her pouch. Ha'kan'ta regarded her strangely as she exhaled, blowing blue-grey smoke out into the late afternoon air, and for the moment Sara worried that the Indian had some taboo about smoking. Then she remembered the peace pipe in Aled Evans's picture and what tobacco had been used for in the Native American culture.

She thought of offering Ha'kan'ta a drag, then realized that she wasn't really sure what the sharing of smoke actually stood for among the woman's people. To be safe, she took another quick drag, then pinched the cigarette out and stuffed it back into her pouch.

Ha'kan'ta looked from Sara back to Kieran.

"If one could return from the Place of Dreaming Thunder," she said thoughtfully, "then indeed I could see some danger. But . . ." She shook her head. "I cannot teach you the Beardance, Kieranfoy—not until we have sought guidance on this matter. The quin'on'a have a lodge near by. I meant to take you there before you brought up these troubling thoughts, Kieranfoy. We will go there now and speak with the elders of their tribe. We will see what the quin'on'a say about Toma'heng'ar's thing of shadows that they have named Mal'ek'a, and you name Taliesin Redhair."

Sara and Kieran regarded each other with misgivings, though each had a different basis for worry. Kieran wondered at the wisdom of placing himself in their hands, if they were Taliesin's friends, or had been, and held him now in some hallowed memory. On the other hand, they were Tom's friends as well. He and Sara were also here on the sufferance of the quin'on'a in the first place. The quin'on'a held the power to send them back, keep them here, or do whatever they wanted to with them.

Sara, for her part, just wanted to get away from all this. She wanted to be back on the seashore where there were only good feelings and good company, where a red-haired harper— who made her feel funny inside whenever she thought of him now—was walking the beach, waiting for her. What was keeping her back? How come she'd been able to go before and couldn't now?

"Do we have a choice?" she asked suddenly.

Ha'kan'ta looked surprised. "You are not my prisoners."

"What about the quin'on'a?" Kieran asked.

"For them I cannot answer, Kieranfoy. But they are honorable. Do not be alarmed about your safety in their hands. They will not harm you. I will stand as your guarantor, if you will. We go only to ask their advice—not to make war."

Maybe you do, Kieran thought, but nothing they say is going to change what I know is true.

He looked about the glade and saw only the forest that enclosed it. So where would he go if he didn't follow Ha'kan'ta? Then he remembered that Sara'd gone off somewhere and met . . . who? All she'd tell him was "a friend." He looked at her now but could read nothing in her face. Who'd given her the guitar and cloak?

He wondered as well what it was that set them so much at odds. And the way she defended the harper. Mother of God! What did she know about any of it? Except she had that ring and there was something about her, some secret assurance, that didn't sit right. He had to wonder what her part was in all of this. Because, like Sara herself, he didn't hold much with coincidence. She was here for a reason. But what was that reason, if it wasn't simply to confound him?

"Come," Ha'kan'ta said. "Their lodge is not far."

Kieran still hesitated, but Sara'd decided she might as well see this through. Logically, she could return to Taliesin as easily from the quin'on'a lodge as from here—just saying that whatever was blocking her eased up. Besides, she'd always wanted to meet an elf. "Let's go," she said.

Now it was two to one, Kieran thought. He touched the bandage on his side. He hadn't had to look at the wound, but from the way it felt he wouldn't be surprised if it hadn't healed already. So. The quin'on'a had taken the time to patch him up. Surely they wouldn't let that effort go to waste? How can so much hang on so little? he asked himself as he nodded to Ha'kan'ta.

"Lead on," he said.

The lodge of the quin'on'a was an hour's trek from the glade. The land began to rise and the stands of larch and pine gave way to thickets of sugar maple, balsam fir and beech.

Higher still were stands of hardwood—red oak, aspens and white birch—mixed with groves of hemlock and jack pines. Ha'kan'ta's mount left them when they reached the steeper slopes, drifting off through the trees like some huge brown specter. The wolves remained, one on either flank, silver fur stark against the tree-covered slopes.

Topping a last ridge, they looked down into a long narrow valley with a small lake at the end nearest to them. Here the forest gave way to meadows on their left. On the right, black ash and cedar met the marshy shores of the lake. Between the two, on a small rise overlooking a series of stone seams that led down to the water, was the village of the quin'on'a.

In its midst was a rectangular barrel-roofed lodge, the longhouse that served as the chieftain's quarters and a place for community gatherings in winter. It was some fifty feet long, eighteen feet in width and sixteen feet high. The entire frame was covered with bark, perforated and lashed together in overlapping layers like shingles. In front of it was a tall totem pole, topped by the carving of a bear's head. Spread out like wings on either side of the lodge were a number of conical tipi covered with hide and bark.

"The lake's name is Pinta'wa," Ha'kan'ta said. "Still-Water."

"I feel like I'm in a remake of *The Last of the Mohicans,*" Sara said. When Ha'kan'ta regarded her quizzically, she shrugged, adding: "Don't mind me. I always loved playing cowboys and Indians when I was a kid."

"The elders await us," Ha'kan'ta said. "We should not keep them waiting."

The wolves remained behind as the three of them began their descent to the lodge. Approaching the village, both Sara and Kieran were surprised by the activities of the quin'on'a. Two were mending a tipi. Others were curing meat over red coals. Women were weaving on looms made of bound branches and one man was sewing a beadwork collar onto a buckskin tunic. Shouldn't they be doing elvish things, Sara thought, like getting ready for dances in mushroom rings?

But if their activities were mundane, their appearance, barring the Indian garb, was more what Sara had imagined. In height they were no more than a slender and delicate five feet, yet there was strength apparent in them. Their faces were sharply featured and high-browed, and many of them had small horns on their foreheads. Their hair was braided for the most part, jet black and hung with feathers and beads.

As they entered the village, the quin'on'a regarded them with dark brown eyes, but said nothing. Sara noticed that many of them carried small drums that hung from braided leather straps at their waists or over their shoulders. She remembered the sound of those drums and the sense of dislocation that had followed their playing. One moment she'd been in Patty's Place, the next waking up here . . . wherever here was. The Otherworld. She wondered if they called it the Otherworld as well? Before she could ask Ha'kan'ta, they reached the front of the lodge. The totem pole towered above them and a quin'on'a woman, older than all the others, stood waiting for them.

"Sins'amin," Ha'kan'ta said respectfully. "I give you greeting." To her companions she explained, "This is She-Who-Dreams-Waking, the Beardaughter of this tribe."

Sins'amin's braided hair was heavy with grey and her dark skin was stretched taut across her facial bones. The beadwork on her collar was shaped into a design that mimicked a strand of bear's claws. Though she stood a head shorter than Ha'kan'ta, she gave the impression of being the taller of the two.

"The word you have sent is troubling," Sins'amin said.

Ha'kan'ta inclined her head. "For that reason we have come to you for true-speech, old mother. I bring you Kieranfoy, craftson of Toma'heng'ar, and his companion Saraken, who your people brought from the World Beyond at the request of the young warrior's master."

"So we did," Sins'amin said. "Yet had we known . . ." She shook her head. "We will speak of this inside—in full council." She stepped aside and motioned them into the longhouse.

"You guys go ahead," Sara said then. "I think I'll go and sit down by the lake until you're done."

Kieran shot her a dirty look. "What do you mean, 'Until we're done'? You're just as involved as I am."

"Hey," Sara said. "Wait a minute. I didn't ask to come here."

"And you think I did?"

"You're the one who's got it in for harpers, Kieran. Not me."

"Lord lifting Jesus! I—"

"She speaks true," Ha'kan'ta said, breaking in. "This council is your concern. Not hers."

"But—"

"The elders are waiting, Kieranfoy."

Kieran clenched his fists at his sides. He looked from Sara

to Ha'kan'ta to the old quin'on'a Beardaughter who stood silently waiting by the entrance of the longhouse. On his face was the look of one betrayed, but Sara ignored it. *The lines are being drawn,* she reminded herself. *Correction: Have been drawn.*

"You don't understand, Sara," he said, trying one last time. "If you only knew—"

"I understand enough to know that I can't stand by while you hurt someone that I . . ." She paused, leaving unsaid: someone that I care for.

"What do you know about Taliesin?" he demanded.

"Nothing," she said, knowing it was as much truth as lie, and looked away.

"Sara," Kieran began. He reached out a hand to her, then let it fall to his side as she stepped away from him. *"Nom de tout,"* he muttered.

He followed Ha'kan'ta into the lodge. Sins'amin let them pass her, then pulled a flap of deerskin across the doorway, leaving Sara standing on her own outside.

She stood for a moment, looking around the village. The quin'on'a had all returned to their various activities and were ignoring her. Smiling uncertainly, she made her way past the lodge and down to the shore of the lake. There, under the shade of a broad-boughed tamarack, she made herself comfortable and stared across the water. She saw a blue heron wing above the marshes on the far side of the lake, heard the hubbub of nesting redwings and swamp sparrows, above them the clear notes of olive-sided flycatchers.

Despite the peaceful scene laid out before her, she sighed, her thoughts circling back to Kieran. If only there was some way she could get through to him. Maybe if he met Taliesin, he could see for himself. . . . But no. There was too much danger in that. What if he tried to kill the harper? Which he probably would do. God, things could get complicated. What would she do if he convinced the council that Taliesin was a threat and they decided to help him out?

"There is little chance of that," a voice said from behind her, "yet still it would be a good thing to be cautious with that one."

Sara whirled around to face a curious individual who was squatting on his heels not three feet from her. At first glance he looked like a quin'on'a child, but a closer inspection proved that, though he might be another of these Indian elves, he was an altogether different sort from the ones she'd seen so far.

Standing, he'd come up to the middle of her chest, and where the quin'on'a's faces were long and finely boned, this fellow had a broad face that seemed all grin and eyes. His hair was more brown than black, and hung not in braids, but in many thin ringlets like the dreadlocks of reggae singers. As she regarded him, she wondered if she'd been thinking aloud. No sooner had that thought come to her, than her unbidden companion shook his head vigorously.

"Oh, no," he said. "But I hear you all the same."

Then that must mean . . . she started to think, and again he nodded.

"Get out of my head!" she cried.

"Can't help it," he said mournfully. "You think too loud. It's not my fault that you think so loud. Why can't you keep your thoughts to yourself instead of throwing them at people, hey? And then you get mad."

Sara just looked at him for a long moment. Every time she thought she was adjusting somewhat, something new had to come along.

"I'm not new," the little man said. "I'm as old as . . . as the land itself."

Sara sighed. "I don't know how to keep my thoughts to myself," she said.

"You should get Redhair to teach you how," he replied. "It's not hard."

Redhair? Remembering what Ha'kan'ta had said, Sara realized the little man meant Taliesin.

"How do you know about him?" she asked.

"We all knew him."

"Well, how did you know that *I* knew him?"

The little man grinned. "This is the first time that you've met me; but not the first time that I've met you. That's how I know!"

"And besides," he added before Sara could ask him to explain that curious statement, "under everything else you're thinking, you're always thinking of him."

And so she was. It bothered her, this fixation she had about the harper. Why was it that she couldn't keep him out of her thoughts?

"Maybe you love him."

"Maybe I do," she said, though it seemed to have happened very suddenly. Maybe that was the way it happened in magic lands—in the Otherworld. She was certainly attracted to him as she'd never been before to anyone else. Maybe he'd put a spell on her. . . .

"What's your name?" she asked the little man.

"Pukwudji."

Sara smiled. "It suits you."

"It should, as it's my own."

"My name's Sara."

"I know," Pukwudji said and grinned.

Well, we'll let that pass, Sara thought. "Are you a quin'on'a?" she asked.

The little man shrugged. "I am what I am."

Sara had to smile as a picture of Popeye came into her head. Pukwudji frowned as he caught the image.

"Not me," he said. "A honochen'o'keh I am—one of Kitche Manitou's little mysteries. When Grandmother Toad first smiled, I was there. I am always alone, but never on my own. The otter is my friend, and the heron. I run with the fox and sleep in the badger's sett. I am Pukwudji and all the world is my home."

Sara laughed. "And what are you doing here?"

"Here?" Pukwudji looked about himself with exaggerated care. Then leaning forward, he said in a stage whisper: "I've come to see if you'll walk with me."

"Where to?"

"Anywhere." He pointed to a pine that stood taller than the others on the ridge behind the quin'on'a village. "There."

"Okay," Sara said. "Let's go."

"And as we walk," Pukwudji added, bouncing to his feet, "I'll tell you a secret."

"A secret? About what?"

"Not yet, not yet. First we walk, then we talk, hey?"

Her curiosity piqued, her heart feeling lighter than it had in ages, Sara scrambled to her feet.

"Lead on, MacDuff," she said.

"Pukwudji MacDuff," he said. "That's me, hey?"

He did a cartwheel, landed with a thump, and turned to face her. From a hidden place amongst the stones, he brought out a small reed flute and tootled a quick tune on it before sticking it in his belt. "Don't forget your music-maker," he said.

Sara shrugged and picked up her guitar case. "And now?" she asked.

"Now we walk, hey?"

"Now we walk, hey!" she agreed, and followed him up the hill.

It was dark and smoky inside the lodge and it took Kieran a few moments to adjust his eyes to the dim light. Looking to Ha'kan'ta for guidance, he sat down cross-legged in the place she indicated and looked around himself. Sins'amin had taken a seat across from the fire that burned in the center of the lodge, ranking herself between the four silent figures who were already there. From the reed mat in front of her, she lifted a wooden mask carved in the semblance of a bear's features, and slipped it on.

"It is because of the bear totem," Ha'kan'ta explained in a soft voice, "that this tribe of the quin'on'a are so close in spirit to my own people, the rathe'wen'a, and so we are all kin to the Great Mother's spiritual vitality—sen'fer'sra. Something-in-movement. That is what your craftfather has termed your 'taw.'"

While the council sat silently communing with each other, she gave him the names of the other elders. To the left, in the long mask of a moose with spring antlers, was Hoth'ans, Elk-Sister, who was the tribe's Creator. On her left, wearing a shorter mask decorated with a doe's small horns, was Shin'sa'fen, She-Who-Drums-Healing, the tribe's Healer. On Sins'amin's right was a broad-shouldered man in the mask of a wolf. His name was Tep'fyl'in, Red-Spear-of-the-Wind, and he was the tribe's War Chief. Lastly, in the mask of a heron, was Ko'keli, Lake-Wise, who was the tribe's Shaper.

By the knee of each elder was a small drum. Lying across their knees were totem sticks. Ko'keli's was bound with blue feathers. Hoth'ans's had a length of curved bone carved with ideographs. Tep'fyl'in's was a tomahawk with wolf claws twined in the leather where the shaft was attached to the head of the small axe. Shin'sa'fen held a length of polished birch, hung with bone beads and three white feathers. Sins'amin's knees were bare, but around the brow of her mask was a headband of bear's claws.

The firelight flickered on the crudely carved and painted features of the masks. There was a sensation of power in the air, as though as invisible presence had settled among them. As the inner silence of his taw flooded him, Kieran found that the masks took on life, as though he faced a council of the beasts that the masks represented.

Shin'sa'fen tossed a handful of crushed bark onto the fire. The flames leaped up, two feet high, then settled down. Ko'keli in her heron mask took up her drum and began to tap out a soft rhythm.

"Kieranfoy," Sins'amin said, "craftson of the spirit-waker Toma'heng'ar. We will hear you speak."

Kieran glanced at Ha'kan'ta and she nodded encouragingly to him. He swallowed dryly and tried to think of where he should begin. He wanted a cigarette very badly. In fact, given his druthers, he wanted to be anywhere else except here, trapped in some Otherworld, Mother Mary only knew where, surrounded by beings that his own mentor had warned him against angering, trying to explain why he wanted to put an end to someone they already thought was dead. Someone further whose memory they appeared to hold in high esteem. He wiped his brow, then clasped his hands together on his lap to stop them from trembling.

What right did they have to demand this of him anyway? Power, he supposed. He was in their power.

"No," one of the masked figures said.

Kieran looked up to see it was Ko'keli who spoke. Her heron mask dipped as she acknowledged his attention.

"Not by the right of power," she said, "but by right of kinship. Taliesin Redhair was drum-brother to A'wa'rathe, who in turn was our brother-in-blood. Just as your own craftfather is." Her fingers continued to tap out a rhythm on her drum, low and insistent.

"We would know," Tep'fyl'in added, fingering his tomahawk, "what war there is between our drum-brothers."

"How can there be war when Taliesin drums in the Place of Dreaming Thunder?" Hoth'ans in the moose mask murmured. She picked up her own drum, adding a counterpoint rhythm to Ko'keli's.

"Let him speak," Sins'amin said.

The others inclined their heads and the masked faces turned back to regard Kieran, eyes glittering bright in their slitholes. Kieran swallowed again, then began to relate in a husky voice all that Tom had told him of Taliesin and Maelgwn's druid and the troubles that had begun on Gwynedd's shores.

"Pinta'wa sleeps," Pukwudji said.

Sara looked down at the lake and nodded. They were sitting on a carpet of pine needles, under the tall pine tree that topped the ridge behind the village, and for the moment she'd put all her troubles aside. It wasn't hard to do in Pukwudji's company.

"I suppose it does," she said lazily.

The simple walk to the pine tree had been lengthened by the roundabout route the little man had chosen that entailed as much cavorting and impromptu dancing as it had walking. Never one to be overly dignified herself, Sara had fallen in with his mood, laughing at his antics, racing to catch up with him, then running back to pick up her fallen guitar case and hurrying to catch up again.

Pukwudji grinned at her response. "Pinta'wa's always sleeping, hey? Except in a storm," he added. "Then she rises and speaks with anger against the shore." He scratched his chin. "Sometimes I wonder if that anger comes because she is confined and the storm reminds her of that."

"You were going to tell me a secret," Sara reminded him.

"I was. I will. Watch."

Rolling up the sleeves of his buckskin shirt and looking like some stage magician, he brushed away pine needles until he'd uncovered a small bit of earth. He dug a shallow hole in the ground, then cupped his hands over it. He blew across his hands and, when he opened them slightly, water began to trickle from his empty palms, filling the hole. When it was full, he blew on his hands again, and, theatrically, opened them wide. They were dry.

"Nice trick," Sara said, impressed.

"No trick."

"Okay. What's next?"

"This."

He spread his hands over the tiny pool of water and it grew dark and still as a mirror. As Sara leaned forward, images formed on the liquid surface. First she saw a heavily forested slope and nothing more. But then, in amongst the pines and larches, she could make out shadowy shapes, thin as the limbs of spiders. Pukwudji made another motion with his hands and the image's perspective narrowed until one of the shapes was brought into sharp focus, filling the image area.

It had skin that resembled a cross between black scales and a boar's bristled hide. Two tusks protruded from either side of its upper canines and a flat, pushed-in nose added to its piggishness. Its body was comprised of spindly limbs and a stocky powerful torso. But it was the eyes that drew Sara's fascinated gaze. They had all the mad cunning of a weasel, but seemed disconcertingly out of place, as the creature had none of a weasel's sleek grace. They reminded her of something, these spidery creatures, though she couldn't place just what. The face, now that she looked at it again, had an ursine quality to it as much as a pig's features—more a wicked cross between the two.

She looked up to find Pukwudji regarding her with interest.

"They are tragg'a," he said.

"So?"

Pukwudji shrugged. "The elders say that when the Darkness coupled with a wolverine bitch, then were the tragg'a brought forth into the world."

Something slipped into place with a click in Sara's mind. She knew where she'd seen these creatures before—or at least something very similar. In her dream. She'd seen the grand-daddy of them all. She bent over the image again, studying the thing. Did it know it was being watched? The perspective drew back again and she saw the whole pack once more. They appeared to be casting for a scent as though they were stalking something.

"They hunt you," Pukwudji said.

"Me?" She looked up to meet his gaze.

Pukwudji nodded. "You don't seem frightened."

"It's hard to be scared," she said, "when the threat's so . . . so intangible. I mean, I've had a couple of bad dreams and. . . . It just doesn't seem very real. How could it be?"

"You're here, aren't you?"

"There's that, isn't there?"

Sara sighed and looked back at the image reflected on the water. "I think I liked you better when you were full of jokes," she said unhappily.

"Me too," Pukwudji said. "But . . ." He pointed at the image. "You had to be warned."

It was disconcerting, Sara thought, the way the little man switched from seeming like a kid out to have a good time, to a wise old man delivering warnings.

Pukwudji sighed, catching the thought.

"Don't you like me?" he asked.

Sara smiled. "Of course I do. You're just full of unexpected surprises, that's all. You fit the name of manitou better than the quin'on'a do."

He made a quick motion with his fingers and the image dissolved. For a moment longer the water remained clear and still, then it started to steam and in the time between one breath and the next, all that remained was a shallow hole in the ground. Standing up, Pukwudji kicked it full of pine needles. When he was done, he turned to regard Sara. She met his gaze steadily, waiting for him to speak.

"What should I do, Pukwudji?" she asked when it seemed he had nothing further to say.

The little man pulled his flute from his belt. He toyed with it and looked away across the lake.

"They will send you back," he said. "The quin'on'a. When they are done with your friend, they will send you both back to the World Beyond."

"That's not so bad," Sara replied. "I can always..." She let her mind fill with an image of her going from her own world to the beach where she'd met Taliesin.

Pukwudji shook his head. "Here you can timewalk," he said. "Here the worlds are thin and close together. They overlap and time flows into time, world into world. It's not the same in the World Beyond, in your world. There the borders are thick and the pathways few that lead between."

"It's only worked once for me so far anyway," Sara said.

"That is because the other times you were trying too hard. To tap the something-in-movement, you must be very still inside yourself. Not try, try, trying. Go softly—like the Wind Children. Then it is easy. If you are here. But if the quin'on'a send you back, you will be trapped in your own world. Trapped and helpless when the tragg'a come for you."

Sara said nothing for a long moment, while she rolled and lit a cigarette.

"What do they want with me?" she asked.

Pukwudji pointed to the ring on her hand.

"But why? What's so special about this ring?"

But as she spoke, she remembered Taliesin and herself exchanging rings, how each ring fitted itself to each finger, how none of this had happened to her until she'd found the ring in the backroom of The Merry Dancers.

"Mal'ek'a wants that ring," Pukwudji said. "Mal'ek'a who is the Dread-That-Walks-Nameless that even the quin'on'a fear. Mal'ek'a who has sent the tragg'a to fetch you to him, even while he searches for you himself."

"What should I do then?" Sara asked again.

"Go to your craftfather. Go back to the time when Taliesin Redhair lived before the quin'on'a return you to your own world. I would go with you, but I am already there.

"Timewalking has its own rules," he explained. "One cannot be in a time when one already exists in it. So it is that you can go back, for in that time you have yet to be born. But I am already there."

"But you won't know me," Sara said.

Pukwudji smiled. "And yet I remember meeting you then. Why else would I warn you now?"

Sara shook her head, trying to clear her spinning thoughts. Everything Pukwudji had said made a certain confused sort of sense, it was true. At the same time the paradox of it seemed to have the same sort of logic that the Mad Hatter or the March Hare from *Alice in Wonderland* might espouse.

"So you think I should go?" Sara asked. "Back to Taliesin?"

"How else can I meet you?" Pukwudji asked with some of his old humor twinkling in his eyes.

"But we just met—oh, nevermind!" She took a last drag from her cigarette and carefully butted it out.

"Don't be afraid of failure," the little man said. "I will help you go back this time."

Sara nodded. "What about Kieran?" she asked, but then she thought to herself, what about him? He was the enemy.

"No," Pukwudji said, wagging a finger at her. "Mal'ek'a is the only enemy—the common enemy that both you and Kieranfoy face."

"Yeah. Except he thinks Mel'ek'a is Taliesin."

"You will have to teach him better then, hey?"

"I suppose so. If I ever see him again." She paused as she remembered something. "I thought you warned me to be careful of Kieran—when I first met you by the lake."

"The only threat Kieranfoy poses to you is that he belittles your potential to grow horns."

"What?"

Pukwudji smiled. "Amongst the quin'on'a, and the hono-chen'o'keh as well, a being who lacks magic is called a herok'a—a 'hornless one.' You will grow horns, but only with encouragement."

"Oh."

Sara wasn't sure that she wanted to have a set of horns protruding from her forehead. She regarded the little man, looking for signs in his features that she was being put on, but he returned her gaze with guileless eyes.

"You think I should go now?" she asked.

"Yes. While you can."

Sara had one more question that she didn't bother to articulate since he could just take it out of her mind: Why should she trust him? But hard on the heels of it, the reason for not asking came: It didn't really matter. She wanted to go back to Taliesin.

She picked up her guitar case and laid it across her knees. Then she leaned across the case, taking a last look at Pinta'wa Lake and the village below.

"Pukwudji?"

"Yes?"

"Thanks," she said, then she closed her eyes.

"Think of where you wish to go," he instructed. "Hold the image of it firm in your mind."

There was a moment's silence, then she heard the little man's flute take up the moonheart tune that Taliesin had taught her.

Now how did he come to know . . . ? She started to ask herself, but then the world rushed away from under her and she hurriedly concentrated on willing herself to the beach under the shadow of Percé Rock. Not being exactly a pro at this sort of transportation, she didn't want to end up . . . well, God only knew where.

The sound of Pukwudji's flute faded, replaced by the sound of waves falling to shore. Filled with anticipation, Sara opened her eyes to find herself sitting at Taliesin's old campsite. Only there was no one there. No trace of where the fire had been. No harp. No dog. No harper.

There was some sort of mistake, she thought. Maybe she'd come at the wrong time. . . . The skin at the nape of her neck prickled uneasily. Oh, Lord! Time. If she was traveling through time, who was to say when she'd end up? It might be years before Taliesin had even come to these shores. Or years after he'd left them.

She bit worriedly at her lip. Had she been mistaken to trust Pukwudji? He might have sent her anywhere. Or did the fault lay with her? She'd concentrated on the beach, but not on Taliesin himself. . . .

The only thing to do was try again. She closed her eyes and whistled the moonheart tune, but this time there was no clearing of her thoughts. No shift of the world underfoot. Pukwudji's powers had brought her this far. Without him. . . . Panic reared, sudden and full, but she fought it back.

Easy, she told herself. Think before you freak out. She had to relax, to clear her head of everything but Taliesin. She thought back to the time she'd managed it successfully. She hadn't had a moonheart tune then. What had she done that was different, that *worked?* And then, as she fiddled nervously with the band of gold on her finger, she knew.

She looked down at the gold ring. It was a twin to Taliesin's, might even *be* his, for all they knew. It was the rings that had called out to each other, or else why had she come to meet the bard in the first place?

Come on, she told the ring. Do your stuff. She rubbed it with her finger and, keeping her thoughts on the harper, started to hum the tune again. And this time the shift underfoot came. The beach fell away behind as the magic took her up and away.

"There *is* an enemy," Sins'amin said when Kieran finished his story, "and it did come from across the Great Water many summers ago, but its name was not Taliesin."

"Mal'ek'a we named it," Ko'keli said. Her fingers, still tapping her drum, rapped out an off rhythm that sent a chill up Kieran's spine. Her blue heron mask bobbed as she nodded her head.

"Nameless, no one may harm it," she added, "though it may harm us. Find its true name, young warrior, and you will gain our favor. Too many of our tribe have fallen prey to it— for too many summers."

"Mal'ek'a is our enemy?" Tep'fyl'in asked, shaking his tomahawk. "It keeps us strong, like the wolves do the caribou, and the fox the grey goose. Is that the work of an enemy?"

"Would you go to the Place of Dreaming Thunder before your time?" the Healer Shin'sa'fen asked. "For that is where the Dread-That-Walks-Nameless would send you were you to meet him, drum as you might, or shake your totem stick until your arm grew too weary to hold it."

Kieran could almost feel the grin behind Tep'fyl'in's wolf mask.

"If I am slain by Mal'ek'a, old woman," he replied, "then my time *has* come."

Sins'amin broke in before the Healer could frame her reply.

"We may argue the good or ill of Mal'ek'a's presence until the day that Grandmother Toad herself Dreams her own Thunder," she said, "and still come no closer to the truth than we are now. Yet it was not for that we gathered in council today."

She looked to either side of her, the bearmask fierce in the fire's highlights.

"Kha," Tep'fyl'in said brusquely. Understood.

Shin'sa'fen tapped her birch totem stick against her knee. The bone beads clicked together until she stilled them with her hand.

"Kha," she said softly. By the intonation she put on the word, she added a further meaning to it. Understood, but unfinished.

"You spoke of dreams," the Creator Hoth'ans said to Sins'amin. She pointed to Kieran. "I have dreamed twice of this herok'a. Once he rode a Stag to the edge of Pinta'wa where a Swan caught him by the shoulders and bore him north. I followed their flight until the Swan alighted on a high cliff. The worlds spun below, layer upon layer of worlds, and the Swan gave him a choice: To take up his own Drum, or to take the life of a caged Wren.

"He chose the Wren."

The others sat in silence when she was done speaking. Kieran, versed as he was in the symbols of the Way, understood as well as the quin'on'a what the dream meant. The Stag and Swan were forces of benevolence and creation. The choice he was offered was to maintain the tradition, or Drum, that his mentor had given him with the Way, or to kill Taliesin, symbolized as the Wren.

Dreams had a power of their own. Unspoken by the quin'on'a Creator, but nevertheless lying there between her words, was the judgment that by choosing to kill the Wren he had closed himself off from the Way. He was about to ask why that should be, to explain yet again that it was not he who sought the harper, but the harper who sought his mentor, but then Ko'keli, her slender fingers still tapping on her drumskin, asked:

"And the second dream?"

Hoth'ans tapped her bone totem stick against the reed mat that floored the lodge.

"In the second dream the herok'a grew horns," she said.

A herok'a who grew horns was a shaman or Wayfarer who filled his or her potential.

"Which dream will you give truth to?" the Creator asked Kieran.

He chose his words carefully. "You say that Taliesin is already dead. How then can I harm him?"

"Time does not flow like a river here," Sins'amin replied.

"Not as it does in the World Beyond from which you came. Here time is like an eddy or a whirlpool. If you seek Taliesin Redhair, you will not be drawn to wherever it is that Mal'ek'a lairs, but back to a time when Taliesin has not yet fared to the Place of Dreaming Thunder."

Kieran was having trouble following her logic. "So he's still alive?" he asked.

"Not in the sense that you use the word," Ha'kan'ta said, speaking for the first time since he'd told the council his story.

"The question I ask," Tep'fyl'in said, "is why do we allow this herok'a to question us?" He fingered his tomahawk and it seemed that the wolf mask bared white fangs for an instant as he turned to Kieran. "Do you consider our words twice-tongued?"

"Ill luck it is to threaten one in council," Ko'keli murmured.

"He is not *of* our council," Tep'fyl'in retorted grimly.

Sins'amin lifted a hand and, except for Ko'keli's soft drumming, all sound ceased in the lodge.

"We have given your enemy what name we have for it," she said to Kieran. "Will you trust us enough to seek the one we have named Mal'ek'a? Or will you persist in seeking Taliesin Redhair's death?"

"And if Mal'ek'a proves to be Taliesin?" Kieran countered.

"If that proves true," the quin'on'a Beardaughter replied, "then we will aid you ourselves in bringing about his death."

"Then I agree."

Sins'amin nodded, then clapped her hands together.

"This council is ended," she said.

Ko'keli's drum stopped abruptly. For a long moment Kieran sat watching the five masked figures who sat silently before him, then Ha'kan'ta nudged him.

"Now we go," she said softly.

"But they haven't said if they'd help me or—"

"The council was not concerned with whether or not it would help you," she replied. "Its concern was whether or not you were a threat."

"A threat? To what?"

Ha'kan'ta shook her head.

"Outside," she said. "There we can talk."

Kieran opened his mouth, then shut it so hard that his teeth clicked together. He stood up on stiff legs and followed Ha'kan'ta outside. Not until the doorflap had fallen back across the opening did they speak again.

"What happened in there?" Kieran asked.

"You were judged." She held up a hand to stop him from interrupting her. "Understand, Kieranfoy. Your craftfather is a drum-brother to the quin'on'a—but so was Taliesin, though in his case it was indirectly, through my father. Mother Bear will not abide blood strife between brothers-in-blood. When such occurs, she withdraws her sen'fer'sra—her spiritual vitality. Without that something-in-movement, the quin'on'a would die and my own people would be struck as if deaf and blind. Imagine yourself without your Wayfarer's taw, Kieranfoy."

"I don't even want to think about that."

"Exactly."

"But what I don't understand is, if Taliesin's dead, why are they so worried about what I might do to him?"

"Don't you ever listen?" Ha'kan'ta asked. She smiled to take the edge from her words.

"Nom de tout! I listen. It's just that nothing I hear makes any sense."

"I will repeat it one last time. In these worlds—what you call the Otherworld—the farther one gets from the World Beyond, the more enmeshed time and space become. Like the layers—"

"Of an onion. I know. Great analogy, only—"

"Only this: If you reach out for Taliesin Redhair strongly enough—you will reach him. But the distance you cross will entail a crossing of years as well as land. And if you were to kill him, if his blood was on the hands of Toma'heng'ar's craftson, it would be the same as though *we* had killed him. My father. The quin'on'a. Myself. All who are true kin or kin-in-drumming. And then we would suffer Mother Bear's judgment."

"So the council was held to see if I could be called off my hunt, is that it?"

"Yes."

Kieran frowned. "And what if I went right on ahead with it? What if I did kill Taliesin?"

"But you won't—not anymore. Not with what you know now."

"I suppose. I'll have to think about it some more, that's for sure. But what about Tom?"

"What Toma'heng'ar pursues is what the council have named Mal'ek'a. He may think he seeks Taliesin Redhair, but he will learn quickly enough when he confronts his thing of shadows just what it is that he faces."

"And what's that? What *is* Mal'ek'a?"

Ha'kan'ta sighed. "An old evil. That is all I know. An old evil from across the Great Water. I think perhaps it might well have its origin in the same homeland as both Taliesin and your craftfather, else why is it so bound to them? But we will see soon enough ourselves, Kieranfoy. Together we will see how Mal'ek'a deals with the Beardance of the rathe'wen'a."

"The council wouldn't help me, so why will you?"

"I have as good a reason as you to hunt Mal'ek'a, Kieranfoy. I told you my father was dead. I did not tell you that he died but a month ago when the tragg'a slew him."

An image of what the tragg'a were leapt from her mind to his and Kieran shivered.

"Why did they kill him?" he asked softly.

"They sought the medicine bag of Taliesin Redhair that my father held in trust for many a year."

"His medicine bag? But after all this time, it'd just be so much dust, wouldn't it?"

Ha'kan'ta touched the pouch that hung at her hip.

"This was my grandmother's," she said. "It is twenty long-summers old—two thousand years. Magics keep it whole—the something-in-movement of Mother Bear."

Kieran looked down at the pouch and then understood why Ha'kan'ta was helping him.

"Sara's pouch," he said. "It's Taliesin's, isn't it? But what does Mal'ek'a want with it?"

"Taliesin's medicines were very strong. Mal'ek'a wants something that was in that pouch and sent his tragg'a to fetch it for him. But my father no longer had it. He gave it Toma'heng'ar—"

"Who gave it to Aled Evans who, when he died, left it in his will to Sara's uncle. He stuck it in a box that sat around in the back of her store until she found it. Lord lifting Jesus!" Kieran shook his head. "But why now?" he asked. "Why, after so many years, would Mal'ek'a suddenly start looking for it?"

"Mal'ek'a was always evil," Ha'kan'ta said, "but not always as powerful as he is now. It is said that he had taken the wolverine as his totem and for that reason the tragg'a serve him, for they are the children of Darkness and the devil-bear."

"But . . ." Kieran was thinking aloud. "Sara left the pouch in her uncle's house. Mal'ek'a will have it by now, unless . . ."

The memory of a gold sparkle on a small hand returned to him. "The ring," he said softly. "It's the ring he wants."

As they'd been talking, they'd wandered down by the lakeside. Kieran looked around, then back at the quin'on'a village. "Where is Sara anyway?" he asked.

Ha'kan'ta closed her eyes and turned her inner vision outward. She stood still for a long moment, then said: "Gone."

"Gone? Well, she can't have gotten far."

"Far enough," his companion said. "She has stepped beyond this world."

"Great," he thought. And she had the tobacco with her . . .

"She's gone home," a third voice said.

They both turned. Pudwudji sat hugging his knees on a nearby rock, a huge grin on his wide face and his eyes filled with a teasing light.

"Who in . . . ?" Kieran began.

"Pukwudji Sarafriend," the little man said. "That's me, hey?"

"What have you done with her?" Ha'kan'ta asked sternly.

Pukwudji simply shook his head, refusing to be intimidated.

"He said she went home," Kieran said. "That must be Tamson House. In the World Beyond."

"I said home indeed." Pukwudji's grin grew broader still. "But home is where the heart is, hey? Do you know her heart well enough, O-would-be-bardkiller? Do you now?"

Kieran took a step towards the little man, but Ha'kan'ta drew him back.

"Remember we spoke of drum-brothers?" she said. "This honochen'o'keh was one of Taliesin's. The bard was loved by many." To Pukwudji she added: "Kieranfoy has sworn council-oath not to harm Taliesin."

Pukwudji shrugged. "Redhair could not be harmed by such a one as he, now could he?"

Kieran frowned. He couldn't remember swearing council-oath. Then he realized that among these people, one's words were taken at face value; by agreeing not to harm Taliesin unless he could prove the bard was Mal'ek'a, he'd as much as sworn an oath.

"No more riddles, Pukwudji," Ha'kan'ta said cajolingly. "Tell us where you sent her. Was it truly to the World Beyond? To her uncle's home?"

"She went," he said. "And where? Did I not say? Then I'll give you one more hint, but just the one and no more, hey?

So listen closely: I sent her to meet my ownself so that I'd know enough to meet her here. How's that?"

"Pukwudji . . ." Ha'kan'ta began, but she was too late.

The little man tumbled off his perch, landed on his feet with a thump, and scampered between them, giving Kieran a pinch on the leg as he ran by. As he neared the lake, he leaped high into the air and did a somersault. By the time he hit the water, he'd turned into a silver-backed trout and disappeared into the lake.

Kieran frowned some more, rubbing his leg. Ha'kan'ta tried to keep a straight face, but failed. Her laughter was clear and sweet and, faced with it, Kieran could only join in.

"It has been many days," she said, when at last she caught her breath, "since I have had reason to laugh. Pukwudji!" she cried across the lake. "I give you thanks!"

Far from the shore, a trout leaped four feet out of the water and landed with a smack on the surface of the lake before vanishing once more. Ha'kan'ta shook her head, still smiling.

"Come," she said to Kieran. "It is time we were on our way."

"But Sara . . ."

"Is a grown woman. She can look after herself."

Their totem masks removed, Sins'amin and her War Chief remained behind in the council lodge long after the others had gone. Tep'fyl'in toyed with his wolf mask, the firelight gleaming on his strong features. He was the youngest elder—his coppery skin unwrinkled, his brow high and smooth, his small horns burnished and gleaming. "Strange use of a council," he said, laying aside his mask.

Sins'amin shrugged. "How so?"

"Such a judgment as we delivered could as easily have been made by one—and she our Beardaughter—as in full council."

"Kha. But think a moment, my Red-Spear. Of Taliesin."

"Taliesin?" he replied. "He drums with our ancestors. What thought does that require?"

Sins'amin smiled. "And yet, Kieranfoy brought with him a companion, and the bard lives now in her."

"You met her; we did not. Tell me, is it true? Has Redhair taken a craftdaughter?"

"Yes. The clasp on her cloak was a twin to his. And she wore his ring. But if final proof were needed, I offer this: Her eyes give my thoughts their truth. She grows her horns, and they are of Redhair's drumming."

"Ah. Then I understand. And you told Kieranfoy nothing. . . ."

"Kha!"

Unspoken between them lay an old quin'on'a prophecy, a power dream thought misinterpreted when the bard did not take an apprentice before he died.

"Kieranfoy and Ha'kan'ta will not prevail against Mal'ek'a," Tep'fyl'in said. "A Beardance, even one Danced by the Drummers of the Bear, cannot prevail against him."

"Perhaps not." Sins'amin's eyes held distant lights. "But it will give Taliesin's craftdaughter time to grow her horns."

Tep'fyl'in smiled, but the humor never touched his eyes. What if the prophecy was wrong? If Taliesin's drumming was never passed on to another? What then? In the Mystery Realms that those in the World Beyond called the Otherworld, time was a strange and malleable thing. In this turn of time's whirlpool, Taliesin never took a craftdaughter and the bard himself was dead. That could change, if the herok'a Sins'amin spoke of grew her horns. But if she did not? Was it such a terrible evil that the quin'on'a had a creature such as Mal'ek'a against which they could test the strength of their bodies and the sharpness of their wit? A tribe was measured by its foes. Did not Mal'ek'a make the quin'on'a of the Bear Clan the mightiest of all the Clans?

But these thoughts he kept to himself.

"Kha," was all he said, his voice soft. "Understood, old mother."

Chapter Five

TUCKER'S BUICK headed a three-vehicle cavalcade that pulled up in front of one of the Patterson Avenue entrances of Tamson House. Before the Inspector stepped out of the car, he shook his head at Collins who was drawing his .45 Colt from its holster under his armpit.

"We're playing this one cool," Tucker said. "While we can. The last fucking thing we need is to have the locals crawling all over us."

Collins shrugged and let the gun drop back into its holster. He shook out a Pall Mall and lit it as he followed Tucker to where Constable Warne was standing guard over a blanket-draped body. Two RCMP paramedics had already brought a stretcher out of the van behind Tucker's car and were laying it down beside the body. Two more constables disembarked from the third car.

"Hold it," Tucker said to the paramedics He looked at Warne. "Give it to me from the top."

"There's not a whole lot to tell, Inspector," Warne replied. "It was going on 0900. I was out, stretching my legs, checking the doors on O'Connor and making my way back to the car, when that"—he indicated the body with a jerk of his head—"just...shit, I don't know. It just appeared there. I ran over, figuring the guy'd been tossed from one of the upper story windows maybe, and then I saw..."

Warne's features seemed a little strained and Tucker knew what was playing through the Constable's head. However used to this line of work you got, there were some things that still hit you hard. Like when they'd brought in Thompson's body last night...Tucker figured he'd start to worry when it *didn't* bother him anymore.

"What'd you see?" Tucker prompted softly.

Warne frowned. "Did you ever pull a bear-mauling detail, Inspector?"

Collins kneeled down beside the body, but Tucker stopped him as he was reaching for a corner of the blanket.

"Anyone around?" Tucker asked. "Witnesses. Anything?"

"The street was empty," Warne said. "If I didn't know better, I'd swear the body just appeared out of nowhere."

Tucker sighed. "Figures. You talked to anyone in the House?"

"Just through the door. They say they'll only talk to you. They did throw out the blanket for me, when I asked."

Tucker looked up and down the street, then turned his gaze to the body. Steeling himself, he nodded to Collins. Warne looked away as Collins lifted the blanket. For a long moment there was silence, then Tucker swore.

"Jesus Christ, Warne! What're you trying to pull?"

"Inspector?"

Warne turned, looked from the mutilated corpse to his superior. The body was the same as it'd been before he'd covered it up. The head half twisted from the shoulders, chest cavity open and intestines spilling out onto the pavement. But Tucker. . . . The Inspector's face was a hard mask. He stepped forward and lashed out at the corpse with his foot. When the leather of his shoe hit the body, Warne winced. The taste of breakfast came rushing up his throat. He started to say something, then saw a vague shimmer flit across the body. Instead of intestines, a lump of mud and twigs went flying under the impact of Tucker's shoe. Where the corpse had been there was only a matted mess of twigs and wet leaves, held together in the shape of a body by drying mud.

Warne stared at the place where the transformation had taken place, his face blank with shock. Where the head would have been, the caricature of features composed of wet leaves appeared to mock him with an evil grin.

"Inspector," Warne began dully. "I swear . . . I *swear* . . ."

Tucker watched the Constable carefully. The shock was genuine. Either Warne was the best fucking actor he'd ever run across, or he sincerely believed that he'd been guarding a mutilated body. The Inspector turned his attention to the House and caught a movement at the curtained windows directly across from them. He remembered the note on his desk. Just what kind of a fucking game were they playing anyway?

"I swear. . . ." Warne was still saying.

Tucker nodded. Warne had seen what he'd seen. He believed that.

"Take him back to headquarters," Tucker said to Collins, "and help him fill out a report. Then send him home." To the paramedics he added: "You guys can take off."

The paramedics shrugged and, hoisting their stretcher, returned to the van with it. The two constables from the third car looked to Tucker for orders.

"You, too," he told them.

"Are you going in?" Collins asked.

"Yeah." Tucker's voice was as grim as the set of his features.

"Maybe you shouldn't go alone—" Collins began, but Tucker cut him off.

"Just get Warne to headquarters, okay? I can handle Jamie Tams."

Collins looked like he wanted to add something, then shrugged. He lit up a cigarette and ushered Warne back to his car that was parked further down the block. Tucker waited until they'd reached the Acadian and the others were gone, before turning back to face Tamson House. His .38 was a comfortable weight on his hip, but he didn't think he'd have to use it. When he heard the Acadian start up, he headed for the door of the House.

Blue let the curtain fall back in place and turned to Jamie with a numb expression on his face.

"We're fucked," he said.

"What do you mean?"

"I mean there's no body out there. Just a heap of twigs and shit."

"But we both saw it," Jamie said.

Blue rubbed his face. "I know. I know what we saw. I know what came down a few hours ago. The whole House shaking like something out of *The Exorcist* and Lon Chaney Jr. clawing at the door. . . . But I'm telling you now, Jamie, there's fuck all out there for your Inspector Tucker to find. I mean, we haven't even got a scratch on the door, and with the body gone. . . ."

"My God! He'll think we made the whole thing up."

"I don't understand," Sally said.

"*You* don't understand?"

"But surely someone would have noticed something?" she

said. "One of the neighbors, or someone just driving by? The sky went *black* and the shaking must have run up and down the street."

Blue shrugged and turned back to the window. "Here he comes," he said. He glanced at Jamie. "You want to do the honors?"

Jamie nodded uncomfortably.

When the door opened and Tucker confronted the five pale faces, the worst of his anger ran from him. Something weird was going down. No doubt about that. But, intuitively, he knew that Jamie Tams and his companions didn't have anything to do with it either. At least they weren't causing it. They were involved, though. No fucking way they weren't.

"Ah . . . Inspector?" Jamie began, stepping back from the door.

Tucker nodded a greeting as he entered. Tams he already knew, but this wasn't the same blustering man he'd met yesterday. Something had been drained out of him. The others were as motley a crew as he might have expected from the files he'd been reading last night. The biker would be Glen Farley. The woman . . . ? And there were two other men; one had a makeshift bandage on his head.

"You wanted to talk to me?" he said to Jamie.

"Ah . . . yes." Jamie was confused. This wasn't how he'd imagined it would go. He'd expected a half dozen policemen to come running in, slapping handcuffs on the lot of them and dragging them downtown, or wherever it was that they took apprehended criminals.

"Who're your friends?" Tucker asked.

Awkwardly, Jamie made the introductions. When they were done, he just stood there, not knowing where to begin. Picking up on Jamie's near-fugue state, Blue spoke up.

"We've got us a problem, Inspector," he said, "that's kind of hard to explain."

Tucker turned his attention to him. "People call you Blue, don't they?"

Blue nodded.

"And you used to ride the Devil's Dragon?"

"Hey. That was a long time ago."

"Yeah. I know."

Jesus, Blue thought. If you know everything, then what the hell are you asking questions for?

"Everybody here involved in this?" Tucker asked.

Blue shook his head. "Just me and Jamie."

"And Ms. Kendell? Where's she?"

"That's part of the problem."

Tucker nodded. "Okay. Why don't you and Mr. Tams and I go somewhere and have ourselves a little talk. The rest of you," he added, speaking now to Sally, Fred and Sam, "hang around, okay? By that I mean, go and do whatever it is that you do, but don't leave the premises. I'll want to talk to you."

Blue and Jamie exchanged glances. Usually, Blue thought, there'd be two cops. One playing Mr. Nice Guy, the other being the hardass. So what was Tucker's game? Was he going to play both parts himself? Knowing what they had to tell him, Blue wasn't looking forward to the next few hours. He knew where they'd end up. Downtown in holding cells, because who the fuck'd believe the story they had to offer? And having a record from his days with the Dragon certainly wasn't going to help.

They retired to the Silkwater Kitchen and there, over cups of coffee, Jamie told the Inspector everything he knew. When he got to the attack on the House this morning, Blue took up the narrative, finishing with the Inspector's arrival.

They both watched the Inspector as they talked, trying to judge his reaction, but he kept a poker face. Only when Blue was finally done did he speak.

"You paint a pretty picture," he said. "Either of you ever think of moving to Hollywood? With imaginations like you've got—"

"I swear it's true!" Jamie said.

Tucker sighed. "I'm so fucking tired of hearing those words. Every two-bit punk or hooker that you pick up is willing to swear to anything, if they think it'll get 'em off."

Here we go, Blue thought. No more Mr. Nice Guy. But Tucker surprised him again.

"Let's just suppose," Tucker said, "that what you've told me is true."

Jamie and Blue looked at each other in astonishment.

"Don't get your hopes up," the Inspector added. "We're just supposing it's not a crock of shit. Now tell me this. Why was the House attacked this morning?"

"But I told you," Jamie said. "It's the ring—the ring that Sara's got."

"Isn't she supposed to be off in Never-never-land?"

"Yes, but—"

"And didn't the elusive Mr. Hengwr go there to look for her?"

"Yes..."

"Then what the hell's this—what? Dead harper? What's he attacking *you* for?"

That stopped Jamie. He'd assumed that the attack was part of the harassment that Tom had told him to expect.

"I...I hadn't thought of that," he said slowly.

"You hadn't thought of that," Tucker repeated, his voice laced with irony. He shook his head wearily.

"Give us a break," Blue said. "Do you think any of this shit makes sense to us?"

"Jesus H.! I'll tell you something, Farley. Even if I believed half of what you've told me, your story's so full of fucking holes it doesn't hold up for dick. You got me?"

Blue bit back a retort and leaden silence descended. He glared at Tucker, who returned the look, not giving an inch. At last Blue looked away and sighed.

"Okay," he said. "So now what. You taking us in?"

Tucker had the warrant for Jamie sitting in the breast pocket of his jacket and knew he could whistle one up for Blue that'd be waiting for him by the time he got to headquarters. The only trouble was, what good would bringing them in do? He couldn't accept the story they'd handed him. But at the same time, it was plain to him that *they* believed it. And something *had* happened here this morning. Why else would Jamie have called him with a story that they had to know wouldn't be believed?

"On what charge?" Tucker asked finally.

"You need a charge?" Blue's voice was sullen.

This guy's done time, Tucker thought. It was there in the file. He'd pulled a year-less-a-day on an assault charge. The Crown report read that he'd been provoked. Other than that he'd never been charged with anything more serious than unlawful possession of firearms and creating a public nuisance. Looking from the biker to Jamie, Tucker came to a quick decision.

"Either of you planning to leave town?" he asked.

"No sir, Marshal Dillon."

"Lay off the shit, Farley. You're in enough trouble as it is." He turned to Jamie. "I'd like to have a look around the House and then talk to the others."

Jamie nodded. "You can look around all you like. We've nothing to hide."

As he started to get up, Tucker shook his head.

"You bring the others in here," he said. "Our hero here can show me around. Right, Farley?"

Blue shrugged.

You could hide a fucking army in here, Tucker thought as Blue led him from room to room. He wasn't really expecting to find anything. He just wanted to get a feel of the place. The route they took led through a lot of broken glass, upset furniture and general disarray—which either lent credence to Jamie's story or proved that they had a lot of really wild parties. Tucker found himself hoping it was the latter.

"What do you really think is going down?" he asked.

They were in the base of the northwest tower, just under Sara's rooms. At the question, Blue paused with his hand on a doorknob and turned to look at the Inspector. A quick retort died on his lips at the set of Tucker's features. The cop wasn't there for a moment. There was just a man, plainly curious. Caring even. And that was a weird thing to think, Blue thought as he framed a reply.

"Up until that thing came through the door at me," he said at last, "I didn't know what to think. Jamie's always been a little off the wall. Different, you know? But not in a way that'd ever hurt anybody. And the same goes for the kind of people that drift into the House. We're down to a core membership right now. There've been up to fifty people staying here at a time and the feeling that goes down is always good. I was into some pretty heavy shit when they took me in—Jamie and Sara. And I'd do anything for them."

"Would you go as far as perjury, if this came to court?"

"Fucking right."

"Well, at least you're being honest."

"We're not bullshitting you, Inspector." Blue tried to think of something, anything, he could say that might drive the point home. "I've seen a thing or two in my time that was . . . well, weird, you know? I lived with some Navajo down in New Mexico for awhile—must've been around '73 or so—and saw some pretty bizarre shit go down."

"Peyote induced?"

Blue shook his head. "I did some mescal—stuff like that. But dope or no dope, there's a lot of things that go on that just can't be explained. I've never really paid that much attention to most of it. But Jamie does. He studies that kind of stuff."

"So what are you trying to say?"

"All I'm trying to say is that there's something more around us, something more than what we can see or even understand. I guess most people never come into contact with it. But some do. And what we've got here is one fuck of a contact. Now you can laugh it off, you can bust us, you can do whatever it is that you're planning to do, but that still won't change the fact that something's going down and it's not something you can put in a neat little box and stick a label on."

Tucker didn't say anything for a long moment. He regarded the biker steadily, then shrugged.

"You could be right," he said at last.

Blue let out a sigh. Well, that was something, at least. Not a commitment, but something.

The rest of the tour went quickly. In the West Library where Sam Pattison worked, Tucker paused long enough to try out the typewriter sitting on one of the desks. He compared its script to a card he took from his pocket, then laughed to himself as he put it away. He hadn't really expected it to match.

Back in the Silkwater Kitchen, he talked to the others, taking an informal statement from each one. Their stories matched, but that didn't mean anything. They'd had plenty of time to put a story together.

"Okay," he said at length. "I've got all I need."

"What happens now?" Jamie asked.

"I've got a few other things to look into. But I'll be back. I'd like you all to stick around, okay?"

"What if it happens again?" Sally asked.

"If what happens again?"

"If that . . . that thing attacks us again," Jamie said.

Tucker raised his hands helplessly. "What do you expect me to do about it?"

Blue laid a hand on Jamie's arm before he could say anything else. "We'll handle it on our own," Blue said.

"If something does come up," Tucker said, "give me a call. You've got my number."

When Blue returned from seeing Tucker out, Jamie asked: "What now?"

"Now?" Blue sat down wearily. "Shit, I don't know, Jamie. We wait some more, I guess."

"Well, I'm going to my study," Jamie said. "Tom entered a program into Memoria that I'd like to have a look at."

"Yeah," Blue said. "Maybe you can make some sense out of all this. Lord knows we need something. I think I'll go and clean my rifle. Just in case, you know?" He glanced at Jamie. "You got any silver bullets?"

Jamie attempted a smile. "Not even one."

He got up and left, looking very old.

Blue drummed his fingers on the table, staring out at the garden. He tried to rationalize what had happened this morning, but it always came down to the same thing: There was no explanation for what had gone down. None, except for what Thomas Hengwr had told Jamie.

Fred left to see what damage his precious gardens had sustained, and Sam trailed along behind him, leaving Blue and Sally alone.

"I'm scared," she said.

Blue looked up, then reached across to take her hand. "You and me both."

"We should go," she said. "Just get away from here."

"I can't leave Jamie to face this alone, babe."

"I meant all of us."

Blue shook his head. "There's Sara to think about. If she comes back, needing us, and we're all gone..."

"I had my pick of the whole city," Sally said, "and I had to choose someone with a white knight complex."

Blue regarded her quizzically.

"I wouldn't want it any other way," she added.

"Yeah. Well—"

Whatever he'd meant to say remained unsaid.

"What's that?" he asked, rising from the table.

"It sounded like Jamie...."

"Je-*sus!*"

Blue was off and running for the east side of the House before Sally could even get up. Tearing down the hallways, he skidded to a stop at the bottom of the stairs that led up to Jamie's study. Jamie stood at the top of them, his face white.

"What happened?" Blue demanded. "When I heard you yelling...."

"It's...I..." Jamie pointed back down the hall toward his study.

Blue took the stairs three at a time and, brushing past Jamie, headed for the study. He wished he'd taken the time to pick up his makeshift club from the hall. Or better yet, gotten his rifle like he'd said he was going to do. But when he reached the doorway to the Postman's Room, with Jamie on his heels, he saw that they didn't need a weapon. What they needed was a doctor. Or a morgue attendant.

"Jesus," he said.

Lying in a sprawl in front of the fireplace was a small man. One half of his face was a bloody ruin, the flesh cut to the bone. All around his head the carpet was stained with blood.

"I thought . . . I thought you and the Inspector went over the House. . . ." Jamie said slowly.

Blue shook his head. "We never got this far. Is he dead?"

"I don't know. I just saw him and . . ."

Blue crossed the room and knelt by the man. He started to reach for him, then dropped his hands uselessly. What the hell was he supposed to do? They had to get this guy to a hospital and fast, except . . . He bent closer.

The edges of the claw marks were already pinking. The wounds appeared to be healing as he stared at them. It was like watching time-lapse photography on a TV documentary. Nervously, he put two fingers to the man's throat and found a pulse. The guy was still alive.

"I don't believe it," Blue muttered.

"What?" Jamie asked, hovering at his elbow.

"Just look at it. The fucking wounds're healing all by themselves." He turned to look at Jamie. "Is this . . . ?"

Jamie nodded. "Thomas Hengwr. We'd better call an ambulance."

"No way."

"But—"

"I told you," Blue said. "The wounds are healing. More of his fucking magic, I suppose."

"That's impossible," Jamie began, then realized what he was saying and who he was saying it about.

"I want to have a talk with this guy," Blue said.

He understood a lot now. Given that all the magics and other bullshit were real, this was the reason for the attack this morning. Something out there wanted Thomas Hengwr. A dead harper, or some refugee from an old Hammer flick—it didn't matter which. Whatever it was, it had given up the attack when the House's defenses had proved too much for it. But that didn't mean it wouldn't try again.

"What if he doesn't get better?" Jamie asked. "What if he dies on us?"

"Oh, he'll get better. All on his ownsome."

"He was going to find Sara," Jamie said. "Oh, Lord! What's happened to her, then?"

"We'll clean Hengwr up and find out," Blue said grimly.

He looked around the room, trying to figure out some way that they could keep Tom here when he woke up. It wouldn't do for him to simply vanish again like Jamie'd said he'd done last night. But what did you use to tie up a wizard?

"We should call Inspector Tucker," Jamie said.

Blue sat back on his haunches. "We'll do that. After Mr. Wizard here comes around and tells us a thing or two."

"I'll go get some hot water and bandages," Jamie said.

"You do that, Jamie. I'll keep watch on our sleeping beauty here."

Jamie almost ran into Sally as he was going out the door of the Postman's Room. "Tom Hengwr's returned," he said in reply to her unspoken question and hurried on.

"Thomas Hengwr? But—" Sally began, but Jamie was already a dozen paces down the hall. She entered the study, not sure she even wanted to know what was going on, and drew a sharp breath at what she found.

"Do you know anything about nursing?" Blue asked, looking up.

She shook her head numbly. "What happened? How'd *he* get in here?"

"I don't know," Blue said. "But I mean to find out."

When Tucker pulled up in front of the Brooke Claxton Building in Tunney's Pasture, he sat in his car for a few moments, composing his thoughts. He wasn't exactly sure what he was doing here. He was sure that Jean-Paul Gagnon had told him all he knew. The main question he wanted to ask— if anything new had come to light—could have just as easily been asked over the phone. What it was, he supposed, was that you could never get a real grip on a person over the phone. You missed all the nuances. The set of the mouth. The look in the eyes. It was easy to lie over the phone. He'd done it himself, the first time he got in touch with Jean-Paul.

Well, he told himself. I won't learn anything sitting out here on my ass. Pocketing his keys, he got out of the Buick and made for Jean-Paul's office. When he reached it, the ADM seemed surprised to see him.

"Salut encore, inspecteur. Have you brought me news of Kieran?"

Tucker shook his head. "I'm afraid not. I was hoping you might have something." He looked at the spread of paperwork across Jean-Paul's desk and added, "I'm not disturbing you, am I?"

"Bien sûr que non. Please. Take a seat."

"Thanks."

"Now. How can I help you?"

As Tucker had discovered often enough in the past: Level with someone and you can drain away ninety-nine percent of their antagonism—as he had done already with Jean-Paul Gagnon. Looking at him, it was hard to remember that this was the same man who'd been ready to call the papers down on them not two days ago.

"I'm trying to get a feel for this case," he said. "There's a whole lot that just doesn't make sense."

"It has become a case now?" Jean-Paul asked.

"Kieran's involved in one death at the moment, Jean-Paul. And perhaps another."

Tucker watched the ADM closely to see what his reaction would be and saw only honest shock.

"Who is it that has died?" Jean-Paul asked.

"One of my men."

"But this is tragic. And how is Kieran involved?"

"He was there when it happened. In fact, if our witnesses are to be believed, it was Kieran who killed my man. With some kind of magical power."

Jean-Paul shook his head slowly. *"Mais c'est incroyable!* How is this possible? I have known Kieran for many years. He is not—how do you say it? He could not do such a thing— *jamais.* He would never kill a man."

"Last time I was here I explained why we were looking for Kieran," Tucker said. "We thought he might have some sort of special abilities, remember? Since then, one constable involved with this investigation has met a violent death, while this morning the head of our Paranormal Research Branch died under rather mysterious circumstances. The verdict that the coroner came up with on Dr. Hogue's death was a heart attack. But he had no history of cardiovascular trouble and on his last medical he was given a clean slate."

"But to link Kieran with these deaths...."

"Until I find him and hear his side of the story, I've no other choice. Tell me, Jean-Paul. Did Kieran ever express an interest in the occult or magic to you?"

"Hocus-pocus?" Jean-Paul asked lightly. "Such as card tricks?" But something passed across his eyes, belying the light tone of his voice.

"Try the paranormal."

"We are all interested in the unknown, are we not, John?" He met Tucker's gaze steadily, then sighed. "You spoke of this before," he said, "and I admit to a certain confusion, *n'est-ce-pas?* It seems somewhat unbelievable that you—the RCMP—would be interested in such things. But I see you are serious." He paused and adjusted some of the papers on his desk. "Was the occult connected to these deaths you spoke of?"

"I'm not ruling it out," Tucker replied. "At this point, I'm not sure what to think."

"And you think Kieran is a...*sorcier?*"

Tucker regarded him for a moment. Then he related some of what had happened in Patty's Place.

"I'm trusting you to keep this to yourself," he added.

Jean-Paul nodded, understanding that such a trust was not given lightly.

"So now you see where we stand," Tucker said.

"Mais..." Jean-Paul began, then shook his head. "How can such a thing be possible?" But as he spoke, his own suspicions of Thomas Hengwr returned in a flood. And if the master, why not the student?

"I don't even know if it is possible," Tucker said. "I was just feeling you out. There's not a hell of a lot in any of this that makes much sense. Not unless you want to accept fairy tales as real."

Jean-Paul looked out the window of his office. Here, in one of the bureaucratic centers of Ottawa, what they were discussing had no place. It had no place in anything either he or the *inspecteur* accepted as real. Considering all that he'd just been told—and there would be so much left unsaid as well—Jean-Paul was more prepared to believe this was all part of some gigantic hoax, except.... Except the *inspecteur* appeared just as uncomfortable as he felt and Jean-Paul could think of no reason on earth why the RCMP would concoct such an obviously unbelievable story.

"D'accord," he said, coming to a decision.

"Sorry?"

Jean-Paul smiled wanly. "I was thinking aloud, John. To reply to your earlier question: Yes. Kieran had a considerable interest in matters not of this world. It was for that reason I believe he took up his relationship with Thomas Hengwr who has something of a reputation of *un sorcier*. Kieran did not speak much of this interest—at least not to me—but often he would give me books on the subject . . . almost as though he was . . . how did you put it? Almost as though he was 'feeling me out.'"

"You think he wanted to get you to join him in . . . in whatever it was that he was involved in?"

"It seems possible, in retrospect, does it not?"

Tucker frowned. He'd broached the subject in the hopes of being laughed out of this office. Instead, Jean-Paul was taking it as seriously as Tucker himself was beginning to. As he *had* to.

"Unfortunately," Jean-Paul added, "I can be of little help to you, still."

"It helps," Tucker said. "Puts things in a little better perspective, if nothing else."

Jean-Paul nodded. "There is a tie between Kieran's interests. His music . . . *la musique celtique*. It is very magical in itself, *n'est-ce-pas?*"

"Celtique?"

"The music of Ireland and Scotland."

"Druids . . . and dead harpers," Tucker said, more to himself, recalling his conversation with Jamie Tams. Jesus *Ker*-ist! "Do you know any of his other friends in town?" he asked. "Anybody involved in this music, say?"

"There was his group—The Humors of Tullycrine. Let me think. They travel about so much, these musicians, the memberships of the groups changing so often. . . ." At length he shook his head. "I am sorry, John. It has been a few years and I was never close with Kieran's friends."

Tucker shrugged. "That's okay. I'll check out some of the clubs that book that kind of music."

"If I think of anyone I will give you a call."

"Do that." Tucker stood. "Thanks for your time."

"I only wish I could be of more assistance. If Kieran is in trouble, I would like to help. He is not an evil man, John."

Tucker thought of how Thompson had looked when they'd brought him in.

"Christ," he said. "I hope not."

Because if that was the work of a good man. . . . He shook his head wearily.

Jean-Paul arose and saw him to the door.

"*Salut*, John," he said. "*Bonne chance.*"

"Yeah. I'm going to need all the luck I can get. See ya. And thanks."

Sitting behind the wheel of his car later, Tucker went over what he had to go on so far and swore. If he could just get a handle, something solid. . . . Sighing, he started up the engine and headed back to headquarters.

Phil Gannon found his employer working out in his private gym. Walters looked up as the big man entered.

"Do you have something to report, Phillip?" he asked.

Gannon nodded and took a seat on a bench press.

"Tucker's hot to trot, Mr. Walters. He knows Hogue's death was no accident. And he knows he could be next."

"Good, good. And the other matter?"

Gannon shrugged. "What do you know about Tamson House?"

"A great deal. What aspect of it are *you* referring to?"

Gannon's shoulders repeated their nonchalant movement. "The place is a loony bin, from all I've been able to gather. I went with a couple of men to pick up Tams when Tucker arrived with a squad of his men, including some medics."

"Ah? And who was in need of medical attention?"

"No one. It looked like they had a body under a blanket on the pavement, but all it turned out to be was a heap of rubbish, molded into the shape of a man. Tucker sent his men off and went into the House. I decided it was a bad time to make my own entrance, so I got in touch with Jack White to see what the score was."

"And what did our Mr. White have to offer?"

"More questions than answers. Security's tight. From what he could gather, Tucker went out to collect Thomas Hengwr's body, only when they arrived it had . . ." Gannon looked embarrassed at relating this particular bit of information. "It had been transformed into the heap of rubbish I mentioned. Sticks and leaves and moss, held together with mud."

"Very interesting. Was there anything else?"

"Not much. Sara Kendell is missing. She's involved with Hengwr's man—something to do with the cover-up at that restaurant last night. White still hasn't been able to get his hands on the files."

"We have Hogue's report."

"If we can believe it," Gannon replied. "Anyway, that's why I decided to pick up Tams. But now with Tucker on the scene at the House...."

"You did well to hold off on him. And how is our intrepid Inspector?"

"He spent a couple of hours in the House, then I followed him out to Tunney's Pasture. I've got a man on stand-by if he leaves headquarters again."

"Find out who he saw at the Pasture, and why."

"I'll get on it."

"And tell our Mr. White to keep us informed. I want a minute to minute update—no matter how trivial the information might seem to him. You might also see about Tams, now that the Inspector's left him on his own again."

Walters turned back to his weights, dismissing Gannon. The big man sat for a moment, then left the gym to carry out his orders.

Jack White wasn't going to like this. He was already nervous. When Gannon told him that Walters wanted a constant update on the situation, he was going to have a fit. But, Gannon thought, that was just too bad for him. You took your money and you took your chances with it. Of course it also helped to have that little matter of White's own indiscretions to hold over his head. He was still selling secrets. Only the man who paid him his money had changed.

"You know what this is beginning to become?" Madison asked.

Tucker shrugged. When he'd reached headquarters there'd been another message on his desk—right on top of a report that Hengwr's bone artifacts had disappeared from the museum last night—but this message was signed. He was to report to Superintendent Madison's office immediately.

"It's embarrassing, that's what it is," Madison finished.

"You gave me a week, Wally."

"A week? Christ, I don't know if I can hold out for another day. Word's starting to filter upstairs, John, and what's coming back isn't pretty. Williams is going to be asking for my resignation if this keeps up—*after* they've drummed you out."

Anger flickered in Tucker's eyes.

"I didn't set up this project," he said.

"I'm not talking about the project itself, John. I'm talking about a report that's sitting here on my desk. What was Warne doped up on, anyway? I'm talking about calling out a mop-up squad to clean up some leaves and shit on someone's front walk."

"I believe Constable Warne saw what he says he saw," Tucker replied evenly.

Madison said nothing for a long moment. Then he leaned back in his chair.

"I think you need a break, John."

"You're not taking me off this," Tucker said, his voice flat.

"You're not being logical," Madison countered.

"Logical?" Tucker broke in before the Superintendant could continue. "There's fuck-all logical about this operation, Wally, and you knew that before you ever assigned me to it. 'Provide security,' you said. Jesus Christ! It's been more like wet-nursing a bunch of assholes who wouldn't know their dicks from a hole in the ground. And security! I've busted my ass and this place is still about as secure as a cedar canoe that's just broken up in white water."

"John, listen to me—"

"No! You listen to me. These are your men I'm working with. And the operation itself...." He shook his head in disgust. "It goes a lot deeper than finding some spook who can read minds or some such shit. I tell you what, Wally. You find out for me how a nobody like Hogue got hired to head this project. You explain to me how Thompson died. And Hogue himself, for that matter. You tell me why Warne sticks to his story when he knows it sounds like the ravings of some doped-up junkie. You tell me where the evidence at the museum disappeared to. You tell me what that fucking note on my desk is supposed to mean."

"John...." he began again.

"You gave me a week to clean this up, Wally. Hold the brass back for that week and I'll do just that. Have I ever let you down before?"

"No. But you've never gone off the deep end before, either."

"Do you really believe that?" Tucker asked softly.

He held Madison's gaze until the Superintendant looked away.

"No," Madison said slowly. "I don't believe it. Only..."

"Oh, I know what you're thinking," Tucker said. "You don't

think it haunts *me?* You don't think *I* feel like I'm setting myself up for a nice long stay in the san'?"

"Okay," Madison said. "But the brass..."

"Stall them. You find out how Hogue got his job. Can you do that?"

"It's not in his file?"

Tucker shook his head. "Just his credentials and some background data. Nothing on how he was contacted, who sponsored him—that sort of thing."

"I'll find out. And in the meantime, what'll you be doing?"

"Me? First off, I'm going to have a talk with whoever's replacing Hogue. You got a name for me?"

Madison pushed aside some files and came up with a sheet that he handed to Tucker.

"Three of them," he said. "Two more researchers—one retired—and an ex-Air Force man who's been specializing in debunking UFO sightings."

"Are you serious?"

Madison smiled. "What's the matter? Don't UFOs fit in with your wizards?"

"Spare me."

"All right. Colonel Chambers isn't even being seriously considered. His name's there to keep the military brass happy."

"That leaves us with the two doctors—Gordon and Traupman. Traupman's retired, so—"

"Not so fast, John. If it was up to me, I'd take Traupman. He's unorthodox—which is what you need right about now. Someone a little twisted. Like yourself." The last was said with a grin. "He had somewhat of a reputation as a ghost hunter in his time. He's written three books—two treatises and one bestseller."

"What was that called?"

"The Last Mistress—schlock horror."

"Guy sounds perfect. Seriously, Wally...."

"I *am* being serious. From his file, Richard Traupman's our man. Gordon's a recent McGill graduate—a lot of talk, no experience."

"How come you've got his name then?"

"Williams has been priming him," Madison said.

"And you want Traupman. You think the Solicitor General's going to go for him when he's got his own boy?"

Madison shrugged. "He's leaning for Gordon, but I think I can convince him to go with Traupman."

Tucker thought about it for a moment. Which of them did *he* want to work with? Hard to say. All he really wanted was to be done with this project and get away for awhile. He glanced at his watch. Getting on to three. He wondered if Maggie was finished in court yet, then shook his head. First things first.

"Have you got addresses for them?" he asked.

"Dr. Gordon still lives in Montreal," Madison replied. "Dr. Traupman has a house in Alta Vista."

Tucker sighed. "So much for a late lunch with Maggie."

"Hey! Are you and Maggie getting back together?"

"Not exactly. But we're working on it." He frowned. "This guy Traupman. Does he know he's being considered for this position?"

"He was aware of the possibility when we were setting up the PRB."

"Okay. Guess I'll drop in on him and see what he's got to say about spooks and stiffs that turn into garbage. How's it going with the reporters?"

Madison shrugged. "We dummied up some witnesses for them—real talkers. It's keeping them busy."

"Well, that's something." Tucker got up and headed for the door. "You know, Wally," he added, pausing at the doorway to look back. "Sometimes it feels like we're living in the middle of a comic book. You know what I mean?"

"All too well."

"Thing I always ask," Tucker said, "is where the fuck's Superman when you need him?"

He let the door swing shut before Madison could reply.

In the Postman's Room, Jamie sat at Memoria's terminal, the screen blank as he rearranged for the hundredth time the artifacts that Sara had found. The bone disc and ring were gone, but everything else was still here. The painting was propped up on one side of his desk. On his blotter, laid out in a neat row, were the pouch and its contents. Fox's claw. Bundle of feathers. Threaded corn kernels. A rounded pebble. In a pile beside them were computer printouts detailing each Weirdin bone and the information that Tom had entered with them.

Closing his eyes, he leaned forward on the desk. In the hall outside his study, he could hear Blue explaining the workings of his rifle to Sally. "You might need to know," Blue was saying.

"I know how to shoot a rifle," Sally protested. "My dad

taught me when I was seventeen. It's just that if I tried to fire that thing, it'd probably take my shoulder off. What're you doing with it anyway? I thought you told me you'd given up this kind of thing."

"Well, I did. Only you don't throw out something like this. I just keep it in the closet, you know. In case."

Neither of them needed to say in case of what.

Sighing, Jamie gathered up the artifacts and replaced them in their pouch. He picked up the painting and stared at it for a long moment. Looking at the incredible detailing of the brushstrokes, it was easier to believe that it was magicked into existence as Tom said it had been than that someone had actually sat down and painted it. Harper and shaman. Taliesin and . . . it took him a moment to remember the Indian's name. A'wa'rathe.

Taliesin didn't look like a threat—not in the painting. And he certainly didn't resemble that creature at the door this morning. Tom's words came back to him. "Every rose hides a thorn . . ."

Wherever Sara was, he hoped it was a million miles from the harper. Sara. Not knowing what was happening to her was what tore him up the most. With the shape Tom was in. . . . He'd been going to find her and . . .

"Any improvement?" he called to Blue.

"Nothing yet, Jamie."

The biker and Sally were sitting in the hall. From where they sat they had a clear view of both the Postman's Room and Gramarye's Clover beside it where they'd laid Tom out on the big four-poster bed. Jamie stood up from his desk and, stretching his shoulder muscles, walked to the other room to have a look for himself. The wound on Tom's face was mostly white scar tissue now. With the blood swabbed away, he appeared to be merely sleeping, not mortally hurt as he'd seemed when Jamie first found him. His breathing was steady, but there was still no color in his face. It was a dead man's face, Jamie thought uncomfortably—a mask of white skin stretched taut over his brow and cheekbones.

Jamie looked down at Tom for a long time, then slowly turned and left the room. At his desk again, he activated Memoria's viewscreen and punched in a request for new data. The computer hummed as it gathered the requested information, spitting it out in neat lines on the screen. He had the key now, Jamie thought. Tom had told him that much. It was there in the weirdin. Now all he had to do was find the right combination of symbols that would unlock his understanding of it all. Shouldn't be hard. He'd already been at it for thirty-odd years. He had a head start, hadn't he?

Frowning, Jamie returned his concentration to the matter at hand. He felt the walls of the room, the entire bulk of Tamson House, lean closer to study it with him. It was a queer, but comforting sensation.

Traupman's house was a plain red brick bungalow, long and rambling. The front yard was cut off from Chomley Crescent by a neatly trimmed cedar hedge, and the lawn between it and the house would have put a golf course to shame. Tucker pulled his Buick into the lane, parked it behind an '81 VW Rabbit, and admired the yard. The flowerbeds alongside the house were bare now in preparation for the winter. Leaning up against the wall of the house were wooden covers for the shrubberies that stood guard on either side of the front door.

Whatever else might be said of him, Tucker decided, Traupman was an organized man.

He met Tucker at the door and his appearance strengthened the Inspector's earlier thought. At sixty-six, Richard Traupman still had a full head of hair and a thick walrus moustache that hung over his mouth. The perfect fit of his tweed jacket and trousers made Tucker feel like a cheap hood.

"Good of you to see me on such short notice, Dr. Traupman," he said. "I hope I haven't disturbed you?"

"Not at all, Inspector. Come in. And please, call me Dick."

Tucker nodded and stuck out his hand. "John Tucker," he said.

Traupman's handshake was firm.

They went through a short hall into a living room that was more a combination library/study than a place to receive guests. Floor to ceiling bookcases lined one wall. Beside them was a broad government-styled oak desk, beside it a battery of file drawers. A worktable cut the room in two. Spread across it were what looked like the pages from a book, dozens of neat stacks of them.

"A book of verse," Traupman said. "I decided to cut down costs and collate it myself. Do you read poetry, John?"

"Not so's you'd notice. Nice place you've got here."

"Thank you. Please have a seat. Can I get you a drink? Or some coffee?"

"Coffee'd be fine."

While he was out of the room, Tucker sauntered over to the worktable and had a look at the poetry. He read a line here and there, but couldn't make a lot of sense out of any of it. That was the trouble with poems. It seemed you had to have a doctorate just to understand the fucking references. Still. Some of it had a nice ring to it.

> ...like Manjushri, I have met death,
> and bear my own victory,
> though not a sword...

Nice. Yeah. If you knew what the hell it meant.

"Been doing this long?" he asked, when Traupman returned.

"The poetry? Yes. But mostly for myself and what friends I have left. This is my first published effort, self-published at that, as the editor who bought *The Last Mistress* wouldn't touch it. He wants the new novel that's been overdue since September. I realize I've been lax about it, but at my age one learns to take things as they come. It seemed more important to see these poems in print. They, unlike a novel, seem a more fitting epitaph."

Tucker nodded and pointed to the line he'd just read. "What's this mean?"

"Manjushri was one of the Bodhisattvas," Traupman explained. "A Buddha-to-be, as it were. He was reputed to have conquered Yama, the god of death, and bore a sword in his hand as a memory of his victory. In the context of the poem, I am using him as an analogy to myself. Presumptuous, but it seemed fitting at the time."

"You mean you've conquered death by living to the age you are now?"

Traupman smiled. "That's one way of looking at it. But no. I'm referring to the fact that so many of my friends and colleagues have passed on. So I have met death, but not conquered him. For I'll die too, when my time comes. Hence I bear no sword."

"I never would have got that out of it," Tucker said.

"It takes work. But enough of my versifications. How can I help you?"

Tucker thought about that for a moment. "It's almost as complex as what you've just explained to me. Are you familiar with the PRB—the Paranormal Research Branch?"

"Vaguely. I was approached by a Superintendant Madison a year or so ago and asked if I would be willing to help out from time to time if my particular expertise was called for. Since then I've heard nothing."

"Well," Tucker said tiredly, "your expertise is damn well needed now. Let me lay out the problem for you and, if you believe even half of it, maybe you can give me an opinion on it. Okay?"

"Is this privileged information? If so, I'm not sure that—"

"You're cleared, if that was what you were worrying about. You were cleared before you were even approached."

"Do I have to swear some sort of oath now?" Traupman asked. He seemed amused by the idea. Tucker smiled with him, but thought of how he'd opened up to Gagnon with nothing but a handshake to keep the ADM quiet. Madison would have his balls if he heard about that.

"That won't be necessary," he said. "But if you could keep it to yourself, it'd be appreciated. You know you're being considered to head up the project now?"

Traupman's eyebrows lifted quizzically.

"Anyway, this is what we've got, Dick."

Traupman was a good listener. He heard the story through, backtracking once or twice to have some point cleared up, saving his own commentary for the end. Tucker liked that.

"Are we nuts, or what?" Tucker asked him when he was through.

Traupman shook his head slowly. "It all sounds so... impossible. I was under the impression that the PRB was involved in paranormal research—hence its name. By that I assumed it would primarily be studies of telepathy, telekinetics... that sort of thing. But this...." He said nothing for a moment, his eyes looking inward. Then he asked: "Why was the whole project centered around the one man, this Thomas Hengwr?"

"We had a lot of people in—primarily, as controls. Hengwr was supposed to be the real thing."

"Yes. But the manner in which he was handled...."

"Tell me about it. But that's past history now. What I have to know now is, where do we go from here? And are you willing to help?"

"I..." Traupman looked at his desk, then his worktable.

"Normally I'd say no, but what you've told me is simply too fascinating to ignore—though heading up the project seems a trifle much to expect."

"Whether you head it up or not, I could still use your help." Tucker decided that he liked this old man. If only they'd had someone like him running the project from the first, instead of that hotshot Hogue. . . .

"I suppose," Traupman said, "that the first item on the agenda would be to discover the validity of what Jamie Tams has told you—though how we might accomplish that is beyond me."

"Well, maybe we could go out and talk to him. What do you think?"

"I think it's an admirable suggestion. I—Lord! I must say that I'm excited. I've dabbled in this field for so many years. But now . . . Just imagine if it could be proved that paranormal abilities *did* exist!"

Tucker smiled. "Feeling like what's-his-name again?"

"Manjushri. But yes. You're right." Traupman regarded the Inspector thoughtfully. "I think I will enjoy working with you, John."

"Well, let's go see if the feeling's mutual." Tucker looked at his watch and stood. "Mind if I use your phone?" he asked.

"Not at all. I'll get my coat."

Tucker got through to the Court House on Nicholas, but had to leave a message for Maggie as she was still closeted with her client. The case had been adjourned to the following day, which meant she'd probably be working late on it anyway. Still, there was no harm in trying. He left the number he had for Tamson House, hoping he wouldn't have to go looking for a phone on his own if she called. Traupman was waiting for him as he cradled the receiver.

"Jamie?" Blue called from the hall.

Jamie looked up from the viewscreen and turned. "Mmm?"

"Fred says that Tucker just pulled up. He's got some old white-haired guy in the car with him. Think it's a shrink?"

"Lord knows we could use one."

Jamie switched off the viewscreen, leaving Memoria to continue the program he'd entered.

"What do we do with Thomas Hengwr?" Blue asked.

Jamie'd been wondering the same thing. Make a clean breast of it? What if the Inspector wanted another tour? Why in God's name were they hiding Tom anyway? Because, the reply came, he was their only link to Sara.

"I don't know," he said at last. "Play it by ear?"

"And lose our heads?"

"What?"

Blue sighed. "Don't mind me," he said, and hummed the line about paranoia from the Buffalo Springfield song "For What It's Worth."

Standing beside him, Jamie laid a hand on the younger man's arm.

"It's getting to you, too, isn't it?" he asked.

"Damn right. When I think of Sara..."

"I think we should just hand him over," Sally said, joining them in the doorway. "The police are set up to handle this sort of thing."

Blue shook his head. "No way the cops are set up to handle anything this weird."

"And we are?"

"There's no clear answer," Jamie said. "Let's just go down and see what the Inspector wants this time. Sally, I'd appreciate it if you'd stay up here and keep an eye on Tom. And Blue?"

"Yeah?"

Jamie pointed to the rifle leaning against the wall.

"Maybe you should put that away," he said.

"It's already done," Blue said and, hefting the weapon, brought it into the study. He looked around, shrugged, then propped it up between two bookcases.

"Good afternoon, Inspector," Jamie said as he entered the kitchen. He glanced at Traupman. "And this is?"

"Dr. Richard Traupman."

Jamie smiled, recognizing the name. "A pleasure, doctor."

"Entirely mine, Mr. Tams. I've read your work on African myths in *Archaeology Today*."

"Traupman?" Blue mused aloud. "Did you write that book—what was it called? *The Last Mistress?*"

"I'm afraid so."

"No shit? I mean, that was a good read. I enjoyed it a lot. I didn't know you lived in Ottawa."

Traupman spread his hands. "I'm surprised to be recognized."

"Thing I was wondering," Blue said, "is when Shaw has that chance to take Chanter when he's human—"

"Blue?"

Blue turned to Jamie, then remembered what they were here for.

"Well, maybe another time," he said with a shrug and took a seat at the table.

Jamie nodded to Fred who took that as an opportunity to leave, and sat down beside Blue. Propping his elbows on the table, he regarded Tucker.

"What can we do for you this time, Inspector?"

"It's your show, Dick," Tucker said to his companion.

"Yes. Well." Traupman smiled. "This is somewhat awkward, as I'm not sure where to begin."

"You're here about Thomas Hengwr, aren't you?" Jamie asked. "And because of what happened—" He caught himself. "Because of what we *say* happened here this morning."

Traupman nodded. "You must admit that it's quite . . . well, unbelievable."

"We've already been all through that with the Inspector," Blue said.

"Blue!"

"Okay, okay."

"I suppose we should begin with this," Traupman continued. "Have there been any new developments?"

Now was the moment, Jamie thought. He caught himself glancing at Blue and knew the biker was thinking the same thing. They could lay it all out now and be done with shouldering the responsibility on their own. That's what Jamie'd like to do, only where would that leave Sara? The RCMP weren't concerned with her. Just with what they could get out of Tom.

Think, dammit, he told himself.

The silence was starting to drag on. Tucker'd know they were hiding something. But it was so hard to think clearly. And then, before he could come to a decision, Sally appeared at the door to the Silkwater Kitchen, a look of poorly disguised worry on her face.

Tucker rose to his feet, his hand streaking to his hip. Shit, that sucker moves fast, Blue thought.

"Okay," Tucker said, letting his hand drop to his side when he saw that there was no immediate threat. "What's up? You people are hiding something and you'd better cough it up. Fast."

Jamie took a steadying breath.

"There have been one or two new developments, Inspector," he said, realizing the irony of that statement.

"Well, spill 'em."

"It's Thomas Hengwr. He showed up here, badly hurt, not long after you left earlier today."

"Hengwr?" Tucker loosed the word like a shot. "How badly hurt?"

"Well, that's one of the developments. His wounds have been healing by themselves while he's been in some sort of a coma."

"And you?" Tucker demanded of Sally. "What's your news?"

Sally swallowed, realizing that she'd blown it. But she'd had to come down. "He's coming around," she said.

Tucker glared at them all. "Jesus H. Christ! What is it with you people, anyway? Do you know what we've been going through trying to find Hengwr? I ought to run the bunch of you in for obstructing justice."

"Justice?" Blue snarled. "What the fuck does someone like you know about justice? You just want Hengwr so that you can play around with his head like he was some kind of guinea pig. You fuck around with him and there goes our chance of finding Sara."

"Now you listen to me, asshole——"

"Gentlemen, gentlemen!" Traupman's voice, though not loud, carried across their argument. "Why don't we go see Mr. Hengwr for ourselves and see what *he* has to say?"

Jamie nodded. "Before he ups and vanishes again."

Tucker sighed. "We're not finished yet," he told Blue.

"Anytime, man. You just set aside that badge you're hiding behind and——"

"Blue!"

"Okay, Jamie."

"Shall we, gentlemen?" Traupman asked. "If you would be so kind as to lead the way, miss."

Sally glanced at Jamie, then nodded.

"This way," she said.

She waited for Blue to catch up to her and took his arm. Leaning close so that the others wouldn't hear, she said: "Don't mess with him, Blue. You've got nothing to prove."

"I know. It's just that guys like him—King Shit with a badge...."

"Blue, please."

"Okay." His features softened. "I'm okay now."

Blue covered her hand with his own. He knew he'd been blowing it. Trouble was, Tucker just rubbed him the wrong way. All cops rubbed him the wrong way. All they had to do was look at him and it got his adrenaline running. It was a bad habit that he couldn't shake. Habit? Shit, it was instinct. Because people like himself always got fucked around. Sara'd told him often enough that it was his own attitude that caused it as much as anything, but. . . . Well, you had to be an outcast in the first place to know what it meant. Some things you just couldn't shake.

Thinking of Sara, he made himself a promise that neither Jamie nor Sally would prevent him from keeping. If Tucker messed up their chances of getting Sara back, he was going to personally kill the fucker. Guaranteed. The ball was in Tucker's court now. Reaching the door to Gramarye's Clover where they were keeping Tom, he glanced back at the others.

"Open the door, Farley," Tucker snapped.

Before Blue could reply, Traupman touched the Inspector's arm.

"This ill will is not really necessary, is it, John?" he asked.

Tucker was about to tell Traupman to mind his own business, then thought better of it. He took a steadying breath instead. "You're right," he admitted.

"Open the door, Blue," Jamie said quietly.

Blue nodded and turned the knob.

Chapter Six

"When you think of a bear," Ha'kan'ta asked, "how do you view its motion?"

She was nursing the coals of her campfire back into life with handfuls of shredded reeds and Kieran, bemused by watching her, was slow to reply. When she looked up, he blinked and found a response.

"Lumbering, I suppose."

Ha'kan'ta shook her head. "Not so. Sometimes they shuffle, but there is always a grace to their every movement. Think of it a moment."

Kieran thought. But Lord lifting Jesus, how often had he had the opportunity to check out how a bear moved?

The journey to Ha'kan'ta's campsite had been strange. Despite Kieran's misgivings, they'd both ridden on the back of Ak'is'hyr, the big bull moose Great-Heart that served Ha'kan'ta for a mount. The ride had taken twelve hours, but the sky above them had turned twice from deep blue to rich purple as they moved through the worlds. After the second sunset, they had reached Ha'kan'ta's camp and it was full night.

"Not far in time," Ha'kan'ta had told him when they left the quin'on'a, "or rather through time. But it lies many worlds from this lodge."

Kieran didn't really know where they were, except that the night had come twice as they moved through different worlds (and different time zones, he supposed), and instead of being near a lake, they were now by a river. Ha'kan'ta's lodge was set back from the river, in amongst the pines that clouded either bank with their dark boughs. The two wolves had awaited them at the camp, silver-furred in the moonlight.

"Shak'syo and May'asa," Ha'kan'ta had named them.
Winter-Brother and Summer-Brother.

"How do you tell them apart?" he'd asked.

"By the way that the sen'fer'sa moves through them. Feel
it. Shak'syo has a winter's breath about him—a piercing spirit
like a sudden north wind—while May'asa dreams a golden
breeze."

Raising his taw, Kieran had reached out to find it so.

"Well?" Ha'kan'ta asked now, drawing him from his intro-
spection.

"I was thinking of the wolves," he said. "Their movements
are more graceful than a bear's to my mind."

"Do you have an affinity towards the wolf?" She had the
shredded reeds burning and had begun to add kindling. "What
is your totem? Surely not that of the wolf?"

"Totem?" An affinity with a certain animal was yet another
of his studies that Tom had been lax in. These many worlds,
the quin'on'a and Ha'ka'ta's people . . . there was so much that
Tom had never told him about.

Ha'kan'ta gave him the time he needed to think, busying
herself with the fire and then in kneading what looked like
unbleached flour on a flat stone by her knee.

"My name," Kieran said. "'Foy.' It comes from the Irish
word 'fiach' which means 'raven.'"

"And do you have an affinity with your flying brothers?"

"I never really thought of it."

Ha'kan'ta stopped kneading for a moment to regard him.

"You are still troubled, are you not?" she asked. "About
your companion, Saraken?"

"Yes and no." Kieran sighed. "It's hard to explain. When
I first apprenticed to Tom, I didn't know anything—about
magic and that sort of thing. But when I began to learn and
found my taw . . . it opened up whole new horizons for me.
Changed the way I perceived the world. I thought I understood
the limits and goals of what Tom was teaching me and tried
to adjust to the one while attempting to attain the other."

"There are few limits," Ha'kan'ta said.

"I'm beginning to see that now. *Nom de tout!* There's so
much more than I was led to believe. And that makes me
wonder: why did Tom tell me so little?"

"How did he withhold knowledge from you?"

"Well, he never showed me how to get to these other worlds,
for one thing."

Ha'kan'ta shrugged. "I think this shows the difference between one who is born to the craft and one who is led into it. From my earliest studies I knew that I must do my reaching for myself. My craftfather—who was my blood father as well—showed me how I could attain the state of sen'fer'sa, the something-in-movement that you call your taw. Once I acquired that ability, I was left to discover whatever else I might on my own."

"He didn't show you anything else?"

"He gave me guidance—when I asked. But often his replies to my questions were cloaked in so much ambiguity that I was left feeling more confused than before I'd asked."

"Lord dying Jesus! Doesn't that sound familiar!"

"So I sought more on my own. Did you not seek?"

"I. . . . No. I suppose I never did. I was content with what I had, with striving for more peace of mind. I suppose that I never really believed in these other worlds, for all that I'd been taught so much that was unbelievable."

"Then there you have it."

Ha'kan'ta returned to her dough. Watching the slow steady movement of her fingers, Kieran thought out loud.

"And that's what's been bothering me about Sara," he said.

"What?"

"Well, everything seems to come so easily for her. Poof! And she can do this. Poof! And there's something else she can do."

"She is a seeker—that much is evident. She reaches out for understanding, for an understanding of everything. And that can be both good and ill, for one can spread oneself too thin. We have a saying. . . ."

"'Accomplished at much, but master of none.' Or something like that?"

"Exactly," Ha'kan'ta said. "Still, she has a skilled craftfather. Taliesin Redhair will not allow her to go too far astray."

"Taliesin? Sara's craftfather?"

"It is to him that she has gone—of that I am sure."

Kieran digested this information and found that it didn't surprise him.

"But as I said before," Ha'kan'ta added, pinning him once more with her steady gaze, "you should put worries of her from your mind for now. You are strong as well. I can feel your taw—bright and shining. And there is as deep a strength in it as anything Saraken will find within herself. Master the Bear-

dance with me. Face Mal'ek'a at my side. Think of this—not
whether or not you are equal to the task. Kha?"

"Understood," Kieran replied.

"Good. We will eat soon. And tomorrow, when the moon
has set, I will take you to my Glade of Study. The medicines
are strong there."

Kieran let out a long breath and the bunched up muscles
around his neck and shoulders loosened as the tension drained
away. Ha'kan'ta was right. Were the quin'on'a right as well?
Had Tom been chasing after shadows?

Ha'kan'ta finished the kneading, shaped the dough into small
loaves, wrapped them in green leaves, and set them by the
edges of the fire. Then she left him and went into the lodge
for a few moments. Returning to sit beside him, she handed
Kieran a small six-holed whistle made of bone.

"Can you play one of these?" she asked.

Kieran began to ask why, but she simply shook her head
and pointed to the whistle. Shrugging, he hefted it, first in one
hand, then the other. He drew up his taw and reached out,
following the instrument's contours with his inner senses as he
ran his fingers along the smoothed bone of its surface. Then
he lifted it to his lips and played—a slow air, haunting and
unfamiliar, that he realized he'd gotten from the whistle itself,
from the instrument's memory of having had that air played
on it many times before.

When he finally took the whistle from his lips and held it
on his lap, Ha'kan'ta asked him:

"Given only the instrument, how would you judge its previous owner?"

"That's a strange thing to ask, but . . ." He closed his eyes,
recalling the air and the feel of the air holes against the pads
of his fingers, the fit of the mouthpiece against his lips, the
spirit that still spoke through it. "I sense a deep quiet. A stillness, like the silence in the heart of my taw. But this instrument's owner had that stillness a thousandfold deeper than
anyone I've ever known."

"An apt description."

"Whose was it?" Kieran asked.

"Taliesin's. Now do you understand what the quin'on'a
meant?"

"Taliesin's? But—"

But nothing. Now he did understand. And if the bard was

anything like this instrument's memory of him, he could well understand how everyone from Sara to the quin'on'a defended him. The spirit he sensed that still touched the whistle could never have become Mal'ek'a, could never have become so evil. But if that was so, why was Tom so convinced that the harper was his enemy?

"Ha'kan'ta..." he began, but she shook her head once more.

"No more talk. Now we eat. And afterwards, you must rest. Your wound still requires time to heal properly. We will have all of tomorrow to speak as much as we will. And in the evening, we will go to my Glade of Study."

The smell of the small loaves lifted from the fire, reminding Kieran of just how hungry he was. Trouble was, bread alone wasn't going to fill him up.

"We must eat lightly," Ha'kan'ta said. "And tomorrow evening we fast in preparation for the Beardance."

Again she seemed to have read his mind. What was it? Did his features give away everything he thought? The discipline of shielding his own thoughts was one of the first things that Tom had taught him, along with how to tune out the static-like mental noise that leaked from the people around him. He bore the skill as unconsciously as he breathed. Yet she seemed to cut right through it.

At the same time that he realized this, he discovered that he could feel the easy rhythm of her surface thoughts as well. He watched the firelight touch her features as she moved the leaf-wrapped loaves away from the fire with a stick. A sense of easy companionship came from her, as though they'd been friends for a long time. She looked up, catching his eye. A fleeting sadness touched her thoughts, then was gone.

"I have been lonely," she said, "for I have sought no companionship since my father journeyed to the Place of Dreaming Thunder. But tonight, sharing my fire with you, I remember what it is I have been missing. My people are solitary folk by choice. Loneliness is rarely a stranger to our lodges. But when the choice is taken away from one... as the tragg'a took my father from me...."

"I'm sorry it happened," Kieran said. "Especially the way it did. It must have been hard on you."

Ha'kan'ta sighed. "I know he is happy, drumming in that place of peace. But still I miss him."

They sat quietly for a long moment. When Ha'kan'ta finally stirred, Kieran started to give the whistle back to her, but she shook her head.

"You must keep it," she said. "I've never played it and I can think of few things more sad than an instrument that is never used. Let my sadness be alone in the night and, with your company to ease it, soon set aside. At least for awhile."

"Thank you," Kieran said, meaning more than just the gift of the bone whistle.

Ha'kan'ta smiled. "You are very welcome, Kieranfoy."

They slept that night on beds of cut cedar boughs, out under the open sky with the scent of the resin strong in the air. Kieran lay awake for a long while, listening to Ha'kan'ta's quiet breathing as she slept a half dozen paces or so from where he lay. He held her gift of Taliesin's whistle in his hand, running a finger across the air holes. An owl hooted in the distance and he had the sudden urge to lift the instrument to his lips and call back to it. Instead, he turned over and, still clutching the whistle, finally fell asleep.

The following morning Ha'kan'ta removed the poultice from Kieran's side and pronounced it healed enough to not require further bandaging. Kieran stared at the scar tissue in mute fascination. All that remained of the wound was a set of four white scar lines raised upon his skin.

That day they spent lazing about Ha'kan'ta's camp, talking of their craftfathers and themselves, exchanging tales of their worlds and their own roles in them as the morning drifted into the afternoon. Late in the day, Kieran took out the whistle and played a few of the Irish tunes he remembered from his days with Toby's band and tried a strathspey that he'd learned from a piper the last time he'd played a club in Halifax. Ha'kan'ta accompanied him on a small ceremonial drum and the jaunty Celtic tunes took on a curious reverence as the music drifted off through the trees.

It drew the wolves in from the forest to lie between them and even Ak'is'hyr, who stood between the riverbank and the camp placidly chewing his cud, appeared to be listening. Kieran had never experienced anything quite like it before. The bone whistle, an instrument he was not overly proficient upon, took on an entirely new dimension for him against the rhythm of Ha'kan'ta's drumming.

At length the twilight came and the moon, floating high

above the pines as darkness fell, turned westward and dipped below the trees. The combination of fasting and the strange resonance of the music that he could still hear inside him worked a spell on Kieran so that he felt light-headed and very aware of his surroundings.

Ha'kan'ta stood. She seemed to float to her feet.

"It is time," she said.

Taking Kieran by the hand, she led him into the forest.

The night skies above Ha'kan'ta's Glade of Study were moonless and grew darker as a spread of cloud cover moved across the stars. A wind touched the boughs of the encircling pines and made a low mournful sound.

"Amongst the rathe'wen'a," Ha'kan'ta explained, "each of us has their own cha'hen'ta—Glade of Study. This is mine. I have named it S'ha'vho'sa—Where-the-Moon-Meets-the-Pines—and it is here, and only here, that I may pass on my knowledge to another. Craftknowledge, such as the Beardance."

Kieran nodded. They were sitting cross-legged, directly opposite each other and so close that he could have reached out and touched her shoulders.

"What exactly is a Beardance?" he asked, remembering their conversation the previous night about how each of them viewed a bear's movement. He was a little uncertain of what was going to be expected of him. Would they daub paint on themselves and dance?

"A Beardance is the ability of shaping one's spirit as a bear's spirit is shaped."

"Shapeshifting?"

A mild sense of alarm touched Kieran. He saw clearly in his mind's eye the man that he'd had to kill in Patty's Place— what? A hundred years ago?

"It is a shapeshifting," Ha'kan'ta said, "but not of the body. Think of the something-in-movement—your taw. You know it as a silence—shapeless, without boundaries. With my people it has the rhythm of a drum and takes on the properties of our totem. With the Beardance, you will learn how to take on the shape of a bear's taw. You will be strong as a bear—stronger than you have ever been. As strong as Taliesin. Strong enough that together we may defeat Mal'ek'a."

"Just like that?"

Ha'kan'ta smiled and shook her head. She had brought a

leather bag with her and her ceremonial drum. She set the bag between them and took from it a necklace of bearclaws and a shallow bowl of carved wood. Next she withdrew what looked like dried mushrooms and a small watersack. She put the mushrooms into the bowl and, using the back of her thumbnail, ground them as with a mortar and pestle. When she was satisfied with the fineness of the powdered fungus, she added water and stirred the mixture with her finger until it became like a paste.

"You must lie down now," she said.

"But. . . ."

"Do not be alarmed. I will be your guide. What we must do now is allow you to meet my totem. But because she is a totem, she is not of this world, nor of any world that can be reached by physical means. She dwells in the world of my heart—deep within. She dwells in Ha'hot'rathe—Where-Walk-the-Bears."

"I'm not alarmed," Kieran said. "I just want to know what to expect."

Ha'kan'ta shook her head. "You must free yourself of all expectations, save this: that you are in my care and that I will keep you from harm, no matter where you go. I will protect your body; my totem will protect your soul."

He lay down, twitched when he felt Ha'kan'ta's finger on first his right, then his left eyelid, but otherwise managed to keep his body still and his mind receptive to what might come.

"That you may see true," Ha'kan'ta said as she daubed the mixture in place.

She followed this by applying it to his ears, his nostrils, on either side of his throat, in the center of his chest, the insides of his wrists and ankles, and lastly on his tongue. It tasted bitter, but by that time the mixture had already begun to affect him as it was absorbed into his skin and entered his bloodstream.

Ha'kan'ta repeated the process on herself, then positioned herself at his head, facing down his body, sitting on bent legs so that either knee touched his temples. Taking up the necklace of bearclaws, she laid it across his chest. Then she took up the drum and began to brush it lightly with the pads of her fingers.

To Kieran, the drum sound was like soft distant thunder, slow and dreamy. It centered his attention on his taw, tightening his focus on that place of inner quiet until his spirit felt free, as though it was sailing out of his body.

He blinked, remembering where he'd been, then saw that
he was no longer in Ha'kan'ta's glade, but rather walking in
a place of low-lying mists. No. They were clouds. He was
walking on clouds and there, through a rift, he could see the
land far below him. Somewhere in that forest his body lay.
Somewhere in amongst all those trees it was hidden from him,
kept from him. Without his soul to guide it, it would die. He
knew that. But how could he return?

"Be calm," a voice said beside him and he saw that he was
no longer alone.

Ha'kan'ta, her face shifting from her own features to those
that were more ursine, then back again, stepped lightly at his
side. Only her eyes remained unchanged. Deep and blue. They
steadied him, turned his panic in on itself until it burned away
and the ashes fluttered groundward. He was calm now. At
peace. And then he remembered why he was here, walking on
clouds, high over the land. He was supposed to meet someone.

"Come," the woman/bear at his side said.

She took his hand and led him on.

He could still hear the drumming. Now it was a familiar
friend, reminding him of the pulse of his blood through his
body where it lay far below, reminding him of it, but without
the earlier panicking fear. He sensed other beings moving around
them, only none of them were as solid as Ha'kan'ta. Solid?
he asked. How can that be? We're walking across the sky. Still
he felt her hand in his own and it was flesh to the touch.

She led him, swiftly and surely. The land unwound below
them, now marsh and cedar, now lakes, now a mountain.

"Do you know this place?" Ha'kan'ta asked him once.

They had paused over a lake and Kieran saw a female figure
on its shore. She looked up and he saw that the woman wore
a stag mask. No. She had the head of a stag.

"Hoth'ans," he said softly. It was the Creator of the quin'on'a.

"She is dreaming," Ha'kan'ta said. "See?"

He saw himself facing the quin'on'a elder. A swan dropped
from the sky above and grasped him by the shoulders, bearing
him aloft. In one hand he held a small bird, in the other a
drum. Before he could see which he chose in this dream of
Hoth'ans, Ha'kan'ta led him on once more, further away still,
to where a great range of mountains rose to cut the sky.

"We are almost there," Ha'kan'ta said.

The drum's beat continued, steady and comforting as a
healthy pulse. They stepped down from the clouds, sank like

feathers to the snow-capped peaks, arrived on one. Kieran's every sense tingled as though an electric current was being fed through them. He saw with sharp-edged clarity, with a deep-sight deeper than any he'd known before. The black stone against the stark white snowdrifts. Every hair on Ha'kan'ta's head, each individual strand standing alone. And her eyes.... Caught by her eyes, he shivered.

There was a musky scent in the air and he could taste the cold on his tongue, though he wasn't chilled. He could feel the blood run through the veins of Ha'kan'ta's hand where their skin touched. The wind that raced across the mountains sped through him, leaving behind a hundred memories of where it had been and what it had seen/smelled/tasted/heard/sensed there.

Letting go of Ha'kan'ta's hand, he turned around and around, marvelling at how the world came ever sharper into focus. When at last he faced his companion again, her eyes caught his once more and she smiled.

"She comes," Ha'kan'ta said.

"She . . . ?"

"My totem," Ha'kan'ta said.

She pointed westward and he followed the direction she'd indicated with his gaze, seeing a golden thread flow from her finger, a bright glitter against the black and grey stones and the stark white snow. He might have become lost, following that thread, except that he then became aware that there *was* something there.

It was enormous. A great black shape with a wingspread so wide it could not be measured except that it seemed to fill the entire sky. Central in that spread of dark feathers were two watchful eyes, blacker still and glittering. The monstrous shape neither approached nor threatened. It merely regarded him un-movingly, spearing him with that intense gaze until Kieran could feel himself withering under it and panic set in once again.

Fear cut through him, sharp as a blade of ice, and just as cold. Where before each delightful sensation had been a mag-ical discovery, now he was gripped by a terror that multiplied a hundredfold and more, and would not let him go. He felt a scream tear from his throat.

"Be calm," Ha'kan'ta said, her voice coming as though from a great distance. "Learn her shape. Let your taw dance the Beardance."

But this was no bear, he wanted to tell her. How could he

learn the shape of her bear totem, when it hadn't come? He
wanted to turn to her, but those enormous eyes pinned him to
the rocks. He wanted to tell her that something else had come
in her totem's place, something dark and filled with...
menace....

His knees gave way suddenly and he would have fallen,
except that a long black feathered wing whispered through the
air and broke his fall. At that touch, his fear dissolved. Understanding leapt in him and he was ashamed that he'd been afraid.

There is no shame in knowing fear, a deep resonating voice
said in his mind. *All know fear when first they meet with me.*

Ha'kan'ta, Kieran began, replying in kind, thought to
thought. *She sees you as...*

Her own totem. And you?

A raven, Kieran said softly. *I see you as a raven.*

As he sent those words, the great bulk of shadows took on
a clearer shape. Kieran shivered, but no longer with fear. He
looked up into those dark orbs, saw the horns gracing the giant
bird's brow, creamy white against the black feathers, and he
shivered again.

Learn my shape, his totem said. *Lift your arms.*

Kieran did. He looked down and saw them shortening, his
fingers elongating, long and slender, skin webbed between
them, feathers forming, row on row. His back hunched, chin
disappearing as his nose and mouth became a beak. His eyes
shifted to the sides of his head. The feathering started as a
cloud of down on his chest and back, then thickened into rich
dark feathers. He tottered on new thin legs until his tail feathers
returned his balance. And all the while, a strange song pulsed
inside him—drum music that spoke with a melody more than
a rhythm, almost with words.

Come, his totem said. *Travel with me awhile.*

I...

Ride the winds, the raven said.

It had lifted its great wings to fill the sky above them. Winds,
set in motion by the movement of that enormous spread opening
tugged and pulled at Kieran until he stumbled, put out his arms
to catch his balance, only to remember they were gone, replaced
by wings. The feathers spread, caught the wind, and he was
lifted into the air.

Come, his totem said. *Learn the use of a Ravendance.*

Kieran looked down. *Nom de tout!* He was airborne! Flying!
Lord dying Jesus. He looked for Ha'kan'ta, but the mountaintop

was bare. He cried her name aloud, but the sound issued forth as a harsh caw that was lost in the wind.

Ha'kan'ta? he asked his totem.

A long wing pointed to the slopes that ran down from the crest of the mountain where Kieran's transformation had taken place. There he saw two bears playing in the snow, frolicking like a couple of young cubs.

Come, the raven said once again.

This time it dipped its wings and the wind bore it away. Copying its lead, Kieran banked his own wings, felt the powerful muscles in his shoulders work against the air's resistance, the rush of the wind through his feathers, and knew a wild peace. His totem cawed, a sound like thunder, and the two of them sped off, dipping and gliding, riding the air currents.

Expect nothing, Ha'kan'ta had told him. What she should have said, Kieran decided, was expect anything. Or everything.

He lifted his own harsh voice and heard the wind shred its echoes against the faces of the mountains. He had never known an experience such as this. Beyond the change in his body, beyond the new shape it wore, he sensed the forming of a mystical bond between himself and the great raven he followed. Now he knew what Ha'kan'ta had meant when she said her totem dwelled in the world of her heart. Deep within. He would never be alone again.

They flew as far and wide as the sky would take them. When they landed at last, on a high craggy tor the sides of which were too steep and wild to climb, but easy enough to reach by flight, Kieran regained his own shape and his totem took manshape as well. He stood tall and proud, with black feathers woven into his dark braids.

"You have been troubled," his totem said. "For some time now."

Memories returned in a flood and Kieran stumbled to sit on a rock before his legs gave way under him.

"I . . . killed a man," he said. "An innocent man."

"I know. And for all that it might seem that you were not directly responsible for that deed, you must still bear the shame of it. Life is precious—all life. But your troubling goes back further still."

Numbly, Kieran nodded. "When the old man disappeared."

"Further back still." His totem smiled sadly. "You chose

the wrong path. You have wasted many precious years. The bard's Way was never yours."

Kieran drew a few quick breaths to steady the drum of his heartbeat.

"What do you mean?" he asked. "I love music...."

"Music, yes. But it was not your Way, for all that you have accomplished with it. Your Way was the Way of the shaman. The magician's Way, though not its mage's aspect. Intuition, rather than ritual. Do you see?"

Kieran shook his head. There was no use in arguing. He knew enough about the Way's various aspects to know that only a shaman could have a totem.

"You are very strong," his totem said. "You could attain great heights and do much good. For others, as well as for yourself."

"By...defeating Mal'ek'a?"

"What will another death gain you?"

Slowly, Kieran nodded. The shock of killing one man already lay heavy on him.

"Nothing," he said softly.

"Just so."

"But what will I do?" Kieran asked.

"Grow."

"And Tom? What of him? And Sara?"

"Teach them how to protect themselves from themselves."

Kieran nodded again. His vision wavered with the motion of his head and he gripped the stone under him with a tight fist.

"It is time you returned," his totem said. "Do you know how to reach me now, should the need arise?"

"The Ravendance. I have to shape my taw to your dance."

"Just so."

The dark eyes glittered in the old man's face his totem wore.

"Tell my daughter, Ha'kan'ta," he said, "tell her that anger ill becomes her. As it ill becomes you, my son. Replenish the world with quiet wonder, not sorceries."

"And Mal'ek'a? What of him?"

"Those whose concern he is will deal with him."

"But what if...what if I can't stop myself or Ha'kan'ta from going after him?"

"You will do what you must," his totem replied. "But think before you hunt. You have killed one being. Will you be responsible for the deaths of more?"

"No," Kieran said. "But I've learned to defend myself."

His totem smiled bitterly. "Perhaps you learned that lesson too well. You struck like a thunderbolt. Acting with great speed on the strength of intuition, rather than thought. That is the warrior's Way, my son."

"But you said I should follow my intuition."

"Just so. But consider before you act."

"But . . ."

"Now it is time for you to go."

The man bowed over him, spreading his arms. As they enfolded Kieran, they became great wings, black-feathered and strong. Kieran knew a sense of dislocation as though the mountain under him had shifted out of sync with his body.

Visit with me again, a voice in his mind whispered, *now that you know the way. There is much I have to show you and always so little time. Always there is so little time. . . .*

The whisper echoed in the deepest recesses of Kieran's mind, as close to him as his own heartbeat. He heard again the sound of Ha'kan'ta's drum. He opened his eyes and looked up into hers. Residues of the drug that had sent him skywalking still remained, casting a magical aura around Ha'kan'ta's features.

"You journeyed far," she said and her voice sounded like soft bells.

Kieran's throat was dry and when he answered, his voice sounded scratchy.

"What did you give me?"

"A shaman's aid," Ha'kan'ta said, "to set you on your journey."

"The mushrooms. They were magic mushrooms?"

Ha'kan'ta nodded. Her hands came away from the drum and a sudden silence filled the glade. She cupped his face, tracing the lines of his cheekbones with soft fingers.

"I saw you fly," she said. "High above me while my totem and I played in the snow."

"You said I'd learn the Beardance."

"I thought you would. I was wrong. Your craftfather was wrong. You have your own totem, my warrior."

"I'm not a warrior. He . . . the raven told me that we should no longer hunt Mal'ek'a."

"I know. She told me as well. Yet we can still be both— shaman and warrior."

"You think we should continue?"

Ha'kan'ta shook her head. Her hands moved up his face to massage his temples.

"Let us leave such talk for another time. I would rather share another dance with you, Kieranfoy. We have journeyed far this evening, part of the way together. Out spirits are close at this moment. There is a dance amongst my people that is danced under blankets. Do you know its steps?"

She took her hands from his face and began to undo her braids. When she shook her hair free and leaned down once more, it fell about their faces in a dark cloud of curls. Her lips brushed against his.

Kieran pulled her down to him. Part of his soul still sang the song of the high winds and feathered flight. It reached out to her, merged into a dusky memory of fur and strength. She moved to lie on top of him and he felt her smile against his cheek.

Chapter Seven

"COLD. So cold."

Thomas Hengwr's eyes were open, but unfocused. Whatever he saw, it was not what those gathered about his sickbed saw. His was the look of one who was experiencing his own private vision of hell. While he trembled from an inner cold, his forehead was slick with perspiration. All Tucker could get out of him were those two words. Cold. So cold.

"Jesus!" he said, lifting his gaze to catch Traupman's. "What the hell's the matter with him?"

Traupman shrugged. "Severe shock, I'd say. Trauma caused by the severity of his injury, though . . ."

His voice trailed off and Tucker nodded. The scars on Hengwr's face looked about two weeks old.

"How long has he been like this?" Traupman asked.

"About fifteen minutes," Sally replied. "I didn't want to come down right away, but then . . . Well, he just kept getting worse. I got him another blanket and then I didn't know what to do."

She shot a glance at Jamie who smiled encouragingly. "You did the right thing," he said.

"Maybe I should get him a hot water bottle."

"I'll get it," Blue said.

"When we found him," Jamie said, "just after you left, Inspector, those scars were open wounds. You could *see* them healing."

"Self-healing or not," Traupman said, rising from the side of the bed, "we have to get this man to a hospital."

As though that was the key to bringing him back, Tom stirred. Tucker saw the glazed look leave the old man's eyes.

264

There was pain in them, but for the first time since they'd come into the room, Tom appeared to be aware of them.

"No . . . no hospital," he said.

Those were the eyes of a frightened man, Tucker thought.

"You're a sick man," Traupman told Tom, returning to sit on the bed. "You need medical attention."

"What is . . . wrong with me . . . no doctor can mend." His eyes clouded over and a violent tremor ran the length of his body. Fighting back the pain, he forced himself to continue speaking, his voice no more than a husky whisper. "I need . . . time. That is all. Time to drive it from me. The . . . shadow. . . ."

"Shadow?" Tucker knelt by the bed, his face near the old man's. "What shadow?"

"Death's shadow. Left a . . . shard of darkness . . . in me. The . . . the House is all that . . . that protects me now. Soon even it . . . won't be enough. If you take its . . . protection from me now . . . I . . . I won't survive the night. . . ."

"What's he talking about?" Tucker demanded.

Traupman shrugged and looked at Jamie.

"I told you," Jamie said. "He thinks the Welsh bard Taliesin is trying to kill him. The *long-dead* Welsh bard. You know. Like in Williams's 'Through Logres' and that sort of thing? That's all I know."

"That's what the Inspector told me," Traupman said. "But it doesn't make any—"

"No," Tom said weakly. "Not . . . not the bard. I was wrong. My foe is more . . . more terrible still. He almost slew me in . . . the Otherworld. Caught me off . . . guard. Would have killed me then had I not . . . not willed myself here. I left a changeling in my place. A thing of mud and twigs . . . made up in my shape, but it won't . . . it won't hold him long. Cold. So cold. . . ."

"Then who is it?" Tucker demanded. "Who did this to you? Tell me and we'll bring him in."

Were it not for the pain, Tom would have laughed. He tried to explain what it was that hunted him, but the words grew tangled with the cold and the pain. He could only repeat himself.

"No hospital," he said. "I . . . feel him near. Soon he will come and . . . nothing will protect me. So cold. Kieran . . . tell him. . . ."

Tucker stood up.

"So what do we do, Dick?" he asked.

Traupman pulled at his earlobe. Looking from the Inspector to Tom, he came to a decision.

"Leave him here," he said. "For now at least."

"You're buying this mumbo-jumbo, then?"

"I'm keeping an open mind." To Jamie, he added: "Are we going to be in the way? I'd like to stay right here with him until we can bring him around."

"Mind?" Jamie said. "Christ, no! It's all in your hands."

He moved closer to the head of the bed and leaned towards Tom.

"Did you find Sara, Tom?" he asked. "Where's Sara?"

For a moment there was no response. Then Tom shut his eyes fiercely as though blocking out some terrible sight.

"Where's Sara?" Jamie demanded, grabbing Tom's shoulder.

"Leave him be!" Tucker said.

"But he knows—"

"The Wren," Tom said suddenly, his voice strong for a moment. "She is with...tell her to beware of...of the... cold...."

His voice drifted off again.

"Come on," Tucker said, pulling Jamie gently but firmly away from the bed. The Inspector looked down at Tom's anguished features and could only shake his head and ask, "What the hell do you think he sees?"

"He knows where Sara is," Jamie tried to explain. "We've got to find out what he's done with her."

"Now's not the time," Traupman said. He moved between Jamie and Tucker and drew Jamie to a chair. "He's delirious. All you're going to get from him are snatches of whatever nightmares he's experiencing."

Jamie opened his mouth, then shut it. Resignedly, he stared at Tom's face and let out a long raspy sigh.

"What did he mean about the House protecting him?" Traupman asked.

Jamie blinked, looked away from Tom to focus on Traupman's features. There was something very calming about Dick Traupman.

"We told the Inspector," he said wearily. "Something attacked the House this morning. I guess it was whoever did that to Tom. It must have known he was here—even if we didn't— and was trying to finish off the job, I suppose. The only thing that kept it out was...well, I can't really explain it. It was as though the House itself was keeping it out. As though there was some sort of psychic shield or barrier that kept it at bay."

"I wish we could know for certain what it was," Traupman said, "if there is something in the House that can stop this—this evil, I suppose we should call it, for want of a better term. If we can find out what it is that stops it, perhaps we can use it to defeat it." He held up a placating hand to forestall Tucker's protest. "No, John. I've not gone off the deep end as you think the rest of them have. You might dissemble, but I know that's what you are thinking."

"I think we're all nuts," Tucker said.

"Be that as it may, there is still something here—something I can almost put my finger on—that lends credence to all the impossible things we've been told thus far. And I'll tell you this, John: If there *is* some Otherworldly monster coming, we'd damn well better be prepared for it when it comes."

"Jesus H. Christ!" Tucker shook his head. "You're serious, aren't you?"

Traupman shrugged. "I'm open to suggestions, John. What would you have us do?"

"I'd . . ."

Tucker looked at their faces. He read the seriousness in Traupman's and the fear that clouded Jamie and Sally's. He knew what Traupman meant. He could feel it too. There was something in the air—like the heaviness that preceded a storm. Something was coming and he couldn't say what. He didn't even want to think about it, except that it was his job and the sooner he got the fucking thing wrapped up, the happier he'd be. If only it didn't seem so . . . plausible. Last night, talking to Maggie, he seemed to have gotten the whole thing into some sort of rational perspective. Now . . . Well, now he just didn't know.

He tried to frame that into a sentence that he could say without coming off sounding like he'd commited himself to this insanity, but the words weren't there. Then Blue returned with the hot-water bottle and the moment was gone.

"Someone's here to see you," Blue told Tucker. "Door on Patterson side—about halfway down."

"To see me?"

"Yeah. A woman. Says her name's Margaret Finch and that you're expecting her. Nice-looking lady." Blue handed Sally the hot-water bottle and added, "You want me to show you the way?"

What the hell was Maggie doing here? Tucker asked himself. He glared at Blue as though the biker was to blame for her showing up. Besides, where did this grease monkey come off, anyway, saying she was nice-looking? What the hell did he know?

Okay, he told himself. Hold it right there. He remembered the message he'd left for her and realized that, rather than calling, she'd probably decided to just come on down. She was probably curious—hell, he *knew* she was curious—and wanted to have a look for herself.

"Yeah," he said to Blue politely, trying to suppress the animosity between them. "I could use a guide."

"The trouble with them," Traupman remarked as they left, "is that they are too much alike."

Sally looked up from the bed.

"You know," she said. "You're probably right."

She placed the hot-water bottle under Tom's feet and wiped his brow with a cloth.

Traupman shrugged.

"What scares me the most," he said, "is if Thomas Hengwr is all he's made out to be . . . well, I don't like to think of how powerful whatever it was that defeated him is."

"You should have been here this morning," Jamie said, then realized that what had almost come through the door then had probably been just a scout of some kind. If it had been the monster itself, he doubted that Blue would ever have gotten the door closed again.

Serge Morin rolled a cigar between his fingers as he watched the House. A half-full plastic container of tea was going cold on the dashboard of his Oldsmobile and the newspaper he'd been reading lay discarded on the seat beside him. Leaning his head back against the headrest, he sighed. He was getting old for this line of work. But it wasn't like the old days anymore. He never used to get bored. Maybe that was what getting old did to you: made you think too much. He was pushing forty-five now. And, *sacrement*, he just couldn't stop thinking. Sometimes at night, when he was looking out the window of his apartment, the faces of the men and women he'd killed came floating up out of the darkness. There was no accusation in their faces. That was what bothered him the most. They just looked like they were waiting. For him.

He glanced at his watch. He'd been here three hours already. He wondered when—

As if on cue, he looked in the rearview mirror to see Phillip Gannon's tan Chevy pull in behind his Olds. Michel Chevier stepped out, and as the Chevy pulled away Gannon raised his hand. Morin nodded to him, then reached across to unlock his own passenger door. Chevier slid in.

"How's it been?" he whispered.

His odd voice was a reminder of a bullet he'd taken in the throat back when he was running a numbers racket for the Pellier Brothers in Montreal. The bullet had been their way of retiring him. Trouble was, he'd survived. The Pelliers—Jacques, Raymond and Phillipe—hadn't.

"Quiet," Morin said. "Tucker showed up with an old guy in tow about forty-five minutes ago. I thought we were moving in before he showed up again?"

"The old guy'll be Traupman," Chevier said. "Gannon was expecting him to show up with Tucker. Anybody else?"

"Nothing since then except for this knockout brunette about five minutes ago. She came in a cab and it didn't wait."

"Wonder who she is?" Chevier thought aloud.

"I don't know, but it's getting congested in there—and people remember faces. What do you know about this place?"

"Not much. But we'll be finding out. Gannon's just gone to give Walters a call. Word is we'll be moving in very soon."

"What about Tucker?"

Chevier shrugged. He popped a mint in his mouth, offered one to Morin before he put them away. "Word on Tucker is that he's outlived his usefulness. Walters wanted him played out on a line, but Gannon's sure that our main target is tucked away in there somewhere, so who needs the horseman now?"

"In there?" Morin asked, indicating the House. "Hengwr's in there?"

"That's what Gannon says. Who's watching the other sides of this place?"

"Bull's on O'Connor. Mercier's parked where he can watch Clemow and the park."

"Five of us, then," Chevier mused. "Enough for everybody."

These days Morin was easy to ruffle and something about Chevier's voice always set his nerves on edge. He figured there were maybe seven or eight people in the House. How many

of them were going to be looking back at him through his
window tonight? "Should be enough," he agreed, keeping his
voice even.

Chevier smiled. "You got anything besides that toy on you?"

Morin looked down at his cigar. The camouflaged blow-
gun was his trademark. It was quick, clean and silent. The
fléchettes were small enough so that even if you didn't retrieve
them, they were rarely found. All you had to remember was
not to inhale when you had the mouthpiece up against your
lips.

He felt like asking Chevier if he wanted a drag from the
cigar, but only nodded. He opened his jacket and pulled a .32
caliber Margolin target pistol a few inches out of his shoulder
holster, then let it drop back into place.

"Nice. Russian training piece?"

"You got it. But I prefer the darts." He wondered if Hogue's
face was already waiting for him at his window.

Chevier shrugged. He carried a Smith & Wesson .38 Chiefs
Special himself. For quiet work, he had a throwing knife strapped
to his left wrist and another hanging between his shoulder
blades. Morin had worked with him twice before.

"So now..." Morin began.

"Now we wait."

Chevier popped another mint into his mouth and chewed it
thoughtfully.

"Maggie, what are you doing here?"

"Come to give my favorite cop some moral support."

"This isn't a game," Tucker said.

"I know," she replied seriously. "That's why I'm here. I
don't want to sit at home, waiting to hear about another 'armed
robbery' on the late news."

"There's not going to be any trouble."

"Then there's no problem with my being here, is there?
Besides, I'd like to meet this Jamie Tams that you've been
talking about." Pointedly she looked at Blue.

"Sorry," Tucker muttered. "This is Glen Far—"

"Blue. Just Blue is fine." He was sick to death of hearing
Glen Farley thrown at him. But he *was* enjoying the Inspector's
discomfort with his ladyfriend; unfortunately, Tucker had one
thing right. "Nice to meet you, ma'am. I'm sure Jamie'd like
to say hello too, but the Inspector's right. This is *not* a good
place to be right now."

"It's all for real then, isn't it?" Maggie asked, looking from one to the other, gauging their reactions with a lawyer's eye.

"Too real." Blue glanced out the window. "Anybody got the time?"

"A little after five."

Blue shook his head. "Well, I hope to hell that it's just the dusk settling in that's making it so dark out there. But I've got a bad feeling..."

Tucker followed Blue's gaze and frowned. "Let's go see how our patient's doing," he said.

"Sure." Blue stopped long enough to pick up a large orange tabby that had wandered into the hall. "Nobody feeding you, big fella?" Then he looked from the cat to Tucker and smiled. "Hey, Inspector. Want to meet a namesake? His name's Tuck."

Tucker glanced at the cat, then caught Maggie's grin.

Blue ruffled the cat's fur, then thought of Sara. The smile on his lips died.

"C'mon," he said.

Letting the cat down, he headed for the stairs.

"Morin?"

Gannon's voice sounded thin coming through the Oldsmobile's cheap speaker grill.

"Yeah?"

"We're heading in. Leave the car where it is and hoof it down to O'Connor. We'll meet you there. Got that?"

"Sure thing."

Switching off the radio, Morin turned to his companion. "You all set?"

Chevier nodded. Morin looked down at the cigar he was still holding and stuck it away in the front pocket of his jacket. "Then let's go," he said.

"Why honey?" Sally asked.

Following Traupman's instructions, she was heating a large tablespoonful by the light of a fat candle.

"It's supposed to impart fertility and vigor," Jamie explained.

Traupman nodded. "The ancients imagined that bees had a parthenogenic origin," he said, "which made honey an uncontaminated sacred food. We'll mix it with mistletoe, which was the Golden Bough of the druids and the followers of Aeneas. It's like we're getting double our money."

Jamie had been surprised they'd had any mistletoe lying around. Though the House was liable to have a bit of everything, stored away somewhere in its labyrinth. You just had to know where to look—and it seemed that the House wasn't above giving you a little nudge in the right direction. He'd gone looking for Fred just now and took a wrong turn that delivered him into the room where the Christmas decorations were stacked in boxes behind a sofa.

"You don't think it's too stale, do you?" Jamie asked, watching Traupman grind the old leaves into an uneven powder.

"Magical things never go stale," Traupman said.

I hope, he added to himself. He wasn't sure why he was going through with this. It wasn't as though he actually expected it to work. But it was good to have a task.

"You have to go about these things just right," he added.

He glanced out the window, then at Jamie. It was getting dark outside. Very quickly. But no one made mention of the fact.

"That's about it," he said. "Is the honey hot yet?"

Sally nodded.

"Bring it here, would you please?"

Jamie watched Traupman stir the mixture of warmed honey and ground mistletoe together in a small glass, not really sure what he expected. A flash of light? A strange smell? But all Traupman ended up with was a cloudy mixture flecked with dark bits of the mistletoe. He held it up to the light, then moved to the bed with it.

"Place feels weird," Morin offered.

"Forget how it feels," Gannon told him. "Just pop that lock so that we can get in off the street."

"Sure. No problem."

There were five of them on one of the House's Clemow Avenue porches, standing around while Morin worked the lock on the door with a set of master keys. The lock was a Weiser— old, but common. The sixth key Morin tried produced a satisfying click.

"Alarms?" he asked.

Gannon shook his head.

"Then we're in."

Morin turned the knob and, standing to one side, eased the door a crack. He remained still for a moment, then pushed it completely open with the toe of his shoe. As he crossed the threshold, an eerie prickling raised the hairs at the nape of his neck. He stood aside as the other four men entered, then shut the door behind them. As they spread out in the hallway, Morin glanced out the small window set high in the door. It seemed a lot darker outside than it had a moment ago—as though a sudden storm had blown up.

"A final briefing," Gannon was saying quietly. "No fireworks. Just keep it clean. Round up anybody you find and bring them back here."

Morin's gaze traveled down the length of the door. The wood looked different than it had a moment ago. He had the weird feeling that if they'd waited a minute or so longer, they'd never have gotten in.

"What about Tucker?" the loose-jowled man called Bull asked. "He's not gonna stand around and pick his nose while we're doing that."

"You let me worry about Tucker," Gannon said.

Bull shrugged. Still at the door, Morin shook his head. Mother Mary, he *was* getting too old for this kind of work. He was never one to get a case of nerves before a job, but that's what the jittery feeling he was experiencing had to be. He reached out a hand to touch the door. The wood was hard and smooth against his fingers. Nothing weird about it. It was just in him.

"What's Walters want with this guy, anyway?" Robert Mercier asked. He was a stocky man, an ex-middleweight fighter who'd gotten too old for the ring, but not too old for a little strong-arm work. Gannon had passed around a photo of Thomas Hengwr earlier and Mercier called the old man's features up in his mind's eye.

"You let me and Mr. Walters worry about that," Gannon told him. "Mike, you take the right corridor. Bob, the left. Serge and I'll handle the upstairs."

"And me?"

"You stay here, Bull. Anybody comes by, collar them. You can store them—" He looked around the hallway and, opening the first door on the right, settled on that room. "Store them in here, okay? Now let's get moving."

Traupman slid his hand under Tom's head and lifted it, bringing the glass with the honey-mistletoe mixture up to the old man's lips. Then the lights went out.

Outside the windows, the sky went utterly black. The candlelight flickered, the one small flame throwing strange shadows across the room. Then a pale luminescence started up along the baseboards and where the walls met the ceiling. That light was all that kept Jamie from losing himself to the sudden fear that gripped him.

His heart pounded, but he knew that the light meant that the House was ready to meet this new attack. It would protect them. He opened himself to the House, reaching out to try and regain that sense of oneness he'd felt with it last night, and it came, quick and sure, like a hand fitting a well worn glove. And then he sensed the presence of outsiders in the House. Not just Tucker and the two that were here because of him, but others . . . scattered through the halls.

"Keep back from the windows," Traupman told Sally.

Sally nodded and moved back. Traupman raised the glass to Tom's lips again, but at that moment the old man sat up, throwing the glass to one side with a reflexive move of his hand. It shattered on the floor.

"It's come!" Tom cried.

He pushed past Traupman to get off the bed, but only sprawled on the floor, shaking with fever. When Traupman grabbed hold of him to pull him back onto the bed, Tom's skin felt like ice to the touch.

Tom fought Traupman's grip. Sparks leaped between his fingers and Traupman threw himself back from the old man. He remembered what Tucker had told him about the constable who had died in Patty's Place. Where *was* Tucker?

He heard a footstep outside in the hall and turned to the door. He only got one glimpse of the stranger that stood framed in the doorway—a tall, broad-shouldered man with a gun in his hand—then the House shook as though someone had let off a bomb under it and he was thrown to the floor.

"Shit!" Blue said as the lights went dead.

He went up the stairs two at a time and burst onto the upper landing to skid on a loose rug. By the pale green light that ran along the baseboards and ceiling ridges, he made out a figure standing by the door of the Gramarye's Clover where he'd left Sally and the others. Jesus Christ! he thought. They're already in! Then he realized it was a man he saw, not a monster. He started down the hall, making for the figure, when the first blast rocked the House.

He caught himself from falling, one hand knocking a painting from the wall in the process. He heard the crash of breaking glass as it smashed beside him. Down the hall, he saw the stranger turn in his direction. Light spat from the end of his outstretched hand and then the boom of a gunshot echoed in the close confines of the hall. Blue threw himself flat and heard the slug whine by over his head.

"Stay down!" Tucker shouted from behind him.

Rolling to one side, Blue looked up to see the stranger running down to the far end of the hall. Tucker fired twice from behind him, but another tremor shook the House and both shots went wild. Before the echoes had died away, Blue was on his feet and running for the bedroom.

"Anybody hurt?" he asked.

The House rocked again, but he saw that though they were as shaken up as he was, nobody had been hurt. He glanced down the empty hall. Who the fuck had that been anyway? Pushing himself back from the door, he ducked into Jamie's study and came out in time to meet Tucker and Maggie. The Inspector looked down at the Weatherby that was now in Blue's hand.

"You know how to use that?" he asked.

Blue nodded. "You keep watch here. I'm going to go nail that fucker."

"Wait a minute—"

"I know the layout. You don't. So I'm going. No arguments, got it? I'm not one of your bully-boys that you can lay orders on."

"Now, listen up—" Tucker began.

"Tucker," Maggie said, laying her hand on the Inspector's arm.

The Inspector nodded. He started to frame what he had to say so it wouldn't come out so abrasively, but it got lost in the sudden turmoil that followed. They braced themselves as another series of shocks ran through the House. Then they heard Sally scream and the room where she and the others were gathered was flooded with a sudden sharp light, as piercing bright as a lightning bolt. Blue turned to see Tom rolling on the floor, the light coming from him, pouring out of the pores of his skin; then abruptly it died and he lay still in the House's faint illumination.

"Jesus," Blue said. "Is he . . . ?"

"Not dead," Traupman replied, gingerly kneeling beside the old man. He pointed to one side of the room that was blackened and charred. "We're lucky he didn't hit one of us."

They spent the next few minutes stamping out sparks, the job made more difficult by the constant shifting of the House under the continuing barrage. The air was close with the smell of burnt wood.

"I'm going," Blue said, picking up his rifle. "You folks stay put."

Tucker looked like he was going to protest again, then said simply, "Keep him alive. Dead, we don't learn anything."

"Hey. I didn't see you aiming for the sky, Inspector."

Before Tucker could reply, Jamie spoke up. "There's more than one of them," he said.

He swallowed, trying to say more, but his link with the House had grown stronger and he felt each barrage of shocks as the House did—as though someone was pummeling every inch of his body. And the blast of Tom's magefire had burned him like a blowtorch, though there was no physical evidence of what he was undergoing.

"How do you know?" Blue asked.

Jamie shook his head. "I . . . I just know. Don't go, Blue. There's too many of them. If they're in league with whatever's attacking us . . ."

He felt the shadows beating at the walls of the House, the claws tearing the wood of its doors, the blind mad hunger of the creatures as they attacked.

"Yeah," Blue said. "And what if they're not? What if they wanted something else and open a door right now and let the monsters in?"

"Yes, but—"

Blue shook his head. "Wizards don't need guns. I don't know who the fuck these guys are, Jamie, but guns I can handle."

Before anyone could raise another objection, he was out of the room, heading down the hall. He hugged the walls, bracing himself when the shock tremors hit. This is fucking crazy, he thought. At each doorway, he paused, waiting for lulls in the attack so that he could check the room out. His familiarity with the House gave him a sense akin to Jamie's new perceptions. He *knew* if there was someone in each one or not, before he ever poked his head around the doorway.

Trusting this instinct, he made good time going down the hall. And while his hands were filled with the weight of his Weatherby, under his breath he muttered the words to the Blessing Way that Charlie Nez had taught him down in New

Mexico. He didn't know how much good it would do, but at this point he'd give anything a try.

Gannon's first thought when the lights died was: They've got the place booby-trapped. He didn't know how or why, but there was a very sophisticated security system in operation here. It had let them get in, but now it was going to play games with them . . . at least until a mop-up squad came to pick them up.

He paused just beyond the door of the room from which he'd heard voices, momentarily indecisive. Then he moved into the doorway and the first shock wave hit. He saw the room full of startled people and registered the fact that they were as surprised by the disturbances as he was, then turned to see a big man in a T-shirt and jeans coming at him from the far end of the hall. He got off one shot, saw Tucker appear behind the first man, and beat a hasty retreat. Tucker's shots ploughed into the walls on either side of him. This wasn't going well at all. What the hell was going on?

The sudden dark, the weird lighting, and the shocks rattling the House just didn't make any kind of sense. He began to get the first inkling then of just what it was that Walters had gotten him into. He'd never believed in what Walters was so intent upon gaining, but for the first time he began to question whether or not such things might actually exist.

When he got to the far end of the hall, he chose a room at random and ducked into it. It gave him an excellent vantage point if Tucker or one of the others decided to follow him. It would also give him a chance to get hold of Morin, who should be retreating as well, and get them all the hell out of here.

He glanced at the room's windows and shook his head. It was so black out there. He couldn't see a thing. How had they opaqued the windows like that? And the lighting. . . . It just didn't make sense. He braced himself as a new series of tremors threatened to spill him to the floor.

Outside the House, the being that the quin'on'a had named Mal'ek'a, the Dread-That-Walks-Nameless, watched its tragg'a storm the structure. Mal'ek'a was weak in the World Beyond, but Tamson House straddled more than one world. Here in a plane of the Otherworld, Mal'ek'a's powers were strong. Here, given time, it could peel the House's defense as though it were no more than a crayfish's shell and tear its enemy from within.

For the druid was here, the enemy. Hurt. Helpless. Mal'ek'a

could taste his presence. He had escaped too often, but would not do so again.

The tragg'a, whose shape Mal'ek'a wore, clawed at the House, rocking its foundations as they swarmed about it. Watching, Mal'ek'a knew that force alone would not tear that protection from his enemy. At least not quickly enough. But there were other methods. Spells to counter spells. The House was here now, in the Otherworld, and here it would stay. There would be no escape for the beings trapped within it, no fleeing into the World Beyond where Mal'ek'a's powers were not strong yet.

Inside, amongst the druid's companions, there would be one whose mind Mal'ek'a could reach. One to control that would crack the shell of the House for it. It need only sift through the minds of those beings to find the one that would suit its purposes.

Bull was staring at the painting of a young woman when the House's lights died. He'd been fantasizing about her, rubbing the wart under his left eye as he imagined her smooth skin under his hands. The skin that would be crisscrossed with welts when he was done with her. He could feel the give in her body as he dug his nails into her, could hear the terror in her voice as she pleaded with him.

A drop of spittle eased out of the corner of his mouth, but then the lights gave out and he was sitting in utter darkness, the fantasy stopped dead as he stood clawing his .32 from its holster under his armpit. The faint luminescence that started up gave him a creepy feeling, but at least he could see. Then the House shook and he was knocked to the floor. Above the din, he heard pistol shots. Three of them.

Crouching on the floor, his revolver ready in his hand, he tried to figure out what was going on. The shots must be bright-ass Gannon running into someone—probably Tucker.

Bull wasn't sure what he should do. Gannon had told him to stay put, but what if Gannon was out of the picture? There was no way he was sticking around to shoot it out with a squad of horsemen. On the other hand. . . . The House rocked again, but this time he was better prepared for it and kept his balance. What the fuck was going on? He was about to start up the stairs when he thought he heard someone call his name.

He turned, looked all around. Nothing. No one. Then why

did he have the creepy feeling that there was someone near? It was like there was someone in his head. "That you, Bob?"

He looked down the left corridor that Mercier had taken. There was no reply. Nothing there. Only that creepy feeling. He swung his gun slowly from left to right, straining his eyes in the dim lighting.

"Stop fucking around!" he ordered. "Who's there?"

Then it came, echoing inside his head like a bad dream. He had a sudden wild feeling, like he was soaring high on coke, aware, but buzzing. He turned to the door and looked into the blackness beyond its windows. Something out there wanted in. The House shuddered as a series of concussions shook it. Regaining his balance, Bull started for the door.

"It's quiet," Tucker said.

There'd been nothing for five minutes now. Just the silence.

"Too quiet," he added, checking the window. It didn't feel like this was the end; more like a lull between attacks.

With Sally and Maggie's help, Traupman got Tom back onto the bed. Jamie was sitting in a chair, his features drawn and haggard, a cold pipe lying forgotten in his hand. Tucker stood by the door, his .38 in his hand; he'd replaced the two spent shells. Sticking his head out the door, he could just make out Blue at the far end of the hallway.

Take it slow, he thought. He looked back into the room. Since it was so quiet now, maybe he should go after the biker. But Jamie had said that there was more than one intruder. He didn't know how Tams knew that, but everything else had been happening like he'd said it would. Blue was doing okay on his own. No point in him going out there and confusing matters.

Just gotta wait, he told himself. But Christ, he hated waiting.

Before Blue turned the corner, he hunkered down against the wall and had a think. One of them was there. He could *feel* him. Not on the landing itself, but in one of the rooms that opened out onto it. The thing was, which room? And how did he plan to handle it? He was just pissed off enough to blow the fucker away, but knew there was no way he could get away with it. Not with the Inspector just down the hall. So how did he flush the guy out and get the drop on him?

The real trouble was, Blue realized, was that he just wasn't cut out for this kind of thing anymore. Physically he could handle it. But his head just wasn't in that space anymore. Six, seven years ago, this would've been a game and he'd have no problem playing his hand. But now, after living with Jamie and Sara all these years . . .

His eyes went flat as he thought of Sara. What if these guys had something to do with her disappearance? In the space of a heartbeat, his whole headspace changed. Not cut out for this kind of thing, was he? He worked the bolt on his Weatherby and the first bullet snapped into place. Like fuck he wasn't.

He came around the corner in a roll, caught a sense of motion behind the door where Gannon was hiding, and fired straight through it. High. The boom of the big rifle was loud in the hall. Before its echoes had died away, Blue worked the bolt again and had the muzzle leveled at the door.

"That was just to show you it was loaded," he called out. "Now are you gonna come easy, or in pieces?"

Well back from the door, Gannon regarded the hole that the Wembley's big 500-grain round-nose bullet had torn through the door. That wasn't Tucker out there, and whoever it was knew how to use his weapon. It'd only be a matter of moments before he got lucky with a shot. There was nothing in this room to stop one of those bullets. Placing his .44 on the floor, he kicked it through the partially open door.

"You've got three seconds to follow that thing," Blue warned. "Hands behind your head. Let's go. One . . ."

The man that came out of the room was a complete stranger to him. He was big and moved with a pantherlike grace. His eyes regarded Blue expressionlessly.

"That's far enough," Blue said. He used the muzzle of the Weatherby to indicate where he wanted Gannon to stop. "Now I want some answers and don't stop to think about them. Who are you and what the fuck are you doing here?"

Gannon had no intention of telling the truth. He opened his mouth, the lie ready, when he caught a movement at the other end of the hall. Thinking back on it later, Blue wasn't sure if he heard something, or if it was the flicker in Gannon's eyes that warned him. All he knew was he had to move. Fast.

Something whispered through the air as he threw himself back, something small and deadly that hit the wall behind him with a slight chunking sound. He was turned around enough to see the man at the other side of the landing. The second stranger spat what looked like a cigar from his mouth and was drawing bead with a .22. There was no way Blue was going to get the Weatherby up in time, no way he could move that fast.

Then he heard Tucker's .38 fire right beside him, saw the man lift into the air a few inches, then smash against the wall, a red stain blossoming on his chest. Gannon dove for the stairs. Shaking his head to clear the thunder from it, Blue brought the Weatherby up from his hip, finger tightening on the trigger.

"We want him alive!" Tucker shouted. "One of them at least!"

The Inspector pushed by him and raced for the stairs, Blue hard on his heels. They saw Gannon reach the bottom, saw another man there with his back to them, his hand on the doorknob.

"The door!" Blue bellowed.

Tucker skidded to a stop, tried to draw bead, but he was too late. Bull opened the door and then all hell broke loose.

The first of the tragg'a tore Bull in two with a crisscross swipe of its taloned forepaws. Gannon froze. His mind went blank for precious seconds as he tried to assimilate what he saw. This. Just. Couldn't. Be. Real.

Then both Tucker and Blue opened fire. The first tragg'a smashed back into the two behind it, but the press of the creatures pushed the slain one aside and they came in with a rush. The stench of them clouded the air. They howled as the two men on the stairs rained bullets on them. Three of them were down, but there seemed to be no end to them. Four down. Tucker's .38 ran out of shells. He leaped down the last few stairs, swinging the useless gun into the face of the nearest monster. It broke all the creature's teeth. Dropping to one side, Tucker rolled out of the way of its talons, drove the gun into its side, his knee into its abdomen.

"The door!" Blue shouted, trying to get Gannon's attention. He couldn't shoot for fear of hitting Tucker. "Shut the fucking door!"

He came down the stairs swinging his rifle like it was a club. At the sound of Blue's voice, Gannon's momentary paralysis dissolved. He moved forward like a tiger, hands moving in a blur. The first tragg'a he hit in the throat with a clawed blow that took out half the creature's windpipe. He broke the taloned paw that was coming for his own chest, sidestepped, dropkicked a second of the monsters, then had his back to the door. Muscles straining, he put everything he had into shutting it, but the press of the tragg'a was too great. There were just too many of the creatures.

For Chevier, who was the first of Gannon's surviving men to reach the foyer, it was like stepping into a scene from Dante's *Inferno*. He took it in, leveled his revolver and opened fire. Mercier, arriving on the further side a half second later, followed suit.

As the ranks of the tragg'a broke under the crossfire, Blue, reeling from a dozen lacerations, fought his way to Gannon's side. Together, they started to shut the door. When Tucker joined them a moment later, they managed to close it all the way. Blue shot the bolt home. Chevier stepped in closer and emptied his gun into one of the tragg'a that Gannon had only knocked down. Snapping out the spent clip, he dug into his pocket for another.

A sudden stillness settled over the foyer. Blue swayed and dropped to one knee. Gannon and his two men eyed the Inspector who was all too aware of his empty .38 lying there on the floor amongst the dead creatures. Then the House shook as though a giant had taken it up in his hand and rattled it.

Not one of them kept his feet. They were thrown against the corpses of the tragg'a, the stench making them gag. They bounced on the floor like rag dolls. The remaining furniture slid around or overturned; broken glass from framed prints and vases spattered against walls and crunched into corners. And then it was over. Silence, pregnant with danger, fell.

"Mary, Mother of God!" Mercier intoned in a dull voice, taking in the chaos about him.

Nobody moved. They waited for it to begin again. Waited for the door to burst open under the press of the creatures. The seconds dragged out and then the House's pale luminescence faded and electric lighting flickered into life.

"Thank Christ," Tucker said. He looked at Blue. "Is it over?"

Blue cocked his head, listening. "That's the reserve generator that's cut in," he said. "I put it on automatic."

"Which means?"

"The House's got its own generators in case of . . . well, power failure or something."

"It's starting to get light outside," Gannon said. He got up and looked distastefully at the mess on his clothes.

"I don't like this," Blue said.

Across from him, Chevier whispered: "Is that so?" His voice was heavy with irony.

Blue shook his head. This . . . this slaughter wasn't what he'd meant. When the door had been open, he'd sensed something outside, something so filled with evil that he'd felt his soul shriveling up inside him. That sensation, though lessened, was still with him. It settled as a deep terrifying dread as he fought his way to his feet. Stepping over one of the dead tragg'a, he looked out the window and went numb. Tucker, sensitive to every nuance at the moment, his whole body still charged with adrenaline, moved towards the biker.

"What's wrong?" he began, then looking outside, he swore. "Jesus H. Christ!" he muttered.

He turned suddenly and Chevier's gun rose to cover him.

"Put it away, Mike," Gannon said. He looked at the Inspector. "I think we better talk."

He too could see what they'd seen. Outside, where O'Connor street should have been, there was a field of tall grass. Beyond it, a forest. He didn't know where they were, but they sure as hell weren't in Ottawa.

Tucker regarded him coldly. With stiff movements, he retrieved his .38, reloaded it and returned it to its holster on his hip. "I don't think you're going to believe it."

Gannon looked from the window to the dead tragg'a. "Try me."

Tucker, following Gannon's gaze, nodded. But before he could speak, Mercier asked:

"How's that door going to hold back these . . . these . . . What the fuck are these things, anyway?"

"The door will hold."

They turned at Jamie's voice to see him coming down the stairs with Traupman.

"You guys okay?" Blue asked. "Sally? Ms. Finch?"

Jamie nodded. "All of us. But only barely. The bookshelf came off the wall and just about did us in." He nodded to the window. "We're in trouble." His voice was tight with strain.

"How's that door going to keep them out?" Mercier wanted to know. "Shit, how come they don't just bust through a window?"

"The House has some form of shield around it that repels them," Traupman explained. "When the door was open, it broke that shield, allowing the creatures entrance. Closed, they can't get at us. They can't get in."

"And we can't get out," Blue said. "Jesus. There's nothing to go 'out' to. Where are we?"

"In Tom's Otherworld, I'd have to say." Traupman looked worn out.

"Thomas Hengwr *is* here?" Gannon asked.

"So that's what you're doing here," Tucker said. "What do you want with him? Who're you working for?"

"We have bigger problems than that at the moment," Traupman said wearily. "Those things will be back. God help us. The horror's real and it's only just begun."

For long moments, no one said a thing. Tucker broke the silence finally.

"We're up shit creek," he said.

Blue nodded. "Without a paddle."

Mal'ek'a allowed his enemy's allies their reprieve. Withdrawing, it left a small pack of tragg'a to keep them from wandering beyond the confines of the House, and turned its attention to other matters.

It did not understand its need to destroy the druid; it only knew that it was a thing that must be done. It had considered itself powerful enough to crack the House, especially attacking it here in its Otherworldly presence, and understood finally that the House was too strong for it still.

Mal'ek'a's perceptions returned to the fall of the Weirdin bones that the druid had thrown in that glade just before Mal'ek'a had cut him down. The other being, the Maiden, had the power it needed. She was small and untutored in the Way. She would be easy prey. And with the power it would take from her, it would return to confront the druid for one last time.

So Mal'ek'a withdrew and cast out its tragg'a to seek a new scent, much as a fisherman might cast his lines. Urgency was not a question. Only fulfillment was. And only with the druid dead would Mal'ek'a be fulfilled.

PART THREE

Warriors and Huntsmen

Things cannot disappear;
they can only change.

—J.W. VON GOETHE

Chapter One

SARA learned, as she willed herself to Taliesin's side for the second time, that traveling between worlds, and especially year-walking, has its own rules. The one she was taught this time was that one shouldn't attempt it too often in quick succession.

Firm ground took shape underfoot, but her legs were too weak to hold her and her senses in too much of a whirl for her to keep her balance. She pitched forward into wet seaweed, her temples pulsing with needle-sharp pains. If she'd had anything in her stomach, she would have lost it. As it was, all she could do was curl up in a fetal position and press the palms of her hands against her temples until the piercing pain subsided to a bearable ache.

When she thought she could move without having her head fall off, she slowly uncurled, sat up even more slowly, and took stock of her surroundings. Her vision blurred through a curtain of tears. Not until she'd wiped her eyes dry on the end of her cloak and then wrapped the damp folds of cloth about her was she sufficiently composed to take stock of her situation.

She was still on the coast, though where on the coast, she wasn't sure. The sky was overcast; she couldn't tell if the still-wet intertidal zone she was in was left behind by a morning or an afternoon tide. Under that grey pall, the sky looked cold and uninviting. Behind her the land rose steeply, a patchwork of fissured limestone cliffs and black spruce. To her right, the cliffs came right down into the water. On her left was a salt marsh. All around her, twisted pieces of driftwood and brackish seaweed dotted the inlet's shore.

Wrong again, she thought, but she wasn't about to try a third time. At least not right away.

She sat quietly for another few moments, pushing back the disappointment that threatened to start a new flood of tears. Back at the quin'on'a lodge she'd felt very brave and sure of herself. But right now, alone God knew where—God knew *when*—she just wanted to give it all up. What was she trying to prove anyway? That she was as much a wizard as Kieran and the rest of them?

She thought of Jamie and Blue and how they must be worrying. She'd been gone for days—at least it had been days for her. Kieran had said something about time passing differently in the Otherworld and the one that they were native to.

God it was confusing.

She bit at her lower lip to stop its quivering, then got angry with herself. Okay, she said. So it didn't work again. It wasn't as though she was an expert. Her major mistake was in expecting everything to work out, one, two, three. She'd rest up a bit and give it another go. But not until this headache was completely gone.

A half-dozen yards from where she sat, a herring gull landed to regard her quizzically. She used to have very romantic notions about gulls—they were the gypsies of the sea, wild and free, housing the ghosts of sailors and smugglers and other such interesting people. That had pretty well vanished the first time she'd traveled east and seen them fighting over garbage around the harborfronts and fishing boats. But sitting here, a million miles and years from the world she knew, that old notion returned.

This gull's feathers looked clean and well groomed. It had a jaunty eye, like an old mariner's, and a lift to its step that made her smile.

Standing on legs that were still a little wobbly, she caught up her guitar case and looked around. Her gull wasn't alone in the sky above her. Others dipped and bobbed in the grey air. She saw black guillemots by the water where the limestone cliffs plunged into the sea. A double-crested cormorant flew straight inland from the sea. She watched its flight and then paused, pulse quickening, when she saw a trail of smoke up on the clifftop.

So she wasn't alone.

Even remembering who her last trail of smoke had led her to, the way her luck was running today, whoever was tending that fire wouldn't be a red-haired bard from old Wales. Indecisively, she stood and stared, weighing her options. There

weren't very many and they didn't take her long to go through.
Either it was Taliesin's fire, or it wasn't. She could either wait
here and never know, or she could go have a look. She glanced
skyward. The sky was darkening more and it was probably
going to rain soon. She sighed. Standing around here wasn't
going to get her anywhere.

Once the decision was made, she almost wished she hadn't
made it. It was one thing to decide to saunter up and have a
look; but quite another to claw her way up through the dense
undergrowth, and slip and slide on the limestone. She wished
she didn't have her guitar to lug around with her. She wished
that whoever'd made that fire could have had the common
decency to build it on a nice convenient beach instead of on
top of the world. She wished that she'd never gotten out of
bed that morning that she'd found the ring, wished she'd never
found the ring in the back of The Merry Dancers. (Well, that
wasn't exactly true, but she was in a grumbly mood.)

Three-quarters of an hour later, breathing hard and more
disheveled then ever, she reached the crest of the cliff. She
pushed her guitar up ahead of her and crawled the last couple
of feet to collapse on a slab of limestone that broke the solid
line of old spruces that stalked the skyline. Like a fool, she
looked back down the way she'd come and almost toppled over
as the sudden feeling of vertigo swam through her.

She'd come up *that?*

She leaned back on the stone to catch her breath, then forced
herself to her feet with a soft groan and headed west along the
clifftop to find the fire. There wasn't as much underbrush up
top as there had been on the way up, but the low branches of
the spruce snarled in her hair and tugged at her cloak. It was
hard to go quietly.

One thing Sara'd learned from her adventures so far was
that one never got what one expected. And so . . . pushing aside
a heavy bough, she found herself looking into a small clearing.
The building that stood just back from the lip of the cliff took
her by surprise.

Of course, she thought, looking at the structure. What else
would I expect to find here?

It was a small round tower, about twenty feet in diameter
and two stories high. The foundations were stone, the walls
timber with wattle chinking, the roof turfed. It was old and
looked as though it belonged on a heathy cliff watching the
sea from the shores of old Ireland, rather than sitting here, the

grey stone greyer still in the dying light, surrounded by black spruce and cedar.

It was very quiet around her. The sea on the rocks far below was a distant sound. Behind the grey cloud cover, the sun finally sank, and twilight edged into night. As though that was a signal, the forest awoke around her.

The trees seemed to stir their earth-laden roots, and rattled their branches like sabers in the wind. Things rustled in the undergrowth. Then a howl tore through the forest—a primal reverberation of savagery given throat and loosed on the world to wake what terror it might. Goosebumps lifted on Sara's skin. Then hard on the heels of that howl, coming like a balm against the pain encompassed in that wailing cry, she heard the clear bell-like notes of a harp, underscored by a soft drumming.

Fear and hope ran through Sara. Heightened senses filled the night with terrors, while the tower beckoned like a sudden haven. She tore across the clearing like an arrow loosed from a bow, her guitar case bouncing against her thigh, her heart in her throat. The howl came a second time, just as she reached the door to the tower, and she threw herself against its hard wooden surface, hand scrabbling for a latch or knob to get it open.

The music stilled. With her face pressed against the door, Sara felt the forest closing in on her. She lifted a hand to pound on the door, and when it swung open she stumbled inside. Her guitar case clattered on the hard wood under the rush-strewn floor. She looked up to see a huge, bearded man towering over her, his blue eyes bright with curiosity, corn-yellow hair braided with beads. As he slowly closed the door behind her, Sara turned to look across the room.

And Taliesin was there.

He sat frozen in the motion of setting aside his harp, his face pale as though he looked on an apparition. At his feet was old Hoyw, as tousled as ever, brown eyes peering through the hair that fell across them as he lifted his head. Sitting across from the bard was an Indian woman whose features were vaguely familiar. Her hair was jet black, braided with beads like the yellow-haired man's, and she wore a dress of white doeskin, decorated with shells and more beadwork. Over her shoulders was a brightly colored blanket worn like a shawl. On her knee was a small drum.

The room itself, undivided by walls, felt spacious. Along one wall was a wooden table, with clayware stacked on it, and

cloak pegs at one-foot intervals, most of which had blankets
or furs dangling from them. A large window overlooked the
clifftop and the sea. The wall behind Taliesin and the woman
was taken up by a large hearth. They sat on piles of bearskins
scattered in front of it.

Sara felt a touch on her arm, started, then allowed the
bearded giant by the door to help her rise. Taliesin finished
laying aside his harp and stood, hands open at his side. The
woman looked from him to Sara with an enigmatic smile.

"Are you a ghost, then, Sara?" Taliesin asked finally.

"No ghost," the man beside her said. "There's flesh on her
limbs, brother, though something's put the fear of Wodan into
her."

"A . . . ghost?" Sara mumbled. "What do you mean?"

"I'd not thought to see you again," the bard said. "I'd thought
you gone—never to return."

The woman across from him laughed in a teasing manner
at that. Taliesin frowned at her, then looked back at Sara. "It
has been a year since last we met."

"A year?" Sara was stunned. "But I just left you yesterday."

"Time is a strange thing in the Otherworld," Taliesin said.

That seemed to be the consensus, Sara thought. She looked
from him to the woman, feeling awkward. What had she expected, though. To be greeted like a long-lost friend?

"Enough," the woman said suddenly. Laying aside her drum,
she stood up and opened her arms in welcome. "They have
lived too long like wolves, these two, to know anything of
manners. My name is May'is'hyr—Summer-Heart. The man
beside you is my husband Hagan Hrolf-get. I bid you welcome
to our lodge. Though its walls be earth-bone more than wood,
and no totem hangs above its door, it still belongs to Mother
Bear, and in her lodge, no guest is unwelcome . . . do they come
as friend or foe, in early morn or on the Night of Hunting
Spirits."

Sara knew who the woman reminded her of now. Ha'kan'ta—
the Moose Girl of the Wild Woods, she thought light-headedly.
The man at the door looked like a Viking. Join them with a
Welsh bard and herself and what did you end up with? A very
weird mixture, that was what.

"Come," Hagan said. "The night's left you shivering. It's
warm by the fire. There's food and drink enough, so don't be
shy."

They were both being friendly—May'is'hyr and the Viking.

But it was the distance she sensed in Taliesin that put her on edge.

"If I'm intruding..." she began in a small voice.

"Drum-brother," May'is'hyr said to Taliesin, "if you do not speak her kindly now you will be forever lessened in my eyes."

Taliesin shook his head as though coming out of a trance.

"I'd not thought it would work...." he began, paused, then only looked at Sara who was standing just a few feet from him now; and suddenly the strangeness ran from him like water from an otter's fur. He smiled and his whole face lit up. "I missed you," he said simply, enfolding her in his arms.

Sara stiffened at his touch. The initial distance, coupled with this sudden warmth left her confused. But as the long fingers of his left hand tousled her curls and he bent his face close to hers, the tension ebbed and she returned the embrace, understanding that, for all that they knew so little of each other, there was something deep inside each of them that recognized a kindred spirit in the other.

"So like a singer," Sara heard May'is'hyr say softly. "They meet like shadows on a ghostly shore—meet and part and he yearns for her like a lovestruck youth in one of his own songs. But when they meet.... Where now are the golden words and heart truths he sang to us for a year and a day?"

Sara felt Taliesin smile against her cheek.

"It's true," he said. "I am a bard and should know by now how to fit words to my feelings, but when I saw you at the door tonight, when you answered the call we sent out and truly came, my tongue went numb. I looked for you for a year, luckless as a 'prentice without a master, and shaped our meeting in my mind. It would go so. I would say this and you would do that. But now..."

His arms tightened and then he stepped back to look her in the eye. "Do you understand?"

"It was a year for you," she said slowly, "but only a day or so for me. I thought of you a lot, but...not like this."

He started to take his hands from her shoulders, but she covered them with her own.

"I'm not saying I don't like it," she said.

And then she had a terrible thought. Both times she'd been with him before, she'd been drawn back, drawn away. Something of what she was feeling must have showed in her features, for Taliesin asked:

"What's wrong?"

"I don't want to go back," she said. "At least not right away. But I never seem to have any choice."

"This time you have a choice," he said quickly. "Before you were like a phantom—in a time not your own. I remember thinking you were one of Gwyn ap Nudd's people; you were like gossamer, for all that I could touch you then and gift you with this." He lifted the collar of her cloak with a finger. "But this time your presence feels strong—though how or why that might be, I can't explain. Perhaps it is because we called you to us, with drum and harp, on this night. I only know that if you went back now, you would be a ghost in your own time."

The relief she'd started to feel washed away and a strange feeling arose from his words. *If* she went back? To stay here forever? What about Jamie and the House, Blue and Julie . . . ? She pressed her face against his shoulder, not really knowing what she wanted, except to be held for a while. There'd be time enough to try to understand it all later.

"Where went the music, then?" Hagan asked gruffly. "Outside the spirits run wild. Will we let them in, or will we play them away?"

My'is'hyr stared daggers at him, then understood that his sudden brusqueness was not without purpose. These two might break their bond before it was woven by the intensity of what they were experiencing. Better to eat and drink and talk of ordinary things awhile. Better to drum a sense of normalcy before the wild of the night settled too deeply in all their souls.

"Kha," she said softly, finding a seat in the furs. She picked up her drum and tapped out a rhythm. Sara and Taliesin stepped apart, stood awkwardly a moment, then sat down together, not touching, but close enough if the need to touch arose.

"Are you hungry?" Hagan boomed. "Do you thirst?"

"A little," Sara said, then realized she was famished.

"Good, good! There's stew left, and ale—though it's strong, mind you, so sip it before you gulp it!"

He grinned at her through his beard. His good humor was contagious and Sara found herself grinning back.

Then, while Sara ate and took small sips of the home-brewed ale, Taliesin and May'is'hyr began to play once more. The harp and drum complemented one another. May'is'hyr's rhythms were complicated and didn't so much support the melodies as add harmonies to them. Hagan played Taliesin's small six-holed whistle. The small instrument looked incongruous in his hands and reminded Sara of Blue with his watercolors.

When Sara finished her stew, she took her guitar from its case. She couldn't play along with every piece, but she played when she could and felt very much at home and amongst friends. She'd catch Taliesin's eye in the midst of a tune and feel again that tingle of recognition leap between them, but it came easily and didn't need to be thought about. All thoughts of danger, all confusion, dissolved away. For now, it was for now, only for the moment. She knew there were people worrying about her, but hoped that they'd understand. How could they not? Jamie and Blue and Julie . . . If they could be here . . .

By the time the music stilled, she was happily content, drowsy from the ale and the excitement and ready for sleep. The strangeness of the night outside the tower was a far and distant thing. If terrors had been lurking out there, the music and its magic had long since soothed or driven them away.

They made their way upstairs in a laughing party. There was one moment of panic when Sara wasn't sure where she was going to sleep but May'is'hyr showed her to her own bundle of furs and Taliesin, after tucking her in and kissing her goodnight, made his way to his own bed. Sara fell asleep almost before her head touched the rolled-up blanket that served for her pillow.

While the others drifted into sleep, Taliesin sat by a window and stared out into the night. On such a night she had returned to him, he thought, wondering at the omen of its timing. A day or so for her, a year for him. But on tonight of all nights. Tonight spirits hunted, the wild awoke and roamed the land, thin-limbed quin'on'a and mischevious honochen'o'keh, the manitous, and beings grimmer still—devils and tragg'a, marsh-creepers and cedar gaunts. All the denizens of the Middle Kingdom, light and dark and grey. And ghosts.

Sara came from a land as strange as any manitous'. So what did that make her? Where the drum-magic and harpspells had kept the other spirits at bay, it had drawn Sara to them. As Mayis had said it would.

In the sky over the sea he saw a quarter moon lifting her horns from the grey waters, though the moon had set hours ago. He knew then that the sleep the others had found would not be his tonight. Not until he walked the night himself.

He cast a last glance around the chamber where the others were sleeping, looked on their slumbering faces with envy, then sighed and arose to go downstairs. He paused for neither harp nor cloak, went out to meet the night, his heart drumming to the tempo of the dark air, walking through stands of spruce and cedar until he came to the tall pointed stone that marked Mayis's Glade of Study. Rathe'feyn, she called this place. The Moon's-Stone-Bear. Here she woke her magics, here they'd exchanged knowledges, and here one night he'd met his own horned grandsire, as easily as though no ocean had separated them from their homeland of the Green Isles.

Tonight he stood alone, his back to the Bearstone and his gaze searching the shadows that lay in amongst the pines, waiting for the one he knew would come. A trembling touched the air, soft as a breath across the strings of his harp. The scent of pine resin and sea were swallowed by the heady odor of apple blossoms, rich and pungent as they are in the spring. Sometimes his grandsire came in the shape of Taliesin's own craftfather—old Myrddin, black hair greying, but still tied back at the nape of his neck, golden eyes deep with dreaming. And sometimes he was the Green Man in a cloak of oak leaves and mistletoe, face like a fox, narrow and brown. Tonight he came as a stag, brow heavy with twelve-pointed antlers, his reddish-brown coat gleaming in the starlight, his eyes heavy with riddles.

Are you content? he asked the bard.

Taliesin inclined his head respectfully. *Content indeed.*

You asked for even an hour in her company. I will give you a handful of days. Are you still content?

Still content.

The stag's riddling eyes smiled, but held a shade of sorrow in their depths. *Will it be enough?* he asked.

Taliesin shook his head. *How can it be enough? It will not be enough until we walk the fields of the Summer Country together with nothing to sunder us.*

She has far and very far to go until that day, the stag replied. *Will you wait all those years for her?*

If I must.

So be it. I chased the moon's shadow for a hundred hundred years before I learned my wisdom. Can I deny you your right at playing the fool for your own moonheart?

Taliesin said nothing.

So be it, the stag repeated. *Cherish your time together, for sundered you must be again. You must send her into danger, son of my son. You must be her Ceridwen's Cauldron and fill her with all the world's knowledge. You must let her earn her place, show her worth. Are you strong enough to watch her strive and suffer and not lend a hand?*

If I must.

The stag sighed and the forest stirred with his breath.

You must, he said softly, *or all will be for naught and she will need to begin her journey again. But what of you? Will you come with me, or will you bide and wait for her?*

I will wait.

Again the stag sighed. *You will die in this land, son of my son. What will keep the moon in your taw when you are shimmering in an Afterworld of Drumming Thunder? What if she loses her path on the Way and leaves you stranded there, forever and always? What if she fails? What will sustain you then?*

My love.

Aye. Your love. So did your father bide in stone for a woman's love; so did I in my own time. Do we tread an endless circle? Must the son always do as the father, as the father's father did?

I will wait for her, Taliesin said simply. *What else can I do?*

Aye. And I will wait for you. So be it. Share your Cauldron with her then, son of my son, that we need wait no longer than we must. But speak not to her of what must be done. Leave that for her to riddle on her own or all the worth of her striving will be undone.

Will you go to her? Taliesin asked.

No need. Her journey is already begun.

As subtly as he had appeared, the stag was gone, and Taliesin stood alone once more. The crag of Mayis's Bearstone pointed skyward behind his back and all around he sensed the spirits of the night, loosed in the sound of wind and creak of tree, brush of leaf against leaf, wing against air, soft padding in the needled carpet.

He thought of Sara, of how he'd first met her that night on the shore when she'd come to him like a fey ghost, how she'd filled his heart. He had been old when he'd left Gwynedd's shores, grown young again as he journeyed by sea to these other shores that his drum-kin named Where-the-Land-Ends. Oh, yes. But through all those years, he'd never experienced the thing that filled him now.

Whether this love was to be returned or not, it did not change what must be done. For that love, for what she'd woken in him, he would give her the Summer Country. She could accept it or not, as she wished. With or without him. The only dowry she must bring to those old hallowed hills was herself. And that dowry was not due to him or his summer kin, but to that Region of Summer Stars itself.

Already she sought it. Long before he'd met her, she'd sought it. It was in her blood, the blood of her forefathers. He sensed that, sensed as well that like them she had reached, without understanding what it was she sought, without being able to put a name to that for which she yearned. But now, because of the gift she had given him, the wonder she'd woken all unknowing in him, he would gift her with that very thing she yearned for: the Summer Country.

The journey was hard, but she had strength enough. And the reward. . . . Was there anything more precious than to be whole? To know the whole of the tune that only echoed faintly in one's heart until one reached the Summer Country?

The stag's first query returned to him as he retraced his steps back to the round tower. Content? Yes, he was content. For had she not returned to him?

Sara was standing in the doorway when he reached the tower, her slender frame and head of tousled curls outlined by the firelight that spilled from within. Taliesin paused a half dozen feet from her, confusion stealing across the calmness that filled him only moments before.

"I couldn't sleep," she said. "I kept dreaming you were a stag. Not a real one—a man with an antlered brow." She shivered. "I've dreamed that before—about you and the shaman. He was a bear and you were a stag. In that dream something horrible came and tried to take me away then—Kieran's demon, I suppose."

"There are no demons here," Taliesin said.

"I know. The night's alive with . . . spirits, I guess. But they don't come near here. Something keeps them away. But I can sense them just beyond the clearing. Are they always there?"

"Yes. But only tonight do they hunt."

Sara shivered again. "That's what I was dreaming about tonight. Hunting. You were a stag-man and you were hunting the moon. You weren't going to hurt it. . . . How could anyone hurt the moon?" She smiled awkwardly. "But you kept chasing it."

Taliesin was astounded at her intuition. "And then?" he asked.

She shrugged. "Then nothing. I woke up. I looked around and saw that you weren't there. I thought maybe you'd gone downstairs, so I came down to talk to you, but you weren't there either. Where did you go?"

"To meet a stag who caught his moon."

Sara laughed. "That's the way a bard would answer me. Or a wizard. Always in riddles. I suppose I should've expected it. Am I supposed to guess what that means?" Before he could answer, she shook her head. "Never mind. I want to ask you something else. What do you see in me, Taliesin? I mean, I'm nobody special. So what do you see in me?"

She'd been thinking about it ever since she'd woken up and she had to know, even though it was a difficult question for her to ask. The words came out in a rush, fed by her own confused emotions.

Taliesin stepped close to her and took her by the hand. "I see the moon," he said, "soft stepping this clifftop and smiling at me. I see the Huntress cast off her war cloak of black feathers and welcome me instead with a maiden's eyes. I see the fairest flower that ever graced the Summer Country, escaped from its borders and blooming in your heart. I see you, Sara, and with you I feel like the gangly country boy I was before Myrddin took me in."

Sara shook her head. "You were never that. First and foremost, you're a bard, and I could never picture you as anything else. Besides, you've already told me that your foster father Elphin was a prince."

"Elphin was a prince," he said, "and the storytellers have made me out more than I am, but I am still no more than a man, who was washed to shore in a coracle and grew up to know the same hopes and fears that touch any man. If we are special, Sara, it is only in each other's eyes."

Taliesin held her gaze steadily. Shyness lay between them for a long moment, then he put his long hands on her shoulders and drew her near. She lifted her face to his, felt the gentle brush of his lips grow fierce, and held him tight, letting herself go with the complex flow and depth of the emotions that filled her. The kiss was long and it left them breathless. A moment longer they regarded each other, the shyness forgotten now. Then hand in hand they entered the tower and made their way to the warm furs scattered in front of the hearth.

The firelight lingered upon their skin, highlighting shoulderblades, arms and brows with a gleam like burnished copper. Their shadows danced on the walls behind them. As their bodies joined, all boundaries fled and, taw to taw, they shared the echoes of the oldest tune of all.

For a long while after Taliesin left May'is'hyr's Bearstone, the glade lay silent in the starlight. Gnarled rootmen passed nearby, chasing shadows. A winged shape drifted over from the forest, circled the stone, then banked sharply to disappear beyond the edge of the clifftop. In amongst the rustlings and stirrings and movements of the many spirits that were free to haunt this night, one small form pushed himself free from the clinging boughs of a thick stand of cedar.

He could wear many shapes at will, but tonight Pukwudji wore his own. His owl-large eyes searched for a lingering trace of stag or bard. Not until he was certain that they were indeed gone did he creep into the clearing to stand under the tall stone. He had been nearby while they'd talked—drawn by the powerful presence of the stag, who was like the Forest Lords of this land, yet not like them. He had listened to them, heard their talk, and not for the first time. They had met before, stag and bard, and each time Pukwudji had listened to them. But tonight . . .

"That was ill done," he muttered, going over their conversation once more in his mind.

He was given to mischief himself, but it was not a mean sort. What these two proposed held too much danger in it for the herok'a they wished to horn. A prank was one thing—especially when it was one of his own devising. But this . . . Ah, they were old and thought themselves wise because they'd grown into their craft through study and trial rather than being born to it. They thought those born to magic were wild, uncontrolled, somehow not deserving of the gifts that they had to work so hard for themselves. Somehow they considered themselves more ennobled for the striving it took them to master their craft.

Bah! Pukwudji spat.

What did it matter how one grew one's horns, or how swiftly? It made him angry, this teaching through riddles and this taking two steps sideways for every one step forward. Tests and testing. What need was there for such? And bad enough it was that they did so in the first place, but worse, they did it to those they loved. What manner of craft-teaching was that?

A sly look came into Pukwudji's eyes then, swallowing his anger. Not for nothing was he Pukwudji, as sly a trickster as his cousin the Coyote. He would show them, these Oh-so-wise wanderers from across the Great Water. He would show them how craft-teaching was done amongst those who followed Grandmother Toad's sen'fer'sa—the something-in-movement. Openly, without secrets. Though he *would* keep his meddling secret from the bard and his unwordly companion. He would warn the herok'a maiden and let the rumor of what the bard and stag did reach Grandmother Toad herself. Hai! And then to see the faces of those two.

Grinning, Pukwudji ran for the clifftop and launched himself into the air. In mid-leap he changed shape, his wide-spread arms becoming black wings to catch the updraft. He winged west along the cliff to where the old round tower of stone straddled the limestone heights. When he reached the glade, he nested in a tall spruce, waiting for sleep to claim the tower's inhabitants.

Ah, see, he thought, sensing Sara and Taliesin's lovemaking. There is such love between you. Already you know her worth, bard, or why would you love her? What need to test her?

It must be some strange custom from across the Great Water, he decided. Some ritual passage like that of the young warriors of the tribesmen that lived in these forests. They were fools. All of them. Pukwudji's eyes sparkled with humor. But he would show them. Soft and subtle. He would go to the herok'a in her dreams.

Sara lay awake for a long while, listening to Taliesin's breathing, savoring the lean length of his body lying against hers.

When she fell asleep at last, the last thing she expected to do was dream. . . .

She stood in front of The Merry Dancers, the shop dark and silent before her, Bank Street devoid of traffic. A great stillness hung over the city and she felt like the ghost Taliesin had said she'd be if she returned to her own time. When she put a hand to the doorknob, the door swung silently open. She hesitated for only a moment, testing the air like some hunting animal, before she crossed the threshold and stood in amongst the familiar odds and ends that still cluttered the shop from wall to wall.

She moved slowly through the shop, touching a vase here, a book there. Books. Lying beside her typewriter was the novel she'd been working on what seemed like ages ago. She picked it up and leafed through the manuscript. It was like someone else had been writing it. With what she knew now, with her own experiences to draw on, she could *really* write something. A fantasy novel to outshine Tolkien and all the others, because it would be written with the authority of actual experience, except . . . She dropped the manuscript back in place. Why write about it when she could live it instead?

It's funny, she thought, moving across the store again. It was as though she was really here. It was hard to tell now what was real and what wasn't. Maybe she should just walk up to the House. Would she meet herself, fast asleep in her bed? Or Jamie? Would he even be able to see her, or was she really a ghost?

A creepy feeling came over her, and she suddenly knew that she was being watched. Visions of Kieran's demon washed over her and the shiver froze into a chill. Slowly she turned, only to see a familiar figure perched on a high-backed chair, curious features reflected in the glow of the streetlights that spilled in through the front window.

"Pukwudji!" she cried happily, her fear turning into relief.

The little man regarded her strangely. How did she know his name? he thought. He had never met her before. But then from her mind came images of his future self, of the two of them playing by Pinta'wa Lake, and later talking on a hilltop. He shook his head. There was something odd involved here. He had told her to go back in time to meet himself?

"Pukwudji?" Sara repeated, a little uncertainly this time.

"That's me," he agreed, nodding.

He'd channeled her dream to grow in a place familiar to her so that she would be more at ease with him when he appeared, more likely to listen to what he had to say. But she already knew him. She was already willing to listen to him, to see what he had to show her. And why not? His future self had given her advice before and things had worked out well for her.

He shook his head, aware that he must speak quickly before it all went awry. Dreams were difficult to shape. They tended

to stray as though blown by a wind unless they were kept firmly
in hand. Then, more to fill an awkward moment, he grinned
and whistled a few bars of a nonsense tune to her.

She smiled back.

"It's funny to see you here," she said. "You don't seem to
fit somehow. But then, I don't suppose I really do any more
either."

"Do you love him?" Pukwudji asked suddenly. "The bard?"

"I . . . I'm not sure. It's strange. When I'm with him, I don't
have any reservations. But when I'm not—like now—it all
seems a little hard to believe. I know he's very special. I know
he says he loves me, but I don't know why. He could have
anybody, so why settle for me?"

"Oh, he loves you," Pukwudji began, then paused.

He was suddenly unsure of the wisdom of his meddling.
She was not of his world, her Way might not be the same as
his. The stag was an Old One—kin to the Forest Lords and
Grandmother Toad. He was Pukwudji . . . clever, yes, but only
a little mystery. Who was he to meddle in the affairs of Forest
Lords and similar beings?

"What's the matter?" Sara asked. "You look so serious. I
hope you don't have any more evil omens for me."

Pukwudji sighed. He saw his future self showing her the
tragg'a and knew that their threat was real. But faced with the
uncertainties that had just come to him, and the sweet presence
of the herok'a who stood before him, he was at a loss as to
what he should do.

"I worry for you," he said at last.

"Why?"

It was a fair question. Pukwudji decided to ignore it. "Among
your bard's tribe, amongst his people, they have certain trials,"
he said instead.

"What sort of trials?" she asked. "What do you mean?"

Suddenly Pukwudji was afraid. Again he sensed that he
meddled in affairs that were not his concern. He pictured the
stag discovering his meddling and grew more fearful still. If
Taliesin's grandsire could be as grim as his own Forest Lords . . .

"Ask him," he said. "Ask the bard. And then we'll talk
again."

He clenched his hands at his side and began to unravel the
threads of the dream. Sara wavered in his sight. The bizarre
surroundings that her dream had drawn them into misted and
smoked.

"Pukwudji?" Sara's voice came from far away.

The little man ignored her. He opened his hands with an abrupt motion and the whole scene dissolved. He was back on the limb of a spruce overlooking the tower's glade, wearing a crow shape once more. In a cloud of feathers, he exploded from his perch and sought the safety of distance, his wings cutting the night air with swift strokes. Behind him, he left Sara to—

—awake in a cold sweat.

She sat bolt upright, heart pounding from the disorientation of waking suddenly in a strange place. Then she felt Taliesin beside her, sensed the quiet that filled the tower, the peace that Taliesin and May'is'hyr had woven into its stones with their magics, and lay back down again.

Just a dream, she told herself and drew closer to Taliesin's warm side. He shifted in his sleep and enclosed her in the safety of his embrace. Just a dream.

In a shirt borrowed from Hagan that hung down past her knees, Sara met the morning humming. The sun was already high as, arms loaded up with her jeans and sweatshirt, she made her way down to the spring-fed pool that May'is'hyr had told her doubled as their bath and laundry basin. Taliesin was still asleep in front of the hearth, sprawled amongst the furs and blankets.

Hoyw followed her down to the pool, flopping down at the edge of the rocks when they arrived. He watched her tentative testing of the water with what could only be amusement. The water was cold. Tugging off Hagan's shirt, she dumped her own clothes in the water. With her teeth gritted in anticipation, she followed them in. The cold water hit her; and it was far worse than she'd imagined. Teeth chattering, she pounded her clothes against a smooth rock and stayed in until she was sure she was turning blue. The soap of white wood ash and fat that May'is'hyr had given her stung her eyes and was hard to wash out of her hair. When she could stand the cold no longer, she clambered out, threw on the shirt and jumped about until the sun and movement warmed her enough to finish with her washing.

May'is'hyr arrived as she was wringing out her clothes. The tall Indian woman wore a simple shift of dark buckskin this morning, her hair pulled back in one long braid that hung down her back. "How is the water?" she asked.

Sara grimaced. "Too cold."

"In the winter," May'is'hyr said, "we fill the tub up by the tower with warm water. And with those two it's best to be first unless you enjoy washing in swamp water. As Mother Bear is my witness, I swear the dirt hides in the snowdrifts just waiting to pounce on them."

She helped Sara wring her jeans dry, then sat back on a rock as Sara dug around in the one big pocket of Hagan's shirt for her tobacco and Kieran's lighter. She looked up to find May'is'hyr studying her. She finished rolling her cigarette, lit it, and offered May'is'hyr a puff. May'is'hyr inclined her head seriously and took the cigarette delicately between finger and thumb. Lifting it in a salute to Sara, she inhaled deeply, then returned it.

First they shared music, the Indian woman thought, now the smoke sacred to Mother Bear. Would they share blood next? She regarded this stranger to her land with open curiosity. Hornless, she still conducted herself with more assurance than the women of the tribes. There was a deepness in her that bore the unmistakable touch of Mother Bear's something-in-movement, but it appeared to move at cross purposes in her. Mayis knew Taliesin's heart—by the First Bear's dark eye, he'd opened it to her often enough. But what of this woman? Who was she, and what did she seek?

"Do you ever have trouble," Sara asked suddenly, "figuring out what's real and what's not?"

May'is'hyr blinked slowly. "How so?"

"Well, you're a shaman too, aren't you?"

"I am a rathe'wen'a—a drummer-of-the-bear—yes."

Sara sighed. "It's hard to explain. It's just that I seem to have trouble working out what's really happening and what's a dream. Dreams become real, or cause things to happen in the real world, but I'm not even sure what the real world is anymore."

"There is only one reality that I know of," May'is'hyr said thoughtfully, "and that is what lies in one's heart. The harmony between oneself and sen'fer'sa. Dreams have their root in reality, but they are important only in how they affect your drumming. We speak to the spirits through our drumming, and that is the final measure of our reality. Do we proceed upon our Way, in our growing close to Mother Bear, then we are real."

"That sounds . . . sort of dogmatic."

May'is'hyr smiled. "Mother Bear is not something dire to be feared. She reflects our joys as well as our sorrows. Yestereve, when we four joined our music, we were close to her. This morning, with her smoke between us and our words questing for truth, we are close to her as well. It need not be dry and serious, Sara. Only true."

"And dreams? They're real too if you . . . learn something from them?"

"They can guide you." May'is'hyr studied her for a moment, then added, "Have you been troubled by dreams?"

Sara nodded. "Only I'm not sure if they actually *are* dreams. The first time I met Taliesin I thought I was dreaming. But then he turned out to be real. And then there's . . ." She motioned vaguely about them. "I'm not sure about anything anymore."

"Tell me what troubles you," May'is'hyr said. "Perhaps I can help."

So Sara did, starting with the day she found the ring and going straight through, leaving nothing out. And the more she talked, the more convoluted the whole mess seemed to her. It was like a ball of yarn made up of a hundred different colors, with odd bits of twigs and straw and dirt caught up in it. You picked up one strand and tried to follow it, but it changed color, got mixed up with two, three, four others, until it was hard to remember which one you'd started with.

"Two things I can tell you," May'is'hyr said when Sara was done. "The first is that, whatever else Taliesin might be, he is still a man and has a man's heart. Who can say what it is that joins a man to a woman? Mother Bear alone can tell us and she remains curiously silent on that subject. This I know: You have been in Taliesin's thoughts since the day you met him on the shore. It is as though he was led astray by one of the honochen'o'keh, so enspelled has he been."

"And the second thing?" Sara asked.

May'is'hyr sighed. "Pukwudji. He is a prankster, that one, cousin to Old Man Coyote. He wears a hundred faces and knows a thousand tricks."

Sara knew a measure of relief. "So I shouldn't take him too seriously?"

"That is more difficult to say. He is like a still pool in that he reflects your heart. If you are mean and small-minded, he will treat with you accordingly. If you are gentle and caring—then he will care for you, be gentle with you."

"So you never can know, can you?"

"In here," May'is'hyr said, touching her breast. "You know in here. For it is *your* heart he reflects."

"I guess I should ask Taliesin then... about these trials."

"I think that would be wise. Taliesin is a strange man—strange to me at least; the Way he follows is different from the Way my own people follow. His people hold great store in an individual's private struggles. It is not so with our Way. With us the knowledge is secret—but only until one asks. We have totems. His people have themselves."

"Oh, boy."

May'is'hyr laid her hand on Sara's arm and smiled. "Don't be afraid. Your tale fills me with forebodings, but know this: You are among friends. We will help you however we can." She stood up and looked at Sara. "Your clothes will be wet for awhile yet. Shall we see if we can find you something more becoming to wear than one of Hagan's old shirts?"

The shift in subject brought a shift in mood.

"I kind of like this shirt," Sara said.

May'is'hyr frowned. "It makes you look fat as a beaver," she pronounced. She puffed out her cheeks and pretended to waddle about. "I saw you more as an otter," she added. "However, you know best...."

Sara laughed. "Okay, okay. What did you have in mind?"

"Something comfortable, I assure you. I have a dress for you. We need only take up the hem a little."

Sara bundled up her clothes and the two of them, with Hoyw trailing behind them, returned to the tower, chatting like old friends.

"No one knows who built this tower," Taliesin said. "Mayis and Hagan lived here for two years before I met them." Mayis was living with her father when they found Hagan washed up on the shore, half dead, big hand clenching that axe of his. A wonder he didn't drown, holding onto its weight! Hagan it was who decided that they should live in the tower. All it needed was some new wattling and turf on the roof. It was surprisingly sound, even after having stood deserted for who knows how many years."

He and Sara sat alone outside the tower, with their backs against the stone wall, a blanket over their shoulders and the broad vista of the ocean spread out before them. Sara wore a dress of soft doeskin that hung to just below her knees and

warm leggings tied to her calves with finely braided grass
thongs. Her wild curls had been tamed into two braids which,
while they weren't as splendid as May'is'hyr's, still made her
feel very much Indian.

They had dined on roasted duck, corn meal cakes garnished
with slivers of pine bark, and rosehip tea that Taliesin had laid
in a supply of over the summer. Now May'is'hyr and Hagan
were inside, Mayis working on a beautiful new blanket that
was already half finished on her loom, while Hagan braided a
fishing net, his big fingers deft and quick as they first worked
the rough hemp into rope, then knotted the rope.

Sara and the bard sat for a long time in the silence of the
wood and the soft drum of the sea on the limestone cliffs below.
The sky was clear, showing a dazzling display of stars. North-
ward, lights danced in the sky, every color of the rainbow,
keeping time to their own magical rhythm. They reminded Sara
of The Merry Dancers shop, which made her think of how
she'd come to be here in the first place, which brought her
around to Kieran's accusations about the bard. And Pukwudji's
strange comment about trials.

The day had been spent quietly, but now, with the night
lying dark and secret about them, Sara decided it was time to
have a serious talk.

"The king's druid who made you leave Gwynedd," she
asked. "What was his name?"

Taliesin's frown was lost in the darkness.

"Tomasin," he said at length. "Tomasin Hengwr t'Hap."

Thomas Hengwr. Sara sighed. So that much of what Kieran
had told her was true. "Do you hate him?" she asked.

"What do you mean?"

"Well, for what he did to you. Do you hate him? Would
you try to kill him?"

Taliesin shook his head, more from confusion than in reply.
"Why should I?" he asked. "He is only a stone now, overlooking the sea."

"But if he was alive. . . ."

"You must understand, Sara," Taliesin said gently. "Tomasin was only the instrument of my exile. I would not say
that he was a good man himself, but . . . how could I remain
when I was no longer welcome in my own land?"

"Kieran said you were born in the Summer Country. Where's
that?"

The bard's eyes almost shone in the darkness. "The Summer

Country. The Region of the Summer Stars. It is everything that is good. It is magic and wild and gentle, fey as starlight, true as a friend's heart. I've only walked its borders, Sara, but how my heart yearns to be there in truth."

For a moment he was quiet, then he added: "I have been told by others that I was born there—but I have no recollection of it. Not in the sense of a homeland that once I knew. Only as a homeland for which I yearn. I thought—when my coracle bore me west on Eil Ton's waves—that it was to the Summer Country I was bound, for legend often spoke of it lying in the west."

Again he was still. When he spoke once more, the yearning had left his voice.

"I do not hate Tomasin. Yet when the sea took my coracle and the Gwynedd shores fell away behind me, I laid that curse of stone upon him. I bade him watch the sea for so long as Gwyn ap Nudd still trod the fields of men. It was ill done, I admit." He turned towards her, his face close to hers. "Why do you ask me this?"

For the first time Sara told him all that had happened to her in the short time since they'd parted on that shore near Percé Rock. The only thing she left out was last night's dream.

"So he lives still," Taliesin said. "In your land, in your time. I can only wish him well, Sara. Truly. This...this Dread-That-Walks-Nameless. . . . It is not I."

"Then what is it?" she asked.

"If it were necessary for me to hazard a guess, I might say it was Arawn, the Lord of the Undead, come to bring Tomasin back to Annwn because he lives beyond his allotted lifespan. So I would say, were it not for this." He held up his hand and his own gold ring winked in the starlight. "Arawn has no use nor need for a bauble such as this. For there is only as much magic in our rings as in any gifting ring. No more. Or if so, only because it was given to me by my master Myrddin who was the greatest bard the Green Isles ever knew. But its magic is a binding magic. It opens the paths of the Way, awaking power that is already present, rather than bestowing it.

"I suppose," he added thoughtfully, "this thing that stalks Tomasin seeks the ring for that purpose: to awake more power in itself."

"But what *is* it?" Sara asked.

"I can't even guess. It's a riddle as tangled as any I've heard; the few clues we have mean nothing to me."

"I thought you were good at riddles."

"So did I," Taliesin said.

Sara sighed.

And there was still another matter that needed talking out. She'd put off asking him about it all day, but she knew she couldn't go to sleep with the question unanswered. Who knew what tonight's dreams might bring?

"Are there some sort of . . . trials in store for me?" she asked finally.

Taliesin stiffened at her side. To his credit, he didn't ask how she knew or what she meant. There was no room for lies between them. But her heart felt cold as though he could sense his grandsire's eyes upon him, could hear again that old voice telling him:

"Leave her to riddle on her own or all the worth will be undone."

"Yes," he replied at length.

"What are they? Or better yet, why are they?"

"All who follow the Way face certain trials, Sara. It is how you face up to them that measures your growth, your worth."

"My worth? To who? To you?"

He turned to her, hurt in his eyes. The darkness hid it from her.

"You need never prove your worth to me," he said.

"Then to who?"

"To the Old Ones. To the Horned Lord and the Moonmother. To the world's taw of which ours is but an echo."

"What's my trial going to be?" Sara asked.

"I fear it's already begun."

"You mean Kieran's demon?"

Taliesin nodded.

"But that thing's got nothing to do with me," Sara protested.

"There is no such thing as chance in the workings of the world," he replied, repeating something he'd told her the second time they'd met on the shore.

"What am I supposed to do?" she asked, her voice bitter. "Play John Wayne with some monster just to score points with your 'Old Ones'?"

"I don't understand," Taliesin said.

Sara pulled away from him and stood up. She walked to the edge of the cliff, her back to the bard.

"Pukwudji was right. He's got good reason to worry about me. Shit, *I* am worrying about me."

"What has Pukwudji to do with this?"

"He told me about your 'trials' last night."

"Sara. It is not through lack of love that this must be. But there can simply be no growth without a struggle of some sort."

She turned to face him.

"Just what exactly am I supposed to do?" she demanded. "Defeat this Mal'ek'a . . . this . . . whatever the hell it is?"

"I don't know. You must seek the answer to that in your own heart."

"Damn you! Just more riddles. Aren't you going to help me at all? I thought after last night that we were lovers—friends at least. I don't understand what's going on, Taliesin. I haven't since this whole mess began. All I want is . . ."

Her voice trailed off. All she wanted was what? She didn't even know anymore.

"What's the big secret?" she asked in a more even tone. "I mean, last night I felt close to you. Like we had something to share with each other. But now you're sitting there like you're a hundred miles away from me. Why, Taliesin? Why does everything have to be a mystery?"

Each word she spoke struck him like a dagger. It was hearing again his own voice raised in protest to his grandsire. He felt the distance between them, sensed the chasm that could become so wide and deep that they might never bridge it if he didn't say something right now.

His own stubbornness rose in him, as it had so many times before. His own arguments with Myrddin returned. He saw himself in Maelgwn's court once more, calling down the moon-silver magic to bind silent the king's bards and druids and so free his foster father after he'd been told to leave well enough alone by both Myrddin and his grandsire. He saw himself wandering the fey borders of the world, always in search of those mysteries that lay ever out of reach. And when he looked at Sara and saw the same struggle beginning in her. . . . Aye, he thought. Bedamned to the Old Ones.

"If you want to follow the Way, you must accept this trial. That is the truth, and no mystery," he said as earnestly as possible. "Decide what it is you want and whatever you decide, I will help you however I can."

For long moments Sara said nothing. She kept her back to him and stared out across the dark ocean. She felt the tension building up in her, muscles knotting in her stomach and shoulders. Please, she said silently. Do more than just sit there.

Then slowly Taliesin arose and came to her. He put his arms around her and she shivered, moved in close.

"I don't know what I want," she said. "I want you. I want to know that feeling again—of being a . . . a moonheart. But I don't want to give up everything I am for it. Jamie. Blue. My old life. That's all part of me still—do you understand, Taliesin? There is a whole lifetime of things and people that made me what I am and I can't just turn my back on them either.

"And then there's the . . . demon. The whatever-it-is. If it's there—if it's been set up to be my trial, then I don't think I want anything to do with your magics or your Old Ones. Mal'ek'a has killed people. It's going to kill more. Your Old Ones shouldn't play with people's lives that way. It's just not right."

Taliesin stroked her hair with one hand, held her tight with his other arm.

"Don't think for a moment," he said. "Set it aside."

"I'm just so confused."

"You must make your decision with a clear head, my moonheart. If you want to go back to your own time, we'll go back together. There will be no headaches this time, either. We'll step across the years with harpmagic, as gently as a soft breeze."

Sara nodded against his shoulder.

"I want to think about it for awhile," she said, pulling away from him. "No. I'm not mad at you any longer. You go on inside. I won't be long."

"Sara. . . ."

She went up on her tiptoes and gave him a kiss. "I'll be okay. Honestly."

He watched her go, indecision making a jumble of his thoughts. Then he told himself: The choice is hers. At least give her the time to make it. He wondered at this night's talk with her, what his grandsire would make of it, how it would affect the outcome of her trial. For he meant what he'd told her. He would help her all he could, even if it meant forgoing the Summer Country for all time.

Truly? he seemed to hear his grandsire ask.

She will show you still, he replied. *There are strengths within her that have no boundaries. You will see.*

Aye, his grandsire replied. *We will see.*

Taliesin entered the tower and closed the door, May'is'hyr

and Hagan looked up at his entrance but, after glancing at his face, said nothing. He crossed the room and took his harp from its case and brought it to the hearth.

He ran his fingers down his harp's strings, adjusting one or two of the tuning pegs with the brass key that hung from a leather thong about his neck. When he was satisfied he began to play, a slow sad air. Neither Mayis nor Hagan knew its name, but they had heard him play it many a time before.

Sara heard the harping as she walked amongst the dark spruce. The night was different tonight—not filled with spirits and movements as it had been yesterday. She hummed the tune Taliesin played, naming it to herself. Lorcalon. Moonheart.

It sounded so sad tonight. Shaking her head, she plunged on into the forest, calling softly: "Pukwudji! Pukwudji?"

She listened, strained her eyes looking through the dark trees, and reached out with that quiet she'd discovered inside herself—her taw. Then she went on.

By the Bearstone of May'is'hyr, a man stood in a cloak of oak leaves and mistletoe, a man who sometimes wore the shape of a stag. He listened to the tune his grandson played, heard the soft call of Sara's voice in the forest, and nodded to himself. As he turned to go, the wind spoke to him, in a voice he alone could hear.

Gwydion, it said. *What are you doing here once more, so far from your own shores?*

Waiting, he replied. *Waiting to see old wrongs righted.*

Then he was gone, and the wind sighed in a voice that only trees understood.

Chapter Two

10:00, Thursday evening.

Superintendent Wallace Madison sat at his desk, chewing on the end of a government issue ballpoint pen and wondering where the hell you started cleaning up a mess like this. Spread across his desk were all the progress reports on Project Mindreach—about as big a crock of bullroar as he'd ever run across. The initial thrust of the operation had never even gotten off the ground. And now . . . now the whole project had fallen to pieces around his ears.

First Hengwr had vanished, then Foy—their only leads. They'd lost Paul Thompson to some boogieman, Dr. Hogue to God knew what. Sara Kendell had vanished. And now both Tucker and Dr. Traupman. Not to mention this other report. There was some kind of force field surrounding Tamson House, denying entry to the squad he'd sent down when Tucker's car had been found abandoned outside.

He shook his head. Jesus, Tucker. I can't give you a week anymore. I can't even give you another hour. But where the hell *are* you?

He'd been called in to see the Solicitor General this afternoon and been told in no uncertain terms that Project Mindreach was being scrapped. There would be no discussion. It was to be dismantled as soon as possible, all personnel being transferred immediately to new positions. Preferably to positions where they would have no contact with one another.

What the hell was that supposed to mean?

Granted, they'd been butting their heads against the wall for the past few months, but now, just when something was breaking, why was the operation being scrubbed? What about

313

Thompson's death? Christ, what about Tucker and Traupman? Was he just supposed to pretend that they'd never existed? And then there was the force field around Tamson House. The implications of its existence put a whole new relevance on the project's importance. But when he'd tried to bring that up with Williams, he'd been cut off before he could even begin.

"Let's understand one thing, Superintendent," Williams had said. "Project Mindreach is finished. In fact it might just as well never have existed." He'd lifted his hand to forestall a further interruption. "There's no need to cry 'cover-up', Madison. It has simply been decided that we've wasted enough of the taxpayer's money on this ill-fated project. There is nothing covert involved, I can assure you."

"But I've got a man out there . . ." Madison began.

"Then I suggest you bring him in."

Madison could feel his blood pressure rising. "Sir," he began again. "If you would just reconsider for a moment this new information I have—"

"No, Superintendent. *You* reconsider. How do you like the Northwest Territories?"

"I . . ."

"If you haven't got this whole affair cleaned up by tomorrow morning, 9:00 AM sharp, I'll have you transferred out to the most godforsaken post we have up there. Do I make myself clear, Superintendent?"

Too clear. But Madison had let it lie. He insisted on having his orders in writing. Once he had them, he'd return to headquarters to begin dismantling the operation. But the whole while he took it apart, half his mind was caught up with Tucker's disappearance.

"Damn!" he cried, snapping his pen in half. He stared at the two jagged ends and pitched them across the room.

"Sir?"

He looked up to see Constable Collins standing in the doorway of his office, his arms weighted down with a carton filled with files.

"Where do you want these, sir?"

"Against the wall, Dan." Madison waited until Collins had deposited his burden, before adding: "Anything new?"

Collins shook out a cigarette and lit it before replying. "Nothing, sir," he said. "Not a damn thing. I did a follow-up on that number you gave me. Margaret Finch hasn't been seen since she left the courthouse on Nicholas Street late this afternoon. One of her co-workers heard her tell a cabbie she wanted to go to Patterson and Bank. That's where—"

"Tamson House is," Madison finished. So they had Maggie, too. "Did you check Traupman's place again?"

"He hasn't turned up. But that's not too unusual, according to his next-door neighbor. She told me that he doesn't keep very regular hours."

Madison nodded. "Thanks, Dan. Is that it for the files?"

"There's one more box."

"Well, when you've brought it up you can go."

"Sure." Collins took a long drag and exhaled, blue smoke wreathing his face. "What about the Inspector, sir?"

"What about him?"

"Well . . . I mean, aren't we going to do anything about what happened to him?"

"What would you suggest?" Damn, Madison thought. He was beginning to sound too much like Williams.

Collins studied him for a moment, then shrugged. "I'll get that last box," he said.

"Dan?"

"Yeah?"

"They've closed the book on Tucker—that's all I know. That doesn't mean I won't be doing what I can for him. And that goes for anyone who wants to lend a hand."

Collins nodded. "I understand, sir. . . . I could use a ride home if you're going my way. I live on Elgin. If you take the Driveway up by the Canal . . . it's a nice ride."

Right by Tamson House, Madison thought. He waved at the paperwork on his desk. "This'll take me a couple of hours," he said.

"Hey. I'm in no hurry. I've got a few things to clear up before my transfer comes through anyway."

"I'd appreciate the company," Madison said.

He nodded to Collins as the constable left, then returned to stare at the files on his desk. Well, here was one for the books. Deskbound Madison hitting the streets again. He drew open a drawer on the left side of his desk and took out a .38 Smith & Wesson in a worn shoulder holster. Christ, he hoped he wouldn't have to use this thing. Then again, considering the bizarre turns this project had taken recently, the gun probably wouldn't be much use even if he *had* to use it.

* * *

"Big place," Madison remarked.

He and Collins stood in Central Park looking at Tamson House. It was just going on twelve-thirty, Friday morning. There still was no word on Tucker, Traupman or Maggie. Nothing on any of them.

"*Weird* place," Collins said. He lit up a fresh Pall Mall from the end of his butt, then ground the butt under his heel. "Not a light on. Nothing. Well, Superintendent?"

"Call me Wally. I've got a court order here from Judge Peterson to search the premises. If no one answers..."

"Yeah. Well, no one's answered. Trouble is I don't think even a court order's going to make much difference. We... ah... already gave it a try earlier this evening—when you sent me down to check out the Inspector's car. But I'm willing to give it another go if you are."

Madison shrugged. "We've come this far. What've we got to lose?"

Crossing the park, they made for the House. All we need, Madison thought, is for someone to come by as we're going in. Williams would have his balls if he found out. But there was no way he was leaving Tucker in there. *If* Tucker was even in there.

"Take a look, Superin...ah, Wally."

Collins shone a pencil flashlight in a window. Madison pushed up against the sill. The .38 was uncomfortable under his arm. His sportscoat wasn't tailored to fit the gun and, even with his jacket open under his overcoat, it was still a tight fit. His hip was bothering him tonight, and his cane was getting in his way.... Peering inside, he tried to make out the features of the room, but the flashlight's thin beam didn't pick up anything.

"Room's empty," he said. "Not even any furniture."

"They're all like that," Collins said. "At least on the bottom floor. But they're not just empty. It's more like there's nothing there."

"And this 'force field'?"

"Watch."

Collins moved to the nearest door, pulling a jackknife from his coat pocket.

"These're old doors, see?" he said. "All you've got to do is slip the blade in between the door and the frame...like this.

Hook it behind the bolt—they're angled on these locks—and pull the blade forward."

He finished the movement, tugging on the doorknob as he did. The door didn't budge.

"They've got it bolted on the inside," Madison said.

Collins didn't reply. He shone the penlight on the end of his knife's blade to show a black scoring on the steel.

"That . . . ?" Madison began.

"Wasn't there before. Something burned it. I could feel a jolt go up my arm when I was working the blade in."

"How about the windows?"

"Same thing happens with the latches."

Madison shook his head. "This just doesn't make any sense. How can there be nothing inside all these rooms? John—Inspector Tucker—described the place to me. Said it was loaded with antiques, books, furniture. . . ."

"There's nothing there now." Collins shook out and lit a new cigarette. "We've got ourselves one weird problem here."

"But a . . . force field? It's like something out of a science fiction movie, for Christ's sake!"

Collins bent down and hefted a good-sized rock. "What do you think?" he asked, indicating the window.

Madison didn't even stop to think about it. "Break it," he said.

Taking off his coat, Collins wrapped it around the stone to muffle the sound of the impact somewhat. The glass didn't break with the first blow. A star of fine lines appeared where he'd hit the window, with long cracks emanating across the glass. He drew his arm back for a second blow, then paused, staring at the glass.

"Je-*sus!*"

"What is it?" Madison demanded.

He shone the narrow beam of the penlight onto the window and felt his stomach muscles tighten. The crack lines in the glass were withdrawing back to the point of impact. As they watched, the cracks smoothed and the window became whole again. The two men stared at each other, neither quite willing to admit to what they'd seen.

Madison grabbed another rock and, heedless of the noise the crash would make, flung it through the window. The rock tore a hole in the glass with a satisfying shattering sound that the night seemed to swallow very quickly. But there was no sound of glass falling to the floor inside the House. No sound of the rock hitting the floor. Collins leaned forward to reach for the latch. As he started to push his hand through the hole in the glass, a bluish-green light flared around his hand. He flung himself backward, cradling the hand against his chest. His eyes watered from the pain and he sank slowly to his knees. Madison dropped to his side.

"Dan!" he cried.

"S'okay." Collins gritted through his teeth. "A little . . . shock. That's all."

"Let me have a look." Madison gently pried the constable's arm away from his chest and shone the penlight on his hand. The skin was peeled and red as though from a burn. The fingernails were black.

"We've got to get you to a hospital," he said, helping Collins to his feet.

"But the . . . Inspector. . . ."

Madison glanced up at the House. It reared up into the night skies like some behemoth; almost he could feel the House watching them, waiting for them to try to gain entry again.

"Tucker's going to have to look out for himself for now," Madison said. "There's no way we're going to get into that place. We don't even know for certain that he *is* in there."

As he led Collins across the park, he wondered how he was going to explain this if word filtered up to the Solicitor General's office, then decided he didn't care. What they'd just seen was proof positive that Project Mindreach hadn't been a waste of time. Only how was he going to convince Williams of that?

Starting the car, he pulled out from the curb and headed for the Riverside Hospital. One thing was for certain, he told himself. He wasn't going to let this lie. Too many men had been hurt to ignore this. And now, now that he knew for himself that the paranormal abilities they'd been investigating in Project Mindreach weren't just some asshole's way of wasting the taxpayers' money as he thought it'd been . . .

He shuddered to think what that kind of weaponry could do in the hands of terrorists and other malcontents. Impenetrable safehouses. Minds that could steal secrets from right out of your head, or fry you with a thought. God alone knew what else these people were capable of.

Maybe Williams wanted the project scrubbed. Fine. He'd just let Williams go on thinking that it had been. But he promised himself this: He wasn't going to let this thing go until he had all the answers for himself. And then...when he had enough documentation to support his claims...well, he'd go right over Williams's head if that was what it was going to take to get some action.

Why was Williams so intent on closing down the project? Madison suddenly remembered something else, something Tucker had asked him before he'd disappeared: "You find out how a nobody like Hogue got hired to head this project...."

Madison had gone over Hogue's file earlier this evening and hadn't found anything in it to make Hogue stand out over any number of other possible candidates. Was that it then? Had Project Mindreach been Williams's private project, set up for his own reasons, and now that his boy Hogue was out of the picture, he wanted to shut it all down?

Well, it didn't matter. He was going to get to the bottom of it. And if it got in the way of Williams's career—that was too bad for Williams. He should have thought of that before he got his hands dirty. Because, the more Madison thought about it, the more it made sense. Williams was playing games and Project Mindreach was one of the pieces. Maybe the whole PRB itself.

Great. So who was he going to go to with what he had right now? Madison shook his head. First some documentation, something hard. Then he'd go after Williams's ass.

Chapter Three

"I'VE never had rabbit stew first thing in the morning before," Kieran said, mopping up the last of it with a chunk of flat bread.

"I would hardly call noon 'first thing in the morning'," she replied.

They'd slept late, only waking when the sun that washed Ha'kan'ta's Glade of Study had become too hot to sleep under. A brisk swim in the river that ran below her lodge served to cool them down and wake them up.

The experiences of the previous night still hung between them, drawing them close. Where yesterday Ha'kan'ta had seemed like a wise woman, unattainable, someone he hadn't even thought of making love with, today Kieran looked on her as a companion, a lover that he couldn't imagine not being with. And the other experience—the time spent with his totem, the raven that he could still feel stirring inside him, dark-feathered and wise—that had left his every sense stretched taut.

Just looking at Ha'kan'ta set tingles running through him. Today he wanted to know what had made her who she was, how her thoughts ran behind those startling blue eyes, the where and when and how and why of her.

"Have you spent time in my world?" he asked suddenly.

"Some. My ancestors came from your world."

Kieran smiled. "Ah! Those blue eyes!"

"My grandfather was a man from across the Great Water—yellow-haired and blue-eyed. His name was Hagan Hrolf-get."

"Sounds like a Viking. How long ago was that?"

"Many, many winters. He was washed up to shore and my

320

grandmother rescued him from the sea. Her name was May'is'hyr and she was, like I am, a drummer-of-the-bear. They lived together in an old stone tower in a place my people called Where-the-Land-Ends—lived there with Taliesin Redhair."

As she spoke the bard's name, she studied his face for a reaction, but Kieran only smiled.

"I've given up all designs on your precious bard," he said. "I'll leave him in Sara's capable hands."

At the mention of Sara's name, Ha'kan'ta grew thoughtful. "I wonder," she said.

"About what?"

"Well, I always remembered Taliesin as being so sad. When I asked my father about it once—he and the bard were very close, closer than Taliesin was to my grandparents even—he told me that Taliesin was sad because he was waiting for a ghost that never came.

" 'I never saw her myself,' he told me, 'but your grandparents knew her—for one day and a night. She came on the Night of Hunting Spirits.' He said her name was Little-Otter, so I always thought she was one of my people. But now I'm not so sure."

Kieran nodded. "It could've been Sara. If she went back in time to meet Taliesin, she might have seemed like a ghost to him. Weird."

"I never had the courage to ask Taliesin about her myself. He became withdrawn as he grew older. When my father was young, they roamed the woods and Taliesin was as wild as my father was then. But while he'd remained youthful in appearance for many seasons, he began to age quite rapidly before he died.

" 'The years fell upon him like winter snows covering a tree stump,' was how my father put it.

"It's sad, isn't it?" she said. "To think of him waiting all that time for her and she never returned to him. I wonder why she didn't go back."

"Maybe that's still going to happen," Kieran said. "Though I'm not sure. I find this time traveling a little unsettling. *Nom de tout!* It makes my head spin, just trying to work it all out."

Ha'kan'ta nodded; her mood had changed. "We need to speak of Mal'ek'a," she said suddenly.

"But the raven told me . . . told us . . . that it wasn't our struggle."

"Still, the quin'on'a set us on the hunt."

"I'm not so sure of that," Kieran said. "I don't think they really expected us to accomplish anything. I don't think they even thought we could find Mal'ek'a, let alone do anything about it. They just wanted us out of the way. The thing we have to ask ourselves is why?"

Ha'kan'ta sighed. "Now this is a thing that makes *my* head spin. Surely there were more simple methods to accomplish that—if such was their intent."

"Not all hyped up like we were. We really wanted to go after him—remember?"

Ha'kan'ta was quiet for a long moment. When she finally spoke, her voice was soft. "I still do."

"But . . ."

"I know," she said before he could continue. "I know what my totem told me. But Mal'ek'a has brought too much pain for me to let it go unpunished. It was Mal'ek'a's tragg'a that slew my father, Kieran. How could I face him when we meet again in the Place of Dreaming Thunder, if I had done nothing?"

Kieran reached over and took her hand, holding it tightly between his own. "It won't solve anything," he said, knowing the emptiness of his words as he spoke them.

"Together we could defeat the monster," Ha'kan'ta said. "Together we are strong. Strong enough even to slay the Dread-That-Walks-Nameless."

"And if our totems take back our strength because we're going against their wishes? What then?" He felt a tension grow between them and added: "I'm not trying to back down, Kanta. It just doesn't feel . . . right."

"Then what do you say on this matter?" she asked, her voice sounding very formal to Kieran's ears.

"We go back to see the quin'on'a."

"And then *they* will not be pleased. They gave us a thing to do."

"If I have my choice between displeasing the quin'on'a or my totem, I think I'll opt for the quin'on'a."

"They can be dangerous."

"But together . . . we're strong. Remember?"

Ha'kan'ta nodded. "I think you are right. Given a choice, I too would rather anger the quin'on'a than my totem." Warmth returned to her eyes, quick as a spring shower. "Forgive my doubting you. I thought—but it is not important. It was ill thought. We know each other well in certain ways, and yet we know so little of each other."

"That's something we'll have to work on."

Ha'kan'ta smiled. "I think I will enjoy 'working on' it. Yet before we begin that. . . ."

"We go see the quin'on'a," he finished for her.

"I will summon Ak'is'hyr and see if he will bear us to their lodge," she said.

She closed her eyes, brow furrowing as she sent out a mental summons for the big moose. Kieran sat back, watching her, glad that the moment of awkwardness between them had passed so quickly. Because if it came right down to it, he'd go against his totem's wishes if he had to. It was a funny thing the way he felt about her. He lifted his hand, fingering the small braids that she'd woven into the hair on either side of his forehead. Lord lifting Jesus, but it felt good to be in love.

In the hills above the quin'on'a lodge, Sins'amin, the tribe's Beardaughter, and her War Chief Tep'fyl'in walked under the pines.

"I should have realized," Sins'amin said softly. "Time is a strange beast, with as little sense as a turtle. *And* as unyielding in its flow as a turtle's shell."

Tep'fyl'in shrugged. "Prophecies have always been open to question," he said. "Why should this one be any different?"

"Because this one we need."

Sins'amin sighed. The prophecy lay unspoken between them. *When the stag's daughter bears the moon's horns,* it ran, *then will the quin'on'a regain their lost forests.*

Once the tribesfolk of the World Beyond honored the quin'on'a with tobacco and rituals. In those days the quin'on'a knew the forests of the World Beyond as well as they knew those of the Otherworld. But then the Europeans came, the round-eyed herok'a with their gift of lies and their need to claim for their own the land that only Kitche Manitou could lay title to, and the quin'on'a were forced to withdraw into the Otherworld.

They withdrew as their counterparts in Europe had withdrawn before them. The quin'on'a were the first to go, but the others followed—the manitous, the little mysteries, the honochen'o'keh—until Grandmother Toad's something-in-movement lay thin in the forests of the World Beyond. Without the belief of the tribesfolk to sustain it, the sen'fer'sa diminished. In time, even the forests of the Otherworld would be empty.

"We grow old, my Red-Spear," Sins'amin said. She paused and took hold of Tep'fyl'in's arm. "We that never knew age. We wither as the tribesfolk drive us further and further from their minds. Without their belief, we will be nothing. Most of them have forgotten the ways into the Otherworld. Year by year their drummers grow fewer. We need them to return to the old ways that we may be sustained by their belief. And without Taliesin Redhair's craftdaughter to open the way for us, we have no hope."

"Pa'teyn'ho was very old when he spoke those words," Tep'fyl'in said. "Who knows whether it was truly his totem speaking through him, or the ramblings of an elder grown too old for his position? Who can even swear that it was Taliesin Redhair he spoke of and not some other? Hoth'ans bears a stag's aspect. Who can say that it is not *her* daughter that the prophecy speaks of?"

"Sometimes I wonder," Sins'amin said, "whether you argue with reason, or simply to hear the sound of your own voice. Hoth'ans *has* no daughter. There has been no child born in our lodge since the Winter of Ko'han'to's passing. Three-and-thirty winters—by the counting of the tribesfolk." She let go of his arm and looked across Pinta'wa's clear waters. "Tell me, Red-Spear. Why must you always take an opposing view?"

"You wait for a prophecy to be fulfilled," he replied. "I would prefer to confront our enemy myself."

"This is not a thing we *can* do."

"Old mother, I fear you are wrong. It is something we *must* do, we must *learn* to do, or we are lost. If we wait too long, the world will pass us by. Then we will be dust indeed—not even remembered in the poorest lodge or tipi."

Sins'amin shook her head. "It was the herok'a who crossed the Great Water that turned the tribesfolk from us, who shrouded their lack of respect for us with their glib tongues and hollow gifts. So it is that those same herok'a must either grow horns themselves and so sustain us, or turn our tribesfolk back to the old ways.

"Pa'teyn'ho knew this. And as he knew that Taliesin's coming would bring us great joy, so he knew that sorrow would come as well. Mal'ek'a is the essence of the lies that the herok'a brought with them. By such reckoning, he is Taliesin's dark twin. So Taliesin, through his craftdaughter, must set it right once more."

"Little remains for us in the World Beyond," Tep'fyl'in said. "The forests have been cut down, the plains seeded with the herok'a's crops. . . ."

"Yet there is enough."

"Taliesin never had a craftdaughter, old mother. He died without passing on his drum."

"No. There you are wrong. I agree that our traditions have not spoken of his taking a craftdaughter, but this I know: his spirit lives on in the one named Saraken. I felt its presence drumming in her."

"That matters not," Tep'fyl'in said. "Mal'ek'a seeks her. He will not give her the time to grow her horns."

"It is only there that we have failed. I had thought to give her time by sending the one named Kieranfoy to face Mal'ek'a. But he learned his dance too well."

"Our only failure," Tep'fyl'in said, "is in not confronting Mal'ek'a ourselves. Time and again I have put it to you. It is *we* who must take action. Are we grown so old that we must cower in fear at the mention of Mal'ek'a's name?"

"No, Red-Spear. But we are the deathless who have come to know mortality. If we were to confront Mal'ek'a, all we would gain is our own deaths. Pa'teyn'ho was the first of us to age and die. Would you follow him?"

"Yes. But with my spear in hand and my wolves at my side. I am stronger than some hornless maiden, old mother. I will not die abed, riddled with time's dreary wounds."

Sins'amin shook her head. "Mal'ek'a was not born to the Way. Only a herok'a who has grown horns, not one who was born to them, has any hope of defeating him."

Tep'fyl'in sighed, his expressionless features masking his frustration. It was an old argument, never resolved.

"Then allow me this," he said at length. "Allow me to confront Ha'kan'ta and her new blanket-mate. Allow me to send them back to buy you the time you tell me you need."

"We must let them speak first," Sins'amin said. "We know only that they return. Not why."

"I will tell you why: Because courage has died in their hearts!"

"You cannot know this."

"In here," Tep'fyl'in replied, tapping his chest. "No matter what words come from between their lips, in here I know why."

"We will see."

* * *

"They know we're coming," Kieran said.

Ak'is'hyr's bulk moved underneath them, the great muscled limbs carrying them as quietly through the forest as the padded paws of the two white wolves that flanked them. It was a curious, but not unpleasant sensation, riding high on the creature's back, ghosting through the trees. Another curiosity was how the return trip from Ha'kan'ta's camp to the quin'on'a lodge took only a third of the time as the trip out had.

"I do not think it is possible," Ha'kan'ta said, "to approach a quin'on'a lodge without their foreknowledge. But this time I sent word ahead that we were coming."

Kieran shook his head. "Not a good idea."

"How so?"

"You've given them time to prepare their story."

"You do not trust the forest spirits, do you?"

"Tom always told me to be careful around them—if the occasion ever arose that I'd have to deal with them. No, I don't trust them, Kanta. They want something from us and I don't think it's going to be something we're willing to give them."

"Perhaps," Ha'kan'ta replied. "They have changed from my grandmother's time. Even from my father's time. Once there were many quin'on'a lodges. Now there are few. And they lie deep within the Otherworld—far from the World Beyond, where once the quin'on'a hunted with as much freedom as any of your own people might."

"Why's that?"

Ha'kan'ta sighed. "My father told me it is because they learned how to die. Once they were held in awe by all the tribesfolk. Now only the rathe'wen'a remember them and we grow very few in number. There might be a handful on your world. No more than thirty others scattered throughout the Otherworld. That is not enough to sustain the quin'on'a. They need belief. Without that belief, they wither."

"Just like elves," Kieran said.

"What?"

But Kieran wasn't listening. His mind had gone back to another conversation, back through the years. "Were they real or not?" he'd asked his mentor.

"Very real," Tom had replied. "But I doubt you'll run across any now. Their time has gone from this world, Kier; this world belongs to mankind now. Elves, the gods of pagan pantheons, hobgoblins and boogiemen, call them what you will—their 'reality' was directly dependent on how much people believed in them.

"When I walk a forest today, I can still hear the drum of Cernunnos's hooves in the long silences. But where once it was a sound like thunder, these days it is a distant echo. Someday it won't be heard at all. The time will come when wizards too will no longer walk our forests. And then ... ah, then what a sorry world it will be."

"But can't something be done?"

Tom had shaken his head. "What can you do against the inevitable? Can you see Pan walking the streets of New York? Diana leading her Wild Hunt through London? There is no more room for them in this world, Kier. When the last of the people we call primitive have been 'civilized' ... with the loss of that innocence, the last magics will disappear."

It had seemed a very depressing prospect to Kieran, for all that the closest he'd been to the beings that Tom described were the tales of the old man himself.

"Don't look so glum," Tom had said. "They disappear from our world, but there are other worlds for them still. World fitting within world, each a little smaller than the next, like Chinese boxes. Each world a little more magical until the last world of all."

"What world is that?"

Tom had smiled then. "Why, the Summer Country, Kier. The Region of the Summer Stars from which all magics come and, in the end, all magics must go."

Kieran remembered thinking it all so much rhetoric—platitudes couched in mythic terms. Jungian symbols that, while perhaps not real in themselves, were still capable of awaking answers in those who understood them. He'd never really pursued them any further. But now. . . . Now he had to accept that the old man had been doing more than setting a few new riddles in front of him. He had only himself to blame for not going further; but, to be fair to himself, he hadn't really wanted more. The deepening of his taw had seemed wonder enough.

"You are very quiet, Kieran."

"I was thinking," he said, "of how close I came to never knowing the real wonder of the world."

"And you know it now?"

He shook his head. "No. But at least I've started to look for it again."

* * *

Three of the quin'on'a elders met them on the slopes just outside the village: Sins'amin the Beardaughter, Tep'fyl'in her War Chief, and the Creator Hoth'ans, who had twice seen Kieran in her power dreams. Strangely enough, for all her earlier antipathy, it was Hoth'ans who seemed the most pleased to see them. When Kieran slid down from the back of Ak'is'hyr, she smiled at him.

"Last night you chose the Drum," she said. "I welcome you, drummer."

Tep'fyl'in scowled at her, but her head was turned and only Kieran and Ha'kan'ta saw the look he gave her. When Ha'kan'ta dropped to the ground beside Kieran, the big moose stepped softly back into the woods, melting in amongst the shadowed pines. The two wolves remained, amber eyes regarding the quin'on'a with suspicion.

"Brothers," Tep'fyl'in said to them. "Do not regard me with such ill wishing."

The guard hairs rose on the wolves' backs and they moved closer to Ha'kan'ta and Kieran. Kieran started at the brush of stiff fur that touched his hand. Looking down, feeling the warmth of the wolf's body close against him, he knew a sudden comfort. He'd raised his taw as they approached the lodge. Now he used it to touch the mind of the wolf at his side, and he knew May'asa, the Summer-Brother, offered his protection.

Tep'fyl'in's scowl grew deeper, but he kept his own counsel. Beside him, Sins'amin touched her necklace of bear claws.

"Why have you returned, drum-sister?" she asked Ha'kan'ta.

In the asking of that simple question, Ha'kan'ta knew that Kieran had been right. The quin'on'a were plainly displeased to see them return. A cold anger rose up in her.

"Did you think never to see us again?" she asked. "Was that your purpose in sending us against Mal'ek'a?"

"We did not send you," Sins'amin replied. "You chose to go of your own will. Our only concern was that you did not trouble the spirit of Taliesin Redhair with your follies. And remember, drum-sister, it was you who brought the outworlder to our council. You that chose to go with him. You that shared your body with him. You that taught him his Totemdance."

"And that was ill done?" Ha'kan'ta demanded coldly.

"It is not our affair," Sins'amin replied.

Ha'kan'ta shook her head. "Warm is the greeting you give a drum-sister. Have I become the enemy as well? What do you see when you look at me? A tragg'a in drummer's flesh?"

"Do not seek to question us," Tep'fyl'in said.

Sins'amin put her hand on his arm, but he shook it off. "Through your ties with the World Beyond," he told Ha'kan'ta, "you have reawoken old griefs. Taliesin Redhair was your father's drum-brother, yet here you are consorting with his self-claimed enemy. You said you would destroy Mal'ek'a, yet you turn back before even setting out. You speak with words of wind. If you would show your worth, bind truth to your words. Return with deeds done, not questions. Then we may speak as equals."

Ha'kan'ta stiffened at Kieran's side. The wolves growled low in their chests, lips drawn back from their teeth.

"Mother of God!" Kieran said, taking a step forward. "Who do you think you're talking to? We're not your lackies, here to run at your beck and call. *Nom de tout!* If you want the demon killed, why don't you do something about it yourself?"

"I do not hear you," Tep'fyl'in said. "You are nothing to me."

The mental scorn that followed hard on the heels of the War Chief's words snapped something inside Kieran. He lunged forward, swinging a fist. Tep'fyl'in smoothly blocked the blow with his left forearm, caught Kieran by the scruff of his shirt, and effortlessly cast him to the ground. The abruptness of his dispatch, coupled with the shock of hitting the ground so suddenly, left Kieran breathless.

"You question my courage," Tep'fyl'in said. "As I question yours."

He drew his tomahawk from his belt and threw it. It landed in the earth between him and Kieran.

"Pick it up," he said, "and we will see who lacks courage and who does not."

It was a challenge to ritual combat. Kieran had only to pick up the tomahawk to accept the challenge. Accept the challenge and get the living shit kicked out of him—if he didn't lose his life.

"Don't," Ha'kan'ta cried.

Don't? Kieran thought. What else could he do?

He knew the whole situation was stupid beyond reasoning. Might makes right. The old law of the jungle. But it didn't matter if he was going to get creamed. Didn't matter that there was no way he could stand up against a trained warrior and hope to win. He had to try. For himself. For Ha'kan'ta. To prove his worth to these so-called higher beings.

He sat up and swallowed drily. His hand shook as it reached out to take the tomahawk's handle. He looked up. Tep'fyl'in's grin was feral, his eyes glittering.

"I forbid this madness," Sins'amin said. "He does not know what he has accepted. You are a trained warrior, Red-Spear. He is not. It will be slaughter, plain and simple."

"I think he understands well enough," Tep'fyl'in replied.

"I . . . I understand," Kieran said.

Sins'amin shook her head. "Still I forbid it."

"Too late, old mother. He has already accepted the challenge."

"He is not the enemy."

Tep'fyl'in's anger spilled from him. "They are all our enemies," he said fiercely. "He and Redhair and all those white-skinned devils that stole the tribesfolk from us. What is Mal'ek'a, but their evil given substance?"

"The tribesfolk had their choice," Hoth'ans said.

Tep'fyl'in shook his head. "If the herok'a had never come from across the Great Water, there would have been no need for the tribesfolk to choose. And what choice is there when the herok'a offered gifts with one hand while concealing the knife blade with the other?"

There was no answer to that old truth. Just as there had been no way to prevent it. The world fared on. Sooner or later, what had come to be would have come about. But that did not lessen the frustration of seeing the tribesfolk turn away from a way of pride and strength. It did not diminish the grief. Never mind that the tribesfolk had made the choice themselves.

But there had been even a semblance of choice only at first, when the herok'a came in small numbers. Later they arrived hundreds to each great ship and swarmed across the land like maggots feeding on an old kill. They were scavengers. Thieves. It was this that built the rage in Tep'fyl'in. And Sins'amin knew that he was not alone in his anger. With the tribes so diminished, many of the quin'on'a felt the same. Grandmother Toad knew that she shared that anger herself, though she tried to temper it with reason.

"So be it," the quin'on'a Beardaughter said wearily. "What will be the weapons?"

"Spears," Tep'fyl'in said quickly.

Kieran stood up, the tomahawk gripped tightly in a trembling hand.

"Not spears," Ha'kan'ta said softly to him. "They are his chosen weapon."

Kieran looked at her and shrugged. What did it matter? his eyes told her. He looked down at the tomahawk—Tep'fyl'in's totem stick. Holding it up in front of him, he spat on it and tossed it at the War Chief's feet.

"Spears," he agreed.

Tep'fyl'in's anger hit him like a physical blow, but Kieran had been expecting it and braced himself.

"This'll look real good," he said contemptuously. "It's going to show everyone how brave you are. The big War Chief. War Chief of a tribe of fools."

Tep'fyl'in's eyes narrowed to slits. But through the red film of his anger, he could feel his own totem stir in agreement to the outworlder's words. Where was the honor in besting one who had no skill? No honor. But honorless or not, he would still glory in the other's defeat.

"To the death," he said.

Sins'amin shook her head. "First blood!"

"Kha," he replied. Understood. What did it matter? First blood would be the same as the outworlder's death when he plunged his spear into him.

"The challenge will be met at moonrise," Sins'amin said.

She looked from Kieran to her War Chief. Her anger was plain. This was not how it had been meant to be. She turned to Ha'kan'ta. "This was never my intention, drum-sister—" she began, but Ha'kan'ta cut her off.

"Drum-sister no more. You have a strange manner of repaying old kindnesses. I am not the enemy. Kieran is not the enemy. But your people and mine are kin no more. Whatever outcome Mother Bear allows tonight, know this: *I* will call a council of the rathe'wen'a and tell them of this madness. The quin'on'a will never outlive the scorn we will hold for you. By the First Bear's dark eye, I wish you ill—now and forever."

Sins'amin bowed her head under the weight of Ha'kan'ta's words. This came of her own intricate plottings. But deserved though it might be, had not those plottings been made with the best for all in mind? Aie! She had been too devious for all their good. Too late, too late now to make amends. The only hope that remained rested on the frail shoulders of Taliesin's craft-daughter—and she had yet to grow her horns.

She lifted her head to regard Ha'kan'ta, opening her spirit

that the rathe'wen'a might understand what and why she had done what she did. But Ha'kan'ta remained closed to her, her heart cold, her desire to understand shattered by anger.

"Until moonrise, then," Sins'amin said softly. Turning, she led her two companions back to their lodge.

When they were gone, Ha'kan'ta sank to the ground, her eyes glistening. Kieran knelt beside her. The two wolves took up guard positions, facing the woods that bordered the quin'on'a lodge.

"He will kill you," Ha'kan'ta said.

She did not ask him to withdraw his acceptance of the War Chief's challenge. She understood that withdrawing would be worse than defeat. Not in what others might think of him, but in what Kieran would think of himself. But her grief threatened to overwhelm her. To lose this precious gift that they held between them, so soon.

Kieran felt strange. His fear had been swallowed by an odd calmness.

"He won't kill me," he said. "It's only to first blood." But they both knew that first blood with Tep'fyl'in meant a spear-thrust deep in the chest.

"I've done a little staff fighting before," Kieran said. "It shouldn't be that much different. Mind you, that was just for fun. But all I've got to do is try to hang in there until he draws first blood. Then it'll be over."

Ha'kan'ta nodded. "I wish we'd never come."

"Too late for that."

Too late for so much, Ha'kan'ta thought. She pulled him close, burrowing her face against his shoulder. Precious afternoon, she wished, last forever.

Alone with her War Chief in the quin'on'a lodge, Sins'amin turned the full weight of her fury on him.

"You are a fool! Worse, you are the greatest of all fools! You are a shame to this lodge. And listen well: You are War Chief no longer!"

"Old mother . . ."

"I know your mind, Red-Spear. You mean to slay him. If you do so, I swear by Grandmother Toad, you will face me. You will face *my* challenge."

The air crackled around the old Beardaughter and Tep'fyl'in knew she made no idle threat. If he had to face her it would be his greatest challenge. And much though he loved her, his heart leaped at the thought. Perhaps it was time for the lodge to have a new leader, one who was not afraid to use his strengths. He would not kill her. Never that. But if he could wrest the chieftainship from her and lead the lodge to glory, then she would see that the old ways might still be restored.

"Old mother..." he began again.

She shook her head. "I do not hear you," she said.

Tep'fyl'in's heart chilled at the insult. This goes too far, he thought.

"Be gone from my sight," Sins'amin said. "Prepare for your great 'challenge.'"

Tep'fyl'in held a sharp retort in check. "I go," he said.

As the flap rustled behind him, Sins'amin sat alone in the lodge. Tep'fyl'in had shielded his thoughts well enough, but not so well that she could not hear them. She was the lodge's Breadaughter. Did he think he could hide what he planned from her? He would discover soon enough that she would not be such an easy victory as the outworlder. Her totem stirred inside her. She thought of Ha'kan'ta's words. She thought of the failure of her own devious plans. She thought of Tep'fyl'in's desperate need for action.

Bowing her head, she wept.

Chapter Four

IT was impossible, but with the proof laid out in front of them, it couldn't be denied. Tamson House had been transported to some other dimension—to Thomas Hengwr's Otherworld. Blue shook his head.

He and Fred and one of the gangster types named Chevier were dragging the last of the bodies out of the House while Tucker, Gannon and Mercier covered them from the porch that had once looked out on O'Connor Street. As they dumped the bodies of the slain tragg'a onto the pile, Sam snagged a ten-gallon tank of gasoline from the porch and sloshed its contents onto the grisly stack. Among the furred and scaly torsos were the bodies of two of Gannon's men—Bull and Serge Morin.

"That's enough," Blue said.

While Sam screwed the cap back on the can and returned to the porch with it, Blue dug in his pockets for a light.

"Better hurry up," Tucker called from the porch. Like all of them, his clothing was torn and smeared with blood. He cradled Blue's Wembley, gaze raking the far fields where the forest marched down into the grass fields. "There's something stirring out there," he added.

Blue nodded. The fire caught with a whoosh and he stepped back from the sudden heat. As the flames raged high, a long wailing howl came from the forest.

"Move!" Tucker shouted. "Here they come!"

He snapped off a shot as Blue and the others ran for the House. Behind them a handful of tragg'a shuffled out of the forest, muzzles lifted to the sky as they keened for their fallen brothers. Blue paused on the porch to have a look at them. A shiver ran up his spine as he watched the pack grow larger as more and more of the creatures came out of the woods.

"Let's just hope the House holds up," said Tucker. The hallway still reeked of the tragg'a.

"It'll hold," Blue said, bolting the door behind them. It had to.

Blue shook his head. Given his druthers at who he'd be stuck with in a situation like this, he certainly wouldn't have picked this crew. But at least most of them were capable of using weapons. He turned back to peer through the leaded windows in the top part of the door. Earlier an alien moon and stars had lit the field as clear as day. But now the fire, though it spilled a blood-red light in a twenty-foot area round the pyre, seemed to call shadows from the wood, a spill of darkness that lay across the field like a black mist.

Near the fire he could see the tragg'a shuffling as close as they dared. Their keening was a terrible din, like the wailing of alleycats—alleycats that were as large as lions. But at least their attention was centered on their slain brothers and not on the House.

"Okay," Tucker said, taking charge. "Time we took stock of our situation. What say we get cleaned up, then have ourselves a meeting and figure things out?"

He studied them, one by one. He knew he could count on Blue, no matter what their philosophical differences might be. Gannon and his two surviving men were an unknown quantity. So long as they were in danger themselves, Tucker thought they'd be allies. But without really knowing what they'd been after in the first place, it was hard to know where they stood. Gannon was in charge, while Mercier was definitely a follower. Chevier, chewing on a mint while leaning casually against a wall, was just a more sophisticated version of Mercier. That left the gardener, Fred, who appeared resilient enough, and Sam, whose eyes had held a look of numbed shock ever since the attack began.

"I figure it's about time," Gannon said.

"Got a place we can use, Blue?" Tucker asked.

The biker nodded. "Take everyone into the Silkwater Kitchen, Fred. I'll go round up Jamie and the others."

"What about those things outside?" Chevier asked. His eerie voice rasped in strange harmony to the noise of the tragg'a. "One of us should keep watch."

Tucker nodded. "Yeah. You're probably right. Want to be elected?"

Chevier glanced at Gannon who nodded. Definitely the boss, Tucker thought. Now who was Gannon working for?

"Sure," Chevier said. "Beats sitting around and listening to a lot of yapping. You want to leave me that Weatherby?"

Tucker handed the rifle to Blue who shook his head.

"I think I'll just hang on to this myself," he said. "You seem pretty good with that handgun of yours."

Chevier shrugged. "Suit yourself. What about the rest of this place?"

"They seem to be gathered outside this door for the time being," Gannon said. He glanced at Tucker. "Maybe we'll get some mobile patrols going after we have our little talk, eh?"

"Sounds good," the Inspector replied. "Let's go."

In Gramarye's Clover, Jamie and Traupman sat across from each other in front of the window. They'd cleaned up the debris as best they could, piling most of it on one side of the room in a great heap of books, broken shelving and the like. The odor of charred wood still hung faintly in the air. Thomas had been returned to the bed, the faint rise and fall of his chest being the only clue that he was still alive. Sally and Maggie sat on the edge of the bed, alternating their attention between the wizard and the two men by the window.

"One just forgets," Jamie was saying. "I've studied the paranormal, the mysteries, for so many years, always looking for the key to unlock all the riddles. When and if I ever found it, I always thought it'd be . . . well, different. I was thinking more in terms of enlightenment. Or higher planes of existence." He looked away from the tragg'a to face Traupman. "I forgot about the evil side. It had to be there. If there was going to be one, there had to be the other."

Traupman nodded. "I still find it . . . difficult to accept. I was willing to go along with telekinetics, telepathy, that sort of thing. But what we're faced with here I always thought of as just so much fiction."

"It isn't as though we never had any clues," Jamie said. "When you think of all the folktales, of all the horrors and monsters that populate folklore. . . ." Jamie shook his head. "God, perhaps it's all real." He glanced at the bed. "I just wish our wizard would be of a little more use than he's been so far. He's managed to get us messed up in it all, but now when we need him. . . ."

Damn, he thought. This is just a grand state of affairs you've brought me into, Tom. Bad enough you had to involve me in it, but what about the rest of them? What about Sara? What has your monster done with Sara?"

"We seem to have two choices," Traupman said. "Try and hold out or—and mind you, I'm not advocating this, merely stating the facts—or give the creatures what they want."

"We can't!" Sally said. "It wouldn't be right."

Why not? Jamie thought. It was Tom that got us into this in the first place. But he knew he wasn't capable of handing Tom over either. "We've no assurance," he said, "that Tom is all they want."

"True. On the other hand, we have his word that it *is* only him they want. Unfortunately, he has yet to be proved wrong."

"Could you do that, Dr. Traupman?" Maggie asked. "Could you deliver another human being to those creatures?"

Traupman regarded her steadily and shook his head. "I spoke only hypothetically," he said. "As Jamie says, we don't truly know what they want. And even if we gave them their wizard, that wouldn't necessarily solve our other problem: How do we get back to our own world?"

"I still can't believe you'd even consider handing him over," Sally said. "You make it sound as though he consciously made things work out the way they have."

"Don't worry, Sally," Jamie said. "Nobody's going to send him out there."

"Send who out where?" Blue asked from the doorway.

"Tom," she said. "They were talking about sending him out to appease the monsters."

Blue thought about it for a moment, then shook his head. "Won't do any good," he said. "Besides. He's all *we*'ve got against them. All we've got to get us back to the real world. How's he doing anyway, doc?"

"Basically, there is nothing wrong with him," Traupman replied.

"Then how come he's just lying there?"

"In a normal case, I would say severe shock. But if he is all he is supposed to be, I would hazard that whatever is controlling those beings outside has gotten to his mind in some way. His body may be self-healing, but his mind? Or his spirit, if you will?"

"You mean he's just out of it?" Blue asked. "We gotta work this thing out for ourselves?"

"So it would appear."

"Shit. How're we—" He shook his head. "Well, we can figure that out downstairs. Tucker wants to have a meeting so that we can talk over the situation. Maybe someone'll have some bright idea."

"I'll stay with our patient," Traupman said.

"No, I'll stay," Sally put in. "You'll be of more help downstairs. I've got nothing to offer except to say that I'm scared and I just want things to get back to normal."

"Amen," Maggie murmured.

"Doc?" Blue asked.

"Well, it doesn't appear that our patient is going anywhere. Just be sure to call us immediately if there is any change whatsoever."

"You going to be okay, babe?" Blue asked.

Sally nodded.

"I'll stay," Maggie offered. "Just send up John when you're done."

"Will do," Blue said.

"Okay," Tucker said when they were all gathered around the big table in the Silkwater Kitchen. "First things first." He turned to Gannon. "Who the hell are you and what are you doing here? Does anyone here know him? Jamie? Blue?"

Before either of them could reply, Gannon held up a hand for silence. "Before we get into these more personal matters," he said, "perhaps we might take stock on exactly where we stand so far as weapons, provisions and the like are concerned."

Weird guy, Tucker thought. He slips easily from talking like some cultural aide to street talk. Well, he might not want to get into his reasons for breaking into Tamson House, but they sure as hell weren't going to just set it aside. The guy was a pro, he *and* the two goons that were left. They weren't here for some simple B&E. They knew about Hengwr and were here to grab him. What Tucker wanted to know was who gave Gannon his orders. And why.

"That might be an excellent place to start," Traupman said, forestalling Tucker's imminent outburst.

"Wait a minute," Blue said. "The Inspector's on the straight and narrow this time. We've got a right to know what these guys are after."

"In good time," Jamie said. He understood Traupman's concern. They were trapped here—all of them together. They needed to stick together if they were going to survive. He wanted to now what Gannon was doing here as much as anyone, but they couldn't risk internal strife right now. Not with the creatures on their doorstep and the House God knew where.

"How are we set for up food and water?" he asked. "And power?"

Blue sighed. Jamie was becoming a right little arbitrator these days, which was a funny position for him to be in seeing how they were all usually trying to calm *him* down. Losing Sara had hit him hard. He took a deep breath to steady the rush of adrenaline and nodded. It was Jamie's House. He'd play by Jamie's rules for now. But God help Gannon if he tried to set them up when they were all supposed to be working together.

"We've got enough fuel," he said, "to run the generator for a month—that's saying we use every light and appliance in the place the whole time. If we conserve it, we should be able to go for some time. We could close off a lot of the place, once the weather turns bad—that'd help on heating and save fuel. How's the wood pile doing, Fred?"

"We have about ten cords," Fred replied. "But water could be a problem. We switched to city hydro back in the fifties. The wells are still operational, but being where we are—I can't promise we'll get anything out of them."

"But there's water right now?" Tucker asked.

Blue left the table and tried the tap. There was a spluttering in the pipes, then the tap spit out a discolored water that cleared quickly. He took a cautious sip.

"Country water," he pronounced. "No chlorine."

"What about food?" Gannon asked.

"Enough to feed an army," Fred replied. "We stored a lot of produce in the cellars this autumn and all the kitchens have canned goods. We might run out of some things . . . but we'll have the basic staples for a long time."

"Well then," Traupman said. "We've established that we won't freeze, starve, nor die of thirst. Perhaps it's time we pooled our information."

He glanced at Tucker as though to say, it's your show. Just take it easy.

"What about weapons?" Gannon asked.

Tucker shook his head. "We can get to that. Let's not mess around anymore, Gannon. We're all stuck here for the duration. Either we work together, or you and your men can get out of the House and try to set up a working arrangement with our friendly monsters. That's the nitty-gritty—just to let you know where you stand. Got it?"

Gannon nodded slowly.

"So give," Tucker said.

The Inspector, Gannon decided, was as abrasive as he'd been made out to be. A throwback to the era of the tough streetwise cop. And, from all the reports that had crossed Walters's desk, a man who got things done. He didn't make idle threats.

Gannon had already decided to go along with Tucker as far as he could, for all that it went against his grain. He just didn't know how much to give. Walters wasn't going to be too happy about having his name given up to the horsemen. On the other hand, Walters wasn't stuck in this weird place. Gannon knew that if he didn't cooperate with Tucker, he might never return to his own world for Walters to chew him out in the first place.

"What do you want to know?" he asked.

"What were you and your men doing in Tamson House?"

"You guessed that much, Inspector. To acquire Thomas Hengwr—if he proved to be on the premises." There was no point, Gannon thought, in mentioning that they were also planning to pick up Jamie Tams and eliminate the Inspector himself.

"Okay," Tucker said. "Then the big question is: Why?"

"My employer wished to have a private conversation with Hengwr."

"And his name is?"

Gannon hesitated, then sighed. "Walters," he said.

"Walters? J. Hugh Walters?"

"The same."

"Jesus H. Christ! Don't tell me. It was him that set Hogue up to run the PRB, wasn't it?"

"For all intents and purposes, it was Mr. Walters who set up the PRB itself."

"But why? Why go through all that trouble? I mean, it was just to get hold of Hengwr, wasn't it? Christ, with his resources, why did he need the Force to do his research for him?"

"Your people were already moving into the area of paranormal research," Gannon explained. "Mr. Walters is a thrifty man. Why should he duplicate research that was already underway? He merely put his own man in charge to ensure that the PRB concentrated on what was valid—rather than the charlatans and frauds that pervade such research."

"And how did he know that Hengwr was the real stuff?"

"Mr. Walters knew Thomas Hengwr in his youth. Hengwr was an old man then. Years later, Walters met Hengwr again, and while he had gone from youth to middle age, Hengwr didn't appear to have aged a single year. Subsequent investigation proved that while a man answering Hengwr's description appeared sporadically over the last few hundred years, he did not exist on paper. There were no records on him—birth certificates, passports, that sort of thing. From what data we could acquire, we discovered that Thomas Hengwr apparently possessed the secret of eternal life.

"Mr. Walters is very concerned with aging. He's in his fifties now. He wants Hengwr's secret of longevity. The rest of Hengwr's supposed paranormal abilities would be only so much topping on the cake."

Tucker shook his head in amazement. Given this information a week earlier, he would have laughed it off. But given what he knew now, that these abilities were real—all *too* real—he went cold at the thought of someone like Walters acquiring them. The man was a voice that was heard in more than one of the world's major nations. He moved high in political, industrial and academic circles. Every day you read something about him—about his acquisition of this, his support of that.

The one thing about Walters that stood out in Tucker's mind was his ruthlessness, an utter disregard for anyone but himself, for anything but what served him. It wasn't something that the average man in the street would be aware of, but to someone like Tucker who knew how to look and what to look for, it was all too plain to see. Give a man like that immortality . . . paranormal powers . . . what could ever stand in his way? Those that he might conceivably not be able to defeat, he need only outlive.

At least Hengwr had kept a low profile. From the skimpy file he had on him, Tucker couldn't really see the old man as a threat. It had always been the possibility of the extraordinary abilities that he might possess that had worried Tucker. Not as they were used by Hengwr, but as they might be used by another. Someone like Walters.

"So," Traupman said, ticking the items off on his fingers. "We've established why Mr. Gannon and his associates came to be in the House. We have provisions. We have the shelter and protection of the House."

"We can't be sure of that last item," Blue said. "We still don't know what it is about the House that keeps those creatures out. It could cut out at any time."

Traupman nodded. "Granted. But that is only a part of our primary concern. Topmost in our priorities should be discovering a way to return to our own world."

"And if we can't?" Gannon asked.

Nobody wanted to think about that.

Well, we've got Thomas Hengwr, Blue thought. All we've got to do is bring him around. Because if they didn't. . . .

"We're going to have to do a little reconnaissance of the area," he said, thinking aloud.

Gannon nodded. "Maybe pick up a local and get some directions—though if those things out there are all we've got to work with.' . . ."

"It's out of the question," Jamie said. "We can't possibly send someone out there to scout around. He wouldn't last five minutes once those creatures caught wind of him."

"There's one bright side we haven't looked on," Tucker said. "At least we don't need silver bullets to kill them. We can hurt them—for as long as our ammunition holds out."

"And then?" Jamie asked. "What happens when we run out of bullets before the enemy runs out of wolfmen?"

"Thomas Hengwr," Traupman said slowly, echoing Blue's earlier thought. "He's what it all boils down to. We've got to bring him around."

Gannon shook his head. From the quick look he'd had at Hengwr after the battle in the front hall with the tragg'a, he wouldn't put much hope in the old man. He remembered being shocked at the frail figure Hengwr was, lying there under the bedclothes, the skin drawn tight across his face, almost translucent, the scars puckering one half of it. He found it hard to picture Hengwr as the immortal sorcerer that Walters had made him out to be. He didn't look strong enough to support his own weight.

"He's all we've got?" he asked Traupman.

"Not unless you have a better suggestion."

"Nothing that comes to mind. This isn't exactly my field of expertise—if you take my meaning. But isn't there something you can do to snap him out of it? What exactly is the matter with him, anyway?"

"As I told Jamie earlier," Traupman explained, "he appears

to be suffering the effects of some severe trauma—the cause of which we can only guess at. Given the creatures that attacked us earlier, I can only shudder to think of what he has had to face."

"So we wait?" Gannon asked. He looked around the table. No one seemed pleased with the idea, but like him they didn't have any advice to offer either.

"Well," he said. "Let's work on our defense. I don't want to be caught sleeping if those creatures manage to break in again."

Blue nodded. "I figure if we patrol the ground floors, that should be enough."

"But no one outside," Jamie insisted.

"No one outside," Blue agreed.

Though sooner or later, someone was going to have to go out there and scout around. Blue didn't have enough patience to sit around and wait for their enemy to make the next move. Come the morning, he'd give serious thought to having a look at what lay beyond the fields around the House.

"I'll take the first shift," Tucker said, glancing at his watch. "It's going on nine. Say three-hour shifts?"

"This is a big place," Blue said. "We better have at least two guards—one to patrol the east and south wings, the other for the north and west."

"Sounds good," Gannon said. "I'll share the first watch with the Inspector."

"Then I'll take the second," Blue said, "with . . ." He looked around the table, settling on Gannon's companion.

"Mercier," Gannon said. "Chevier and Fred here can have the three-to-six shift, then the Inspector and I'll take over."

"What about us?" Jamie asked.

Tucker shook his head. "We'll need you and Dick alert enough to deal with Hengwr."

"And me?" Sam asked.

"You can share the dawn shift with Chevier and Fred," Blue said.

For a long moment after that they sat and looked at each other. The full implications of what had actually happened to them still had to sink in. Intellectually, they prepared for the coming confrontation with Hengwr's enemy who had now become their own enemy. It was easier to put aside the shock of the unreal being real when they were all in a group like this.

It would be later, when they split up, when some tried to sleep and others patrolled the House's lonely corridors, that they would each have to cope as best they could.

They were trapped in a situation where logic had no perimeters, where all their experiences meant nothing. They didn't know the rules. If there were any rules.

"Well?" Chevier asked when Gannon and Mercier met him back in the front hall.

"Better get some sleep," Gannon said. "You've pulled the dawn shift."

"Yeah. Sure." He took out a mint and popped it into his mouth. "But how're we handling this, Phil?"

"We play along with them. What else can we do? We're in a no-give situation."

"And Walters?"

Gannon shrugged. "We'll worry about him when and if we get back to the real world. But then . . . well, we'll grab Hengwr and make our break."

"Tucker's mine," Mercier said.

"Yeah? Where'd you get a hard-on for him?"

"Well, we can start with him wasting Serge."

Gannon nodded. He was remembering his own confrontation with Blue in the hallway moments before Serge got hit. It irked him to have been taken so easily by an amateur.

"Okay," he said. "The Inspector's all yours. But the biker's mine." He grinned. "What about you, Mike? You got a preference?"

Chevier shook his head. "Sounds to me like you don't want to leave any witnesses," he said in his whispery voice. "If that's the case, there'll be plenty for all of us. I'll just take whatever's left."

"I don't think we should wait," Mercier said. "It's when we get back to Ottawa that they'll be expecting us to make our move."

"He's got a point there," Chevier said.

"We wait," Gannon said decisively. "I've got the feeling that we'll need every hand that can hold a gun before we get out of this place."

"I wish you hadn't come," Tucker said to Maggie. She was accompanying him on his rounds along the south side of the House.

"There are times when you infuriate me with your protecting-the-helpless-female attitude. You know that, Tucker?"

"Yeah?"

"Yeah," she replied, mimicking him. Then she sighed. "But this isn't one of them. I just couldn't stand the thought of phoning you just to have you ask me to wait for you at home."

"I know. In your shoes, I'd've done the same."

"You wouldn't fit into my shoes, Tucker."

Tucker smiled, for the first time in hours, and put his arm around her waist to draw her close.

"I thought we were supposed to be patrolling," Maggie said, snuggling against him.

"We are, we are. This is all part of the job."

"Oh, really? Maybe I should've been a cop."

"What? And miss out on the high drama of playing Perry Mason?"

A look of mock horror passed over her face and she patted her stomach.

"Do you think I'm putting on weight?" she demanded.

Tucker shook his head. "Your weight's in all the right places."

"Betcha can't wait till twelve," she said with a grin.

"You just won yourself a bet."

Alone for the first time in hours, Jamie paced the length of his study, pausing from time to time to glare at the blank viewscreen of his computer. There was a solution to their problem in it. He knew it. Just as Tom's program had been hidden away in it for so many years. What else had Tom entered into its memory banks? And what was the code he needed to call it up? It was going to be something simple. Something obvious. So obvious that he probably wouldn't know it even if he tripped over it. Damn Tom, anyway, for being so obtuse. It wasn't right to play around with people's lives like this.

Turning from the desk, Jamie settled in one of the easy chairs in front of the hearth. He took out his pipe and filled it, searched for a match on the table beside him. His manuscript for the *International Wildlife* article was still sitting there, Sara's blue pencil on top of it. Setting aside his unlit pipe, Jamie stared into the cold hearth.

Sara, he thought, his chest tightening. He could sense an answering tension in the walls of the House. Through all that had been happening, her disappearance had been in the forefront of his mind—a sharp ache for which there was no remedy.

Was this the Otherworld that Tom had sent her to? Was she still safe with his apprentice, or had this Mal'ek'a thing captured her? Maybe she was just beyond the edges of the field that encircled the House, being held by the creatures. Held? Lord, if they had her, she wasn't even alive.

The realization brought a cold chill. Cursing Tom Hengwr again, he rose and went to his desk. He switched on Memoria, hand poised above the terminal. Where did he start? A random search? Try for a key word? A phrase? He knew they were supposed to be conserving energy in case they were in for a long stay, but he didn't really care. They had to do something about their position *now*. There might not be a later.

Sighing, he had Memoria call up the Weirdin bone file. One by one he left each bone on the screen, staring at it with his mind open, trying for an instinctual understanding, some leap of intuition that would help him where logic had failed.

Sally wanted to accompany Blue on his turn of guard duty and, thinking of the scouting expedition he had planned for himself in the morning, he made no protest. He planned to take his trail bike—the big chopper wouldn't be worth a damn in this kind of terrain. But even with the bike and his Weatherby, he knew he was asking for trouble. Still, they couldn't just sit around the House, waiting for a solution to present itself to them. They had to get out of here. Back to Ottawa.

He didn't have much faith in Thomas Hengwr being of much help to them—even if he did come round. Hengwr was the one who'd gotten them into this fucking mess in the first place. And there was another thing. Echoing the worry that was running through Jamie's head, he too had the feeling that Sara might be out there somewhere—maybe stumbling through the bush, lost, waiting for them to find her. The wolfmen mightn't have a clue what the roar of a trail bike was, but she'd know. If she was out there, near enough and able to move, she'd come to him.

"Heavy stuff," Sally said. "What's going to happen to us, Blue?"

Blue sighed. "We're going to kick ass and get out of this mess, that's what's going to happen. No way we're going to roll over and die just to please those things outside."

"It's not even just them," Sally said. "Those men—the one called Gannon and the other two. They give me the creeps."

"They are creeps," Blue said. "I'm not even all that sure

about Tucker. They're all in the same headspace—Tucker, Gannon, the others."

"I don't think you can put the Inspector with those other men. He may be straight, but I think he's pretty upfront."

Blue never got a chance to reply. They had just turned the corner of the hall that led from the east wing to the south side that would have faced Central Park if they were still in Ottawa. A crash of breaking glass came from the third room on the right. Working the bolt of the Weatherby as he ran, Blue burst into the room, Sally hard on his heels. He lifted the rifle as she panned the flashlight across the window. There was a stone on the floor, jagged shards of glass scattered across the carpet. Something came through a hole in the window—a paw, maybe a hand—and Blue's finger tightened on the trigger. Before he could fire, blue light flared and whatever had been trying to get in was gone.

Sally took a step forward.

"Hold it!" Blue said. He kept the rifle leveled at the window, his gaze never wavering from it. They both watched, with a mixture of astonishment and fear, as the window began to repair itself.

"Blue . . . ?"

"That didn't look like any monster's paw," he said. "That looked like a hand."

"The window, Blue."

"Yeah. I know."

Whatever it was about the House that protected them was still operating. Shaking his head, Blue lowered the rifle. The House had always been a little strange, but this was freaky.

"I gotta go out and have a look," he said. "Give me the flashlight, babe."

She shook her head. "I . . . I'm going with you."

"Don't be crazy," he began, then paused at the look of determination on her face.

She was scared. Shit, *he* was scared. But she wasn't going to back off. That was part of what had drawn him to her in the first place. She didn't seem like she'd back off from anything. She might've been a little weirded out when all of this started—hell, who hadn't been?—but she was pulling like a trouper now.

"Okay," he said. "Let's go."

They made their way to the nearest southside door, eased it open and stepped out onto the porch. Sally held the flashlight at her side, the light turned off. For long moments they stood there, waiting for their eyes to adjust to the starlight, listening, watching. When Blue was satisfied that there was nothing out there, at least nothing close, he led off towards the window. When they reached it, Blue studied their surroundings again, receptive to the slightest pinprick warning of danger. But the night was still. The only scent in the air was that of wildflowers and the tall grass. The only sound was that of the wind and their own quick breathing.

"Take a look around the window," Blue said. He kept his back to the House, gaze darting left and right, and out to the open expanse of field.

"What am I looking for?"

"For some sign of whatever was trying to break in. A footprint. Whatever."

"There's nothing," she said after a moment. "Have we got the right window?"

"What's the ground like?"

"Soft."

So it would've held a print. Whatever had tried to get in had to have left some sign.

"You keep watch for a sec," he said.

He passed her the rifle and, using the flashlight, hunkered down to have a look. Sally was right. There was nothing there. The ground lay undisturbed. So what the hell had been trying to get through the window before the House fried it?

"Let's check a couple more," he said.

They investigated the ground under three more windows, then double-checked them in their return to the door. The story was the same under each one—nothing had left a track. Not even a scuff. Blue had set his own weight in the dirt and left a bootprint. Sally, weighing in at a hundred and two pounds, had tried as well with the same results.

"Let's go back inside," she said suddenly. "I'm starting to feel creepy—like we're being watched."

"We probably are," Blue said, but he motioned for her to go on ahead of him.

He stared off into the darkness for a long time, lips pursed as he thought, before following her inside. "What do you think it was?" he asked as he locked the door once more.

Sally shook her head. "I haven't a clue. With everything so mixed up, it could've been anything. A ghost?"

"You know what I think? I think it was someone from our world, trying to get in."

"What?"

"It makes sense," he said, "in a weird sort of way. And everything's so mixed up that anything's possible. What if the House is in two worlds at the same time? If it's just the inside of the House that goes world-hopping? Remember the attack this morning? When we went outside, there was nothing on the doors or the walls. Not a scratch. But this afternoon, when we found ourselves here. . . . Well, you saw the sides of the House where the wolfmen attacked. The wood's all clawed to ratshit. The place is a mess. The way it *should* have looked this morning."

Sally nodded. "I think you're right. But what does that mean? And how could there be two Houses as strange as this one is?"

"I don't know. Jamie's grandfather had this one built. Maybe there's something in old Anthony Tamson's journals that can tell us. Jamie'd know where to look."

"But wouldn't he already have thought of that by now? If he knew?"

"Not necessarily. All the Tamsons are heavy-duty writers. They pump out reams of the stuff, from Jamie's grandfather all the way down to Sara. Who'd have time to go through it all?"

"Well, let's go ask him."

Blue shook his head. "After we've finished our patrol."

"Maybe there'll be something in those journals that will tell us how to get back."

"You got it," Blue said.

But if there wasn't, that made it even more imperative for him to scout around tomorrow. Because if one structure could straddle two worlds, there might be others. And if he found another one, there was a chance that he might find someone in it who could give them a hand. It'd be dangerous, but he wouldn't walk into anything blind.

He slung his rifle over his shoulder, adjusting the strap so that it hung comfortably, ready at hand. The Weatherby could be awfully persuasive, if push came to shove.

Traupman dozed in a chair in Gramarye's Clover, wakening from time to time to have a look at the patient. Tom's breathing had evened out as the night progressed and while his skin was still pale, it was not so transparent. He wondered what it was that could have affected Tom in such a way—what sort of a being this Mal'ek'a creature was.

Traupman found this entire situation extremely disturbing. Here he was, he thought, closing his eyes again, a writer of macabre fiction, a pursuer of "forbidden lore" for all these years, but never a believer. There had always been a wide streak of cynicism running through him—just enough to keep the papers he'd had published free of the baseless enthusiasm that invalidated so much paranormal research. He had only let himself go in his fiction. But he'd never believed in any of it. Not for a moment. It had just come out of the dark side of his imagination. It was a healthy catharsis to relieve his own fears of dying as the years took their toll on him. For he was getting old now. Too old for this. Too old to have fiction become reality.

A footstep in the doorway brought him out of his reverie. He saw Phillip Gannon leaning against the doorjamb.

"How's the patient, Dr. Traupman?"

"Still unconscious. But he's resting easier."

"Any chance we can pry a few words from him tomorrow?"

"I'm hoping."

Gannon nodded. "Just a little guy, isn't he. A funny-looking little guy. If you passed him on the street, you'd never think he could cause such a fuss. Well, you take care of yourself, Dr. Traupman. It's going to be a long day tomorrow."

The words were pleasantly spoken, but there was a dead look in Gannon's eyes. This was a dangerous man, Traupman realized. He stared at the empty doorway for a long time after Gannon was gone. A very dangerous man, he amended. He hoped John had some way of dealing with him and his companions, when and if they got out of their present predicament.

Mal'ek'a waited in a place of darkness.

It gave no thought to the passing of time. Its patience would be rewarded. It had its tragg'a scouring the worlds, past and present, for the small hornless one who kept the bard's power-object from it. They would find her. And when they did, they would bring Mal'ek'a the ring. What they did with her afterwards was of no concern to it. All it needed was the ring to crack open Tamson House that it might take its rightful prey—the druid.

The only other method of gaining entrance to that cursed House had failed dismally. Mal'ek'a thought of reaching for another mind in the House, but the creatures that remained within were stronger and the House had strengthened its protection.

No. There was time enough. There was forever. It need only be patient. It had already waited through a thousand years of darkness to free itself. It had waited to gather strength enough to fashion itself a body, to bend the wills of the devil-bear's children to its own purposes. It could wait longer. It was mortals who lived to die. Beings such as itself and the druid would go on forever. Until they were slain.

Mal'ek'a's power flickered in its eyes as it savored the thought of its enemy's death. There would be no Summer Country for him. He was to know the same wintry void that lurked in Mal'ek'a's own heart.

"You both saw this?" Jamie asked.

As he looked from one to the other, Sally nodded.

"And it was a hand? A human hand . . . not a paw?"

"It happened pretty fast," Blue said. "But I'm sure it was a hand. When we checked around outside, we couldn't find anything. I tell you it fits."

"I don't know," Jamie said. He rubbed his eyes, weary from the hours he'd spent hunched over Memoria's terminal and viewscreen. "I suppose it could be possible," he conceded.

"It fits, Jamie. Where do you keep your grandfather's journals? There's got to be some reference in them to what makes the House so strange. After all, he had the place built."

"I've been through them," Jamie said.

"But you weren't looking for this," Sally said.

He'd come up with nothing himself. It was the same frustration that had dogged him for years. He *knew* the answer was in reach. He just couldn't focus on it. Blue's theory warranted looking into, but he just didn't have the energy. He needed to catch a couple of hours of sleep before he simply passed out where he was sitting.

"All the journals are in the Library in the west wing," he said. "Where Sam works."

Blue nodded. "In the glass shelves—on the right as you go in?"

"That's them."

"Maybe we should get Sam to go through them. I don't

think he's really cut out for guard duty. You get some sleep, Jamie. We'll go ask him if he's up to it and then we're hitting the sack ourselves."

"All right."

"Come on, Jamie," Sally said. She helped him to his feet, then glanced at Blue. "You go talk to Sam while I get Jamie to his room."

"Gotcha. You hang in there, Jamie. We'll work this thing out yet."

It was past four by the time Blue made it back to the Firecat's Room. Sally was still awake when he got into bed and drew him close.

"Hold me," she said.

Their lovemaking was slow and tender, a reaffirmation of life among the death and horrors that they'd faced. Lying beside her afterwards, Blue looked at her sleeping face and ran a finger down her cheek. This was real. Hell of a time for it to happen. But at least they had this much. Some people went their whole lives through never finding it.

He lay awake for a long while, thoughts drifting from the woman at his side, to Sara and where she might be, to what tomorrow had in store for them. At length he fell into a fitful sleep, awakening two hours later.

It was light outside. Just going on seven. On a Friday morning in Never-never-land. Did they even have days of the week in this place? He tried to get back to sleep, but he was too wound up. After a while he slipped out of bed, drew the covers up around Sally, and got dressed. He hung a knapsack over one shoulder, his Weatherby over the other.

"Blue?" a sleepy voice asked from the bed.

"It's okay, babe. I'm just going to scout around a bit. You try and get some more sleep, okay? I'll see you later."

He bent over her to give her a kiss, then straightened slowly. Jamie and Tucker'd look after her. There was no one to look after Sara. Catching up his motorcycle helmet, he left the room. Sally was already asleep again.

Gannon and Tucker would be on patrol now. He'd have to make sure he didn't run into either one of them because he wasn't in the mood for either arguments or explanations. He made his way downstairs without being spotted, then paused when he heard a sound in the library. Walking silently on the carpeted hall, he made his way to the door and peered in. Sam was sitting on the floor in front of the glass bookshelves that held Anthony and Nathan Tamson's journals. He had them stacked on either side of him and was bent over one, hand pushing the hair back from his face, his lips pursed as he studied the neat printing on the page before him.

"How's it going?" Blue asked.

"Wh-what?" The book fell from Sam's hand as he started.

"Hey! Easy, man. I didn't mean to startle you."

"Oh, it's you." He put his hand against his chest. His eyes were bloodshot, gaze darting left to right. "You almost gave me a heart attack."

"Sorry, Sam. You find anything in those yet?"

"I've found a lot—only nothing we can use. Not yet anyway."

"Well, keep plugging at it. How's the head?"

Sam touched the bandage on his forehead and shrugged. "It's there," he said.

"You get any sleep?"

"I'm planning to. But first I want to finish this pile."

"Don't wear yourself out, man. It looks like a long job."

Sam nodded. Then he took in Blue's knapsack and helmet. "Where are you going?" he asked.

"Just for a little scout around. Nothing serious."

"I don't think that's such a good idea, Blue. Have you told Jamie?"

"Hey, I'm not going far. You take it easy, Sam. I'll see you in an hour or so."

He pushed off before Sam could continue the discussion, making for the kitchen. There he loaded his knapsack with some provisions and a canteen that he filled at the sink. He dug a small compass out of a tool drawer and clipped it to his belt, then, chewing on a piece of cheese, headed for the garage facing O'Connor where he kept his bikes. He made it there without running into either Gannon or Tucker, which made him wonder about how much good these patrols were doing in the first place. Well, he'd put more faith in whatever it was about the House that was protecting them, than in either Tucker or Gannon and his crew.

Once in the garage, he wheeled his trail bike out into the open space in front of the big doors and loaded up his knapsack and a spare can of gas on the back. The bike was a Yamaha YZ 250—nothing too big. He only used it for tooling around in the bush, keeping his chopped-down Harley for street use.

When he had the gas can and knapsack strapped in and had balanced their weights, he topped off the gas tank. Ready to go. He was just picking up his rifle, when a voice spoke from behind him.

"Well, well, well."

Shit! He turned slowly to find one of Gannon's men standing in the doorway that led into the House. Mercier, he thought. Whatever glib explanation Blue might have come up with died as he saw the gun in Mercier's hand. It was a .22 Margolin target pistol that had belonged to one of the two men that had died yesterday in the attack. Mercier's own .38 was stuck in his belt.

"What do you want?" Blue asked.

"Well," Mercier said, enjoying the moment, "when Gannon saw you creeping through the halls—all loaded up for a trip, it seemed—he asked me to go have a look-see, just to find out what it was all about. You got some place you're going, biker-boy? Some friends you're calling in, maybe?"

Blue's eyes narrowed, but he kept a smile on his face. "Hey, what is this shit, man?" he said. "I'm just going to scout around a little, you know?"

"Can the bullshit. Nobody's going to scout around with those monsters still on the prowl—not unless they've got some place to go. Now where is it?"

"I already told you—"

Mercier lifted the .22 and shook it back and forth slowly. "Uh-uh. You're going to have to do better than that. I always figured you folks knew more than you were letting on. If you know a way back, you better spill it now, biker-boy. Before I spill your brains all over the back of that wall. Got it?"

This was just great timing, Blue thought. Even if he could get his rifle up in time, he didn't have a shell in the chamber. He had to think of something, and think fast. If Gannon had sent his goon to go have a look, it wasn't hard to bet that Gannon'd be along himself real soon. About nine feet separated Mercier from him. There was no way he could cross that distance before Mercier got off a shot. And Mercier, being what he was, wasn't likely to miss.

"Okay," he said, letting his shoulders sag slightly. "There's a way out."

Mercier smiled. "Keep talking, friend. Keep them words rolling. Where is it? How far?"

"Just past the forest—" Blue began, lifting his hand to point, but Mercier cut him off.

"Not so fast. You keep those hands moving slow, biker-boy. And why don't you lay down that rifle? Your hand must be getting awfully tired just hanging onto it like that. Just ease the barrel down on the floor and bend down slowly and lay it out. *Now,* friend."

Now? Damn right, "friend." It was now or never.

Something Blue hadn't felt in years rose up in him. It was the who-gives-a-shit attitude that he'd worn as proudly as his colors back when he rode with the Devil's Dragon. It was that anger that Jamie and Sara had showed him how to diffuse, to focus that energy on creating rather than destroying. But every-thing they'd given him disappeared in that moment, leaving the savagery that he'd never quite gotten rid of.

Mercier knew that look, but the suddenness of Blue's attack, its sheer viciousness, took him off guard for the precious sec-onds the biker needed. Mercier's first shot went over Blue's head and he never got the opportunity for a second one. The butt of the Weatherby came up out of the air and drove into his jaw with all the force of Blue's arm behind it, shattering bone. The blow threw him back against the wall, his jaw hang-ing askew. Fire poured through him, nerve ends seared with pain. He tried to bring up the Margolin, but Blue stepped in close and smashed the rifle down again. The .22 spilled out of lifeless fingers and Mercier slumped to the ground, his skull staved in. A red stain spread across his shirt, leaked to the floor.

"Stupid fucker," Blue said, standing over him.

There was a wild singing in his ears and he shook his head, trying to get rid of it. I don't want to feel like this anymore, he told himself. I'm not *like* this anymore. Even with those fucking monsters I wasn't like this.

But it was there inside him, the savage side of himself freed again. He took a deep breath. Another. The sudden rush of oxygen helped to clear his head. He knew that the one shot Mercier got off was going to bring people down here. And there wasn't time for any of the crap that would come in their wake. He wasn't up to being diplomatic with Gannon or Tucker. And he sure as fuck wasn't ready to face either Jamie or Sally.

Shifting the Weatherby to his left hand, he took Mercier's .38, stuck it in his own belt, and put the Margolin in his jacket

pocket. He looked down at the corpse. What was he supposed
to do with the body? God damn Mercier! If he could just've
left him alone. . . . Blue shook his head, breathed deeply. Slow
down, he told himself. We've got a ways to go still. Now
think. Leave it here or take it? Fuck it! He'd take it. Let them
try to figure out what had happened to Mercier. Let Gannon
do a little sweating, seeing's how he always seemed so cool.

The decision made, he moved quickly. He got the garage
doors open and wheeled the bike out. Returning to the garage,
he carried Mercier's body out and dumped it unceremoniously
beside the bike. Inside again, he threw a tarpaulin over the
bloodstained floor, then stepped outside, locking the doors shut
behind him. He balanced Mercier on the gas tank and handlebars, hit the ignition and the bike roared into life. The body
was awkward and he zigzagged across the field, heading for a
break in the woods that was due east. He didn't bother to look
back. The bike's noise would've alerted anyone in the House
that something was up. He just hoped he could make it into
the woods before someone caught a look.

As he was nearing the trees, he saw the black shapes shuffle
from the forest on the right. He gunned the bike to the trees
and skidded to a stop. The bike tipped and he wrestled it back
upright by brute force. Sucker weighed a lot with two people
on it. Glancing at the tragg'a, he dumped Mercier's body on
the ground and took off again.

"Play with that for a while!" he called back over his shoulder.

Then he was in amongst the trees and needed all his attention
focused on the obstacle course they made. He just hoped he
didn't run into another pack of the wolfmen in a place where
he couldn't maneuver. They didn't move fast and he knew he
could outdistance them, given the room to move. But all he
needed was to lose the bike and have to face a pack of them
on foot. He'd take one or two with him, but after facing them
yesterday, he knew he wouldn't last long. They'd have him
then and that'd be all she wrote.

"What the hell was that?" Tucker demanded.

He came running up to where Gannon stood, about to put
his shoulder to the door that led to the garage.

"Seems like one of the birds has flown the coup," Gannon
replied. "Locked the door from the inside of the garage." He
hit the door with enough force to pop the lock and they both
stepped in.

"Was it Blue?" Tucker asked.

Gannon nodded. "I saw him heading down the hall, all loaded up and ready to travel. I sent Mercier after him while I went and checked to make sure it wasn't a mass exodus."

"What does it matter to you who comes and goes here?"

"Well, Inspector. Remember your pretty little speech about us all sticking together until we got through this? I just didn't want to be left out on the flight home. That's all."

"Well, he's gone now. Where's your man Mercier?"

Gannon shrugged. There was a familiar smell in the air. Gunsmoke mixed with blood. Once you smelled them, you didn't forget. He kicked aside the tarpaulin and they both stared at the blood.

"Not a whole lot left of him," Gannon said. "I wonder where your biker friend stored the body. He probably took it with him and dumped it in the field for the wolfmen's breakfast."

Looking at the blood, Tucker shook his head. Something didn't fit here. Though he and Blue had had their differences, he just couldn't see the biker gunning someone down in cold blood. And Gannon's answers were all just a little too pat.

"Just what did you tell Mercier to do when he caught up with Blue?"

"To detain him, Inspector. Nothing more."

"And if he wasn't into being 'detained'?"

"I left that up to Mercier's discretion. From the looks of things, he made the wrong decision. Unless, of course, the biker got the drop on him and just blew him away."

"No way. That's the way you people operate."

"And you know the people of Tamson House well enough to give them all such sterling character references? Let's not play games, Inspector. They know far more about all of this than they're telling us. They can't have lived in this place for so many years without learning how to control this hopping between worlds."

"I don't buy that, Gannon. They're in this with us. Their lives are in as much danger as our own."

"It appears that way...."

"It *is* that way. You've got one man left, Gannon. Keep him in line—keep yourself in line—or it'll be my pleasure to send you both out to say hello to your dead buddies. Got me?"

Gannon regarded him steadily, cold eyes glinting with amusement. "And what would your superiors say if they knew what a bloodthirsty man they have representing them?"

"If you've got a grievance, Gannon, you're welcome to go

find one of my superiors and take it up with them. There's a
door to the outside right behind you."

"I think I would rather see what Dr. Traupman has managed
to come up with in regards to our sorcerous Mr. Hengwr, if
it's all the same to you."

Keep it up, Tucker thought, as he followed Gannon out into
the hall. Just keep it up, asshole.

But as they made their way upstairs, he had to think about
Blue himself. What was the biker trying to pull with this fool
stunt? They'd agreed yesterday that any exploration of the
Otherworld was going to wait until they had a bit of a better
idea as to what they could expect out there. Blue had better
have a damn good explanation ready, or he'd find himself in
deep shit when he got back. If he got back.

Tucker paused at a window and looked out across the fields
to the forest. Trouble was, the law didn't mean dick out here.
The words "out of my jurisdiction" had come to take on a
whole new meaning for him.

Traupman awoke with a start, wondering sleepily what had
roused him. His back was stiff from having stretched out in a
chair for most of the night and there was a buzzing in his ears.
He glanced at Tom, then realized that the sound came from
outside. It sounded like a motor. Rising awkwardly from the
chair, he made it to the window just in time to see Blue's trail
bike with its double load weaving drunkenly across the field.
At the edge of the forest, the bike stopped. Traupman watched
the biker relieve himself of a limp body, then head off, deeper
into the woods.

Strange, Traupman thought.

He stood looking out the window, trying to work out what
was going on. When the tragg'a reached Blue's burden, Traupman turned from the window and shivered. You couldn't pay
him enough to go out there. Blue was either a brave man or a
fool. He wondered what had sent the biker into the forest.
There was nothing out there but the wolfmen, Hengwr's mysterious enemy, and bushland. Or at least, that was what they
had all assumed. Perhaps Blue was simply going out to establish
the validity of those observations.

Who knew what lay beyond the forest? Traupman admitted
a strong curiosity himself. But his prime concern was the well-
being of Thomas Hengwr. He would simply have to wait until

Blue returned with the information. He wondered briefly whose body it was that the biker had left for the tragg'a. If it was another casualty, he hoped it was one of Gannon's men.

Sitting on the edge of the bed, he studied Tom. It was frustrating not being able to do anything. Hengwr was resting easily, but he still couldn't be roused. The wounds on his face were simply old scars now. Traupman put his fingers against Tom's throat. The pulse was steady. He lifted one eyelid, then the other. The eyes were still rolled back. Traupman couldn't understand what it was that kept Tom in this catatonic state.

He looked up as the door opened.

"Good morning, John," he said. "Mr. Gannon."

"Morning, Dick. Any change?"

Traupman shook his head. He perceived the tension that crackled between the two men and wondered if Blue's burden had anything to do with it. He decided to wait until he and John were alone before asking.

"I can't seem to bring him around, John."

"Can't you give him a shot of something?" Gannon asked.

"I'm afraid that a stimulant might just trigger a more regressive response. We're dealing with a very delicate situation here. With the proper facilities, there might be something we could do. But here . . . I suggest we continue waiting."

"What if he never comes around?" Gannon said.

"Then we figure another way out of this mess," Tucker growled.

Gannon shrugged. "Let me know when you've figured it out, Inspector," he said and left the room.

Tucker glared at his back.

"What was all that about?" Traupman asked.

"We had a little argument," Tucker replied. "The biker— Blue—killed one of Gannon's men and took off on a trail bike."

"Killed . . . ?"

Traupman had realized that Blue's burden was dead, but the question of murder hadn't entered his mind.

"I don't think Blue had a choice, Dick. I suspect Gannon's man just leaned too hard on him."

"And now Blue's fled and we're short two more men."

"He'll be back," Tucker said. "The way Gannon told it, Blue looked like he was going on a scouting mission. Remember he talked about that yesterday?"

"Yes. But with this killing. . . ."

"That won't stop him from coming back. His friends are here. No matter what he thinks of Gannon or us, he won't leave his friends to fend on their own. Besides, where the hell can he go out there?"

As he spoke, Tucker remembered his recent conversation with Gannon. He mentioned Gannon's suspicions to Traupman.

"It's possible, John. What do we really know about these people?"

"Don't you start on me, too! They're in as much danger as we are, for Christ's sake."

"I suppose," Traupman allowed. "But at this point in the proceedings, we should keep our eyes open and not settle into any assumptions. It's easy to side with the residents of Tamson House against both the wolfmen and Gannon. But we have to remember that we really don't know these people."

"I'll keep it in mind," Tucker muttered.

Walking back down the hall, he shook his head. This he didn't need. He knew Dick was right—it just wasn't something he wanted to think about. Because if Jamie and Blue were taking him for a ride as well. . . . Goddamn! He *really* didn't need this. But he couldn't get away from it either.

"Lived here long?"

Sally looked up, then smiled at Maggie and made room for her on the couch. She'd been trying to straighten up the long room that ran off the Silkwater Kitchen without a lot of luck. This was where she and Blue had spent a lot of time. The Sony Betamax and 20″ screen TV were in here. Blue's worktable was up against the window overlooking the garden. The opposite wall was taken up by bookcases that held souvenirs of Blue's sojourn in New Mexico and stacks of old *Popular Mechanics* and biking magazines.

At the moment, the contents of the bookcases and shelves were heaped under them. Sally had been straightening the paint containers and sketchbooks on the worktable, then found herself sitting on the couch going through a sketchbook that was mostly filled with studies of herself. Blue had never shown these to her. A lot were head and shoulders, sketched from a number of different angles. A half dozen more were of her doing her tai chi.

Looking at them, remembering the news that Jamie had given her this morning about Blue taking off on his bike, she'd felt a lump rising in her throat. There were two different men living in that big lug's body. She wondered what he would have been like if he'd never gotten mixed up with that biker gang. Then she wondered if she'd still care for him as much— for he wouldn't be the same person. That was part of what drew her to him. Not the violence. Just the intensity, the assurance that went into everything he did, whether it was making love, working on a bike, or painting.

Laying aside the sketchbook, she brought her knees up under her chin and turned so that she was facing Maggie.

"It feels like I've lived here forever," she said, "though it can't have been for more than a few weeks. A lot happened in a little time in this place."

"Too much," Maggie agreed. "Where are you from originally?"

"Granville, O-hi-o. It's a small college town. I ended up here by way of California and Vancouver."

"I saw some of your artwork up in Jamie's study. I like it very much—especially the washes. Is that your sketchbook?"

"No. It's Blue's."

"May I?"

Sally hesitated for a moment, then shrugged. Why not?

"These are beautiful," Maggie exclaimed as she leafed through the book. "There's so much expression in them, and yet there's a . . . stillness, a sense of peace, at the same time. It's hard to imagine—" She broke off. "I'm sorry. I didn't mean . . ."

"That's okay. He doesn't look the part, that's for sure. And with what he pulled this morning. . . . It's not like him. I'm not saying that because I care for him or because I haven't known him for that long. Sara and Jamie both told me the same thing— back before all this mess started. He's got to be pushed pretty hard to let himself go like that . . . to . . ." She couldn't quite bring herself to say the words "to have killed somebody."

"Everybody's been under a lot of tension," Maggie said.

"I know. But. . . . You know, he told me he was going this morning and I was too sleepy to register what he was saying. I don't know if I even said goodbye to him and now . . . now I might not see him again. Not if those monsters get a hold of him. I was trying to clean up in here and found that sketchbook with all those studies of me in it and . . . I just feel so lost."

Maggie laid a hand on Sally's knee. "Your friend Jamie's been brooding about it all morning as well," she said. "I can't say everything's going to work out, because I don't know what's going on in the first place, but maybe if you talk to Jamie you'll feel a little better. It might make you both feel better."

"I don't feel I know Jamie well enough, to be honest. And now, first with Sara disappearing, then this mess, and Blue taking off...Jamie really depends on Blue. I think that's what's kept Blue straight for so long. Because both Jamie and Sara depended on him. Him and Fred. Have you met Fred?"

"Briefly. He doesn't say much."

A small smile tugged at Sally's lips. "Ask him about his gardens."

Maggie looked out the window. "I find it strange that they're still there," she said.

"Blue and I were talking about it last night. We figure that there's a Tamson House on two worlds and when this shift came, just the inside of the House and the gardens were moved into this Otherworld."

"So the House is still standing back in Ottawa?"

Sally shrugged. "Well, at least the outside of it is. And maybe the inside of the one on this world."

"It all sounds very confusing and highly unprobable—if it wasn't for the fact that we *are* here."

They sat quietly for a few minutes, then Maggie asked: "Want a hand with this room?"

"Sure. Thanks."

Sally got up and replaced the sketchbook on the table, then the two of them started in on the bookshelves.

"You're a lawyer, aren't you?" Sally asked as they worked.

"Mmhmm. That's how I met John—the Inspector."

"What's he really like?"

"Stubborn as a mule and about as patient. He's got his own way of looking at things, and woe be to the person who tries to tell him different. But under all his bluster, he's a good man. Much like Blue in many ways—though a lot straighter."

"That's what I told Blue. Not that they were alike, but that although the Inspector's straight, he's not a gangster like that Gannon."

Maggie paused, with a book in her hand. "He gives you the creeps, too?"

"Does he! It's bad enough being pulled out of our own world and dropped God knows where, without having to put up with those guys at the same time."

Maggie put away the book she was holding, then regarded

Sally seriously. "It's not a nice thing to say," she said, "but they're as much monsters as those creatures outside. I know their type and I don't like them. I can feel their eyes on me when I walk by. . . ." She shivered. "I'm almost glad that Blue shot one of them."

Sally nodded. The thought had crossed her mind as well. But all she wanted was to have him back. She couldn't bear to think of what might be happening to him out there.

"The fucker's dead," Chevier whispered. "If the wolfmen don't get him, I will."

"In time," Gannon said, "in time. I have the feeling he's gone for help. That there's someone or something out there that he knows of, that they can go to for support. The more I think of it, the more it seems to me that Tams and the lot of them know exactly what they're doing. I wouldn't be surprised if Hengwr's 'coma' isn't just one more little fix-up to keep us guessing."

Chevier popped a mint into his mouth and chewed slowly. He'd found a new supply in one of the kitchen cupboards.

"I've had it," he said. "I'm sick of this place, sick of those things that howl outside, sick of it all. Don't you think it's about time we just grab one of them—say the old man who plays with the computer, or one of the women—and cut the truth out of them?"

Gannon shook his head. "Not yet. We'll give it until night-fall. But if we don't get some answers by then . . . well, we'll just have to make sure we get the midnight shift and take Mr. Tams off to the cellars or some place where no one can hear him. Meanwhile, we'll just mingle. Have you noticed any place that they treat like it's off limits?"

"What do you mean?"

"Well, the way I see it," Gannon explained, "is there's got to be some mechanism that moves this place around from world to world. If their 'magics' were all that great, they would have gotten rid of us and the monsters a long time ago."

Chevier thought about it for a moment.

"It's Tams's computer," he said finally. "Got to be. Either that, or the gardener's got it stashed away in with his flowers somewhere. He plays dumb, but he's always watching. Didn't want me to go out in the garden this morning. Said it was for 'guests' and not the likes of me."

"Do you know anything about computers?" Gannon asked.

Chevier shook his head.

"Then you go check out the garden while I pay another visit to Tams's study. I just wish I knew what I was looking for."

After leaving the House behind, Blue found that the forest swept north and south, giving him a few hard moments as he headed due east, then thinned into hilly meadows where all he had to keep a watch out for were fieldstones. The roar of the bike was loud in the still woods, but for the first time he didn't give a shit; he had a little angst to burn off. He'd had another run-in with the tragg'a—about ten minutes into the woods—but soon left them behind, turning left for long miles before circling back to the hills again. He hadn't seen a trace of them now for a couple of hours. Come to think of it, he hadn't seen a trace of anything since he'd left the House. Just virgin woodland.

Drawing up on a knoll, he found a level piece of land, shut off the motor and put the bike on its kickstand. He got off, working his stiff muscles loose. The sudden silence that fell echoed the quiet that had finally settled inside him. The hard riding he'd forced himself through had done its job. It always did.

That moment of sheer unadulterated rage had left him shaken and scared. He hadn't realized he was still capable of that kind of a killing frenzy. It was okay when you were riding with a gang, if you didn't care who you fucked with or what happened to you. But he'd mellowed out, and to have it come back just like that. . . .

Okay, he'd thought as he'd pitted himself and the bike against the rough terrain, choosing the routes that had him fighting just to keep the damn machine on its wheels. It happened. It's happened before and now it's happened again. But the fucker had it coming. The man he'd killed, Gannon, Chevier—they all had the same eyes. They didn't care about anything except themselves. That's where the old gang and men like Gannon differed.

Right or wrong, the Devil's Dragon still had one loyalty, a thing they held above themselves. They rode for the club and the club meant more than the individual. But the Dragon lost his loyalty when they left him to catch the tab in a little backwater town between North Bay and Toronto. He'd barely gotten out of there with his ass in one piece.

He'd been stuck there, out on old Highway 17, with the

crap beaten out of him and no bike, trying to make it home. To get a ride, he'd thrown away his vest with the Dragon colors stitched onto its back. All the way home he'd thought about what he'd do, how he'd get even, but hitching out of T.O., he'd gotten a ride with some dippy author and ended up in Tamson House and everything had changed for him.

Sara'd been—how old? Just a kid. Thirteen tops, and treated him like a pal from the word go. Jamie hadn't blinked an eye when he'd told him about the Dragon. They never tried to change him, but somehow just being in that House, he'd changed. Because of them. For them.

He'd left for awhile, riding down through the American midwest to stay with Charlie on the reservation, then up through Florida, New England, the Maritimes, thinking all the time, finding he liked the change; and came home. Home. Funny word. But that was what Tamson House had become.

It was stress that was messing him up right now, he realized. Worrying about Sara, about what was going on around them, about Gannon and Tucker and Thomas Hengwr. He wished he hadn't killed Mercier, but if Mercier'd had his way, it would've been Blue lying there. And where would that leave Jamie and Sara? They were going to need him against men like Gannon. Against those weird wolfmen that Hengwr had either conjured up or drawn to them. No, he didn't regret what he'd had to do. And he knew he'd do it again if the situation arose again. They weren't in Ottawa anymore. They weren't anywhere where they could call in the cops to give them a hand.

Mercier's .38 was digging into his stomach, so he trans- ferred it to his pack, grabbing some bread and cheese out of it while he had it open. He topped off his tank from the spare gas container, then removing the scope from his Weatherby, he used it as a makeshift telescope to check out the country around him.

He had to give the Otherworld this much: it sure was a wild and pretty land. Too bad they didn't know how to shift the House back and forth themselves, because it would be awfully nice to have access to country like this just by stepping out of the House. Of course they'd have to get rid of the wolfmen.

Remounting the scope, he finished his sandwich, swallowed a mouthful of water, and climbed back on the bike. He used his compass and the sun to fix the House's position and decided to make a southern sweep, returning to it by the west. It looked like his hopes weren't going to pan out. There was nothing out here but bush. But the lack of success hadn't been from lack of trying.

Two hours later he hit some heavy bushland. He didn't like the look of the dense thickets of cedar, brush pine, aspens, birch and maple. There were too many places where he could get ambushed, assuming he could find a way thorugh with the bike. He decided to take a break and give the engine a chance to cool down while he stretched his legs. Topping off the tank again, he hefted his Weatherby, working the bolt to get a shell in the chamber, and set off to do a little scouting on foot. Thirty paces or so into the forest, he came upon a game trail running roughly southwest.

Returning to the bike, he started it up. He bent low over the handlebars, taking it slow. Branches rattled against his helmet, snapped against his back and sides. He was glad he'd brought his leather jacket and wished he'd thought to have brought some gloves. Once the rifle got caught and he had to back up to work it free. Then he was on the trail and, giving the bike some gas, he shifted gears and was rolling again.

The trail meandered. He stopped from time to time to check his compass and found the trail had a tendency to run almost northwest at times. Well, that was all right. That was roughly in the direction of the House. He only hoped the trail hadn't been made by the shuffling of many padded monster feet.

He was fifteen minutes on the track when he came to a clearing. He saw the trail head on out the further side back into the woods. In the middle of the clearing a second trail joined it, coming up from the south. But what made him bring up the bike sharply and kill the engine was a pole in the center of the clearing. It stood about six feet high. On top of it was a bear skull with the twelve-tined antlers of a stag tied to it. Hanging in streams from the antlers were a series of braided leather thongs, decorated with large beads and feathers.

"Jesus."

Blue swung the rifle from his shoulder, checked to make sure he still had a cartridge in place. Leaving his helmet hanging from the handlebars of the bike, he slowly moved forward. Well, somebody lived here. He studied the sides of the clearing before stepping closer. The question was who? The wolfmen? Didn't have the right feel about it for them—though he wasn't sure how far he could trust instinct here.

He thought he heard something move in the undergrowth

to his right and swung the rifle in that direction, finger tightening on the trigger. Then a voice spoke gutturally, from directly behind him. His stomach muscles tightened. He turned, slowly so as not to startle whoever it was that had spoken.

He stood face to face with an old Indian. The man was grey-haired, the thick locks bound up in two braids, interwoven with feathers. He wore unadorned buckskins, with a bone carving hanging from his neck. The carving was of a bear's head—so realistically portrayed that Blue got the weird feeling that the carving was staring at him. The old man's eyes were deep brown and searching. He carried no weapon, though thrust into his belt was a thin rod of what looked like birch. It, too, had feathers on its end. Hanging on the opposite side of his belt, as though to balance the weight, was a small medicine bag.

The old man spoke again. He was plainly unafraid of Blue.

Blue shook his head. Still moving slowly, he leaned his rifle butt on the ground, the barrel propped against his legs, and tried to remember the sign language that Charlie Nez had taught him.

Don't understand, he signed. *Stranger. These woods. Friend.*

The old man nodded and his fingers moved fluidly in reply. Blue had always been better at understanding the signs than at shaping them himself.

Who are you? the old man signed. *What has brought you to me, Rider-of-Thunder?*

My name— No. That was tribe. Move the hand in, Blue told himself. *My name is Blue. I come from . . .* House. How did you sign house? He made a sweeping motion with his hands and used the Navajo shape for dwelling place. *. . . big hogan.* He pointed in the general direction of the House, wondering how much he'd gotten across.

The Indian nodded. *I know that place. It is always empty though the—*He shaped an unfamiliar sign—*are camped near it now. They seek entry but the medicine of the Great Lodge is too strong for them.*

Your name? Blue signed.

Ur'wen'ta I am called. Blue translated that to: "Bear-of-Magic." *I am of the wandering people. The drummers-of-the-bear. What has brought you to this land, Blue-Rider-of-Thunder?*

We're doing good so far, Blue thought. His hands and fingers felt somewhat stiff from lack of practice. It was hard, thinking of what he was trying to say, translating it into motions, reading the old man's signs, translating again. He got good vibes from the old fellow. But just how much did he want to pass on?

Well, you were looking for help, he told himself.

Shaking his fingers to loosen them, he signed:

The . . . He tried to copy the Indian's sign for the wolfmen, flubbed it and was corrected. This time he got it right. Roughly translated, it came out to: "Offspring-of-the-Devil-Bear." Something to do with wolverines. Blue nodded. Yeah, them. Except they had a lot of snake in them too. *They are attacking us,* he continued. *We have a . . . sick man. Medicine man. He needs help. Can you help him?*

How is your drummer sick?

Blue tried to explain, but the concept was too difficult for him to get across.

He sleeps? Ur'wen'ta signed.

Blue nodded.

A power dream?

Blue thought about that for a moment, not sure he understood the term. When Ur'wen'ta repeated the question, Blue shrugged. *Don't know. Can you help us?*

Ur'wen'ta looked uncertain. *I am bound to a summoning of my people. The daughter of my drum-brother has called me to her side.* He searched the sky, took the hour from the sun; and made a noncommital motion. *I will go with you to the Great Lodge and try to help your drummer. But by nightfall, I must be gone.*

Blue signed his thanks, then glanced at his bike. No way it was going to carry the both of them that far. Ur'wen'ta caught his look.

Ride your Thunder, he signed. *I will meet you at the Great Lodge. Beware the* . . . Again that unfamiliar sign. Tragg'a. Ur'wen'ta pointed to the Weatherby. *That is your totem stick?*

Blue wasn't sure how he was going to explain the rifle's function through fingerspeech, so he simply nodded.

It will not be strong enough, Ur'wen'ta signed.

He took the birch rod from his belt and offered it to Blue. *But you will need this,* Blue signed.

Ur'wen'ta smiled and shook his head. He pressed the totem stick into Blue's hand. *I have my drum,* he signed.

What? Blue replied.

Again the Indian smiled. He made a pass with his hands and smoke wreathed between his fingers. A moment later and

a small ceremonial drum hung at his belt. He tapped it twice
and Blue, already startled by the drum's appearance, was taken
aback at the deep resonance that the small instrument produced.
Go, Ur'wen'ta signed. *I will meet you there.*

Still uncertain, Blue nodded and returned to his bike. He
thrust the totem stick in his belt, shouldered the Weatherby,
and put on his helmet. He glanced at the Indian again. Ur'wen'ta
nodded and smiled. Blue shrugged. All right. His bike roared
into life and he put it into gear. As the machine shot forward,
he saw Ur'wen'ta tapping on his drum once more. He thought
he could hear the sound of the instrument over the noise of his
bike, but that was patently impossible . . . wasn't it? Still, the
sound pulsed to the tempo of his own pulse. Then he was in
the woods, following the trail again. But for all the distance
between himself and Ur'wen'ta, the sound of the drumming
never left him.

"What's that?" Maggie said.

They were taking a well deserved rest in the Silkwater
Kitchen—she, Sally and Tucker. Chevier had been hanging
around, bothering them, until they made it plain that he wasn't
welcome. The last they'd seen he was making his way into the
garden with Fred on his heels, shaking his head and complain-
ing.

"That's Blue!" Sally cried as the sound registered. She jumped
to her feet and ran for the side of the House it was coming
from. The other two followed at a more subdued pace.

"Over here!" Jamie called.

He was standing by a window in the hall and pointing.
Together they watched the trailbike come across the field, four
or five tragg'a moving to cut Blue off. Tucker glanced out the
window, then headed for the nearest outside door.

"Gannon!" he called as he reached the door.

Gannon entered the foyer, a question in his eyes.

"It's Blue," Tucker explained. "We've got to give him some
covering fire."

"Let him find his own way in," Gannon said and wandered
off.

Tucker swore at his retreating back, then flung the door
open and took out his .38. He waited for the creatures to come
close enough for him to make his shots count. Two of them
were closing in on the bike. He fired once, more to let Blue
know that he had some support than with any hope of hitting

one of the creatures. He saw Blue's bike skid, the two tragg'a rush at him, then shy away as the bike righted and sprang forward with a roar.

Now Blue was ahead of even the closest tragg'a. Tucker lowered his pistol and stepped out on the porch. Blue drove right up to the porch, up the steps and into the House. The roar of the bike thundered in the confined space. As Tucker slammed the door shut, Blue cut the engine and silence descended. Turning, Tucker saw Blue pull a stick with feathers attached to one end out of his belt and look at it.

"What do you know?" Blue murmured. "Sucker actually worked."

"Just what the hell did you think you were—"

"Hey! Easy, Inspector. Before you go jumping all over me, did an old Indian show up here?"

"An old . . . ?"

"Blue!"

Sally came pounding down the hall and flung herself at him. Blue closed an arm around her and pulled her in tight. The hall began to fill up as Jamie and Maggie approached. Traupman descended the stairs. Gannon appeared from further down the hall. The latter had a grim look on his face and Blue knew he was in for some hard questioning. Tucker, though he seemed relieved to see him, had a grim look about his features as well.

"Suppose you tell us what you were trying to prove," Tucker said, "going out—"

"I'd like to hear about Robert Mercier," Gannon said. He fixed his cold eyes on the biker.

Like a shadow, Chevier appeared at Gannon's elbow, methodically chewing a mint, one hand in the pocket of his sports jacket. Clearly, Chevier had a gun in there. Tension crackled in the air. Blue was caught between the implicit threat he read in the eyes of Mercier's companions and the need to know what had happened to Ur'wen'ta. He could still feel the drumming inside him, only where was the Indian?

"We're waiting," Gannon said.

Tucker stepped forward, but before he could speak, Chevier whispered: "Keep the fuck out of this, Inspector. This is between us and Mr. Wonderful here. Got it?"

"So this is it, then?" Blue said softly.

He moved Sally aside and wished he'd stopped and thought about this happening before he'd come roaring in. His Weatherby was strapped to his back. Mercier's .38 was in his pack.

The Margolin pistol was in his pocket. All three of them might as well be on the moon. Tucker had his own gun still in his hand, but it was hanging down by his leg. By the time he got it up, Chevier could gun him down just by firing through his pocket.

"Just talk," Gannon said. "If you make it good, there doesn't have to be any trouble. For the rest of them, that is. You . . . well, you've got a problem."

Gannon hadn't meant to start something now. There were too many people hanging around, getting in the way. But he'd gotten edgy, doing nothing but waiting all day. He'd found nothing in Jamie's study. Chevier'd come up with dick-all. And there was the biker, roaring into the hallway just asking to be hassled.

What was there to say? Blue thought. He could feel the sweat start up on his forehead, could sense the anger just waiting to rip out again. But this time he wasn't going to be so luckly as he'd been with Mercier. There were too many people around, too many chances for someone to get hurt. He couldn't risk it.

"Better put the gun down, Inspector," Gannon said quietly. "No point in playing the hero at this point in the proceedings. The biker's dead meat."

Tucker weighed his chances and they weren't good. Chevier was a pro. He hadn't taken his eyes off of Tucker once since this little drama started up. That was because Tucker was the only one holding a piece.

"Uh . . . Mr. Gannon. . . ." Jamie began.

"Shut your mouth, Tams."

As Tucker started to drop his gun, the front door opened. All eyes turned to see Ur'wen'ta standing there in a totem mask of a bear's head topped with stag's antlers, looking like a demonic figure out of a Bosch painting. Smoke wreathed about his clothing, smoke the color of his hair. The sound of his drumming filled the air. For long moments no one spoke, no one moved. Then the drumming stopped and the spell lifted.

"Jesus!" Tucker said and lifted his gun.

"No!" Blue lunged for the Inspector's arm, belatedly remembered Chevier's gun, but neither action was played through.

Ur'wen'ta's drum spoke again, but this time it spoke its rhythm on its own, the drum skin resonating without a hand tapping against it. It breathed calm throughout the hall, stole the tension from each of those gathered there. The Inspector lowered his gun. Chevier took his hand from his pocket. The tightness even in Gannon's features eased as the drumming thundered inside him, inside them all.

Ur'wen'ta regarded Blue. *This is your tribe?* he signed.

Yes and no, Blue replied.

There is much anger present.

I know.

Blue frowned, wondering how to translate an explanation of what was going down.

It does not matter, Ur'wen'ta signed. *Where is your drummer?*

I will show you.

As Blue took the shaman upstairs to where Thomas lay, the others finally stirred.

"What happened?" Jamie asked. "One minute we were all set to kill each other, and in the next. . . ."

"He stopped us," Traupman said. He looked up the stairs, features thoughtful. "Just like that. As though we were merely children that needed to be silenced. To him, we probably *are* children."

"We better go see what they're up to," Tucker said.

"I don't think it would be wise to disturb them just now," Traupman said. "It seems that Blue's found a shaman to cure Thomas Hengwr. We've done what we can with Hengwr. Let's give the shaman his chance."

"Fuck that!" Gannon said.

He started for the stairs but pulled up sharp as Tucker lifted his .38. The Inspector looked at Gannon, then at the gun. The drumming still resonated in him, so when Gannon backed off, Tucker holstered the weapon. He should have taken Gannon's and Chevier's while he had the drop on them, but something in the rhythm of the drumming stopped him.

He could see Chevier and Gannon trying to work it out as well.

"Who was that Indian?" Maggie asked. "Where did he come from?"

"Blue found him, I guess," Tucker replied. "Though where he found him. . . ." He glanced out the open door, slowly shut it. "Somewhere out there, I suppose."

"Can we trust him?"

"I don't know, Maggie. I don't know if we have a choice."

"I think we can trust him," Traupman said.

"Did you understand what they were saying?" Tucker asked. "Waving their hands around like that?"

Traupman shook his head. "No. But it begins to lend credence to our earlier suspicions."

"What suspicions?" Jamie wanted to know.

"That you people know more than you're letting on," Gannon said.

The vehemence had left his voice and he looked uncomfortable. Tucker knew just how he was feeling. It was weird being just . . . shut down like this. It was like every time you started to get angry, something cut in and mellowed you out. The drumming.

"It's not true," Jamie replied. "I've never seen that . . . man before."

"Then where did Blue find him?" Tucker asked. "How come they can communicate?"

"I don't know. Blue's got a thing about Indians—he used to live with some down in New Mexico. Maybe he picked it up there."

Tucker nodded. He remembered Blue mentioning that. But that still didn't explain what the Indian was doing here or how Blue had got in touch with him.

"I think we'd better go up," he told Traupman. "We won't interrupt or anything, but I've got to know what's going on up there."

Traupman hesitated, then stepped aside. One by one they went up the stairs.

Ur'wen'ta paused in the doorway of Jamie's study, his attention caught by the painting that was propped up on the desk beside Memoria's terminal. Glancing at Blue, he crossed the room to study it, removing his totem mask as he did so.

How can this be? he signed. *This is my drum-brother A'wa'rathe—He-Who-Walks-With-Bears. My drum-brother and Redhair from across the Great Water.* He reached out to touch the painting, drawing his fingers back before actual contact. Turning back to Blue, he signed, *Powerful are the medicines of the Great Lodge. They drum all around us.*

Remembering how easily Ur'wen'ta had stopped the confrontation downstairs, Blue signed back, *Powerful are the medicines of Ur'wen'ta as well.*

The old Indian smiled. *This is so. Come. We will see your drummer.*

Ur'wen'ta's humor died away as he approached the bed where Tom lay. Whatever it was that kept his drum playing by itself quickened its tempo. Ur'wen'ta replaced his totem mask. For long minutes he stood studying Tom's pale features. Then he climbed on the bed and knelt beside him. He took a pinch of pollen from the medicine bag at his side and, murmuring, touched it to each of the wizard's eyelids. Then he laid his hand on Tom's brow, fingers spread so that his thumb and little finger each gripped a temple. Abruptly, the drumming ceased and Ur'wen'ta moved away from the bed.

I know this drummer, he signed. *He is a man driven by devils. Always it has been so. He stalks Mal'ek'a—the Dread-That-Walks-Nameless—and it stalks him. He was my drum-brother's brother, and so is kin to me. But I cannot help him.*

What is wrong with him?

He has confronted that which he hunted and that meeting has sent his soul fleeing. It hides deep within him, lost and shaken. Given time, I could draw him back, but time I do not have now, Blue-Rider. A'wa'rathe's daughter Ha'kan'ta has summoned our tribe to a meeting that I must attend. When I am done there, I will return.

When?

Before moonset, Ur'wen'ta signed.

Thanks are given to you, Blue replied. His hands were moving more deftly as the half-forgotten movements returned to him. *We will wait for you until that time.*

I will return. Ur'wen'ta paused, then added with a quick cutting motion: *The Others—your people. They do not trust you. Some of them mean you ill. I tell you this because I sense in you an echo of my totem.*

You honor me.

Ur'wen'ta shook his head. *It is Mother Bear who honors us both. I will return, Blue-Rider, perhaps with others of my tribe. Toma'heng'ar is known amongst my people. Many have drum-ties with him, though there are some who frown on his enmity with—*He made an unfamiliar sign that translated into "Silver-Brow." *Redhair. It is an evil time when enemies are blooded to the same tribe.*

He looked to the door where Tucker and the others were now gathered.

Your own people have come, Blue-Rider.

Ur'wen'ta's drum began to speak once more and smoke arose to wreathe about him.

Until moonset.

Until moonset, Blue signed. He pulled Ur'wen'ta's totem stick from his belt and offered it back.

Keep it until my return, the shaman signed.

The smoke billowed and then he was gone, taking the drumming with him. In the ensuing silence, Blue knew a sharp sense of loss. Ur'wen'ta had filled him with a sense of peace. Of control. Sighing, he turned to face the door, knowing what he still had to go through and not looking forward to it.

Tucker stepped back as Blue turned, eyes locked on the totem stick still in the biker's hand. Blue grinned. So it made them nervous, did it? Well, he'd play that up for all it was worth. Maybe it would stop them acting like such a bunch of assholes.

"I guess we'd better talk," he said.

"You've got a real glow about you," Sally told him hours later. "Ever since you got back."

Blue nodded. He felt it too. It was like the rhythm Ur'wen'ta had played that twinned the pulse of his blood through his own body and never stopped. He heard it like a soft drum echoing still. Like the distant sound of a horse's hooves against the ground.

His confrontation with Tucker and the rest of them had come off a lot smoother than he'd though it would. A *lot* smoother from the way it had been shaping up before Ur'wen'ta showed. The shaman had left them all subdued, which suited Blue just fine. They'd brought up Mercier and quietly accepted his version of what had happened. Even Gannon and Chevier did— though there was a flicker of something in the latter's eyes. Gannon remained impassive.

"You scared me, going off like that," Sally said.

"I scared myself. But we had to do something. We're just lucky things worked out the way they did."

"You really think he'll come back?"

"He'll be back, babe. He's the kind of guy that plays it straight."

"I don't know how you can be so sure."

Blue tapped his chest. "In here. He reads okay in here. Just like you do."

"Well, in that case," she said, snuggling closer to him, "he's got to be okay."

Blue grinned. "I kinda thought you'd see it that way."

* * *

"I wish you didn't have to do that."

Tucker looked up from the table where he was dismantling and cleaning his gun.

"Why not?" he asked.

Maggie shrugged. She was wearing a blue workshirt and some jeans that Fred had found for her. "It just reminds me of too much that's ugly," she said at last.

Tucker sighed. "I can't take a chance on it not working at its optimum performance level. Especially not now. You know that."

"I know. I'm sorry. I'm just all on edge."

"Still thinking about this afternoon?"

Maggie nodded.

"Well, Gannon worries me, too," Tucker said. "He's a dangerous man and I'm getting the feeling that he's getting too jumpy. That just makes him more dangerous. Him and his whispering goon. I haven't seen them around for awhile, have you?"

"No. And I'd like to keep it that way."

"We'll get out of this," Tucker said.

He peered down the inside of the .38's barrel. Satisfied, he set aside the swab and cleaning cloth.

"How?" Maggie wanted to know. "There's a feeling of . . . wrongness in the air tonight."

Tucker nodded. "I know. I can feel it too. That's why I'm cleaning this sucker. Something's going to break tonight."

"I just hope it isn't us," Maggie said softly.

"Are we still going through with it tonight?" Chevier asked. "Now that the biker's got himself a magic wand. . . ."

"The biker does, but Tams doesn't."

"There's that."

Gannon looked out of the window into the darkness and frowned. "Did you find a place we can work on him?" he asked.

"It's got to be the cellars. Nobody goes down there and the walls are so thick that no one'll hear anything. Even if they miss him, in a place this big they'll never find us. At least not before we get what we need from him."

"Good," Gannon said. "Good."

But he kept thinking about the biker. The anger that gripped him wasn't very professional and he knew it. But nothing had

been professional about this operation. Still, the biker would
have to wait. And Tucker. Until Jamie Tams gave them what
they needed.

"What are you thinking about?" Jamie asked Traupman.

Traupman looked up from where he'd been studying Thomas
and shrugged. "Just trying to work out how the shaman did
it—calming us all down without speaking a word. And the
way he diagnosed what's the matter with our patient here."

"We don't know that he's right," Jamie said.

Traupman shook his head. He crossed the room and took a
chair across from Jamie.

"I believe he went right into Thomas Hengwr's mind," he
said. "He went right in and, mind to mind, found the problem."
He looked beyond Jamie, eyes slightly unfocused. "It's so
frustrating. To find out after all these years that it's all real,
all possible. After sifting through so much garbage looking for
even a shred of evidence. I'd give anything to be twenty years
younger so that I could begin again with what we've learned
in these past few days."

Jamie nodded. "Perhaps it was simply our own inability to
come to terms with the reality of it all that was holding us
back."

"Perhaps," Traupman agreed.

"I'm going down to talk with Sam," Jamie said, rising from
his chair. "I think I'll give him a hand with those journals."

"Why don't you bring a few up and I'll go through them
while I'm babysitting our patient."

"All right. Want a drink to go with them?"

"Tea would be fine."

Blue sat up suddenly, looking around.

"What is it?" Sally asked. "Your medicine man?"

"Don't know, babe. I just have this feeling."

He crossed to the window and looked out into the darkness.
There was something out there. Not just the tragg'a, not just
the night. He could see the moon from where he stood, still
above the trees. He didn't think it was Ur'wen'ta coming. He
didn't know what it was. He just had this feeling inside
that . . . something was coming.

"I'm going to check out the windows and doors," he said.
"Want to come?"

"We're not going outside?"

"I'm not planning to, babe."

He shouldered the Weatherby and went to his pack, taking out Mercier's .38. He'd already given Tucker the Margolin. He handed the weapon to Sally.

"Use both hands, okay?" he said. "It's got a hell of a kick if you're not expecting it."

Sally swallowed and took the gun. It was heavy and looked huge in her small hands.

"You okay, babe?"

She nodded.

"Don't shoot until you know what it is you're shooting at, okay?"

"I don't know about this, Blue...."

"It's probably nothing," he replied.

"I'll be all right," Sally said.

"Then let's go."

Blue didn't know what they were looking for. He just knew he had to get moving, because something else was moving. They ran into Tucker and Maggie in the Silkwater Kitchen. Tucker had just finished cleaning the Margolin.

"What's up?" he asked, taking in their weapons and their attitude.

"Don't know," Blue said. "It's just a feeling I've got."

Tucker nodded. There it was. He wasn't the only one. He regarded the biker steadily, realizing that his attitude towards him had changed over the past few days. He was glad they were on the same side—whatever was shaping up.

"I'll take the west side of the House," he said.

Blue nodded. "Something's coming," he said, "but I don't know what it is."

Tucker waited for him to explain.

"What I'm trying to say is, don't shoot first and ask questions later. It could be Ur'wen'ta."

"That's not making it easy," Tucker replied. He'd been about to tell Blue that he didn't need to be told a thing like that, but he'd bit the comment back.

"Nothing about this is going to be easy," Blue said.

Chapter Five

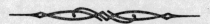

SARA followed the clifftops east. Her moccasins whispered against the rocks. Low-growing twigs brushed against the soft leather of her dress. The wind tugged loose hairs from her braids to tickle her cheeks. The tang of the sea was strong in the air, mixed with the heady rich resin scent of the spruce and cedars. Stars glimmered like distant candles and the Northern Lights danced.

She came out of the woods into May'is'hyr's Glade of Study—Rathe'feyn, the Moon's-Stone-Bear. Here the night was silent. Standing under the height of the Bearstone, she had the sensation of entering a cathedral whose lofty ceiling was the night sky itself, whose walls were the forest and the cliffs. Stepping close to the Bearstone, she laid her cheek against its rough surface and thought she felt the earth breathe through it.

For the first time since Taliesin and Pukwudji had spoken of them, she began to get a true sense of those shadowy Old Ones that moved just beyond the borders of one's everyday perceptions. It didn't matter then whether or not they were testing her, nor what their reasons might be. All that was important was that she be found worthy of their continued interest. What she'd told Taliesin was true: everything she'd been before, all her friends and her life up to now, had made her what she was. But the desire to become a moonheart, she realized suddenly, did not invalidate what she'd done thus far. Nor did it make her a different person.

What did she want? She repeated Taliesin's question to herself. To reach her full potential. And if that entailed going back to her own time and facing the danger of Kieran's demon, then that was what she had to do.

She'd come this far, mostly by drifting along with events,

like a leaf on the wind. It was time she took to the Way using her own endeavors, with a clear goal in mind.

Closing her eyes, she drew up Taliesin's tune in her mind and sent a silent call through the forest. Against her back, the Bearstone seemed to grow warm, adding its own deep resonances to her small thought-voice.

Pukwudji was no longer sure what it was he'd attempted to do by entering Sara's dreams and drawing her to him. To prove something to the bard and his stag-browed Forest Lord from across the Great Water. Yes. To show them that there were many Ways and all of them true. And in doing so, he'd be helping Sara—which was no selfish deed in its own right. So. Given such motives, why did he sense such foreboding?

He knew the feeling well enough, for this would not be the first time he'd meddled in the affairs of those more powerful than himself—but none of them had been Forest Lords. It would be wise, he was once told by an old tribal Shaper of the quin'on'a, not to meddle in the affairs of the Old Ones. For they were powerful and quick to anger.

Miserably, Pukwudji stared at his toes and wondered what he'd begun. Should he go to the bard and tell him what he'd done? Thinking a moment, the honochen'o'keh mournfully shook his head. No. It was too late for that. Oh why, oh why, had he meddled?

Because, he told himself, such was his nature.

He lifted his head with sudden resolve. He was Pukwudji. Not so powerful as a Forest Lord, but he had strengths still. Not so wise as the quin'on'a, but cunning still. Yes. He was Pudwudji and he was what he was. Always alone, but never on his own, for all the world was his home.

His fears washed from him like tidal foam flowing from the shorebound rocks. His owlish eyes gleamed bright in the darkness as he stood up and looked about. He heard it then—Sara's sen'fer'sa calling to him. Ah, he thought, feeling the strength of her call. Grandmother Toad herself might call like this, solemn as the mysteries of the old stones that once walked and now were still.

Hai-nya!

He liked this herok'a whom he'd only met in a dream, but had watched from afar all through the day. His future self had liked her as well—or so her memory showed him. There was in her something that was neither bear nor wolf nor any beast he knew. It was as delicate as the moon's light, yet rooted deep in the earth's bones. When she grew her horns. . . .

He lifted his head and called to the night sky: *See her, Mother Moon? She is your daughter, this hornless one. And she will not be hornless for long.*

The wind stirred the leathery cedar leaves and rattled the slender spruce needles one against the other.

Hai-nya-hey!

Pukwudji grinned. He opened his arms wide and took an owl's shape. Silent wings beat the night air as he sailed above the dark trees, following the call back to its maker.

Other beings heard that silent call.

In the round tower overlooking the sea, Taliesin's harping faltered for a moment, then began anew. *Call him then,* he thought. *Perhaps a manitou can help you where I can not.* His harping took on an edge, reflecting his disappointment.

May'is'hyr nodded over her weaving. *Yes, Little-Otter. Call Old Man Coyote's cousin to you. But remember what I told you. What he will be will depend on what is inside you.*

She glanced at Hagan who'd looked up, regarding first her, then the harper, before returning to his net. He heard nothing but the wind, but he'd lived with these two long enough to know that for them the night held more than he could sense. Something was brewing. The little maid was gone, Taliesin brooded like a lovesick bird, and Mayis was too quiet for his liking. But that was the way of druids—be they harper or shaman. They were always hearing things on the wind, reading import into the flicker of a fire's honest flames, the turn of a bird's wing in the sky. Bah! It was no concern of his.

Further afield, in the camp of Ko'si'tye, Tall-Deer, who was the chieftain of the tribal folk whose hunting lands bordered closest to the round tower, the tribe's old Healer lifted his grey head from his blankets and left his lodge to learn what had called him from the paths of sleep. His name was Ho'feyn'to, Wind-That-Shakes-the-Moon, and he had seen sixty-three winters. Stamping his feet in the dewy grass, he lifted his head to regard the night skies, his nostrils flaring like a hare's. For a long moment he stood, listening with his sen'fer'sa, before he returned to his lodge.

"What is it?" his craftdaughter asked from her blankets.

"Spirit talk."

"But what do they say?"

The old man regarded her through the lodge's darkness, his old eyes bright and seeing as clearly as if the sun had already risen.

"If you must ask," he said, "then there is no need for you to know. Kha?"

His craftdaughter sighed and turned, seeking sleep once more. "Kha," she said softly.

Ho'feyn'to sat awake for along while, his gnarled fingers toying with the rough fringes of his medicine bag, as he considered what he had heard. At length, he too returned to his blankets, but sleep was long in coming.

Further afield still, three tragg'a paused in the midst of their hunt.

Their heads swiveled on their thin necks. Yellowed tusks gleamed in the starlight and long talons clicked loud in the still night air as they opened and closed their clawed hands.

Listening, they regarded each other, weasel grins tightening their lips into grimaces of amusement. This herok'a they sought would not be so hard to find if she kept up this call. Instinct gave them a direction and, judging the distance between themselves and the call, they began a shuffling lope towards it. If they kept to this pace they would reach the herok'a long before sunrise.

The talismanic medicine she carried they would deliver to Mal'ek'a. But her hornless soul would be theirs. They would feed on her body and make a medicine necklace from her bones.

For a long time Sara was simply a part of her call. It was like an old stately tune that kept tempo to the rhythmic rise and fall of her chest, to the drum of her heartbeat. The call grew fainter, fainter, then died away. She opened her eyes. Pukwudji had come.

The little man stood a few feet away, regarding her with his big solemn eyes.

"You came," she said.

Pukwudji nodded.

"I am like the tide. I always keep my trysts."

Sara smiled. "I didn't know we had one."

"Oh, yes." He sat down, taking his time about crossing his legs.

"You seem at peace," he said at last. "At least, more so than the last time I saw you."

"It's very peaceful here. Something about this stone and the air and . . . well, everything. But all my fears and worries are still there, underneath the calm, banging around against each other in a big jumble. I don't really want to think about them, to be honest, but now that you're here, I suppose I should." She was quiet for a moment, gathering her thoughts. "Pukwudji, if I was just dreaming the last time we met, how come you remember it too? Was it real?"

"It was real. I came to you as a totem would come: through a dream to warn you. I thought what they did was wrong. What they expected of you was unfair if they would not allow you foreknowledge."

"They?"

"Taliesin and *his* totem. The stag. The Forest Lord from across the Great Water."

Sara remembered what Taliesin had told her last night after he'd come walking out of the forest. He said he'd met with a "stag who caught the moon." So it hadn't been just bardic doubletalk, or rather, it had been, only she hadn't pursued it far enough. An image came to mind of a small bone disc with a stag's antlers inscribed on one side and a quarter moon on the other.

"You were very vague last night," she said.

Pukwudji nodded. "I was . . . afraid."

"Of what? Taliesin?"

"Of him? No. Of his totem. Forest Lords are very powerful, Sara. I knew I was meddling in what didn't concern me. They can be quick to anger."

"What changed your mind?"

The honochen'o'keh looked uncomfortable.

"That's okay," Sara said. "You don't have to tell me any more if you don't want to. I don't want you getting into trouble because of me."

Pukwudji remained serious for a long moment, then a broad grin blossomed. "I changed in here," he said, tapping his chest. "Who are the Forest Lords, I thought, to tell Pukwudji what to do? I have been here as long as they have. And especially a Forest Lord from across the Great Water! What have I to fear from him?"

Watching him, Sara knew that what he said was ninety

percent bravado. Still there was nothing wrong with that. Bravery was in knowing the odds and still going against them.

"Thank you for helping me," she said.

The little man continued to grin, then asked: "What have you decided to do?"

"Go back to my own time. Now that I know the way here, I can always come back, can't I?"

Pukwudji shook his head. "Magics don't work so well in the World Beyond. You will not find the going hard. But returning? That will take more strength than you have now."

"I kind of thought it'd work out that way. But I've got to go back. I don't feel I have much choice. I just disappeared as far as my friends and family are concerned. They must be worried sick. And then there's this test of the Old Ones. . . ."

"But if you go back," Pukwudji said, "you do what they want you to do. It will be dangerous for you."

"I know. Kieran's demon. But I have to try."

Pukwudji stole the reference from her mind and shivered when he saw what Kieran's demon was. Mal'ek'a did not yet exist in this time. He did not think he would like a time when it did exist.

"That thing is worse than a tragg'a," he said. "You mustn't go, Sara. Here you are strong and have the potential for greater strength. In the World Beyond the learning will be all that much harder."

"I know that too." Sara sighed. "Why's it so important to the Old Ones that I face this thing of Kieran's anyway?"

"It is not the demon itself," Pukwudji explained, "so much as the challenge. Redhair's people seem to set great store by personal challenges."

It was then that he related the conversations he'd overheard between Taliesin and his grandsire.

"Taliesin sounds as confused as I am," Sara said when the honochen'o'keh was done.

Pukwudji nodded. "His heart and his reason war with one another."

"This makes it worse than ever," Sara said. "If he's willing to give up so much for me . . . the least I can do is see this thing through. The demon isn't even after me—it's after Thomas Hengwr, Kieran's mentor." But then she remembered what the future Pukwudji had shown her, and the little man caught the image from her mind. They both knew she was glossing over the truth.

"Don't go," he said. "Look at yourself. You belong here."

He referred to the dress that Mayis had given her. With her moccasins, leggings and braids, perhaps she did fit it. Then she shook her head.

"No, I don't. I don't know where I belong. I did before. I belonged right where I was. But that was before I knew what I know now. How can I go back to being so . . . so mundane, when I know that magics are real and there are worlds upon worlds to explore? When I can have that deep quiet inside me and be at peace, how could I ever be happy not striving to attain it?"

They were quiet then, wrapped in their own thoughts. From a sidepocket of her dress, Sara took out her tobacco pouch, rolled and lit a cigarette. When she offered a puff to the hon-ochen'o'keh, he shook his head.

"Sharing Mother Bear's smoke is for tribesfolk," he said, "not for folk such as I am. I bind my vows heart to heart, without need of the sacred smoke or the mingling of blood. Besides, my blood and the blood of mortal folk do not mingle well."

"Why not?"

"It changes them. Fills them with a . . . wildness . . . like. . . ." He projected an image to explain what he lacked words to tell. For a moment, Sara felt as though she was on acid. A rush of sensation filled her, sight and smell and sound all so strong that her head spun. Then the moment was gone, but she leaned back against the Bearstone, still feeling weak.

"Like being high," she said. "Only all the time."

Pukwudji caught the thought behind her words and nodded.

"It brings madness to some," he said. "To others, a certain fey wisdom."

He paused, regarding her for a long moment, then shook his head. Sara didn't need the ability to read minds to know what had passed through his. If Pukwudji and she mixed blood. . . .

"No thanks," she said. "That'd be all I need. I feel certifiable as it is."

"We will be heartfriends," Pukwudji said. "Heartkin."

"I'd like that."

"And now. . . . You will go?"

"I think so."

"Without bidding farewell to Redhair?"

"I think he already knows what I'm going to do."

Pukwudji nodded. "I will help you. I cannot yearwalk myself, but I can lend you the strength to make your passage easier."

"Will you do something for me?" Sara asked. "After I'm gone?"

"What thing?" he asked, but he already knew.

"Be Taliesin's friend. I think he's going to need a few. Tell him that I think I love him and if I don't come back it won't be through want of trying. We'll meet again somewhere."

"I will tell him. He too will be my heartkin. For your sake."

They stood up and Sara looked down at what she was wearing. She should have changed before coming out. Well, it was too late now. She turned to ask Pukwudji if she was supposed to stand in a certain way or something, then froze. The honochen'o'keh's head was cocked as though he listened to something, and a strange expression settled on his features.

"What is it?" she asked, for she too knew a sudden foreboding.

"You must go quickly."

"What *is* it?"

"Tragg'a," he replied, pulling his whistle from his belt. "Gather your sen'fer'sa. Quickly!"

Sara couldn't concentrate. The air in the glade was oppressive now, where it had filled her with peace before. All her fears and confusions came roaring back and she didn't feel brave or prepared enough to do anything except perhaps collapse where she stood.

"Sara!" Pukwudji called.

Her thoughts spilled from her mind to his and he knew what was happening inside her. "I will work the sending," he said. "Farewell."

He leaned forward and, standing on his toes, kissed her cheek. She was aware of the dryness of his lips and the sudden warmth she felt emanating from him. It stirred the sluggish cold blood in her veins. She drew in a deep breath as he lipped his whistle, playing Taliesin's Lorcalon tune. Finally she could move. The music set up a resonating reply in her own mind and she focused on home, on Tamson House and her own room. On safety.

"Goodbye," she whispered.

Pukwudji's form began to mist in her sight. That familiar sense of spinning away through nothing came back. Then the blackness came rolling over her mind and she was gone.

The honochen'o'keh stared at where she'd been for long moments, stirring at last when he sensed the nearness of the tragg'a. He changed shape to that of a woman whose curly hair was captured in braids, who wore a beaded white dress and pale tan leggings. On her finger was a gold ring.

He waited until the tragg'a broke from the woods and let them catch sight of him before he fled into the forest. He could have easily lost them, but he held his pace back to match theirs. Down the hill he led them, careening against the spruce, pretending to weaken, then rushing on when they drew too close. Not until he thought he'd led them far enough along this chase, did he allow them to catch up.

The smell came first, roiling through the air like the stagnant water of a swamp that had been stirred up. The wildness of their feral thoughts, half formed and weasel fierce, struck him like a blow. He let the first draw near enough to reach out for him, saw the taloned paw sweep toward him.

"Hai-nya!" he cried.

He changed shape and was a sparrow hovering in the air above them, out of reach, taunting. Their growls rocked the forest as they leaped for him, raking the air with outstretched claws.

Pukwudji grew weary of the sport. Sara was safe now and that was enough. Time he himself was gone. But just as he was about to leave, the creatures themselves paused. Their boarish snouts sucked the air, reading the wind. Suddenly, the largest of them roared and, with a *whfft* of displaced air, vanished. Moments later the other two were gone as well and all that remained of them was the sour reek in the air that they'd left behind.

Pukwudji fluttered to the ground and returned to his own shape. *Oh, Sara,* he thought fiercely. *Beware, beware.*

But he knew his warning wouldn't reach her. She was too far away now, gone through the years to her own time, and he couldn't follow. And what was she to do, hornless in a world of faded magics, when such creatures as the tragg'a confronted her?

Mournfully, he headed off through the forest, making for the round tower. What lies should he tell Redhair? Oh, yes, she's safe and all's well, never fear. He knew what he'd like to tell the bard: Redhair, it was by your need of testing that she is endangered. But he remembered his promise to Sara. He was heartkin now. Well, there deserved to be truth between

heartkin. Let the bard share his grief. Perhaps Redhair's precious Forest Lord from across the Great Water would have a
solution to offer them.

Sick at heart, Pukwduji changed to his swiftest shape. High
above the forest he winged to where the tower kept its watch
across the sea. He dropped from the sky like an eagle, regained
his own shape and stood before the door. He could hear the
harping inside, and nothing else. Blinking back tears, he lifted
his hand and rapped on the stout wooden beams that made the
door.

The yellow-haired man who opened the door stepped hastily
back at the sight of a honochen'o'keh on his doorstep. Inside
the harping died. Fierce-eyed as the tragg'a that had pursued
him, Pukwudji stepped within.

Sara was a little weak-kneed when the solid ground formed
underfoot once more, but that was all. Her heart continued to
thump from the scare she'd gotten in the Otherworld—and
from her own hit and miss efforts at this strange mode of
traveling, so she was a little afraid of opening her eyes. When
she did, she found herself standing on Patterson Avenue, with
Tamson House rearing out of the darkness in front of her. The
street was quiet and there was only the faint murmur of traffic
from the Queensway and Bank Street to tell her that she was
back in a city again.

She wasn't sure whether she felt happy or sad. Too much
kept happening too quickly. What had Pukwudji done when
the tragg'a came? Was he all right? Would Taliesin understand
why she'd gone so suddenly without saying goodbye?

She started to reach for her keys, then realized they'd be
back in the Otherworld still. Much good they'd do there. Stepping up to the door, she leaned on the buzzer. It was late, but
somebody'd come down to let her in. Blue or Jamie, or one
of the Houseguests.

When a couple of minutes passed and there was still no
reply, that all too familiar sense of foreboding returned to her.
Why was no one answering? She peered through a window,
trying to see if anyone was coming. It looked strange inside.
Like there was nothing there. Fear began its quick march through
her once more. What if there was something wrong? After all
that had happened to her in just two days. . . . Oh, God! What
if Kieran's demon had shown up here?

Feeling very panicky, she ran along Patterson until she came to the tower that housed her own rooms. She picked up a stone and, convincing herself that a window wouldn't cost too much to replace, smashed one in. The breaking glass sounded loud to her ears and she hoped one of the neighbors across the street wouldn't call the police, thinking she was a burglar.

She'd used too much force with her blow and her stone fell inside. As she started to reach in for a latch, she realized that she'd never heard it hit the floor inside.

She stood there, with her hand poised in front of the window, unable to move. Her throat was dry and she had difficulty swallowing. There was something terribly wrong here. Steeling herself, she reached in, but the latch wasn't there. Heedless of the glass on the windowsill, she leaned forward to brave a look and withdrew in shock. There was nothing inside. The House simply wasn't there.

It was too much to take on top of everything else. How could everything have been so normal just a few day ago and now be as senseless as the worst nightmare imaginable? Houses. Simply. Didn't. Disappear. It had to be her. She just thought it wasn't there anymore. If she went in through the window, everything'd be okay again. Except there was no way she was going in through that window.

She looked along Patterson again. It looked so bloody normal. So why had the House suddenly gone all surreal on her? The House was always there, no matter what else happened. When things had gotten weird these past few days, one of the things that had kept her going was knowing that the House at least existed. It was her anchor to reality.

She backed away from the broken window. It had the look of an endless tunnel that went nowhere. The jagged edges of the glass looked smoother and the hole seemed smaller, as though the House was alive and healing itself. Where *had* the stone and broken glass gone to?

No. Don't think about it, she told herself. Don't think about what's happening to the window. Just step back on the sidewalk. Go back the way you came—

She froze. Down the street, their shadows elongated by the streetlights, she saw them appear, first one, then another, then a third. She didn't need Pukwudji to tell her what they were.

Tragg'a.

"Listen!" Blue cried.

He took Sally's arm and stopped dead, head cocked. They heard the sound of breaking glass and something hard hitting the floor, bouncing.

"That came from Sara's tower," Blue said. "Let's go!"

He took off at a loping run, working the bolt of his Weatherby. Stopping at the door to Sara's rooms, he pushed it open with his shoulder and entered at a crouch, the rifle leveled. Sally flicked on the lights. The first thing Blue saw was the broken window. The edges of the glass were already smoothing as the House healed itself. More glass was scattered on the floor. At Blue's feet was a stone the size of two fists.

"Blue?" Sally asked.

"They didn't get in," he replied, coming to his feet. "Not yet, anyway."

He approached the window cautiously, staring at the regenerating glass. Through the opening that still remained he could see nothing. But that feeling was still there. Something was coming. Where was Ur'sen'ta? And Hengwr . . . They needed him more than ever now.

"Come on," he said to Sally. "Let's see if Tucker's found anything."

Mal'ek'a stirred in its place of darkness.

Its patience came to a sudden end. That damnable House! It would tear it up by its stony roots and smash it until not a piece of it remained that was larger than its own fist. The House's defenses were strong, but not impenetrable. It had breached them once. It needed only another mind. Another mind to grasp and twist until it cracked open a second breach. And this time it would not fail.

"Mr. Tams?"

Jamie looked up from the fridge to see Gannon and Chevier standing in the doorway of the Silkwater Kitchen. Chevier held a handgun negligently in his hand.

"Let's go for a walk, Mr. Tams," Gannon said.

Jamie looked left and right. Where was everybody else? What did Gannon want with him? Maybe he should try to make a break for it. . . .

"I wouldn't try what you're thinking," Gannon murmured. "Mike's awfully good with that gun of his."

Chevier's lips shaped a feral grin. His voice was bad enough.

His silence at the moment made things seem even worse.

"Look, Mr. Gannon," Jamie began, "I. . . ."

Gannon shook his head. "Uh-uh. We've got a quieter place to talk. Just come along nice and easy and you won't get hurt."

"What was that racket?" Tucker asked.

Blue shrugged. "Something tried to get in but didn't quite make it. The House is still blocking them, but something's gotta give. Anything happening on this side?"

"It's been quiet. Too . . ."

Tucker paused, looking from Blue to Sally.

"Do you hear it?" he asked.

Blue nodded. "Howling. They're going to attack again. Sounds like it's coming from the south side."

"Christ! I left Maggie sleeping on a couch in one of those rooms."

"Well, what're we waiting for?"

Mal'ek'a found the mind it needed. It paced through the forest, nearing the House, and with each step it took, it tightened the bindings of its will about that other mind.

Do not fight me, it whispered with its thoughts. *We were one before. We shall be one again. Welcome me, and I will swallow you with my power. Fight me, and I will scatter the shards of your soul across the worlds.*

The mind was weak, shattered once and scarcely mended. Earlier Mal'ek'a had sought it with all the power at its control, to no avail. But something had changed. Something had drawn that mind up from out of its abyss, left it weak and approachable, where Mal'ek'a could find it.

You are mine, it whispered. *Welcome me.*

Gannon opened the cellar door and motioned for Jamie to go down.

"Wait a minute," Jamie began.

Gannon backhanded him across the mouth, making every tooth in his head rattle. The force of the blow threw him against a wall. Gannon grabbed him by an arm and propelled him down the stairs.

"Move!"

Jamie fell to his knees at the landing. Before Gannon could push him again, he drew himself upright and went on down. What in God's name was going on?

"Get the door," Gannon said as he followed Jamie into the first cellar.

As Chevier kicked the door shut, Gannon pointed to a high-backed wooden chair that Jamie recognized as coming from one of the dining rooms in the west wing, standing among the rows of wine racks.

"Sit," Gannon said.

Jamie sat.

"Now talk."

"A—about what?"

Gannon hit him again, snapping Jamie's head against the back of the chair. The jolt took Jamie's breath away.

"Please," he said. "I don't know what you want with me, but—"

Again the big fist lashed out.

"You're talking," Gannon said quietly, "but you're not saying anything I want to hear. I'll put it to you simply: How does this place work? How did we get here and how do we get back? Where are the fucking controls?"

Jamie's head rang and he could hardly see straight. He opened his mouth, but nothing came out. There was nothing he could tell them. He heard Chevier chewing on a mint behind him and shuddered. Gannon reached forward and lifted Jamie's chin with his fist.

"Talk," he said, his voice soft and dangerous.

Traupman had been in Jamie's study. He left it and entered Gramarye's Clover, drawn by the sound of Thomas Hengwr's thrashing. To conserve what power they had, there was only one light on in the room, and that was over by the chairs near the window. It cast a pale light on Tom's anguished features. He whipped back and forth on the bed, limbs entangled in the blankets that had covered him.

"No," he muttered. "No. No!" His face glistened with perspiration. His back arched and fell. His hands were clenched into fists.

Traupman hesitated in the doorway. Should he call for some help or do what he could on his own? Jamie was due back at any minute. That decided him. He moved across the room.

"It's all right," he said softly. "Everything's going to be all right."

Tom's eyes snapped open at the sound of his voice and

Traupman stopped dead in his tracks. He saw the look of a wild beast caged in those eyes. And those eyes began to glow.

Sara started to shake. There was no way she could handle tragg'a, not with the House gone. What in God's name had possessed her to take up this stupid challenge? She didn't know what to do. She had to run, but run to where? What could protect her in this world? She couldn't return to Taliesin's tower. The moonheart tune wouldn't work here.

The tragg'a hadn't spotted her yet. If she could just get around the corner. . . .

One of the creatures sighted her and they headed her way. They lifted their hideous snouts to the sky and howled. The sound stopped the blood in Sara's veins. For long moments she watched the tragg'a draw near, numb with terror. Then her adrenaline cut in with a rush and she was off and running. It didn't matter where to, just so long as she got away from those . . . things.

Skidding around the corner of the House, she hiked up her dress and vaulted over the low fence that separated the park from Patterson Avenue. She landed badly and tumbled in a sprawl, clawing her way to her feet. Running along the parkside of the House, she kept glancing back, hoping that by some fluky miracle she'd lost her pursuers. But then they rounded the corner, the largest a few paces ahead of its companions, and they were gaining on her.

She heard the squeal of burning rubber from Patterson, then a car door slamming. A voice called out commanding them to stop.

A quick look back showed her that the lead tragg'a was steadily closing the distance between them. There was no way she could outrun them. She was halfway down the side of the House now and tiring, while the tragg'a seemed unaffected. She saw a window open with nothing but a screen between her and whatever was inside the House now. Better the danger you didn't know than the sure death you did, she thought, as she hurled herself at the screen. It broke under her weight and she tumbled in.

There was a moment of frightening disorientation, when up seemed like down and the whole world spun, then she landed on a rug that slid out from under her. She heard a gunshot outside, saw the lead tragg'a thrust its face at the ripped screen.

The rank stench of the creature assailed her. She tried to move, but could only stare helplessly as the tragg'a made as if to follow her in. Then a piercing blue light flared in the window. She heard the tragg'a's roar of pain, heard sounds behind her, voices, running feet.

"Don't shoot!" a vaguely familiar voice cried.

She tried to recall why it sounded familiar, where she knew it from. Her eyes hurt from the glare of the blue fire. Spots danced in front of her eyes. She turned from the window. She tried to stand, got halfway up.

"Oh, God!" she muttered as she crouched on the floor. Her hands were slick with perspiration. She lifted her head and attempted to focus on the silhouetted form in front of her.

"I understood that," another voice said. "She speaks Eng—"

"Ho-lee shit!" the first voice broke in. "It's Sara!"

"Blue?" she asked.

She was still half blind. She'd only been a few feet from the flare at the window. She reached out with her taw, searching for a familiar presence.

"Is that you, Blue?"

Blue knelt in front of Sara, but she still couldn't see him. "Is that you, Blue?" she asked again.

"It's me, Sara." Gently, he reached for her and drew her into his arms. "It's okay now, Sara."

"The tragg'a . . ."

"It's dead," he said. "Or hurt bad. The House fixed it. It won't be coming in after you."

She shuddered against him. Awkwardly, Blue patted her shoulder, and tears of relief welled up in his eyes. For a long moment, all he could do was hold her. Then slowly he disengaged his arms and helped her to her feet.

"Can you stand up now?" he asked. "Christ, look at you! You're a regular Pocahontas. Where'd you dig up those threads?"

The beginnings of a smile tugged at Sara's lips. "You . . . you wouldn't believe me if I told you," she said.

"Want to bet?"

She blinked as what he'd just said settled in her. The spots in her eyesight were fading, and she saw she was in one of the downstairs rooms on the south side of the House—facing the park. Seeing Sally, she smiled, then her eyes widened as her gaze swung around to Tucker. What was he doing here? She took a step forward. Her legs were still a little wobbly, but her panic had subsided. She turned to face Blue and saw the torn window screen.

"There . . . there were two more, Blue."

"Two? There's a whole fucking army of them out there."

"A whole . . . ." She shook her head slowly. "But . . . I thought they followed me here from the Otherworld. There were only three of them chasing me. They appeared just behind me on Patterson." She stopped when she saw the looks on their faces. "What's the matter?" she asked. "Why are you looking at me like that?"

"Patterson's not out there anymore," Sally said. "There's nothing out there but forest."

"Forest? But I was just out there. They were chasing me through the park. . . ." Her voice trailed off as she neared the window and saw the moonlit fields running off into the darker shadow of the forest. "Oh, God! Where are we?"

But she already knew. This explained why the House had seemed empty earlier. It wasn't there anymore. At least its insides weren't. But how had she ended up here? If they stepped out, would they be back in Ottawa?"

"I've been a long way into the woods," Blue explained when she asked. "There's nothing out there but bush. And monsters. Trags."

"Tragg'a."

"Whatever."

At that moment the howling started up again. Sara shivered, stepping back from the window. The hole in the screen was half the size it had been and growing smaller.

"They can't get in," Tucker said. He handed the Weatherby back to Blue. "But that hasn't stopped them from trying."

Sara wasn't listening. Her small taw was raised and she threw out her senses, searching until she touched what she sought—the thing that led the tragg'a. Kieran's demon. Mal'ek'a. It was drawing near.

"He's out there," she said softly.

"Who is?"

"Mal'ek'a—the Dread-That-Walks-Nameless. I can feel him." She shivered. "He's so strong. So evil. I don't think these walls are going to stop him. Not this time. He won't stop until—"

She stumbled as though she'd been hit, fell to her knees and clapped her hands against her temples.

"Get out! Get out of my head!"

* * *

I remember you, Mal'ek'a whispered. *When I am done with the druid I will return for you.*

Mal'ek'a felt its words hit the small hornless one like so many blows. It grinned, then returned its attention to the other mind, thrusting sharp commands deep into the wounded soul of its enemy, the druid.

We are one, it hissed, overriding the other's protests. *But I am the stronger now. Welcome me....*

"No!" Tom screamed.

He came off the bed, eyes blazing. Mal'ek'a's commands were like fires in his brain, dragging him from the cool darknesses deep inside him into the harsh light of reality.

You know me, Mal'ek'a told him. *You are me!*

"No!"

Tom tore at his shirt, gulped air, shook his head from side to side. Motion caught his eye. He saw Traupman backing out of the room, only it wasn't Traupman he saw. He saw his own evil twin mirrored across the room. He lifted his hands and gold magefire blossomed in his palms, arcing towards the man in the doorway. Traupman was lifted into the air as though by a great fist and hurled against the wall. The air smelled of cooked flesh. Traupman's body smoked as it slid to the floor, lifeless eyes staring at Tom with a glassy accusation imprinted in their retinas.

Tom stared numbly at the dead man and sank to the ground. Mal'ek'a pounded at his mind. Tom wanted to hide—from what he had done, from what he was—but there was no escape.

He saw again the tall longstone on Gwynedd's shores that had been his prison for a thousand years. He had changed, forced the evil festering in his soul away through meditation and other mental disciplines. But the evil, rather than dissipating, had taken on a life of its own. It had escaped their imprisonment in the standing stone long before Tom himself had. It was the lie that Tom had named Taliesin. It was the Dread-That-Walks-Nameless that the quin'on'a named the white man's curse. It was what had struck him down in the Otherworld when he'd been reading the Weirdin he'd thrown to find Sara. It was his own twin and, deny it though he might, he had always known it existed.

"No!" he cried, staring at Traupman's charred corpse.

Yes. Accept it.

Tom saw himself in the Otherworld again, throwing the Weirdin bones, bent over the reading cloth, turning to face his enemy, turning to face himself. . . .

"No!"

He twisted and faced the window now.

"No!"

He lifted his hands, drawing up the last shreds of his waning power. The fire in his hands burned like a miniature nova and he flung it at his enemy.

You are mine! Mal'ek'a cried.

The entire side of the room blew outward. Flaming debris rained on the field, burning and crushing the nearest tragg'a. The House rocked. A voiceless wail pierced Tom's mind. The House! He'd wounded the House and left a breach for his enemy to enter. He pressed his face against the floor. Where now his vaunted wisdom? Where his powers and strengths? Where now his humanity? Gone. All gone.

He fled as the first tragg'a came clawing up through the hole in the House's side. Feeble flickers of blue light ran along the edges of the hole, but the gap was too big for the House to defend.

The tragg'a were inside. And with them came their master.

Gannon drew back his arm to hit Jamie again.

"Talk, damn you!"

Jamie looked up through swollen eyes. Feebly he tried to shake his head, but Chevier held him by the hair and he couldn't move. Blood dripped from cuts above his eye, blinding him. A broken tooth was stuck in his throat, choking him.

"Hit him again, Phil," Chevier said in his whispery voice.

Gannon nodded. But then the House shook to its very foundations. The stones seemed to grind against each other and Jamie screamed.

Christ! Gannon thought. I never even—

Jamie lunged out of the chair, leaving a handful of hair in Chevier's fist. He bowled Gannon over and thundered up the stairs, moaning. It was not his own pain he felt at the moment, but a deeper pain. Now he knew what this bond was that existed between the House and himself, and the knowledge shook him to the depths of his soul. There was a sharp stab in his abdomen, like a knife wound piercing him. He had to pause at the top of the stairs to lean against the wall.

Gannon appeared at the bottom of the stairs.

"You can't get away," he said. "I've got the key to the door. Now get down here and—"

"Fools!" Jamie shouted through bloodied lips. His voice echoed and re-echoed in the confined place. "They've broken in. We're all dead now!"

As Gannon lifted his gun, Jamie turned and hit the door with his shoulder. It should have held. It was locked. It was made of stout oakwood and heavily hinged. Instead, it gave way. As Gannon fired, Jamie was already through the door and off down the hall. He ran to the right and had disappeared around the corner by the time Gannon topped the stairs.

The big man paused, listening. He heard sounds coming down the corridor to his left and ran that way, Chevier following close behind. When they rounded the corner, they came face to face with the first wave of tragg'a.

Sam rubbed at his eyes, stretched his neck, then returned to the journal. Anthony Tamson's handwriting was crabbed and difficult to read after a time, but he thought he'd found what they were looking for. It just didn't make any sense. He reread the passage again, shaking his head.

> *It will be my flesh, my bone. It will House my soul. Already I can feel it bind me to it. We will straddle the worlds. My flesh may be too weak, my years too many, but I will still live on. My son I will protect, and my son's son, and all my line hereafter. So long as my line lives on, so long as we stand, bones of stone, flesh of wood, we will endure and redress the wrongs of our ancestor's evil.*

There was nothing in the pages before that passage to give any indication as to what had led up to it. By comparing the dates of the entries, the only inconsistency Sam could find was a two-week gap between the last entry and this one. Checking the binding, he didn't think any pages had been torn out. He bent over the old journal, meaning to read on, when he heard the blast and felt the House shake under him.

God! Not again.

He glanced at the book, then at the door. Better get this up to Jamie, he thought. Maybe he can make some sense out of it.

* * *

Blue helped Sara to her feet.

"Jesus!" Tucker said. "What was that?"

They heard the blast from upstairs, followed by the rocking of the House.

"It's alive," Sara said. "The House is alive and something's just . . . just . . ." She couldn't go on. The House's pain touched her like the thrust of something sharp under her ribs.

"What did she say?" Tucker asked.

"They're in," Blue said. "The tragg'a have broken in."

He knew it. This was what he'd been feeling all night. The fuckers had broken in. So now what did they do?

"Maggie!" Tucker cried.

He headed for the door only to collide with her.

"Tucker," she began. "Upstairs. . . ."

He nodded. "Where do we go?" he asked, turning to Blue.

"It's no good," Blue said. "They're already in this time. You heard them. They must've blown off half the House."

"We're not giving up now. Maggie, give Sara a hand. Sally, do you know how to use that gun?"

"Yes, but—"

"Blue. Blue! For Christ's sake. Pull yourself together!"

"Okay. All right."

Blue tried to think. He'd been gone there for a moment. They'd put too much faith in the House holding the tragg'a back. Hadn't really thought through what they'd do once the suckers actually broke in.

"We've got to get everybody together and hole up somewhere," he said. "In one of the towers."

"Okay." Tucker herded them out of the room. "Let's *go!*"

"But Jamie. . . ."

"Let's just get moving."

Jesus, Tucker thought. What he wouldn't give for his squad right now.

Sally went out first, followed by Maggie and Sara. Tucker looked at Blue. Don't go to pieces on me now, he thought.

"I'm okay now," Blue said, reading the look on Tucker's face.

He went out the door with Tucker bringing up the rear. Ahead of them, Sally gave a startled yelp. Blue pushed ahead, his rifle leveled, and saw it was Jamie. He took one look at Jamie's face and the last vestiges of shock drained from him. Somebody was going to burn tonight!

"What happened to you?" he asked Jamie.

"Gannon and . . . the other guy. They . . . it doesn't matter. The creatures are in. They're . . ."

"We know, Jamie."

For the first time, Jamie saw who Maggie was supporting. "Sara!"

He started for her when Tucker bellowed: "Let's *move!*"

Blue led them down the hall. Glancing over his shoulder, Tucker caught a glimpse of motion at the other end of the hall. Jesus H. Christ! It was Hengwr. He took a step in the old man's direction, then saw the tragg'a swarming behind the wizard. Blue and the others were turning a corner ahead of Tucker. The Inspector hesitated, then headed after them. He didn't want to risk a shot down the hall for fear of hitting Hengwr. But he wasn't going to hang about waiting for him either. Sucker got them into this mess in the first place.

They picked up Sam as they rounded a second corner and made the safety of Sara's tower without running into the tragg'a. When everyone was in—thank God the towers only had one entrance each, Tucker thought—he took up a stand by the door. Inventory time. Who was missing? Gannon and Chevier. Well, fuck them. Traupman. Jesus! And the gardener—what the hell was his name? Fred.

Tucker stared at the corner they'd just come around, but Hengwr never showed. What came first was the smell of the creatures, rolling down the hallway ahead of them. Then the first tragg'a shuffled into view.

"Give me some room," Blue said in the Inspector's ear.

Tucker moved to one side. The big Weatherby boomed once and the first tragg'a was thrown against the wall behind it when the bullet hit it. Blue worked the bolt again and shot the second creature. When a third and fourth rounded the corner, Tucker opened up. He emptied his gun, then pushed Blue back inside and slammed the big oak door shut.

"The dresser," he said.

With Maggie and Blue's help, he manhandled it in front of the door, added a chest on top of it and a table in front of the dresser. While Blue stood in front of the makeshift barricade, Tucker turned to face the room, reloading his .38. Jamie was slumped on a couch, all strength drained out of him. His face was bruised, one eye swollen shut, dried blood caked in his beard. Sara sat beside him, holding his hand. Sally stood facing the window, the handgun Blue had given her large in her trembling hands.

Lastly he looked at Maggie. She was holding up well, but there was a grim look in her eyes that Tucker wished he'd never had to see.

"I'm sorry it had to be like this," he began, but she shook her head.

"It's not your fault I'm here, Tucker."

"Never could talk you out of anything anyway," he said.

Her lips shaped a smile that never touched her eyes. Her knuckles were white around the handle of the Margolin, but her hand was firm.

The tragg'a reached the door. They clawed at its wood and filled the hall with the terrible din of their howling. It might hold them for awhile, Blue thought. But what about when the big cheese showed up? What the hell were they going to do then?

"I thought we'd make it," Blue said without turning. "Through all the shit, I really thought we'd pull through."

"We're not dead yet," Tucker said.

"No," Blue agreed. "Not yet."

He felt like firing a couple of rounds through the door, just to discourage the creatures a bit, but didn't want to waste the shells. When they broke through he wanted to take as many of them as he could before they took him down. He especially wanted a shot left for this Dread-whatever-the-fuck-it-was that Sara spoken of.

He glanced at where she was sitting beside Jamie. She was looking better, head lifted, a fierce look in her eyes. She looked different—all duded up in her Indian gear. Looked good.

"Listen," Sara said.

"I can hear them," he said.

"No. *Listen*."

But he didn't know what she meant. He didn't know that it was her taw reaching out that let her hear . . . beyond the cacophony of the tragg'a, beyond the weird moaning of the House, beyond the railings of Mal'ek'a as he stalked the corridors that were empty of life save for his own creatures. Beyond all that, Sara heard the sound of drumming.

Chapter Six

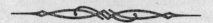

11:15, Friday morning.

Madison left his car in the parking lot at the Riverside Hospital and, after checking in at the information desk, found his way to the room where Dan Collins was. The antiseptic smell of the hospital followed him up the elevator and down the corridor, making him nervous.

Collins was smoking a cigarette and staring up at the ceiling when Madison came through the door. His hand was wrapped in white gauze and lay stiffly at his side. Madison took the chair near the head of the bed, laid his cane on the floor and massaged his thigh.

"Good morning, Dan," he said. "How are you feeling today?"

"Rotten." Collins grinned and butted out his cigarette. "This place is driving me batty. Think you can pull a few strings and get me out of here? Christ! It was only a burn."

"That's why I'm here. The doctor's signing you out at noon."

"Did you talk to Williams?" Collins asked. "Has he decided to reconsider closing down the operation?"

"I didn't ask him to."

"But . . ."

"Whatever's going down," Madison said, "the Solicitor General's in the thick of it. He's got to be. So I'm not going back to him without something hard I can show—something that he doesn't dare ignore. Until then, I'm playing it like he wants it. The PRB's shut down. Transfers are in effect as of Monday morning. And the files are all boxed in my office, waiting to be sent down to Archives."

"So what are we going to do?"

"We? You're going home. You're out of this, Dan. I'm—"

"No way I'm out of it," Collins said firmly. "You got anybody to lend you a hand?"

"No. But—"

"Shit, Wally. You haven't been on the street in years. You can't just waltz around out there expecting everything to fall neatly into place. When was the last time you fired that .38 of yours?"

Madison glanced down at the bulge under his left armpit. "It shows that bad, eh?"

"It shows if you're looking for it," Collins said. "When was the last time you used it?"

Madison shrugged. "I don't know. Out in the practice range, I suppose. Last spring, maybe."

Collins shook his head. He took out a cigarette one-handedly, tossed the package onto the table beside his bed and picked up his lighter. "So what's *our* plan, Wally?" he asked.

Madison sighed. "Okay. I want to stake out Tamson House tonight. All weekend if necessary. I dropped in on a friend of mine this morning who runs a video store and picked up a camera. Then I borrowed a couple of battery-operated spots from another friend who owns a photo supply shop. Told him I was filming something kinky in my garden tonight."

Collins laughed. "And he believed you?"

"Said he wanted a print of the film when it was done."

"Figures. So what are you going to do with all that stuff?"

"Break another window."

"Break . . . I get it." Collins thought about it for a moment. "They'll just think it was faked. Have you seen what they can do with special effects these days?"

"But this is different. This is real."

"Yeah. Only how do we prove it to them?"

Madison shook his head. "It's a start, Dan. Maybe we'll be lucky for once and something will break. The way the project's gone so far, something's got to give."

"Okay." Collins butted out his new cigarette and sat up. "So get me out of here already."

"Call for you, Mr. Williams. On line two."

Michael Williams pushed aside the report he was reading and picked up the phone.

"Williams here."

"Glad I caught you, Mike. Do you have a minute?"

Williams frowned as he recognized the voice. J. Hugh Walters. Respected businessman and political advisor. Patron of the arts. He was also the headhunter who had Williams by the balls.

It had been his first and only time—one slip that would never have been picked up if it hadn't been for the accident. . . He didn't know how Walters had known about it. But knowing what he knew now of the magnate, it didn't take a lot of guesswork to realize that the whole incident had probably been a set-up. But of course it was far too late to do anything about it by that time. Everything. What kept Williams from throwing away his entire career was the fact that Walters never asked for much. Nothing that jeopardized national security. All Walters required was a word here, a favor there.

"I'm just checking on the Project," Walters said. "How's the clean-up going?"

"We're almost done."

"Good, good. And no leaks?"

"No leaks."

"What about our intrepid Inspector Tucker? Any word on him?"

Williams still wasn't sure if Tucker was in Walters's employ or not. "He's still missing," he said.

"That's a shame. Tucker's a good man—a credit to the Force." Walters paused for a moment, then added: "I've got another little problem that you might be able to help me with, Mike."

"All you have to do is ask."

One day, Williams promised silently, he'd end this. He'd expose Walters no matter what it cost him. It just wasn't the right time. He wasn't sure that it would ever be the right time.

"It has to do with my business associate, Phillip Gannon." Walters asked.

"What about him?"

"I seem to have misplaced him. I sent him around to Tamson House yesterday with a few men and he hasn't been back in touch with me since."

"What would you like me to do?"

"Nothing. It's just if one of your men should get a trifle over-zealous and pick him up—well, I don't want him on any official record. It would rather spoil his usefulness to me."

"That shouldn't be any problem. As far as the Force is concerned, Tamson House is no longer a going concern."

"Good, good. Well, I've got to run, Mike. Give my love to Joan and the children."

Walters hung up and for a long moment Williams listened to the dial tone. Then he slowly cradled the phone and stared off across his office. Unlocking his desk drawer, he reached in the back and took out an envelope. It was unaddressed on the outside. But inside, on the letter's heading, the address was plain. It was to be sent to the Prime Minister's office. All it required was a date and his signature on it. The wording was simple. It stated that for personal reasons, he was resigning his post as Solicitor General. Nothing more. But it would be enough. It would end the nightmare. End a part of it at any rate. He would still have to live through Walters's retribution.

How could he face Joan and the children if Walters made the entire sordid affair public? Slowly he returned the letter to its place and relocked the drawer.

"Bingo!" Madison said.

Collins looked up from the cigarette he was lighting and glanced down Patterson Avenue. They'd been staked out for about three hours, watching the House. In the back seat of Madison's four-door Volkswagen Rabbit, the third member of their team stirred. Doug Jackson was a blond, husky man that Collins had worked with before. He was just finishing off a two-week vacation when Collins had called him in on a favor.

"Looks like an Indian," Jackson said. "Do we grab her?"

Madison shook his head. "Not yet. Let's see what she does first."

He drew the straps of the portable Sony VCR up around his shoulder. Jackson would take care of the lights.

"Doesn't have a key," Collins murmured as they watched the woman ring a doorbell. "Just some visitor, I guess."

"We're not leaving anything to chance, Dan."

"Sure. She's leaving. Do you want me to—"

"Not yet. She's on foot. She won't get far." Madison leaned closer to the windshield, watching the woman slowly walk along the House. "What's she doing?"

"Looks like she picked up a rock."

The woman threw the rock at the window, then staggered back.

"Okay," Collins said. "We've got her on a B&E."

"Hold it!" Madison said. "She just reached inside the window. How come she didn't get burned?"

They were so intent on following the woman's actions that they were unaware that she was no longer alone on the street. It wasn't until she turned that Jackson noticed the three figures further down Patterson.

"Heads up," he said. "We've got company. I wonder how they got this far up the street without our . . . Jesus!"

"They're wearing some kind of masks," Madison said.

Jackson shook his head slowly. "Those aren't masks."

They stared at the unnatural beings, unable to believe what they were seeing. It was one thing to be sitting in a theater and watching the wonders of modern special effects technology make the impossible real, but quite another to be confronted by these things in the middle of an Ottawa street. Madison remembered reading the statements of the witnesses in Patty's Place.

"Just like Thompson," he began.

Howls lifted from three inhuman throats, blending into one horrific wail.

"They're after the woman!" Collins cried.

Madison started up the car. They watched the woman bolt around the corner of the House, into the park, the creatures following at a deceptively quick shuffling pace. Madison stamped on the gas pedal, coming to a squealing stop as they reached the spot where the figures had disappeared into the park. Collins winced as he put pressure on his wounded hand, opening the door.

"Jesus H. Christ!" he muttered.

"Let's go!" Madison cried.

He took off at a limping run, drawing his .38 from its shoulder holster, hands damp with sweat.

"Stop!" he shouted as he turned the corner.

He paused there, waiting for the other two to catch up.

"Give me that camera," Collins said.

He took the sack that held the lights from Jackson, allowing the other men to hurry on, unburdened. He followed at a slower pace.

As Madison rounded the second corner, he saw the woman throw herself at a window. She disappeared inside the House just as the first of the creatures reached the place where she'd been. Aiming his revolver, he fired a shot. The second creature stumbled, shrieking with pain. The first hit the window and flew back in an explosion of blue fire. Madison drew bead on the last of them, while Jackson fired three shots in rapid succession. The third creature twisted as it was hit, fell in a sprawl. The second had spun back against the House where it too had dropped.

The two men approached the scene cautiously. When they reached the dead creatures, Madison looked down at them, then away. He felt sick at the reek rising from their corpses.

"Just three of them," Jackson said.

He searched the park with a careful gaze as he replaced his spent shells.

"What in God's name are they?"

As Collins came up, Madison glanced at the window. Still nothing there. Just the grey inside and the edges of the screen....

"Set up those lights," he said.

He took the camera from Collins and set it up on its tripod, focusing it on the window. In the distance he could hear sirens. He wondered how the window had come to be open in the first place. When the cold glare of the spotlights threw the regenerating screen into bold relief, he let the videotape roll.

"This place is going to be crawling with locals in another minute," Jackson remarked. "If we're still playing this one low-key, we'd better get our asses in gear."

"We don't have to pussyfoot around anymore," Madison said. "Not even with Williams."

He nodded to the corpses of the three dead creatures. The one that had tried to get in the window was still smoking.

"We've got these things now," he said. "I'd just like to see Williams say that this never happened. We're going to wait right here for the local police and cooperate with them as fully as possible. He won't be able to stop it now."

Lights were coming on throughout the neighborhood. An Ottawa Police cruiser pulled up on Bank Street, its cherry lights flashing. The wail of other sirens approached.

"Still doesn't tell us what happened to Tucker and the rest of them," Collins remarked.

"But it's more than we had a few hours ago," Madison replied. He put away his gun, motioning for Jackson to do the same. "We don't want anyone with itchy fingers to get the wrong idea about us."

A second car pulled up behind the first cruiser. Spotlights stabbed the night, weaving back and forth across the park until their lights picked out the three men. While one of the policemen remained by the cars, the others started across the park, weapons in their hands. As they drew near, Madison called out:

"I'm reaching for identification."

The first officer nodded and Madison gingerly withdrew his billfold, flipped it open and let his badge glint in the light of the spotlights. Visibly relaxing, the policeman put away his sidearm and approached, wrinkling his nose at the smell that came from the bodies of the creatures.

"What the hell's going on?"

"I'm Superintendent Madison and these two men are—"

Before he had a chance to finish, an explosion rocked the air. The men turned to see a great piece of the second story's walls blow outward to rain flaming debris on the park.

"Ho-lee fuck!" the first patrolman muttered.

"Well, we've got ourselves a way in," Jackson said and headed for the hole, sidestepping the debris.

"Careful!" Madison called as he followed.

Shinnying up a support, Jackson made it to the porch's roof. He reached for a handhold higher up, cursed and drew back his hand.

"Jackson?"

"I'm okay. Just a little shock."

He drew a pair of gloves from the sidepocket of his windbreaker and reached up again. He had the feeling, just for a moment, of being crowded. As though he wasn't alone on this perch. He shook off the feeling. Prepared for the sting of the shock this time, he heaved himself up. Now the feeling was stronger. He stood in the opening and stared into an empty greyness. He thought he felt something brush by him and he stepped aside. There was nothing there. He could still smell the reek of the dead creatures. It was stronger somehow.

The greyness in front of him wavered. He caught a brief glimpse of a devastated room, furniture and goods thrown about as though by a whirlwind, then it was gone. Taking a step in, the grey wavered once more. A sensation like static electricity ran through him. He had a sudden feeling of vertigo, as though the building had shifted under him. He turned to go back, saw not the park with the house lights beyond it, but dark fields and forests. Then he was in the midst of a swarm of howling creatures.

* * *

"Jackson? Jackson!"

Madison turned to the policeman beside him, but before he could speak, something was flung from the gap torn in the House's wall. He followed its descent and knew, without having to look, what it was. Jackson's body, what was left of it, hit the ground with a dull slapping sound. Madison's stomach lurched.

"Oh, Christ!" he mumbled, leaning against the porch for support. He looked at the patrolman standing beside him. The man's face was as white as his own. Get a grip on yourself, Madison thought. He swallowed drily. "We . . . uh, we've got to cordon this place off," he said.

The patrolman started to nod, then stepped quickly to the side of the House where he lost the contents of his stomach. More patrol cars were pulling onto Patterson and Clemow. Their flashing lights crisscrossed, adding to the hellish quality of the moment. Burning debris threw smoke into the air. The place reeked with the stench of the monsters. Along the park railing that bordered Bank Street, civilians were gathering.

Someone had to take control, Madison thought. He hurried to where the others were still staring open-mouthed at the dead creatures and began to bark orders. The men, out of their depth in a situation this bizarre, were quick to follow them.

Walters sat in his den staring at the confusion on his television screen.

"Although the actual cause of the explosion has not yet been . . ." the commentator was saying when Walters shut off the sound with his remote control and continued to regard the picture in silence.

He had to give them this. They were fast. Like vultures. The entire area had been cordoned off. The place was swarming with reporters, television crews, RCMP, local police and spectators. He had seen the pictures of the dead creatures that had been broadcast thus far and tried to understand exactly what it was that had taken place at Tamson House.

Was still taking place, he amended. According to the TV commentator, the police had not yet entered the building. Earlier attempts had left two officers dead, a third seriously wounded. They were now waiting for reinforcements. The next assault would be on the gap high in the building's south wall, where an RCMP officer had been thrown out earlier in the evening, torn to ribbons.

He wondered what it was that they expected to find. One thing he knew—they were going about this all wrong. If he had been in charge, he would have had the tightest possible security clamped down on it from the first moment. By the time he had found out, however, it had been too late for him to do anything. He toyed with the idea of calling Williams, then shook his head. The man was beginning to feel the pressure. Perhaps dismantling the PRB had been too hasty a decision—especially with what was transpiring tonight.

Frowning, Walters brought the sound back up.

It was too late to reconsider. What was necessary now was to salvage what he could from the present. Because no matter who he had to step on, he was going to come out ahead. What was on the TV screen at the moment proved beyond the shadow of a doubt that the parameters of science would have to be stretched to encompass an entire new field of knowledge.

Walters expected to be at the forefront of that pioneering. And he expected to keep it for himself if it was at all possible.

Jean-Paul Gagnon was at a friend's house in Alta Vista when the first news bulletin interrupted the regular programming. He stared aghast at the screen. That was Tamson House. When the camera panned across the three dead monsters, he shuddered, remembering his conversations with Inspector Tucker. Making his apologies, he left as soon as he could, pointing his VW down Bank Street, to the Glebe and Tamson House.

After what he'd just seen on the television, he couldn't discount any of what the Inspector had told him. And if the Inspector was only partially correct, it still meant that Kieran was in a great deal of trouble. Because somehow Jean-Paul knew that he would find Kieran there. The Inspector had been certain that Jamie Tams and his strange House were central to the problems that had been plaguing him.

Jean-Paul wasn't sure what he hoped to accomplish by going to the House now. Was it to lend moral support to the Inspector or Kieran? To make up for not trusting Kieran enough to tell him about the investigation as he should have in the first place? *Seigneur!* He only hoped that he wouldn't arrive just to identify a corpse.

Chapter Seven

"THERE is still time to stop this madness," Ha'kan'ta said.

Kieran shook his head. He looked across the circle of hard-packed dirt to where Tep'fyl'in stood. The quin'on'a War Chief wore nothing but a loincloth. His greased skin shone in the firelight. His eyes were bright and eager; his body relaxed. Ready. Thrust into the dirt beside him was a six-foot spear, point upward, a handful of white feathers tied where the leather bound the sharp flint head to the shaft.

A similar spear pointed out of the earth beside Kieran. He too wore only a loincloth. His skin was greased and his hair tied back in a short braid. He didn't think he cut nearly the impressive figure that the quin'on'a warrior did.

"I'll let him knock me around a bit," Kieran said, "give him the first blood—and that'll be that."

Ha'kan'ta turned to him, caught the nervous self-deprecation in her lover's features. "Lord lifting Jesus!" Kieran murmured. "You know I'll do my best."

"He will try to kill you," Ha'kan'ta replied.

Kieran knew that. He looked at the circle of watching quin'on'a and didn't see much sympathy in their faces. But here and there amongst the slender, horned beings, he saw other men and women standing—physically hornless, stockier in build, taller.

"Who are those others?" he asked.

"They are rathe'wen'a," Ha'kan'ta said. "They came in answer to my summoning."

"There's not too many of them," Kieran said. He counted perhaps a dozen—fourteen at tops.

"We have never been a large clan. And many of my people have not come. Some are too far to answer. Some want no

411

part of the quin'on'a—in friendship or enmity. Some . . ." She shrugged. "Some are elsewise occupied. But these will be enough."

"What are you planning? Don't go starting something. . . ."

"We will not interfere, Kieran. But we will see that this combat goes no further than first blood."

Kieran shook his head. *"Nom de tout!* Having them here is just asking for trouble, Kanta. He'll play it straight. He has to."

"I believe that Red-Spear has moved beyond honor."

"Sins'amin, then. She'll keep an eye on him."

"The quin'on'a Beardaughter has her own trials in store, I fear. But they are not my concern. My only concern is keeping you alive, beloved."

Kieran looked away, and caught Tep'fyl'in's gaze. A flicker of amusement ran across the War Chief's features. They will not stop me, his eyes seemed to say, indicating Ha'kan'ta's people. Only you can stop me and you have not the strength. Nor the skill. Nor the courage.

"Kieran . . ." Ha'kan'ta began.

But then the moon lifted above the trees and the trial was to begin.

"I love you," Kieran said softly.

The intensity of feeling that came with those words surprised him, but gave him the strength he needed. Ha'kan'ta stepped forward, brushed her lips against his.

"Good hunting, my warrior," she whispered, then stepped back.

Kieran nodded. Grasping the haft of his spear, he pulled it from the dirt and strode forward. Father Raven, he thought, lend me skill.

If his totem heard him, it made no reply.

Pukwudji crept from the woods and moved to a position from which he could see both the circle of dirt and Ha'kan'ta. He was here because, whatever thoughts Sara had had when she'd left the rath'wen'a and Kieran, they were still her friends. She might not know it, but he could see it, as plain as the slap of a beaver's tail on the still waters of Pinta'wa.

They were in danger. Kieran's was easy to see. It lay in the strength of Red-Spear's arm, in the bright edge of flint at the end of the War Chief's spear. For Ha'kan'ta it was a more subtle thing. She and her people might stop Tep'fyl'in for a

moment, but honor or no honor, the quin'on'a would not allow
their interference. Kieran would have to face his trial on his
own. Pukwudji meant to stay by Ha'kan'ta's side and keep her
from doing more harm than good.

It was up to the Forest Lords to see that justice was done.
It was up to the quin'on'a elders to uphold their honor.

As he neared Ha'kan'ta's side, he saw an old rathe'wen'a
approach her from the other side. Pukwidji knew that one:
Ur'wen'ta. Bear-of-Magic. The old man, looking past Ha'kan'ta,
saw and recognized Pukwudji.

"Do you bring ill or good with you, Trickster?" he asked
softly.

"I am a mirror," Pukwudji replied. "Is that not a saying of
your people?"

Ur'wen'ta nodded thoughtfully. "It is indeed. But still I
wonder."

Shrugging, Pukwudji turned to watch as Sins'amin stepped
out to speak.

Kieran heard little of the Beardaughter's speech. He caught
a phrase or two—such as "trial by combat... honor will be
upheld... first blood...." He concentrated instead on what
was to come. He drew up the stillness inside him, let the silent
drumming of his taw narrow the focus of his attention until all
that concerned him was the beardless warrior who stood opposite him. He weighed his spear. The heavier spearhead end
made the weapon feel unbalanced. What little experience he
had was only with plain staves.

There was a huge concentration of power in the circle of
dirt. The quin'on'a and Ha'kan'ta's people focused their own
magics on what was to come, setting the air crackling with
their attention.

"The Forest Lords watch," Sins'amin was saying in conclusion. "Conduct yourself with fitting honor."

She stepped back and the two men were alone in the circle.

Kieran balanced lightly on the balls of his feet, the spear
held like a staff in a two-handed grip before him. For long
moments they faced each other, still as the granite stones that
dotted the slopes behind them. Then suddenly Tep'fyl'in was
in motion, his spear a blur. Kieran barely brought his own
weapon up in time to block the blow. The crack as wood struck
wood was loud in the silence, and the vibration of the spear's
shaft made his hands sting. Blow followed blow in a rapid

flurry, and Kieran backed away under the onslaught, conscious only of the two ends of the War Chief's spear that darted for him with all the speed of a snake's strike. Sweat ran into his eyes, mingled with the grease on his back and chest, as he drove his body to meet the challenge. But block each strike though he did, he knew he was already slowing.

Tep'fyl'in withdrew, stood poised, a look of quiet amusement in his eyes. It was then that Kieran realized that the War Chief had yet to exert himself. This first series of quicksilver moves had only been the quin'on'a's method of drawing out his opponent's skill. And now that he knew—

"Hai!" Tep'fyl'in cried.

The head of his spear flashed towards Kieran's eyes. Kieran whipped up his own weapon to block it, saw too late the reverse end of the other man's spear lashing for his legs. He took a hard blow on his calf that knocked him from his feet. As Tep'fyl'in's spearhead darted for his face, he rolled frantically out of the way in the dirt. Again the sudden reverse. This blow took him as he was rising, high in the chest, and sent him tumbling back onto the dirt.

Once more Tep'fyl'in withdrew, allowing Kieran to get to his feet. His leg and side ached, the leg already stiffening under him. He knew he had to move on the offensive before he took a worse hit.

He came in at a low crouch, feinted high, then low, managed to slip the head of his spear in above Tep'fyl'in's block, but the quin'on'a was already out of the way before the blow could strike home. Kieran spun, following the momentum of his attack, caught a glancing blow across his upper arm, but his own strike came whirring down, landing with a satisfying crack against Red-Spear's hip. The hit caught the quin'on'a by surprise and Kieran followed up his momentary advantage, but Tep'fyl'in recovered before another blow landed.

His spear struck with a crack against Kieran's left hand, then his right. As Kieran's weapon fell from numbed fingers, Tep'fyl'in brought the blunt end of his spear up and in. Kieran took the blow in the stomach, buckled over. Moving in, the quin'on'a caught Kieran with a glancing blow to the side of his head.

The skin broke under that blow and Sins'amin rose to call an end to this mockery of a trial. The young warrior had acquited himself well against Tep'fyl'in, for all that Red-Spear had been merely toying with him, holding back until that final exchange of blows. Ha'kan'ta gasped as Kieran pitched forward senseless into the dirt, blood smearing his brow. But relief leaped across her worry. At least it was ended. At least he lived.

"The combat is ended," Sins'amin said. "You have won, Red-Spear. Let the youth be."

"He is mine!" Tep'fyl'in cried. "His life is mine to take away or give."

"The combat was to first blood."

Tep'fyl'in shook his head. "Again you are wrong, old mother. The combat ends with this!"

Tep'fyl'in whirled his spear in his right hand so that the flint head pointed directly at his motionless adversary. The haft of the weapon slapped against the waiting palm of his left hand. Two-handedly, he poised the spear above his foe, ready to drive the point home.

But Ha'kan'ta's taw was as poised and ready as Tep'fyl'in's spear. Her power was a golden spark of magefire held in check by her closed fist. She opened her hand to loose it, to blast the War Chief's weapon from his hands, but Pukwudji threw himself against her, spoiling her aim. Magefire seared the night air, shooting harmlessly into the sky. Unbalanced, Ha'kan'ta and the honochen'o'keh tumbled to the ground in a tangle of limbs.

"No!" Sins'amin cried in a voice like thunder.

She knew she was too late. The spectators, quin'on'a and rathe'wen'a alike, leaned forward.

Tep'fyl'in brought his spear down. But before it could taste Kieran's flesh, the weapon twisted to one side of its own volition and sank deep into the packed earth. Tep'fyl'in cried out in surprise and pain as the haft of the spear burst into flames, searing his hands.

"Who dares?" he roared, turning to view the spectators.

Through a red blaze of anger he saw only stunned looks on each face, from Sins'amin and his own people, to the rathe'wen'a and Ha'kan'ta and Pukwudji who were struggling to their feet. His gaze settled on Kieran, who was beginning to rise. Tep'fyl'in's anger snapped the last vestiges of his sanity. He reached down and caught Kieran by the throat, dragging him up in a powerful grip. His fingers tightened on the pale throat.

So complete was his rage, he did not hear the murmur that ran through those who watched, did not hear the rumble of deep drumming that suddenly filled the air. He saw only Kieran's bulging eyes, felt the weak blows of Kieran's fists against his chest and forearms. Then to his horror, his hands began to open of their own accord. He fought to control them. Muscles jumped out in knots on his arms and shoulders, but slowly his fingers were pried apart as though a hand of iron pulled them from about Kieran's throat. When Kieran fell gasping for air in the dirt, Tep'fyl'in no longer saw him. For the first time he was aware of what the others saw.

A tall figure stood across the circle from him. It had the body of a man, with a wolf's head, raven's feathers that streamed down his neck and shoulders like a mane, and a stag's antlers thrusting above the lupine features. Dangling from the horns were more feathers, entwined with thin strips of braided leather and beads. About his loins was a pelt of foxskin.

"You have forsaken your honor, Red-Spear-of-the-Wind," the apparition said. His voice boomed above the solemn drumming that filled the air. His eyes were gold and merciless. "So you have forsaken your right to live."

Tep'fyl'in's gaze darted left and right, but he could find no sympathy—from his own people or the rathe'wen'a. Only Sins'amin's face held pity for him. From her he turned away.

"He is not of our people, Father," he said.

"He is more my son this night than you are."

"No!" Tep'fyl'in cried. "He cannot be your son! The stink of evil flows through his veins. He runs with the hare. His acceptance into our Way is a mockery of all we hold true. Because of him and his people, the tribes are gone and we dwindle, forsaken by them. Will you have us wither away into memories?"

"I would have you accept a new Way. Truth wears many faces, Red-Spear. Many paths lead to one destination. It is the spirit that will not accept change that will dwindle and be lost."

"We dwindle *because* of change," Tep'fyl'in said bitterly. "We must return to the old ways if we are to grow strong again. You of all of us must know that best, Father. See yourself. See how the Forest Lords themselves have withered. How many were you once? How many are you now? Like the quin'on'a, you have learned to die."

The Forest Lord shook his head. "There can be no return to the old ways. Life goes on, as the wind crosses the plains, as the forests that grow to die and in dying are reborn. If it were otherwise, life would be stagnant. Would you grow rank and sour like a marsh? Is that what you wish for your people, Red-Spear?"

"It will not end so," Tep'fyl'in said. "It cannot end so. We must remain true, if no other will. If even the Forest Lords allow the white-skinned hornless strangers to force them from the true Way, it is time that they go themselves to drum in the Dreaming Thunder."

He moved suddenly, snatching up Kieran's fallen spear and flinging it one smooth motion. The weapon flew true, striking the Forest Lord in his deep chest. But the strange figure simply stood, the spear thrusting from him like an extra appendage. The drumming never faltered. Then slowly he lifted a hand and pulled it free. Blood, dark and green as the needles of the surrounding spruce, flowed from the wound, coagulated, clotted. The wound closed.

"We *are* the Dreaming Thunder," the Forest Lord said softly.

The drumming that pulsed through the night air fell silent.

"Farewell, my son," he said. "Remember this lesson when you are born again. Remember, or be doomed to live it all again. Remember, or you will never drum in the Place of Dreaming Thunder."

Tep'fyl'in howled like a wolf as the power arced between the Forest Lord's eyes and his own. As he fell to his knees, he heard his furred brothers answer in the distance. They paused in their hunting to lift greyed muzzles skyward, keening with sorrow. Only two wolves remained silent. Silver-furred, they stood watching, attention divided between the dying War Chief and the honochen'o'keh who had dared to attack their drum-sister.

Tep'fyl'in's life leaked from him. He howled, not in pain, but in sorrow. Then in anger. His head grew too heavy to hold up. Lowering it, his dark eyes looked into Kieran's. The hatred in the quin'on'a's eyes struck Kieran like a physical blow.

"I . . . I curse . . ." Tep'fyl'in began, but died before he could complete the thought.

He sprawled face down into the dirt and then it was over. The cries of the distant wolves faded and silence returned. Sins'amin regarded the Forest Lord. She saw him as a she-bear, tall and amber-eyed, fur grizzled and brown. She shaped words in her mind but could not connect them to express what lay inside her.

I understand, the bear's low voice rumbled in her mind. *No shame has been brought to your lodge.*

He meant no ill.

The bear shook her head. *Yet he brought great ill with his actions.*

Sins'amin bowed her head, accepting her totem's gentle rebuke. When the bear spoke of Red-Spear, Sins'amin knew that she spoke for her as well.

Kieran saw the Forest Lord as a raven.

Again you acted without first considering, the raven said to him. *What had you hoped to gain with this madness? Was it for love that you accepted this challenge?*

Kieran shook his head. *No,* he replied slowly. *It was for pride.*

The Forest Lord's unblinking gaze weighed Kieran's words against what his soul held.

If you can admit that much, the raven said at length, *perhaps there is still hope for you.*

Why did you help me? Kieran asked.

I did not aid you. I came to aid Tep'fyl'in. He broke from our Way, forsook his honor. Left to his own, he would have set as much sorrow into motion as your Mal'ek'a has. Worse, he would have done so with the best of intentions. There is nothing so pitiable as a misguided soul.

Still, I thank you.

As you will. What will you do now?

Kieran said nothing.

I ask you this, little brother, the raven said. *Remember the quiet wonders. The world has more need of them than it has for warriors. And this I will tell you as well: One cannot seek to uphold honor in a being that has none. In seeking Mal'ek'a you will bring only sorrow to yourself. There is a price for every action. Regard what Tep'fyl'in has paid.*

But Mal'ek'a is evil, Kieran said. *And Tep'fyl'in was right, it was my people that loosed him in the world. Mal'ek'a came from across the Great Water, did he not?*

He did. Do what you must do, the raven replied. *Farewell, my son. I will look for you again when you seek peace, not war.* Turning, the Forest Lord stepped in amongst the trees and was gone.

Kieran lifted himself painfully from the dirt. He put a hand up to his throat, and winced from the pain. It was difficult to breathe. Looking about himself, he saw that the quin'on'a had departed as silently as his totem. Only Ha'kan'ta and her people remained. And one other: Pukwudji.

"You knew he would come," Ha'kan'ta said to Pukwudji. "That is why you stopped me from interfering."

The honochen'o'keh had not known. All he *had* known was that if Ha'kan'ta or any of her people had interfered, the quin'on'a would not have stood idly by. One death was in the wind. Kieran or Tep'fyl'in would die. He had come to stop others from dying. But that a Forest Lord would come.... He shrugged, not bothering to reply. Let her read her own meaning into what had transpired tonight.

Ha'kan'ta crossed the circle and knelt by her lover, smiling down into his face. She touched his brow with feather-light fingers.

"Now we can know peace," she said. "The quin'on'a no longer have a hold on our lives."

Kieran shook his head. "There's still Mal'ek'a to deal with."

"No."

"Nom de tout, Kanta!"

But now their roles had been reversed and it was she who would have no more to do with it.

"It is ended," she said. "For us it is ended. Let others deal with the dread one. He was never ours to pursue."

And your father? Kieran thought, but he left it unsaid. It was unfair to throw that at her. If she had come to grips with that debt, it was not his right to place her in its grip once more. But he ... he still had a debt to repay. Mal'ek'a came from the same lands across the Great Water as his own ancestors had; it was by their immigration to these shores that Mal'ek'a had gained a foothold, riding the tall-masted sailing ships like an ill wind.

Those ancestors no longer lived, so it was up to him to make good their debt.

"I have to go after him," Kieran said.

Ha'kan'ta said nothing for a long moment, then shook her head. "We share one future," she said. "If you go, so must I."

"There is another reason we must act," Ur'wen'ta said. Neither of them had heard him approach.

"I never thanked you for coming," Ha'kan'ta said.

"Thanks are not required. There was just cause. You summoned us, we came. You could have done no less. There was little enough for us to do, though if the Forest Lord had not intervened...."

"What's the other reason?" Kieran wanted to know.

Ur'wen'ta drew a pouch from his belt and took out a handful of small bone discs.

"Do you know the man that these belong to?" he asked Ha'kan'ta.

But it was Kieran who replied. "Those are Tom's bones! Where did you get them?"

"I found them in a glade, in the part of the Otherworld that lies closest to the World Beyond. They lay scattered in the grass. And there was blood."

"Mother of God!" Kieran passed a hand across his eyes. His chest constricted. "Is he . . . he's not . . . ?"

"Dead? No. But Mal'ek'a has finally trapped him. He is in a Great Lodge in the forests near my hunting grounds—sorely hurt. He has companions with him, but Mal'ek'a's tragg'a have encircled the place and soon they will strike."

Kieran got to his feet, tested his leg to see if it would hold his weight. It would do. "We've got to go to him," he said.

"You must rest," Ha'kan'ta protested.

Ur'wen'ta shook his head. "If you take time to rest, there will be nothing left of our drum-brother to give aid to."

"I'll manage, Kanta. I have to. It's Tom we're talking about."

Ha'kan'ta nodded, remembering her own craftfather who had been both father of her flesh as well as the teacher of her spirit.

"How many tragg'a does he have with him?"

Ur'wen'ta sighed. "How many branches has the pine? They are many. But we are rathe'wen'a. We have fourteen drums. Fourteen drummers. It is Mal'ek'a we must fear—not the packs of the devil-bear's offspring that run with him."

"How fast can we get there?" Kieran asked.

"Too swiftly for what we must face."

Kieran was stunned. He stood with the rathe'wen'a and Pukwudji amongst the trees that bordered the fields surrounding the Great Lodge.

"Tamson House," he said. "Lord dying Jesus! It's Tamson House!"

"You know the place?" Ur'wen'ta asked.

Kieran nodded numbly. What was it doing here? "That's where Sara lives," he said to Ha'kan'ta. "In my world. How can it be here?"

At the mention of Sara's name, Pukwudji pushed forward.

He stared at the strange lodge, reached out with his mind and found her.

"That lodge borders more worlds than one," the honochen' o'keh said. "It has a soul of its own. I have spoken to it—but not here. Not in these forests."

"How is it possible?" Kieran murmured.

The familiar peaks and gables of Ottawa's most curious structure didn't fit into this setting. He looked around, half expecting the concrete and lights of the Nation's capital. But the dense bushland remained.

"The tragg'a have breached the lodge," one of the rathe' wen'a said, a tall woman of middle age, cheeks painted with white lines.

"Then we are too late," another said.

"No!" Pukwudji cried. He shifted shape. Eagle wings cut the air as he raced toward the House. When he reached it, he banked in a long sloping glide, seeking entrance. He came to the hole torn in the wall of Gramarye's Clover. The opening was blocked with tragg'a. The eagle hesitated, then it dove for the opening, talons and beak slashing left and right as it broke through the creatures. Once inside, its wing size hampered its movement. A tragg'a raked the air with its claws, came away with a fistful of feathers. Pukwudji shifted shape again.

For a moment he wore the furred body of Ha'kan'ta's totem. He barreled through the tragg'a with the sheer power of the shape's bulk. Then a lynx charged down the hallway, heading for the northwest tower.

Kieran followed the eagle's flight with the farseeing of his taw, then sent his thoughts ahead. The House was filled with a torrent of anger/bloodlust/fear/determination. He sifted through the minds he touched, searching for Tom. His taw touched a familiar presence that struck him like a dagger blow. A sense of darkness washed over him, reminiscent of that thing he'd sensed in the back of the pub in Ottawa when he'd been forced to kill an innocent horseman.

"He's in there," Kieran said. "Mal'ek'a." His soul twisted at the dread one's touch. How could he ever have believed this to be Taliesin? The soul that had left its memory on the whistle he carried in his belt and this thing of evil were poles apart. The one stood for life. The other was the antithesis of life.

"The tragg'a are many," Ha'kan'ta said.

Ur'wen'ta nodded. "But still we must try."

One by one they set off through the calf-high grass. They were fourteen drummers and one drum-brother, and with them ran two silver wolves. Few enough to pit against Mal'ek'a and his devil-bear offspring. Tom's bag of Weirdin bones slapped against Kieran's thigh as he ran. Forgotten were the aches in his leg and temple; at that moment, it seemed that his whole life had been in preparation for this final conflict.

The sound of drumming followed their passage across the field and he let its rhythm fill him. He had thought himself a peaceful man, one who sought harmony in place of battle. But tonight he was a warrior, a huntsman, and evil was his prey. Who could say what path the service of peace might take? Tonight the drumming was the sound of war, and he was one with its sounding.

PART FOUR

Grandmother Toad's Circle

Had we known in the beginning,
the tune would twist our fingers so
and drive our feet across the borders
the way the north wind drives the snow

...all that's been has led us hither,
all that's here must lead us on.

—ROBIN WILLIAMSON

Chapter One

"WHAT'S she talking about?" Tucker demanded.

Blue shook his head, his gaze on the door. That sucker was going to give way any minute. He tried to listen like Sara had asked him to, but all he could hear was the tragg'a. Clawing at the door. The thud of their bodies as they threw themselves against it. The howls and snarling.

"Sara?" he asked.

Her eyes were unfocused, looking beyond him, beyond the room. "Drumming," she said. "Can't you hear it?"

"Drumming?" Then he remembered Ur'wen'ta, and the old shaman's drum. Blue couldn't hear anything, but if Sara heard it, that meant Ur'wen'ta was on his way back.

"That's the way the quin'on'a work their magics," Sara was explaining. "They use their drumming to call up their—" Her eyes went wide, her face paled, as she felt the touch of a familiar mind. "Pukwudji!" she cried.

She ran for the door. The little honochen'o'keh was approaching fast, sending his thoughts on ahead to her. She put her shoulder against the dresser that Blue had pushed against it and tried to move it.

"Sara!" Blue cried. "Are you nuts?"

He tugged at her arm, but she shrugged it off, returning to her task.

"Pukwudji's out there. My friend's out there, Blue!"

"Get a hold of yourself, Sara. There's nothing but fucking monsters out there."

He pulled her away from the dresser and she turned on him. The rifle fell from his grasp and hit the floor. Tucker started towards them, when Blue suddenly leaped aside. Sparks flickered weakly from Sara's hands. Blue slapped at his chest. Burn

425

holes smoldered in his T-shirt. Before either of them could get a hold of her, Sara grabbed the dresser again and heaved. The wood smoked where she touched it, but the dresser shifted enough for her to get at the door.

As she opened it, a sudden turmoil sounded outside in the hall. Mixed with the howls of the tragg'a was the screech of a wild cat, then a hissing and spitting. Tragg'a howls turned to cries of pain. The cat screams deepened into a roar like a giant grizzly bear's.

"Sara!" Blue yelled, but she stepped into the doorway.

Madness ruled in the hall. Tragg'a were flinging themselves at the gigantic bear that was hurling them against the walls with great sweeps of its paws. Thunder rumbled in the beast's chest. Its fur was clotted with blood—both its own and that of its foes. It was holding its own, but would finally give way under the press of the tragg'a's numbers.

As Sara stepped into the hall, some of the tragg'a turned to face her. Lifting her hands, she drew up her taw, a nerve jumping in her temple as she concentrated. Small sparks continued to flicker about her hands. Then the first of the tragg'a reached her and swept her aside with a glancing blow of its paw. She bounced against a wall and skittered down the hall where she landed in a heap, half stunned.

"Jesus Christ!" Tucker bellowed.

He lifted his .38 and opened fire. The first tragg'a went down, but two more filled the doorway. He got another, but the third was in the room and lunged for Blue who was retrieving his rifle. As the creature launched itself at the biker, Sally drew bead and fired. The big gun kicked in her hand, throwing off her aim. She missed, gritted her teeth and fired again. The bullet caught the tragg'a high in the shoulder and spun it around. Blue, his rifle in hand, twisted out of the creature's way and smashed the butt of the Weatherby into its face.

"The door!" Tucker cried. "Somebody help me with the door!"

Maggie and Sam ran to put their shoulders against it and shove. Tucker stood by the open door, firing until he emptied his gun. He saw the bear go down in the hall as he turned to help them.

"Tucker!" Blue yelled. "Sara's still out there!"

Sara? Tucker hesitated for a moment and the tragg'a burst in again, flinging the door wide. Sam and Maggie stumbled, as Tucker grabbed the monster, locking his hands on its wrists, and tried to throw it to the floor. A second beast charged in. Blue's Weatherby boomed in the confined space and the creature was flung back into the hall.

Before Blue had a chance to work the bolt on the rifle, another was inside, howling, talons flashing. It tore off half of Sam's face with a sweep of its paw, flung him aside and moved for Maggie. Sally fired, drilling the tragg'a high in its chest, then turned to help Tucker. She couldn't find a clear target. The tragg'a and Tucker rolled over and over, moving too much for her to risk a shot. She heard the boom of Blue's rifle again and her gaze flicked to the door.

Maggie shot the next creature as it entered—firing three times with the .22 until it dropped. Behind the felled monster, Sally could see the tragg'a tearing at the fallen bear. The bear seemed to shimmer before her eyes, changing shapes. It was a wolf, a bird, a small man, a wildcat, a bear again. Its struggles grew weaker.

Blue charged the door, swinging his rifle like a club. It cracked against the skull of one tragg'a, leaped for another. This creature tore the rifle from his hands, flung it aside and closed in.

The tragg'a Tucker was fighting gained an advantage, rolled on top of the Inspector. He held it back, muscles straining with the effort of keeping its jaws from his throat. As it began to overpower him, Sally blinked the sweat from her eyes, aimed and fired.

Throughout the assault, Jamie had sat on the couch, staring blankly into nothing. The beating he'd undergone at Gannon's hands, the shock of the tragg'a's renewed attack, not even Sara's reappearance could intrude on the sudden understanding he'd gained of Tamson House.

It was more than wood and stone, towers, roofs and rooms, cellars and gardens, miles of corridors. It sheltered more than an ordinary dwelling did, protected on more levels than might mundane walls and doors. It housed the soul of his grandfather and his father. The House's soul *was* theirs.

Hunched on the couch, withdrawn into himself, Jamie shared its deepening pain, offered what strength he had to the House's soul to overcome the evil that stalked through it like a spreading cancer. There was no time to try to understand how such a thing could be—that his father and grandfather should still live on in the wood and stone of the House. There was only the struggle to survive, to repel the cancer that had entered, to make of the House a haven once more. There was only the evil to exorcise. Nothing else mattered.

"Let's try here," Kieran said as they came up to the west side of the House. He drew back his spear to break the glass, but Ur'wen'ta stopped him.

"This lodge has a protecting spirit," the rathe'wen'a explained. "I have seen it repel tragg'a with sorcerous blue fires."

Kieran could hear the battle inside. There were guns firing, tragg'a howling. What sounded like the roar of a bear. He didn't sense Tom's spirit at the moment, but if the old man was in there, he needed help *now*. Not later.

"The protective spirit is hurt," Ur'wen'ta said. "We must convince it that the small hurt we will bring it as we break in is meant for its good, not further harm, else it will attempt to slay us as well."

Ur'wen'ta turned to the others. At his unspoken signal, the drumming picked up in tempo. Kieran felt the magics gather, the drumming deepen. He didn't know what Ur'wen'ta meant by a protective spirit, but he could sense something stir as the old shaman sent forth a silent call.

Jamie sat up suddenly. His pulse pounded with a sound like drums and the drums seemed to speak.

We crave entrance, they said.

Together, the House's spirit and Jamie's searched for the source of the sound, found the rathe'wen'a. The drumming eased the pain of the tragg'a's entrance, of the evils that strode their halls. It promised hope.

Enter, Jamie and the House said with the same voice.

The window in front of Kieran swung open by itself. He turned to Ur'wen'ta, received a nod and went in over the windowsill. The others followed. Kieran crossed the room, flung open the door to the hall and saw the tragg'a swarming at its far end. Ha'kan'ta's wolves pushed at his legs and followed Kieran as he went limping into the hall, shouting at the tragg'a. He raised his spear as the first tragg'a turned. He threw, saw the spear plunge into the monster's side, and then realized that he'd left himself defenseless. A second and third tragg'a turned to face the new attack. Lord dying Jesus! Kieran thought. Now what?

"Down!" a voice cried from behind him.

He dropped to the floor and an arc of power ionized the air above him, striking the first rank of tragg'a. The stench of burning flesh joined with the reek of the creatures, making him gag. As though the magical attack was a summons, the tragg'a turned from whatever their earlier target had been and charged the rathe'wen'a. Their howls filled the air.

They passed Kieran in a rush. One dropped on him and he gathered his taw, burning the creature when it touched him. Weaponless? Hardly. He pushed the charred creature aside, half expecting it to turn into a man, then met a renewed attack.

Two tragg'a leaped at him, the force of their momentum throwing them all through a door into an empty room. Power crackled from Kieran's hands as he gripped the creatures. But his leg buckled under him and he fell. He took a blow on his shoulder that bit deeply into the flesh, another down his side, before he could finish the first of the monsters. The second fell under the attack of Ha'kan'ta's wolves.

Staggering to his feet, he made for the door, then pitched headlong to the floor. The leg wouldn't hold him anymore. The pain of his wounds made it hard to concentrate, to hold his taw firm, to raise the power. He saw Shak'syo, the Winter-Brother, lying still beside him, the silver fur matted with blood. May'asa, the Summer-Brother, hobbled to stand between Kieran and the open door, growling low in his chest. Kieran lifted his head to see the bulk of another tragg'a filling the door.

Tucker pushed the creature Sally had shot off his chest and clawed his way to his feet. He saw Blue closing in with a tragg'a, then the creature leaped from the biker as though burned. The Inspector's gaze followed Blue's to his belt where Ur'wen'ta's totem stick was thrust. They both realized the significance at the same moment.

A shout came from the hall. That came from a man's throat, Blue thought, not a monster's. Tugging the totem stick from his belt, he stepped into the hall, the stick held out in front of him. The tragg'a around the bear backed off, snarling. He saw Sara lying still against the wall, then heard another shout and turned.

At the far end of the hall he saw what looked like Indians. There were three of them—no, four. Others crowded behind them. The foremost held out their hands and by now Blue knew what to expect. He threw himself to the floor as the power blast surged down the hall, frying tragg'a.

Behind him in the room, he saw Tucker moving to the door. "Get back!" he called.

As Tucker backed off, Blue began to inch his way to where Sara lay. What the hell had gotten into her? She could've gotten them all killed. Then he remembered she'd been saying something about a friend. Had she meant the Indians, or. . . . He glanced at the bear, but it was a bear no longer. As he watched, it changed into an eagle, wings twisted at awkward angles, to a lynx with its life dying in its eyes, to a small weird-looking man with a face meant for laughing that was now twisted in pain. The small being was bleeding from dozens of wounds.

Most of the tragg'a were now involved in attacking the strangers down the hall. The few that remained kept their distance from him because of the totem stick. Blue looked to Tucker in the doorway but, before he could ask the Inspector to give him a hand, he sensed movement from where Sara lay. He turned to find her struggling up, her face pressed against the wall. She looked at him, her eyes blank for a moment. Then she saw the little man and a moan came from her throat.

Clutching her head with one hand, she crawled to where Blue lay, passed him to press her face against the small being's cheek. Tears streamed from her eyes. She tore at her leggings, got one free and tried to stauch the worst of the little man's wounds with it.

"Let me give you a hand," Blue said, keeping a wary eye on the nearest tragg'a. "We'll move him into the room."

Sara nodded numbly.

Pukwudji stared at her. His breathing was ragged and uneven. "We . . . we showed them . . . hey?"

Sara blinked back tears. "We did, Pukwudji. Don't try to move. We're going to . . . to . . ."

"Redhair . . . I was his . . . friend. . . ."

"Don't talk," Sara murmured to Pukwudji. She gathered his head onto her lap, looked pleadingly at Blue, then back at the little man as he spoke again.

"I see him . . . in the . . . the Thunder. . . . He stretches his . . . hand. . . ."

"Easy does it," Blue said. He lifted the little man gently, wondering how someone who could become a bear could weigh so little.

"Careful," Sara said, standing up with Blue, her eyes never leaving Pukwudji's face. "He . . . he . . ."

Until we meet again . . . hey . . . ? Pukwudji mindspoke.

She felt his soul slip away first, then saw the light die in his eyes. "No," she said, touching the little man's cheek. "No. No!"

Something snapped inside her. The power she'd reached for as she'd stepped out into the hall, the power that had eluded her and allowed the tragg'a to strike her down, surged through her now. It flamed in her eyes, crackled at her fingertips, blossomed in the palms of her hands.

Blue threw himself against the wall as Sara loosed her power down the hall at the remaining tragg'a. Caught between two fires, hers and that of the rathe'wen'a, they finally broke. Not until the last of the creatures was dead or had fled did she stumble to her knees, the magefire fading from her hands.

"Jesus!" Tucker said, stepping into the hall, "I wish to fuck she'd give a little warning when she's going to pull that kind of—"

"Ease up," Blue said sharply. He laid his frail bundle on the floor and went to Sara, helping her to her feet.

"He always wanted to . . . to help me," she said through her tears.

Blue didn't know what to say. He looked at the body of the little man and blinked. The corpse shivered, grew transparent, then was gone. All that remained where it had lain was a small medicine pouch. He picked it up, hefted its weight. Its contents jingled.

"Sara," he began.

Her shoulders heaved with her sobbing and she didn't hear him. He put the pouch in the pocket of her dress and drew her close, wishing there was some way he could comfort her. Someone had a lot to answer for. He looked down the hall. They might have managed to pull through another skirmish, but the fucking war was still on.

Kieran tried to lift himself from the floor. May'asa growled low in his chest. The tragg'a, half in, half out of the room, grinned. It began to make its move when it was pulled out of the room, its matted fur aflame with magefire. As its howl died in its throat, it tumbled to the floor. A sudden silence fell, broken only by the sound of weeping.

Gritting his teeth, Kieran hobbled to the door. He looked to the right to see two men. One was standing, the other was comforting a woman that he recognized with a shock. Sara!

He understood her grief when he saw Pukwudji's body, drew in a quick breath as the body faded where it lay and disappeared. Kieran didn't know either of the men, but the one standing with a revolver in his hand seemed to recognize him. Didn't matter. What was important now was . . .

He looked the other way and saw her coming to him, one arm hanging limp at her side, her dress torn and stained with blood. Mother Mary! Let the blood not be hers!

She came to him and they held each other awkwardly. Her eyes held unshed tears and not until she pressed her face against his unhurt shoulder did they fall. "They slew all but three," she said in a voice tight with sorrow. "Ten of my kin lie dead, Kieran. How could I have asked so much of them?"

"We chose to come," Ur'wen'ta said, coming up to them.

He was bleeding and leaned heavily on Kieran's spear. Behind him came the other two survivors, neither of them unhurt. Ur'wen'ta touched Ha'kan'ta's shoulder.

"Mal'ek'a still lives," he said. "I can feel him. He is here. In this lodge. It has not ended yet."

Ha'kan'ta shook her head. "This is how we fared against his tragg'a—how can we hope to prevail against him?"

"We must," Ur'wen'ta said. "Or our drum-kin will have died in vain."

"The tragg'a came at them from two sides," Kieran said, telling Blue and the rest of them what Ur'wen'ta had told him. "They were facing you, concentrating their attack on the pack you folks were holding off, when a second pack came swarming up the other corridor. That's when most . . . that's when we took our losses."

They were holed up on the second floor of the northwest tower, in Sara's sitting room. The four rathe'wen'a sat silently behind Kieran, tending their wounds, following the flow of the conversation with their sen'fer'sa so that while the details remained obscure, they understood the intent. The herok'a—the hornless ones—were unable to receive thoughts, else they might have all spoken mind to mind.

Tucker sat by the door that opened onto the stairs leading down. His gun lay on his lap and he divided his attention between the stairs, what Kieran was saying, and cleaning an ugly gash on Maggie's forearm. Blue and Sally sat side by side on a couch, holding hands, attentive. The biker glanced from time to time at Sara, who knelt beside a silver wolf, one hand on his back. He'd seen her start when the beast came up to her, but now they seemed like old friends. Maybe they'd both lost something today. There'd been two silver-furred wolves in the House. There was only one of them now.

Sam's body had been left downstairs—he'd died before he even hit the ground, Tucker'd said. Jamie'd had to be half carried upstairs. They'd put him in a big easy chair and there he sat now, incommunicado. Blue glanced back at Sara. "What do we do now?" he asked aloud. "We're not going to survive another attack."

If we do not slay Mal'ek'a, Ur'wen'ta signed in fingerspeech, *we will not live to see the coming dawn.*

Blue nodded. Great. All they had to do was go down there and finish off this demon or whatever the fuck it was, and off they could go. What could be simpler? Only half of them were dead or missing, and there just happened to be a House full of tragg'a as a complication. He wondered then about the fate of the others who hadn't made it to the tower with them. He didn't really care what had happened to Gannon and his goon; if the tragg'a'd got them it would just save him the trouble of having to deal with them. Old Tom Hengwr had gotten them into this, so he could get himself out before Blue was going to worry about him. It was Fred and Dr. Traupman that concerned him now. They were probably dead as well by now, but he couldn't be sure. And if they were out there, cut off and alone. . . .

"Where is this Mal'ek'a?" Blue asked, using sign language as he spoke the words aloud.

Ur'wen'ta shrugged. He was about to reply when Jamie spoke up, startling them all. "He is in the east wing. We . . . I . . . don't know what he's doing." Jamie's brow furrowed as he concentrated. "It's hard to see. It's so dark there. . . ."

Tucker and Blue exchanged glances. The inspector lifted his eyebrows questioning, but Blue shrugged. "Jamie," he said. "Can you see Fred? Or anybody else?"

"Gannon and Chevier are dead." Jamie's voice was hard as he spoke their names. "Tom is . . . we . . . I can't see Tom. Dr. Traupman is dead. Fred is in the garden."

"Alive?"

"Alive."

"Okay," Blue said. "This Mal'ek'a's in the east wing. So do we wait, or do we go after him?"

Tucker cleared his throat. "Ah . . . Jamie," he said. "Do you see any of the . . . wolfmen?"

"They are prowling through the House—mostly on the ground floor."

"How close?"

"There are many in the corridor below."

Tucker stared down the stairs, listening hard. He could hear them now, shuffling around down there. Maggie moved aside and he picked up his gun. He glanced back at Jamie. Something had happened to Tams that was more than just getting beaten up by Gannon. It was weird how all these "powers" kept popping up out of the woodwork. Was Blue going to sprout wings next? Christ, was he?

"Hold it," Tucker said suddenly. "There's something on the stairs."

Blue was on his feet and across the room in an instant, the gun he'd given Sally in his big hand. The stock of the Weatherby had been broken earlier and he hadn't gotten around to rigging something else to fit it yet.

"That's no monster," he said. "It's Thomas Hengwr!"

Kieran arose, his pulse drumming. Blue was down the stairs, helping the old man up. His clothes hung in ribbons from his back and were wet with sweat and blood, and his eyes had a haunted look to them. But at least he was alive, Kieran thought. He helped Tom up the last few steps and settled him on the couch beside Sally. Ha'kan'ta and Ur'wen'ta exchanged glances as they watched the old man enter. They'd reached out with their sen'fer'sa, but there was nothing there to touch.

"How else could he escape Mal'ek'a's detection?" Ur'wen'ta murmured, but he looked troubled.

Tom looked around the room. "Kieran?" he asked as his gaze touched his apprentice's face. "Is it truly you? Thank all the gods that live, you're unharmed!"

"What happened to you?" Blue asked. "You've been out cold for about two days."

"Two days?"

Blue nodded. "You showed up all bloody and battered in Jamie's study two days ago and were dead to the world except for muttering a few words now and again. What gives?"

"Never mind that," Tucker said. "Can you kill him?"

"Kill . . . ?"

"Mal'ek'a," Kieran said.

"What is it anyway?" Blue asked.

Tom sighed. He passed a hand across his brow and seemed to grow smaller as he sat there on the couch.

"He is evil incarnate. And no, I cannot kill him. I am too weak. There is not enough power in this room to even...." His voice trailed off as his gaze lit on Sara. He looked down at her hand. Taliesin's ring glittered, gold and beckoning. "Gods!" he cried. "There is hope! We have the bard's ring."

Sara looked up as though just aware of Tom's presence. She recognized him from his infrequent visits to The Merry Dancers, and more recently from the photograph that Tucker had shown her. With an effort, she lifted her thoughts from her sorrow and reached across to Kieran's mentor with her taw—an automatic gesture now, she realized. She met the same nothingness that the rathe'wen'a had experienced when Tom first entered the room.

"What are you?" she asked. "I can see you with my eyes, but there's nothing there for my taw to touch."

Tom looked taken aback for a moment, then nodded with understanding.

"I cannot let my defenses slip for a moment," he explained. "Mal'ek'a is hunting me. If I let my guard down, he will be upon us in moments. We need time to plan our attack, to prepare. For with the ring, we have a chance."

"Let your guard down for a minute. Mal'ek'a's clear across the House."

Oh, Christ! Blue thought. Don't start being difficult again. He tried to catch Ur'wen'ta's eye, succeeded, signed:

Help me convince her not to be a hindrance.

"Are you mad?" Tom said. "We have a chance. Would you throw it away?"

"I don't trust you," Sara said.

Blue's heart sank at that, sank further when Ur'wen'ta indicated that he would not help him in this.

"Sara," Blue began.

"What do we know about him?" Sara asked, turning to the biker. "He's the reason we're in this mess in the first place."

Tom's eyes narrowed, but he said nothing.

"All he's done," Sara continued, "is bring harm to everything I care for. Jesus Christ, Blue! For all I know he *is* the problem. All I'm asking is for him to show a little faith—that's all."

"You don't understand," Tucker said, taking a step towards her.

Sara turned to the rathe'wen'a. "What do you feel when you reach out to him?" she asked Ha'kan'ta.

"Nothing, Little-Otter."

Sara blinked, hearing Mayis's pet name for her on Ha'kan'ta's lips. Then she nodded. Why not? Ha'kan'ta was Mayis's grand-daughter. "Will you stand by me?" she asked.

"What're they saying?" Tucker asked Kieran.

Kieran shook his head. He waited to hear what Ha'kan'ta would say.

"No one will force you to give up your ring against your will," the rathe'wen'a said.

Kieran opened his mouth to protest, then paused. He looked from Tom to Ha'kan'ta. Suddenly his loyalties were being divided. He loved them both. But Tom had been wrong—so very wrong—once already.

"What's so important about the ring?" he asked Tom.

"With it, Mal'ek'a will be unstoppable. Used against him— used properly against him—and it will be the means of his defeat."

Sara swallowed. What if she was wrong? She was running on tension now, following her intuition. She had no reason to suspect Tom of anything. On the other hand, she suspected him of everything. He'd spent the better part of his life hunting down the man she'd come to love. But if the ring had to be used against Mal'ek'a. . . .

"I'll use it against him," she said.

"Don't play the fool," Tom said sharply. "It must be wielded by one who understands its use. Please." He turned to the others. "Convince her. It is our only hope. With the ring I can defeat Mal'ek'a. Without it we are doomed."

"Give him the fucking ring," Tucker said.

Blue frowned. He wanted to stand by Sara, but she'd proved that she wasn't running on all cylinders. Though that wasn't quite fair. He was judging her recent actions by the person he'd known. Not by who she was now. She was changed now, older somehow. Stronger. And the Sara he'd known hadn't been able to call up fire with her hands either.

"Ease up," he told Tucker.

"Ease up? For Christ's sake, Blue! We're running out of time. Now she either gives him the ring, or we take it from her and give it to him ourselves."

Blue looked from Tucker to Sara. He saw her jaw tighten, glanced at her fingers for a telltale trace of flickering. Her hands were balled up into fists. And—was that magefire or the ring glinting?

"Kieran!" Ha'kan'ta said suddenly. "Why do we argue amongst ourselves when we have a common foe?"

Before he could reply, Blue turned to Tom and asked:

"How come you're okay all of a sudden when a few hours ago you were out like a light? We couldn't've roused you if we'd let a bomb off under you."

Tom closed his eyes wearily, then opened them to look directly into Blue's. "Do I look 'all right' to you?"

"I'm tired of fucking around," Tucker said. "We've got a chance to hit the enemy. Let's use it. Or else..."

"Or else what?" Blue demanded.

Tucker started to lift his gun and Blue mirrored the action with his own weapon. Before either of them could bring their guns to bear, Ur'wen'ta loosed a pale light from his hands that knocked the weapons to the floor. The two turned to face the old shaman—a threat plain in Tucker's face, Blue's features uncertain. The old Indian shook his head and reached for Sara's shoulder.

"If you will allow me to speak through you?" he asked in the language of the rathe'wen'a.

Sara hesitated, then reached out with her taw. The old shaman's sen'fer'sa, his own taw, met hers openly. She heard the drumming that never stilled inside him, knew that this was somebody she could trust. She reached out with her hand and the old man spoke through her, taw to taw, the words coming from her mouth.

"My name is Ur'wen'ta and I am of the drummers-of-the-bear. Will any here deny me my right to speak?" He paused for a moment, then continued. "The test that is asked for is not asked lightly. I, and my people, demand the same, else we will leave you now. You," he said to Tom, "have nothing to fear. We will shield your presence from Mal'ek'a. He need never sense you. We are drummers—not children who play at the craft."

For a long moment there was silence, then Tom sighed.

"I agree to the test," he said. "I have nothing to hide from you. I fear only that your cloak of hiding will fail to shield me from Mal'ek'a's gaze. But if a test is needed that we might save ourselves, then I agree to it. Only in this do I warn you: Mal'ek'a is more powerful than you might imagine. I truly fear that he will strike at you through me when I let my defenses fall."

"Are we so much weaker than you, Toma'heng'ar? We are

four—five if we include your craftson. Shall we fail where you succeed?"

"I have warned you," Tom said. "If you fail, we are all dead."

"Jesus Christ!" Tucker said. "We don't have time to play these games. Blue, use a little common sense. Help me!"

Blue looked pointedly down at their guns. Maggie took the Inspector's arm, felt his tension.

"It's out of your hands," she said softly. "You're not in charge, Tucker. You're not responsible for what happens here anymore. No more than any of us are. I say let them test him."

That was the problem, Tucker realized as she said it. He was used to being in charge, being responsible. But here, he was out of his depth. He didn't even have Traupman to help him make sense of it all. Traupman. Christ! "Okay," he said, moving aside. "Do what you want."

Tom nodded and stood, offering his hand. The rathe'wen'a moved forward. One stood by the door, looking down the stairs, but was joined with her drum-kin through their sen'fer'sa. The other three surrounded Sara and Tom.

"Kieran?" Ha'kan'ta asked.

He wanted to refuse, to have nothing to do with this test of his mentor, but knew he couldn't. He stepped forward, let his taw join their sen'fer'sa. Drums appeared at the belts of the rathe'wen'a and their sound filled the room with a resonating rhythm. Sara suppressed a shiver and reached out with her right hand. Tom shook his head.

"The hand of your heart," he said.

She let the one hand fall and lifted the other. She remembered what had happened when she'd touched Kieran. It wasn't the same with the rathe'wen'a or Taliesin. They followed a different path, she supposed. She wasn't sure she could stand sharing taws with this strange little man. He had been her enemy—or at least her lover's enemy. She didn't know if she could bear what she'd find inside him. Then Tom's hand closed around her own, closed around her ring hand, around Taliesin's ring, and she felt a darkness come swelling across her mind.

"Now it is mine," a gravelly voice said through Tom's lips, and a hiss of amusement followed the words.

The blood in Sara's veins went cold. She stared at Tom, but it was no longer Kieran's mentor that stood there. This was a darker Thomas Hengwr, a shadow that wore the shape of the monster from her dream. She tried to cry out, but her voice had died, had been stolen away. She pulled at her hand, but the muscles of her arm would no longer obey her commands.

"I needed only its touch," Mal'ek'a said. "I will wear your hand about my neck in memory of this gift you have given me."

Chapter Two

It took Jean-Paul the better part of fifteen minutes to reach home. He parked his VW and hurried back to Bank Street on foot. The situation was worse than it had appeared on the TV. Crowds blocked the traffic on Bank trying to get a glimpse, sirens and police loudspeakers roared, and there was a general hubbub that fluttered between panic and confusion. It took him another ten minutes to work his way through the mass. When he finally reached the makeshift barriers that were set up along the entrance to the park, he had to vie with television and newspaper news crews for attention from the guards.

He finally caught a city policeman's eye. He flashed his government ID—just enough to let the patrolman think that he was here on official business. "I'm here to see RCMP Special Inspector John Tucker," he shouted.

"Wait here."

The officer returned with a tall man in corduroys and a windbreaker. His right hand was wrapped in bandages. His left held a cigarette. "My name's Constable Dan Collins," he said. "Who did you want to see?"

"Inspector Tucker. John Tu—" Before Jean-Paul could finish, Collins had turned aside to the policeman.

"Let him through," he said. "If you'll come with me, Mr . . . ?"

"Gagnon. What exactly is going on here, Constable?"

"Maybe you could tell me what you're doing here first."

Collins recognized Jean-Paul's name, but made no mention of it.

"I was at a friend's home when I saw all of . . . this on the television. *C'est incroyable!*"

"And what made you think the Inspector would be here?"

"He was investigating a case that he thought might have

440

some connection with Tamson House, *n'est-ce pas?* When I saw this chaos on the news bulletin, I had to come."

They reached the part of the park that faced the gap blown out of the side of the house. Three men were having an animated discussion that stopped abruptly as they came up to them.

"Who's this?" Madison demanded.

"Jean-Paul Gagnon," Collins said. "He's looking for the Inspector."

Madison regarded Jean-Paul for a few moments. "We think he's in there, Mr. Gagnon," he said finally. "Do you have some information for him?"

"No. I saw this on the news and. . . . My friend—Kieran Foy. The Inspector wanted him for questioning and I thought they might both be here."

Madison recalled Tucker's report. Gagnon had been very cooperative, but he didn't need civilians cluttering up the landscape.

"I appreciate your coming down, Mr. Gagnon, but if you have no information for us, I'm afraid I'll have to ask you to stand clear with the other spectators." He said the word as though it was a disease. "What we've got here is so far off the wall. . . ." He turned to Collins. "Did you get a preliminary report back from the morgue yet?"

"Yeah. But they've got nothing definite yet. They pulled in a couple of experts from Agriculture Canada and the National Museum—biologists and a couple of hotshot naturalist experts."

"And?"

"They won't be quoted on this, but their initial probes show that these things are literally not of this world. They're sending one of their men down here and asked if we could 'refrain from killing any more of them.'"

"Jesus!" Madison turned to Jean-Paul. "Do you see what we're dealing with?"

"*Mon dieu!* It is as John said then? You are dealing with *des sorciers?*"

"We don't know what we're dealing with. But we're going to find out. We're just getting ready to send a team in through that hole—specialists from our anti-terrorist squad. Now, if you'll excuse us, Mr. Gagnon?"

Jean-Paul nodded and backed away. The men immediately fell into a discussion as to their best method of operation and he found himself unobserved. That was fine. He would stay out of their way, but close enough to watch the proceedings. If they brought Kieran out, he would make sure that he wasn't spirited away to some hidden detention center for questioning. If Kieran was involved in this, he would need a friend.

Dismissing Gagnon from his mind, Madison returned to his briefing. The two men with him were Corporal Karl Holger, RCMP Anti-Terrorist Squad, and Lieutenant Tom Deverell of the Ottawa City Police Department. Madison had already been in touch with his superiors and been given the go-ahead.

"Your men ready, Corporal?"

"Yes, sir."

"Tom, can you get your men to clear a few more blocks? Once the squad goes in there's no telling what they'll stir up. We don't know how many of those things are in there. If they break out through the cordon. . . ."

"We're working on it, Wally. But we're walking a thin line now between the normal gawkers and outright panic. Bad enough the TV crews got shots of those monsters of yours. We're playing it like you asked—terrorists in monkey suits. They tried to hit the Embassy over on O'Connor, failed, and took refuge in this House of yours. The media's not buying it, but they're willing to play it our way for now."

"I don't care about the media," Madison said. "Not right now. I'm just worried about what'll happen if more of these monsters break free of the cordon and get into that crowd."

"We're doing what we can."

"Okay."

Madison looked up at the House. Already the gap was starting to look smaller. It hadn't closed up as quick as the windows, but it was still closing. Sooner or later someone was going to notice. And when word of this leaked out, there'd be hell to pay.

"Take your men in, Corporal," he said. "And watch yourselves. I don't know what they've got those walls pumped up with, but you take a bad burn off of them."

Holger tipped a finger to his forehead and crossed the grass to where his squad was waiting for him. They were dressed in dark khaki and bullet-proof vests, with combat helmets that had gridded face-guards that could be snapped down in place. Each man carried an SMG—standard military issue, 9mm, with twenty rounds per magazine. They had folding stocks to extend the carbine's closed length and spare magazines clipped to their belts. The squad would have preferred Israeli UZIs.

"Hey, Holger," a big black man asked the Corporal. "Are we going in?"

"You got it, Wilson."

"'Bout fucking time."

. Madison and Collins watched the squad make their approach. Two ladders slapped against the edges of the gap and men were going up them almost before they were in place. Three of the squad had remained behind, standing well back from the ladders, carbines aimed at the hole. When the last of their comrades had entered, they followed suit.

Madison waited, found he was holding his breath, let it out slowly. A minute ticked by. When a voice squawked from the walkie-talkie he was holding, he jumped.

"You read me, Superintendent?" Wilson's deep voice sounded tinny coming from the small speaker.

"Loud and clear," Madison replied. "What have you got?"

"We've got a mess. Place looks like it was torn apart by a fucking anti-tank gun. We've got one·body—an old man, Caucasian, looks to be in his early sixties, severe burns about his face and chest. We— Just a moment. Corporal Holger says the corridors appear to be clear. Do you want to come up and take a look for yourself?"

"I'm on my way."

Madison handed Collins the walkie-talkie and started for the House.

"I don't think this is such a good idea," Collins said, trailing after the Supertintendent. "You going up there."

Madison paused with his hand on the ladder and looked back. "I don't see as we have a whole lot of choice, Dan," he said. "We don't know where Tucker is. We don't know what's going on in there, but we've got a better idea than Holger and his men do. One of us has got to be on hand. You've got your burn, so that leaves me."

"And you've got your leg."

"But at least I can fire a weapon. Look, Dan. Neither one of us knows exactly what we're up against, but at least we know some of the whom better than Holger and his men do. One of us has to be in on this."

"Okay," Collins said. "Just don't play the hero."

"You've got a bargain, Dan."

They clasped hands, and then Madison started up the ladder.

By the time he was nearing the top, Madison was a bundle of nerves. Gingerly he left the last rung and stepped into the rubble. He felt a mild shock—it touched his bad leg most strongly—but saw nothing in front of him. Just a wall of grey. He looked back. The crowds and police barricades seemed very far away. It was almost quiet up here, the crowd noise just a faint murmur. Turning back to the House, he took a deep breath and stepped into the greyness.

A sensation hit him, like a feeling of vertigo. He would have stumbled, but someone caught him by the arm, steadied him. He looked up to see one of Holger's men holding him and nodded thanks.

"Weird shit, isn't it?" Wilson said. "I forgot to warn you 'bout it."

Madison looked back, but instead of the wall of grey, or the park, he saw wild bushland bordering a field. The House appeared to be in the middle of it.

"I forgot to warn you 'bout that, too," Wilson said.

"What in God's name. . . ."

"I don't know 'bout you," Wilson said, "but I don't think God's got a whole lot to do with this place. You recognize the victim?"

Madison followed the man's finger with his gaze and nodded. Christ! It was Traupman. "Have you found any other bodies?"

"Not so far, Superintendent. Holger's waiting for you in the hall. C'mon." Wilson turned to the two other men that were in the room. "You guys hold this place, right? One at the gap, one at the door. Let's go, Superintendent."

They found Holger at a landing on their right. The Corporal looked up as they approached, frowned when he saw that Madison wasn't wearing any protective gear.

"We found some more of your monsters down below, Superintendent," he reported. "From what we can tell, it looks as though they were burned to death—like the man upstairs."

"Anything . . . human?"

"One more man," Holger said. "But these things . . . I've never seen anything like this. What the hell *are* they?"

"Where's the other body? The human body?" Madison's stomach was starting to react again. God, the stench in this place. It was like a charnel house.

Holger led him to one of the doors leading outside. In front of it lay the remains of a man who had been literally torn in half. Madison's stomach gave a lurch, but he forced himself to look. His gaze stopped at a severed head, then he looked away.

"Hengwr," he said. "That...was Thomas Hengwr."

"Whatever did that—I don't think it was the same as those creatures we've found so far."

Madison saw the strain in the man's features. He was doing a good job of maintaining a professional air of detachment, but it was costing him, "What makes you say that?"

Holger shook his head. "Can't put my finger on it. It's more just a feeling. The creatures look fairly strong, but to tear a man in two like that—I just don't think they're big enough. Look at the size of their paws and talons. They might've torn him to bits, but they couldn't have cut him in two like that." He lifted his face-guard and wiped his brow before replacing it. "Jesus. Let's get a move on. I just hope the rest of this place isn't filled up with more of the same."

"You want me to call up forensics?" Wilson asked. "Let 'em get a start on the two we've found so far?"

"Not yet," Madison replied. "Let's have more of a look around first."

He didn't know if he was going to make it through this. The smell was bad enough. But seeing Traupman back in the other room, and now Hengwr...

"Upstairs or down?" Holger asked. "We could split up and—"

"No. We stick together."

They followed the corridor north, to the side of the house that would have faced Patterson and made their way to the ground floor.

"Christ," Holger murmured. "How big is this place anyway?"

"Too big," Madison replied.

Rounding the corner, they found more of the dead creatures, though not as many as with the first group. There were two human bodies here. They looked like they'd been savaged by the creatures, but not dealt with as Hengwr had been. That added fuel to the argument that something else had killed Hengwr. What kind of something else?

"You recognize them?" Holger asked.

Madison shook his head.

"I've got a real bad feeling 'bout this place," Wilson said softly. "Like something's watching us, you know?"

One of the other men started to nod, then froze. "Down there," he said. "I saw something move."

"I don't see anyth—"

Suddenly the corridor, behind and in front of them, was swarming with the creatures. The SMGs chattered, dropping the first line of them in a spate of bullets.

"In here!" Wilson shouted.

The men moved for the comparative safety of the room he indicated where at least the creatures could only attack them a few at a time, but before the echoes of gunfire had faded, the halls were empty once more. All that remained were the creatures that had been gunned down.

"We've got to get out of here," Holger said. "The place must be crawling with them."

Madison nodded. "We need more firepower. Christ! We need an army."

"I think I'd prefer a few mad-dog terrorists," Wilson muttered as they made their way cautiously back to the stairs. "Leastways, they like to yap a bit before they jump you."

"Amen," one of the men said.

"Anything?" Lieutenant Deverell asked Collins.

The RCMP constable shook his head.

"Hasn't been a thing," he said as he shook out a Pall Mall and accepted a light from Deverell. "How're things on the front lines?"

The Lieutenant grinned. "The rabble are restless. But they're starting to thin out some." He pointed to the walkie-talkie that Collins had stuck in his pocket. "Why don't you give them a call?"

"Sure."

As he started to reach for it, one of Deverell's officers came up to them.

"Lieutenant?"

"Watcha got, Zurowski?"

"Guy wants to see you. A Mr. Walters. J. Hugh Walters." Deverell blinked. "*The* J. Hugh Walters?"

"That's what he says."

"Where is he?"

"Over there." The officer pointed back towards Bank Street. "Standing between those two goons. Business associates, he calls them, but I know goons when I see them. What do you think a guy like him's doing with a pair like that?"

"I don't know. But I mean to find out."

"Wait a minute," Collins said. Something clicked inside him. Nothing he could pin down—just an intuitive feeling that he knew he had to play out. "Do me a favor, would you?" he asked Deverell. "Stick to the story we've been giving the press—no matter what he says. Can you do that?"

"Yeah, but . . ."

Collins drew him aside, out of the patrolman's hearing. "I'm going to level with you. But you'd better keep this under your hat or there'll be all hell to pay. We've got a leak—a big leak and high up."

Deverell held up a hand. "I don't want to hear any more."

"But you'll do as I ask?"

"By the book. No matter who he is, until your people give me a release, this has got nothing to do with civilians. Period."

"Thanks, Deverell. That's one I owe you."

As he watched the two policemen confer, Walters knew that he had made a mistake in coming here. He had been unable to sit at home, waiting for something to break, and with Gannon gone, there had been no one he could trust to come in his place. Not that he was even certain what he would do, once he was here. He had planned to play it by ear—some combination of concerned citizen with a liberal mix of the informed advisor. Instead, all he had managed to accomplish was to tie himself to what was happening here tonight. Not a good move. Definitely not one of his best ideas.

As Deverell approached he knew the best thing to do now was to make a strategic retreat. He would have Williams make sure that he remained unconnected to this incident. It would be simple enough if he left immediately—before speaking to the Lieutenant. He turned to one of the men with him.

"Stall him," he said, indicating Deverell and turned rapidly away, his other bodyguard flanking him.

From his own position, Collins saw the move and nodded to himself. Right, he thought. Gotcha. He pulled out his walkie-talkie. "Give me Superintendent Madison."

There was a moment's silence, then: "Hang on."

"Dan?"

"I've got something for you, Wally. J. Hugh Walters made an appearance here not a few minutes ago. Tried to bully his way in, but as soon as we went to talk to him he took off like a scared rabbit."

"Walters?" Madison's voice sounded strained.

"You okay, Wally?"

"We're . . . yeah. We're okay. We're on our way out, Dan. You'd better get on the blower and call up more men. A lot more men."

"What the hell did you find in there?"

"You don't want to know."

"What about Tucker—"

"I'll tell you all about it when we're out."

Madison cut the connection, leaving Collins staring at the silent communicator. Wally sounded in a bad way. Collins knew he wasn't going to like what the Superintendent had to tell him. He wasn't going to like it one bit.

Chapter Three

TUCKER reacted first. He'd been leaning against a wall, half watching the proceedings, the other half of his mind planning on how they'd get by the tragg'a to have their showdown with Mal'ek'a. But before Tom changed, before he spoke, before the others were even aware that something was wrong, he *knew*.

He swept his gun up from the floor, aimed between the rathe'wen'a and fired. The bullet passed through Mal'ek'a, not bothering it in the least. Blue started for Tucker, Maggie was hauling at his arm trying to hold the Inspector back, and then they all knew and understood what he'd been doing.

Tucker flung himself between Ha'kan'ta and another of the rathe'wen'a and hit Mal'ek'a with a shoulder block. Something . . . some force . . . picked him up and flung him across the room. He smashed into the wall, his breath whooshing out of him. He tried to sit up, but he couldn't see straight. There was a sharp jabbing pain under his heart. One or two ribs were cracked—maybe broken. He couldn't use his left arm.

He pushed himself up with his right arm, but his legs wouldn't hold him. The room spun in his sight. Get up, he told himself. Get the fuck up, Tucker! But there was a pounding in his head. Concussion, he told himself, as he still fought to get up. You've got a fucking concussion. You've—

Everything went black and he collapsed where he lay. The rathe'wen'a at the door turned from her post to face Mal'ek'a's sudden threat, pouring her concentration into the battle of wills between her drum-kin and the dread one.

Blue started for Mal'ek'a, hesitated when he saw what happened to Tucker. Got to be some way, he was thinking as he turned to see the Inspector hit the wall. He still had Ur'wen'ta's totem stick thrust into his belt. He took it out to use against

Mal'ek'a, then saw the tragg'a coming up the stairs.

He meant to shout a warning, but it never left his lips. The tragg'a tore the rathe'wen'a from her post by the door and dragged her down amongst them. The warning left Blue's throat as an inarticulate roar of anger. As the creatures came up the stairs, pounding the rath'wen'a woman under their paws, he lunged at them. The first caught a boot in the face and fell back into the others, but they were swarming like rats on the stairwell.

"Goddamn motherfucking sons of stinking bitches!" Blue roared. He had the advantage of being above them, of holding a small opening where they could only get at him one at a time. He matched their fury, howl for howl, savage as the devil-bear that was said to have sired them on the darkness.

Sally had been coming to his aid, the .38 held in a sweaty hand, but at the sudden berserker rage that overtook him, she stepped back, stunned. She looked to where Maggie crouched beside Tucker, the Margolin pistol in her hand, to the ra-the'wen'a that encircled Mal'ek'a and Sara, to Jamie sitting slack-jawed in the easy chair, his eyes unfocused.

"Oh, God," she mumbled, and the gun shook in her hand.

"Blue," she pleaded, not daring to touch him in case he turned on her. He frightened her more than the tragg'a did. "Please ... Blue. . . ."

He never heard her. His entire being was focused on each tragg'a that met him at the stairtop. He was beyond fear now— just as the creatures had overcome their fear of Ur'wen'ta's totem. He struck one or two of them down with it, choked on the stench of searing flesh as the stick burned them, felt the stick break, fought then with his bare hands.

The rathe'wen'a fought a battle of another sort. In the realms of the spirit the drumming of their sen'fer'sa was locked in a struggle against the power of the being they called the Dread-That-Walks-Nameless. Named, they could have power over it, for names have power. Unnamed, they could only try to hold their own against it. They worked to keep the spark that was Sara's soul from being snuffed out, to keep the ring of power from the monster's grasp. They fought inside Sara, used the ring's power to aid them. But the ring, clasped in Mal'ek'a's hand, was also used against them.

When their drum-sister died at her post by the door, the loss of her sen'fer'sa at first strengthened rather than weakened them. As they felt her soul spin away, their anger grew and fed their hearts; but the struggle slowly turned against them. While they grew weaker, Mal'ek'a seemed to grow more potent, and his darkness seeped into their souls, stilling the drumming note by note. Mal'ek'a grew blacker still, grew like the heart of all darkness.

Soon, they knew, he would have them—as surely as his tragg'a had taken their drum-sister. And then indeed all would be lost. For Mal'ek'a would emerge stronger still, and all the worlds would be his battleground. The dark of his soul would spread until nothing remained but shadow. His shadow. And he would still be unnamed.

Jamie had felt Mal'ek'a's presence vanish in the east wing and reappear in Sara's tower. It was a puzzle that his mind stored away for later reference. For now he was concentrating on the House, and the souls of his father and grandfather that inhabited it still.

How can you still exist? he asked.

It was a gift, the House's spirit replied. *From a Horned Man. A gift and a curse.*

I don't understand.

The druid is our kin, James. We are his only descendants. It is we that must set his evil right.

Thomas Hengwr is our ancestor?

The House shifted in agreement. *He sired the first of our forefathers—on a serving woman in King Maelgyn's retinue. From that small bastard boy our line sprang. Our people lived in Wales—then called Gwynedd. They moved to Cornwall— then called Kernow. Finally they came across the Atlantic to settle in the Ottawa Valley. That was Simon Tamson, your great-great-grandfather.*

But why did you have to wait so long to tell me this?

The time was not right, James. It would have served no purpose. That was what the Horned Man said. It was not until Hengwr came to you a few nights past that I knew the moment had come, but your soul was closed to me. I did what I could to keep the evil at bay, but I needed you, before the monster could be confronted.

This . . . Mal'ek'a?

It is not Mal'ek'a we face, but the evil of our ancestors given a life of its own. Mal'ek'a is Thomas Hengwr—separated from him these many long years, but still one half of the druid's soul.

No!

The House sighed.

When the bard Taliesin imprisoned Thomas Hengwr in the longstone, only one half of Hengwr remained trapped. The other half escaped to wreak its evil on the world. But sooner or later they had to meet again, the one to destroy the other, for there could not be two of them in the world. It upsets the balance. Twice the Horned Man slew Hengwr's evil half, and twice it rose again—more powerful than before. It can only be killed by one of us, James. Only one related to it by blood can destroy it forever.

But . . .

We must stop it, James. Though it costs us our admittance into the Summer Country.

Stop it? Jamie asked. *How?*

Enough, Mal'ek'a cried to itself. With the ring attached to both Sara and it, with the rathe'wen'a augmenting Sara's strengths with their own to sustain her, this struggle could go on for too long, serving no purpose.

Mal'ek'a moved toward the rathe'wen'a and they backed away. It dragged Sara with it, slowly crossing the room to where Blue fought the tragg'a. Sally shouted a warning and threw herself against the biker, pushing him against the wall, out of the doorway. Blue turned to her, eyes blazing, hesitated.

"Dear God!" Sally cried at the blind battle-rage in his eyes. She backed away, saw him take a step toward her, arm uplifted, stagger, then collapse to the floor.

Mal'ek'a reached the doorway.

It must not escape my confines! the House cried to Jamie.

The moment for understanding was past. Jamie knew he could only act now and question those actions later. Together with the House, he called up the blue fire that took its birth where the stone cellars rooted deep in the earth, called up the earth currents and set its magefires crackling through the House.

The door slammed shut as Mal'ek'a reached it.

Blue fires leaped from the door knob as it closed its free hand about the brass fitting. The House's power was not strong enough to damage it, but combined with the attack of the rathe'wen'a, it was enough to weaken the dread one. The drum magic increased as Ha'kan'ta and her kin took advantage of the opening in Mal'ek'a's defenses, but the creature recovered too quickly.

Enough, Mal'ek'a roared to itself a second time. It bent its will to the small hand trapped in its own scaled paw. Under its power, the skin began to blister and blacken. Mal'ek'a meant to sever the hand from Sara's arm, so severing the rathe'wen'a's connection to itself. And then, with the ring fully in its power, Mal'ek'a would deal with drumming and drummers.

Terror was all that Sara knew when Mal'ek'a invaded her mind. Terror and pain. Helplessly she fled before Mal'ek'a, deep and deeper inside herself. The monster followed relentlessly.

They sped down a dark corridor of her mind, towards a golden spark that flickered at its further end. The very core of her being wavered there like a guttering candle. They raced towards it, Sara and the evil thing that had invaded her, dropped through layers of memories and thoughts. Like in a bad dream, the spark never seemed to come any nearer.

Sara took the pain of her body and used it to propel her further. She took the degradation that Mal'ek'a brought into her mind and fed it to her own need for speed. And then the spark was a hand's-breadth away. Mal'ek'a's fetid breath was on her neck. She could feel its claws tear at the back of her soul's body-shape. And then she was inside the spark, holding that last barrier against her tormentor.

And there, in that last secret place, she found hidden away, the moonheart air. Lorcalon. Taliesin's first gift to her. Mal'ek'a hadn't taken it from her yet. To Mal'ek'a it would be nothing. It was such a small thing. But it soothed the raw edges of her nerves, gave her a moment to breathe. For one brief instant she held the sound of harping close to her, a harping that was as sweet as summer rain, deep as the echoing drums, peaceful as a forest pool, bright as a star.

She faced Mal'ek'a from that innermost core, looked into the features of the man she'd once known, briefly, as Thomas Hengwr. The moonheart tune gave her a last strength, and as Mal'ek'a cut her to her soul's marrow she raised what last strengths she could and joined minds with the monster.

The thrust of her soul caught Mal'ek'a by surprise, though it did not hurt it. But in that moment she knew Mal'ek'a as well as he knew her, and the same truth that Tamson House had revealed to Jamie was hammered home. They were kin. She and his monster. She was descended from it, from its evil.

You are *Thomas Hengwr*, she moaned. *Dear God in heaven.*

The same blood that flowed through the monster, that quickened the cancerous life in it, flowed through her veins. Once only half alive, it had swallowed Thomas Hengwr, buried the old druid's spirit in a welter of its own evil, and now it was whole. Her ancestor. Her blood! She remembered something about the sins of the fathers being reaped by their children.... She was doomed. By Mal'ek'a's blood, she was damned.

Tomasin Hengwr t'Hap, her soul murmured, giving Mal'ek'a its true name.

As its physical form squeezed the life from her hand, so its soul reached for her. She waited for its touch without struggling. She welcomed death.

And then she heard voices. In that last moment where she balanced on the keen edge between life and death, saw faces merging with the demonic features of her tormentor.

She saw Pukwudji, his face lifted to the sky as he cried: "See her, Mother Moon? She is your daughter, this hornless one. But she will not be hornless for long!"

Mother Moon. And then there were bone discs spinning through the air between Mal'ek'a and herself. One was the image of a quarter moon. On its reverse was a stag's horns. A head formed under the antlers and a voice that seemed familiar, though she didn't know it, murmured: "What if she loses her way and leaves you stranded there, forever and always? What if she fails? What will sustain you then?"

The face changed and Taliesin's features were there. "My love," he replied to that other voice.

The bard's image changed, became a seascape, lonely trees standing guard on limestone cliffs, and the voice of the wind in them asking: "What are you doing here ... so far ..."

Again the antlered man.

"Waiting," he said. "Waiting to see old wrongs righted."

"We will see," the wind replied. "We will see."

They spoke of her, Sara realized. They spoke of what she must do, but they expected too much. They couldn't know what Mal'ek'a was, who it was, what it made her. All she wanted was to die. She remembered her dream, so long ago, when she lay in her own bed, in her own rooms, and the feral thing had reached out for her, jaws closing on her—

No! she cried.

Magefire blossomed between her and the monster, throwing it back. She heard the drumming then, felt the rathe'wen'a lending their aid.

A name, the drums muttered. *If we had a name . . .*

A name? She knew Mal'ek'a's true name. But before she could speak it, Mal'ek'a lunged, quenching her magefire in a flood of darkness.

Is that it? she demanded. *Is that all they require—your name?*

Mal'ek'a smothered her soul-shape's mouth with horrors. She choked on the things that crawled across her face and skin, burrowed into her flesh until her skin rippled with their passage. This wasn't her real body, she told herself. It was all illusion. But the pain was real. And the maggots, as they burrowed through her flesh, felt real. . . .

Yes, Mal'ek'a said, speaking for the first time. *We are kin. For you to have survived so long, we must be kin. Blood of my blood. Joined to me . . . when I swallow you . . . that will bring me more power than all the rings that Gwyn 'ap Nudd might fashion.*

It wasn't real! If she could only—

Too real, Mal'ek'a hissed. *Too real for you.*

The drums pounded, magefire crackled like lightning, but nothing could penetrate Mal'ek'a's defenses. While the rathe' wen'a fought on, Kieran despaired. He was only half aware of the room around them. He saw some of Blue's berserk battle with the tragg'a, Tucker lying still against the wall. When the blue fires rose up and the door closed, he knew a moment's hope. The House could help them! But understood in the next instant that all the House could do was contain Mal'ek'a. And when the creature finally had the ring, nothing would contain it. Not the House. Not the drumming. Not the worlds themselves.

He saw then the blistering on Sara's arm, the skin bubbling and charring. Name of all! Mother Mary. . . .

He lunged forward, took hold of Sara's arm to try to pull her free, and was suddenly overwhelmed by small pale squirming horrors that burrowed into his body. He heard the hiss of Mal'ek'a's evil voice like a roar in his skull, knew the sensations of a body not his own. He and Sara were sharing a body once more. He felt the final vestiges of hope give way in her, and so in him, pulling both down into endless despair. Then he found, in amongst it all, a name he'd always known.

He threw it out to the drummers before Mal'ek'a could contain him as well. The drums caught the name, wove it into their spell, channeled it back through Sara, through the ring.

Tomasin Hengwr t'Hap howled.

Suddenly Kieran and Sara were free. Sara was thrown back, the ring on her finger glowing white, healing the blistered and burned tissue of her flesh while it pierced Mal'ek'a with its unearthly radiance. Kieran shuddered, then lifted his own hands to join his magefire to hers. He heard, above the sound of the drumming, the sound of harping—here for a moment, then gone.

We can only hold him, Ha'kan'ta cried in despair. *He is still too strong.*

Already the white flare of the ring was dimming. Sara's legs gave out from under her and she slowly slid to the floor. The rathe'wen'a attempted to continue alone, but exhaustion was beginning to take its toll on them. The drumming wavered.

You know what you must do, the House said.

Jamie nodded. He crawled from the chair to where Ur'wen'ta's discarded spear lay. As the first of the rathe'wen'a fell under Mal'ek'a's rejuvenated power, he stepped forward, the weapon raised awkwardly in a two-handed grip. He plunged it straight into the monster's chest.

Black blood sprayed from the wound, burning like acid where the hissing drops landed. Mal'ek'a's clawed paw grasped the spear and it pulled itself along the weapon's length, reaching for Jamie. The monster's eyes bulged. Blood trickled between its jaws. The face was half Tom's, half the distended features of a tragg'a. Jamie held on grimly as the thing clawed its way closer. He could see the life leaking from the monster, knew he must only hold on another moment. Only one more moment.

"Blood . . . for blood!" Mal'ek'a roared.

Its talons tore into Jamie's chest and the two fell, one atop the other, red blood mingling with black, smoking and hissing in tiny pools. Then silence fell in the tower room.

Collins watched Madison and the squad come out of the House. He could hear the murmur of the crowd on Bank Street swell in anticipation. Fucking ghouls, he thought. He ran forward, hesitated when he saw the looks on the faces of the men.

"Jesus! What did you find in there?"

"Hell," Madison said.

The spotlights that stabbed the park with their brilliant glare accentuated the pallor of his skin.

"Just what the hell were those things?" Wilson was muttering.

"I don't know," one of the other squad members said. He swallowed thickly. "I'm just glad that a bullet can kill them. God! Did you see that guy by the door. . . ."

Madison stared beyond Collins to where the crowd pushed at the barriers. TV cameras whirred, zoomed in to capture on video the reactions of the men as they stood around, breathing deeply of the clean air, soaking up the dark green of the nighttime park to ease the memories of what they'd so recently viewed.

"Get rid of them, Dan," Madison said. "Get rid of them all. I want this whole area cleared."

"Do you want to call in the military?" Corporal Holger asked.

"We'll call up whatever it takes to clean that place out. I don't know if anyone's still alive in there, but if they are, we've got to get them out."

"Shee-*it*," Wilson said. "We're going back *in* there?"

"What about Tucker?" Collins asked.

"We didn't . . . find him." Madison rubbed his temples. His leg was throbbing. "Christ! After what we've found so far, I'm not sure I even *want* to find him."

Collins put a hand on Madison's forearm. "You better take it easy, Wally. You look all done in. We've got some coffee over there by the—"

His voice broke off and he stared numbly behind the Superintendent at the House. Madison turned and took a step back, stunned.

When Jean-Paul saw the Superintendent emerge from the House, his first thought was to walk over and speak with him. But when he saw the grim looks on the faces of the men, he hesitated. Mother of God! What had they found in there? He looked at the House and stared at it in morbid fascination. The building looked dead. Ancient. Unlived in. Then his eyes widened.

Blue fire ran up the walls, sheathing the House in eerie flames. They ran crackling up to the eaves, swept across the roof, leaped up into the dark night sky. There they took the shape of two men. Jean-Paul recognized them both. One was *le sorcier* Thomas Hengwr. The other was Jamie Tams.

They were joined by a thick thread that, as Jean-Paul looked more closely, appeared to be a spear. Jamie Tams held one end. The other was plunged into Hengwr's chest. A howl ripped across the sky, cutting through the noise of the sirens and the crowd and the two figures flickered in the fires that engulfed the House. Suddenly the figures joined, elongated. The shriek dwindled into an unearthly moan that shook the ground, rattled the houses for blocks away. Then the elongated single figure rushed straight up into the air, vanishing in a trail of flickering blue light like a comet's tail.

It left in its wake a silence broken only by the wailing of the sirens. The men operating them shut them off, one by one. The watching crowds were silent. The House stood black and empty beyond the park.

"Mary, Mother of Jesus," Collins murmured in awe.

Madison walked slowly towards the House, followed by Collins and the squad. Nervous fingers curled around the triggers of their SMGs. As they neared the House, they saw that the walls appeared to be wrapped in some sort of black sheathing that stretched from the ground at their feet up to the roof. Madison nodded to Holger who sent a couple of his men back up a ladder.

There in the gap of the wall, the black sheathing seemed like smoky glass, covering every inch of the hole.

"Sealed up tighter than a nun," one of the men called down.

"What the hell was that we saw?" Collins asked.

Madison shook his head slowly. "I don't know, Dan. I don't know if we'll ever know." He drew a hand along his face, stared blankly at the House, then turned away. "Let's get rid of these crowds and call up some more men—see if we can't find a way in again."

For those still living in the northwest tower, the ensuing silence was a sweet balm that they clung to for long precious moments. Kieran looked around at what was left of them. The tragg'a had fled. Tucker lay by the wall where he'd been thrown, Maggie bent over him, but staring at the still body that lay in the center of the room. Sally was helping Blue lean up against the wall. She wiped the blood from his eyes. When he saw

Jamie's corpse, he looked away, weeping. Sara lay against the other wall, white with shock, her eyes unseeing.

Remembering what she'd undergone, Kieran shuddered. Only two of the fourteen rathe'wen'a remained. With guilty relief, Kieran realized that one of them was Ha'kan'ta. He drew her close to him. The other was Ur'wen'ta, who slowly hobbled to the couch and dropped onto it with a bitter sigh. May'asa lifted his head and nudged the shaman's hand with his muzzle. The wolf's silver fur was red with dried blood, but it had survived.

"How could it have been . . . Tom?" Kieran asked. He looked at where Jamie lay. The spear was still clutched in his hands. His head was tilted to one side. His torn chest was hidden from view, but blood leaked into pools on either side of him. There was no sign of Mal'ek'a. No sign of Thomas Hengwr who had been the Dread-That-Walks-Nameless.

"*Nom de tout!*" Kieran murmured. "Did it escape? Is it *still* alive?"

Beside him, Ha'kan'ta slowly shook her head. "He has been cleansed from this world—but at such a cost."

She pulled away from Kieran and crossed the room to where Sara lay. The arm that had been burned was healed, but the ring had changed. The gold had been burned black in that last desperate attempt to hold the monster back. Kneeling by her, Ha'kan'ta took Sara's face in her hands and spoke a pain-easing spell. Her sen'fer'sa was at its lowest ebb, but she forced it to answer her. Her drum tapped a soft rhythm, weak and distant. Slowly the glazed look left Sara's eyes, and color returned to her ashen cheeks. She looked over Ha'kan'ta's shoulder, saw Jamie, remembered. . . .

"Hush, Little-Otter," Ha'kan'ta murmured. "It is over now." She drew Sara's head to her shoulder, ran her hand down her back. "Hush."

"It . . . it's not over. You don't know. It . . . Mal'ek'a's blood . . . it's still in me. The evil is still here . . . in me."

Ha'kan'ta shook her head. "We all have good and ill within us. Such is the way that Mother Bear formed us. That is why we strive for peace—we who follow the Way. We strive to keep the one at bay while we add potency to the other. It can take many lives to accomplish that, Little-Otter. The road to the Place of Dreaming Thunder is not a short or easy one. And no one will take you there. You must fare on your own, with your own strengths, quelling your own weaknesses. Others can guide you, or share your burdens awhile, but in the end it is you who must choose between the one and the other. Only you can decide which you will be—a Thomas Hengwr or a Mal'ek'a. For though they sprang from the same source, they were never the same."

"I wanted to die so bad," Sara said. "Just to know that the same blood flows through me. . . ." She shivered.

Ha'kan'ta glanced at Kieran. "We must take them from here—all that are hurt. Then we must cleanse this lodge. I think Sins'amin will aid us in that. She owes us that much."

Kieran nodded.

"My arm was all burned," Sara murmured, sitting back. She looked at her hand, at the black ring.

Ha'kan'ta reached forward and scraped a fleck of black charring free. Under it, the gold still gleamed yellow.

"See?" the rathe'wen'a said. "Evil can cloak us, can do all it can to cover us with its own corruption, yet if the heart remains true, it cannot prevail. It can slay the body, but it cannot slay the soul. There is no shame in sharing Mal'ek'a's blood. The shame would be in fleeing life. In giving truth to Mal'ek'a's lies. Show the world that Mal'ek'a's blood means nothing. That it is what is in here"—she touched her breast— "that counts. The silence within. The stillness born of the something-in-movement that we call up with our drumming."

"I. . . ."

"You must be strong, Saraken, Little-Otter. You must be strong enough to give meaning to the sacrifices offered this night."

"I . . . I'll try."

"It will not be easy," Ha'kan'ta said sorrowfully.

Sara stared at her uncle's body, remembered Pukwudji. No, it would not be easy at all.

Chapter Four

2:30, Sunday afternoon.

Madison and Collins pulled in beside a police cruiser on Patterson Avenue and looked at Tamson House. The crowds had dispersed, but the House remained the same. No way in. Nothing came out. The local residents were starting to complain about the police barricades. No one seemed to remember Friday night anymore. Or if they did, they weren't talking about it. The film crews from CJOH and CBC could add nothing. The last searing flash of blue fire had wiped clean their video tapes. The newspaper photographers only had shots of the police barricades, the dark House.

But it had been real. There was no question of it in Madison's mind. Collins still had his hand in bandages—try to convince him it hadn't happened. And they had the three bodies of the whatever-they-weres back in the labs.

"You think anyone survived in there?" Collins asked.

Madison knew by anyone, Collins meant Inspector Tucker.

"I don't know, Dan," he replied.

On the seat between them lay yesterday's edition of *The Citizen*—the headlines screaming: "SOLICITOR GENERAL DIES WHILE SIGNING RESIGNATION". The body of the article gave the cause of death as a heart attack, but Madison wasn't buying it. It was too much like Hogue's death to suit him. And Williams had been connected to what went down at Tamson House and the PRB. Just like Walters was. Madison knew it. He just didn't have anything hard to prove it. He needed physical evidence, documentation, and he didn't have it. But he'd keep digging.

The events at Tamson House had made the front page, but strangely enough, the paper was still using the press release

that Madison had drafted on Friday night—even though their
reporters had been right on the scene. He supposed what couldn't
be explained was forgotten. By Monday's edition the story
would probably be buried somewhere inside the paper. There
was also the possibility that Walters had his hand in the silence.
He could be pulling a few strings, only what the hell he hoped
to gain from it Madison still couldn't figure out.

They had made a connection between Walters and Hogue.
The connection between Walters and Williams was even easier
to make. After all, a man who was known to advise the Prime
Minister was just as likely to know someone in Williams's
position. What they didn't have was Walters's hold on Williams. There had to be something, but so far it was eluding
them.

Madison sighed. "All we've got is questions. No answers."

"Maybe we're asking the wrong questions."

Madison lifted his eyebrows quizzically.

"Look at it this way," Collins said, lighting up a cigarette.
"Walters is the one we want to talk to. Maybe we should just
pay him a little visit—off the record."

"The end justifies the means?"

"You don't hear about him quibbling because he's got to
dirty his hands. Remember that natural gas deal last year, when
he—"

Madison shook his head. "We're not stooping to his level.
We'll get him. It'll take a while, but—"

"—we always get our man." Collins laughed bitterly. "Shit,
Wally. Do you think he'd hesitate for a minute if he knew we
were onto him?"

Madison looked away. "Is that . . . ?" he asked, pointing to
a man walking down Patterson from Bank Street.

"Gagnon," Collins agreed. He accepted the change of subject. "He lost someone in that fucking House as well."

Blue found Sara in the garden, sitting on the stone benches
by the fountain. He was supposed to be resting, but though he
ached from head to foot, he couldn't lie in bed any more. He
was afraid if he didn't start moving soon, he'd never get up.

Sara didn't look up as he approached. Her gaze was on a
row of graves, five freshly turned mounds of dirt that were all
that was left of the ones they had lost. Jamie. Sam. Thomas
Hengwr, whose body they'd found in the east wing. Traupman.
And Fred, who'd been found in the garden.

Someone had cleaned the dress that May'is'hyr had given her and she was wearing it now. The pouch that Blue had found when Pukwudji's body had vanished was in a pocket. In it were the House keys that she'd left behind in the round tower and a curious Y-shaped tuning key made of brass. It was the tuning key to Taliesin's harp.

The quin'on'a had come in answer to Ha'kan'ta's summoning. They had dug the graves and lowered the bodies in, covered them with the thick dark earth. Gannon and Chevier's bodies had been burned with those of the tragg'a. This second pyre, built on the ashes of the first, burned twice as high and for twice as long as the one Blue and the others had made a few days ago. The bodies of the slain rathe'wen'a had been carried away—so that their own people might honor them in their own way, Blue supposed.

He sat stiffly down beside Sara. The quin'on'a had been able to do a lot with their healing medicines and drumming, but he'd been cut up so bad that he knew it'd be a long time before he felt up to par again. They'd had better luck with Tucker. Left arm broken. They'd set it and put it in a sling. Three cracked ribs. They'd bound up his chest in a tight swath of bandage and told him to take it easy for awhile. Leg sprained—it had twisted under him when he hit the wall. More bandaging.

"Mind some company?" Blue said after a bit.

Sara turned to look at him. Her face was all hollow angles. Dark rings circled eyes that were red from crying and lack of sleep. She reached out a small hand and he took it in his own.

"I can't believe they're all dead," she said softly. "I can't believe what we went through. How come they died and we survived? I *wanted* to die. I'm still not sure if that's the way I feel now because I don't know who I was that night, Blue. I don't know who I am."

"I know," he said.

And he did. He didn't remember much about his berserker stand on the stairs—just flashes that still left him shaken. Sally had never told him how close he'd come to attacking her, but somehow he remembered that the clearest of all. He'd been asking himself the same questions as Sara did ever since. How come he was alive and Jamie was dead? Jamie and Fred. Sam. Traupman.

"I don't think there is a reason," he said finally. "Not one that we'll ever understand."

Sara nodded mournfully. "But, Blue. Will it ever stop hurting? I look over there and see those graves and it hurts so bad. . . ."

"They'd want us to carry on," Blue said.

The words sounded as hollow to him as they probably did to her. He wasn't sure there was any point in carrying on.

They stood in amongst the garden's trees, observing Sara and Blue on the bench. One was the Forest Lord who had come to Kieran's trial by combat. The other was a grey-haired man, his eyes solemn, deep and old. He had a cloak over his shoulders that looked like it was made of oak leaves, woven together.

"See what sorrow you have wrought, Gwydion?" the Forest Lord said heavily. "It might have been a game to you, but it has sundered the fabric of their lives. So many hurt. So many dead. You might have prevented this. You had but to act."

"And you did not?"

The Forest Lord turned to face him. "Do not seek to entangle me with your riddles. Had I known what Mal'ek'a's death would entail, I would have slain him myself. I take no pleasure from sorrow—be it my own children's or that of another's."

"And you think I do? You think it was all but a game? Twice I slew him and twice he returned, stronger than before. Only one of his own bloodline could cleanse the world of his presence forever. I knew that, but twice I intervened nevertheless. Each time he came back, he left more sorrow in his wake. Should I have let him return a third time?"

"You might have warned them."

"I could not. You saw yourself how she reacted when she learned the truth. She was willing to die rather than accept it. Even now she hovers between life and the kiss of forgetful death. Do you think she could have faced him, knowing what she knows now?"

"She would have been the stronger for it," the Forest Lord said.

"No. It would have weakened her."

"Did your grandson know as well?"

Gwydion shook his head. "He would never have let her go."

The Forest Lord sighed. "I do not like you, Gwydion. You take a simple thing and make of it a tangled web. You take a truth and hide it behind riddles. I think it is time you left my lands. Left them to return nevermore."

"Still you fail to understand."

"I understand," the Forest Lord said. "All too well. Mark what I say: Strength comes from knowledge, from understanding and from truth. Deny your children those, and you deny them their right to grow. I admire this Sara, for striving still, for reaching when her right to know was denied her. And I admire her uncle who gave his life to end Mal'ek'a's evil. But you, you I do not admire. I understand your fears. I understand why you did what you did. But I believe you underestimated the woman; underestimated them all. Had they known what they faced, they might have planned their attack better. So many need not have died. Many of *my* children died, Gwydion."

"Still I maintain," the grey-haired man said, "that faced with the truth, they would have been overwhelmed by it."

"You are a fool. It was not until they learned the truth that they prevailed. Now I ask you again: Leave my lands."

"Your lands? How many people remember you in the World Beyond? There are as many of my people dwelling in what remains of your forests and plains as there are of yours. More!"

The Forest Lord frowned. "You forget yourself, Gwydion. You and I are not the same. I am kin to the lords who rule you—not kin to you. I ask you for a third and final time: Begone."

"I go. My work here is done."

"Aye," the Forest Lord sighed. "While mine begins."

He stood alone under the trees then, rueing the day he ever allowed Taliesin to set foot on his lands. It was not the bard's fault. He was a good man. But he came with threads that still bound him to his homeland. Threads that drew Mal'ek'a, drew Gwydion, and brought with them the one's evil and the other's misguided ideals. It would have been better if he'd not listened to his sea-brother and allowed Taliesin to land on his shores.

He looked again to where Blue and Sara sat. Her small form was almost hidden by his larger one, yet both of them were diminished by sorrow and confusion.

"Come, my sister," he called with a voice like wind. "The one is a warrior and the other a child of your own heart. Yet they both need your healing touch."

For a long moment the leaves of the trees in the garden were still. Then there was a sound like the whisper of distant thunder, a low drumming, and in amidst its rhythm, he heard his sister reply.

"I come, brother."

* * *

Blue saw them first, the tall woman walking towards them and the child she held by the hand. The woman's hair was the pure white of moonlight, her coppery skin smooth and young, her body slender under the white doeskin dress, moving with a supple grace. The child was broad-faced, with a horned brow and dark brown hair that hung in a Rastaman's dreadlocks. He moved with a skip to his step, his eyes twinkling and a grin splitting his features.

One moment they weren't there and the next they were. Blue had been looking in that direction and he could swear that they'd just appeared out of nowhere.

"Heads up," Blue murmured to Sara. "We've got company."

Sara looked up. She saw the woman first and felt the moon-heart air start up inside her. She was suddenly aware of a low drumming. It had been there for some time, she realized, only she hadn't noticed it until this moment. And then she saw the woman's companion.

"Puk—Pukwudji?" she said in a small voice.

She stood, wanting it to be him so badly, but knowing that it couldn't be the little honochen'o'keh. But the little man's grin grew wider. He pulled his hand free of the woman's and cartwheeled the remaining distance before throwing himself into Sara's arms.

"Hey!" he whispered in her ear as she tightened her arms about him.

"Oh, Pukwudji. . . ."

They sat down together on the bench. Sara was crying and laughing at the same time. Blue looked up to see that the woman had stopped a half dozen paces from the bench. She was smiling at him.

"You must be he that Ur'wen'ta names Blue-Rider-of-Thunder," she said.

"Yeah. I . . . I'm Blue, all right."

"And you are Sara Little-Otter who befriended the bard Redhair."

Sara nodded. Pukwudji had grown very still at her side. He held her hand tightly.

"May I sit with you awhile?" the woman asked.

Sara smiled uncertainly and nodded again. "Who are you?"

"I have been called Ketq Skwaye by some. Most name me Grandmother Toad."

Blue started to say that she certainly didn't look like either a grandmother or a toad, but decided to keep his thoughts to himself. Grandmother Toad smiled at him again, as though she'd read his thoughts, but she said nothing, and sat down in the grass and regarded both Sara and Blue in turn. For a long while they sat in a silence that no one felt obliged to break.

"It was indeed a terrible night," Grandmother Toad said finally.

Sara squeezed Pukwudji's hand. "How did . . . ?" she began.

"Pukwudji survive?" Grandmother Toad smiled. "The little mysteries never die. They were born in the world's heart, from the drumming of stone against stone, of root against earth, the crack of antlers against a tree trunk. But the others . . . they did not fare so well.

"You both lost those you loved last night. As did my brother—so many of his drummers. And Red-Spear. He would have been a great leader, that one, if he had not been so filled with anger. You would have understood Tep'fyl'in," she said to Blue. "You are much the same as he was. There is a storm in you as there was in him—only you have learned to bind your thunder."

Blue shook his head. In control? When he almost killed Sally?

"But there was a need for it to be loosed then, was there not?" Grandmother Toad said. "Do you stride across the face of the world like a thundercloud, or do you keep that storm bound? And you did not strike the woman. You have no need to know shame. Rather, know a certain pride that you are what you are. A strong man who does not need to flaunt his strength."

"I used to. . . ." Blue began, then hesitated. She wouldn't know what he meant if he told her about the colors of the Devil's Dragon, and the bikers he used to ride with. But . . .

"You used to indeed," she said, "but no longer. And I know," she added, "that you ask yourself, what use is this strength if it could do nothing to aid those who died? Think of this, Blue-Rider, when that question arises to trouble you: Are you responsible for all that goes on in the world? Even the Great Spirit allows its children to be responsible to themselves. You may not have saved all, but what of those you did save?"

"But Jamie . . ."

"Ah." She sighed. "Him you could not have aided, unless he had asked you to. He knew what he did. He chose to do it. Remember him with gladness and know that he has found a place amidst the Dreaming Thunder."

There was something so comforting about her words, that Blue felt himself truly relax for the first time since this had all begun.

"Grandmother Toad?" Sara asked. "Is Jamie really in . . . in the Place of Dreaming Thunder?"

"Indeed, child of my heart. He and the rathe'wen'a—all save the druid. I know not what fate awaits that one's spirit. As the one half did great evil, so did the other great good. He is gone, I think, to the afterworld of his own people."

"Is that where I'll go now? We're the same bloodline. . . ."

"But you are not dead."

"I'm not so sure that what I am is all that much better," Sara replied.

Pukwudji shifted uncomfortably beside her, upset at the turn that the conversation had taken, but before he could speak, Grandmother Toad said softly: "It ill becomes you to speak so, Little-Otter."

Sara felt that Grandmother Toad didn't understand, but didn't know how she could explain what she meant when she wasn't exactly sure what she meant herself. She felt betrayed. By her ancestry. By Jamie for dying and leaving her behind. By Taliesin who'd tried to bind her to him with his moonheart air.

Taliesin. He'd let her go to confront Mal'ek'a as part of some test. Certainly she'd left the tower on her own and, with Pukwudji's help, made it back to Ottawa. But how could the bard have expected her to confront Mal'ek'a and survive? What kind of a test was that? In God's name, how could he say that he loved her on the one hand and throw her to—to such an evil on the other? How could she even care about this mystic Way anymore, when to follow it she had to lose her friends and her family first? Were they the cost of enlightenment?

"He never knew," Grandmother Toad said. "He could not tell you, because he never knew. He did not know what Mal'ek'a had grown to be—if he had he would never have let you go on your own to confront him. He thought it was a test like the one he faced when he was a youth, when he faced his greatest danger, and that danger was himself. If one failed that test, one didn't die. It only meant that one did not know oneself well enough and so must delve the deeper and attempt it again."

In a way, Sara thought, that was exactly what had happened to her. "But—"

"And Lorcalon was never a gift," Grandmother Toad said. "You were already a moonheart, my daughter. He but woke it in you. His only gift to you was his love."

"Do you think I should go back to him?"

"You cannot go back to him."

"Why not?"

Grandmother Toad sighed. "The past is closed. The past already is. It has been. Three times you went to him, twice as a ghost. That much is written in the Tale of Time. But there will be no fourth time."

"But that means—"

"That he drums in the Place of Dreaming Thunder. Yes."

Sara shook her head. "I don't understand. Why is he there? Why not in . . . in his own afterworld? Like Thomas Hengwr. Why isn't Taliesin in the Summer Country?"

"I did not say that the druid went to the Summer Country, though for his sake, for all that he suffered, I can only hope that he has indeed found that final peace."

"I did this for Taliesin," Sara said softly. "For us. This stupid test. I never knew what was going on. What Mal'ek'a was. What was the point of it? All that's come out of it is Jamie's dead. Jamie and the others. . . ."

"And the worlds were rid of a great evil. Did you expect a reward?"

"No . . . that is . . ." Sara sighed. "I suppose I did. I didn't know what I was getting into, but I guess I did expect to be with Taliesin when it was all over. I thought we'd be together. But I guess I don't even know if we'd get along."

No, she thought. That was another lie. She'd been uncertain once, but she knew now. She looked at Grandmother Toad, met the woman's solemn gaze for a long moment, then looked away.

"I don't know why I'm saying all this," she said. "I'm just looking for something to hold onto, I suppose. Even if I was with Taliesin, that wouldn't bring Jamie or the others back."

"You cannot go to Taliesin Redhair," Grandmother Toad said. "But you can still call him to you."

It didn't register at first. Then the words sank in and Sara looked up with hope in her eyes. "It's true? I can call him to me? But how?"

Pukwudji touched the pocket that held the pouch with the tuning key to Taliesin's harp in it.

"Ring and key," he said.

Sara glanced at him. The honochen'o'keh grinned. "And your love makes three, hey?" he finished.

Sara looked from the little man to Grandmother Toad. The tall woman rose from her place in the grass and nodded.

"There is strength in threes," she said. "But he will not come to you unless you truly want him to."

"But. . . ."

"We must go now," Grandmother Toad said.

"I know the way to the World Beyond," Pukwudji said as he rose to go. "Perhaps I'll come and play a trick or two with you, hey?"

He leaned close and his dry lips brushed her cheek. Sara held him close for a moment, then slowly let him go.

"Be well, daughter of my heart," Grandmother Toad said. "Remember us in the World Beyond, remember the mysteries great and small, for we diminish without your love."

"Who is that woman?" Kieran asked, looking down into the garden from the tower.

"What woman?"

"That one . . . coming out of the garden with that strange little man that was at the quin'on'a lodge."

Ha'kan'ta crossed to the window to have a look for herself. Her eyes widened slightly and she nodded, knowing who it was and who Sara had been speaking with. This was what Sara and Blue needed to draw them out of their despair. She turned to Kieran, but he no longer needed to know the woman's name.

Across the distance that separated them, he met Grandmother Toad's gaze and felt the last pain inside him withdraw. Like Sara, he'd felt betrayed. Intellectually, he knew that the old man who'd been his mentor was not the same being that they'd fought two nights past in the tower. But his heart could not separate the two.

Remember what was good, the woman's eyes seemed to say to him, and he did.

"Grandmother Toad," he said softly, turning to Ha'kan'ta.

He looked out the window, meaning to thank the strange woman for what she had eased inside him, but both she and Pukwudji were gone.

Ha'kan'ta smiled. "I think you have severed your last bond with the World Beyond," she said.

Kieran nodded, then asked: "Did you ever think I wouldn't stay?"

Ha'kan'ta kissed him for her reply.

* * *

As Blue got up from the bench, Sara stared at the graves.
A stillness settled over her. She'd wanted to ask Grandmother
Toad one last question: If she could call Taliesin back, then
why not Jamie? Why not all of them?

A quiet drumming spoke to her. *There are some whose final
resting place the Dreaming Thunder is*, it said.

But who decided that?

There was no reply.

She looked down at the ring on her finger, thought she saw
Taliesin's features reflected in miniature in the glint of the
gold. She turned her finger and the image was gone. A trick
of the light. She drew Pukwudji's pouch from her pocket and
took out Taliesin's tuning key. Ring and key. And her love.
What if it wasn't enough?

She reached inside for the silence deep within her, reached
for her taw; but it was still shaken and weak from her ordeal
with Mal'ek'a. Grandmother Toad might have brought some
small measure of comfort with her, but it could only heal so
much. It could not touch the guilt that she was alive while
others were dead, or the lonely aching.

"I'd call you, Taliesin," she said softly, "but I don't know
how."

She twisted the harp's tuning key in her fingers, tapped it
against her ring.

"I want to come back," she said, "but they say I can't. They
say the past is closed to me now—except in my memory. I
need more than that right now. I'm sorry that you had to wait
so long. Wait for nothing. Ha'kan'ta told me about...about
how sad you were. She knew you. I wouldn't have left the
tower if I'd known, but I thought I had to. I thought that was
what you wanted me to do. I did it for us. But now..."

Oh, she loved him. She knew that now. But...She stared
at the tuning key, at her ring, not knowing what to do.

"I need you so badly," she said. "But I don't...know how
to call you...."

She bowed her head. Her throat constricted, dry as sand-
paper. She turned to the fountain to get a drink, dipped her
hand in and paused with it halfway to her mouth. The water
trickled from her fingers when she heard it. A spray of harp
notes...a spill of music, flowing like water.

Lorcalon. The moonheart tune.

It rose in her. Her taw drummed with it.

She looked up beyond the fountain and saw a familiar figure

standing there. He was wavery, like a mirage. Almost transparent. But the sun lifted highlights from his red hair, his green eyes were deep with sadness as he shared her sorrow, and he smiled for love of her. He let his fingers fall from the harp strings, drew the strap from his shoulder and set the instrument on the grass beside him.

"Taliesin?" Sara asked hesitantly.

She was afraid it was another trick of the light. If she moved, he would waver and be gone. She hadn't called him. She didn't know how.

"Please don't go," she said.

The moonheart tune thrummed inside her and she willed him to be real, to stay. She gripped the tuning key with white knuckles. It was warm in her hand—almost hot. She held it tighter.

"I never knew," he said. His voice had a slight echo to it, a distance, as though he spoke to her from a long distance away. "I never knew what he had planned for you—my grandsire Gwydion. If I had, I would never have let you go alone. That was a horror we should have faced together." He seemed to grow more transparent as he spoke, fading.

"But we did face him together!" Sara cried. "The tune you gave me was all that kept me safe in the end."

"I did not give it to you. It was always there."

He was almost gone—just a gossamer shape, a ghostly outline. She could see the trees through him.

"I failed you," he said.

His voice was sad. Fainter.

Sara wouldn't listen anymore. She ran around the fountain and reached for him. It was like touching mist.

"You didn't fail me," she said. "*You* gave me the moonheart tune. You *were* with me!"

Was the mist more solid? The music inside her leaped through her fingers to reach for him, to draw him to her. She heard the sound of drumming all around them. One moment they were in the garden, the next on a high flat rock atop a mountain, with rocky crags stretching for leagues in all directions. There were dark clouds in the sky. They had faces. Like bears...ravens...deer...otters...cranes. Animal heads on human bodies. Dark cloud bodies that played ceremonial drums.

"Don't go," she said fiercely. "I love you, Taliesin."

There was a swirl and a spinning underfoot. She lost her balance as the ground shifted under her.

"I love you," she said again.

Arms caught her from falling. She blinked and the mountainscape was gone, the sound of drumming diminished, fading, gone. Only the moonheart tune remained, moving to the rhythm of her heartbeat, of her breathing. She felt Taliesin's arms around her and buried her face against his shoulder. For the first time since her ordeal, she wanted to live again.

She leaned back to look up into his face. His eyes glistened. There were lifetimes in those eyes. Mysteries. Wisdom and folly. But most of all there was her love returned.

They held each other for a long time. Taliesin looked over her shoulder at the line of graves.

"I wish I had known him," he said softly. "Your uncle."

Sara swallowed, nodding. "He'd've liked you, Taliesin. I know Jamie would've liked you."

As though the words were a signal, they stepped apart. There was a moment's awkwardness.

"What . . . what happens now?" Sara asked.

"I think you should return to your own world, Sara."

"And . . . and you?"

"I would like to come with you—if you'll have me."

"If I'll . . ." She stepped close again and drew her arms tightly around him. Taliesin returned the embrace.

"How're you feeling, Inspector?" Blue asked.

"A hell of a lot better than you look. What's up?"

"The quin'on'a are ready to ship us back."

"Yeah?"

Blue nodded.

"What's on your mind, Blue?" Tucker asked.

The biker looked from Maggie and Sally to the Inspector, then sighed.

"I want to know how we're going to play this," he said.

"You give it any thought?"

"No. I'm just starting to get my head tied on a bit straighter, to tell you the truth."

"I know the feeling." Tucker glanced at Maggie. "I think we should play it like it never happened."

"What?"

Tucker shrugged. "What else can we do? Hengwr's gone. Foy's staying. I'm sure as hell not going to ask Sara to do a demo for the boys in the PRB labs—she'd probably fry me, if you didn't get to me first."

"I'd've thought . . ." Blue began, then nodded. "Okay. I'll go tell 'em we're ready."

"One thing, Blue."

"Yeah?"

"What Gannon told us . . . about Walters. It goes no further than us. Got it?"

Blue frowned. "You're not going to cover up for him, are you? Shit, ninety percent of this fuck-up's got to do with him. If he hadn't been hounding Hengwr. . . ."

"Ease up, Blue. I don't want Walters touched because he's mine. Plain and simple."

Blue studied the Inspector for a long moment, then shrugged. "I can handle that," he said.

When he and Sally left, Maggie regarded Tucker with a certain amount of alarm. "You can't mean that," she said.

"It's got to be that way, Maggie. We'll never pin anything on him. I believe in the law—without it we're in deep shit. But you know as well as I do that we can't touch him. And he's just going to start this crap all over again and fuck up some more lives. He didn't get where he is by kissing ass. He got there by breaking it."

"And then what?"

"Then I'm going to carry on."

"Like nothing ever happened?"

Tucker sighed heavily. "No. Like everything happened."

"I'm not going back with you," Kieran said to Sara.

They stood alone on the field outside her tower, sharing a last cigarette.

"I know," she said.

Kieran looked past her to where Taliesin and Ha'kan'ta stood just inside the door. "I still can't face him," he said.

"He understands why you thought the way you did."

Kieran fiddled with the whistle Ha'kan'ta had given him— Taliesin's whistle. He started to pull it out of his belt, but Sara stopped him with her hand.

"Keep it," she said. "To remember him. To remember us both. Kieran. I'm sorry I was such a shit to you."

"You and me both. But it all worked out."

"We'll be back," Sara said. "Taliesin and I. We'll want to see you and Kanta again. Sooner or later you'll have to talk to him."

"Lord lifting Jesus, Sara. you make it hard. We'll wait until then, *d'accord?*"

"Sure."

She stepped forward and kissed him lightly on the cheek. "See ya, Kieran."

He caught Ha'kan'ta's eye. As the rathe'wen'a came to where he stood with Sara, a low drumming started up.

"That's the quin'on'a," he said. "We've got to run. *Salut*, Sara."

Ha'kan'ta embraced her.

"If you see Pukwudji," Sara said, "tell him I'll be showing up to play a few tricks on him."

Ha'kan'ta smiled "I will tell him, Little-Otter. Be well."

Sara watched the two of them walk to where Sins'amin and her people were gathered. She stood for a long moment, staring up into the skies of the Otherworld. Then she ground her cigarette underfoot and went in to where Taliesin and the others were waiting.

3:15, Sunday afternoon.

Madison and Collins were doing the rounds of the guards watching the House.

"I don't know what you're expecting, Wally."

"Something's got to give. Sooner or later, we're going to get in, or something's going to come out."

"After what you told me you found in there, I don't know if I *want* anything to come out—if you know what I mean." He stopped to light a cigarette, but never had a chance to bring his lighter up. "Wally?"

"I hear it, Dan. Shit! We've got to get more men down here, pronto!"

"Too late."

The drumming seemed to come from all around them. They stood and watched as the black sheen faded from the House. It lost its dead look. Sunlight that had simply disappeared when it touched the House now glinted on windows and set off the highlights on its sills and eaves. Slowly the drums died away. Madison and Collins moved closer. There was a door opening on one side of the building. Uniformed city police and plain-clothes RCMP officers came at a run, drawing their weapons. Madison pulled his own .38, transferring his cane to his left hand.

Jean-Paul joined the pair of them as he reached the cluster of policemen. The door opened wide and twelve fingers tightened on their triggers.

"Tucker!" Madison roared as the first figure stepped into the light. "Put away those guns. Jesus H. Christ—Tucker! You made it!"

Tucker grinned, albeit wanly.

Jean-Paul stood to one side watching the people emerge. When the last of them had come out of the House and there was still no sign of Kieran, he began to turn, stopped when Tucker called out his name. Slowly he joined the others that crowded around the survivors.

"Were you looking for Kieran?" Tucker asked.

Jean-Paul nodded.

"We found him. He's okay, but he won't be coming back. To Ottawa at any rate."

"Where is he, John?"

Tucker turned to look at the House.

"In an Otherworld, Jean-Paul," he said. "In *the* Otherworld." As Jean-Paul nodded and started to leave again, Tucker caught his arm. "I told Kieran what went down—between you and me."

"Yes. And?"

"He sends his love, Jean-Paul."

Epilogue

IN mid-December, when the streets were cold enough for snow but the snow had yet to come, there were two items of interest in *The Citizen*. The first was on the front page, and the headline read:

J. HUGH WALTERS SLAIN BY BURGLAR

The body of the article went on to describe how the business magnate had been slain by a burglar who had ransacked his house late the previous evening. Police had no suspects as yet.

The second was in the entertainment section. There was a photograph of four rather scruffy-looking individuals, under which it said:

THIS WEEK AT FACES:
MUSIC IN THE CELTIC TRADITION FEATURING:

COBBLEY GREY

Under that was a small symbol of a quarter moon with two antlers rising up from behind it. Beneath the symbol it read:

WITH A SPECIAL OPENING SET FROM

TAL GWION & SARA KENDELL
ON WELSH HARP AND GUITAR

Nowhere did it make mention that Special Inspector John Tucker had left that morning on an extended holiday to Jamaica with his long-time friend and companion, Margaret Finch.

Author's Note

THE preceding novel is a work of fiction. All characters and events in this book are fictitious, and any resemblance to actual persons living or dead is purely coincidental.

I might especially note that while there is neither a Tamson House nor an antique shop called The Merry Dancers in Ottawa, at the same time the RCMP does not have a Paranormal Research Branch, a position on its force of Special Inspector such as depicted in the character of John Tucker, nor has any past or present Solicitor General been even rumored to have committed the indiscretions ascribed to *Moonheart*'s Michael Williams.

And, for those curious in such things, this book was written under the influence of Alan Stivell, Andreas Vollenweider, Neville Marriner, Ann Triskell, Edgar Froese, Klaus Schultz, Radio Silence, Robin Williamson, Silly Wizard, the Fureys, and Kate Bush—to name the most prominent.

Ottawa, Winter 1983.

APPENDIX: *A Brief Description of the Weirdin*

DESCRIPTION:

Sixty-one, two-sided flat round discs, made of bone, with an image carved on either side; one hundred and twenty-two images in all. Divided into thirteen Prime; twenty-three Secondary (fifteen First Rank; eight Second Rank); and twenty-five Tertiary (nine Static and sixteen Mobile).

METHODS OF USE:

Questioner selects twelve Weirdin from Bag, at random, and holding hand directly above center of the Triskell on the Reading Cloth, lets them fall. (Alternately, the Weirdin may be taken from the Bag, one at a time though still randomly, and laid on the Reading Cloth in numerical order.)

READING CLOTH:

The positions on the Cloth read as follows (see accompanying diagram):

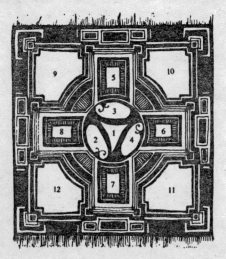

THE TRISKELL:

The Questioner is in the center (1), the three arms signifying: Marrow, or Health (2), Attitude, or Will (3), and Heart, or Spirit (4).

THE CROSS:

These are the direct influences that affect the Questioner: North, known as the Foundation, or Past (5); East, known as Change, or the Present (6); South, known as Forthcoming, or the Direct Future (7); and West, known as Destiny, or the Far Future (8).

THE OUTER CIRCLE:

These are the peripheral influences that affect the Questioner: Future Allies or Adversaries (9); Present Allies or Adversaries (10); Course of Action (11); and General Conclusion (12).
Note: Particular care must be accorded to both the position of the Weirdin to one another, as well as their positioning on the Reading Cloth.

THE MEANING OF THE WEIRDIN:
Prime:

1.a) *The Horned Lord*—Lord of Animals and the World's Wood; aspect of Cernunnos, Pan, etc.; supernatural power, protection.
 b) *The Moon Mother*—the White Goddess in all her aspects; immortality, perpetual renewal, enlightenment.

2.a) *The Grey Man*—autumn, west, twilight, mystery, elf-friend.
 b) *The Blue Maiden*—spring, east, dawn, rebirth.

3.a) *The Yellow Tinker*—winter, north, night, obscurity.
 b) *The Red Queen*—summer, south, day, warmth, youth.

4.a) *The Bearded King*—strength.
 b) *The Scapegoat*—delegated guilt.

5.a) *The Queen of Otters*—sovereignty, healing, fidelity.
 b) *The Old Fern Man*—mortality, solitude, sincerity.

6.a) *The Mage*, or *Knight*—creative power.
 b) *The Apprentice*, or *Young Man*—neophyte, initiate.

7.a) *The Maiden*—primordial innocence.
 b) *The Dwarf*—unconscious and amoral forces of nature.

8.a) *The Trickster* (depicted as *Cat* or *Fox*)—stealth, desire, liberty, choice.
 b) *The Shepherd*—protector, guidance.

9.a) *The Harper*, or *Wren*—spiritual, change, guide to Otherworld.
 b) *The Piper*—harmony.

10.a) *The Wanderer*—aimless movement.
 b) *The Pilgrim*—follows a direct and purposeful path.

11.a) *The Dancer*—creative energy, reinforcement of strength.
  b) *The Huntsman*—pursuit of worldly ends, death.

12.a) *The Warrior*—antagonistic force, or defender.
  b) *The Imp*—disorder, tormenting.

13.a) *The Weaver at Her Loom*—fate, time.
  b) *The Enchantress*—self-delusion, binding/destroying.

Secondary: First Rank

14.a) *The Hazel Staff*—magic power, journeying, wisdom, inspiration.
  b) *The Iron Sword*—justice, courage, authority, inflexibility.

15.a) *The Thistle Cloak*—disguise, austerity, defiance.
  b) *The Mirror*—truth, self-realization.

16.a) *The Necklace,* or *Garland*—both binds and limits; diversity in union; dedication; beads or links—bring the multiplicity of manifestation; thread and connection—the non-manifest.
  b) *The Bear's Cauldron,* or *Honey Cup*—nourishment, heart, life, inexhaustible sustenance.

17.a) *The Circle,* or *Serpent*—self-contained, having no beginning and no end; death and destruction, or renewing its skin—resurrection, self/created taught.
  b) *The Scales*—balance, justice.

18.a) *The Book*—quest, learning, knowledge.
  b) *The Net*—entanglement.

19.a) *The Shield*—preservation.
  b) *The Flint Knife*—hardiness of heart, indifference, sacrifice, vengeance, death.

20.a) *The Flute*—anguish, extremes of emotion.
  b) *The Harp*—calls up the seasons; malleability of Time; Change, if not Progress.

21.a) *The Mask*—protection, concealment, transformation, non-being.
  b) *The Wand*—power.

22.a) *The Sheaf of Corn*—awakening, life, unity, harvest.
  b) *The Acorn,* or *Hazelnut*—hidden wisdom, friendship.

23.a) *The Bell*—charm against destruction.
  b) *The Candle*—illumination, or uncertainty of life.

24.a) *Fire*—transformation.
  b) *Ice*—rigidity, brittleness, impermanence.

25.a) *The Cedar Crown*—sovereignty, honor, reward, nobility, incorruptibility, or stasis.
  b) *The Ship*—adventure, exploration.

26.a) *The Ring*—power, dignity, delegated power, completion, cyclic time.

b) *The Key*—axial symbol of opening and closing. binding and loosing.

27.a) *The Tides*—reciprocity, opportunity.
   b) *The Drum*—speech, revelation, tradition.

28.a) *The Bag*—secrecy, winds of chance.
   b) *The Glove,*or *Marigold* —evidence of good will, fidelity.

Secondary: Second Rank

29.a) *The Forest*—place of testing and unknown peril.
   b) *The Hearth*—home, spiritual center.

30.a) *The Mountain*—constancy, eternity.
   b) *The Ocean*—chaos, endless motion.

31.a) *The Wood*—shelter.
   b) *The Mist*—error, confusion.

32.a) *The Standing Stones*—prophecy, eternal, cohesion.
   b) *The Crossroads*—choice, or union of opposites.

33.a) *The Island*—isolation and loneliness, or safety and refuge.
   b) *The Lake*—receptive wisdom, absorption.

34.a) *The River*—the passage of life. flowing.
   b) *The Chasm*—separation.

35.a) *The Field*—place of nourishment.
   b) *The Labyrinth*—attaining realization after ordeals.

36.a) *The Cave*—entrance to Otherworld.
   b) *The Door*—hope, opportunity.

Tertiary: Static

37.a) *The Oak*—durability; is also MAN in microcosm, in its branches, are two *Ravens*—Thought and Memory.
   b) *The Mistletoe*—neither tree nor shrub; all-healing, new life.

38.a) *The Hemlock*—death, deceit, ill luck.
   b) *The Rose*—heavenly perfection twined with earthy passion.

39.a) *The Apple,* or *Silver Bough*—fertility, love, joy, knowledge.
   b) *The Willow*—mourning, unhappy love, loss.

40.a) *The Mandrake Root*—power of magic.
   b) *The Rowan Bough*—protection against magic.

41.a) *The Alder,* or *Fairy Tree*—divinity, resurrection.
   b) *The Elm*—dignity.

42.a) *The Ivy*—revelry, clinging dependence.
   b) *The Mallow*—quietness, rusticity.

43.a) *The Hawthorn*—chastity.
   b) *The Birch*—fertility, light.

44.a) *The Ash*—modesty, prudence.
 b) *The Juniper*—protection, confidence, boldness.

45.a) *The Pine Cone*—good fortune.
 b) *The Thorn*—trial, without spiritual danger.

Tertiary: Mobile

46.a) *The Swan*—benevolence, magic, purity.
 b) *The Wolf*—fierceness.

47.a) *The Hare*—intuition, resurrection.
 b) *The Falcon*—aspiration, victory over lust.

48.a) *The Goose*—war.
 b) *The Boar*—preservation from danger.

49.a) *The Stag*, or *Unicorn*—renewal, creation, innocence.
 b) *The Toad*—evil power.

50.a) *The Heron*—vigilence, quietness.
 b) *The Crow*—beginnings, the first step.

51.a) *The Dragon*—sovereignty, untamed nature.
 b) *The Sparrow*—insignificance, lowliness.

52.a) *The Crane*—herald of death, trouble.
 b) *The Dolphin*—saviour, guide.

53.a) *The Kingfisher*—calmness, beauty.
 b) *The Mouse*—incessant movement, senseless agitation.

54.a) *The Elk*, or *Moose*—supernatural power, whirlwind.
 b) *The Spider*—weaver of destiny.

55.a) *The Robin*, or *Swallow*—hope, resurrection.
 b) *The Swine*—gluttony, greed, anger.

56.a) *The Bee*—industry, order.
 b) *The Salmon*, or *Trout*—foreknowledge.

57.a) *The Badger*—mischief, playfulness.
 b) *The Owl*—wisdom, darkness, death.

58.a) *The Horse*—intellect, wisdom, reason.
 b) *The Winged Deer*—swiftness, truth.

59.a) *The Goat*—superiority, vitality.
 b) *The Sheep*—helplessness.

60.a) *The Eagle*—release from bondage.
 b) *The Rat*—plague, decay.

61.a) *The Woodpecker*—prophecy
 b) *The Lizard*, or *Salamander*—silence.